LOVE COMES
SOFTLY 1–4

LOVE COMES SOFTLY 1-4

Four Bestselling Novels
in One Volume

JANETTE OKE

BETHANYHOUSE
a division of Baker Publishing Group
Minneapolis, Minnesota

Published by Bethany House Publishers
11400 Hampshire Avenue South
Bloomington, Minnesota 55438
www.bethanyhouse.com

Bethany House Publishers is a division of
Baker Publishing Group, Grand Rapids, Michigan
www.bakerpublishinggroup.com

Printed in the United States of America

ISBN 978-0-7642-1520-9

Library of Congress Control Number: 2015952285

Cover design by Eric Walljasper

Cover image of woman: © Brad Wrobleski, MasterFile

16 17 18 19 20 21 22   7 6 5 4 3 2 1

LOVE COMES
SOFTLY

To my dear friend and former teacher,
Mrs. Irene Lindberg

ONE

The Grim Reaper

The morning sun shone brightly on the canvas of the covered wagon, promising an unseasonably warm day for mid-October. Marty fought for wakefulness, coming slowly out of a troubled and fitful sleep. Why did she feel so heavy and ill at ease—she who usually woke with enthusiasm and readiness for each new day's adventure? Then it all came flooding back, and she fell in a heap on the quilt from which she had just emerged. Sobs shook her body, and she pressed the covering to her face to muffle the sound.

Clem is gone. The truth of it was nearly unthinkable. Less than two short years ago, strong, adventurous, boyish Clem had quickly and easily made her love him. Self-assured and confident, he had captured her heart and her hand. Fourteen months later, she was a married woman out west, beginning a new and challenging adventure with the man she loved—until yesterday.

Oh, Clem, she wept. Her whole world had fallen around her when the men came to tell her that Clem was dead. Killed outright. His horse had fallen. They'd had to destroy the horse. Did she want to come with them?

No, she'd stay.

Would she like the missus to come over?

No, she'd manage.

She wondered how she had even gotten the words past her lips.

They'd care for the body, one of them had told her. His missus was right good at that. The neighbors would arrange for the burying. Lucky the parson was paying his visit through the area. Was to have moved on today, but they were certain that he'd stay over. Sure she didn't want to come with them?

No, she'd be all right.

Hated to leave her alone.

She needed to be alone.

They'd see her on the morrow. Not to worry. They'd care for everything. Thank ya—

And they had gone, taking her Clem with them, wrapped in one of her few blankets and fastened on the back of a horse. The kindly neighbor should have been riding it, but he was now leading the animal slowly, careful of its burden.

And now it was the morrow and the sun was shining. Why was the sun shining? Didn't nature know that today should be as lifeless as she felt, with a cold wind blowing like the chill that gripped her heart?

The fact that she was way out west in the fall of the year with no way back home, no one around that she knew—and she was expecting Clem's baby besides—should have filled her with panic. But for the moment the only thing her mind could settle on and her heart grasp was the overwhelming pain of her great loss.

"Oh, Clem! Clem!" she cried aloud. "What am I gonna do without you?" She buried her face again in the quilt.

Clem had come out west with such wild excitement.

"We'll find everything we want there in thet new country. The land's there fer the takin'," he had exulted.

"What 'bout the wild animals—an' the Injuns?" she had stammered.

He had laughed at her silliness, picked her up in his strong arms, and whirled her around in the air.

"What 'bout a house? It'll be 'most winter when we git there," she worried.

"The neighbors will help us build one. I've heered all 'bout it. They'll help one another do whatever needs to be done out there."

And it was true. Those hardy frontiersmen scattered across the wilderness would leave their highly valued crops standing in the fields, if need be, while they gave of their time to put a roof over a needy if somewhat cocky and reckless newcomer, because they would know far better than he the fierceness of the winter winds.

"We'll make out jest fine. Don't ya worry yourself none, Marty," Clem had assured her. With some reluctance, Marty had begun preparations for the long trek by wagon train to follow her beloved husband's dream.

After many weeks of travel, they had come upon a farmhouse in an area of rolling hills and pastureland, and Clem had made inquiries. Over a friendly cup of coffee, the farmer had informed them that he owned the land down to the creek, but the land beyond that, reaching up into the hills, had not yet been claimed. With an effort, Clem had restrained himself from whooping on the spot. Marty could tell that the very thought of being so near his dream filled Clem with wild anticipation. Thanking their soon-to-be neighbor, they hurried on, traveling a bit too fast for the much-mended wagon. They were within sight of their destination when another wheel gave way, and this time it was beyond repair.

They had camped for the night, still on the neighbor's land, and Clem had piled rocks and timbers under the broken wagon in an effort to make it somewhat level. In the morning they had discovered more bad luck. One of the horses had deserted them during the night, and his broken rope still dangled from the tree. Clem had ridden out on the remaining horse to look for it. And then the accident, and now he wouldn't be coming back. There would be no land claimed in his name, nor a house built that would stand proud and strong to shelter his wife and baby.

Marty sobbed again, but then she heard a noise outside the wagon and peeped timidly through the canvas. Neighbors were there—four men with grim faces, silently and soberly digging beneath the largest spruce tree. As she realized what their digging meant, a fresh torment tore at her soul. *Clem's grave.* It was really true. This horrible nightmare was

11

actually happening. Clem was gone. She was without him. He would be buried on borrowed land.

"Oh, Clem. What'll I do?"

She wept until she had no more tears. The digging continued. She could hear the scraping of the shovels, and each thrust seemed to stab deeper into her heart.

More sounds reached her, and she realized that other neighbors were arriving. She must take herself in hand. Clem would not want her hiding away inside the wagon.

She climbed from the quilt and tried to tidy her unruly hair. Quickly dressing in her dark blue cotton frock, which seemed to be the most suitable for the occasion, she snatched a towel and her comb and slipped out of the wagon and down to the spring to wash away her tears and straighten her tangled hair. This done, she squared her shoulders, lifted her chin, and went back to meet the somber little group gathered under the spruce.

There was a kindness, a caring, in all of them. She could feel it. It was not pity, but an understanding. This was the West. Things were hard out here. Most likely every person there had faced a similar time, but one didn't go under. There was no time or energy for pity here—not for self, not for one another. It took your whole being to accept the reality that death was part of life, that the sorrow was inevitable, but that you picked up and carried on.

The visiting pastor spoke the words of interment, committing Clem's body to the dust of the earth, his soul into the hands of God. He also spoke to the sorrowing, who in this case was one lone, small person, the widow of the deceased; for one could hardly count the baby that she was carrying as one of the mourners, even if it was Clem's.

Pastor Magnuson spoke words that were fitting for the occasion—words of comfort and words of encouragement. The neighbors listened in silent sympathy to the familiar Scriptures they had heard on similar occasions. When the brief ceremony was over, Marty, her head bowed, turned from the grave toward the wagon, and the four men with the shovels went back to the task of covering the stout wooden box they had brought with them. As Marty walked away, a woman stepped forward and placed her hand on the slim shoulder.

"I'm Wanda Marshall," she said, her voice low. "I'm sorry we don't have any more than the one room, but you'd be welcome to share it for a few days until you sort things out."

"Much obliged." Marty spoke in almost a whisper. "But I wouldn't wanta impose upon ya. 'Sides, I think I'll jest stay on here fer a while. I need me time to think."

"I understand," the woman answered with a small pat, and she moved away.

Marty continued toward the wagon and was stopped again, this time by an older woman's gentle hand.

"This ain't an easy time fer ya, I know. I buried my first husband many years ago, and I know how you're feelin'." She paused a minute and then went on. "I don't s'pose you've had ya time to plan." At the slight shake of Marty's head, she continued, "I can't offer ya a place to stay; we're full up at our place. But I can offer ya somethin' to eat, and iffen you'd like to move yer wagon to our yard, we'd be happy to help ya pack yer things, and my Ben, Ben Graham, will be more'n glad to help ya git to town whenever yer ready to go."

"Thank ya," Marty murmured, "but I think I'll stay on here fer a while."

How could she explain that she had no money to stay, not even for one night, and no hope of getting any? What kind of work could a young, untrained woman in her condition hope to get? What kind of a future was there for her, anyway?

Her feet somehow moved her on to the wagon and she lifted a heavy hand to the canvas flap. She just wanted to crawl away, out of sight, and let the world cave in upon her.

It was hot in there at midday, and the rush of torrid air sent her already dizzy head to spinning. She crawled back out and down on the grass on the shady side of the wagon, propping herself up against the broken wheel. Her senses seemed to be playing tricks on her. Round and round in her head swept the whirlwind of grief, making her wonder what truly was real and what imagined. She was mentally groping to make some sense of it all when a male voice suddenly made her jump with its closeness.

"Ma'am."

She lifted her head and looked up. A man stood before her, cap in hand, fingering it determinedly as he cleared his throat. She vaguely recognized him as one of the shovel bearers. His height and build evidenced strength, and there was an oldness about his eyes that belied his youthful features. Her eyes looked into his face, but her lips refused to respond.

He seemed to draw courage from somewhere deep inside himself and spoke again.

"Ma'am, I know thet this be untimely—ya jest havin' buried yer husband an' all. But I'm afraid the matter can't wait none fer a proper-like time an' place."

He cleared his throat again and glanced up from the hat in his hands.

"My name be Clark Davis," he hurried on, "an' it 'pears to me thet you an' me be in need of one another."

A sharp intake of breath from Marty made him pause, then raise a hand.

"Now, hold a minute," he told her, almost a command. "It jest be a matter of common sense. Ya lost yer man an' are here alone." He cast a glance at the broken wagon wheel, then crouched down to speak directly to her.

"I reckon ya got no money to go to yer folks, iffen ya have folks to go back to. An' even if thet could be, ain't no wagon train fer the East will go through here 'til next spring. Me, now, I got me a need, too."

He stopped there and his eyes dropped. It was a minute before he raised them and looked into her face. "I have a little 'un, not much more'n a mite—an' she be needin' a mama. Now, as I see it, if we marries, you an' me"—he looked away a moment, then faced her again—"we could solve both of those problems. I would've waited, but the preacher is only here fer today an' won't be back through agin 'til next April or May, so's it has to be today."

He must have recognized in her face the sheer horror Marty was feeling.

"I know. I know," he stammered. "It don't seem likely, but what else be there?"

What else indeed? raged through Marty's brain. *I'd die first, that's all. I'd rather die than marry you—or any man. Get out. Go away.*

But he didn't read any more of her rampaging thoughts and went on. "I've been strugglin' along, tryin' to be pa an' ma both fer Missie, an' not doin' much of a job of it, either, with tryin' to work the land an' all. I've got me a good piece of land an' a cabin thet's right comfortable like, even if it be small, an' I could offer ya all the things thet a woman be a needin' in exchange fer ya takin' on my Missie. I be sure thet ya could learn to love her. She be a right pert little thing." He paused. "But she do be needin' a woman's hand, my Missie. That's all I be askin' ya, ma'am. Jest to be Missie's mama. Nothin' more. You an' Missie can share the bedroom. I'll take me the lean-to. An' . . ." He hesitated a bit. "I'll promise ya this, too. When the next wagon train goes through headin' east to where ya can catch yerself a stagecoach, iffen ya ain't happy here, I'll see to yer fare back home—on one condition—thet ya take my Missie along with ya." He paused to swallow, then said, "It jest don't be fair to the little mite not to have a mama."

He rose suddenly. "I'll leave ya to be a thinkin' on it, ma'am. We don't have much time."

He turned and strode away. The sag of his shoulders told her how much the words had cost him. Still, she thought angrily, what kind of a man could propose marriage—even this kind of a marriage—to a woman who had just turned from her husband's grave? She felt despair well up within her. *I'd rather die,* she told herself. *I'd rather die.* But what of Clem's baby? She didn't want death for their little one, neither for her sake nor for Clem's. Frustration and anger and grief whirled through her. What a situation to be in. No one, nothing, out in this Godforsaken country. Family and friends were out of reach, and she was completely alone. She knew he was right. She needed him, and she hated him for it.

"I hate this country! I hate it! I hate him, the cold, miserable man! I hate him! I hate him!" But even as she stormed against him, she knew she had no way around it.

She wiped her tears and got up from the shady grass. She wouldn't wait for him to come back in his lordly fashion for her decision, she thought stubbornly, and she went into the wagon and began to pack the few things she called hers.

A Mama for Missie

They rode in silence in his wagon. The preacher was at the Grahams',
where he had gone for dinner. Missie was there, too, having been left
with the Graham family for the older girls to look after while her pa
was at the funeral. They'd have the preacher speak the words, pick up
Missie, and then go on to the homestead. Marty sat stiff and mute
beside him as the wagon jostled on. She struggled to lift a hand and
push breeze-tossed hair back from her hot face. He looked at her with
concern in his eyes.

"Won't be too long now. It's powerful hot in the sun. Ya be needin'
a bonnet to shade yer head."

She sat silent, looking straight ahead. What did he care about the
hot sun on her head? What did she care? Nothing worse could possibly
happen to her. She turned her face away so he couldn't see the tears
forming against her will. She wanted no sympathy from this stubborn
man beside her.

The horses trudged on. Her body ached from the bouncing of the
wagon over the track of ruts that had to make do as the road.

She was relieved to see the homestead of the Grahams appear at the
base of a cluster of small hills. They drove into the yard, and he leaped

lightly down and turned to help her. She was too numb to refuse, fearing that if she tried it on her own, she'd fall flat into the dust. He lifted her down easily and steadied her on her feet before he let her go. He flipped a rein around the hitching post and motioned her to precede him into the house.

She noticed nothing of her surroundings. In her befuddled state, her mind refused to record anything. She remembered only that the door was opened by a surprised Mrs. Graham, who looked from the one to the other. Marty was vaguely aware that others were there, apparently waiting for the call to the midday meal. In the corner she saw the preacher in conversation with a man, who, she supposed, was Ben. Children seemed to be all around. She didn't even try to ascertain how many. The man—Clark Davis, he'd said his name was—moved toward the two men in the corner while he talked to Mrs. Graham.

Including the preacher and Ben in his explanation, he was saying, "We've decided—"

We! she stormed within herself. *Ya mean you.*

". . . to marry up while the preacher be still here to do the honors. It will mean a home fer Mrs. Claridge here an' a mama fer my Missie."

She heard Mrs. Graham's "It's the only sensible thing to be a doin'" and the preacher's "Yes, yes, of course."

There was a general stir about her as a spot was cleared, and in what seemed almost an immorally brief span of time she was hearing the familiar words. She must have uttered her own responses at the proper times, for the preacher's words came through the haze, ". . . now pronounce you man and wife."

There was a stirring about her again. Mrs. Graham was setting extra places at the table and encouraging them to "set up an' eat with us afore ya go on." And then they were at the table. The children must have been fed by the older girls before the grown-ups arrived home from the funeral. The preacher blessed the food, and general talk continued on around her. She probably ate something, though she later could not remember what it was or anything else about the meal. She felt like a puppet, moving, even speaking automatically—being controlled by something quite outside of herself.

They were moving again. Getting up from the table, making preparations to be on their way. The preacher tucked away a lunch that had been prepared for him and said his farewells. One of the older Graham boys led the man's horse up from the barn. Before the preacher left the house, he turned to Marty and in a simple, straightforward manner took her hands in his and wished God to be very near her in the coming months. Marty could only stare dumbly into his face. Ben and Clark followed him to his waiting horse, and Mrs. Graham said her good-bye from the open door. Then he was gone. Mrs. Graham turned back into the room, and the men went toward the hitching rail and Clark's team.

"Sally Anne, ya go an' git young Missie up from her nap an' ready to go. Laura, you an' Nellie clear up the table an' do up these dishes."

Mrs. Graham bustled about, but Marty was aware only of the movement about her as she sat limp and uncaring.

Sally returned, carrying a slightly rumpled little figure, who, in spite of her sleepiness, managed a happy smile. Marty noticed only the smile and the deep blue eyes that looked at her, being a stranger to the little one. *This must be Missie,* she thought woodenly. This was verified when Clark stepped through the door and the girl welcomed him with a glad cry and outstretched arms. He swept her up against his chest and for a moment placed a cheek against hers. Then, thanking his host and hostess, he turned to let Marty know that they'd be on their way.

Mrs. Graham walked out with her. There were no congratulations or well-wishing on the new marriage. No one had made an attempt to make an occasion of it, and Marty breathed a sigh of relief for that. One misplaced word, no matter how sincerely spoken, would have broken her reserve and caused the tears to flow, she was sure. But none had been spoken. Indeed, the marriage was not even mentioned. These pioneer people were sensitive to the feelings of others.

They said good-bye only as one neighbor to another, though Mrs. Graham's eyes held a special softness as she looked up at Marty on the wagon seat and said simply, "I'll 'llow ya a few days to be settlin' in an' then I'll be over. It'll be right nice to have another woman so close to hand to visit now an' then."

Marty thanked her and the team moved forward. They were again at the mercy of the dusty road and the hot sun.

⟳

"There it be—right over there." Marty almost jumped at Clark Davis's words, but she lifted her eyes to follow his pointing finger.

Sheltered by trees on the north and a small rise on the west was the homestead that belonged to this man beside her.

A small but tidy cabin stood apart, with a well out front and a garden spot to one side. A few small bushes grew along the path to the door, and even from the distance Marty could see colors of fall blooms among their stems.

Off to one side was a sturdy log barn for the horses and cattle, and a pig lot stood farther back among a grove of trees. There was a chicken house between the barn and the house and various other small buildings scattered here and there. She supposed she must learn all about each of them, but right now she was too spent to care.

"It's nice," she murmured, surprising herself, for she hadn't intended to say any such thing. Somehow, in her mind, it looked so much like the dreams that she and Clem had shared, and the knowledge hurt her and made her catch her breath in a quiet little sob. She said nothing more and was relieved when Missie, seeing that they were home, took all of her pa's attention in her excitement.

When they pulled up at the front of the cabin, a dog came running out to meet them and was greeted affectionately by both Clark and Missie.

Clark helped Marty down and spoke gently. "Ya best git ya in out of the sun and lay yerself down a spell. Ya'll find the bedroom off'n the sittin' room. I'll take charge of Missie an' anythin' else thet be needin' carin' fer. It's too late to field work today anyway."

He opened the door and held it while she passed into this strange little house that was to be her home, and then he was gone, taking Missie with him.

She didn't take time to look around her. Feeling that she must lie down or else collapse, she made her way through the kitchen and found the door off the sitting room that led to the bedroom. The bed looked inviting, and she stopped only long enough to slip her feet from her shoes before falling upon it. It was cooler in the house, and her weary body began to demand first consideration over her confused mind. Sobs overtook her, but gradually her churning emotions subsided enough to allow her to sink into deep but troubled sleep.

THREE

Marriage of Convenience

Marty awoke and stared toward the window, surprised to see it was already dusk. Vaguely aware of someone stirring about in the kitchen, the smell of coffee and bacon made her acknowledge she was hungry. She heard Missie's chatter, and the realization of why she was here swept over her again. Without caring about anything, she arose, slipped on her shoes, and pushed her hair back from her face. She supposed she looked a mess, but what did it matter? She was surprised in the dim light to see her trunk sitting against the wall by a chest of drawers. Everything she owned was in there, but that thought failed to stir her.

She opened the trunk, took out her brush, and stroked it over her hair. Then she rummaged for a ribbon and tied her hair back from her face. She had made some improvement, she hoped. She smoothed her wrinkled dress and moved toward the bedroom door and the smell of the coffee. Clark looked at her inquiringly as she entered the room, then motioned her to a chair at the table.

"I'm not much of a cook," he said, "but it be fillin'."

Marty sat down and Clark came from the stove with a plate of pancakes and another with a side of bacon. He set it down and went back for the steaming coffee. She felt a sense of embarrassment as she realized he was taking up what she should have been doing. Well, it would be the last time. From now on she'd carry her load. Clark sat down, and just as Marty was about to help herself to a pancake, she was stopped by his voice.

"Father, thank ya fer this food ya provide by yer goodness. Be with this, yer child, as Comforter in this hour, an' bless this house an' make it a home to each one as dwells here. Amen."

Marty sat wide-eyed looking at this man before her, who spoke, eyes closed, to a God she did not see or know—and him not even a preacher. Of course she had heard of people like that, various ones who had a God outside of church, who had a religion apart from marryin' an' buryin', but she had never rubbed elbows, so to speak, with one before. Nor did she wish to now, if she stopped to think about it. So he had a God. What good did it do him? He'd still needed someone to help with his Missie, hadn't he? His God didn't seem to do much about that. Oh well, what did she care? If she remembered right, people who had a God didn't seem to hold with drinkin' an' beatin' their women. With a little luck she maybe wouldn't have to put up with anything like that. A new wave of despair suddenly overwhelmed her. She knew nothing about this man. Maybe she should be glad that at least he was religious. It might save her a heap of trouble.

"Ain't ya hungry?"

His words made her jump, and she realized she had been sitting there letting her thoughts wander.

"Oh yeah, yeah," she stammered and helped herself to the pancake he was holding out to her.

Little Missie ate with a hearty appetite, surprising in one so tiny, and chattered to her father at the same time. Marty thought she picked out a word or two here and there, but she really couldn't put her mind to understanding what the child was saying.

After the meal she heard herself volunteering to wash up the dishes, and Clark said fine, he'd see to putting Missie to bed, then. He showed Marty where things were and then, picking up Missie, he began washing and readying her for bed.

Marty set to work on the dishes. As she opened doors and drawers of another woman's cupboards, a further sense of uneasiness settled on her. She must force herself to get over this feeling, she knew, for she had to manage in this as if it belonged to her. She couldn't restrain the slight shudder that ran through her, though.

As she returned from emptying her dishwater on the rosebush outside the door, Clark was pulling a chair up to the kitchen table.

"She be asleep already," he said quietly.

Marty placed the dishpan on its peg and hung the towel on the rack to dry. *What now?* she wondered in panic, but he took care of that for her.

"The drawers in the chest all be empty. I moved my things to the lean-to. Ya can unpack an' make yerself more comfortable like. Feel free to be a usin' anythin' in the house, an' if there be anythin' thet ya be needin', make a list. I go to town most Saturdays fer supplies, an' I can be a pickin' it up then. When ya feel more yerself like, ya might want to come along an' do yer own choosin'." He paused a moment, then looked into her face.

"I think thet ya better git ya some sleep," he said, his voice low. "It's been a tryin' day. I know thet it's gonna take ya some time before it stops hurtin' so bad—fer ya to feel at home here. We'll try not to rush ya."

Then his gaze demanded that she listen and understand. "I married ya only to have Missie a mama. I'd be much obliged if ya 'llow her to so call ya."

It was an instruction to her; she could feel it as such. But her eyes held his steadily, and though she said nothing, her pride challenged him. All right, she knew her place. He offered her an abode and victuals; she in turn was to care for his child. She'd not ask for charity. She'd earn her way. Missie's mama she would be. She turned without a word and made her way to the bedroom. She closed the door behind her and stood for a few moments leaning against it. When she felt more composed, she crossed quietly to look down on the sleeping child. The lamp gave a soft glow, making the wee figure in the crib appear even smaller.

"All right, Missie," Marty whispered, "let's us make ourselves a deal. Ya be a good kid, an' I'll do my best to be a carin' fer ya."

The child looked so tiny and helpless there, and Marty realized that here was someone barely more than an infant whom life had already hurt. What deserving thing had this little one done to have the mother she loved taken from her? Marty's own baby stirred slightly within her, and she placed a hand on the spot that was slowly swelling for the world to know that she was to be a mother. *What if it were my little one, left without my care?* The thought made near terror take hold of her. Again she looked at the sleeping child, the brown curls framing her pixie face, and something stirred within Marty's heart. It wasn't love that she felt, but it was a small step in that direction.

Marty was up the next morning as soon as she heard the soft click of the outside door. Clark must have come into the kitchen before going to the barn. Quietly she dressed so as not to disturb Missie and left the room, determined to uphold her part of the "convenience" marriage which was now her lot. So she had a roof over her head. She'd earn it. She would be beholden to no man, particularly this distant, aloof individual whose name she now shared. She refused, even in her thoughts, to recognize him as her husband. And speaking of names, she cautioned herself, it wasn't going to be easy to remember that she was no longer Martha Claridge but Martha Davis. Listlessly she wondered if there was a legal difficulty if she stubbornly clung to her "real" name. Surely she could be Martha Lucinda Claridge Davis without breaking any laws. Then with a shock she realized her baby would have the Davis name, too.

"Oh no!" She stopped and put her hands to her face. "Oh no, please. I want my baby to have Clem's name," she whispered her horror.

But even as she fought it and the hot tears squeezed out between her fingers, she knew she'd be the loser here, as well. She was in fact married to this man, no matter how unwelcome the idea; and the baby who would be born after the marriage would be his in name, even though Clem was the true father. She felt a new reason to loathe him.

"Well, anyway, I can name my baby Claridge iffen I want to," she declared hotly. "He can't take thet from me."

She brushed her tears on her sleeve, set her chin stubbornly, and moved into the kitchen.

The fire was already going in the big black cook stove. That must have been what he came in for, and Marty was glad she wouldn't have to struggle with that on top of her almost insurmountable task of just carrying on. She opened the cupboard doors and searched through tightly sealed cans until she found the coffee. She knew where the coffeepot was, she thought thankfully. Hadn't she washed it and put it away herself? There was fresh water in the bucket on a low table near the door, and she had the coffee on in very short order.

"Well, thet's the first step," she murmured to herself. "Now what?"

She rummaged around some more and came up with sufficient ingredients to make a batch of pancakes. At least that she could do. She and Clem had almost lived on pancakes, the reason being that there had been little else available for her to prepare. She wasn't going to find it an easy task to get proper meals, she realized. Her cooking experience had been very limited. Well, she'd learn. She was capable of learning, wasn't she? First she'd have to discover where things were kept in this dad-blame kitchen. Marty rarely used words that could be classed as profane, though she had heard plenty in her young lifetime. She sure felt like turning loose a torrent of them now, though. Instead she chose one of her father's less offensive expressions—about the only one she'd ever been allowed to use.

"Dad-blame!" she exploded again. "What's a body to do?"

Clark would expect more than just pancakes and coffee, she was sure, but what and from where was she to get it?

There seemed to be no end of tins and containers in the cupboards, but they were all filled with other basic ingredients, not anything that could work for breakfast.

Chickens! She'd seen chickens, and where there were chickens there should be eggs. She started out in search of some, through the kitchen door, through the shed that was the entry attached to the kitchen. Then her eye caught sight of a strange contraption at the side of the shed. It looked like some kind of pulley arrangement, and following the rope down to the floor, she noticed a square cut in the floorboards, and one end had a handle attached. Cautiously she approached, wondering if she might be trespassing where she did not belong. Slowly she lifted the trapdoor by the handle. At first she could see nothing; then, as her eyes became more accustomed to the darkness, she picked out what appeared to be the top of a large wooden box. That must be what the pulley and rope were for. She reached for it and began to pull on the ropes, noticing that the box appeared to be moving upward. It took more strength than she had guessed it would, yet she found she could handle it quite nicely.

Slowly the box came into view. She could feel the coolness that accompanied it. At last the box was fully exposed, and she slipped the loop of rope over a hook that seemed to be for that purpose. The front of the box was fitted with a door, mostly comprised of mesh, and inside she could see several items of food. She opened the door and gasped at the abundance of good things. There were eggs in a basket; crocks of fresh cream, milk, and butter; side bacon and ham. On the next shelf were some fresh vegetables and little jars containing preserves and, of all things, she decided after a quick sniff, fresh honey. Likely wild. What a find! She'd have no problem with breakfast now. She took out the side bacon and a few eggs. Then she chose some of the jam and was about to lower the box again when she remembered Missie. The child should have milk to drink as long as it was plentiful, and maybe Clark liked cream for his coffee. She didn't know. In fact, she didn't know much at all about the man.

Carefully she lowered the box again and replaced the trapdoor. Gathering up her finds, she returned to the kitchen feeling much better about the prospect of putting breakfast on the table.

The coffee was already boiling, and its fragrance reminded her how hungry she was. She took the dishes from the cupboard and set the table. She'd want the food hot when Clark came in from chores, and she didn't know how long they took him in the mornings.

FOUR

Morning Encounter

Marty had just turned back to mixing her pancakes when she heard Missie stirring. Best get her up and dressed first, she decided, and she left her ingredients and bowl on the table. As she appeared at the bedroom door, Missie's bright smile above the crib railing faded away, and she looked at Marty with surprise, if not alarm.

"Mornin', Missie," Marty said and lifted the child from the crib to place her on the bed.

"Now, I wonder where yer clothes be?" she asked the child, not really expecting an answer.

They were not in the large chest of drawers, for Marty had already opened each drawer when she unpacked her own things the night before. She looked around the room and spotted a small chest beneath the room's one window. It was Missie's, all right, and Marty selected garments she felt were suitable for that day. Missie did have some sweet little dresses. Her mama must have been a handy seamstress.

Marty returned to the tiny one who, wide-eyed, was watching every move. Marty laid the clothes on the bed and reached for Missie, but as the child realized this stranger was about to dress her, she made a wild grab for her shoes and began screaming.

Marty was sure her shrieks would pale a ghost.

"Now, Missie, stop thet," she scolded, but by now the little girl was howling in either rage or fright, Marty knew not which.

"I wan' Pa," she sobbed.

Marty conceded defeat.

"Hush now, hush," she said, picking up the child. Gathering the clothes against the squirming little body, she carried her to the kitchen, where she placed girl and belongings in a corner. Missie possessively pulled her clothes to her, still sobbing loudly. Marty turned back to the pancakes just as the coffee sputtered and boiled over. She made a frantic grab for the pot, pushing it farther to the back of the stove. She'd put in too much wood, she now realized. The stove was practically glowing with the heat. She looked around for something to clean up the mess, and finding nothing suitable, she went to the bedroom, where she pulled a well-worn garment from her drawer. The thing was not much more than a rag anyway, she decided, and back she went to the kitchen to mop up. Missie howled on. It was to this scene that Clark returned. He looked from the distraught Marty, who had by now added a burned finger to the rest of her frustrations, to the screaming Missie in the corner, still clinging furiously to her clothes.

Marty turned from the stove. She had done the best she could for now. She tossed the soggy, stained garment into the corner and gestured toward Missie.

"She wouldn't let me dress her," she told him, trying to keep her voice even. "She jest set up a howlin' fer her pa."

Marty wasn't sure how she expected Clark to respond, but certainly not as he did.

"I'm a-feared a child's memory is pretty short," he said, so calmly that Marty blinked. "She already be fergettin' what it's like to have a mama."

He moved toward the cupboard, not even glancing Missie's way, Marty noted, lest it encourage her to a fresh burst of tears.

"She'll jest have to learn thet ya be her mama now an' thet ya be in charge. Ya can take her on back to the bedroom an' git her dressed an' I'll take over here." He motioned around the somewhat messy kitchen and the partially prepared breakfast. Then he opened a window to let some of the heat from the roaring stove escape, and he did not look at either Marty or Missie again.

Marty took a deep breath and stooped to scoop up Missie, who reacted immediately with screams like a wounded thing, kicking and lashing out as she was carried away.

"Now, look you," Marty said through clenched teeth, "remember our bargain? I said iffen ya be good, I'd be yer mama, an' this ain't bein' good." But Missie wasn't listening.

Marty deposited her on the bed and was shocked to hear Missie clearly and firmly state between hiccuping sobs, "I . . . wan' . . . Mama."

So she does remember. Marty's cold anger began to slowly melt. Maybe Missie felt the way Marty did about Clark—angry and frustrated. She didn't really blame the little one for crying and kicking. She would be tempted to try it herself had not life already taught her how senseless and futile it would be.

Oh, Missie, she thought, *I knows how ya be feelin'. We'll have to become friends slow like, but first*—she winced—*first, I somehow have ta git ya dressed.*

She arranged the clothes in the order she would need them. There would be no hands to sort them out as she struggled with Missie, she knew. Then she sat down and took the fighting child on her knee. Missie was still throwing a fit. No, now it wasn't fear. Marty could sense that it was sheer anger on the child's part.

"Now, Missie, ya stop it."

Marty's voice was drowned out by the child's, and then Marty's hand smacked hard, twice, on the squirming bottom. Perhaps it was just the shock of it, or perhaps the child was aware enough to realize that she had been mastered. At any rate, her eyes looked wide with wonder and the screaming and squirming stopped. Missie still sobbed in noisy, gulping breaths, but she did not resist again as Marty dressed her.

When the battle was over, the child was dressed, and Marty felt exhausted and disheveled. The two eyed each other cautiously.

"Ya poor mite," Marty whispered and pulled the child close. To her surprise, Missie did not resist but cuddled in Marty's arms, allowing herself to be held and loved as they rocked gently back and forth. How long they sat thus Marty did not know, but gradually she realized the child was no longer sobbing. Detecting the smell of frying bacon coming from the kitchen, she roused herself and used her comb, first on her own unruly hair and then on the child's brown curls. She picked up Missie and returned to the kitchen, dipping a cloth in cool water to wash away the child's tears and also to cool her own face. Clark did not look up. *There he is, doing again what I should be doing,* Marty thought dejectedly as she sat Missie at the table. The pancakes were ready, the eggs fried, the bacon sizzling as he lifted it from the pan. The coffee steamed in their cups, and a small mug of milk sat in front of Missie. There was nothing left to do but to sit down herself. He brought the bacon and sat across from her.

She wouldn't be caught this time. She remembered that he prayed before he ate, so she bowed her head and sat quietly waiting. Nothing happened. Then she heard faint stirrings—like the sound of pages being turned. She stole a quick glance and saw Clark, Bible in hand, turning the pages to find the place he wanted. She could feel the color rising slowly to her cheeks, but Clark did not look up.

"Today we'll read Psalm 121," he said and began the reading.

"'I will lift up mine eyes unto the hills, from whence cometh my help.'"

Marty solemnly wished her help would come from the hills. In fact, she'd take it from any direction. She brought her mind back to catch up to Clark's reading.

"'The Lord is thy keeper: the Lord is thy shade upon thy right hand. The sun shall not smite thee by day, nor the moon by night. The Lord shall preserve thee from all evil: he shall preserve thy soul. The Lord shall preserve thy going out and thy coming in from this time forth, and even for evermore.'"

Gently he laid the book aside on a small shelf close to the table, and then as he bowed his head and prayed, Marty was again caught off guard.

Dad-burn him, she fumed, but then her attention was taken by his words.

"Our God, fer this fine day an' yer blessin's, we thank ya."

Blessin's, thought Marty. *Like a howlin' kid, spilled coffee, an' a burned finger? Blessin's like that I can do without.*

But Clark went on. "Thank ya, Lord, thet the first hard mile with Missie be traveled, an' help this one who has come to be her new mama."

He never calls me by my name when he's talkin' to his God, thought Marty, *always "this one." If his God is able to answer his prayers, I sure hope He knows who he's talkin' 'bout. I need all the help thet I can git.*

Marty heard the rattle of spoon against a bowl and realized her mind had been wandering and she'd missed the rest of the prayer, including the "amen," and still she sat, head bowed. She flushed again and lifted her head, but Clark was fixing Missie's pancake, so her embarrassment went unobserved.

At first breakfast was a quiet meal. Little Missie was probably too spent from her morning struggles to be chatty, and Clark seemed pre-occupied. Marty, too, sat with her own thoughts, and most were not very pleasant ones.

What after breakfast? she wondered testily.

First she'd have to do up the dishes, then properly clean the messy stove. Then what? She'd jump at a chance to wash up the few pitiful things that comprised her wardrobe. She'd also like to wash the quilts she had and pack them away in her trunk. She'd need them again when she joined the wagon train going east.

Her mind flitted about, making plans as to how she might repair the few dresses she possessed if she could just find a little bit of cloth some-place. Clark said he went to town on Saturdays. This was Wednesday. She'd have to take stock of the cupboards and have a list ready for him. She stole a glance at him and then quickly looked back at her plate. He certainly did not look like a happy man, she told herself. Brooding almost, one could call it. At any rate, deep thinking, as though trying to sort through something.

Then Missie cut in with a contented sigh and a hearty, "All done, Pa." She pushed her plate forward. The face was transformed.

"Thet's Pa's big girl." He smiled lovingly, and the two shared some chattering that Marty made no effort to follow. Clark rose presently and refilled his coffee cup, offering her more, too. Marty scolded herself for not noticing the empty cup first.

Clark pushed back his plate and took a sip of the hot coffee. Then he looked steadily across at her. She met his gaze, though she found it difficult to do so.

"S'pose ya be at a loss, not knowin' where to find things an' all. I see ya found the cold pit. Good! There be also a root cellar out back. Most of the garden vegetables are already there. Only a few things still be out in the garden. A shelf with cannin's there, too, but ya need a light along to do yer choosin', since it be dark in there. There's also a smokehouse out by the root cellar. Not too much in it right now. We plan on doin' our fall killin' and curin' next week. Two of the neighbors and me works together. There be chickens—fer eggs an' fer eatin'. We try not to get the flock down too low, but there's plenty to spare right now. There won't be fresh meat until it turns colder, 'ceptin' fer a bit of the pork. When the cold weather comes we try an' get some wild game—it keeps then. Sometimes we kill us a steer if we think we be needin' it. There be fish in the crik, too. When the work is caught up I sometimes try my hand at a bit of loafin' an' fishin'. We're not bad off, really."

It was not a boast, simply a statement.

"We have us real good land and the Lord be blessin' it. We've had good crops fer the last four seasons. The herd has built up, too, and the hogs an' chickens are plentiful enough. All the garden truck thet we can use can be growin' right outside the house, an' there's lots of grain in the bins fer seedin'. We has some cash—not much, but enough, an' iffen we do be needin' more, we can always sell us a hog.

"We're better off than a lot of folks, but the neighbors round about here are makin' good, too. Seems as how our move to the West's been a good one. Got me some cuttin's a few years back from a man over acros't the crik. An' in a couple of years, if all goes well, we should have some fruit on 'em. The apples might even be a settin' next year, he tells me. I'm a tellin' ya this so's ya be knowin' the lay o' the land, so to speak. Ya don't need to apologize fer askin' fer what ya be needin', both fer yerself an' fer Missie. We've never been fancy, but we try an' be proper like."

He pushed back from the table after his long speech and stood silently for a moment, as if sorting out in his thinking if there was anything else he should tell her.

"We've got a couple o' good milk cows at present an' another due with an off-season calf, so we have all the milk an' butter we be needin'. There's a good team of horses an' a ridin' horse, too, iffen ever ya want to pay a visit to a neighbor's. Ma Graham be the closest, an' she's 'bout as good company as anybody be a wantin'. I think ya'll find her to yer likin', even if she be some older than you.

"Most of my field work is done fer the fall, but I do have me a little breakin' I aim to do yet, iffen winter holds off awhile. First, though, I plan to spend a few days helpin' one o' the neighbors who ain't through yet. He got 'im a slow start. Plan to go over there today—Jedd Larson—an' give 'im a hand. I'll be asked to stay to dinner with 'em so won't be home 'til chore time. Ya can make yerself to home, an' you an' Missie git to know one another like, an' maybe we won't have any more of those early mornin' fusses."

He turned to Missie then and swung her up easily into his arms. "Ya wanna come with Pa to git ole Dan an' Charlie?"

She assented loudly and the two set off for the barn.

Marty stirred herself. *"No more early mornin' fusses."* Looked like this short statement would be his only reference to the incident. He hadn't seemed to pay much heed at the time, but, she reflected, maybe it had bothered him more than he let on.

She began to clear the table. Clark had told her so much that it seemed difficult to sort it all out at one time. She'd shelve it for now and draw on it later as she had need. She began to make plans for her day.

She'd scout around and find a tub to heat water and then wash clothes and quilts as she had hoped she could. Maybe she'd be able to find a needle and thread and do the much-needed repair work, as well.

By the time she had started on the dishes, Clark was back to deposit Missie with her. He had to work to detach her clinging arms. Missie had by now become used to going everywhere with her pa, and it wasn't going to be easy for the first while to make her understand that things would be different now.

"Pa's got to go now, and yer gonna stay with yer mama. I'll be back later," he explained carefully to her over her sobs. After Clark had left and Missie had finally ceased her crying, Marty put away the last of the dishes and set to work cleaning the stove. That done, she swept up the floor and felt ready to turn to her other plans for the day.

She had never had much practice at keeping a real house, but she was determined she would do a good job of it. Clark was never going to be embarrassed about the home that he lived in as long as she was earning her keep as Missie's mama. As soon as she had her own things in order, she'd turn her attention to the house, which had been a bachelor's quarters for too long. Even though Clark had been better than most in keeping things up, still it wasn't as a woman would have it. Just give her a few days. She'd have things looking homey.

FIVE

Iffen I Can Jest Stick It Out . . .

By late afternoon Marty had finished washing everything that belonged to her and some of Clark's and Missie's clothes, as well. The day was much cooler than the previous one, she noted with relief. She didn't think she could have tolerated another one like that. This felt more like mid-October, a glorious Indian summer day.

Standing at the clothesline, Marty gazed out toward the west. Far beyond the rolling hills, blue mountains rose in majesty. Was it from those peaks that Clark was seeking the help of his God?

The trees along the hillside were garbed in yellows and reds. Indeed, many of the leaves were already on the ground or being carried southward by a gusty breeze.

It was a beautiful scene, and how happy she would have been to share it with Clem. *If only Clem and I could have had this together.* Her heart ached even more than her tired back as she emptied the water from the washtubs.

Missie was having a nap. Marty was glad to be free of the child for a while—almost as glad as she was that Clark was away for the day. How relieved she had felt at his announcement that morning. Maybe with luck the neighbor's work would keep him away for several days.

She hardly dared hope for so much. She had planned to look around the farm today to learn where things were, but she felt far too tired just now. She'd just sneak a few minutes of rest while Missie was still sleeping and then take her scouting trip a little later.

She threw out the last of the rinse water, replaced the tubs on the pegs at the side of the house, and extremely weary, went in to stretch out on her bed. She cried a bit before drowsiness claimed her, but the sleep that followed was the most restful she'd had since Clem had died.

Marty awoke with a start—not sure what had roused her but already sensing that something was amiss. Maybe Missie had cried. She propped herself on one elbow and looked at the crib. No, it wasn't that. Missie wasn't even there. *Missie isn't there? But she must be.*

Marty scrambled up, her heart pounding. Where was Missie? Maybe Clark had come home and taken the child out with him.

"Don't panic," she whispered fiercely. "She's got to be somewhere nearby."

Marty checked the little cabin quickly, then the corral, but the team was not back. She looked all around the buildings, calling as she went. No Missie. *She must have climbed right over the crib railing,* she said to herself between shouts for the little girl. *I must have been awfully sound asleep.* Marty ranged farther and farther from the buildings, but still no Missie. She was getting frantic now in spite of her efforts to keep herself under control. Where could Missie be? What should she do?

By now tears were streaming down Marty's cheeks. Her dress had suffered another tear near the hem, and she had thorns in her hands from the wild rosebushes through which she had forced her way. She checked the creek—up and down its banks, searching the clear, shallow water, but no sign of Missie or of anything that belonged to her.

Maybe she followed the road, Marty thought frantically, and she set off at nearly a run down the dusty, rutted roadway. On and on she stumbled. *Surely Missie couldn't have gone this far,* Marty tried to reason, but she hurried on because she knew of nothing else to do. Then over the hill in the road ahead she saw Clark's team coming toward her.

She didn't even consider stopping by the side of the road and waiting for him to approach but plodded doggedly on toward the wagon.

Whatever could she say to Clark? How could she tell him? She could
not even be trusted to care for one small child. Would Clark have some
idea of where to search that she had not already tried?

Soon she had to step aside to allow the team to draw up beside her.
Heart constricting with remorse and fear, she turned her dirt- and tear-
streaked face up to Clark—and there sat Missie big as life on her pa's
knee, looking very proud of herself.

Clark whoaed the horses to a stop and reached down a hand to help
Marty into the wagon. She climbed up reluctantly, her head spinning.
Oh, what must he think? They traveled toward home in silence. Why
didn't he say something? He'd not spoken, other than a giddup to the
team. Missie was quiet, too. Well, she'd better be, the little rascal. If she
said one word, Marty knew she'd feel like smacking her. Her great relief
at seeing the child safe and sound was now replaced with feelings of
anger. Marty's face felt hot, both from the efforts of her frantic search
and her deep humiliation. Then her chin went up. So he wasn't talking.
Well—neither was she. He could think what he would; she wasn't doing
any explaining. She hated him anyway, and she didn't think much more
of his undisciplined child.

*Iffen I can jest stick it out fer thet wagon train, then I'll be leavin' this
wretched place so fast ya won't even find my tracks*, she railed silently.

The woman in her wanted desperately to resort to tears, but the
woman in her also refused to give in to even that small comfort.

Don't ya dare, she warned herself, *don't ya dare allow him thet
satisfaction.*

She held her head high, eyes straight ahead, and remained that way
until they reached the house. She disdained any help Clark might have
offered and quickly climbed down over the wheel, managing to tear
her dress even further.

He placed Missie on the ground, and Marty scooped the child up
rather brusquely and went into the house. Missie seemed unaffected
by it all and paid no attention as her new mama noisily went about
starting another fire in the kitchen stove.

Another meal to prepare—but what? It caused her additional embarrassment, but Marty knew it would have to be pancakes again. That was about the only thing she really knew how to make. Well, let him choke on them. She didn't care. Why should she? She owed him nothing. She wished she had stayed in her wagon and starved to death. That's what she wished.

Amazingly enough, Marty's fire took, and the fine cook stove was soon spilling out heat. Marty didn't even think to be grateful as she stormed about the kitchen, making coffee and preparing the second batch of pancake batter for the day. She'd fry a few pieces of ham rather than bacon, she swiftly decided.

She really couldn't understand why it bothered her so much that all her efforts since coming to this house had met with such complete failure. She shouldn't care at all, and yet she did—much as she didn't want to acknowledge it. Marty felt deeply that failure was a foe to be combated and defeated. It was the way she had grown up, and it was not easily forsaken now.

While the griddle was heating, she cast an angry look at Missie.

"Now, you stay put," she warned, then hurried out to bring in all her washing before the night's dampness set in.

When Clark came in from the barn, supper, such as it was, was ready. If he was surprised at pancakes again, he did not show it. Marty's cheeks again burned to realize that his pancakes had been just as good as hers.

So what? she raged to herself. *My coffee be a sight better.*

It must have been, because when she again missed noticing Clark's empty cup and he got up to refill it, he remarked, "Good coffee," as he poured her a second cup. Marty turned her face away and simply shrugged.

After supper she cleared the table and washed Missie up for bed. She still felt like shaking the little tyke each time she touched her but refrained from doing so.

When Missie had been tucked in and Marty had washed her own hot, dusty feet, she excused herself with a murmur. Gathering her clothes she had brought in from the line, she took the items to her bedroom and shut the door. She carefully folded her worn but clean dresses and undergarments, laying them on her bed. If only she had a needle and some thread. But she wouldn't ask him, she determined. Never!

She sat down on the bed to allow herself time for some well-earned self-pity. It was then she noticed a small sewing basket in the corner behind the door. For a moment she couldn't believe her amazing find, but upon crossing to the basket, she discovered far more than she had dared to hope.

There were threads of various colors, needles of several sizes, a perfect pair of scissors, and even some small pieces of fabric.

Determinedly Marty settled down. Sewing—now, that was one thing she could do. Though mending hardly fit into the same category as sewing, she felt a surge of anticipation.

She was soon dismayed, though, as she tried to make something decent out of the worn things before her. The longer she worked the more discouraged she became. She had attacked the least-worn items first, but by the time she reached the last few articles, she was completely dejected. They'd never last the winter, and it was a sure thing she'd never ask him for anything. Even if she was forced to wear nothing but rags.

"We've never been fancy, but we try an' be proper," she remembered him saying.

"Well, Mr. Proper, what would ya do if ya had nothin' to make yerself proper with?" she demanded through gritted teeth as she pulled the tattered dress over her head and replaced it with a carefully mended nightdress.

Marty fell into bed, and the events of the day crowded through her mind—the too-hot stove and the coffee boiling over, the tantrum-throwing Missie, the frantic search for the child, more pancakes. A sob arose in her throat. *If only Clem were here . . .* and again she cried herself to sleep.

SIX

Housecleaning

The next morning presented a cloudy face as Marty looked toward the window. The weather was changing. It wouldn't be long until the beautiful Indian summer would give way to winter's fury. *But not yet,* she told herself, determined to be cheerful in spite of her wretched circumstances. The day was still warm and the sky not too overcast. Perhaps the clouds would soon move away and let the sun shine again.

Slowly she climbed from bed. Surely today must be an improvement on yesterday, she hoped. Already yesterday seemed a long way in the past—and the day before, the day she had buried Clem. Marty could hardly believe it was only two days ago. But two days that had seemed forever.

Marty slipped into the gingham she had mended the night before, cast a glance in Missie's direction, and quietly moved toward the door. She did hope that the morning scene of yesterday would not be repeated. She didn't know if she could face it again.

She put on the coffee and set the dishes on the table, then started preparations for the morning pancakes.

Dad-blame it. She bit her lip. *I'm tired of pancakes myself.*

It hadn't seemed so bad to have pancakes over and over when that was all that was available, but with so many good, fresh provisions at her disposal, it seemed a shame to be eating pancakes. She'd have to figure something out, but in the meantime they needed a meal to start the day. She went out for another piece of side bacon.

Missie awoke and without incident allowed Marty to dress her. So that battle seemed to have been won! She placed the tot in the home-made chair and pulled it back from the table to keep small fingers from getting into things.

When Clark came in from the barn, the breakfast was ready and Missie was sitting well behaved in her chair. Clothed and in her right mind, Clark's expression seemed to say, though he made no comment, to Marty's relief.

They sat down together at the table, and after the morning reading and prayer, breakfast proceeded with nothing out of the ordinary occurring.

Marty watched surreptitiously for Clark's coffee cup to need a refill, but when she jumped up for the pot he waved it aside.

"I'd like to but I'd better not take time for a second cup this mornin'. The sky looks more like winter every day, an' Jedd still has him some grain out. I'm gonna git on over there as quick as I can"—he hesitated—"but thet's right good coffee."

Marty poured her own second cup and put the pot back. The only thing he could say about her was that she made good coffee. Well, maybe she was lucky—and he was lucky—she could do that much!

Clark stopped at the door and said over his shoulder, "I'll be eatin' my noon meal with the Larsons agin." Then he was gone.

This time Missie's whimpering lasted only a few minutes. Marty's thoughts turned to his parting announcement. "Bet he's tickled pink to be able to have 'im one meal a day to the Larsons. Wouldn't it be a laugh should Mrs. Larson give 'im pancakes?"

In spite of herself Marty couldn't keep a smile from flitting across her face. Then she sat down to leisurely enjoy her second cup of coffee and plan her day.

First she would completely empty and scrub out the kitchen cup-boards, and then she'd go on to the rest of the kitchen, including the walls, window, and curtains. By night, she vowed, everything would be shining.

She didn't spend as long over her coffee as she had intended, for she became anxious to begin her activities and see everything fresh and clean.

She hurriedly washed up the dishes and found some things she hoped would keep Missie amused for a while. Then she set to work in earnest. She might lack in a lot of ways, she thought, but she could apply herself to work—and apply herself she did.

By the time the ticking clock on the mantel told her that it was twelve-thirty, the cupboards were all scrubbed and rearranged to suit her own fancy. She had discovered several items, too, like ground corn for muffins and grains for cooked cereals. Maybe breakfast wouldn't always have to be pancakes after all.

She stopped her cleaning to prepare a meal for herself and Missie. Fried ham and a slice of bread with milk to drink satisfied them both. She was glad that milk was plentiful. Along their way west, Clem had fretted that she should be drinking milk for the baby. Now there was milk in abundance, and Clem's boy would be strong when he arrived.

After Marty tucked Missie in for her nap, she set to work again. She felt tired, but under no circumstances would she lie down and give Missie a chance to repeat her performance of yesterday. That little mite must have walked over a mile before she met her pa. At the thought of it Marty felt again the fear and sting of humiliation. No sirree, there was no way she would let that happen again, even if she dropped dead on her feet.

On she worked, washing the curtains and placing them out in the breeze to dry. Then she tackled the window until it shone, and went on to the kitchen walls with more energy than she knew she possessed. It was hard, slow work, but she was pleased with her accomplishment. As she scrubbed away at the wooden log walls, she was amazed at the amount of water it took. A number of times she had to stop and refill her pan. Remembering the curtains, she stopped her scrubbing and went in search of anything resembling an iron so she could press the curtains before rehanging them. She found a set of sad irons in the shed's corner cupboard and placed them on the stove to heat. She then realized that in her preoccupation with her scrubbing, she had let the fire go out, so the task of rebuilding it was hers once more. She scolded herself as she fussed with the small flame to try to coax it into a blaze. When finally it began to sustain itself, she returned to her scrubbing. She refilled her pan many more times and had to take the buckets to the well for more water. Finally the task was finished. The logs shined, even if they had soaked up the water.

By the time she brought in the curtains, the irons were hot enough to press them. The renewed curtains looked fresh and crisp as she placed them at the window.

Missie wakened and Marty brought her from her bed and got a mug of milk for each of them. Missie seemed cheerful and chatty after her sleep, and Marty found her talkative little companion rather enjoyable. It kept her mind off other things—just as her hard work had been doing.

She placed Missie in her chair with a piece of bread to nibble on and set to work on the wooden floor with hot soapy water and scrub brush. By the time she was through, her arms and back ached, but the floor was wondrously clean. She gave the rug at the door a good shaking outside and replaced it again, then stood and surveyed the small kitchen. Everything looked and smelled clean. She was proud of herself. The kitchen window gleamed, the curtains fairly crackled with crispness, the walls—well, now, the walls looked sort of funny. Oh, the logs looked clean and shiny but the chinking—somehow the chinking looked strange, sort of gray and muddy instead of the white it had been before.

Marty crossed to the nearest wall and poked a finger at the chinking. It didn't just look muddy. It *was* muddy—muddy and funny. Marty wrinkled her nose. What had she done? The water, of course! It wasn't the logs that had drunk up the water; it was the chinking! It had slurped up the scrub water thirstily and was now gooey and limp. She hoped with all of her heart that it would dry quickly before Clark got home. She looked at the clock. It wouldn't be long, either. She'd better get cracking if supper was to be more than pancakes.

She had noticed that the bread was as good as gone. Then what would she do? She had never baked bread before, nor even watched her mother do it that she could remember. She hadn't the slightest idea how to start. Well, she'd make biscuits. She didn't know how to bake them, either, but surely it couldn't be too hard. She washed her hands and went to the cupboard. She felt that it was more "her" cupboard now that she had put everything where she wanted it.

She found the flour and salt. Did you put eggs in biscuits? She wasn't sure, but she'd add a couple just in case. She added milk and stirred the mixture. Would that do it? Well, she'd give it a try.

She sliced some potatoes for frying and got out some ham. She supposed that she should have a vegetable, too, so she went to work on some carrots. As she peeled them she heard Ole Bob welcome home the approaching team. Clark would care for the horses and then do the chores. He'd be in for supper in about forty minutes, she guessed, so she left the carrots and went to put the biscuits in the oven. They handled easily enough, and she pictured an appreciative look in Clark's eyes as he reached for another one.

She went back to her potatoes in the frying pan, stirring them carefully so they wouldn't burn.

"Oh, the coffee!" she suddenly cried and hurried to get the coffeepot on to boil. After all, she could make good coffee!

She sliced some ham and placed it in the other frying pan, savoring the aroma as it began to cook. She smelled the biscuits and could barely refrain from opening the oven door to peek at them. She was sure they'd need a few minutes more. She stirred the potatoes again and looked anxiously at the muddy chinking between the logs. It wasn't drying very fast. Well, she wouldn't mention it and maybe Clark wouldn't notice it. By morning it would be its old white self again.

The ham needed turning and the potatoes were done. She pulled them toward the back of the stove and put more wood in the firebox. Then she remembered the carrots. Oh dear, they were still in the peeling pan, only half ready. Hurriedly she went to work on them, nicking a finger in her haste. Finally she had the pot of carrots on the stove, on what she hoped was the hottest spot to hurry them up.

The potatoes were certainly done, rather mushy looking from being overcooked and overstirred, and now they sat near the back of the stove looking worse every minute. The biscuits! Marty grabbed fiercely at the oven door, fearing that the added minutes may have ruined her efforts, but the minutes had not ruined them at all. Nothing could have done any harm to those hard-looking lumps that sat stubbornly on the pan looking like so many rocks.

Marty pulled them out and dumped one on the cupboard to cool slightly before she made the grim test. She slowly closed her teeth upon it—to no avail; the biscuit refused to give. She clamped down harder; still no give.

"Dad-burn," murmured Marty, and opening the stove, she threw the offensive thing in. The flames around it hissed slightly, like a cat with its back up, but the hard lump refused to disappear. It just sat and blackened as the flame licked around it.

"Dad-blame thing. Won't even burn," she stormed and crammed a stick of wood on top of it to cover up the telltale lump.

"Now, what do I do with these?"

Marty looked around. How could she get rid of the lumpy things? She couldn't burn them. She couldn't throw them out to the dog to be exposed to all eyes. She'd bury them. The rotten things. She hurriedly scooped them into her apron and started for the door.

"Missie, ya stay put," she called. Then remembering her previous experience, she turned and pulled the coffeepot to the back of the stove.

Out the door she went, first looking toward the barn to make sure that her path was clear. Then she quickly ran to the far end of the garden. The soil was still soft, and she fell on her knees and hurriedly dug a hole with her hands and dumped in the disgusting lumps. She covered them quickly and sprinted back to the house. When she reached the yard, she could smell burning ham.

"Oh no!" she cried. "What a mess!"

She washed her hands quickly at the outside basin, and the tears washed her cheeks as she raced for the tiny kitchen, where everything seemed to be going wrong.

When Clark came in for supper, he was served lukewarm mushy potatoes and slightly burned slices of ham along with the few slices of bread that remained. There was no mention of the carrots, which had just begun to boil, and of course no mention of the sad lumps called biscuits. Clark said nothing as he ate. Nothing, that is, except, "That's right good coffee."

SEVEN

A Welcome Visitor

Friday dawned clear and bright again, though the air did not regain the warmth of the first part of the week. Marty lay in bed remembering their supper the night before. She had carefully avoided any comment on the muddy chinking, but one small chunk in the corner had suddenly given way. It lost its footing between the logs, falling to the floor and leaving a bit of a smear on the way down. Clark had looked up in surprise but then had gone on eating. Marty prayed, or would have prayed had she known how, that the rest of it would stay where it dad-burn belonged. It did, and she thankfully cleared the table and washed the dishes.

Lamplight was needed in the evenings, as the days were short. The men worked in the fields as late as they could before turning to chores, so it was full dark before supper was over. Marty was glad when darkness had fallen that night. The lamplight cast shadows, obscuring the grayish chinking. As she washed Missie up before bed, she thought she heard another small piece give way, but she refused to acknowledge it, raising her voice to talk to Missie and try to cover the dismaying sound.

That had been last night, and now as Marty tried to prepare herself to face another day, she wondered what new and dreadful things it held for her. One thing she had already confronted. The bread crock was empty, and she had no idea of how to go about restocking it. She supposed Clark knew how to bake bread, but she'd die before she'd ask him. And what about the chinking? Had the miserable stuff finally dried to white and become what it was supposed to be? She dreaded the thought of going to look, but lying there wasn't going to solve any problems.

She struggled up from her bed. Her muscles still ached from her strenuous efforts of the day before. She'd feel it for a few days, she was sure. Besides, she hadn't slept well. Her thoughts had again been on Clem and how much she missed him. Now she dressed without caring, ran a comb through her hair, and went to the kitchen.

The first thing she noticed was the chinking. Here and there all around the walls, small pieces lay crumbled on the floor. Marty felt like crying, but little good that would do. She'd have to face Clark with it, confess what she had done, and accept her well-deserved rebuke for it.

She stuffed a couple of sticks into the fire and put on the coffee. Suddenly she wondered just how many pots of coffee she would have to make in her future. At the moment those pots seemed to stretch into infinity.

She found a kettle and put on some water to boil. This morning they'd have porridge for breakfast. *But porridge and what?* she wondered crossly. What did you have with porridge if you had no biscuits, no muffins, no bread, "no nuthin'," Marty fretted out loud. Pulling the pot off the stove in disgust, she went to work again making pancakes.

Missie awakened and Marty went in to pick her up. The child smiled and Marty found herself returning it.

"Mornin', Missie. Come to Mama," she said, trying the words with effort to see how they'd sound. She didn't really like them, she decided, and wished she hadn't even used them.

Missie came gladly and chattered as she was being dressed. Marty could understand more of the baby words now. She was saying something about Pa, and the cows that went *moo,* and the chickens that went *cluck,* and pigs—Marty couldn't catch the funny sound that represented the pigs, but she smiled at the child as she carried her to her chair.

Clark came in to a now-familiar breakfast and greeted his daughter, who squealed a happy greeting in return.

After the reading of the Bible passage, they bowed their heads for Clark's prayer. He thanked his Father for the night's rest and the promise of "a fair day for the layin' in of the rest of Jedd's harvest."

Marty was surprised at the next part of the prayer.

"Father, be with the one who works so hard to be a proper mama for Missie an' a proper keeper of this home."

The prayer continued, but Marty missed it. Everything she had done thus far had been a failure. No wonder Clark felt it would take help from the Almighty himself to set things in order again. She didn't know if she should feel pleased or angry at such a prayer, so she forcefully shoved aside the whole thing just in time for the "amen."

"Amen," echoed Missie, and breakfast began.

At first they ate rather silently, only Clark and Missie exchanging some comments and Clark scolding Missie.

"Don't ya be a throwin' pancake on the floor. Thet's a naughty girl an' makes more work fer yer mama."

Marty caught a few other references to "yer mama," as well, and realized that Clark had been using the words often in the past two days. She knew he was making a conscious effort at educating the little girl to regard her as mama. She supposed she'd have to get used to it. After all, that's what she was here for—certainly not to amuse the serious-looking young man across the table from her.

Another piece of chinking clattered down, and Marty took a deep breath and burst forth with, "I'm afeared I made a dreadful mistake yesterday. I took to cleanin' the kitchen—"

"I'd seen me it was all fresh and clean lookin' an' smellin'," Clark said quickly.

Now, why'd he do that? she stormed inwardly. She took another gulp of air and went on, "But I didn't know what scrub water would be doin' to the chinkin'. I mean, I didn't know thet it would all soak up like an' then not dry right agin."

Clark said nothing.

She tried once more. "Well, it's fallin' apart like. I mean—well, look at it. It's crumblin' up an' fallin' out—"

"Yeah," said Clark with a short nod, not even lifting his eyes.

"Well, it's not stayin' in place," Marty floundered. "Whatever can we do?"

She was almost angry by now. His calmness unnerved her.

He looked up then and answered slowly. "Well, when I go to town on Saturday, I'll pick me up some more chinkin'. It's a special kind like. Made to look whiter an' cleaner, but no good at all fer holdin' out the weather—the outside chinkin' has to do thet job. There still be time to redo it 'fore winter sets in. Water don't hurt the outer layer none, so it's holdin' firm like. Don't ya worry yerself none 'bout it. I'm sure thet the bats won't be a flyin' through the cracks afore I git to 'em."

He almost smiled and she could have gleefully kicked him. He rose to go.

"I reckon ya been pushin' yerself pretty hard, though, an' it might be well if you'd not try to lick the whole place in a week like. There's more days ahead, an' ya be lookin' kinda tired." He hesitated. "Iffen ya should decide to do more cleanin', jest brush down the walls with a dry brush. All right?"

He kissed Missie good-bye after telling her to be a good girl for her mama and went out the door for what he said might be the last day of helping Jedd Larson with his crop. Marty supposed he'd be around the place more then. She dreaded the thought, but it was bound to come sooner or later.

She put water on to heat so she could wash up the rag rugs before winter set in and then found a soft brush to dust the sitting room walls.

It didn't take nearly as long to brush them as it had to scrub the kitchen, and it did take care of the cobwebs and dust. She was surprised to be done so quickly and went on to the windows and floor, as well.

The sitting room curtains were still fluttering in the fall breeze and the rugs drying in the sun when she heard the dog announce a team approaching. Looking out of the window, she recognized Mrs. Graham, and her heart gave a glad flutter as she went out to welcome her. They exchanged greetings, and Ma Graham put her team in the shade and gave them some hay to keep them content with the wait. Then she followed Marty to the house.

The dog lay on one side of the path now, chewing hard on a small, bonelike object. Marty saw with dismay that it was one of her biscuits. The dad-blame dog had dug it up. With a flush to her cheeks, she hurried Mrs. Graham on by, hoping the older woman would fail to recognize the lump for what it really was.

As they entered the kitchen, Marty was overcome with shyness. She had never welcomed another woman into her kitchen. She knew not what to do or say, and she certainly had little to offer this visitor in the way of refreshment.

Marty noticed that Ma Graham kept her eyes discreetly away from the crumbled chinking and remarked instead about the well-scrubbed floor.

Marty bustled about self-consciously, stuffing wood in the stove and putting on the coffee. Ma talked easily of weather, of delightful little Missie, whom her girls loved to care for, and the good harvest. Still Marty felt ill at ease. She was thankful when the coffee had boiled and she was able to pour them each a cup. She placed Missie in her chair with a glass of milk and put on the cream and sweetening for Ma in case she used it. With a sinking heart, she realized she didn't have a thing to serve with the coffee—not so much as a crust of bread. Well, the coffee was all she had, so the coffee would have to do.

"I see ya been busy as a bee, fall cleanin'," Ma observed.

"Yeah," responded Marty.

"Nice to have things all cleaned up fer the long days an' nights ahead when a body can't be out much. Them's quiltin' an' knittin' days."

Yeah, that's how she felt.

"Do ya have plenty of rugs fer comfort?"

She was sure they did.

"What 'bout quilts? Ya be needin' any of those?"

No, she didn't think so.

They slowly sipped their coffee. Then Ma's warm brown eyes turned upon her.

"How air things goin', Marty?"

It wasn't the words, it was the look that did it. The expression in Ma's eyes said that she truly cared how things were going, and Marty's firm resolve to hold up bravely went crumbling just like the chinking. Words tumbled over words as she poured out to Ma all about the

51

pancakes, Missie's stubborn outburst, the bread crock being empty, the horrid biscuits, Missie's disappearance, the chinking, the terrible supper she had served the night before, and, finally, her deep longing for the husband whom she had lost so recently. Ma sat silently, her eyes filling with tears. Then suddenly she rose, and Marty was fearful that she had offended the older woman by her outburst.

"Come, my dear," Ma said gently, her tone putting any fear of offense to rest. "You air gonna have ya a lesson in breadmakin'. Then I'll sit me down an' write ya out every recipe thet I can think of. It's a shame what ya've been a goin' through the past few days, bein' as young as ya are an' still sorrowin' an' all, an' if I don't miss my guess"—her kind eyes traveling over Marty's figure—"ya be in the family way, too, ain't ya, child?"

Marty nodded silently, swallowing her tears, and Ma took over, working and talking and finally managing to make Marty feel more worthwhile than she had felt since she had lost her Clem.

After a busy day, Ma departed. She left behind her a sheaf of recipes with full instructions, fresh-baked bread that filled the kitchen with its aroma, a basketful of her own goodies, and a much more confident Marty with supper well in hand.

Marty breathed a short prayer that if there truly was a God up there somewhere, He'd see fit to send a special blessing upon this wonderful woman whom she had so quickly learned to love.

EIGHT

It's a Cruel World

Saturday dawned clear and cooler. The breakfast of porridge and corn muffins was hurried so Clark might get an early start to town. Marty presented him with the list that Ma Graham had helped her prepare the day before.

"Mind ya," Ma had told her, "in the winter months it be sometimes three or four weeks between the trips we be a takin' to town because of winter storms, an' ya never know ahead which Saturdays ya be missin', so ya al'ays has to be stocked up like."

So the list had turned out to be a lengthy one, and Marty inwardly was concerned, but Clark did not seem surprised as he skimmed quickly through it. He nodded his agreement with the list, then bent to kiss Missie good-bye, promising her a surprise when he returned.

Marty sighed in relief at another day without him about and turned her thoughts to planning what she would do with it. Clark had cautioned her to take things a bit easier, and Ma Graham said she feared that Marty was "overdoin' for a woman in her state," but Marty knew she must have something demanding to fill her hours or the sense of her terrible loss would overwhelm her. She looked around to see what to tackle on this day. She'd finish her cleaning, she decided. First she'd put water on to heat so she could wash the bedding. Then she'd do the window, walls, and floor in the bedroom, and if time still allowed, she'd do the shed. She did not even consider cleaning the lean-to. *That's Clark's private quarters,* she told herself, and she would not intrude.

Setting Missie up with her little rag doll and a small handmade quilt to wrap it in, Marty began her tasks, forcing her mind to concentrate on what she was doing. A nagging fear raised its head occasionally. If she finished all the hard cleaning today, what would she do tomorrow, and the next day, and the day after that? Marty pushed the thought aside. The tomorrows would have to care for themselves. She couldn't face too far into the future right now. She was sure if she let her mind focus on the weeks and months ahead of her in this tiny cabin with a husband she had not chosen and a child who was not hers, she'd break under the weight of it all.

She finished her final task of the day just in time to begin supper preparations. Clark had said he should be home for the usual chore time. She thumbed through the recipes Ma had left. She'd fix biscuits and a vegetable stew, she decided, using some of the meat broth Ma had brought to flavor the stew. She went to work, discovering that she had overlooked stoking the fire again.

"Dad-burn it. Will I never learn?" she fretted as she set to work to rebuild it. Missie, clutching her doll, watched it all with wide eyes.

"Da'-bu'n it," Marty heard the little girl murmur and couldn't help but feel a bit sheepish. She took a deep breath to calm herself, and the vegetables were simmering nicely when the team pulled up outside. Clark unhitched the wagon near the house to make it easier to unload the supplies, then went on to the barn with the horses.

Marty continued her supper preparations. This time, thanks to Ma Graham, the biscuits looked far more promising.

She noticed that Clark looked weary when he came in from his chores. He gave Missie a warm hug before he sat down at the table, but Marty thought his shoulders seemed to droop a bit. Was shopping really that hard on a man, or had she made the list too long and spent all his money? Marty mulled it over from her place at the table, but there didn't seem to be an answer, so she concentrated on cooling Missie's stew.

"'Fraid the totin' in of all of the supplies will sort of mess up yer well-ordered house fer the moment." Clark's voice interrupted her thoughts.

"Thet's okay," Marty responded. "We'll git them in their proper place soon enough."

"A lot of the stock supplies will go up in the loft over the kitchen," Clark went on. "Ya reach it by a ladder on the outside of the house."

Marty felt her eyes widen. "I didn't know there'd be a loft up there," she told him.

"It's nigh empty right now, so there wasn't much use in yer knowin'. We stock it up in the fall so's we won't run out of sech things as flour an' salt come the winter storms. I'll carry the stock supplies direct up so's I won't have to clutter yer house with 'em. The smaller things, though, I'll have to bring in here so's ya can put 'em all away in the place where ya want 'em. Do ya be wantin' 'em in the kitchen or in the shed?"

Marty knew it would be handier in the kitchen, yet if they were in the shed, there wouldn't be such a clutter until she got them put away. She decided on the shed, and they hurried through their supper in order to get at the task.

After they had finished eating, Clark pulled from his pocket a small bag of sweets and offered one to Missie. Then he gave the sack to Marty, telling her to help herself and then tuck it away in the cupboard for future treats. Missie sucked in noisy enjoyment, declaring it "num" and "Pa's yummy."

Marty washed the dishes, and Clark brought the supplies into the shed as they had agreed.

As she filled cans and crocks, Marty felt heady with the bounty of it all. She could hear Clark as he labored under the heavy bags, climbing again and again up the ladder to the kitchen loft.

At last it was all done. The cupboards were bulging. Imagine if she and Clem could have stocked up like that. Wouldn't it have been like Christmas and picnics and birthdays all wrapped up in one? She sighed and wiped away an unexpected tear.

Marty was tucking Missie in for the night, wondering if Clark was going to come hear the little girl's prayers as he usually did, when she heard him struggling with a rather heavy load. Marty's curiosity led her back to the kitchen to investigate. Clark, hammer in hand, was removing a crate enclosing some large object. She stood watching silently from the door while Clark's tool unmasked the contents. Her breath caught in her throat, for there, shining with metal and polished wood, stood the most wondrous sewing machine she had ever seen.

Clark did not look her way but began speaking, his voice sounding as weary as his shoulders had looked. But he seemed to feel that some kind of explanation was in order.

"I ordered it some months back as a surprise fer my Ellen. She liked to sew an' was al'ays makin' somethin' fancy like. It was to be fer her birthday. She would have been twenty-one—tomorrow." Clark looked up then. "I'd be proud if ya'd consider it yourn now. I'm sure ya can make use of it. I'll move it into yer room under the window iffen it pleases ya."

Marty swallowed back a sob. He was giving her this beautiful machine. She had always dreamed of having a machine of her own, but never had she dared to hope for one so grand. She didn't know what to say, yet she felt she must say something.

"Thank ya," she finally was able to murmur. "Thank ya. Thet . . . thet'll be fine, jest fine."

Only then did she realize that this tall man before her was fighting for control. His lips trembled and as he turned away, she was sure she saw tears in his eyes. Marty brushed by him and went out into the coolness of the night. She had to think, to sort things out. He had ordered the machine for his Ellen, and he was weeping. *He must be suffering, too,* she thought, stunned by the realization. The weary sag of his shoulders, the quivering lips, the tear-filled eyes. *He . . . he must understand something of how I'm feeling.* Somehow she had never thought of him as carrying such deep sorrow. Hot tears washed down Marty's cheeks.

Oh, Clem, her heart cried. *Why do sech things, sech cruel things, happen to people? Why? Why?*

But Marty knew there was no easy answer. This was the first time Clark had mentioned his wife. Marty hadn't even known her name. Indeed, she had been so wrapped up in her own grief she had not even wondered much about the woman who had been Clark's wife, Missie's mama, and the keeper of this house. Now her mind was awake to it. The rose by the door, the bright cheery curtains, Missie's lovingly sewn garments that she was too quickly outgrowing, the many color-ful rugs on the floor. Everything—everything in this little home spoke of this woman. Marty felt like an intruder. What had she been like, this Ellen? Had she ever boiled the coffee over or made a flop of the biscuits? No, Marty was sure she hadn't. But she had been so young—only twenty-one tomorrow—and she was already gone. True, Marty was even younger—nineteen, in fact—but still, twenty-one seemed so young to die. And why did she die? Marty didn't know. There were so many things she didn't know, but a few things were becoming clear to her. There had been a woman in this house who loved it and made it a home, who gave birth to a baby daughter whom she cherished, a young woman who shared days and nights with her husband. Then he had lost her, and his loss had left him in grief and pain—like she was experiencing over losing her Clem. She had assumed she was the only one who bore that kind of sorrow, but it wasn't so.

It's a mean world, she mused as she turned her face upward. "It's mean an' wicked an' cruel," she said out loud as she gazed upward.

The stars blinked down at her from a clear sky.

"It's mean," she whispered, "but it's beautiful." What was it Ma Graham had said? *"Time,"* she'd said, *"it is time that's the healer—time an' God."* Marty supposed she meant Clark's God.

"Iffen we can carry on one day at a time, the day will come when it gets easier an' easier, an' one day we'll surprise ourselves by even bein' able to laugh an' love agin." That's what Ma had said.

It seemed so far away to Marty, but somehow she had confidence that Ma Graham should know.

Marty turned back to the house. It was cool in the evening now, and she realized she was shivering. When she entered the kitchen she found that all traces of the machine and the crate had been removed.

On the kitchen table was a large package wrapped with brown paper and tied with store twine. Clark motioned toward it.

"I'm not sure what might be in there," he said. "I asked Missus McDonald at the store to make up whatever a woman be needin' to pass the winter. She sent this. I hope it passes."

Marty took a deep breath. Just what did he mean? She wasn't sure.

"Would ya like me to be movin' it in on yer bed so's ya can be a sortin' through it?"

Without waiting for her answer, which may have taken half the night, she felt so tongue-tied, he carried it through to her room and placed it on her bed. He turned to leave.

"It's been a long day," he said quietly. "I think I'll be endin' it now," and he was gone.

Marty's fingers fumbled as she lit the lamp. Then she hurried to untie the string. Remembering the scissors in the sewing basket, she hurried to get them to speed up the process. She could hardly wait, but as the brown paper fell away she was totally unprepared for what she found.

There was material for undergarments and nighties and enough lengths for three dresses. One piece was warm and soft looking in a pale blue-gray; already her mind was picturing how it would look done up. It would be her company and visiting dress. It was beautiful. She explored further and found a pattern for a bonnet and two pieces of material. One lightweight and one heavier for the colder weather.

There was lace for trimming, and long warm stockings, and even a pair of shoes, warm and high for the winter, and a shawl for the cool days and evenings, and on the bottom, of all things, a long coat. She was sure no one else in the whole West would have clothing to equal hers. Her cheeks were warm and her hands trembled. Then with a shocked appeal to her senses, she pulled herself upright.

"Ya little fool," she muttered. "Ya can't be takin' all this. Do ya know thet iffen ya did, ya'd be beholden to thet man fer years to come?"

Resentment filled Marty. She wanted the things, the lovely things, but oh, she couldn't possibly accept them. What could she do? She would not humble herself and be beholden to this man. She would not be a beggar in his home. Tears scalded her cheeks. Oh, what could she do? What could she do?

"We are not fancy, but we try an' be proper" came back again to haunt her.

Could it be that he was embarrassed by her shabbiness? Yes, she decided, it could well be. Again her chin came up.

Okay, she determined, she'd take it—all of it. She would not be an embarrassment to any man. She would sew up the clothes in a way that would be the envy of every woman around. After all, she could sew. Clark need not feel shame because of her.

But the knowledge of what she knew—or thought she knew—drained much of the pleasure from the prospect of the new clothes.

In his lean-to bedroom, Clark stretched long, tired legs under the blankets. It had been a hard day for him, fraught with difficult memories.

It used to be such fun to bring home the winter supplies to Ellen. She had made such a fuss over them. Why, if she'd been there today she would have had Missie sharing in the game and half wild with excitement. Well, he certainly couldn't fault Marty, only five days a widow. He couldn't expect her to be overly carried away about salt and flour at this point. She must be in deep hurt, in awful grieving. He wished he could be of some help to her, but how? His own pain was still too sharp. It took time, he knew, to get over a loss like that, and he hadn't had enough time yet. The thought of wanting another woman had never entered his head since he'd lost Ellen. If it weren't for Missie, this one wouldn't be here now; but Missie needed her even if he didn't, and one could hardly take that out on the poor girl.

At first he had resented her here, he supposed—cleaning Ellen's cupboards, working at her stove—but no, that wasn't fair, either. After all, she hadn't chosen to be here. He'd just have to try harder to be decent and to understand her sorrow. He didn't want Missie in an atmosphere of gloom all the time. No, he'd have to try to shake the feeling, and in time maybe Marty could, too, so that the house would be a fit place for a little girl to grow and learn. *It's going to be harder for Marty,* he thought, *as she is all alone.* She didn't have a Missie, or a farm, or anything really. He hoped Mrs. McDonald had selected the right items for Marty. She really was going to need warmer things for the winter ahead.

The idea that he was doing anything special for her in getting her the things she needed did not enter his thinking. He was simply providing what was needed for those under his roof, a thing he had been taught was the responsibility of the man of the house when he was but a young'un tramping around, trying to keep up with the long strides of his own pa.

NINE

The Lord's Day

Sunday morning dawned bright and warm with only enough clouds in the sky to make an appealing landscape. At breakfast, hoping she wasn't too obvious, Marty asked Clark if he was through at Jedd's or if he'd be going back for the day. Clark looked at her with surprise.

"Jedd has him a bit more to finish off," he said, "an' I wouldn't be none surprised iffen he'd work at it today. Me, though, I al'ays take a rest on the Lord's Day. I know it don't seem much like the Lord's Day with no meetin', but I try an' hold it as sech the best I can."

Now it was Marty's turn for surprise. She would have known better if she had given it some thought, but in her eagerness for Clark to be away from the house, she hadn't considered it at all.

"'Course," she whispered, avoiding his eyes. "I'd plumb fergot what day it be."

Clark let this pass without further comment. After a moment or two, he said, "I been thinkin' as how me an' Missie might jest pack us a lunch an' spend the day in the woods. 'Pears like it may be the last chance fer a while. The air is gettin' cooler an' there's a feelin' in the air thet winter may be a mite anxious to be a comin'. We kinda enjoy

60

jest spendin' the day lazyin' an' lookin' fer the last wild flowers an' smart-lookin' leaves an' all. Would thet suit yer plans?"

She almost stuttered. "Sure . . . sure . . . fine. I'll fix yer lunch right after breakfast."

"Good!"

It was settled, then. Clark and his little Missie would spend the day enjoying the outdoors and each other, and she, Marty, would have the day to herself. The thought both excited and frightened her. She wasn't too sure how she would do with no little girl around to help keep her thoughts from dwelling on her loss.

Clark went out into the shed and returned with a strange contraption that appeared to be some sort of carrier to be placed on his back.

"Fer Missie," he answered her unspoken question as she gazed at it. "I had to rig this up when I needed to take her to the fields an' a chorin' with me. She's even had her naps in it as I tramped along." He smiled faintly. "Little tyke's gotten right heavy at times, too, fer sech a tiny mite. Reckon I'd better take it along today fer when she tires of walkin'."

Marty realized she was giving them far more lunch than they needed, but the fresh air and the walk through the hills was bound to give them a hearty appetite.

Missie was beside herself with excitement and called good-bye over and over to Marty as they left. Ole Bob joined them at the door, and Marty watched the trio disappear behind the barn. As she turned back to clear the table and do up the dishes, she remembered that today would have been Ellen's birthday. Maybe their walk would include a visit to her gravesite. Marty somehow believed that it would.

She hurried through the small tasks of the morning and then fairly bolted to her bedroom and the waiting material and shiny new machine. She wasn't sure if she was breaking Clark's Sabbath with her sewing or not. She hoped not, but she was not sure she could have restrained from doing so even if she had known. She did hope she would not offend Clark's God. She needed any help He was inclined to give her. She pushed the thoughts aside and let her mind be completely taken up with her task—almost. At times she nearly caught her breath with feelings that came from nowhere.

Wouldn't Clem be proud to see me in this?
This is Clem's favorite color.

And later she whispered, "Clem al'ays did poke fun at what he called 'women's frivols.'" She couldn't help a little smile, but soon it got caught on the lump in her throat.

No, it seemed there was just no getting around it. Clem was there to disquiet her thoughts, and his absence still made her throat ache. Stubbornly she did not give in to the temptation to throw herself on her bed and sob, but she worked on with set jaw and determined spirit.

In the afternoon she laid her sewing aside. She hadn't even stopped for anything to eat. She hadn't missed it, though, and her sewing had been going well. The machine worked like a dream, and she couldn't believe how much faster seams were turned out with its help. She decided, however, that her eyes could use a rest, after staring so long at the machine foot. And her legs and feet were tiring after pumping the treadle all this time.

She walked outside, stretching her arms toward the sky. It was a glorious fall day, and she almost envied Clark and Missie's romp through the crackling leaves. Slowly she walked around the yard. The rosebush had one single bloom—not as big or as pretty as the earlier ones, she was sure, but beautiful just for its being there. She went on to the garden. The vegetables, for the most part, had already been harvested. Only a few things remained to be taken to the root cellar. At the end of the garden was the hole she had dug to bury her biscuits. It had been redug by Ole Bob, who felt it was his duty to unearth them again. A few dirty hard lumps still lay near the hole—even Ole Bob had abandoned them. It no longer mattered as much, Marty thought as she gave one a kick with her well-worn shoe. Funny how quickly things can change.

She walked on, savoring the day. The fruit trees that Clark had told her of looked promising and healthy. Wouldn't it be grand to have your own apples? Maybe even next year, Clark had said. She stood by one of the trees, not sure if it was an apple tree or not, but should it be, she implored it to please, please have some apples next year. She then remembered that even if it did, she would be long gone for the East by then. She didn't bother to inform the apple tree of this, for fear that it would lose heart and not bear after all. She turned and left, not caring as deeply now.

On she walked, down the path to the stream just behind the smokehouse. She found a stone platform that had been built into the creek bed where a spring, cold from the rocky hillside, burst forth to join the waters below. The perfectly shaded spot cooled crocks of butter and cream in the icy cold water on hot summer days. Clark hadn't told her about this, but then, there had been no reason to, it not being needed this time of year. She paused a moment, watching the gurgling water ripple over the polished stones. There was something so fascinating about water, she told herself as she moved away, and this would be a choice place to be refreshed on a sultry summer day. But of course she wouldn't be here then, she reminded herself once again.

She went on to the corrals, reaching over the fence to give Dan, or was it Charlie, a rub on his strong neck. The cows lay in the shade of the tall poplars, placidly chewing their cuds while their calves of that year grew fat on meadow grass in the adjoining pasture. *This is a good farm,* Marty decided—just the kind Clem and she had dreamed of having.

Giving her head a quick shake, she started for the house, past the henhouse. She suddenly felt a real hunger for panfried chicken. She hadn't realized how long it had been since she had tasted any, and she remembered home and the rich aroma from her ma's kitchen. At that moment she was sure nothing else would taste so good. Preparing chicken was one thing she had watched her mother do. Whenever they were to have fried chicken, she would station herself by her ma's kitchen table and observe the whole procedure from start to finish. Her mother had never begun with a live bird, though. Marty had never chopped off a chicken's head before, but she was sure she could manage somehow.

She walked closer to the coop, eyeing the chickens as they squawked and scurried around while she tried to pick out a likely candidate. She wasn't sure if she should first catch the one she wanted and then take it to the axe, or if she should go to the woodshed for the axe and bring it to the chicken. She finally decided she would take the chicken to the axe, realizing that she would need a chopping block as well.

She entered the coop and picked out her victim, a cocky young rooster that looked like he would make good frying.

"Come here, you, come here," she coaxed, stretching out her hand, but she soon caught on to the fact that a chicken would not respond like a dog. In fact, chickens seemed to be completely something else. They flew and squawked and whipped up dirt and chicken droppings like a mad whirlwind whenever she got to within grabbing distance of them. Marty soon decided that if she was to have a chicken for supper, full pursuit was the only way to get one into the pan. She abandoned herself to an outright chase, grabbing at chicken legs and ending up with a faceful of scattered dirt and dirty feathers. Round and round they went. By now Marty had given up on the cocky young rooster and had decided to settle for anything she could get her hands on. Finally, after much running and grabbing that had her dress soiled, her hair flying, and her temper seething, she managed to grasp hold of a pair of legs. He was heavier than she had expected, and it took all her strength to hold him, since he was determined he wasn't going to be supper for anyone. Marty held tight, just as determined. She half dragged him from the coop and looked him over. This was big boy himself, she was sure, the granddaddy of the flock, the ruler of the place. So what, she reasoned. He'd make a great panful, and maybe the bird hated the thought of facing another winter, anyway.

Panting with exhaustion as she headed for the woodshed, Marty nonetheless felt very pleased with herself to have accomplished her mission.

She stretched the squawking, flopping rooster across a chopping block, and as he quieted, she reached for the axe. The flopping resumed, and Marty had to drop the axe in order to use both hands on the fowl. Over and over the scene was repeated. Marty began to think it was a battle to see who would wear out first. Well, she wouldn't be the one to give up.

"Ya dad-blame bird—hold still," she hissed at him and tried again, getting in a wild swing at the rooster's head.

With a squawk and a flutter, the rooster wrenched free and was gone, flopping and complaining across the yard. Marty looked down at the chopping block and beheld in horror the two small pieces of beak that remained there.

"Serves ya right!" she blazed, kicking the pieces off the block into the dirt.

Still determined not to be beaten, she headed again for the coop, while one short-beaked rooster still flapped about the farm, screaming out his wrath to a dastardly world.

Marty marched resolutely to the coop and began all over again. After many minutes of chasing and gulping against the flying dust, she finally got what she was after. This fellow was more her size, and again she set out for the chopping block. Again things didn't go well there. She stretched him out and reached for the axe, dropped the axe and stretched him out, over and over again. Finally she got inspired, and taking the chicken with her, she headed for the house. Into her bedroom she went, bird firmly under her arm, and took from a drawer the neatly wound roll of store string. Back at the woodshed, she sat down on a block with the chicken in her lap and securely tied the legs together. Then she carried him outside and tied the other end of the string to a small tree. Still holding the chicken, she tied another piece of string to his neck. She tied the second string to another small tree. She brought the chopping block from the woodshed and placed it in the proper spot beneath the chicken's outstretched neck.

"There now," she said with some satisfaction and, taking careful aim, she shut her eyes and chopped hard.

It worked—but Marty was totally unprepared for the next event. A wildly flopping chicken—with no head—covered her unmercifully with spattered blood.

"Stop thet! Stop thet!" she screamed. "Yer s'pose to be dead, ya—ya dumb headless thing."

She took another swing with the axe, relieving the chicken of one wing. Still it flopped, and Marty backed up against the shed as she tried to shield her face from the awful onslaught. Finally the chicken lay still, with only an occasional tremor. Marty took her hands from her face.

"Ya dad-blame bird," she stormed and wondered briefly if she dared pick it up.

She looked down at her dirty, bloodstained dress. What a mess, and all for a chicken supper.

Out in the barnyard an indignant short-beaked rooster tried to crow as Marty picked up the sorry mess of blood and feathers and headed for the house.

All of those feathers had to come off, and then came the even more disgusting job of cleaning out the innards.

Somehow she got through it all, and after she had washed the meat in fresh well water and seasoned it, she put it in the frypan with savory butter. She decided she'd best get cleaned up before Clark and Missie returned. A bath seemed to be the simplest and quickest way to care for the matter, so Marty hauled a basin into her room and filled it with warm water. When she was clean again, she took the dreadfully dirty dress and put it to soak in the bath water. She'd deal with that tomorrow, she promised herself as she carried the whole mess outside and placed it on a wash table beside the cabin.

Feeling refreshed and more herself after her bath, Marty resumed her preparations for supper. When Clark and Missie arrived, tired but happy from their day together, they were greeted by the smell of frying chicken. Clark's face showed no surprise, and their exchanges were matter-of-fact as Marty welcomed the two in for supper.

Indeed, Clark could hardly contain his surprise during the meal and had been on the verge of asking Marty if she'd had company that day, so sure was he that she must have had help to accomplish what a chicken for supper would require. But he'd thought better of such a question. After supper, on the way to the barn, he saw the soiled dress in the red-stained water and the mess by the woodshed. The chopping block was still where Marty had left it, though Ole Bob had already carted off the chicken's head. The store twine was there, too, still attached to the small trees.

As he passed the coop he could tell there had been some general upheaval there as well. It looked like the chickens had flopped in circles for hours—feathers and dirt were everywhere, including in the overturned feeding troughs and watering pans.

What really topped all was the old rooster angrily perched on the corral fence with his ridiculously short beak, clacking away to beat the band.

"Well, I never," muttered Clark, shaking his head in amazement.

He couldn't help but smile at the sight of that rooster. Tomorrow he'd do something about him. Tonight he was thankful for Marty's meal of fried chicken.

TEN

Neighborly Hog Killin'

Marty mentally braced herself for the new week, hoping with all her heart that it would be packed full of activity.

Monday morning, Clark brought in the big rooster, beheaded and plucked. He advised Marty to boil rather than try to fry the patriarch of the flock, and Marty didn't mind taking his advice. After cleaning the bird and putting him on to cook in her largest pot, Marty set to work washing up all the clothing she could find that needed washing. Her back ached from the scrub board, and she was glad to spend the rest of the day at her sewing. She was surprised at how easy it was to care for Missie. The little one was quite content with a big wooden spoon and a bowl to stir up pretend meals for her dolly. Marty decided she'd make some new doll clothes when she had time.

The rest of the week was packed full, too. She went with Clark to Ben Graham's for the killing of the hogs. Todd Stern and his near-grown son, Jason, were there, too, and Marty recognized them as the kind neighbors who had brought Clem's body back and supplied his burying place. The pain was there, sharp and hurting again, but she made a real effort to push it from her. She was glad to be with Ma Graham.

She felt able to draw so much strength, wisdom, and advice from the older woman.

As the day went on, Marty could not help but notice the looks that were exchanged between young Jason and Ma's Sally Anne. If she didn't miss her guess, something was brewing there.

She had little time to ponder on it, however, for the cutting and preparing of the meat was a big job. After the menfolk had done the killing and the scraping and had quartered the animals, the women were hard pressed to keep up with them.

The job that Marty found hardest to stomach was the emptying and preparing of the casings for the sausage meat. Floods of nausea swept over her, and several times she had to fight for control. When they were finally done, Marty went to the outhouse and lost all her dinner. She was glad to be rid of it and went back to work feeling some better.

The men looked after preparation of the salt brine for curing the bacon and hams and readied the smokehouse for the process. The women ground and seasoned the sausage meat and had the slow, rather boring task of stuffing the casings and tying them into proper lengths. It helped to be able to chat as they worked; still the job seemed a tedious one. On the second and third days, Hildi Stern came with her menfolk, and the extra hands aided much in getting the job done.

Lard had to be chopped up and rendered, some kept for cooking and frying and some put aside to be used in the making of soap.

By the end of each day, those involved were tired and aching. Marty noticed that Ma tried to assign her the less-demanding tasks, but Marty would have none of it, wanting to do her full share.

At the end of the third day, the meat was divided up and things were cleaned up and put away for the next year's killing. Ma's Sally Anne put on the coffee for them all. They needed to renew their strength for the work that waited at home at day's end. Marty noticed Jason look in Sally's direction and saw her face flush beneath it. She couldn't fault Jason. Sally Anne was a very pretty seventeen-year-old, and just as sweet as she was pretty, Marty thought. Was Jason good enough for her? Marty hoped so. She knew nothing of the boy to make her think otherwise. He looked strong, and he certainly had been carrying his share of the work the last few days. He seemed mannerly enough. Yes, she summed it up—maybe he'd be all right. Anyway, it looked like he'd have to be, the way they were mooning over each other.

She remembered again how it had been when she had first met Clem— when his eyes turned toward her, she could feel him watching even when she wasn't looking directly at him, and her cheeks would flush in her excitement. She had known right away that she would love him, and she guessed he had known it, too. His very presence had sent fireworks through her. She had felt she couldn't wait to see him again, but she could hardly bear it when she did. She had thought she'd explode with the intensity of it, but that's what love was like. Wild and possessing, making one nearly burst with excitement and desire—being both sweet and painful at the same time. Yes, that's how love was.

Clark was excusing himself from the table and Marty got up, too. She said the necessary thank-yous and good-byes to Ma Graham and eyed the crocks of lard she was to take home for making soap.

"No use us both gittin' ourselves in a mess makin' soap," Ma Graham said. "Marty, why don't ya leave them crocks here an' come over in the mornin' an' we'll do it all up together like?"

Bless ya, Ma Graham, Marty's heart cried. *Ya know very well I'd be downright lost on my own tryin' to make soap fer the first time.*

She looked at Clark for his reaction.

"Sounds like a good plan ta me," Clark responded.

"Thank ya, Ma," Marty said with feeling. "I'll be over in the mornin' jest as soon as I can."

Thank-you seemed very inadequate for the gratitude she felt.

ELEVEN

Togetherness

Marty kept her word and hurried through the morning household chores so she could do her rightful share of the work at Ma's. As she went for Missie's coat and bonnet, Clark spoke up.

"I've nothin' pressin' to take my time today. Thought I'd be doin' the caulkin' here in the kitchen. Why don'cha jest leave Missie to home with me, an' then ya won't need to worry ya none 'bout her gittin' underfoot around those hot pots."

Marty nodded her appreciation and agreement and hurried to the team and wagon that Clark had waiting.

It was cooler today. In fact, there was almost a chill to the air. Maybe winter would soon be coming. Marty did not look forward to those long days and even longer evenings that stretched out before her.

The soapmaking was a demanding, hot job, and Marty was glad when they were finished. The soap mixture was placed in pans, ready to be cut into bars after it had cooled.

The two women sat down for a much-needed cup of coffee and one of Ma's slices of johnnycake. There did not seem to be much chance for confidential talking at Ma's place. What with eleven children crowding every corner of the small house, there was seldom an opportunity to be alone. But Ma talked freely, ignoring the coming and going.

She told Marty that her first husband, Thornton Perkins, had been the owner of a small store in town, and when he had come to an early death, he had left her with the business and three small children to provide for. When Ben Graham came along with good farmland and the need for a woman, he appeared to be the answer to prayer, even though he had four small ones of his own tagging along behind him. So they had joined forces, the young widow with three and the widower with four. To that union had been born six more children. One they had lost as a baby and one at the age of seven. The seven-year-old had been one of Ma's, but Ben, too, had felt the loss deeply. Now the children numbered eleven, and every one of them was special.

Sally Anne and Laura were both seventeen, only two months apart, with Ben's Laura being the older. Next came Ben's Thomas, then Ma's Nellie. Ma's Ben had been next, and Ma supposed one of the reasons Ben had become so attached to this boy was that they both bore the same name. Ben's twins were next in line, Lem and Claude. They were named after their two grandfathers. The younger children Marty still didn't have sorted out by name. There was a Faith and a Clint, she knew, and she believed she had heard the little one called Lou.

It was the two older girls that most interested Marty. Sally Anne was one of the prettiest young things Marty had ever seen, and the girl seemed to simply adore her stepsister Laura. Laura, though capable and efficient, was plain and probably knew it, for she seemed to always be trying to outdo Sally Anne. *Why does she do it?* Marty puzzled. *Can't she see that Sally Anne practically worships her? Laura has no earthly reason to lord it over her.* In watching more closely, she decided that Laura was unaware of what she was doing, probably driven by a deep feeling of being inferior to her pretty sister.

She doesn't need to feel thet way, Marty reasoned silently. *She has so much to offer jest the way she be.*

She supposed there was nothing she could do about it. However, she promised herself that she'd try to be especially nice to Laura and maybe help her realize she was a worthwhile person.

It was getting to be late afternoon, and Marty knew she must be on her way.

She thanked Ma sincerely for all her help with the soap. Now she felt confident that she'd be able to do it on her own the next time. She told Ma that if she could spare the time, she'd sure appreciate another visit from her before the snow shut them in. Ma promised to try and, giving Marty a hearty hug, sent her on her way.

When Marty reached home, Clark came out of the cabin to take over the team, and he brought Missie with him for the brief trip to the barn. As Marty entered the kitchen, she saw that all of the old crumbled chinking had been replaced with new and was rapidly turning to the proper attractive white. Now she wouldn't be sweeping up pieces of it each time she cleaned the kitchen floor. Though she was still embarrassed about her inadvertent error, she was glad the chinking was fixed and noted with appreciation that Clark had even cleaned up any mess he had made in completing the job.

Marty was tired as she began supper preparations, and she knew she would be very glad when it was time to go to bed. Tomorrow was Saturday, so she must first make a list for Clark, since he would want to leave for town early the next morning.

TWELVE

Finishin' My Sewin'

Clark did leave early for town the next day, and Marty sighed with relief as she watched him disappear with the wagon and team. She still felt him to be a stranger to avoid whenever she could; though, without realizing it, some of her emotional turmoil was seeping away simply because, deep down, she realized her anger toward Clark was unfounded. They were victims of circumstances, both of them, forced to share the same house. Notwithstanding, Marty still was much relieved when his duties took him elsewhere.

The supply list hadn't been as long this time, but Clark had asked her to check through Missie's clothing to see what the child would be needing for the winter. Marty did this and carefully added some items to the list. Then Clark stood Missie on a chair and traced a pattern of her small foot so he could bring back shoes for her growing feet.

Marty busied herself with her morning routine. She still felt tired from the day of soapmaking. In fact, she wondered if the emotionally driven hard work of cleaning, cooking, and sewing during the preceding days was not taking its toll. She felt drained and even slightly dizzy as she finished up the dishes. For the sake of the little one she was carrying, she must hold herself in check and not pour all her energy into frenzied activity. She had lost her Clem. Now, more than ever, she wanted his baby.

74

Marty decided she would make this day an easier one. She did household chores for the day, sweeping and tidying each small room. Her bedroom had become quite crowded with her bed, Missie's crib, two chests, her trunk, the sewing basket, and the new machine. She wouldn't complain, she thought, as she looked at the beautiful shining thing. There really was more room for it in the sitting room, but she was sure that for Clark to have to see it continually would be a hurtful reminder. No, she'd be glad to spare him that much, and she ran a loving hand over the polished wood and gleaming metal.

"Today, Missie," she spoke to the child, "I'm gonna finish my sewin'."

She moved across to the garments she had already made and fingered them with pride. There hung the newly made bonnets, one of light material, a little more dressy, the other of warm, sturdy cloth for the cold days ahead. There were the underclothes, some trimmed with bits of lace. She had never had such feminine things before. She almost hated to wear them and take away their fresh newness. Two nighties lay folded in the drawer. She had put extra tucks and stitching on them, and one had some dainty blue trim. Two dresses hung completed. They were not fancy, but they were neat and attractive, and Marty felt confident that Clark would deem them "proper."

Beside her chest stood the new shoes, still black and shiny. She had not as yet worn them. As long as she could, she would wear her old ones and keep the new ones to admire. Her new coat and shawl, so very new and beautiful, hung on pegs behind the door.

Marty sighed. She had only the blue-gray material left to make up. She had saved it until last because it was to be special. She let the beautiful material lay against her hand, then lifted one corner to her cheek.

"Missie," she half whispered, "I'm gonna make me a dress. Ya jest wait until you see it. It's gonna be so grand, an' maybe—maybe when I be all through, there be enough material left to make ya somethin', too."

Suddenly that was important to Marty. She wanted, with all her heart, to share this bit of happiness with someone, and Missie seemed the likely one to share it with.

"Maybe I'll even have enough for a dolly dress," Marty added as Missie patted the material and proclaimed it "pwetty." Marty went to work. Missie played well on the rug by the bed, and the sewing machine hummed along. When Missie became restless, Marty was shocked to find the clock said ten past one.

"Oh dear!" Marty exclaimed, picking up the child. "Missie, I'm plumb sorry. It be long past yer dinnertime. Ya must be awful hungry. I'll git ya somethin' right away."

They ate together and then Marty tucked Missie in for her nap. The child fell asleep listening to the steady whir of the machine.

The new dress took shape, and when she had carefully finished each tuck and seam, Marty held it up. It nearly took her breath away. She was sure she had never had one quite so pretty. She had added some width for her use now, but she would easily be able to take it in after her baby arrived. She couldn't resist trying on the dress and frankly admiring herself. She removed it reluctantly and carefully hung it with her other dresses, arranging each fold to hang just right.

Eagerly she set to work on the small garment for Missie. She decided to make a small blouse from the white material that was left over from her underthings, with a jumper for over it from the blue-gray wool. She had enough to do the same for the worn little doll.

The blouse was soon completed, and with great care Marty set to work on the tiny jumper. The tucks were fussed over to make sure they were just so, and each seam was sewn with utmost care. When Marty was finished she made small decorative stitches across the yoke with needle and thread.

Missie, who had long since awakened from her nap, kept demanding to see the "pwetty," and Marty's work would be interrupted while she showed her.

Suddenly Marty jumped from her chair as she heard Ole Bob welcoming Clark home.

"Dad-burn," she said, hastily laying her sewing aside and hurrying to the kitchen. "I haven't even thought me about supper."

The stove was cold to her touch. She had forgotten all day to replenish its fuel.

Clark had driven on down to the barn. The supplies would not take as many trips to carry this time, nor would they be as heavy to tote.

Marty rushed about the kitchen. She remembered an old secret of her ma's. If the menfolk come looking for their supper and you're caught off guard, quickly set the table. That will make them think supper is well on the way.

In a mad flurry, Marty hastened to throw on the plates and cutlery. Then she flushed at her foolishness. That wouldn't trick Clark. He had nearly an hour of choring ahead and wouldn't be looking for plates on yet. A stove with a fire in it might be a bit more convincing. When Clark came in, Marty was building the fire and wondering what she could have ready for supper in a very short time.

After depositing his armload of purchases, Clark went back out to do the chores, and Marty set to work in earnest preparing the supper.

When Clark returned from the barn, the meal was ready, simple though it was. Marty made no apology. After all, she told herself, it wasn't as though she had whiled away the whole day. Nevertheless, she promised herself not to let it happen again.

After the supper dishes had been cleared away, Clark brought out his purchases for little Missie. She was wild in her excitement, hugging the new shoes, jumping up and down about the new coat and bonnet, and running around in circles waving her new long stockings in the air. She exclaimed over the material to be sewn into little frocks, but Marty was sure the tiny child didn't really understand what it was all about. She returned to the shoes, pulled her bonnet on her head, back to front, and whirled another long stocking. Marty couldn't help but smile, understanding how the little girl felt.

Suddenly Missie turned and headed for the bedroom, a pair of the new stockings streaming out behind her. *She's going to put them in her chest,* Marty thought. In a moment the flying feet came running back and one of the tiny hands carried over her head the small jumper Marty had been working on. Marty watched as Missie pushed the garment onto Clark's lap, pointing at the fancy stitching and exclaiming, "Pwetty. Mine. Pwetty."

Clark carefully picked up the jumper in his big work-roughened hands. His eyes softened as he looked across at Marty. She held her breath. For a moment he did not speak but sat quietly stroking the small garment. His voice sounded a bit choked as he responded, "Yeah, Missie, very pretty," but it was to Marty that he spoke, not the excited child.

Clark had more surprises. For Missie he had a picture book. She had never seen such a wondrous thing before and spent the rest of the evening carefully turning the pages, exclaiming over and over her excitement at finding cows and pigs and bunnies in such an unlikely place. Clark had bought himself some books, too, for the long winter evenings ahead. This was the first time Marty was aware that Clark was a reader. She then remembered the shelf in the sitting room with a number of interesting-looking books on it. No doubt some of them had been favorites of Missie's mama. Maybe she herself would have time of a winter evening to read one or more of them.

Clark had a package for her, as well, that would help pass the months ahead. It contained wool and knitting needles and pieces of material for quilt piecing, and he told her he had a sack of raw wool that he had stored until such time as it was needed.

Marty was very thankful. She loved to knit, and though she had never quilted before, she was anxious to try her hand at it.

Missie was too excited to go to bed, but with a firmness that surprised Marty, Clark informed her that she'd had enough excitement for one night and all her things would be there in the morning. After Marty washed the child up and got her ready for bed, Clark tucked her in and heard her short prayer. Marty carefully folded the new things and picked up the pieces of material. *This will fill up a few more days,* she thought with relief. If only she could keep herself busy, perhaps she wouldn't feel so lonely and bereft. She placed everything in Missie's chest for the night, planning to go to work on sewing the little garments the next day.

Oh no, she suddenly remembered. *Tomorrow be another Lord's Day!*

She couldn't expect Clark and Missie to tramp off into the outdoors two Sundays in a row, especially when it was getting a bit chilly.

"Dad-burn!" she exclaimed softly.

How in the world would she be able to suffer through the long, miserable day anyway? Maybe she should wrap up well and take to the woods herself. Well, no use fretting about it now. She had a small amount of work to do yet on the jumper, and then she'd take her tired self off to bed. It seemed a usual thing these days for her to feel weary.

THIRTEEN

Ellen

Sunday was a cool day with a wind blowing from the west. After their morning reading and prayer, Marty's mind kept puzzling over the Scripture passage. "'The Lord is my shepherd,'" she heard Clark read from the Psalms. *How could the Lord be a shepherd?* she wondered. She gradually was listening more closely, and she found herself wanting to ask Clark a question or to repeat some portion so she might ponder its meaning. But she could not bring herself to ask him.

Could this God Clark was reading about be a comfort to others as He had been to the writer?—David, Clark said his name was. Marty acknowledged that she knew very little about God, and sometimes she caught herself yearning to know more. Bible reading hadn't been a part of her upbringing. She wondered in a vague way if she had missed out on something rather important. On occasion Clark would add a few words of his own as a background or setting to the Scripture for that day, telling a bit about the author and his troubled life at the time of his writing. Marty knew that the explanation was intended for her, but she didn't resent it. Indeed, she was pleased with whatever added to her understanding.

During the morning prayer time, Marty found herself wondering if she dared to approach Clark's God in the direct way that Clark himself did. She felt a longing to do so, but she held back.

When Clark said "amen," Marty's lips also formed the words.

Breakfast began after Missie declared her loud "'men," too.

What on earth are we gonna do with this long day in front of us? Marty wondered silently. She knew that on this Lord's Day she should not sew. She had made that blunder once, but to repeat it would be tempting God's anger to fall upon her, and she couldn't risk that. If He could spare any help at all for her, she desperately needed it.

Clark interrupted her thoughts. "On the way to town yesterday, I stopped me at the Grahams' to see if there be anythin' thet I might be gettin' them in town. Ma asked thet we come fer a visit an' dinner today. Who knows how many nice Sundays we be a havin' afore winter sets in? I said I'd check with ya on it."

Bless ya, Ma, thought Marty. *Oh, bless ya!*

Out loud she quite calmly said, "I'd be likin' thet," and it was settled.

She hurried with the morning dishes, and while Clark went to get the team, she quickly got Missie and herself ready to go.

She dressed Missie in the new blouse and jumper with a pair of the new stockings and the little black shoes. She brushed out Missie's curls until they were light and fluffy. The child truly did look a picture as she twirled and pirouetted, admiring herself and clapping her little hands with excitement.

Marty then turned to her own apparel. She took the new blue-gray dress from the hanger and held it up to herself. It should have been for Clem, and somehow she just couldn't bring herself to put it on. If Clark failed to notice it, she would be disappointed, and if by some strange chance his eyes showed admiration, that would hurt even more. She didn't want admiration from him or any other man. She could still clearly see Clem's love-filled eyes as he pulled her to him. She smothered the sob in the folds of the dress and put it back on its hanger. She chose the plainer navy dress with the bit of lace trim at the throat and sleeves. Surely this one would be quite acceptable, even proper, for Sunday dinner with the neighbors.

She dressed in the new undergarments and long stockings, put on the new shoes, and slipped the dress over her head. She'd wear the lighter bonnet and her new shawl. It wasn't cold enough to be needing the heavy coat.

Carefully she brushed out her curly hair and then decided to pin it up fashionably. She had been dreadfully neglectful of it lately, she knew. It took her several minutes for her to arrange it appropriately. She was peering critically at herself in the small mirror on the wall when she heard Clark call from the door asking if they were ready.

Missie burst from the room to meet her pa and was informed that she looked like a "real little lady an' your pa is right proud of you."

Marty followed, avoiding Clark's eyes. She didn't want to read anything there, whether real or imagined. She noticed as he helped her up to the seat of the wagon that he had changed from his work clothes and looked rather fine himself. As they traveled to the Grahams', she gave her full attention to the young Missie and the lovely crisp fall day.

Marty helped Ma Graham and the girls get the dinner on. In contrast to the first time she found herself in the Graham home, Marty now was able to concentrate, and she found Ma to be a very good cook, a fact that was no surprise to her after all the recipes she had provided. Following dinner, the men left for the sunny side of the porch for some man talk.

Young Jason Stern put in an appearance, much to the blushing of Sally Anne. The two went for a walk, always staying properly in full sight of the house.

The two women made quick work of the dishes, and then Ma and Marty sat down for their own chat. It felt so good just to sit and talk with Ma. Marty didn't mind the unusual idleness half so much with such pleasant company. After discussing general women's topics, Marty took advantage of the fact that the rest were outdoors and the two young ones down for a nap to raise a question.

"Ma," she ventured, "could ya tell me 'bout Ellen? Seems thet I should be knowin' somethin' 'bout her, since I be takin' over her house an' her baby."

Marty made no reference to "her man," and if Ma noticed, she made no sign of it. Marty told Ma about the sewing machine and Clark's reaction to it.

Ma sighed deeply and looked off into space for a moment. When she spoke, her voice was a mite shaky. "Don't hardly know what words to be a tellin' it with," Ma said. "Ellen was young an' right pretty, too. Darker than you, she be, an' taller, too. She was a merry and chattery sort. Loved everythin' an' everybody, seemed to me. She adored Clark, an' he 'peared to think her somethin' pretty special, too." Ma paused and looked into Marty's face, probably wondering how she was responding to this sensitive topic. Nodding thoughtfully, she continued her narrative.

"When Missie was born, ya should have see'd the two of 'em." Ma shook her head and smiled gently. "Never see'd two people so excited— like a couple of kids, they were. I delivered Missie. Fact is, I've delivered most babies here 'bouts, but never did I see anyone else git quite thet excited over a newborn, welcome as they normally be.

"Well, Ellen, she was soon up an' about an' fussin' over thet new baby. She thought she was jest beautiful, an' Missie be right pretty, too. Anyway, the months went by. Clark an' Ellen was a doin' real good. Clark's a hard worker, an' thet's what farmin' is all about. Ya git what yer willin' to pay fer in sweat an' achin' back. Well, things was goin' real good when one day last August Clark came ridin' into the yard. He was real agitated like, an' I knew thet somethin' was wrong. 'Ma,' he says, 'can ya come quick? Ellen is in awful pain.' Thet's what he says. I can hear him yet.

"So I went, yellin' to the girls what to do while I be gone. Ellen was in pain, all right, tossing an' rollin' on the bed, holdin' herself an' groanin'. She refused to cry out 'cause she didn't want Missie to hear her. So she jest bit her lip till she near had it a bleedin'.

"Wasn't much thet I could do but try to keep her face cooled. There was no doctor to go fer, an' we jest watched, in such pain ourselves over the fact thet we couldn't be doin' anythin' fer her. Clark was torn between stayin' with Ellen an' carin' fer Missie. I never been so sorry fer a man.

"Well, the night dragged by, an' finally 'bout four in the mornin' she stopped thrashin' so. I breathed a prayer of relief, but it wasn't to be fer long. She kept gettin' hotter an' hotter an' more an' more listless. I bathed her in cool water over an' over again, but it were no use."

82

Ma stopped for a moment, then took a deep breath and went on. "Thet evenin' we lost her, an' Clark—" She stopped again.

Ma brushed away a tear and stood up. "But thet be in the past, child, an' no use goin' over it all agin. Anyway, ya be there now to care fer Missie, an' thet's what Clark be a needin'. Was awful hard fer him to do all his fall work while totin' thet little one round on his back. I said I'd keep her on here, but I reckon Clark wanted her to know thet she be his an' somethin' special, not jest one of a brood. Besides, he never did want to be beholden to anybody. There was a childless couple in town who would have gladly took her, but Clark would have none of it. Said she needed her pa right then; that's what Clark said. Anyway, Clark's prayers seem to be gittin' answered, and Missie has you now an' a right good mama ya be a makin', too—sewin' thet sweet little dress an' all."

She patted Marty's arm. "Yer doin' jest fine, Marty. Jest fine."

Through the whole speech of Ma's, Marty had sat silent but listening with her heart as well as ears. The hearing of Clark's sorrow had opened afresh the pain of her own. She wanted to weep, but she sat dry eyed, feeling anew the sorrow of it all. It indeed had been a shock for her to hear that Clem was dead, but she hadn't had to sit by him for hours watching him suffer, not able to lift a hand to relieve him. She decided she probably'd had a mite easier suffering of the two.

Oh, Clem, her heart whispered. *Clem, I'm glad thet ya didn't have to bear pain like thet.*

She roused herself as Ma scrambled up, exclaiming that time had just flown and the menfolk would be looking for coffee.

FOURTEEN

Missie

The next morning at breakfast Clark informed Marty that the coming Thursday Missie would have her second birthday. Marty immediately felt concerned. She wasn't sure how Ellen would have celebrated the event. She didn't want to let Clark down, but how was she to know what the family chose to do about birthdays? She silently weighed the matter for the rest of the meal.

Clark must have sensed her mood because he finally inquired, "Somethin' be a troublin' ya?"

"No," Marty lied and remained silent for a few more minutes, then decided that would never do. If they had to share the same house, they'd just have to be frank and honest with each other, so she blurted out, "It's jest thet I don't know what ya would want planned fer Missie's birthday. Do ya have company? Have a party? Do somethin' different?" She shrugged. "I don't know."

"I see," Clark said, and she felt he really did understand. He got up and refilled their coffee cups.

Dad-blame, Marty scolded herself, *I missed thet second cup agin with my deep thinkin'.*

Clark didn't appear to be bothered by it. He sat back down and creamed his coffee, pushing his plate back and pulling his cup forward as though preparing for a lengthy stay.

By this time little Missie was getting restless and wanting down from her chair. Clark lifted her down and she ran to find her new book.

"Funny thing," Clark continued then, "but I don't rightly remember any fixed thing thet we be a doin' fer a birthday. Seems in lookin' back thet they were all a mite different somehow. Missie, now, she only had one afore, an' she was a bit young then to pay it much mind." He hesitated. "I think, though, thet it would be nice to be a havin' a cake fer her. I got a doodad in town last Saturday while I was there. I hope it pleases her. Jest a silly little thing, really, but it looks like it would tickle a little'un. I don't think thet we be needin' company's help in celebratin'. She'll enjoy it as much on her own with jest"—he paused slightly and finished quickly—"jest us."

Marty was relieved. That kind of a birthday celebration she felt she could manage. She sat quietly for a moment and finally raised her eyes to Clark's and said, "I been thinkin'. Seems thet I don't know much 'bout Missie, an' seems as though I should be a knowin' a sight more iffen I be goin' to raise her an' all. Ya know how young'uns be. They like to hear their folks tell of when they did this an' when they said thet, an' how cute an' clever they was, an' quick in their ways an' all. Someday soon Missie's goin' to be wantin' to hear sech things, an' I should be able to tell her. The only thing I really know 'bout her is her name."

Clark surprised her by laughing quietly. It was the first time she had heard him laugh. She liked it, but she couldn't figure out the reason for it. He soon explained.

"I be thinkin' thet ya don't really know even thet," he said with another chuckle. "Her real name be Melissa—Melissa Ann Davis."

"Thet's a pretty name," Marty said. "I don't be goin' by my real name, either. My real name be Martha, but I don't much like it. All my family an' friends called me Marty, 'cept my ma when she was upset. Then it was Martha, real loud like. Martha Lucinda—" She had nearly finished it with Claridge but caught herself in time. "But tell me 'bout Missie."

"Well, Missie be born on November third, two years ago, 'bout four o'clock in the mornin'."

Clark's face became very thoughtful as he reflected back. Marty remembered Ma telling of the great excitement that Missie's appearance had brought.

"She weren't much of a bundle," Clark went on. "Seemed to me she was rather red an' wrinkled an' had a good head of dark hair. She seemed to grow fast an' change a lot right from the start, an' afore ya knowed it she was a cooin' an' smilin'. By Christmastime she was most givin' the orders round here, it seemed. She was a good baby as babies go an' slept through the night by the time she was three months old. I thought I'd picked me a real winner. Then at five months she started to cut her teeth. She turned from a sweet, contented, smilin' darlin' into a real bearcat. Lucky fer us, it didn't last fer too long, though at the time it seemed forever. Anyway, she made it through. So did we, an' things quieted down agin.

"When she had her first birthday, she could already say some words. Seemed right bright for a little tyke, an' al'ays, from as far back as I can remember, she loved pretty things. Guess thet's why she took so to the little whatever it be thet ya sewed fer her.

"Started walkin' 'fore her first birthday an' was soon climbin' to match it. Boy, how she did git around! One day I found her on the corral fence, top rail, when she be jest a wee'un. Got up there an' couldn't git down. Hangin' on fer dear life, she was.

"She was gettin' to be a right good companion, too. A lot of company she was. Chattered all the time, an' more an' more there was gettin' to be some sense to it.

"One day she came in with a flower. Thrilled to pieces with it, she was. Picked it right off the rosebush. The thorns had pricked her tiny fingers an' they was a bleedin'. But she never paid them no mind at all, so determined she be to take the 'pretty' to her mama. Thet flower is pressed in her mama's Bible."

Clark stopped and sat looking at his coffee cup. Marty saw him swallow and his lips move as though he meant to go on, but no sound came.

"Ya don't need to tell me any more," she said quietly. "I know enough from this to be able to tell young Missie somethin' 'bout her young days."

She searched for something further to say and found that anything she could bring to mind seemed inadequate, but she stumbled on. "I know how painful it be—to remember, an' anyway when the day comes thet young Missie need hear the story of her mama—an' she should hear it, to be sure—but when thet day comes, it's her pa thet she should be hearin' it from."

Marty rose from the table then so that Clark need not worry about saying more. Slowly he finished his coffee, and she set to getting her water ready to wash the dishes.

The day was quite cool, but Clark announced that he planned to see how much sod he could get turned on the land he was claiming for spring planting. Marty hoped the weather would hold, not just so that he could finish the plowing but also so that he would continue to be busy away from the house. She was getting more used to him, but she still felt awkward and at loose ends if he was in the house very long.

Sometimes the days went too slowly for Marty, but she was relieved when she could always find work with which to fill them. What with washing, cleaning, bread baking, and meal getting, she had to look for time in which to do Missie's sewing. Little garments did take shape under her capable hands, however, and Missie exclaimed in delight over each one of them.

Marty had a secret project in the works, as well. Missie's birthday had sent her mind scrambling over what she might be able to do for the little girl. She didn't have a cent to her name, even if she could have found a way to spend it. She then thought of the beautifully colored wool Clark had brought and the brand-new knitting needles. Each night she retired to her room as soon as her day's tasks were taken care of, and with Missie sleeping soundly in her crib, the knitting needles clicked hurriedly. She must work quickly to be done in time. When she finally crawled into bed each night, she was too tired to even lie for very long and ache for Clem. She thought of him, and her last wish of the night was that he could have been by her side, cuddling close in the big double bed. But even though her thoughts turned to him, her tired body demanded sleep, and she mostly felt too weary to even cry.

Thursday dawned cold and windy. Clark was still determined to carry on with his plowing. Marty hoped he would not take a chill by so doing.

He paid no mind to her worries and went anyway. She wondered secretly if he wished to be away from the house as much as she wanted that.

After dinner was over and Missie had been put down for her nap, Marty went to work on the birthday cake. She felt much more confident now, having practiced with Ma's recipes. Carefully she watched her fire on this day. It would not do to have it too hot, nor to let it die out as she so often did.

She sighed with relief when she lifted Missie's cake from the oven. It appeared to be all that she had hoped for.

The wind was colder now and Marty found herself fussing about Clark. What in the world would she ever do if he took sick and needed nursing? *Dad-burn man! He shouldn't be taking such chances,* she scolded mentally. She'd keep the coffeepot on so whenever he decided to come in she'd have a hot cup waiting. She'd do almost anything, she figured, to keep him on his feet and walking. Why, if he went down sick, she wouldn't know where to start on the chores. She'd never even set foot in the barn, she realized. Some womenfolk had to do the milking all of the time, and for that matter, some did the slopping of the hogs, too. Clark hadn't even turned the feeding of the chickens over to her. Maybe he had expected it and she just hadn't done so. She had been so mixed up and confused when she came to this place that she hadn't given it a thought. Well, she'd ask. Maybe tomorrow at breakfast if the time seemed right. She was willing to do her rightful share.

She heard the team coming and cast a glance out the window.

"He be lookin' cold, all right," she murmured as she pushed the coffeepot forward on the stove.

When Clark came in, he stood for a few moments holding his big hands over the kitchen stove.

Marty poured his cup of coffee and went for some cream. She decided to also bring some muffins and honey in case he wanted a bite to go with the hot drink.

He watched her from the stove and said nothing until she had set it by his place at the table.

"Won't ya be a joinin' me?" he asked, then, "I hate to be a drinkin' coffee all alone."

Marty looked up in surprise but answered evenly, "Ya be the one thet be needin' it. Ya be chillin' yerself fer sure workin' out in thet wretched wind an' all. Lucky ya be iffen ya don't be a puttin' yerself down over it. Come, ya'd better be drinkin' this while it be hot."

It was a mild scolding, but something in it seemed to tickle Clark. He smiled to himself as he crossed to the table. She could hear his good-natured complaining. "Women—honestly, one would think a man was made o' sugar frostin' the way they can carry on." He looked at her directly and said, "I may be the one a needin' it, but I doubt thet a few minutes at the table an' off yer feet be a hurtin' ya much, either. You're doin' too much, I be a thinkin'." But his tone was kind.

"No," Marty said solemnly. "No, I don't do too much. I jest find thet workin' sure beats moanin', thet's all. But as ya say, a cup of coffee might be right good. I do declare, hearin' thet wind howl makes my blood chill, even though it be warm in here."

She poured herself a cup of coffee and joined him at the table.

After their coffee, Clark said he had come home early from the plowing because he thought a storm might be on the way and he wanted to have the rest of the garden things in the root cellar before it struck. So saying, he left the house.

Marty turned to Missie's now-cooled cake. She wanted it to look special for the little girl, so she used all her ingenuity and ingredients available for that purpose. When she was finally done, she looked at it critically. It wasn't great, she decided, but it would have to do. She placed it in the cupboard behind closed doors to await the proper moment. She set to work on plans for a little something extra for supper. Missie's call from the bedroom interrupted her, and she went in for the little girl.

"Hi there, Missie. Come to Mama," she said.

She had said the words before and hadn't liked them, so she had not referred to herself as such since. But as she spoke them now, they didn't seem nearly so out of place.

She lifted the wee one from the bed, noticing as she did so that her own little one was demanding more room. She was glad she had put plenty of fullness in the new dresses she had made.

Missie ran to get her shoes, and Marty carried child and shoes to the kitchen, where she put them on. Already it was chilly in the bedroom. She did not look forward to the cold winter ahead. How glad she was not to be in the covered wagon. The very thought made her shiver.

She gave Missie a mug of milk and half a muffin and went back to preparing the evening meal.

Clark finished up the work in the garden and did the evening chores a bit earlier than usual. Marty sensed an excitement he had not shown before. She knew he must have dreaded the arrival of his little girl's birthday without Ellen there to share it, but she also knew he wanted to make the most of it for Missie's sake.

After they had finished their supper, Marty went to the cupboard for the cake. Missie's eyes opened wide in wonder, but she did not understand its meaning.

"Pwetty, pwetty!" she cried over and over.

"It's Missie's birthday cake," Clark explained. "Missie's havin' a birthday. Missie was one," he indicated with one upright finger, "now Missie be two." Another finger joined the first.

"See, Missie," her pa continued the explanation, "you're two years old. Here, let me help ya."

He took the small hand in his big one and helped Missie hold upright two fingers.

"See, Missie, ya be two years old."

"Two—old," Missie repeated.

"Thet's right," said Clark, sounding well pleased. "Two years old, an' now we'll have some of Missie's birthday cake."

Marty cut the cake and was surprised at how good it was. As she took a bite she thought of her first effort with the biscuits. Now, thankfully, with practice and Ma's recipes, she could turn out things that she need not be ashamed of. Three weeks had made quite a difference. And Clark asked for and received a second piece of cake.

When they had finished, Marty was about to wash the supper dishes, but Clark suggested they first see what Missie thought of the gift he had purchased.

Clark went out to the shed and returned with a small box; then lifting Missie out of her chair, he presented it to her.

90

"Fer Missie's birthday," Clark said.

Missie turned and looked at the cake, as though wondering if she was to put "the birthday" in that small box.

"Look, Missie," Clark told her, "look here in the box. This is fer Missie on her birthday."

He helped the child lift the top lid, and Missie stared in wonder at the item in the box. Clark lifted it out, wound it firmly, and placed it on the floor. When he released it, it began to spin, whirling out in many colors of red, blue, yellow, violet—too many to name.

Missie clasped her hands together excitedly, too awestruck to say anything.

When it stopped whirling she pushed it toward Clark, saying, "Do it 'gin."

Marty watched for some time before she turned to the dishes, and then suddenly she remembered her own gift. It certainly wasn't anything as delightful for a little girl as Clark's, she thought as she carried it from the bedroom. Maybe Missie wouldn't care for it at all. Well, she'd done what she could with what she had.

"Missie," she announced as she entered the kitchen, "I have somethin' fer ya, too," and she held out her gift.

"Well, I be," Clark muttered in astonished tones. "Missie, jest look what yer mama done made ya."

Marty knelt in front of the child and carefully fitted 'round her shoulders the small shawl over which she had labored. It was done in a soft blue, with pink rosebuds embroidered on it. Tassels lined the edge, and they seemed to especially intrigue the little girl, whose hands kept stroking them.

"Oh," said Missie. "Oh, Mama."

It was the first time she had used the term, and Marty found herself swallowing a lump in her throat. She tried to hide her feelings by adjusting the shawl to hang right.

Suddenly she was aware that Clark was looking at her, and there was a puzzled look on his face. Marty glanced down self-consciously and in so doing saw with horror the reason for the look. In kneeling before the child she had knelt on her skirt, pinning it down firmly so its tightness outlined her growing body. Flushing, she scrambled to her feet.

Now I've gone an' done it, she thought angrily. Well, she couldn't have gone on hiding it forever anyway. Besides, why should she feel any shame? It was Clem's baby, conceived in wedlock and love. She couldn't help that he was no longer here to share parenthood with her. Still, she didn't know why, but she just wished that this man who had taken her in didn't have to know about it until it had arrived. Well, there was no use fretting about it. He knew now and there was nothing she could be doing about it.

She turned to the dishes and Clark went back to playing with Missie.

FIFTEEN

Disclosed Secret

Next morning the sky was dark and scowling. The wind still blew from the north, telling the world it was now in charge. The horses huddled together, backs to the storm, and the cows gathered in the shelter of the barn, trying to escape the chill of the gale. Very few chickens appeared outside of the coop, and those that did soon dashed back to the warmth of the building. As Marty noted their flight from the blast, she remembered her resolve to speak to Clark about assuming the care of them.

"Dad-burn," she exclaimed under her breath, "I sure did pick me a grand time to be startin'."

Clark's prayer at breakfast that morning included a thanks to the Almighty for the warm shelter that was theirs, both for man and beast, and for the fact that they need not fear the cold of winter, due to the mercies of their great God. *An' to this hardworking man hisself,* added Marty mentally. However, she did acknowledge the truth found in the prayer. It was comforting to know they were prepared for the cold weather ahead.

Marty was just getting around to wondering once again what on earth she would do with Clark around the house all day, when he took her completely off guard.

"I be leavin' fer town right away," he said. "Is there anythin' thet ya be needin'?"

"But it's only Friday," Marty responded.

"Yes'm, I know thet, but I have some business there thet I'd like to be a seein' to right away like, an' if a storm comes up, we might jest have to sit tight a spell."

Marty couldn't help but feel the idea was a rather foolish one. This time he'd take a chill for sure. He'd managed to somehow sneak past his last tempting of fate without appearing any the worse for it, but surely he couldn't be that lucky again. But who was she to argue, and with a man? If they made up their minds, there just wasn't much a body could do about it. She left the table and checked out her list to see if anything else should be added.

Clark sat with his last sips of coffee, then finally spoke, his voice low. "Me bein' a man and all, I didn't notice what I s'pose a woman would have see'd long ago. I had me no idea thet ya was expectin' a young'un."

Marty did not look up from her list. She did not want to meet his eyes.

"I'm right sorry thet I didn't know. I might have saved ya some of the harder things. From now on, ya'll do no more totin' of them heavy water pails. When ya be needin' extra water fer washin' an' sech, ya be lettin' me know."

How silly, thought Marty. *If this baby gonna be harmed by totin' water, the damage be done long ago.*

But she said nothing, and Clark went on. "We be blessed with lots of good fresh milk. I hope ya be takin' advantage of it. If there be anythin' ya need or anythin' I can do, I'd be obliged if ya let me know."

He paused, then said, "Seein' as how I be goin' to town today anyhow, I figured as how maybe Mrs. McDonald would fix up a bundle of sewing pieces thet ya be needin' to sew baby things. If there be anythin' in particular thet ya be settin' yer mind on, then try to describe it fer her on the list."

Marty stood tongue-tied, and she felt her stomach knot. She hadn't gotten around to worrying yet how she would clothe the new young one. It had seemed so very far off in the future, but Clark was right. She must start sewing or she'd never be ready.

"Thank ya," she finally answered Clark. "I'm sure Mrs. McDonald be knowin' better'n me what I be needin'," and she handed him the completed list.

She looked out of the window, still anxious about the weather. Storms came suddenly out here on the prairie sometimes, she was told, and she hated to see Clark set out when there was a chance that one was on the way. He seemed to read her thoughts.

"Plenty of time to git to town an' back," he said. "Iffen a storm should catch me, there be plenty of neighbors livin' between here an' town, an' I'd be able to take shelter with one of them if I be needin' to."

"But . . . but what 'bout the chores?" Marty stammered. "I don't even know what to do, or where to find the feed, or nuthin'."

Clark swung around to face her, and it was clear from the look on his face that he had not considered the question of her with the chores.

"Iffen a storm be comin' an' I have to shelter an' don't make it home, ya don't leave this house. Do ya hear?"

Marty heard, loud and clear.

"Don't ya worry none 'bout the hens or the hogs or even the milk cows. Nuthin'—I mean nuthin'—out there be so important thet I want ya out there in a storm tryin' ta care fer it."

So that's the way it be, thought Marty, hiding her smile. *Well, he needn't get so riled up 'bout it.*

It was the closest to upset she had ever seen Clark, and she couldn't help but be surprised. He turned from her, buttoned his heavy jacket, and reached for his mitts. He hesitated. "Might be a fine day to be a piecin' a quilt. The little feller will be a needin' a warm 'un."

Yeah, Marty thought, *he—or maybe she—most likely will.*

"I'll be back fer chore time," Clark assured her as he moved to go out the door; then he paused a moment and said quietly, "I be right glad thet ya'll have a little'un to remember 'im by"—and he was gone.

SIXTEEN

Thoughtful and Caring

Clark did return in time for the chores, much to Marty's relief. By then the snow was falling, swirling around angrily as it passed the window. Clark went right on down to the barn to take care of Dan and Charlie.

"He be settin' more stock on them horses than on his own self," Marty murmured to herself as she watched from the kitchen window. "He's been out in the weather as long as them two."

She moved to the stove and pushed the coffee closer to the center of the firebox so that it would be sure to be hot.

Missie had been playing on the floor, but when she heard Ole Bob's joyous bark of welcome, she jumped up, eyes shining.

"Daddy comin'," she said excitedly.

Marty smiled, noting again the fact that Missie often said "Daddy" even though Clark referred to himself as "Pa." Ellen must have preferred "Daddy," Marty decided. Well, then, for Ellen's sake, she would talk about Daddy to Missie, too.

Clark was soon in, arms full of bundles and face red from the cold wind. At the sight of her pa, Missie danced around wildly.

"Daddy here—Daddy here. Hi, Pa."

Clark called to her and, when he had rid himself of his parcels, swung the little girl up into his arms. She exclaimed over his cold face as she patted his cheeks.

"Best ya be warmin' up a bit 'fore ya start the chores," Marty suggested as she poured a cup of coffee.

"Sounds like a right good idea," he responded, taking off his heavy coat and hanging it by the fire to let it warm until he had to go out again. He stood for a moment with his hands over the stove and then crossed to the table. Marty poured cream in the coffee and placed it before him.

"Thet there fair-sized bundle be yourn," Clark said. "Mrs. McDonald was right excited 'bout fixin' it up. Think she was a mite confused. Seemed to think it was my young'un. It bein' none of her business, I didn't bother none to set her straight."

He swallowed a few more gulps of hot coffee. Marty's thoughts whirled.

His young'un? How could it be his young'un, us not even bein' true man an' wife? 'Course, Mrs. McDonald wouldn't be knowin' thet. She felt her face coloring in embarrassment.

Clark put down his cup and calmly continued, "I got ta thinkin' later, though, thet maybe I should've said somethin', so I went back. 'Mrs. McDonald,' I says, 'true, my missus be havin' a young'un, and true I'll be a treatin' it as one of mine, but also true thet the pa be her first husband an' thet bein' important to her, I wouldn't want folks gettin' things mixed up like.'"

Clark finished his coffee. "Well, I best be gettin'."

He shrugged into his coat and was gone before Marty had time to get her scrambling thoughts in order.

He understood. He'd gone back to the store to set Mrs. McDonald straight because he knew, as Ma Graham had told Marty, that her tongue was the busiest part of her anatomy. Give the woman a day or two of fair weather and everyone in the area would know of the coming baby.

Clark understands that it be important to me that the new baby be known as Clem's. Her mind continued to try to sort out this man as she began to put away the supplies he had purchased.

She turned with anticipation to her bundle and decided to take it in on her bed to examine the contents. It was cold in the bedroom now, and she shivered, partly from excitement, she was sure, as she unwrapped the brown store paper.

Mrs. McDonald certainly had gone all out. Marty's hands went to her face as she looked at the beautiful materials. Surely a young'un didn't need that many baby things. Her cheeks flushed at the thought of the days and evenings ahead when she could sit and work on the small garments. She wished she had someone to talk with about her feelings and was tempted to pour it all out on Missie. No, she'd best wait awhile for that. The remaining months would seem far too long for a two-year-old. Oh, if only Clem were here to share it with her. Her eyes filled once again, and a hot tear trickled down. She brushed it away with the back of her hand. If only it were that easy to get rid of the pain in her heart.

When Clark came in to supper, he was noticeably shivering in spite of his heavy coat. He remarked that he couldn't believe how much the temperature had dropped in a few short hours. The wind no doubt had a great deal to do with it, he added.

Before he sat down to the table, he lit the fireplace in the sitting room.

"Guess it's time," he observed, "to be havin' more heat than jest the cook stove."

When he prayed that night, he asked God to be with "people less blessed than we," and Marty was reminded of her covered wagon with the broken wheel. She shivered to think of what it would be like to be huddled in it now, trying to keep warm under their scant blankets.

After the meal Clark moved to the sitting room to check and replenish the fire, and Missie brought in her few toys to the rug in front of it.

Marty did the dishes, feeling warm and protected in spite of herself. How else could she feel in a snug cabin while the wind screamed around its corners, unable to get in?

The evening was still young, and Marty was anxious to get started on her sewing, but she realized how cold her room would be. She was still trying to figure out some answer to her problem as she emptied her dishpan and replaced it on its peg.

"It'll be right cold in yer room from now on," she heard Clark say from behind her. "Do ya be wantin' yer machine moved out to the sittin' room? There be plenty of room there fer it."

Marty turned and looked directly at him as she asked slowly, "Do ya mind seein' it sittin' there?"

"S'pose I do some," he answered frankly. "But it's not as hard now as it was at first sight of it, an' 'twould be only foolhardy not to put it where it can be of best use. I'll git used to it." So saying, he went to do as he had suggested.

Yes, Marty thought to herself, *this man will do the right thing even if it hurts.*

She felt a bit selfish about her anticipation of sewing in the warm room. If things had to be as they were, caught in a marriage she certainly would not have chosen on her own, she could have done worse. She still ached for her Clem. She wished him back, even if it meant having far less than what she had now. Still, she would be unfair if she refused to see the goodness in this man whose name she had taken and whose home she shared. That he was a real worker and a good provider was apparent, but she was discovering other things about him, too—things like thoughtfulness and caring. Certainly she couldn't fault him in his demands on her. She was only expected to be Missie's mama and to keep up the little home. He hadn't even complained about her cooking. No, she decided, even though she didn't like her situation, she could have done much worse.

She set her mind on her sewing. She would give Missie a bit more playing time before she tucked her in for the night. Clark had settled himself near the fireplace with one of his new books. Marty thankfully picked up a pattern that Mrs. McDonald had included. She had never sewed for one so small before and would have been hard put to know how to cut the material without the pattern. Her hands fairly trembled with excitement. She'd do the cutting on the kitchen table, where she had more room. She couldn't help but think the three of them seemed almost like a real family.

SEVENTEEN

Mysterious Absence

The days of November brought more storms, and snow lay heavy on the fields and big drifts rose around sheltered spots. Occasionally the wind ceased blowing and the sun shone, but the temperature always stayed below freezing. There was still much to do, however, and activity on the small homestead did not cease because of the weather. Whenever the snowstorms abated, Clark hitched up the horses and spent his time with faithful Dan and Charlie in the wooded backcountry gathering logs for their fuel supply.

On the more miserable days, extra time spent in the barn eased the animals through the inclement weather with as little discomfort as possible.

Marty filled her days caring for Missie, keeping up the house, baking bread, washing, mending, ironing—the list seemed endless to her, yet she was thankful to have each of the long days occupied, particularly ones that held her indoors.

In the evenings she went gladly to her sewing, adding each stitch on the tiny garments with tender care. She had laid aside the quilt she had begun. It could wait. She wanted to concentrate on preparations for the baby.

She had noticed Clark often referred to the coming infant as "he." The baby could surprise them both and be a girl, she knew, but Marty was rather determined to think of a son for Clem.

She'd already decided on a name—Claridge Luke. Claridge after his pa's last name, and Luke in honor of her father. How proud her pa would be to know he had a grandson bearing his name. But that would have to wait for the first wagon train going east, when she'd pack up her son—maybe even Missie—and head back home.

The thought of taking Missie along with her was of more and more concern. What was best—both for the little girl and for Clark? She saw the great love Clark had for his daughter, and she wondered when the time came if he'd really be able to let her go. Or if he should. Marty herself was getting awfully attached to the child. Saying "Mama" came easy now to both of them. Indeed, sneaking up quite unawares was the feeling she was just that, Missie's mama. Each day she enjoyed the young child's company more, laughing at her silly antics, marveling at her new words, and even sharing some of them with Clark when he came home at night.

With Marty hardly realizing it, Missie was becoming very much a part of her life. She could barely wait for the new year, the time she had planned for telling her secret to the little girl. She was sure the child would share her anticipation of the new baby. But Marty didn't let herself stop to think too deeply about it all or to analyze her gradually changing feelings. It was enough just to tick the slow days off, discarding them casually like something that had served its purpose, and move forward; for indeed, Marty was still marking time.

As November drew to a close, Marty realized that Clark seemed to have made an unusual number of trips into town, especially for that time of year. It wasn't as though they had need of specific supplies. They had stocked up in preparation for winter's confining grip. And indeed Clark sometimes returned with very few purchases, even using the saddle horse on occasion rather than the team. Marty hadn't thought to wonder about it at first, but this morning's breakfast conversation had gotten her to puzzling over it. Clark had announced casually enough that he would be gone for three or four days. There appeared to be a break in the weather, he explained, so he had decided now was the time to make a trip to a town much larger than their small local one. Clark had arranged for young Tom Graham to come in the evening and stay the night to look after the evening and morning chores, he told her. If the weather should turn sour, Marty could ask him to stay on through the day, as well. If she was in need of anything, she could send word with Tom to the Grahams.

His words had puzzled Marty. He indeed had taken an unusual number of trips, now that she thought about it, but really it was none of her business. He was probably looking for new machinery to till the land, or better seed, or a place to sell his hogs. Anyway, it was his doings, so why should she worry over it? Young Tom would be over. There was nothing further with which to concern herself.

Still, as Clark gave Missie a good-bye hug and admonished her to be a good girl for her mama, Marty couldn't help but feel at least curious and maybe a bit uneasy.

"I'll be back Saturday night in time fer chores," he promised and went to the barn for Dan and Charlie. As Marty watched him leave the yard, she noticed that the crate was in the wagon box and a couple of hogs were having a ride along to town.

What had he said a while ago? *"If we be needin' more cash, we can al'ays sell a hog."*

He must be shoppin' for 'nother plow or more seed, she decided with a shrug. Still, on the other hand, she had cost him a powerful lot of extra money, what with the winter clothing for herself, the wool for knitting and the pieces for quilting, and then to top it off, the things for the baby.

Marty fretted over the realization, something she usually kept herself from doing. Finally, with real effort she pushed it aside.

"No use takin' on so," she murmured to herself. "Guess I'm jest a mite off my feed or somethin' to be stewin' 'bout it so. Wish I could have me a good visit with Ma. Thet'd set things to right. By the time Clark gits back, it'll be December already."

Time was indeed moving on, no matter how slow it could seem, and hadn't Ma said that it was time that healed? She hoped the days would go quickly while Clark was away.

Marty was more relieved than she would admit to see the team coming on Saturday as the sun was setting. She didn't know why she should feel that way. Young Tom had done a fine job of the chores, she was sure, and she hadn't at all minded his company in the evenings. After supper he played with Missie or read and reread her book to her. He was proud of the fact that he had learned his letters and knew how to read, as did each of Ma's children. He loved to show off to Missie and—Marty smiled—to her, as well, she wagered. By now Missie could repeat many of the lines of her book and loved to pretend she was reading herself.

They had gotten along just fine while Clark was away, so that had no bearing on her sense of relief to see him come home. Perhaps deep within was the haunting memory of a casual good-bye to Clem and a later discovery that it had been the last, but she shook off that possibility and went to tell Missie that her pa was home.

Missie was overjoyed at the sight of her daddy and began a dance as soon as she spotted him from the chair at the window.

Marty noticed the crate was now empty, but she could see no purchase that might have been made from the proceeds. Only a few small packages sat on the seat beside Clark. Dan and Charlie looked weary, she thought, as she watched them plod toward the barn, but their steps picked up as they drew near warm stalls and a full manger.

Clark looks tired, too, she decided as she watched him climb down and begin to unhitch the team. He wasn't moving with the same energy that usually accompanied his activities.

"Well, your pa's here now an' he'll be wantin' some hot coffee," Marty remarked as she helped Missie down from her perch at the window.

Coffee presented no problem, for Marty had it at the ready. She had made it in between her pacings back and forth to the window watching for the first glimpse of the team.

Things, she hoped, would continue on now in their usual way. This wasn't the life she had wanted or planned, but at least her days had taken on a pattern now familiar to her, and there was a certain amount of comfort in the familiar.

Clark came in with a few groceries, and Marty welcomed him with a cup of coffee and a happy little girl to greet him.

EIGHTEEN

Christmas Preparations

"Our God," Clark addressed the Almighty in his morning prayer, "as we be nearin' the season of yer Son's birth, make our hearts thankful thet He came, an' help us to be lovin' our neighbor with a love like He showed us."

He's talkin' 'bout Christmas, Marty thought with a sudden awareness of the season. *Oh my, it be only two weeks away, an' I haven't even been thinkin' on it.*

Her mind went plunging from thought to thought, so again she had missed the rest of the prayer and sat with eyes still closed after the "amen." Missie pulled at her sleeve, wanting her breakfast.

Marty lifted a flushed face and hurriedly fixed Missie's porridge for her, blowing on it to cool it before giving it to the child.

"Ya know," she ventured a little later, "I had fergot all 'bout how close Christmas be."

Clark looked up from his own bowl of porridge. "I know Christmas be a mite hard to be a thinkin' on this year. Iffen it be too hard fer ya, we can most ferget the day, 'cept fer the reading of the Story an' maybe a sock fer young Missie."

Marty thought for a few minutes.

"No," she finally answered. "Thet wouldn't be right. Missie needs her Christmas—a proper one like, an' I reckon it may do us good, too. We can't stay back in the past nursin' our sorrow—not for her sake, nor fer our own. Christmas, seems to me, be a right good time to lay aside hurtin' an' look fer somethin' healin'."

Clark stared at her for a while, then dropped his eyes back to his bowl. He finally said quietly, "Seems I never heard a better sermon from any visitin' preacher than the one I jest heard." He paused a moment, then said, "Ya be right, of course. So what ya be plannin'?"

"Well . . ." Marty turned it over in her mind, trying to recall exactly what had happened at her home to prepare for Christmas. There hadn't been the reading of the Scripture story, but they could add that easy enough. And there had been a good supply of corn liquor, which they could do without. Otherwise, there must be several things she could do the way her mother had. This would be her first Christmas away from home—the first Christmas for her to make for others, rather than have others make for her. The thought made her feel both uneasy and excited.

"Well," she began again, "I'll git me to doin' some Christmas bakin'. Maybe Ma has some special recipes she'll share. Then we'll have a tree fer Missie. Christmas Eve we'll put it up after she be tucked in, an' we'll string popcorn an' make some colored chains, an' have a few candles fer the windows, an' we'll kill a couple of the finest roosters, an' I'll find me somethin' to be makin' fer Missie—"

The excitement growing in her must have been infectious. Clark joined in with his own anticipation of the coming Christmas.

"Roosters, nuthin'," he announced. "I'll go myself an' buy us a turkey from the Vickers. Mrs. Vickers raises some first-rate 'uns. Maybe there be somethin' we can be makin' fer Missie together. I'll ride over to Ma's today an' git the recipes—or better still, it looks like a decent day. Ya be wantin' me to hitch ole Dan an' Charlie so ya can be goin' yerself?"

"Oh, could I?" Marty's tone held the plea in her heart. "I'd love to see Ma fer a chat—iffen yer sure it be all right."

So it was decided that Marty would go to the Grahams'. But Clark added another dimension to the plan. If it was okay with her, he'd drive her to Ma's, and then he and Missie would go on to the Vickers's and get the turkey. That way they'd be sure to have it when the big day arrived. Missie could do with some fresh air, too, and some time with her pa.

Marty hurried through the dishes as Clark went to get the team. She bundled Missie up snugly and slipped into her long coat. It was the first time she had worn it, and she thought, looking at herself with a grin, perhaps the last for a while. Two of the buttons refused to meet their matching buttonholes. She sighed. "Well," she told Missie, taking her shawl, "guess I'll jest have to cover up the rest o' me with this."

The day spent with Ma was a real treat. They pored over Ma's recipes, Marty selecting so many that she'd never get them all baked. She would choose some from among the many at a later date. She also wrote down careful instructions on how to stuff and roast the turkey, it being her first attempt at such an endeavor. They shared plans and discussed possibilities for the holiday ahead. Marty felt a stirring of new interest within her at the anticipation of it. For too long she had felt that the young life she carried was the only living part of her. Now for the first time in months she began to feel alive again.

Before she knew it, she heard the team approaching. Clark was called in for a cup of coffee before setting off for home, and he came in carrying a rosy-faced Missie, excited by her ride and eager to tell everyone of the "gobble-gobble" they had in the wagon for "Christ'as."

Marty could hear the live turkey vigorously protesting his separation from the rest of the flock. Clark had said he would be placed in the hens' coop and generously given cracked corn and other fattening things until a few days before Christmas.

Missie romped with young Lou while the grown-ups had their coffee, too excited to even finish her glass of milk.

On the way home Marty got up the nerve to voice a thought that had gradually been taking shape. She was a bit hesitant and hardly knew how to express it.

"Do ya s'pose—I mean, would ya mind iffen we had the Grahams come fer Christmas dinner?"

"All of 'em?" Clark's shock was evident.

"'Course, all of 'em," Marty rejoined stoutly. "I know there be thirteen of 'em an' three of us; thet makes sixteen. The kitchen table, stretched out like, will hold eight. Thet's the four grown-ups an' the four youngest of the Grahams. Missie'll be in her chair. Thet leaves seven Graham young'uns. We'll fix 'em a place in the sittin' room an' Laura an' Sally Anne can look after 'em."

She would have babbled on, but Clark, with a laugh and an upright hand, stopped her. "Whoa." Then he said, "I see ya got it all sorted out. Did ya speak with Ma on it?"

"'Course not," said Marty. "I wouldn't be doin' thet afore I checked with you."

He looked sideways at her, and his voice took on a serious note. "I don't know." He hesitated. "Seems to me it be a pretty big order, gettin' on a Christmas dinner fer sixteen, an' servin' it in our small quarters, an' ya bein' the way ya are an' all."

Marty knew she must fight for it if her idea was to be.

She scoffed at his protest. "Pawsh! There be nuthin' wrong with the way I be. I feel as pert now as I ever did. As to fixin' the dinner, I'll have as much of thet done ahead as I can, afore the house packs jam tight. Then 'twon't be sech a problem. When they gits there, Ma and the girls will give a hand—an' with the dishes, too. Oh my—"

She stopped and fairly squealed. "Dishes! Clark, do we have enough dishes to set so many?"

"I don't know, but iffen ya don't, Ma'll bring some of hers along."

"Good!"

She smiled to herself. He had as good as said that they could come. She had sort of swung him off track by diverting his attention to the dishes. She felt a bit guilty but not enough to be bothered by it. "It be settled, then," she ventured, more a statement than a question.

NINETEEN

Snowbound

Clark went back to his days in the hills felling trees, and Marty went to work in her kitchen. She pored over the recipes and, after finally making her choices, spent day after day turning out tempting goodies. In spite of Missie's attempts to "help," baked goods began to stock up almost alarmingly, and she was having a hard time finding places to put all of them.

Missie sampled and approved, preferring the gingerbread boys Marty had made especially for the children.

In the evenings she and Clark worked together on a dollhouse for Missie. Clark had constructed a simple two-room structure and was busy making wooden chairs, tables, and beds. Marty's part was to put in small curtains, rugs, and blankets. "Those things a woman usually be makin'," Clark had said. She found it to be fun helping with the project, watching it take shape. The kitchen had a small cupboard with doors that really opened, a table, two chairs, and a bench. This was Clark's work. Marty had put up little kitchen curtains, added a couple of bright rugs on the floor, and put small cushions on the chairs.

The sitting-bedroom had a small bed complete with blankets and pillows, a tiny cradle, two chairs, a footstool, and a trunk with a lid that lifted. Marty still had to fix the blanket and pillow for the cradle and the curtains for this room. Clark was working on a stove for the kitchen.

"Wouldn't be much of a kitchen without a stove," he reasoned.

Marty was pleased with their efforts and glad that the dollhouse should easily be finished in time for Missie's Christmas.

Clark had made several more trips into town, stopping the first time to invite the Grahams to Christmas dinner. He seemed to feel these trips were important, yet as far as Marty could see, he had nothing to show for them when he returned. She shrugged it off.

The last time he had brought back some special spices for her baking and a few trinkets for Missie.

"She be needin' somethin' fer her Christmas sock," he said as he handed them over to Marty's care.

Marty reviewed all this in her thinking as she laid cookies out to cool.

Would Clark be expecting a gift from her? She supposed not. It would have been nice to have some little thing for him, but she had no money for a purchase and no way of getting someplace to buy it. And what could one sew for a man?

As she worked she remembered the piece of soft blue-gray wool that still lay in her sewing basket. After she finished the cookies, she'd take a look at it and see if it were possible to make a man's scarf out of the material.

When she later checked the material, she decided it was quite possible. Knowing that Clark wouldn't be in from cutting trees until chore time, she set to work. She finished the stitching, finding it necessary to do a bit of piecing, and then tucked it away. Tomorrow while Clark was away she would hand embroider his initials on it.

Christmas would soon be here. She wondered if the day itself would be half as exciting as the preparations for it had been.

Only three days to go now. They had finished their gift for Missie the night before and complimented each other on the outcome. Now breakfast was over, and Clark had gone back to cutting wood. Marty asked him to keep an eye open for nice pine branches bearing cones so she might form a few wreaths. He said he would see what he could do.

Clark would work in the morning in the hills, and in the afternoon he would kill the gobbler, who at the present was going without his breakfast. Marty hurried through her tasks, then took up the scarf for Clark. Carefully she stitched a bold C. D. on it and had it tucked away in her drawer before Clark arrived for dinner.

Now just two days until Christmas, but the day was the Lord's Day, and any further preparations would have to wait. Marty conceded to herself that perhaps a day of rest was not such a bad idea, and when Missie was tucked in for her afternoon nap, she stretched out on her own bed, a warm blanket drawn over her. She felt weary, really weary, and the weight of the baby she carried made every task she took on doubly hard. She closed her eyes and gave herself up to a delightful sleep.

Day one—the morrow would be Christmas. The tom was killed, plucked, cleaned, and hung to chill in preparation for stuffing. Marty had carefully formed her wreaths, pleased with Clark's selected branches, and tied them with her cherished store twine. She had placed one in each window and one on the door. A small tree had come from the hills with Clark's last load of wood and waited outside until the time when Missie would be tucked in bed and it would be placed in a corner of the sitting room. The corn already had been popped and strung, and Marty had made chains from bits of colored paper that she had carefully saved. She had even made some out of the brown store wrap that had come from town.

The scarf lay completed, but as Marty looked at it a feeling of uneasiness overtook her. Somehow it didn't seem the thing to be giving a man like Clark. She wondered if she'd really have the courage to go through with it.

Well, she said, mentally shelving the matter, *I'll have to be handlin' thet when the time comes, an' jest keep my mind on what I'm doin' now.*

What she was "doin' now" was peeling large quantities of carrots, turnips, and potatoes for the Christmas dinner. There would be cabbage to dice, as well. The batch of bread was rising and would soon be ready for baking. The beans were soaking and would be flavored with cured ham later. Canned greens and pickles were lined up on the floor by the cupboard, waiting to be opened, and wild nuts were placed in a basket by the fireplace to be roasted over the open fire.

Mentally Marty ticked off her list. Things seemed to be going as scheduled. She looked around her at the abundance of food. Tomorrow promised to be a good day, and tonight they'd have the fun of decking the tree for Missie and hanging her sock.

Christmas Day! Marty opened her eyes earlier than usual, and already her head was spinning. She must prepare the stuffing for the turkey, put the vegetables on to cook in her largest kettles, bring in plenty of the baking from the shed, where it was sure to be frozen in this weather. Her mind raced on as she quickly dressed.

The room felt so cold she'd be glad to get to the warm kitchen. She silently bent over Missie to check that she was properly covered, then quietly tiptoed from the room.

It was cold in the sitting room, too, and she hurried on to the kitchen. There was no lamp lit there, so Clark was not up. She shivered as she hastened to light it and moved on to start the fire. It was so cold that her hands already felt numb. She could hear the wind whining around the cabin as she coaxed the blaze to take hold. It would be a while before the chill left the air. She moved into the sitting room to light the fire there. She must have it warm when Missie got up.

When both fires were burning, she checked the clock. Twenty minutes to six. No wonder Clark wasn't up yet. He usually rose about six-thirty in the winter months. Well, she needed every minute she could get. She had so much to do.

She turned to the frost-covered window and scratched a small opening with her fingers to look out on Christmas Day. An angry wind swirled heavily falling snow, piling drifts in seemingly mountainous proportions. She could not even see the well for the density of it.

Marty didn't need to be told that she was witnessing a dreaded prairie blizzard. The pain of it all began to seep in. She wanted to scream out against it, to curse it away, to throw herself on her bed in a torrent of tears. Her shoulders sagged and she felt weary and defeated. But what good would it do to strike back? The storm would still rage. None in their right mind would defy it simply for a Christmas dinner. She was licked. She felt dead again. Then suddenly a new anger took hold of her. Why? Why should the storm win?

"Go ahead," she stormed aloud as she stared out through the window. "Go ahead and howl. We have the turkey ready to go in the oven. We have lots of food. We have our tree. We have Missie. We'll—we'll jest still have Christmas!"

She wiped angry tears on her apron, squared her shoulders, and turned back to add more wood to the fire. Then she noticed Clark sitting there, boots in hand, watching her.

He cleared his throat, and she looked steadily at him. She had worked so hard for this day and now she was cheated out of it. She hoped he would not try to say something understanding or her resolve might crumble. She quickly moved to stand in front of him as he sat lacing his boots, and with a smile she waved her hand toward the laden cupboard. "My word. What're we ever gonna be doin' with all this food? We'll have to spend the whole day eatin' on it."

She moved back to the cupboard and began work on preparing the turkey for roasting.

"I do hope thet the Grahams haven't been caught short-fixed fer Christmas. Us sittin' here with jest us three an' all this food, an' them sittin' there with so many. . . ." She drifted to a halt and glanced over at Clark, who sat there openmouthed, a boot dangling from his hand.

He shook his head slightly, then said, "Ma's too smart to be took off guard like. She knows this country's mean streak. I don't think they be a wantin' at all."

Marty felt relieved at that news. "I be right glad to hear thet," she said. "The storm had me worryin'."

She finished stuffing the turkey, then opened the oven door.

"Best ya let me be liftin' thet bird. He's right heavy," Clark said and hurried over to put it in.

Marty did not object. With it safely roasting and the stove gradually warming the kitchen, Marty put on the coffeepot and then took a chair.

"Seems the storm nearly won," she acknowledged slowly, "but it can't win unless ya let it, can it?"

Clark said nothing, but as she looked at him his eyes told her that he understood her disappointment—and more than that, her triumph over it.

He reached out and touched her hand. When he spoke his voice was gentle. "I'm right proud of ya, Marty."

He had never touched her before except for helping her in and out of the wagon, and something about it sent a warm feeling through her. Maybe it was knowing that he understood. She hoped he hadn't noticed her response to his touch and quickly said, "We'll have to cook the whole turkey, but we can freeze what we can't eat. I'll put the vegetables in smaller pots an' cook only what we be needin'. The rest will keep fer a while in the cold pit. The bakin'"—she stopped and waved a hand to all the goodies stacked around and laughed—"we be eatin' thet till spring iffen we don't git some help."

"Thet's one thing I don't be complainin' 'bout," Clark said. "Here I was worryin' 'bout all those Graham young'uns with their hefty appetites comin' an' not leavin' anythin' fer me, an' now look at me, blessed with it all."

"Clark," Marty said in mock dismay, "did you go an' pray up this storm?"

She'd never heard him laugh so heartily before, and she joined in with him. By then the coffee was boiling, and she poured two cups while he went for the cream. The kitchen was warmer now, and the hot coffee washed away the last of the chill in her.

"Well," she said, getting up as quickly as her extra burden would allow, "we may as well have some bakin' to go with it. Gotta git started on it sometime. What ya be fancyin'?"

Clark chose a spicy tart and Marty took a simple shortbread cookie.

They talked of the day ahead as they shared their coffee. Clark wouldn't go out for the chores until after Missie was up. That way he wouldn't miss out on her excitement. Then they would have a late breakfast and their Christmas dinner midafternoon. The evening meal would be "the pickin's," Clark said. That would save Marty from being at the stove all day. It sounded like a reasonable plan to her, and she nodded her agreement.

"We used to play a game when I was a kid," Clark said. "Haven't played a game fer years, but it might be fun. It was drawed out on a piece o' paper or a board, an' ya used pegs or buttons. While ya be busyin' about, I'll make us up one."

The clock ticked on and the snow did not cease nor the wind slacken, but it didn't matter now. It had been accepted as a fact of prairie life, and the adjustments had been made.

When Missie called from her bed, Clark went for her. Marty stationed herself by the sitting room fire to watch the little girl's response to their Christmas preparations. They were not disappointed. Missie was beside herself with excitement. She rushed to the tree, went from the small toys in her sock to the dollhouse, then to the sock, back to the dollhouse, exclaiming over and over her wonder of it all. Finally she stopped, clasped her tiny hands together, and said, "Oh, Chris'as bootiful."

Clark and Marty laughed. She was off again, kneeling before the dollhouse, handling each small item carefully as she took it out and placed it back again.

Clark finally stood reluctantly to go do the chores. The storm was still raging, and he dressed warmly against it. Caring for the stock would be difficult on such a day, and he murmured to Marty that he was glad the animals were sheltered from the wind.

Marty felt some concern as she watched him go out. The snow was so thick at times that you couldn't see the barn. She was glad he took Ole Bob with him, as the dog could sense directions should the storm confuse Clark. He also left instructions with her. If he wasn't in by midmorning, she was to fire the gun into the air and repeat, if necessary, at five-minute intervals. Marty fervently hoped it wouldn't be necessary.

Much to Marty's relief, Clark was in before the appointed time, chilled by the wind but reporting all things in order.

She put the finishing touches on breakfast, and they sat down to eat. Missie could hardly bear to leave her new toys and came only with repeated promises that she could return to them following the meal.

They all bowed their heads and Clark prayed. "Sometimes, Lord, we be puzzlin' 'bout yer ways. Thank ya, Lord, thet the storm came well afore the Grahams be settin' out. We wouldn't want 'em caught in sech a one."

Marty hadn't thought of that, but she totally agreed.

"An', Lord, thank ya fer those who share our table, an' bless this day of yer Son's birth. May it be one thet we can remember with warm feelin's even if the day be cold. Thank ya, Lord, fer this food thet ya have provided by yer goodness. Amen."

"Amen," said Missie, then she looked up at her pa. "The house"—she pointed—"thanks—house."

Clark looked puzzled. Marty, too, felt bewildered but tried to understand what the small child meant.

"I believe she be wantin' ya to say thanks fer her dollhouse," Marty finally ventured.

"Is thet it? Okay, Missie, we pray again. An' thank ya, Lord, fer Missie's dollhouse. Amen."

Missie was satisfied, and after her second "amen," she quickly began work on her breakfast between quick glances over at the beloved dollhouse.

They roasted nuts at the open fire, played the game Clark had made, which Marty won with alarming consistency, and watched Missie at her play. When the child was later tucked in for a nap, a tiny doll chair firmly grasped in hand, Marty got busy with the final dinner preparations. After the child awoke they would have their Christmas dinner. She wanted everything to be just right. From those early days of only pancakes to a bountiful table spread with all manner of good things in just a little over two months. Marty was rather pleased with herself.

After they had eaten more than enough of the sumptuous meal, Clark suggested they read the Christmas story in the sitting room while their food settled.

"Yer turnin' out to be a right fine cook," he observed, and Marty could feel herself flush at the compliment. "I think Ma Graham would be even more impressed than me," he went on, "and we'll jest have to plan us another get-together so she can find out fer herself."

They moved to the sitting room, and Clark took Missie on his knee and opened the Bible. He first read of the angel appearing to the young girl, Mary, telling her that she had been chosen as the mother of the Christ child. He went on to read of Joseph and Mary's trip to Bethlehem, where no room was found in the inn, so that night the infant Jesus was born in a stable and laid in the cattle's manger. The shepherds heard the good news from the angels and rushed to see the newborn king. Then the wise men came, following the star and bearing their gifts to the child, going home a different way for the protection of the baby.

Marty thought she had never heard anything so beautiful. She couldn't remember ever knowing the complete story before as it was given in the Scriptures. A little baby born in a stable was God's Son. She placed a hand over her own little one.

Wouldn't be carin' fer my son to be born in a barn, she thought. *Don't suppose God was wantin' it thet way, either, but no one had room fer a wee baby. Still—God did watch over Him, sendin' angels to tell the shepherds an' all. An' the wise men, too, with their rich gifts. Yes, God was carin' 'bout His Son.*

The story captured Marty's imagination as she waited for the birth of her own first child, and she thought on it as she did the dishes. After she was through in the kitchen she returned to the sitting room. Clark had gone out to do the evening chores before it got too dark. It was hard enough to see one's way in the daylight in such a storm.

Marty sat down and picked up the Bible. She wished she knew where to locate the Christmas story so she might read it again, but as she turned the pages she couldn't find where Clark had read. She did find the Psalms, though, and read one after the other as she sat beside the warm fire. Somehow they were comforting, even when you didn't understand all of the phrases and ideas, she thought.

She read until she heard Clark entering the shed and then laid the Book aside. She'd best put on the coffee and get those "pickin's" ready.

Later that evening, after Missie had been put to bed, Marty got up the courage to ask Clark if he'd mind reading "the story" again. As he read, she sat trying to absorb it all. She knew a bit more about it this time, so she could follow with more anticipation, catching things she had missed the first time. She fleetingly wondered if Clem had ever heard all of this. It was such a beautiful story.

Oh, Clem! her heart cried. *I wish I coulda shared sech a Christmas with you.* But it was not to be, and Marty took a deep breath and concentrated on the story from the Book.

After the reading, Marty sat in silence, only her knitting needles clicking, for she did not enjoy idleness, even on Christmas.

Clark put the Bible away and went out to the lean-to. He returned with a small package.

"It ain't much," he said, looking both sheepish and expectant at the same time, "to be sayin' thank ya fer carin' fer Missie an' all."

Marty took it from him with a slight feeling of embarrassment. Fumbling, she took off the wrapping to reveal a beautiful dresser set, with ivory comb, brush, and hand mirror. Hand-painted flowers graced the backs in pale golds and rusts. It nearly took Marty's breath away.

She turned the mirror over in her hand and noticed letters on the handle, M.L.C.D. It took a minute for her to realize they were her initials: Martha Lucinda Claridge Davis. He had not only given her the set, he had given her back her name. Tears pushed out from under her lids and slid down her cheeks.

"It's beautiful," she whispered, "really beautiful an' I . . . I jest don't know how to thank ya."

Clark seemed to understand what had prompted the tears, and he nodded slowly.

Marty went to put the lovely set on her chest in her room. She remembered the scarf. She lifted it out of the drawer and looked at it. No, she decided. She just couldn't. It wouldn't do. She shoved it back in the drawer. It just wasn't good enough, she decided. Not good enough at all.

TWENTY

A Visit From Ma Graham

Thinking back, Marty declared it a good Christmas in spite of having to overcome her keen disappointment. It would have been so much fun to have shared it with the Grahams, but as she had concluded there was nothing that could be done about that, somehow she felt sure Clark's prayer had been answered and that in years to come they would remember it with warm feelings.

After the storm, the wind stopped howling and the sun came out. The stock moved about outside again, and the chickens ventured from their coop to their wire enclosure for a bit of exercising. Ole Bob ran around in circles, glad to stretch his legs. Marty envied him as she watched. How good it would be to feel light and easy moving.

Looking carefully at herself for the first time in months, she studied her arms and hands. They were thinner than they used to be, she realized. She hiked up her skirt and looked at her legs. Yes, she definitely had lost weight, except for the one spot where she decidedly had put it on. She'd have to eat up a bit, she chided herself. She'd been quite thin enough before. After the baby arrived, she'd "blow away in the wind iffen she wasn't tied down," as her pa used to say. Well, she was sure enough tied down now, she concluded. The baby seemed to be getting heavier every day. She felt bulky and clumsy, a feeling she wasn't used to. Well, she realized, it was to be expected. December was as good as spent. Even as she thought of that, the month of January stretched out before her, looking oh so long. She wondered if she could endure it. Well, she'd just have to take it one day at a time.

January dawned with a bright sky and no wind, something Marty had learned to be thankful for. She hated the wind, she decided. It sent chills right through her.

This was the new year. What did it hold for her? A new baby for sure. Then a faint anxiety pressed upon her, and she implored Clark's God to please, please let everything be all right.

Clark had been to town again the day before and returned home with a rather grim expression. Marty was about to ask the meaning of all of the trips but checked her tongue.

Iffen it be somethin' I be needin' to know, he'd be sayin' so, she told herself as she went to get the breakfast on the table.

Seems on a new day of a new year, somethin' good should be happenin'.

When she checked out the kitchen window, she felt that it truly had, for there were three graceful and timid deer crossing the pasture. Marty ran back to the bedroom for Missie.

"Missie," she roused the little girl, "come see."

She hurried back to the kitchen, hoping the deer hadn't already disappeared. They had stopped and were grazing in an area where horses had pawed the snow from the grass.

"Look, Missie," Marty said, pointing.

"Oh-h," Missie's voice expressed her excitement. "Doggies."

"No, Missie," Marty giggled, "it's not doggies. It be deer."

"Deer?"

"That's right. Ain't they pretty, Missie?"

"Pretty."

As they watched, Clark came in from the barn, Ole Bob bounding ahead of him, barking at whatever took his fancy. The deer became instantly alert, long necks stretched up, legs tensed, and then, as though on a given signal, they all three leaped forward in long, graceful strides, lightly up and over the pasture fence and back into their native woods.

It was a breathtaking sight, and Marty and Missie were still at the window gazing after them when Clark entered.

"Pa!" cried Missie, pointing. "Deer—they jump."

"So ya saw 'em, eh?"

"Weren't they somethin'?" Marty said in awe.

"They be right nice, all right, though they be a nuisance, too. Been noticing their tracks gettin' in closer an' closer. Wouldn't wonder that one mornin' I be a findin' 'em in the barn with the milk cows."

Marty smiled at his exaggeration. She finally pulled herself away from the window and busied herself with breakfast.

Later in the day, after the dinner dishes had been cleared away and Marty was putting some small stitches on a nightie for the new baby, she heard Ole Bob suddenly take up barking again. Someone was coming, she decided, and him not a stranger. She crossed to the window and looked down the road.

"Well, my word," she exclaimed, "it be Ma an' Ben!"

Joy filled her as she put aside her sewing and ran to make them welcome.

Clark came in from the yard, seeming not too surprised. He and Ben took the horses to the barn for sustenance and rest after their hard labor to buck some large drifts across the road. The two men then seated themselves in the sitting room by the fire and talked of next spring's planting and of their plans to extend their fields, and other man-talk.

Imagine thinkin' of plantin' now with ten-foot drifts standin' on the cornfields, Marty thought as she put on the coffee.

The women settled in the kitchen. Ma had brought along some knitting, and Marty brought out the sock she was knitting for Clark. She needed help in shaping the heel and was glad for Ma's guidance.

They discussed their Christmases and their disappointment, but both admitted to having a good Christmas in spite of it all. Ma remarked that they were more than happy to say yes when Clark had stopped by yesterday, inviting them to come for coffee New Year's Day if the weather held.

So thet's it, Marty thought. *An' he didn't tell me fer fear it might be ruined agin by "mean" weather, as he calls it.*

The visit took on even more meaning for her. Ma told Marty the news that young Jason Stern was there "most ever' time I turn me round." With misty eyes she told how Jason had come Christmas Eve and asked permission for Sally Anne and him to be "a marryin' when the preacher come for his spring visit."

"He seems a right good young man," she added, "an' I should feel proud like, but somehow it be hard to give up my Sally, her not yet bein' eighteen, though she will be, jest by the marryin' time."

Marty thought back to her own tearful pleas, begging her ma and pa for permission to marry young Clem. She had been about the age of Sally Anne. She suddenly saw her own ma and pa in a different light. No wonder they were hesitant. They knew life could be hard. Still, she was glad she had those few happy, even though difficult, months with Clem.

"Thet Jason," Ma went on, "he already be cuttin' logs fer to build a cabin. Wants 'em ready fer spring so there can be a cabin raisin' an' a barn raisin', too. Workin' right hard he is, an' his pa's a helpin' him. He's gonna farm the land right next to his pa. Well, we couldn't say no, Ben an' me, but we sure gonna miss her happy ways an' helpin' hands. I think it be troublin' Laura, too. She jest not been herself the last few days. Moody an' far off like. She always was a quiet one, but now she seems all locked up in herself like. Bothers me, it does."

Ma stopped and seemed to look at something a long way off. Then she pulled her attention back to the present. "We's all gotta settle in an' add to Sally Anne's marriage things—quilts an' rugs an' sech. Got a heap to do 'twixt now an' spring.

"How be things a comin' with the doc?" Ma asked, changing the subject and catching Marty completely off guard.

"What doc?" puzzled Marty.

"Why, the one Clark be a workin' on to git to come to town. The one he be makin' all the trips fer an' gettin' all the neighbors to sign up fer. He's most anxious like to git him here afore thet young'un of yourn makes his appearance."

At Marty's dumbfounded look, Ma finished lamely, "Hasn't he been tellin' ya?"

Marty shook her head.

"Hope I haven't spilled the beans," Ma said, "but ever'one else in the whole West knows 'bout it, seems to me. Thought you'd be a knowin', too. But then maybe he thought it best ya not be gettin' yer hopes up. Might be ya jest not mention my big mouth to him, huh?" Ma Graham smiled a bit sheepishly, and Marty nodded her head, dumbly agreeing.

So that was it. All the urgent trips to town and sometimes beyond, even in poor weather, coming home cold and tired, to get a doctor to the area before her baby was due. She shook her head as she got up to put on the coffeepot. She had to move away quickly before Ma saw her tears.

Their morning coffee together was a sumptuous affair. Marty thought back to the time of Ma's first visit when all she could offer her was coffee. How different this was with the abundance of fresh bread and jelly, fancy cakes, tarts, and cookies. Ben remarked several times about her good cooking, and she responded that she should be—his cook had taught her. Missie wakened and joined them in her chair, asking for a gingerbread boy. Time passed all too quickly as they shared table and conversation.

Marty was reluctant to see them go but thankful for the unexpected time together, and she did want them to arrive home before nightfall.

After they had gone their way, she cheerfully began to clean up. She turned to Clark. "Thank ya so much fer invitin' them."

At his surprised look, she explained, "Ma let it slip, not knowin' thet I didn't know you had invited them." She couldn't resist adding, "I noticed, though, thet ya didn't invite all of those young'uns with the hearty appetites."

They shared a laugh together.

January's wintry days crawled by. Clark made more trips to town, or wherever he went. Marty was no longer puzzled, and she felt quite sure he was going off on these cold days on her behalf. Her sewing was nearly completed now, and she looked at the small garments for her coming baby with much satisfaction. She would be so happy to be able to use the baby things, so new and sweet smelling.

Clark fretted about the lack of a cradle, and Marty assured him one wasn't needed yet as she planned to take the wee one into her bed until he grew a bit. Clark was satisfied with that, saying that come better weather he'd get busy on a bigger bed for Missie and let the baby take over her crib.

As the month drew to a close, Marty felt the time had come when she could share her secret with Missie. Clark had gone away again, and the two of them were alone in the house.

"Come with Mama, Missie," Marty said. "Mama wants to show ya somethin'."

Missie didn't have to be coaxed. She loved to be "showed somethin'." Together they went to the bedroom, where Marty lifted the stack of small garments from the drawer. She couldn't help but smile as she held the top one up for Missie to see.

"Look, Missie," she said. "These are fer the new baby. Mama's gonna get a new baby fer Mama and Missie. Jest a tiny little baby, only 'bout so big. Missie can help Mama take care of the baby."

Missie intently watched Marty's face. She obviously wasn't sure what this was all about, but Mama was happy, and if Mama was happy, it must be good.

"Ba-by," Missie repeated, stroking the soft things. "Ba-by, fer Mama— an' Missie?"

"Thet's right." Marty was wildly happy. "A baby fer Missie. Look, Missie," she said, sitting on her bed, "right now the baby is sleepin' here."

She laid Missie's hand on her abdomen, and Missie was rewarded with a firm kick. Her eyes rose to Marty's in surprise as she quickly pulled away her hand.

"Thet's the baby, Missie. Soon the baby will sleep in Mama's bed. He'll come to live with Mama and Missie an' we'll dress 'im in these new clothes an' bundle 'im in these soft blankets, an' we can hold 'im in our arms, 'stead of how Mama be holdin' 'im now."

Missie didn't get it all, that was sure, but she could understand that Baby was coming and Mama was glad, and Baby would use the soft things and live in Mama's bed. Her eyes took on a sparkle. She touched Marty timidly and repeated, "Mama's ba-by."

Marty pulled the little girl to her and laughed with joy. "Oh, Missie," she said, "it's gonna be so much fun."

Clark returned home that night with a strange-looking lump under a canvas in the back of the sleigh.

Well, Marty thought wryly, *I'm sure thet be no doctor,* and her curiosity was sorely roused.

After Dan and Charlie had been fed and bedded, Clark came through the door carrying the surprise purchase.

Marty could scarcely believe her eyes. "A new rocking chair!" she exclaimed.

"Right," said Clark. "I vowed long ago thet iffen there ever be another baby in this house, there's gonna be a rockin' chair to quiet it by."

He grinned as he said it, and Marty knew the words really were a cover-up for other feelings.

"Well," she answered lightly, "best ya sit down an' show Missie how it works so you'll know how to use it when the baby's needin' ta be quieted." They shared a smile.

Then Clark pulled Missie up onto his lap and snuggled her close. They took two rocks, and the child popped up to stare at this wondrous thing. She watched, swaying, as Clark rocked a few more times, then settled back contentedly, enjoying the new marvel.

Clark soon had to leave for chores, and Missie crawled up on her own to try to make the chair respond correctly.

It's gonna be so much fun to have, Marty told herself. *Jest imagine me with my young'un all dressed up fancy like, an' me sittin' there rockin' 'im. Probably is room enough for Missie beside me, too. I can jest hardly wait.*

The baby seemed impatient, too, for it gave a hard kick that made its mother catch her breath and move back a mite from the cupboard where she was working.

When Clark came in from choring, Missie scooted down from the chair and ran to take his hand.

"Daddy, come," she urged him.

"Hold on, Missie, 'til yer pa gits his coat off," Clark laughed. "I'll come—I'll come."

Missie stepped back and watched him hang up his coat, then took his hand again. "Come see."

Marty thought she was still excited about the chair, and it looked like Clark assumed that, too, as he turned toward it. But Missie tugged at his hand to lead him over to Marty.

"Look—ba-by," she cried, pointing at the spot. "Ba-by fer Missie. Mama let Missie touch 'im."

Marty flushed and Clark grinned.

"Well, I reckon it be awful nice," he said, picking up the little girl. "So Missie's gonna git ta have a new baby, an' we'll rock 'im in the chair," he continued, walking away with the child as he spoke. "We'd better be gittin' some practice, don't ya s'pose. Let's rock a mite while yer mama gits our supper."

And they did.

TWENTY-ONE

A New Baby

It was mid-February, and Marty sat opposite Clark at the table, both absorbed in their own thoughts. Clark's shoulders drooped, and Marty knew he probably was feeling discouraged over the outcome of all his efforts. A doctor indeed had been secured for the town and surrounding community, but he wouldn't be arriving until sometime in April. This was too late for what Clark—and Marty—had wanted him for.

Marty sat quietly, her own thoughts rather despondent. The little one was getting so heavy, and the last few days things just seemed different. She couldn't name what it was, but she knew it was there. She was troubled in her thinking. This was the time when a woman needed a "real" husband, one she could talk to. *If only Clem were here*—the eternal refrain again. She wouldn't have felt embarrassed to talk it over with Clem.

"I've been thinkin'," Clark interrupted her thoughts, "seems yer time must be gettin' perty close. Seems ya might feel more easy like iffen Ma could come a few days early an' be a stayin' with ya fer a spell."

Marty hardly dared to hope. "Do ya really think she could?"

"Don't know why not. Sally Anne an' Laura be right able to care fer the rest. Good practice fer Sally Anne. Hear she be needin' to know all that afore long. I'll ride over an' have a chat with Ma. I hope we won't be keepin' her fer too long."

Oh, me too—me too. Marty's thoughts were a jumble of relief and concern. But she was so thankful for Clark's suggestion that she had to struggle to keep back the tears.

And so it was that Ma came that day, bringing with her a heavy feather tick and some quilts with which to make up a bed for herself on the sitting room floor. She was an old hand at this, and Marty took much comfort in her presence there.

Marty didn't keep her waiting long. Two mornings after, on February sixteenth, she awoke from a restless sleep sometime between three and four o'clock. She tossed and turned, not able to find a comfortable position, feeling generally uneasy.

What was uneasiness gradually changed to contractions—not too close and not too hard, but she recognized them for what they were. Around six o'clock Ma must have sensed more than heard her stirrings and came into her room to see how she was.

Marty groaned. "I jest feel right miser'ble," she muttered.

Ma gently laid a comforting hand on Marty's stomach and waited until another contraction seized her. "Good," she said. "They be nice an' firm. It be on the way."

Ma told Marty that she was going to make sure the fire that had been banked the night before was still alive. Marty could hear her put in more wood and fill the kettle and the large pot with water. "No harm in plenty of hot water," Ma said to Marty through the bedroom door. "It probably won't make an appearance for a while yet, but might as well be prepared." Her cheerful calm and obvious know-how were greatly assuring to Marty as another labor pain bore through her.

No doubt hearing some stirrings, Clark emerged from the lean-to. Even through her own distress, Marty could see that he was pale and already worried.

"Now, ya stop a frettin'," Marty heard Ma say to him. "I know thet she be a little thing"—her voice dropped a notch—"but she be carryin' the baby well. I checked a minute ago. He dropped down right good an' he seems to be turned right. It only be a matter of time 'til ya be a holdin' 'im in thet rockin' chair."

Marty couldn't hold back a groan at the next contraction, and Ma hurried into the room to soothe her and lay a cool cloth on her forehead. When Marty could catch her breath and relax some, she could see Clark, looking even whiter, sitting in a kitchen chair with his head bowed and lips moving. She knew he was praying for her and for the baby, and that was even more comforting than Ma's experienced hands.

Clark bundled Missie up and took her out to the barn with him so she might not hear the agonizing groans of her mama.

Marty held on, taking one contraction at a time, her face damp from the effort, her lips stifling the screams that wanted to come. Ma stayed close by, giving words of encouragement and administering what she could in advice and comfort.

Time ticked by so slowly—for Marty, who now marked time by contractions; for Clark, who, Ma told her, was trying with Missie's help to work on harnesses out in the barn; and for Ma herself, who obviously wanted the ordeal safely over for all of them.

The sun swung around to the west. Would this never end? wondered Marty between pains. It was agonizing. Ma kept telling her that from her years of experience, she knew the time was drawing near. Everything was in readiness. Then at a quarter to four, Marty gave a sharp cry that ended as a baby boy made his appearance into the world.

With a sob Marty lay back in the bed exhausted, so thankful that her work was done and that Ma's capable hands were there to do what was necessary for the new baby. A tired but joyful smile couldn't help but appear on Marty's face as she heard her son cry.

"He's jest fine," Ma said. "A fine, big boy."

In short order she had both baby and mother presentable and, placing the wee bundle on Marty's arm, went to bring the good news to Clark.

"He's here," Marty heard her call out the door, "an' he's a dandy."

Clark's running footsteps were clearly heard, and he soon came panting into the cabin, carrying Missie with him.

"She's okay?" His anxious eyes moved from Ma to the bedroom door as he set Missie down.

"Fit as a fiddle," Ma responded. Marty knew Ma was relieved, too. "She done a great job," Ma continued, "an' she's got a fine boy. Iffen ya slow down a mite an' take yerself in hand, I may even let ya git a small peek at 'im."

Clark took off his coat and unbundled Missie.

"Here, Missie, let's warm a bit afore we go to see yer mama," Marty heard him tell the little girl. They stood together at the fire, and then he lifted her up and followed Ma to the bedroom.

Clark stood by the bed and looked down at Marty. She was tired, and she knew she probably didn't look her best after this long, difficult day, but she smiled up gallantly. His gaze shifted to the small bundle. Marty held the baby so Clark could see him better. He was a bit red yet, but he sure was one fine boy. One small clenched fist lay against his cheek.

"He's a real dandy," Clark said, the awe he was feeling showing in his tone. "What ya be a callin' 'im?"

"He be Claridge Luke," Marty answered.

"Thet's a fine name. What the Luke be for?"

"My pa."

"He'd be right proud could he see 'im. His pa'd be right proud, too, to have sech a fine son."

Marty nodded, a lump hurting her throat at the thought.

"Claridge Luke Davis." Clark said it slowly. "Right good-soundin' name. Bother ya any iffen I shorten it to Clare sometimes?"

"Not a'tall," said Marty. Indeed, she wondered if anything would ever bother her again.

They had both forgotten Missie during the exchange, and the little girl remained silent in her pa's arms, staring at the strange, squirming bundle. At last she inquired, as though trying to sort it out, "Ba-by?"

Clark's attention turned to her. "Yah, Missie, baby. That's the baby thet yer mama done got ya. Little Clare, he be."

"Rock . . . baby?" Missie asked.

"Oh no, not yet a while," laughed Clark. "First the baby an' yer mama have to have a nice long rest. We'd best be goin' now an' let them be."

Marty responded only with a slight smile. She was a strange mixture of delirious happiness intermingled with sadness and was oh, so very tired.

I do declare, she thought as the two left the room, *I think thet be the hardest work I ever did in my whole lifetime,* and after slowly sipping some of Ma's special tea, she drifted off to sleep.

In the sitting room, Clark and Missie cuddled close in the rocking chair. "Missie, let's pray fer yer mama and the new baby." At her nod, he closed his eyes and prayed, "Thank ya, Father, thank ya for helping Ma, and fer Marty's safe birthin', an' thet fine new boy." His "amen" was echoed by the small girl in his lap.

TWENTY-TWO

Ma Bares Her Heart

Ma stayed on with Marty for several days after the arrival of little Claridge Luke.

"I wanna see ya back on yer feet like afore I leave ya be," Ma declared. "'Sides, there be nothin' pressin' at home jest now."

Marty was more than pleased to have the older woman's company and help. She was thrilled with her new son and eager to be up and around. Not being one who is happy when kept down, she was after Ma to let her get up from the second day on. Ma, reluctant at first, allowed her small activities that gradually grew with each day.

Missie, excited about the new baby, loved to share Marty's lap with him as they rocked in the chair. Clark seemed to take on a new air of family pride, declaring, "That little tyke has already growed half an inch and gained two pounds. I can see it by jest lookin'."

The day came when Marty felt sufficiently able to cope with managing the house and the children on her own. She was sure that even with Ma's kindness and generosity, she must be anxious to get home and look to her own.

Ma nodded her agreement. "Yeah, things do be goin' fine around here. Ya take care o' yerself an' things be jest right. I'll have Clark drive me on home tomorrow."

Marty would miss Ma when she left, but it would be good to have her little place all to herself again.

That afternoon as the two women had coffee together one more time, their conversation ranged over many topics. They talked of their families and their hopes for the future. Ma again expressed her need to adjust to Sally Anne's soon departure from the family nest.

"She seems so young yet," Ma said. "But ya know ya can't say no once a young'un has the notion."

"But she's not jest bein' a strong-willed girl," Marty countered. "She jest be in love. Don'cha remember, Ma, what it was like to be so young an' so in love thet yer heart missed beatin' at the sight o' him an' yer face flushed when ya wasn't wantin' it to? 'Member the wild feelin' thet love has?"

"Yeah, I reckon," Ma responded slowly. "Though 'twas so long ago. I do remember, though, when I met Thornton, guess I didn't behave myself much better than Sally Anne." Ma gave a short chuckle but quickly looked serious again.

"What was it like, Ma, when ya lost Thornton?"

"When I lost Thornton?" repeated Ma. "Well, it be a long time ago now. But I 'member it still, though it don't pain me sharp like it used to. Myself—way down deep—wanted to die, too; but I couldn't let that happen, me havin' three little ones to look out fer. I kept fightin' on, yet all the time I only felt part there. The rest of me seemed to be missin' or numb or somethin'."

"I know what ya mean," Marty said, her voice so low she wasn't sure she was heard. More loudly she said, "Then ya met Ben."

"Yeah, then I met Ben. I could see he be a good man an' one ya could count on."

"An' ya fell in love with 'im."

Ma paused, then shook her head. "No, Marty, there was no face flushin' an' fast heart skippin'."

Marty stared.

"No, it be different with Ben. I needed 'im, an' he needed me. I married 'im not fer love, Marty, but fer my young'uns—an' fer his."

Ma stopped talking and sat studying her coffee cup, turning it round and round in her hand. "Fact be, Marty—" She stopped again, and Marty knew this conversation was very difficult for her. "Fact be, at first I felt—well, guilty like. I felt like I be a . . . a loose woman, sleepin' with a man I didn't feel love fer."

If Ma hadn't seemed so serious, Marty would have found that statement humorous. It was hard to imagine Ma, a steady, solid, and plain woman, with a faith in God and a brood of eleven, as a "loose woman." But Marty did not laugh. She did not even smile. She understood some measure of the deep feelings being expressed by Ma Graham.

"I never knowed," Marty finally whispered. "I never woulda guessed thet ya didn't love Ben."

Ma's head came up in an instant, her eyes wide.

"Lan' sake, girl!" she exclaimed. "Thet were *then*. Why, I love my Ben now, ya can jest bet I do. Fact is, he's been a right good man to me, an' I 'spect I love 'im more'n I love myself."

"When—when an' how did it happen?" Marty asked, both fascinated and a little frightened by what she might hear. "The head spinnin' an' the heart flutterin' an' all?"

Ma smiled. "No, there's never been thet. See . . . I learnt me a lesson. There's more than one way thet love comes. Oh, sure, sometimes it comes wild like, makin' creatures into wallerin' simpletons. I've seed 'em, I've been there myself; but it doesn't have to be thet way, an' it's no less real an' meanin'ful iffen it comes another way. Ya see, Marty, sometimes love comes sorta stealin' up on ya gradual like, not shoutin' bold words or wavin' bright flags. Ya ain't even aware it's a growin' an' growin' an' gettin' stronger until—I don't know. All the sudden it takes ya by surprise like, an' ya think, 'How long I been a feelin' like this an' why didn't I notice it afore?'"

Marty stirred. It was all so strange to get a peek inside of Ma like this. She pictured a young woman, widowed like herself, with pain and heartache doing what she had felt was best for her children. And Ma had felt . . . guilty. Marty shivered.

I do declare, she thought, *I couldn't have done it. Thanks be to whatever there be in charge of things thet I wasn't put in a position like thet. Me, I've jest had to be a mama.*

She pushed away from those thoughts and rose to get more coffee. She didn't want to even consider it anymore. Now Ma was happy again and she needn't feel guilty anymore. She now loved Ben. Just how or when it happened, she couldn't really say, but it had. It just—well, it just worked its way into her heart—slowly, softly.

Marty took a deep breath, pushed it all aside, and changed the subject.

<hr />

Little Clare was getting round and dimpled, cooing at whoever would talk to him. Missie took great pride in her new baby "brudder." Clark was happy to take the "young fella" and rock him if he needed quieting or burping when Marty was busy getting a meal or cleaning up or doing the dishes. Marty was often tired by the end of the day, but she slept well, even though her nights were interrupted with feedings.

Clark was working doubly hard on the log cutting. He had told Marty that their cabin was too small, and come spring, he planned to tear off the lean-to and add a couple of bedrooms. Marty wondered if he had forgotten his promise of fare for her trip back home. Well, there was plenty of time to remind him of that. It was only the first of March.

TWENTY-THREE

Visitors

A new baby gave the neighbor ladies a delightful excuse to put aside their daily duties and go calling. So it was in the weeks following the arrival of little Clare that Marty welcomed some of her neighbors whom she had not previously known, except perhaps fleetingly as a face at Clem's funeral.

The first to come to see Marty and the baby was Wanda Marshall.

Marty set aside the butter she was churning and welcomed her sincerely. "So glad thet ya dropped by."

Small and young, with blond hair that at one time must have been very pretty, she had light blue eyes that somehow looked sad even as she smiled. Marty recognized her as the young woman who had spoken to her the day of Clem's funeral, inviting her to share their one-room home.

Wanda smiled shyly and presented a gift for the new baby.

When Marty opened the package, she found a small bib, carefully stitched and with embroidery so intricate she could scarcely understand how one could do such fine work. It looked delicate and dainty, like the giver, Marty thought. She thanked Wanda and exclaimed over the stitching, to which Wanda gave a slight shrug of her thin shoulders.

"I have nothing else to do."

"Lan' sake," said Marty, "seems I never find time fer nuthin' since young Clare came along. Even my evenin's don't give me much time fer jest relaxin'."

Wanda did not respond as her eyes gazed around the house. Eventually she spoke almost in a whisper. "Could I see the baby?"

"My, yes," Marty answered heartily. "He be havin' a sleep right now—he an' Missie—but iffen we tippy-toe in, we can have us a peek. Maybe we'll be able to have us coffee afore he wakes up wantin' his dinner."

Marty led the way into the bedroom. Wanda looked over at the sleeping Missie with her tousled curls and sleep-flushed cheeks. "She's a pretty child, isn't she?"

"Missie? Yeah, she be a dolly thet 'un," Marty said with feeling.

They then turned to Marty's bed, upon which little Clare was sleeping. He was bundled in the carefully made finery his proud mama had sewn for him. His dark head showed above the blanket, and stepping closer, one got a look at the soft pink baby face, with lashes as fine as dandelion silk on his cheeks. The small hands were free and one tiny fist held a corner of his blanket.

Marty couldn't help but think he looked beautiful, and she wondered that her visitor made no comment. When she looked up, it was to see her guest quickly leaving the bedroom.

Marty was mystified. Well, some folks you never could figure. She placed a tender kiss on Clare's soft head and followed Wanda Marshall back to the kitchen.

When Marty reached the kitchen, the young woman stood looking out of the window. Marty quietly went to add more wood to the fire and put on the coffee. Finally Wanda turned slowly and Marty saw with surprise that she had been struggling with tears.

"I'm sorry," she said with a weak attempt at a smile. "He's . . . he's a beautiful baby, just perfect."

She sat down at Marty's table, hands twisting nervously in her lap, her eyes downcast, seemingly to study the movement of her hands. When she looked up again, Marty thought she looked careworn and older than her years.

With another effort at a smile, she went on, "I'm sorry. I really am. I didn't know it would be so hard. I mean, I had no idea I'd react so foolishly. I'd . . . I'd love to have a baby. My own, you know. Well, I did. I mean—that is, I have had babies of my own. Three, in fact, but they've not lived—not any of them, two boys and one girl, and all of them . . ." Her voice trailed off; then her expression hardened. "It's this wretched country!" she burst out. "If I'd stayed back east where I belong, things would have been different. I would have my family—my Jodi and Esther and Josiah. It's this horrible place. Look . . . look what it did to you, too. Losing your husband and having to marry a . . . a stranger in order to survive. It's hateful, that's what—just hateful!"

By now the young woman was weeping in broken, heartrending sobs. Marty stood rooted to the spot, holding slices of loaf cake. *Lan' sakes,* she thought frantically, *the poor thing. What do I do now?*

She took a deep breath for control and crossed to Wanda, laying a sympathetic hand on her shoulder. "I'm so sorry," she said softly. "So sorry. Why, iffen I'd lost young Clare, I don' know . . . I jest don' know iffen I could've stood it."

She made no further reference to her loss of Clem. This woman was battling with a sorrow Marty had not faced—bitterness. Marty continued. "I jest can't know how ya must feel, losin' three babies an' all, but I know ya must hurt somethin' awful."

By now Marty had her arms around the shaking shoulders and pulled the young woman against her. "It's hard, it's truly hard to be losin' somethin' thet ya want so much, but this I know, too—ya mustn't be blamin' the West fer it all. It could happen anywhere—anywhere. Womenfolk back east sometimes lose their young'uns, too. Ya mustn't hate this land. It's a beautiful land. An' you. Yer young an' have yer life ahead of ya. Ya mustn't let these tragedies bitter ya so. Don't do a lick o' good to be fightin' the way things be, when there be nuthin' a body can do to change 'em."

By now Wanda had been able to quiet her sobbing and seemed to allow herself the comfort of Marty's words and arms.

"Life be what ya make it, to be sure," Marty murmured. "No woman could find good in buryin' three of her babies, but like I said, you is young yet. Maybe"—she was about to say maybe Clark's God—"maybe the time thet lies ahead of ya will still give ya babies to hold an' love. Ya jest hold on an' keep havin' faith an' . . . ."

Marty's voice trailed off. *Lan' sakes, I didn't know I could talk on so without stoppin'.*

"An' 'sides," Marty said as another thought overtook her, "we're gonna have a doc in town now, an' maybe with his help . . . ."

She let the thought lie there with no further comment.

Wanda seemed at peace now. She lay against Marty for a few more minutes, then slowly straightened. "I'm sorry," she said. "I'm very foolish, I know. You're so kind and so brave, and you're right, too. I'll . . . I'll be fine. I'm glad . . . about the doctor."

The coffee was threatening to boil over, and Marty ran to rescue it. As they sat with their coffee and cake, Marty began their chat by asking Wanda about her background.

Marty learned that Wanda had been a "city girl," well bred, well educated, and perhaps a bit spoiled, as well. How she ever had gotten way out west still seemed a puzzle even to her. She shook her head as though she still couldn't quite fathom how it had all come about.

Clare fussed and Marty went to bring him out, nursing him as they continued their visit over coffee. Not knowing just what effect the baby's presence might have on Wanda, Marty kept him well hidden with the blanket.

Wanda talked on about having so little to do. She did beautiful stitching, that Marty knew, but she didn't have anyone to sew for. She didn't quilt, she couldn't knit or crochet, and she just hated to cook, so didn't do any more of that than she had to. She loved to read but had read her few books so many times she practically could recite them, and she had no way of getting more.

Marty offered the practical suggestion that she would teach her to quilt, knit, or crochet if she cared to learn.

"Oh, would you?" Wanda enthused. "I'd so much love to learn."

"Be glad to," Marty responded cheerily. "Anytime ya care to drop in, ya jest come right ahead."

Young Clare finished nursing and set himself to squirming. Marty turned her attention to the baby, properly arranging her clothing and lifting him up for a noisy burp.

Wanda laughed quietly, then spoke softly. "Would you mind if I held him for a minute?"

"Not a'tall," Marty responded. "Why don't ya jest sit ya there in the rockin' chair a minute. He's already spoiled by rockin', I'm thinkin', so a little more won't make no difference."

Gingerly Wanda carried the baby to the rocking chair and settled herself with him snuggled up against her. Marty went to clear the table.

When Missie called a few minutes later and Marty crossed through the sitting room to get the little girl, she noticed Wanda gently rocking, eyes far away yet tender, baby Clare looking like he fully enjoyed the attention.

Poor thing, Marty's heart responded. *Poor thing. I be jest so lucky.*

Ma Graham came next, bringing with her a beautiful hand-knit baby shawl. Marty declared she'd never seen one so pretty. Ma brought her youngsters with her on this trip. They all were eager for their first look at their new little neighbor. Ma seemed to watch with thoughtful eyes as Sally Anne, eyes shining, held the wee baby close. Each one of Ma's children took a turn carefully holding the baby—even the boys, for they had been raised to consider babies as treasures indeed.

The group lunched together, and before it seemed possible, the afternoon was gone.

The next day an ill-clad stranger, with two equally ill-clad little girls, appeared at Marty's door. At Marty's welcoming "Won't ya come in," the woman made no answer but pushed a hastily wrapped little bundle at Marty.

Marty thanked her and unwrapped the gift to find another bib. Quite unlike the one that Wanda Marshall had brought—in fact, as different as it could be; the material was coarse, perhaps from a worn overall, though the stitches were neat and regular. There had been no attempt to fancy it up, and it looked rather wrinkled from handling. Marty, however, thanked the woman with simple sincerity and invited them once more to come in.

They came in shyly, all three with downcast eyes and shuffling feet.

"I don't remember meetin' ya afore," Marty ventured.

"I be . . ." the woman mumbled, still not looking up. Marty didn't catch if it was Rena or Tina or what it was, but she did make out Larson.

"Oh, ya be Mrs. Larson."

The woman nodded, still staring at the floor.

"An' yer two girls?"

The two referred to flushed deeply, looking as though they wished they could bury themselves in the folds of their mother's wrinkled skirt.

"This be Nandry an' this be Clae."

Marty wasn't sure she had heard it right but decided not to ask again.

As they waited for the coffee to boil, Marty took a deep breath and attempted to get the conversation going. "Be nice weather fer first of March."

The woman nodded.

"Yer man be cuttin' wood?"

She shook her head in the negative.

"He be a bit down," she finally responded, twisting her hands in her lap.

"Oh," Marty quickly grasped at this, hoping to find a connection with her withdrawn visitor. "I'm right sorry to be hearin' thet. What's he ailin' from?"

Mrs. Larson hunched a shoulder upward to indicate it was a mystery to her.

So be it fer thet, thought Marty sadly, picturing a husband and father driven to drink.

"Would ya like to see the baby?" she inquired.

The trio nodded.

Marty rose. "He be nappin' now. Come along."

She knew there was no need to caution for silence. This ghostly trio was incapable of anything louder than breathing, she was sure.

They reached the bed where the infant slept, and each one of the three raised her eyes from her worn shoes just long enough for a quick look at the baby. Was that a glimmer of interest in the younger girl's eyes? She probably imagined it, Marty decided, and she led the way back to the kitchen.

Marty was never more thankful to see a coffeepot boil in all of her life. Her visitors shyly helped themselves to a cookie when they were passed and seemed to dally over eating them as though to prolong the enjoyment. Marty got the feeling they didn't have cookies often. Marty wrapped up as many as she dared for them to take home. "We'll never be able to eat all these afore they get old," she assured the girls, carefully avoiding eye contact with their mother. She did not want to offend this poor woman.

They left as silently as they had come, watching the floor as they mumbled their good-byes.

Marty crossed to the kitchen window and watched them go.

They were walking. The drifts made the road difficult even for horses, and the air was cold with a wind blowing. She had noticed that none of her visitors were dressed very warmly. She watched as they trudged through the snow, leaning into the wind, clasping their too-flimsy garments about them, and tears formed in her eyes. She reached for the gift they had brought with them, and suddenly it became something to treasure.

Hildi Stern and Mrs. Watley came together. Hildi was a good-natured middle-aged lady. Not as wise as Ma Graham, Marty told herself, but a woman who would make a right fine neighbor.

Mrs. Watley—Marty didn't hear her given name—was a rather stout, boisterous lady. She didn't appear to be overly inclined to move about too much, and when Marty asked if they'd like to go to the bedroom for a peek at the baby, Mrs. Watley was quick with a suggestion. "Why don't ya jest bring 'im on out here, dear?"

They decided to wait until Clare finished his nap.

Each lady brought a parcel. Hildi Stern's gift was a small hand-knit sweater. Marty was thrilled with it.

Mrs. Watley presented her with another bib. This one, well sewn and as simple and unfussy as it could be, would be put to good use along with the others. Marty thanked them both with equal sincerity.

When they had finished their coffee, Mrs. Watley, looking like she enjoyed her several helpings of cookies and loaf cake, exclaimed what a grand little cook Marty was. Next they inspected the new baby. After they pronounced him a fine specimen, saying all of the things that a new mother expected to hear, Mrs. Watley turned to Hildi Stern.

"Why don't ya run along an' git the team, dear, an' I'll be a meetin' ya at the door?"

It was done.

Mrs. Vickers was the last of the neighbor visitors close enough that a new baby merited a drive on the winter roads. She had her boy, Shem, drive her over and sent him on to the barn with the horses while she came bustling up the walk, talking even before Marty got to the door to open it.

"My, my, some winter we be havin'. Though, I do declare, I see'd me worse—but I see'd me better, too—ya can jest count on thet—heerd ya had a new young'un—must be from the first mister, I says when I hears it—ain't been married to the other one long enough fer thet yet. How it be doin'? Hear he's a healthy 'un—an' thet's what counts, I al'ays say. Give me a healthy 'un any day over a purdy 'un—I al'ays say—take the healthy 'un ever'time."

She kicked the snow from her boots and came on into the kitchen. "My, my, ain't ya jest the lucky 'un—nice little place here. Sure beats thet covered wagon ya was livin' in. Not many women hereabout have a home nice as this, an' ya jest gettin' it all a handed to ya like. Well, let's see thet young'un."

Marty tactfully suggested they have coffee while Clare finished his nap, and Mrs. Vickers didn't turn the offer down. She settled herself on a kitchen chair and let her tongue slide over her lips as though adding oil to the machinery so it would run smoothly.

Marty had opportunity for little more than a slight nod of her head now and then. She thought maybe it was just as well. If she'd been given a chance for speech, she may have said some unwise things to her visitor.

Between Mrs. Vickers's helpings of loaf cake and gulps of coffee, Marty heard that:

"Jedd Larson be nothin' but one lazy good-fer-nothin', al'ays gettin' started when ever'one else be done—'ceptin' when it come to eatin' or drinkin' or raisin' young'uns—they been married fer ten years—already had 'em eight young'uns—only three thet lived, though—buried five—his missus—so ashamed an' mousy like—wouldn't no one 'round even bother to go near—"

Marty made herself a promise that come nice weather she'd pay a call on Mrs. Larson.

"Thet Graham clan—did ya ever see so many kids in the self-same family? Almost an insult to humans, thet's what it be—bad as cats or mice—havin' a whole litter like thet—"

Marty found herself hard put to hold her tongue.

"See'd thet young Miz Marshall yet? I declare me—thet young prissy woulda been better off to stay her back east where she be belongin'—her an' her first-class airs—an' not even able to raise her a young'un—woman's got no business bein' out west if she can't raise a young'un—an' confident like—I think there be somethin' funny there—hard to put yer finger on—but there all the same—doesn't even give ya a proper welcome when ya call—me, I called, neighbor like, when each of the young'uns died—told her right out what she prob'ly be a doin' wrong—well, ya know what—she most turned her back on me—"

Poor Wanda, thought Marty, aching once more for her new friend.

"Well, now—if that's the way she be, I says, leave her to it. Have Hildi and Maude been over? I see'd 'em go by t'other day—goin' over to see thet new young'un of the Davises, I says to myself—well, Hildi be a fine neighbor—though she do have some strange quirks—me, I'm not one to be a mentioning 'em. Maude Watley, now—thet be another matter—wouldn't do nothin' thet took any effort, thet one—she wasn't always big as the West itself—be there a time afore she catched her man thet she be a dance-hall girl—she wouldn't want one knowin' it o' course—but it be so—have ya been to town yet?"

At Marty's shake of her head, she hurried ahead.

"Well, mind ya, when ya do go, don't ya be tellin' nuthin' to thet there Miz McDonald thet ya don't want spread 'round thin like. She be a first-rate tongue wagger, thet 'un."

Marty also found out that Miz Standen, over to town, had her a Saturday beau.

"I'm bettin' thet the visitin' parson had him somethin' to hide, or he'd settle himself to one place." The woman dropped her voice as if someone else might hear the dark secret.

"The Krafts are expectin' them another young'un—makin' five."

"Milt Conners, the bachelor of the area, seems to be gettin' stranger ever'day. Should git 'im a woman—thet would be doin' him some good—he's gettin' liquor somewhere, too—nobody knows where, but I do have my s'picions."

And on and on she went, like a walking newspaper. The new doc would be arriving in April—folks saying Clark bought him—well, they needed a doc—hope he was worth it and not here just to make money on people's woes.

Young Sally Anne was hitching up with Jason Stern—supposed those two families be pairing off regular like in the next few years.

The woman finally stopped for a breath, and Marty wondered aloud that Shem had not come in from the barn and supposed he was getting cold and tired of waiting. Well, she'd send a slice of cake and a gingerbread cookie or two out with Mrs. Vickers.

Mrs. Vickers must have taken the hint and made her way out the door, still chattering as she left. Marty's head was spinning and her ears tingling. The visitor hadn't even looked at the baby.

TWENTY-FOUR

New Discoveries

The days of March were busy ones for Clark. Marty watched as he pushed himself hard at the logging, working as long as there was light and then doing the chores with the aid of the lantern. Each night at the supper table he tallied up the total logs he'd felled for the new addition, and together they kept track of how many more were needed.

Marty's days were full, too, doing the usual housework and caring for the new baby and Missie. With the increased laundry needs, she found it difficult to get the clothes dry between one washing and the next.

In the evenings after the children were down for the night, both Clark and Marty were happy to sit quietly before the open fire, Marty with her quilt pieces or knitting, Clark with one of his books, working on some project, or mending some small tool of one kind or another. Marty found it increasingly comfortable to talk with Clark. In fact, she looked forward to relating the events of the day and reporting on Missie's conversations with her.

Clark had spent many evenings fashioning a new bed for Missie so the fast-growing Clare would be able to take over the crib. Marty enjoyed watching the bed take shape. She noticed the few simple tools Clark worked with responded well to his capable hands. She carefully pieced the quilt that would go on the bed and felt a growing sense of a shared accomplishment.

As they worked, they talked about the people and happenings that made up their little world. The early fall and long winter had brought animals down from the hills in search of food. Lately a couple of coyotes had been moving in closer and closer at nights, and Clark and Marty chuckled together about poor Ole Bob's noisy concern at the intrusion.

The neighbors were rarely seen during the winter months, so news was scarce. Clark said measles had been reported in town, but no serious cases had developed.

The two talked of spring planting and plans for the new bedroom, hoping that spring would be early rather than late in coming. They laughed about Missie's attempts at mothering her "brudder Clare." It wasn't any particular conversation or subject, but they probably were discovering deeper things about each other without actually being aware of the fact. Feelings, dreams, hopes, and, yes, faith were shared in a relaxed, ordinary way.

One evening as Marty quilted and Clark sanded the headboard for the bed, their talk turned to the Scripture passage he had read aloud at breakfast that morning. Having no background in such things, Marty found that a lot of the truths she heard from the Bible were difficult to understand. Over time Clark had explained about the promises to the Jewish people of a Messiah who would come. But their perception of His purpose in coming was far different from what He actually came to accomplish. They wanted freedom from their oppressors; He came to give freedom from self and sin. They wanted to be part of a great earthly kingdom, but His kingdom was a heavenly one.

Marty was beginning to understand some of the things concerning the Messiah, but there were still a lot of unanswered questions in her mind.

"Do ya really think thet God, who runs the whole world like, be knowin' you?" she asked forthrightly.

"I'm right sure thet He do," Clark responded simply.

"An' how can ya be so sure?"

Clark looked thoughtfully at the Book carefully placed on the shelf near the table. "I believe the Bible, and it tells me thet He does. And because He answers my prayers."

"Ya mean by givin' ya whatever ya ask fer?"

Clark thought a minute, then shook his head. "No, not thet. Oft times He jest helps me to git by without what I asked fer."

Marty shook her head. "Thet seems ta be a strange idea."

Clark looked at her a moment, then said, "I'm thinkin' not so strange. A lot of times, what folks ask fer, they don't need a'tall."

"Like what?"

"Like good crops, new plows, an extry cow or two."

"What about iffen ya lose something thet ya already had an' had sorta set yer mind on?"

He didn't hesitate. "Ya mean like Clem or Ellen?"

Marty nodded slowly.

"He don't take away the hurt, but He sure do share it with ya."

"Wisht I woulda had me someone to share mine with."

"He was there, an' I'm thinkin' thet He helped ya more than ya was aware."

"But I didn't really know to ask Him to."

"I did."

TWENTY-FIVE

Catastrophe!

On March sixteen little Clare marked his first month in the family. So far he had been a first-rate baby, but Clark kept warning, "Jest ya wait 'til he starts cuttin' his teeth."

Marty told Clark she hoped he would be wrong—and Clark fervently hoped so, too. "Missie had herself a plumb awful time with them teeth," he told her.

The day had turned colder again after some hints of spring, and it looked like another storm might be hitting soon. Clark had left early in the morning to restock their supplies.

He was back earlier than usual, and the anticipated storm was still holding off. Mrs. McDonald had sent a small parcel for the baby. Marty opened it and found another small bib.

"I do declare," she laughed. "Thet boy sure be well set up fer bibs. Guess he be well fixed fer droolin' when those teeth come in."

Clark laughed with her.

Missie's bed had been completed by now and set up in the bedroom, and the small crib was moved into the sitting room, where it was warmer for the baby during the day. He was awake more often now and liked to lie and look around, waving his small fists frantically in the air. Marty still took him into the bed with her at night.

When the day ended and evening fell, Clark and Marty both noticed a shift in the wind. Clark commented, "Guess we not be gettin' thet storm tonight after all."

The thought was a welcome one. Large drifts of snow still lay over the ground, and their hopes for an early spring were disappointed regularly. The weather mostly stayed cold with occasional snow flurries, and the arctic winds made winter's long stay even drearier.

With Clark's hurried trip to town and Marty having baked bread as well as done the washing for the baby, they were both tired from a long day's work, so Clark said good-night and headed for the lean-to.

Marty tucked herself in, stretching her toes deep into the warm blankets. She nursed young Clare so he would sleep as far into the night as possible and settled down with him tucked in beside her. She thought she had barely fallen asleep when she was awakened with Clark bending over her, hurriedly pulling on his jacket.

"The barn be ablaze. Ya jest stay put. I'm goin' fer the stock," and he was gone.

Marty's head felt foggy with sleep. Had she had a dream? No, she was sure he really had been there. What should she do? It seemed to take forever before she finally was able to move, though in truth it no doubt was a matter of seconds. She scrambled from the bed, making sure Clare and Missie were both sleeping, and then, without stopping to dress herself or even slip into her house socks, she ran through the house to the kitchen window. Before she even pulled the curtain aside she could see the angry red glow. Horror filled her as she looked at the scene. The barn's roof was on fire, with leaping flames towering into the dark sky and smoke pouring upward, and there was Clark silhouetted against the frightening scene. He had swung open the barn door and smoke was billowing out.

As Marty realized what he had actually said to her and saw him about to enter the inferno, her own voice choked out, sounding as desperate in her ears as she felt, "No, Clark, no. Don't go in there, please, please—"

But he had gone—for the animals. *We can get more animals, Clark,* her heart silently cried.

Marty stood at the window—watching, straining, dying a thousand deaths in what seemed forever, praying as best she could. And then through the smoke plunged Charlie—or was it Dan?—and right behind him came the other horse, rearing and pawing the air. The saddle horse came close behind, dragging his halter rope and tossing his head wildly. He ran until he crashed stupidly into the corral fence, falling back only to struggle up again to race around frantically.

Marty stared unblinking at the barn door. "Oh, Clark, Clark, please, please. God, iffen ya can hear me, please let 'im come out," she whispered through teeth clenched tightly together.

But the next dark shape to come through the smoke was a milk cow, then another, and another.

"Oh, God!" sobbed Marty. "He'll never make it."

The walls of the barn were now engulfed in flame, too. The fire licked hungrily along the wall, reaching terrifying fingers toward the open door. And then she saw him, stumbling through the entrance, dragging harnesses with him and staggering along until he reached the corral fence. She could see him clinging to it for support and pulling a wet towel he must have grabbed on his way out away from his head and face.

"Oh, God!" cried Marty as she collapsed in a heap on the cold kitchen floor.

Somehow the long night blurred together from then on. Marty simply couldn't take it all in. Clark was safe, but the barn was gone. Neighbor men, with water and snow, seemed to be everywhere, now fighting to save the other outbuildings.

Women were there, too, bustling about her, talking, giving the men a hand by turns, making up sandwiches and coffee. Marty felt numb with emotional exhaustion. Someone placed baby Clare in her arms.

"He's cryin' to eat," she said. "Best ya sit ya down an' nurse 'im."

She did. That much she could understand.

When morning came, the barn lay in smoldering ruins, but the sheds had been saved.

Tired, smoky faces gathered around a hastily made campfire in the yard for the coffee and sandwiches. Their clothes and boots were ice crusted, and their hands cupped around mugs for warmth. They talked in hushed tones. Losing one's barn and feed, with winter still in full swing, was a great loss, and each one knew it only too well.

Eventually the men quietly gathered their women, anxious to be home and out of frozen clothing. Just as the first team left the yard, Jedd Larson arrived with his team.

"Good ole Jedd." Marty heard an annoyed whisper. "Prob'ly be late fer his own buryin'."

Jedd took over where the others had left off, helping himself to a cup of coffee and grabbing up a sandwich. As the neighbor families, one by one, took their leave, he appeared to be settling in for a long chat.

Poor Clark, Marty thought as she glanced anxiously out the kitchen window. *He jest be lookin' beat. All ashes an' soot an' half frozen, an' now Jedd wants to sit an' jaw him to death—no sense a'tall, thet Jedd. Well, I won't 'low it,* and pulling her shawl about her shoulders, she marched out.

"Mr. Larson," she greeted the man, keeping her voice even. "Right good of ya to be comin' over to give us a hand. Guess things be under control like now, thanks to all our fine neighbors. Have ya had coffee? Good! I'm sorry to be interruptin' like, but right now I'm afeared thet my husband be needed indoors—iffen ya can be excusin' 'im."

She had never referred to Clark as her husband before, and Clark's cup paused midway to his mouth, but he said nothing. She gave a meaningful nod toward the door, and Clark added his thanks to Jedd and went into the house.

"Give yer missus our greetin's," Marty told the man. "We won't be keepin' ya any longer, ya havin' chores at home waitin' on ya an' all. Ya'll be welcome to come agin when ya can sit an' chat a spell. Bring yer family along. Thank ya agin. One really 'preciates fine neighbors. I'd best be gettin' in to my young'uns. Good day, Mr. Larson."

Marty turned to the house, looking over her shoulder as Jedd Larson crawled into his wagon and aimed it for home. She noticed he didn't have the wagon box moved to the sleigh runners yet. No doubt he had kept planning on getting to it but just hadn't found the time.

Marty entered the house to find a puzzled Clark. "I was thinkin' Missie would be in some kind o' state and would need some comfortin' from her pa, but she's still sleepin' sound like," he said. "Clare's awake, but he don't look none the worse for wear." Clark grinned down at the contented baby in the crib. "Who be needin' me?" he asked wryly.

She stared at him dumbly, seeing his lips were cracked and bleeding from the heat of the fire. She had bravely, if nearly frantic with worry, held on through the night, answering questions about where to find the coffee and all and was she okay. She had restrained herself from running out into the barnyard to see if Clark was really all right. She had kept herself from angrily lashing out against whoever or whatever had let such a disastrous thing happen to Clark, he who worked so hard, who helped his neighbors, who was so patient and talked quietly and never lost his temper, who didn't drink and mistreat his family, who believed in God and prayed to Him daily, who lived by the Book and what it said.

Why, why did this have to happen to Clark? she railed silently. *Why not lazy Jedd Larson or—or . . .* After having lived through this tragic night, and now seeing Clark safe in front of her, Marty could hold it all in no longer. She turned away, leaned against the wall, and let the sobs overtake her.

She felt his hands on her shoulders, and he turned her to him, then pulled her gently into his arms. He held her close like he would a weeping child, stroking the long hair falling over her shoulders. He said nothing and simply let her weep against his chest.

Finally she was able to stop, all the confusion and anger drained from her. She pulled herself away, wiping her face on her apron. "Oh, Clark," she whispered, "whatever air we gonna do now?"

He didn't answer for a moment, and then he spoke so calmly she knew he felt sure of his answer. "Well, we're gonna pray, an' what He sees us to be needin', He'll give; an' what He sees we don' need, He'll make us able to do without."

Marty led the way to the table, and they sat and bowed their heads together. Then Clark reached for the Book, quietly opened it, and began reading, "'The Lord is my shepherd; I shall not want. . . .'"

When Clark came in for breakfast after chores that morning, Marty learned that the cows had run off in terror. The horses, too, had scattered. The pigs were safe in their pens, as were the chickens, but Clark was hard put finding enough to satisfy them without delving too deeply into the precious seed grain that had escaped the blaze. The grazing stock, one pasture over, stood in their shelter bawling to be fed, but with what? All their feed had gone up in smoke. "I jest did the best thet I could fer now," Clark commented with a shrug.

Marty fretted over his cracked lips and blistered hands, but Clark lightly brushed aside her concern.

Missie was strangely quiet as they ate, no doubt sensing something was amiss as she looked between her pa and mama.

Finally Marty could hold the question in no longer. "What ya plannin' to do?"

"First off, I'm goin' over to Ben's," Clark answered matter-of-factly. "He said he'd be right glad to take two of the milk cows. He'll feed 'em both in exchange fer the milk from the one thet's still milkin'. When I have me feed again, we'll get 'em back."

"An' the rest of the stock?"

"We'll have to be sellin' the fifteen head in the grazin' pen."

"An' the hogs?"

"Most of 'em will have to go. I hope to spare me a young sow or two."

"How ya be feedin' 'em?"

"The seed grain wasn't lost. It's in the bins by the pig lot. I'll have to hold me off plantin' thet new land I'd been countin' on 'til another year an' use some of the grain to feed a sow through to spring."

"An' the horses?"

"Horses are fair good at grazin' even in the winter. They can paw down through the snow. I'll take me a bit of money from the sellin' of the stock to git me enough feed to look to the one milk cow thet we keep."

"Ya got it all figured already," Marty said in awe.

"Not quite all, but I been workin' on it. We maybe have to skimp a bit here an' there, but we'll make it. Iffen all goes well, come crop time, we'll be gettin' on our feet agin."

An' the fare back east? Marty didn't ask the question out loud, but Clark somehow must have seen the question in her eyes.

He looked steadily at her for a moment, then spoke slowly. "When I asked ya to set yerself in here to care fer Missie, I made a promise to ya. I'm not goin' back on it now. To tell ya the truth, I would be a missin' ya should ya go, you an' the young'uns"—he stopped and Marty could see his Adam's apple move as he swallowed—"but I'll not be a holdin' ya iffen it's what ya be a wantin'."

For the first time, Marty was no longer sure.

Clark carried through his plans for the stock. The hogs, except for two promising young sows, were sold, as was the grazing stock. He decided to buy enough feed for the milk cow and the two sows and to save the seed grain so the new field could be sown after all. They would need the money from the crop more than ever to help with expenses until the livestock built up again. Only a few hens were saved. The rest were put in crates and taken to town.

Clark now was faced with even more logs to cut since, come spring, a new barn would have to be built.

"Don't worry none about the extry room," Marty told him. "We'll need the barn first." But he said he thought he could manage both with only a slight delay on the house.

The corral fence was repaired, and the single cow and team of horses were placed in the grazing pen, where there was shelter for them. The saddle horse was lent to Jason Stern, who seemed to have great need of it for the present.

Somehow life fell into a routine again. No one was wishing for spring more fervently than Marty, but she found herself wanting it for Clark more than for herself.

TWENTY-SIX

Barn Raisin'

March blew itself out in an angry snarl of wind and snow; then April's arrival promised better things. As the month progressed, the snow began to melt into lacy crystals, the sun took on new warmth, and patches of green gradually appeared in sheltered places. Dan and Charlie greedily sought out each bit of green, eager for easier feeding after foraging through the snow since the fire. The Guernsey had ceased giving milk, readying herself for calving. Milk for Missie and for cooking now had to be brought by pail from the Grahams' every few days.

Near the end of the month, Marty looked out at the nearly bare garden. How eager she was to get at its planting. Cooped up all these months, she could hardly wait to get to some tasks that could be done out-of-doors.

However, Clark had other things that must be done before getting the ground ready for Marty's garden. Over the last month, the neighbor men had brought their teams and given Clark a hand with the logging. Now the logs were stacked and ready for the raising of the new barn. If they had a good day, they'd even give a hand with the two new bedrooms, they promised.

Marty looked out now, envisioning the new barn standing where the old one had been. How good it would be for Clark—and the animals—to have a barn again. The bedrooms—she'd wait on them as long as she had to.

But the first big event for the community was to be the house raising for young Jason Stern and Sally Anne Graham, a house being even more important for the two than a barn. Tomorrow was set aside for the "raisin'," and Marty had been busy draining kraut, cooking ham, and baking extra bread and pie. The men would offer their labors, and the womenfolk would open their larders. Marty looked forward to the day. It would be so welcome to have a visit with her neighbors.

The house raising went well, and the men finished the task in the late afternoon. The women enjoyed a day chatting about their families and sharing recipes and patterns. The Larsons were late, and when they did arrive, Mrs. Larson timidly set her pot of potato stew on the table laden with good things. For the most part no one seemed to pay her much mind, but Marty crossed over to at least say a "howdy" and a welcome to the obviously lonely woman.

Her husband, Jedd, was there to give a hand only on the last few logs, then seemed to consider his advice of far more worth than his brawn. He did, however, manage to down a hearty meal along with the rest.

Marty went home contented with the outing and what was accomplished. Sally Anne would have a nice little cabin in which to set up her first housekeeping. True, there was still a lot that needed to be done, but Marty was sure that Jason would soon take care of that.

During the day, Marty had had a nice long visit with Wanda Marshall, showing her a simple crochet pattern and finding her a keen student of the handwork.

Mrs. Vickers had buzzed about, whispering choice bits of news in various ears, and Mrs. Watley had planted herself in a sunny spot by the desserts and busied herself with drinking coffee and "keepin' the young'uns outen the food."

It was all fun, Marty decided, and next week would be their turn to host the neighbors and be the recipients of their cheerful efforts.

True to their word, the group started arriving on Tuesday morning, determined to get the job done. Log by log the barn began to take shape.

Clark and Todd Stern manned the axes that skillfully cut the grooves so one log might fit the next. Clark had decided to build the barn a mite larger to accommodate the animals he anticipated in the future.

By the time the women banged the pot to announce dinner, the barn had nearly reached the rafter stage. The men were eager to get back to their work, so did not tarry long over their meal.

While the women were doing up the dishes, Tommy Graham came in and casually announced, "Pa said iffen ya be movin' the things from the lean-to, we be tearin' it off an' makin' the bedrooms."

Marty fairly flew. She had never been in the lean-to before and was rather shocked at its spartan furnishings. The bedframe held a coarse straw tick. Marty laid her hand on it and thought it hard and lumpy. Remembering her own soft feather tick gave her a bit of a pang. *It must've been awfully cold out here all winter,* she thought guiltily as she moved the few articles Clark had into the sitting room, as well as his clothes from the pegs.

Marty was scarcely finished when she heard the hammers and crowbars have at it. The men went to work with a will, and by supper the logs were in place.

Supper was almost festive. The men were well pleased—and rightly so—with all that had been completed in just one day. Marty could tell that Clark Davis was a favorite neighbor. There wasn't a man there he hadn't helped out at one time or another, and it pleased them to be able to lend a hand in return.

When the meal was over, the men visited while the women cleaned up the tables and sorted out their own crockery and pans for the return to their homes.

Jedd had set a new record for himself on that day. He had made it in time for both dinner and supper, partaking freely of both meals. His missus couldn't make it. "Feelin' poorly," he said. Marty felt genuinely sorry for the poor woman and their daughters.

At last the group had all said their good-byes and clambered into their various farm wagons and onto horses, some promising to be back to help with the roof and floors.

Clark was almost half dead on his feet, having attempted to carry more than his share of the load at his own "raisin'" and then having to go out for choring after it was all over. He stretched out on the straw tick now lying on the sitting room floor, announcing he meant to just rest a bit before he went to bed "proper like" in the new addition. In next to no time he was sound asleep, snoring softly while Marty put the children to bed.

Marty came into the room and stopped short. "Lan' sakes," she exclaimed softly, "he be plumb beat."

She went over to gently ease a pillow under his head and slip off his shoes, then placed a blanket over him and moved in to her own bed.

TWENTY-SEVEN

Laura

In less than two weeks' time the visiting preacher would be paying his spring visit, and Sally Anne would be marrying. Ma still mourned to think of her oldest moving out of the family circle, but she told Marty she guessed it was a part of life, and from now on she'd be losing them one by one.

But second daughter Laura's strange behavior troubled her mother. The girl had been acting so different lately, sullen and resentful around the house, then slipping away for long walks. At times she even rode off on one of the workhorses.

Marty didn't find all this out till some time after the fact, but finally Ma could take it no longer and knew she must have a talk with the girl. She waited for a time when they were alone, then began as gently as she could.

"Laura, I be thinkin' thet somethin's troublin' ya. I'd be right glad to be a sharin' it iffen ya'd like to lay it on me."

Laura seemed to look at Ma with rebellion in her eyes.

"Nothin' the matter with me," she responded resentfully.

"I think there is. Maybe it's a natural thing—with all the fussin' an' fixin' fer Sally Anne."

Laura's chin went up. "What do I care 'bout Sally Anne?"

"She be yer sister—"

"No, she ain't."

Ma looked fully at the girl now. Anger began to stir within her.

"Ya listen here, missy. Sally an' you been close like ever since I be yer ma."

"Ya ain't my ma."

Ma stopped short, and she told Marty later that she was sure her mouth was hanging open. She had known things were bad but had not guessed they were this bad. Finally she started over slowly. "Laura, I'm sorry, really I am. I never knowed ya was feelin' this way—so strong like. I've tried to be a ma to ya. I love ya like ya was my own, and yer pa—he'd do most anythin' fer ya."

"Won't need to be a doin' fer me much longer now," declared Laura.

"Whatcha meanin'?"

"I'm gettin' married, too."

"Yer gettin' married? But ya ain't even had ya a beau."

"Have too."

"Well, we never knowed it. Who be—?"

"Milt Conners." Laura stared back with stubborn determination in her face, no doubt well aware of the Grahams' view of the young man in question.

Ma reeled inwardly, turmoil and consternation making her nearly weak with the announcement from Laura. Never in her life would she give one of her daughters to Milt Conners. Not if her life depended on it. His drinking and carousing were well known in these parts, and not just hearsay.

When finally she could speak again, she tried her best to be firm yet gentle. "Oh no, ya ain't," she began. "No one in this house be takin' themselves up with Milt Conners. Iffen I didn't stop ya, yer pa sure would."

"Ya can't stop me!" Laura's assertion seemed to shock her as much as Ma. The girl took a tentative step backward.

"Oh yes'm, we can," said Ma, equally determined.

"It be too late," flung out Laura.

"Whatcha be meanin'?"

"I'm . . . I'm gonna have his baby." Now Laura's eyes were downcast, and she wouldn't look Ma in the face.

Ma told Marty she felt a weakness go all through her and thought she'd have a faint. Finally she staggered forward and steadied herself on the back of a chair. "Whatcha be sayin', girl?" she managed to ask.

But Laura stood her ground. Let Ma and Pa fume and fuss or anything else. Come time for Sally Anne to be standing before the preacher, she'd be there, too.

"I'm gonna have his baby," she repeated, more firmly this time.

Ma stepped forward, tears streaming down her face. She reached out for Laura and pulled her gently into her arms, holding her close, her head bowed against the long brown hair.

"Oh, my poor baby," she wept. "My poor, poor baby."

Ma's genuine love and care seemed to touch Laura, but the girl stoutly insisted that she loved Milt and was going to marry him come what may.

The two weeks until the preacher's visit were full of wedding preparations as well as deep sorrow in the Graham home. When Sally Anne heard of Laura's planned wedding, she generously offered to share some of her own household articles she had been stitching and preparing. Laura would have none of them, declaring she wouldn't need much, as Milt was already set up for housekeeping. Nevertheless, Ma sat up late each night, making a quilt and hemming towels and curtains.

Ben carried on with his usual farm work, but his shoulders sagged, and his face appeared drawn. The joy of the big day had been stolen from them. Even Laura did not seem to carry the glow that a new bride should, but she set her jaw determinedly and helped in preparations for the double wedding.

TWENTY-EIGHT

The Big Day

The preacher's visit would occur on Easter Sunday morning. The community would first have an outdoor service together, then the wedding ceremonies would follow. Later the neighbors would all join for a potluck dinner to honor the new couples and to have a chance for a neighborly visit before spring work would demand much of their time.

Marty looked forward to the day. She was very grateful for the neighbors she had come to know and the friends she had made. With winter behind them and the feeling of spring in the air, she was restless to get out somewhere—for something. She also was curious about the church service and what the preacher would have to say. Her only connection with church had been for marriages and funerals, and the last time she had seen this preacher, she had been in such grief and emotional turmoil she could hardly remember the event or him.

She felt happiness for Sally Anne with the sparkle of love on her face, but her heart ached for Laura. After Ma had confided the reason for their consent to the marriage, Marty shared Ma's deep concern over the coming union and felt such helplessness, knowing there was nothing any of them could do to prevent further heartache for this strong-willed girl or her family.

Marty busied herself embroidering two sets of pillowcases for the new brides. She was fearful lest her true feelings show themselves even in her stitching. The one pair was so much joy to work. The other made her fingers feel as heavy as her heart.

Soon enough the big day arrived. The sun promised a warm spring day as Marty bustled about readying the pots of food that she would be taking and getting Missie and Clare dressed in their finest.

She decided she would wear her as yet unworn blue-gray dress. She finally accepted that she would "feel right" in it. Clark did look at her with admiration, and she found she didn't mind it. She felt herself flush under his gaze.

Marty's eyes cast joyfully about the yard and the surrounding hills as they packed up the wagon. A child at her side and babe in arms, she faced the bright morning beside Clark, pointing out each new sign of spring. Though the fields were now bare, with only patches of soiled snow left in hidden places, the first flowers were slowly lifting their heads to the sun. Returning birds occasionally made an appearance on a fence post or tree limb. But the surest sign of spring was the feeling within her as she breathed in the warm, fragrant air.

They were one of the first families to reach the Grahams', and Marty wanted to help Ma with the last of the preparations. Clark assured her that Missie and Clare would be fine left with him; the fresh air would do them all good. As Marty turned to hurry into the house, she heard Ben's comments on what a fine-looking son Clare was and Clark's gentle boasts of the tiny boy's already apparent strength and awareness. Marty smiled to herself.

Makeshift benches had been placed around for the church service, and long tables were arranged for the meal.

Ma's house was soon a hive of activity, for a visit from the preacher and two weddings on the same day were cause for any amount of flurry.

The Stern family arrived, causing Sally Anne to flush a becoming shade. Marty was glad to see Jason look at her with pride and love in his eyes.

Just before the service was to begin, Milt Conners appeared, looking as cocky and troublesome as ever. The men sociably made room for him on the bench, but Marty could understand the distress of the Grahams. She could not feel at ease about this man, either.

After all were seated on the benches, Ben Graham stood to his feet and welcomed the neighbors to his farm on this "fine spring day." He trusted they would find the Easter service a "real blessin'" and invited them to share in the weddings of his two eldest daughters, thanking them kindly "fer all the good food appearin' on the tables."

He then introduced the visiting preacher, Pastor Simmons, and expressed how "fine it is to have 'im here on Easter Sunday mornin', an' I know we's all lookin' forward to sharin' in the mornin' meetin'."

The pastor took charge of things then, and he commented on the "beautiful day that the Lord hath made," expressed his delight at seeing them all in attendance, and led the group in prayer. They sang a few hymns from memory, not having any hymnals. Marty didn't know the words to any of the hymns, but she enjoyed listening to the others sing. She must get Clark to teach her some of the tunes and words to the songs, she decided.

When Pastor Simmons began to speak to the people, Marty listened intently. The simple but powerful story of Easter began with Christ's ministry to the people of His day, His arrest, and the false accusations that sentenced Him to die. The preacher told of the political factions of the time and the historical reasons for His death, but he then explained the real purpose in the Father allowing, yea, planning for His beloved Son to die.

Marty's heart was torn as she listened. She had heard before how cruel men of Christ's day had put Him to death with no just cause, but never before had she realized it had anything at all to do with her. Now to hear the fact that He personally took the punishment for her sins, as well as for the sins of all mankind, was a startling and sobering discovery.

I didn't know—I jest didn't know thet ya died fer me, her heart cried as she sat on one of the benches, Clare held tightly in her arms and Missie and Clark on either side. *I'm sorry—truly I am. Lord, I asks ya to be doin' what yer intendin' in my heart.* Tears slipped from her eyes and down her cheeks. She didn't even bother to wipe them away. She could feel Clark's eyes on her when he occasionally glanced her way.

But the preacher did not stop there. He went on with the story of that first Easter morning when the women went early to the tomb and found the Lord had risen.

"He lives," said the preacher, "and because He is victor over sin and death, we, too, can be."

Marty's heart filled with such a surge of joy she felt like shouting—but not here, not now, she cautioned herself. She would eventually, though. She had to tell someone that now she understood. *I've given myself to be a knowin' Clark's God,* she told herself, awed by the thought.

She reached over and slipped her hand into Clark's. When Clark looked at her, she returned his gaze. He must have read the difference in her face, and the big hand firmly squeezed her smaller one. Marty knew he shared her joy, as she now shared his God. It was enough.

The weddings followed the worship service. Laura and Milt stood together first in front of the pastor. Sally Anne had wanted it that way. Milt looked down at his feet, shifting back and forth with regularity. He looked rather careless in demeanor and attire, though he had trimmed his beard and had a haircut. Laura looked shyly at him in a way that made Marty hope maybe, with the help of a good woman's love, this man could indeed change. She wanted with all her heart for the two of them to find happiness together.

Jason and Sally Anne stood next, and Marty knew the joy and love showing on their faces was reflected in the Grahams' as well as her own heart. How easy it was to share in their happiness.

As soon as the ceremonies were over, the neighbors began the merry-making, throwing rice, ringing cowbells, and lining up to kiss the brides. The two couples were finally allowed to sit down at the table piled with gifts, and while the womenfolk made preparations for the noon meal, the brides unwrapped their presents.

As the good-natured talk and laughter continued during the meal, the Larsons arrived. Jedd swaggered over to the tables, not even bothering to tether his team. Mrs. Larson placed a pan of corn bread with the other dishes and, with eyes to the ground, ushered her youngsters to a safe-looking place at a far table. Marty rose and, with a pretense of refilling the water pitcher, passed close to the woman.

"Ya all be welcome. So glad ta see ya agin'," Marty said softly. The woman did not lift her eyes, but a small spot of color appeared in each cheek as she nodded in answer. "The good Lord has done so much fer all of us," Marty continued, reaching out to tousle each child's hair. "Preacher talked 'bout it this mornin', how God can clean up folks' hearts and change their ways. He's put me on that path," she added, not exactly sure how to express what she was feeling.

Marty's feelings soared with satisfaction as she noticed Mrs. Larson's upward glance. Wasn't that an expression of hope? Meanwhile, Jedd just loaded his plate and settled down to eat. Further visiting with Mrs. Larson could come at another time.

When the tables had been cleared away, the two new young couples loaded their wagons and kissed Ma good-bye. Ma bore up bravely, but there was a longing in her eyes as she kissed Sally Anne good-bye, and an expression of deep concern as she pulled Laura close to her, holding her at length before she released her. Marty turned away lest her own tears spill over.

Clark and Marty lingered for a while, sensing how a difficult time in the Grahams' lives had been made even more so, then collected their children and got themselves on home.

"All in all, this was a good day," Marty told Clark, and he nodded his agreement.

TWENTY-NINE

Planting

The sun carried more warmth each day, and Marty was very glad to get the children outside into the fresh air. Clark had finished work on the new bedrooms, and Marty had added her own touches with curtains and rugs. They did appreciate the additional areas for work and play. Clark's days began early and ended only when it was too dark to see any longer in the fields he was tilling, and every day more land was ready for the carefully guarded seed that had survived the fire.

Enough grass was now finding its way out of the earth for the three cows to graze. A young calf was in the weaning pen, the second cow was still to calf, and a third would come much later.

One of the sows already had offspring at her side. Missie was especially captivated by the squealing little piglets trying to get their fair share at mealtimes. The sow had not given them as good a litter as they had hoped, bearing only six and losing two, but they thought the second sow might do better. Three of Marty's eight hens were sitting on eggs. She hoped to replenish the chicken coop again.

The new barn stood straight and strong, a bit larger than its predecessor. As yet it was still unchinked, but that could be done during slack time later in the year. The roof was on and the floor in. It would do as it was until after the crop was in the ground.

Marty was humming one of the new hymns she was learning as she worked on breakfast preparations. Missie had specifically asked for pancakes, and as Marty stirred the batter she remembered those early weeks in this little house when all she knew how to make was pancakes. Then she thought of the two new brides and wondered how they were making out with their cooking responsibilities. She was sure they would do much better, with Ma having trained them well.

Sally Anne was well settled in. She and Jason had driven over one evening to return the saddle horse. Jason's eyes shone with pride as he boasted of how Sally Anne had hung the curtains, spread the rugs, and set her little kitchen in order. She was a right fine cook, too, he went on, and Sally Anne's cheeks had flushed with pleasure. Clark and Marty chuckled about it later. Marty smiled now as she pictured the young couple so content in their love for each other.

Then her thoughts shifted to Laura. How was Laura really doing? she wondered. Clark had seen her recently when he had driven up over the brow of a hill, and there was Laura walking down the road. She had seemed startled at his sudden appearance, he said, and had turned sharply away. When he stopped the team to offer her a lift, she looked back at him to say, "No thanks, walkin' be right good for me." But her eyes looked troubled and there was a bruise on her cheek. He had gone on his way, but as he related his story to Marty that evening she could tell he was deeply troubled by it all. *Poor Laura*, Marty thought, shaking her head. To be expecting a child with this man and seeming so unhappy and alone. Her heart ached for her—and for Ma Graham.

She could hear Clark whistling as he came from the barn, so she called Missie to come quickly to the table. *I wonder*, she thought as she helped the child into her chair, *if spring plantin' always makes a man so happy like.*

Spring was getting into her blood, too, and she was anxious to sink her own hands into the soil. It was so wonderful to feel slim and comfortable again. She felt like she was gliding about, no longer weighted down and clumsy "carrying a young'un everywhere I go," as she had expressed it once to Ma. She was thankful to have baby Clare out where she could hug him close or lay him down at will.

During their morning reading and prayer, Marty almost smiled as Clark read, "'Come unto me, all ye that labour and are heavy laden, and I will give you rest.'" She felt she understood the meaning of Jesus' words in a special way.

I thank ye, Lord, that ye be teachin' me how to rest in you, she prayed inwardly. *Ya be comfortin' me, and I be grateful for that.*

After Clark had finished praying and committing their day to God, Marty asked, "Be it about time to plant the garden?"

"Some of the seeds should go in now. I be thinkin' this mornin' thet I best put the plow to work turnin' the ground. Should be ready fer ya in short order. Ya wantin' to plant it today?"

"Oh yes," Marty answered enthusiastically. "Me, I'm right eager to get goin' on it. Only . . ."

When she couldn't think of how to tell him, Clark urged, "Only what?"

Marty flushed. "Well . . . I never planted before."

"Planted what?"

"Planted anythin'."

"Didn't yer folks have themselves a garden?"

"My ma said 'twas a nuisance, thet she'd as leave buy off a neighbor or from the store. She didn't care none fer the soil, I reckon."

"An' you?"

"I think I'd love to git into makin' somethin' grow. I can hardly wait to try. Only . . ."

Clark looked across at her. "Only what?" he prompted again.

"Well," Marty gulped, "I know thet the garden be a woman's work, but I was wonderin' . . ." She hesitated. "Jest this one time, could ya show me how to plant the seeds an' all?"

Clark looked as though he was trying not to smile and answered slowly, "I reckon I could . . . this once, mind."

Marty looked at him and the twinkle in his eye and took a deep breath of relief. It was the first time she had been able to bring herself to ask him for something, and he seemed to be pleased rather than offended by it. She said, "The best time be right after dinner while the young'uns be havin' their naps. Will the ground be plowed an' ready by then?"

Clark nodded. "I think I can oblige that schedule," he said with mock seriousness as he got up for the coffeepot. Marty nearly choked on a mouthful of pancake. It was the first time she had missed getting his second cup of coffee for some months. Clark seemed unperturbed as he poured for both of them and returned to his place.

Over their steaming mugs they discussed what seeds she would plant; then he reached for his hat. "Thet be good coffee," he said as he went out the door.

At noon after the dinner dishes were done and the children settled, Clark and Marty spread the garden seeds out on the kitchen table to decide what was to be put in at first planting and what left until later. Clark patiently showed her the different seeds, telling her what they were and the peculiarity of their growing habits. Marty listened wide-eyed. He knew so much, Clark did, and as he talked about the seeds, they seemed to take on personalities right before her eyes—like children, needing special care and attention.

They soon gathered up the seeds and headed for the garden. The sun warmed the ground, making the freshly turned soil smell delightfully inviting. The two laughed together about how Missie, and soon Clare, too, would want to be getting their hands—as well as the rest of their little bodies—into the dirt.

Marty reached down and let a handful of the soil trickle through her fingers. *It's beautiful,* she wanted to say, but it seemed such a foolish word to describe dirt. She suddenly stopped, and turning her back to Clark, she slipped off her shoes. Then lifting her skirt modestly, she peeled off her stockings and tucked them carefully into the toes of the shoes. Standing barefoot, feeling the luxury of the warm earth, she dug her toes deeply into its moist richness. She felt like a child again—young and free, with burdens and responsibilities stripped away for the moment.

No wonder horses like ta lie down and roll when their harness is taken off, she thought. *Me, I'd love to be doin' the same thing.*

Clark was already busy preparing rows for her to plant. She went down on her knees and began to drop seeds into the fertile ground.

"Someday soon, I'll be watchin' ya grow," she said quietly as the tiny carrot seeds spilled from her hand.

Clark returned to cover the row after she had placed the seed.

He looks to be enjoyin' it 'most as much as I am, thought Marty. Then she caught sight of their gamboling calf and wished she herself had the nerve to skip around like that. *It's good jest to be livin' on sech a day.*

The two worked on together, for the most part in silence, and Marty was feeling a new comradeship with the earth and with this tall, patient man whom she called her husband. Nearing the end of their task, Clark squatted down to carefully pat earth over the sweet corn Marty had just dropped into the ground.

Seeing his rather unstable position, Marty sneaked up behind him and gave him a playful shove. He went sprawling in the loose dirt as he took a quick look at her trying to hide her laughter behind her hands.

"Me thinks there's someone askin' fer sweet corn down her neck," he said, scrambling up and reaching for a handful of corn.

Marty was off at a run, but even though she was rather nimble, Clark's long strides soon overtook her. Both long arms went about her, halting her escape. She writhed and twisted against him, seeking to loose herself, but her laughter made her efforts most ineffectual. Clark tried to hold her close so he could free one hand with the corn kernels, but his own laughter was hampering his efforts.

Marty was conscious of his nearness in a way she had never been before. The strength of the arms that held her, the beating of the heart against her cheek, the clean smell of shaving soap that still clung to him—everything about this man who held her sent warm tingles all through her. Her breath was beginning to come in little gasps, and she was powerless to struggle any longer.

The one strong arm pinned her securely against him, and his other hand dumped its load of kernels down the front of her dress. Marty looked up into laughing eyes bent over her, uncomfortably close to her own. The breath caught in her throat as a strangely familiar emotion swept through her. The expression on Clark's face was somehow changing from teasing to something else.

Marty pulled back abruptly, an unreasoning fear filling her heart and her body going weak.

"Thet be Clare?" she said quickly, pushing with trembling hands against Clark's chest.

Clark let her go, and she half ran, half stumbled to the house, her cheeks aflame.

Inside she leaned her head against the bedroom door, trying to sort out the reasons for her throbbing heart and troubled spirit. She could find no answer, and after giving herself several minutes to get herself in hand, she picked up her courage and returned to the garden. But Clark was just putting away the tools. The job was done.

THIRTY

Sorrow

Marty looked out the window each morning to check on the progress of the garden. Tiny green stalks were starting to push through, and Missie was nearly as delighted as Marty as they watched them grow. The little girl quickly learned that she should not step on the tender plants or pull them up to inspect their roots.

The activities and conversations in the household seemed to be normal, but deep down Marty knew something had changed. Clark was as considerate as ever, and they still talked things over and enjoyed the children. But there was an uneasy acknowledgment that things were different. She would not let herself think too deeply about it. It was fairly easy to go through the motions of the day in the same orderly fashion she had learned to follow.

She rose early, fed baby Clare, prepared breakfast, and dressed Missie. Then they read Scripture, prayed, and ate the morning meal. She could sit across from Clark, could talk to him and share her plans for the day in as ordinary a way as ever, but she did not let her eyes linger on his for very long. She longed for things to stay as they had been and at the same time feared that they might. *Oh my,* she mourned, *what's happenin'? What's gonna happen . . . ?*

Marty wandered out to the garden to see the growing things and hopefully take her mind off all the perplexing thoughts and feelings. Somehow the garden always gave her a sense of accomplishment and joy. She even found herself talking to the corn, then pushed a little dirt around a potato plant, coaxed the onions and lettuce to hurry a bit, and wondered why she had bothered with so many beans.

She walked over to the fruit trees and was admiring each new leaf when she noted that one of the trees bore blossoms. Her heart leaped—apples. Imagine, apples! Oh, if she could only show Clark, but he was in the fields planting. Then she was surprised to see him coming toward her in long, purposeful strides.

"Clark," she called eagerly. "Clark, come see."

With her eyes fixed on the tree, she reached for his hand to draw him closer.

"Look, Clark," she enthused. "Apple blossoms. We're gonna have apples. Jest look."

There was no answer. She looked up in bewilderment at the silence. Clark stood looking down at her, his face pale, and she could read such sorrow in his eyes. Her heart contracted with fear.

"What . . . what be wrong?" she whispered through trembling lips.

He reached for her then, placing a hand on each shoulder, and looked deeply at her as though willing her some of his strength to help her bear the news he was bringing.

"It's Laura. They done found her in the crik over by the Conners' cabin."

"Is she . . . is she . . . ?"

"She be dead, Marty."

She sagged against him, her hand pressed to her mouth. "An' Ma?" she finally asked.

"She be needin' ya."

And then she was sobbing, her face against his chest. His hands smoothed her hair as he held her close. She cried for Ma, for Laura, for Ben, even for Sally Anne.

Oh, God, she prayed. *Ya be the only one to be helpin' at a time like this. Help us all now. Please, God, help us now.* Somehow she knew Clark was silently praying the same prayer.

Marty was there when Laura's body was brought to the Grahams'. She would never forget the heartrending scene. Ma gathered the lifeless body into her arms, weeping as though her heart would break and rocking back and forth, saying over and over, "My poor baby, my poor little darlin'." After a time, she wiped her tears, squared her shoulders determinedly, and began to tenderly prepare the body for burial. Ben's grief certainly matched Ma's, but he did not feel the same freedom to express it. Marty had never seen such an ashen face, such bewilderment and grief, as she saw in Ben. She was even more concerned for Ben than for Ma.

Ben insisted on riding over to the Conners' cabin. Unbeknownst to him, Clark had already been there. He had found a very drunk Milt, who swore he knew nothing of Laura's death. He may have roughed her up a bit, he admitted. But she was quite alive when he'd last seen her, he insisted. Clark had convinced Milt in no uncertain terms that he would be wise to move farther west and to do so immediately.

Clark rode over again with Ben, making no mention of his previous visit. The cabin looked to be deserted for good and in a great hurry. Clark told Marty later that he was very relieved Milt had already gone, fearing what Ben might have done in his present state.

Neighbors came, and they lovingly set to work. The coffin was built and the grave dug, and the frail body of the girl was committed to the ground. In the absence of a preacher, Clark was asked to say the "buryin' words." Marty could sense how difficult it was for him as he held the Bible open and read the ancient words, "'For dust thou art, and unto dust thou shalt return. . . .'"

Solemnly they all turned from the new mound, leaving Ma and Ben to sort out and adjust to their grief. Ma, whose wisdom and care had comforted many a neighbor in tragic circumstances, once again said through her tears that time was the answer. This time she was saying it to herself.

THIRTY-ONE

New Strength

By June the second cow had calved and, to Clark's great surprise, bore twin female calves—a special gift from God, he announced. "We sure be able to make use o' one more," he told Marty. He was carrying Clare, and Marty held firmly to Missie's hand as they watched the calves awkwardly trying to stand up. Missie thought it was quite funny and would have loved to climb in the pen with them.

A week later the other sow had her pigs, not an exceptional litter but an acceptable one, and she had kept all eight of them.

The hatching of the chicks meant three proud mothers were strutting around with a total of twenty-seven chicks fluttering between them. Missie was quite insistent that the chicks would want to be held, but fortunately they were able to keep away from her chubby hands.

Marty still had not been able to shake off the sorrow of Laura's tragic death. It seemed to hang about her, choking out the happiness she wanted to feel.

Missie came down with the measles, and even though she was not awfully sick, Marty hovered over her, worried lest another tragedy strike. But the child was rather quickly up and around again, pretending that her doll had the measles "an' needs a wet cloth on her head, too."

It was while Missie was still red-blotched and feverish that news came of the first wagon train passing through town, heading east. Marty was busy with doctoring Missie, and there would be other trains, she told herself.

On a warm June day after Missie was back to health, Marty tucked the two youngsters in for their afternoon nap and decided to step outside for a breath of fresh air. She had been cooped up long enough and felt rather restless and uneasy.

She walked through her much-loved garden, noticing how much the plants had grown during the time of Missie's illness. The blossoms on the apple tree had dropped their petals, making room for the fruit forming on the branches.

She walked past the buildings and down to the stream. She seemed drawn to that quiet spot she had discovered long ago when she had needed comfort—then because of her own loss, and now because of Ma's.

She really needed a place to think, to sort things out. Life was so confusing—the good mixed with the bad; such a strange combination of happiness and sorrow.

She sat leaning against a tree trunk, watching the clear water gurgling by.

"God," she whispered, "what be it all about? I don't understand much 'bout ya. I do know thet yer good. I know thet ya love me, thet ya died for me; but I don't understand 'bout losin', 'bout the pain thet goes so deep I can't see the end. I don't understand at all."

She closed her eyes, feeling the strength of the sturdy tree trunk behind her, listening to the rustling of the leaves, feeling the slight breeze ruffling her hair.

She closed her eyes more tightly, drawing from the peace and beauty of the woods. When she opened them, Clark was there, leaning against another tree, his eyes on her face.

She was startled at first and quickly stood.

"Sorry to be frightin' ya," he told her. "I seed ya comin' over here, an' I thought ya'd maybe not mind me joinin' ya."

"'Course not."

Silence fell between them. Clark picked up a branch and broke off small pieces. Marty watched the stream carry them swirling away in the current.

"Guess life be somethin' like thet stream," Clark commented quietly.

"Meanin'?"

"Things happen. Leaves fill it up—animals waller in it—spring floods fill it with mud." He hesitated. "Bright sunshine makes it like a mirror glass; sparklin' rain makes it grow wider, but it still moves on—unchangin' like—the same stream even with all the things thet happen to it. It breaks through the leaves, it clears itself of the animal wallerin'—the muddy waters turn clean agin. The sunshine an' the rain it accepts, fer they give life an' strengthen it like, but it really could have done without 'em. They're extries like." He broke another branch and added more to the stream.

"Life's like thet," he picked up again. "Bad things come, but life keeps on flowin', clearin' its path gradual like, easin' its own burden. The good times come, too; we maybe could make it without 'em, but the Lord knows we need 'em to help give meanin'—to strengthen us, to help us reflect the sunshine.

"Guess one has to 'spect the good an' the bad, long as we be livin', an' try one's best to make the bad hurt as little as possible, an' the good—one has to help it grow like, make all the good things count."

Marty had shut her eyes again as Clark was speaking. She stood there now, eyes closed, breathing deeply of the woods and the stream.

Life was like that stream. It went on, whatever happened to it. She was ready to go on now, too. She had drawn strength from the woods. No, not that. She had drawn strength from the God who had made the woods.

THIRTY-TWO

Love Comes Softly

Marty hurried through her mending, wanting to have it all finished before she had to get supper ready. She was working on a pair of Clark's overalls, the last item in her mending basket. As she handled the garment, she was reminded again of what a big man she was married to.

"Why, they'd swaller me," she chuckled as she held them up in front of her. Missie thought it was funny, too.

Missie was trying to copy her mama in everything she did. Marty had given her a scrap of cloth and a button. She threaded a blunt needle for Missie and showed the little girl the art of button sewing.

"Ya may as well learn how it be done," she told her. "Ya'll need to be knowin' how to do this afore we know it."

Missie busied herself pushing the needle in and out of the material. Marty smiled at the child's efforts—the thread showed up in some very strange places, but Missie was quite happy with her newly learned skill.

Baby Clare lay on a rug, cooing and talking to himself and anyone else who would care to listen. He was four months old now, a bright, happy, healthy child, who as yet had not fulfilled Clark's dire predictions of "wait until the teeth come in." All three of his family members doted on him, so why shouldn't he be content?

Missie talked to him as she worked. "See, baby. See big si'ter. She sewin'. Do ya like it? Look, Mama. He smiles. Clare likes it—my sewin'."

Marty nodded at them both and went on sewing the overall patch. A loud crash made her jump and Missie exclaimed, "Dad-burn!" as she looked at the spilled button box.

"Missie, ya mustn't say thet."

Missie stared up at her mama. "You did."

"Well, I don't say it anymore, an' I don't want ya sayin' it, either. Now, let's git down an' pick up all them buttons on the floor 'fore Clare gits 'em in his mouth." Missie obeyed, helping put the buttons back in their container and placing it on the sewing machine.

Marty finished her patch and hurried to get supper ready. Clark would be in shortly from chores, and she planned to talk with him about moving the children's beds to their new bedroom. This would give her a bit more space to move around in her own small bedroom. Clark had moved his things into the other one just as soon as he'd been able to get a roof over it and the floor in. With Clare sleeping through the night now and the warmer weather, Marty didn't need to worry about the children becoming uncovered. It would be nice to be able to reach her things without banging her shins on a small bed or tripping over Missie's doll.

She almost had the meal on the table when Missie came flying through the door.

"Mama—Mama—Clare sick!"

"Whatcha meanin'?" Marty spun around to look at her.

The child grabbed her hand, jerking her toward the sitting room.

"He sick!" she screamed.

Marty ran toward the rasping, gurgling sound.

She snatched up the baby, who was struggling furiously, his little fists flailing the air as he fought for breath.

"He's chokin'!" Marty cried. She turned him upside down and smacked him on the back between his tiny shoulder blades.

Clare still struggled.

"Run fer yer pa," Marty told the small child, trying to keep the panic out of her voice. Missie ran.

Marty reversed the baby and carefully pushed a finger down his throat. She thought she could feel something, but the end of her finger just ticked it. Clare was gagging, but nothing came up.

Clark came running through the door, his eyes wild with concern.

"He's chokin'!" Marty told him.

"Slap his back."

"I did." Marty was in tears now.

"Put yer finger—"

"I tried."

"I'll git the doc."

"There's no time."

"Wrap 'im up," Clark instructed her, his voice firm. "I'll git the horses."

The baby was still breathing—struggling, gasping little breaths, but he was still breathing.

"Oh, God," Marty prayed desperately. "Please help us. Please help us. Jest keep 'im breathin' 'til we reach the doc."

She grabbed a blanket and wrapped it about Clare. Missie stood, eyes wide, too frightened to even cry.

"Missie, git yer coat on," Marty ordered, "an' bring a blanket from yer bed so thet ya can lay down in the wagon."

The child hurried to obey.

Clark raced the team toward the house. Marty ran forward with the baby in her arms and Missie by the hand. Without speaking, Clark hauled Missie up, putting her and her blanket in a safe place on the wagon floor; then he helped Marty and the baby over the wheel, and they were off.

The long trip to town was a nightmare. The ragged breathing of the baby was broken only by his fits of coughing. The horses plunged on, harness creaking as sweat flecked their necks and haunches. Clark urged them on and on. Marty clung to Clare; the wagon jostled her bones, sweat from the horses dotting her arms and face.

We'll never make it—we'll never make it, Marty cried inwardly as Clare's gasping breath seemed to be weakening and the horses' breakneck speed slackened. But on they galloped, seeming to draw on a reserve Marty would have never guessed they had.

The baby's breathing was even more erratic as lights from the town finally came into view. Clark spoke again to the horses and they sped forward. How could they continue on at this pace? They must be ready to fall in the harness, but Clark's coaxing voice seemed to strengthen them.

Straight to the doctor's they galloped, and Clark pulled the heaving horses to a stop and jumped down before the wagon had stopped rolling. He reached up for little Clare, and Marty surrendered him, watching Clark head for the door on the run. Marty turned to help Missie up from the floor of the wagon. For a moment Marty clung to the little girl, wanting to assure her that all would be well—but would it? She climbed over the wheel and held up her arms for the child.

By the time Marty entered the room that served as the doctor's office, the baby had been placed on a small table under, what seemed to her, a very bright light. The doctor was bending over him, appearing to completely overwhelm the small gasping figure as he examined him.

"He has a tiny object stuck in his throat," he said matter-of-factly, just as though Marty's whole world did not revolve around that very fact.

"I'm going to have to go after it. We'll have to put him to sleep. Call my missus, will you? She helps with this—has special training."

Clark rapped loudly on the door separating the office from the living quarters, and a woman came into the room. On seeing the small baby fighting for every breath, her eyes showed instant concern.

"Oh my! What's his problem?"

"He has something in his throat. We're going to have to put him to sleep and remove it."

The doctor was already in action as he spoke, and she quickly joined him, the two working as a well-matched team.

The doctor seemed to have forgotten the rest of the family as he hurriedly prepared himself; then he looked up suddenly. "You folks can just take a chair in our living room. This won't take long, but we work best alone."

Clark took Marty's arm and led her from the room. She went reluctantly, hating to leave the precious little baby, fearing every breath might be his last.

Clark helped ease her numb body into a chair. She was still clinging to

Missie. He suggested that Missie could sit on another chair beside her, but she shook her head. Clark himself did not sit down but paced the floor with an anxious face. Marty knew he was petitioning his God. His hand trembled as he removed the hat he had forgotten. Watching him, Marty realized just how much he loved the wee baby. *He loves him as though he were his own,* she thought and didn't find this strange at all. After all, she loved Missie in the same way and had as good as forgotten there ever was a time when the little girl had been only a tiny stranger.

Centuries seemed to drag by, and Missie finally wriggled out of Marty's arms and fell asleep on her blanket in a corner. But eventually the doctor appeared at the door. Clark crossed to Marty, placing a hand on her shoulder as if to protect her from hearing the worst, but the doctor smiled at them.

"Well, Mr. Davis," he said, looking at Clark, who was, after all, the one responsible for his coming to this town. "Your boy is going to be just fine. Had this button lodged in his throat; luckily it was turned sideways or—"

"It weren't luck," Clark responded.

"Call it what you may"—the doctor shrugged—"it's out now. You can see him if you wish."

Marty stood up. *He is all right. My baby is all right.* She wasn't sure her legs could hold her upright. "Oh, God, he's all right. Thank ya. Thank ya!" she exclaimed.

If it hadn't been for Clark's arms about her, she would have gone down in a heap. He pulled her to him, and they wept in thankfulness together.

Clark and Marty stood looking down at the relaxed but pale little face, relief flooding through them. Marty had not released Clark's hand and his arm still steadied her.

"He's been through a lot, poor little fellow," the doctor said sympathetically, and Marty felt she would be forever beholden to this kindly man.

"He needs a long, restful sleep now," the doctor said. "He's still under the effect of the sleeping draught we gave him. I expect he'll sleep through the night without stirring. My wife and I will take turns sitting with him. You folks had best try to get some rest. I'm sure the hotel across the street will have a room."

"Shouldn't . . . shouldn't we stay with 'im?" Marty finally found her voice.

"No need, ma'am," the doctor answered. "He'll sleep, and seems to me you could be using some yourself."

"He's right," Clark said. "Ya be needin' some rest—an' some supper, too. Come on. Let's get across to the hotel."

With a last glance at the sleeping baby, stroking his cheek to assure herself that he was really all right, Marty allowed herself to be led out. Clark picked up the tired and hungry Missie and carried her across the street.

Marty was glad to sink into the chair and hold Missie close, crooning words of love to her, while Clark made arrangements at the desk.

Clark returned to her. "They'll rustle up some supper an' then show ya to a room."

"What 'bout you?"

"I'll be needin' to care fer the horses. They need a good rubdown an' a bit of special care."

Marty nodded. Right now she dearly loved old Dan and Charlie.

"We'll wait fer ya," she nodded.

"Be no need—" Clark started.

"Yes, we'll want to wait for ya."

Clark agreed and went out. While he was gone, Marty told Missie what a brave girl she had been, and how she had helped baby Clare by calling her mama and getting her pa, and lying still on the wagon floor and not crying at the doctor's. She was a big girl and her mama loved her very much.

To Marty's bewilderment, large tears filled Missie's eyes and she began to cry.

At Marty's prompting, she finally sobbed, "But . . . I spill . . . buttons."

Marty pulled her close, rocking her gently. "Missie, Missie, it weren't yer fault that baby Clare found a button thet got missed in our pickin' up. It jest happened, thet's all. Don't ya be frettin' 'bout it. Mama an' yer pa love ya so very much, an' you was a brave girl to be so good. You hush ya, now."

She finally got the little girl comforted.

Clark returned, reporting that Dan and Charlie would be fine after a good rest. And they'd get it, too, he declared—they'd earned it.

The three went in together to the hotel dining room. But none of them felt much like eating. Missie was too tired, Marty too spent, and Clark too relieved to be much interested in food.

After making an effort to down a light meal, they requested that they be shown to their room.

A small cot had been placed in one corner, and the first thing Marty did was prepare Missie for bed as best she could. There was no soft, warm nightie, but Missie didn't mind. She fell asleep almost before she finished her short prayer.

Marty sat beside her until she was sure the child was asleep, then kissed her again and went over to a very weary Clark, who was trying to relax in a large chair.

What could she say to this man who sat before her? This man who comforted her when she sorrowed, understood her joys, gave her strength when her own strength was spent, shared with her his faith, and introduced her to his God. There was so much she felt. That strange, deep stirring within her—she understood it now. It was a longing for this man, his love. She wanted him; she knew that now. But how . . . how could she tell him?

She stood there mute, wanting to say it all, but no words came. Then he rose and reached for his hat.

"Where ya be headin'?" She found her voice then.

"I'm thinkin' thet I'll spend me the night over at the doc's. Iffen little Clare be wakin', I'm thinkin' thet he should wake to some of his own 'stead of strangers."

"But Doc says he won't wake till morn."

"Maybe so. All the same, I'll find comfort jest watchin' him sleep peaceful like. I'll be over in the mornin' to be sure ya not be needin' anythin'."

He turned to go, but she knew she mustn't let him. If he went now without knowing . . .

Still her voice would not obey her command. She reached out and took his sleeve. He turned to her. She could only look at him, imploring him to read in her eyes what she could not say with her lips.

He looked into her face searchingly; then he stepped closer and his hands went to her shoulders, drawing her toward him.

He must have read there what she wanted him to see, but still he hesitated a moment.

"Ya bein' sure?" he asked quietly.

She nodded her head, looking deep into his eyes, and then she was in his arms, being held the way she ached to be held, feeling the strength of his body tight against her, raising trembling lips to his.

How long had she wanted this? She wasn't sure. She only knew that now it seemed like forever. She loved him so much. She must later find the words to tell him so, but for now she would content herself with being held close, hearing his words of love whispered tenderly against her hair.

How did it all come about—this miracle of love? She didn't know. It had come upon her unawares . . . softly.

LOVE'S
ENDURING
PROMISE

Dedicated with love to
Edward
Terry, Lavon, Lorne, and Laurel
—my wonderful family

ONE

New Beginnings

Marty stirred restlessly. The dream had possessed her, and now she felt an uncontrollable shiver run through her body.

With her gradual wakefulness came an intense relief. She was here, safe and belonging, in her own bed.

Still, an uneasiness clung to her. It had been a horrible dream, so real and frightening. Why, she asked herself, did she even have this dream after all this time? And it had been so real—so very real.

She could feel the dream's frightening details close in about her again as she thought about it. The broken wagon, a howling blizzard pulling and tearing at the flapping canvas, and she, Marty, huddled alone in a corner, vainly clasping a thin, torn blanket about her shivering body in an effort to keep warm. Her despair at being alone was more painful than the cold that sought to claim her.

I'm gonna die, she had thought during the dream, *all alone. I'm gonna die*—and then, thankfully, she had awakened and had felt the warmth of her familiar four-poster and looked through the cabin window at a sky blessed with twinkling stars.

But she could not suppress another shiver, and as it passed through her body, a strong arm went about her, drawing her close.

She hadn't meant to waken Clark. His days were such busy ones, full of farming and care of the animals, and she knew he needed his sleep. As she studied his face in the pale light from the window, she realized he wasn't really awake—not yet.

A flood of love washed over her. Whenever she needed assurance of his love, it was readily given to her, even from the subconscious world of sleep. This was not the first time that, even before he awakened, he had sensed her need and held her in his arms.

But wakefulness was coming to him now. He brushed a kiss against her loose hair and whispered, "Somethin' wrong?"

"No, I'm fine," she murmured. "I jest had me a frightenin' dream, thet's all. I was all alone an'—"

His arm tightened. "But yer not alone."

"No, an', Clark, I'm so glad—so glad."

As he held her close, she knew her shivering had ceased and the reality of the dream was gone.

She reached a hand to his cheek. "I'm fine now—really. Go back to sleep."

His fingers smoothed her hair, then gently rested on her shoulder. Marty lay quietly, and in a few moments Clark's breathing assured her that he was asleep again.

Marty had control of her thoughts now. With the terror of the dream pushed aside, now she used the quiet moments before the dawn to think through and plan for the activities of the day.

Over the winter months, every moment the community menfolk could spare from their own work had been given to felling and skidding logs. The families in the area felt strongly the need for a school for the educating of their children, and they knew the only way they would get one would be to build the structure themselves and find a teacher to go with it.

It would be a simple one-room affair, built near the creek on a piece of property donated by Clark and Marty Davis.

Gradually the piles of logs had grown. The men had been anxious to bring in the required number in front of the spring thaw, and then before the land would be beckoning to their plows, there would be time for a work bee or two.

The log count had been taken—the requirement filled. Tomorrow was the day set aside for the "school raisin'." The men hoped to complete the walls and perhaps even add the rafters. The building would then be completed through the summer as time allowed. By fall the children would have a school of their own.

Marty's thinking jumped ahead to the teacher. They still needed to find a teacher, and they were so difficult to locate and interest in coming out to the frontier. Would they build their school only to discover that they were unable to obtain a qualified teacher? No, they must all pray—pray that the little group working on the search would be fruitful, that their efforts of building the school would not be in vain, that a suitable teacher would be found.

Little Missie would not attend the school for its first term. She would be five come November and probably too young to join the others starting in the new school. Marty felt torn—she wanted Missie at home with her for another year. Still, in all the excitement over the new school, it was hard to not be actually involved with a child in attendance. She reminded herself again that Clark and she had decided Missie should wait—a hard decision, for Missie talked about the new school constantly.

At first the school had seemed so far into the future, but now here they were on the threshold of its "birthin'." The thought of it stirred Marty, and she knew she would be unable to go back to sleep, even though she should. It was too early to begin the day's work. Her moving about might waken the other members of the family.

She lay quietly, sorting out in her mind what food she would prepare for the school work crew on the morrow and what would need to be done in preparation today. She mentally dressed each of her children and even mentally noted which of the neighbor women she might want to have a chat with when the work would allow it. The opportunity to gather together, even if it meant hard work and extra effort, was something Marty treasured, and she knew the others of their community shared her anticipation.

The minutes seemed to tick by slowly, and finally her restlessness drove her from under the covers. She lifted herself carefully and slowly, for the child she carried made most movements cumbersome.

Jest another month, she reminded herself, *an' we will see who this is.*

Missie was hoping for a baby sister, but little Clare didn't care. A baby was a baby to his small-boy way of thinking; besides, a baby stayed in the house, and he, at every opportunity, marched along with his pa, trying to match his steps with Clark's. So Clare couldn't see a baby adding much to his world.

Marty slipped into her house socks and wrapped a warm robe about her. The little house was cold in the morning.

She went first to look in on the sleeping Missie and Clare. It was still too dark to see well, but through the light from the window their outlines assured her that they were covered and comfortable as they slept.

Marty went on to the kitchen and as quietly as possible lit the fire in the reliable old kitchen stove. Marty felt a kinship with her stove—almost like a man with his team, she reckoned with a little smile. The stove and she worked together to bring warmth and sustenance to this home and family. Of all the things their home held, the stove, she felt, was really hers.

The fire was soon crackling, and Marty put the kettle on to boil and then filled the coffeepot. It would be a while before the stove warmed the kitchen and the coffee began to boil, so Marty pulled her robe about her for warmth and lifted Clark's worn Bible from the shelf. She'd have time to read and pray before the family began to stir.

She felt especially close to God this morning. The dream had made her aware again of how much she had to be thankful for, and the anticipation of the new school added to her feelings of well-being. As close and cared for as she felt with Clark, only God truly understood her innermost self. She was glad for the opportunity to pour it all out to the One she had come to know only recently.

Marty sat slowly sipping the hot coffee, enjoying its warmth spreading through her whole being. She felt refreshed now, both physically and spiritually. Again her eyes sought out the passage on the pages open in her lap. The verse had seemed meant especially for her at this particular time. *Be strong and of a good courage; be not afraid, neither be thou dismayed: for the Lord thy God is with thee whithersoever thou goest.*

The words were rich in promise and a comfort to her, particularly after her troubled dream. *Alone.* The word was a haunting one. She was so thankful she was not alone. Once more in deep humbleness and gratitude she acknowledged the wisdom of her Father in bringing Clark so quickly to her after the tragic death of husband Clem. She realized now that as soon as she had inwardly healed sufficiently to be able to reach out to another, Clark was already there, eager to welcome her. Why had she fought God's provision for her for so long—with every fiber of her being? Ma Graham had said it took time for the heart and the emotions to be restored, and Marty was sure that was the reason. Given that time—and Clark's gentle patience—she had been able to love again.

To love and be loved, to belong, to be a part of another's life—what a precious part of God's plan for his creation, she thought as she poured herself another cup of coffee.

Had she ever been able to really tell Clark all she felt? Somehow to attempt putting it into words seemed never to do her true feelings the proper justice. Oh, she had tried to express it verbally, but words were so inadequate. Instead she sought to say it with her eyes, her actions. Indeed, her very being responded to him daily in a hundred ways.

The little life within her gave a sudden kick.

"An' you," Marty whispered, "you are one more expression of our love. Not jest the creatin' of ya, but the birthin' an' the raisin'. Thet's love, too. Yer special, ya know. Special 'fore we even know who ya are. Special because yer ours—God-given. God bless ya, little'un, an' make ya strong of body, mind, an' spirit. Might ya grow tall an' straight in every way. Make yer pa proud—an' he will be proud. Long as yer beautiful an' strong of soul—even if yer body should be weak or yer mind crippled—jest be upright of spirit. I know yer pa. Thet's what's most important to 'im. An' to yer ma, too."

A stirring from the bedroom interrupted Marty's inner conversation with her unborn child, and a moment later Clark appeared.

"Yer up early," Marty said, welcoming him with a smile. "Couldn't ya sleep, either?"

"Now, who could lay abed with the smell of thet coffee floatin' in the air? I declare, iffen those ladies anxious to catch themselves a man would wear the aroma of fresh-perked coffee 'stead of some Paris perfume, they jest might git somewhere."

They chuckled together, and Marty made to rise from her chair.

"Jest stay sittin'." Clark laid his hand on her shoulder. "I know where the cups are. Don't usually have the pleasure of a cup of coffee afore chorin'. Maybe ya could make this a habit." He grinned companionably and reached for a mug. She knew he didn't really want her getting up any earlier, considering her busy days keeping up with two lively young'uns and another on the way.

Clark poured his coffee and came to the table where he sat across from her. He seemed to study her carefully, and Marty read love and concern in the look.

"Ya be all right?"

"Fine."

"Junior behavin'?"

Marty grinned. "When ya got up and came out here, I was jest sittin' here havin' a chat with her."

"*Her,* is it?"

"Accordin' to Missie, it daren't be anythin' else."

"Had me a bit worried there in the night."

"Thet weren't nothin' but a silly dream."

"Wanna talk 'bout it?"

"Not much to be sayin', I guess. It was the awful feelin' of bein' alone thet frightened me so. Don't rightly know how to be sayin' it, but, Clark, I'm so glad thet I never had to really be alone—even after I lost Clem. There was you an' Missie right away to fill my life. Oh, I know I shut ya out fer a time, but ya were there. An' Missie gave me someone to think about, a purpose, right away. I'm so glad, Clark. So thankful to God thet He didn't even give me a choice but jest stepped in an' took over, even when I wasn't thinkin' of Him."

Clark leaned across the table and touched her cheek. "I'm glad, too, Mrs. Davis." There was teasing in his eyes, but there was love there, too. "Never met 'nother woman thet could make better coffee."

Marty playfully brushed his hand aside. "Coffee—pawsh."

Clark's expression grew more serious. "Guess I was kinda hooked even 'fore I smelled the first potful. Never will fergit how little an' alone ya looked headin' fer thet broken-down wagon, tryin' so hard to hold yer head up when I knew thet inside ya jest wanted to die. The inside of me jest cried right along with ya. Don't s'pose there was another person there who understood yer feelin' better than I did. I ached to somehow be able to ease it fer ya."

Marty blinked away a tear. "Ya never told me thet afore. I thought thet ya were jest desperate fer someone to be carin' fer yer young Missie."

"True, I was, an' true, thet was what ya were s'pose to think. I tried hard fer the first couple of months to convince myself of it, too. Then I finally had to admit thet there was more to it than thet."

Marty reached out and squeezed his hand. "I got me a rascal," she teased.

"An' then ya up an' put me through the most miserable months of my life—wonderin' iffen ya'd ever feel the same 'bout me or iffen ya'd jest pack yer bags an' leave. Guess I learned more 'bout prayin' in those days than I ever had afore. Learned more 'bout waitin', too."

"Oh, Clark, I didn't even know," Marty whispered, choking up a little. She lifted his hand and placed a kiss on his fingers. "Guess all I can do is try to make it up to ya now."

He rose from his chair and bent over her, planting a kiss on her forehead. "Ya know—I jest might hold ya to thet. Fer starters, how 'bout my favorite stew fer supper—thick an' chunky?"

Marty wrinkled her nose. "A man," she said, "thinks the only way to prove yer love is to pleasure his stomach."

Clark rumpled her loose hair.

"I best be gittin' to those chores or the cows will think I've fergotten 'em."

He kissed her on the nose and was gone.

TWO

Ponderin's

The sun stretched and rose from its bed the following day, scattering pink and gold upon the remaining winter snow and the white-and-green fir trees. It promised to be a good day for the school raising. Marty breathed a prayer of thanks as she moved from her bedroom. She had been concerned that they might have another early spring storm, but here was a day just like she had hoped and prayed for. She apologized to the Lord for doubting His goodness, whether it rained or shone, and went quickly to the kitchen.

Clark had beat her to it this morning and had already left the house to do the chores. The fire he had built for her spread its warmth through the farm home. Marty hurried to get the breakfast on the table before the children appeared.

As she worked at the stove, stirring the porridge and making toast, a sleepy-eyed Clare walked into the room. His shirt was untucked and the suspenders of his overalls were twisted and fastened incorrectly. One shoe was on but still untied, and he carried the other under an arm.

"Where's Pa?" he questioned immediately.

Marty smiled as she looked at the tousle-haired boy.

"He's chorin'," she answered. "Fact is, he should be most done. Yer gonna have to hurry to git in on it this mornin'. Here, let me help."

She tucked in the shirt, fastened the suspenders correctly, and placed him on a chair to do up his shoes.

"This the day?" he wondered.

"Yep—this is the day. By nightfall we'll have us a school."

Clare thought about that for a while. He had already told Marty he wasn't sure he'd like school, but everyone else seemed excited about it. He smiled good-naturedly.

"Well, I better hurry," he said as he slid off the chair. "It's a good thing me not goin' ta school—Pa needs me."

Marty smiled. *Sure he does,* she thought. *Pa needs ya—needs ya to git in his way when he's feedin', needs ya to insist on draggin' along a pail thet's too big fer ya. He needs ya to slow his steps when he takes the cows back to pasture, needs ya to chatter at him all the time he's workin'.* She shook her head but the smile remained. *Yeah, he needs ya—needs yer love an' yer hero worship.* She bent to give the little boy a hug, then helped Clare into a warm coat, put his hands into his mittens and his cap on his head, and opened the door for him. He set out briskly to find his pa, Ole Bob prancing around him with delighted barks.

Marty returned to her breakfast preparations, glancing occasionally at the children's bedroom doorway. She'd have to call for Missie. She was a late sleeper and didn't bounce out of bed like Clare did each morning. Missie, too, liked adventure and discovery of what the day might hold, but she was willing to wait for it until a little later. Already she was a good little helper and was especially looking forward to assisting Marty with the new "little sister" on the way. For Missie's sake, Marty hoped the new baby would be a girl. She couldn't have loved Missie any more if she had been born of her own flesh and blood.

Marty set the table for their breakfast, wondering how many of the neighbor women were doing the same with similar excitement coursing through them at the thought of the new school. Their young'uns would not have to grow up ignorant just because their folks had dared to travel west to open up the frontier for farming and ranching. The children could grow up educated and able to take their place in the community—or other communities, if they would so choose.

Marty's thoughts turned to the two Larson girls, daughters of her friend Tina. Husband Jedd hadn't felt that the new school was all that necessary, calling it "plain foolishness—girls don't need edjecatin' anyway." But Tina Larson's eyes had silently pleaded that her girls be given a fair chance, too. They were getting older, thirteen and eleven now, and they needed the schooling before it got too late for them.

As she moved about her kitchen, Marty prayed that Jedd might have a change of heart.

In the midst of her praying, she glanced out the kitchen window and saw her *men* coming from the barn. Clark's normally long strides were restrained to accommodate the short, quick steps of little Clare. Clare hung on to the handle of the milk pail, sure that he was helping to carry the load, and chattered at Clark as he walked. Ole Bob bounded back and forth in front of them, assuming that he was leading the way and that without him the two would never reach their destination.

Marty swallowed a lump in her throat. Sometimes love hurt a little bit—but oh, such a precious hurt.

⁓

The Davis family was the first to arrive down by the creek, but then, they didn't have far to go, the land for the school having been set aside by Clark from his own homestead. Clark unhitched the team and began to pace out the ground, pounding in stakes as he went to mark the area for the school building.

Clare scampered around after him, grabbing up the hammer as soon as it was laid down, handing out stakes, and being a general help and beloved nuisance.

An old stove had been placed in their farm wagon, and Marty busied herself preparing a fire and putting water on to heat. This stove didn't work nearly as well as the one in her kitchen, but it would be better than a campfire and would assist the ladies greatly in preparing a hot meal.

Missie pushed back her bonnet and let her light brown curls blow free. She enjoyed the feeling of the warmth of the sun on her head as she moved the team to a nearby clump of trees, where she tied them and spread hay for their breakfast.

Soon other wagons and sleighs began to arrive, and the whole scene took on a lively, excited atmosphere. Children ran and squealed and chased. Even Clare was tempted away from dogging his father's activities.

The women chattered and called and laughed as they greeted one another and fell in with the meal preparations.

Businesslike, the men began eyeing logs, organizing and choosing those best suited for footings, and mentally sorting the order in which the logs should be used. Then the axes went to work. Muscled arms placed sure blows as chips flew, and strong backs bent and heaved in unison as heavy logs were raised and placed. Marty noted with some pride Clark's acknowledged leadership among the men and their respect for him.

It was hard work, made lighter only by the number who shared it and the satisfaction that it would bring. An occasional hearty laugh or shared chuckle broke through the sounds of the work itself. And soon the shape of their schoolhouse was clearly seen as the walls gradually grew with each log set in place.

The early spring sun seemed almost hot, and the workers discarded jackets as their bodies grew warm from effort.

The old stove cheerily did its duty—coffee boiled and large kettles of stew and pork and beans began to bubble, spreading their welcome aroma throughout the one-day camp.

A child running by stopped in midstep to sniff hungrily and ask if dinner was ready yet, and a man, heaving a giant log, called over his shoulder to find out how soon the meal would be set out. At the stove, the woman who stirred the pot called that he should hold his horses, and she gave the little boy a smile and pat and admonished him to run along, no doubt imagining her child doing sums at a yet unseen blackboard.

The sun, the logs, the laughter—but most of all, the promise—made the day a good one. They all would go home weary yet refreshed—bodies aching but spirits uplifted. Together they would accomplish great things, not just for themselves, but for future generations. They had given of themselves, and many would reap the benefits.

Marty and Clark thought Ben Graham said it best as the group stood gazing at the new structure before turning teams toward home.

"Kinda makes ya feel tall like."

THREE

Little Arnie

Marty forced herself to set about getting supper. Clark would soon be in from the field and, thankfully, chores would not take him long.

In the sitting room Missie was busy bossing little brother Clare.

"Not thet way—like this!" Marty heard her exclaim in disgust.

"I like it this way," Clare argued, and Marty felt sure he'd get his own way. The boy had a stubborn streak—like her, she admitted ruefully to herself.

She stirred the pot to be sure the carrots were not sticking to the bottom and crossed mechanically to the cupboard to slice some bread. She wasn't herself at all—and she knew the reason.

She glanced nervously at the clock and held her breath as another contraction took hold of her. She really must get off her feet. She hoped Clark would be back soon.

As the contraction eased, Marty moved on again, placing the bread on the table and going for the butter.

She was relieved to hear the team arrive to Ole Bob's welcome and proceed on to the barn.

Clare must have heard the team, too, and ran through the kitchen, no doubt happy to be released from Missie's demanding play and return to a world where men worked together without interference from the womenfolk. Marty shook her head and chuckled in spite of herself as he grabbed his jacket from a hook and excitedly shoved an arm in the wrong sleeve. He would later discover his mistake and correct it as he ran, Marty knew.

Chores did not take long and Clark was soon in, bringing a foaming pail of milk that Clare assisted in carrying.

Marty dished up the food and placed it on the table as the "menfolk" washed in the outside basin. She sank with relief into her chair at the table and waited for the others to take their places.

Clark finished the prayer and began to dish food for himself and Clare. He glanced at Marty, then stopped suddenly and looked steadily into her face.

"What's troublin'?" he asked quietly.

She managed a weak smile. "I think it's time."

"Time!" he exclaimed, setting the potatoes on the table with a thump. "Why didn't ya say so? I'll get the doc." He was already on his feet.

"Sit ya down an' have yer supper first," Marty told him, but he was shaking his head before she could finish.

"Best ya git yerself to bed," he said, then turned to the children. "Missie, watch Clare." He looked into the little girl's face. "Missie, the time's close now fer the new baby. Mama needs to go to bed. Ya give Clare his supper an' then clear the table. I'm goin' fer the doc. I won't be long, but ya'll have to be a big girl and take care of things 'til I git back. If yer ma needs anything, ya get it for her, ya hear?"

Missie nodded solemnly.

"Now," Clark said, assisting Marty to her feet, "into bed with ya, and no arguin'."

Marty allowed herself to be led away. Bed was the thing that she wanted most—and second to that, she suddenly realized, was Ma Graham.

"Clark," she asked as he pulled back the quilt for her, "do we hafta get the doc?"

"'Course," he responded, stopping to look at her. "Thet's what he's here fer."

"But I'd really rather have Ma, Clark. She did fine with Clare, and she could—"

"The doc knows what to do iffen somethin' should go wrong. I know Ma has delivered lotsa babies, and most times everythin' goes well, but should somethin' be wrong, Doc has the necessary know-how and . . . and all."

A tear slid down Marty's cheek. She had nothing against the doc, but she wanted Ma.

Don't be silly, she told herself, but the thought remained, and as the next contraction seized her, the desire for Ma to be with her grew.

Clark handed her a nightie from the peg behind the door and helped her slip out of her dress and into the soft flannel gown.

He tucked her in and assured her with a kiss that he'd be right back. Marty noted his pale face and his quick, nervous movements. He left the room almost on the run, and a moment later Marty heard the galloping hoofbeats of the saddle horse leaving the yard.

From the kitchen came the voices of the children. Missie was still bossing Clare, telling him to hurry and clean his plate and to be very quiet 'cause Mama needed to rest so she could get the new baby sister.

Marty wished she could sleep, but of course none came as the contractions steadily increased in strength and frequency.

Missie rather noisily cleared the table, though Marty could tell she was trying to do it quietly. Then it sounded like she was busy putting Clare to bed. He protested that it was not bedtime yet, but Missie refused to listen and eventually won, to Marty's surprise and relief. Clare was bedded down for the night.

Missie poked her head into the bedroom to report on things, and fortunately it was between contractions, so Marty was able to converse normally with her. Marty hugged her with one arm, thanked her for her help, and directed the little girl to get herself into bed. Missie nodded solemnly, then obediently went along to do her mother's bidding.

The moments, then the hours, crawled by slowly. The contractions were awfully close together now and harder to bear without crying out.

Ole Bob barked and Marty, relieved, wondered at the doc getting there so quickly. But soon it was Ma who bent over her.

"Ya came," said Marty in disbelief and thankfulness. Tears immediately and unashamedly ran down her cheeks. "How did ya know?"

"Clark stopped by," Ma answered. "Said ya was needin' me."

"But I thought he was goin' fer the doc."

"He did. The doc will do the deliverin'. Clark said ya needed me jest fer the comfortin'." Ma smoothed back Marty's hair. "How ya doin'?"

Marty managed a wobbly smile. "Fine . . . now. I don't think it'll be as long this time as with Clare."

"Prob'ly not," Ma responded. She patted Marty's arm. "I'll check on the young'uns and get things ready fer the doc. Call iffen ya need me."

Marty nodded. "Thank ya," she said. "Thank ya fer comin'. I'll be fine . . . now."

Ma came and went, and then Marty was dimly aware of more voices joining Ma's in the kitchen. The words floated on the air toward her, and then Doc was beside the bed, talking to Ma in low tones, and Clark was bending over her, whispering words of assurance.

Marty was rather hazy about the rest of it until she heard the sharp cry of a newborn.

"She's here," Marty murmured quietly.

Doc's booming voice answered her.

"*He's* here. It's another fine son."

"Missie will be disappointed," Marty almost whispered, but Doc heard her.

"No one could be disappointed for very long over this boy. He's a dandy," and a few minutes later the new son was placed beside her. In the light of the lamp, Marty could see he was indeed "a dandy," and love for the new wee life beside her spread through her being like warm honey.

Then Clark came, beaming as he gazed at his new son and placing a kiss on Marty's hair.

"Another prizewinner, ain't he, now?" he said proudly. Marty nodded and smiled wearily.

Clark left, soon to return with a sleepy child in each arm. He bent down.

"Yer new brother," he whispered. "Look at 'im sleepin' there. Ain't he jest fine?"

206

Clare just stared big eyed.

"A boy?" Missie asked, sounding incredulous. "It was s'posed to be a girl. I prayed fer a girl."

"Sometimes," Clark began slowly, "sometimes God knows better than us what is best. He knows what we want might not be right fer us now, so sometimes, 'stead of givin' us what we asked Him fer, He sends instead what He knows is best fer us. Guess this baby boy must be someone special fer God to send him instead."

Missie listened carefully; then a smile spread over her face as the baby stretched and yawned in his sleep.

"He's awful cute, ain't he?" she whispered. "What we gonna call him, Pa?"

They named the baby Arnold Joseph and called him Little Arnie right from the first.

Clare seemed to find him a bit boring and complained that "Arnie don't *do* nothin'," though he would have defended him to the death. Missie fussed and mothered and wondered aloud why she'd ever felt a sister would've been any better.

Things settled down again to a comfortable routine. The crops and the gardens were planted. And Marty was going from early morning till late into the evening, for the new baby, along with the joy, also brought more work. Marty's days were full indeed—full, but overflowing with happiness and love.

FOUR

Visits

By fall of that year, Baby Arnie had grown steadily into a healthy and strong little boy. He had firmly established his rightful spot in the family, laughing and cooing his way into their hearts. He ignored Missie's instructions about the proper way to crawl and scooted around on his tummy.

When the crops were harvested, Clark declared the year's yield the best ever.

Marty somehow managed to keep up with the produce of her garden. Having Missie's helpful hands to entertain Arnie and keep an eye on Clare was greatly appreciated.

The only disappointment that fall was the new school. Over the busy summer months the men had found enough time to shingle the roof, install the windows, and put in the floor. A potbellied stove had been ordered and installed and simple desks had been built. The area farmers had each contributed to a pile of cordwood that stood neatly stacked in the yard. A crude shelter for the farm horses and the necessary outbuildings had been erected. Even the chalkboards were hung—but the school stood empty and silent. In spite of the diligent work done by the search committee, no teacher had been located.

Marty had lain awake restless and fretful more than one night because of it. It seemed so unfair that they would dream and work so hard to construct the fine little building only to have it stand vacant and the children left another year without formal education. Now the talk was of next year, but next year seemed an awful long time to wait. Especially for youngsters such as the Larson girls for whom opportunity for schooling was slipping away.

Marty was busy canning one morning when she heard the sound of an approaching team. With neighbors some distance away, visitors were all too few and very welcome. She wiped her hands on her apron and looked out the window to see Clark greeting Wanda Marshall and taking the team for her.

When Wanda headed for the house, Marty was immediately aware of her vegetable-spattered apron and her work-stained hands. She quickly threw the apron from her and drew a clean one from a drawer. Tying it about her as she went to the door, she could feel a smile already turning up the corners of her mouth.

She welcomed Wanda with a glad embrace, and both began to talk at once in their eagerness for a visit.

"I'm so glad thet ya came," Marty said. "'Scuse my messy kitchen. Cannin', ya know."

"Don't ya mind," Wanda assured her. "I shouldn'ta come at such a busy time, but I just couldn't stay away. I just had to see you, Marty."

"Don't ya ever wait fer a time thet's not busy. My land, seems all the days are busy ones, an' I sure do need me a visit with a friend now an' then."

Marty supposed she should wait and let Wanda tell her news, but the glow on her face prompted Marty to question further. "But what's yer news? I can see yer fairly burstin'."

Wanda chuckled—almost a girlish giggle, Marty thought. She had never seen Wanda look so happy.

"Oh, Marty!" Wanda said. "That's right, I'm fairly bursting." Then she laughed, took a deep breath, and rushed on, "I've just been to see Dr. Watkins. I'm going to have a *baby*!"

At Marty's exultant "Oh, Wanda!" she continued her report.

"Dr. Watkins says he sees no reason why I shouldn't be able to keep this one. No reason why it shouldn't live. Cam is so excited—says our son is going to be the handsomest, the strongest, the smartest boy in the whole West."

"Well, I'm guessin' Clark might have himself somethin' to say about thet," Marty laughed.

Wanda laughed, too. "When I asked him, 'What if it's a girl?' he said she would be the prettiest, the sweetest, and the daintiest girl in the whole West. Oh, Marty, I'm so happy I could just cry." And she did.

Marty went to put her arms around her, and they cried together, unashamed of the tears of joy that trickled down their cheeks.

"I'm jest so happy fer ya, Wanda," Marty finally was able to say. "An' with Doc here, everythin' will go all right, I'm jest sure. Ya'll finally have thet baby you've been wantin' so bad. When will it be?"

Wanda moaned, "Oh, it seems so far away yet. Not until next April."

"But the months will go quickly. They always do. An' ya can have the winter months to be preparin' fer 'im. Sewin' and quilting an' all. It'll make the winter sech a happy time. It'll go so fast ya'll find it hard to be doin' all ya want."

"I hope so. Marty, can you show me the pattern for that sweater Arnie was wearing last Sunday? I'd like to make one."

"Sure. Ya'll have no problem at all crochetin' thet."

Over coffee and sugar cookies, Marty and Wanda worked out the pattern—Wanda taking notes as Marty showed her the sweater and explained the crochet stitches.

The afternoon went quickly, and when Arnie and Clare awoke from their naps, Wanda said she must be on her way.

Missie was sent to ask Clark if he would bring Wanda's team. He complied at once, and with another embrace and well wishes, Wanda was on her way home.

Marty walked back to the grain bin with Clark. "Wanda had the best news," she enthused. "She is finally gonna have thet baby she wants so badly. She's so excited. Oh, I pray thet everythin'll be okay this time."

Marty could tell Clark was pleased for Wanda. She went on, "An' Cam says iffen it's a boy, it'll be the smartest, handsomest, and best in the West, and iffen it's a girl, the prettiest. I told her you might give him some argument on that," and the two laughed together.

Then Clark's eyes became thoughtful.

"Ya prob'ly don't know Cameron Marshall too well yet, do ya?"

"I've hardly met the man—only seen 'im a few times at neighborhood meetin's. Why?"

Clark's expression became even more serious. He said, "He's a rather strange man." He paused a moment. "It's jest like Cam to feel thet his boy's gotta be the smartest, his girl the prettiest. Thet's like Cam." He waited a moment. "I think thet's the reason he married Wanda. He figured she was the prettiest girl he'd ever laid eyes on—so she jest had to be 'his.' The problem with Cameron Marshall is the importance he puts on 'mine's the best.' I 'member one time Cam saw a fine horse. He jest had to have it 'cause he figured it a little better'n any other horse in these parts. Sold all his seed grain to git thet horse. Set him back fer years, but he had him a better-lookin' horse than anybody 'round about. Guess he figured it was worth it.

"Ever notice his wagon? All painted up an' with extry metal trimmin's. Could have had a bigger place to live. Men of the neighborhood figured on being neighborly a few years back and helped him log so's he could build. 'Stead, he saw thet wagon, so he sold the logs an' bought it—an' he an' Wanda still live in thet one little room. The way Cam sees it, a house belongs to the woman, not the man. Often wished he'd take him a notion thet he had to have the best house, too—might find 'im a way to git one. Sure would be easier fer Wanda—an' now with a baby comin', they sure do need more room."

Clark was looking off at the distant hills as he finished. Marty had never known before what kind of a man Cameron Marshall was. She felt helpless and wished there was something she could do to help her friend.

Clark mused, "Often wondered what would make a man feel so unsure of himself like, thet he had to prove himself by gittin' *things*. Somethin' deep down must be troublin' Cam to have made 'im like he is."

Clark took a deep breath and seemed to bring himself back from a long way off. "Sure do hope thet the young'un be a dandy, or it's gonna be awful hard on his pa."

He turned to face Marty and smiled then. "Didn't mean to put a damper on yer good news. I'm sure Cam will have reason to be proud— an' Wanda—I'm real happy fer Wanda. It'll wake her life up to have a baby in it."

The day held a chill with reminders that winter was around the corner. As Marty packed a box with bread, soup broth, vegetables, and molasses cookies, she was thankful no wind was blowing.

Word had come that morning that Mrs. Larson was ill. It sounded like something far more serious than a common cold or flu, and Marty felt she should go and see her neighbor, even though the cold wind was rather daunting.

Clark did not like to see her go alone, but with the fact that Missie was far too young to be left in charge of Clare and Little Arnie, there was nothing for him to do but remain at home with the children.

Marty dressed as warmly as she could. Then, carrying her box with her, she went out to where Clark waited with the team.

"Don't let yerself to be kept over-late," he cautioned. "An' should it start to really blow, head home quick like."

Marty promised, tucked the blanket carefully around herself, and started off.

When the rather unkempt Larson homestead came into view, Marty noticed only a tiny wisp of smoke rising from the chimney of the cabin.

No one met her in the yard to assist her with the team, so she tethered Dan and Charlie to a nearby post and hurried, with her box, to the house.

There was a stirring at the window, and the tattered curtain fell back into place as she approached. Her knock was answered by the younger daughter, Clae, who quietly motioned her in.

Her sister, Nandry, was washing dirty dishes in a pan of equally dirty water. A stubby broom leaning against the table indicated to Marty that Clae had been making an effort to sweep the floor.

Well, at least they are trying, Marty thought with thankfulness. After greeting the girls, she turned to the almost-cold stove. The room was cold, too, and sent shivers through her, in spite of the fact she had not yet removed her coat.

She opened the lid of the stove to observe one lone piece of wood smoldering in the firebox.

"Where's yer wood?" she asked hopefully.

Clae answered, "Is none. Pa didn't get it cut, and we can't split it."

"Do ya have an axe?"

"Yeah . . . sort of."

Marty discovered what the "sort of" meant when she went out to the scattered heap that made up their meager winter supply. Never had she seen such a dull and chipped tool. With a great deal of effort she was able to chop enough wood to take the chill off the house.

After she had built up the fire and placed a kettle on to boil, she went in to see Mrs. Larson.

The woman lay huddled under some blankets on a narrow bed in the second room of the small cabin. Marty was relieved to see that at least clothing was not strewn all over the room. Then she realized with despair that probably everything they owned was on their backs, in an effort to keep out as much of the cold as possible. Mrs. Larson lay white and quiet beneath the scant covers.

Why didn't I think to bring a heavy quilt? Marty reprimanded herself, and even as the thought went through her mind, she saw the shiver that passed through Mrs. Larson. Marty stood close to the bed, reaching out to gently smooth the hair back from the thin white face.

"How are ya?" she whispered.

Mrs. Larson attempted an answer, but it was muted and low.

"I'll git ya some warm broth right away," Marty said and hurried back to the kitchen. She put the broth on to heat, then went out to the sleigh and returned with the blanket she had tucked around herself for the drive over. She warmed the blanket at the stove before she took it in to Mrs. Larson and wrapped it close about the shivering body.

The broth was soon warm, and Marty asked Clae for a dish and a spoon. She took the bread from the box and handed it to the girl.

"Why don't you an' Nandry have ya some broth while it's hot, an' some bread to go with it?" she said.

213

The hungry looks in the girls' eyes told her they would do so eagerly.

Marty carried the hot broth to Mrs. Larson. She realized the woman was already too weak to feed herself and hoped she would not object to being spoon-fed. There was no need to worry. Mrs. Larson accepted the food with thankfulness showing in her eyes.

"The girls . . ." she whispered.

"They're eatin'," Marty assured her quickly, and Mrs. Larson looked relieved.

Marty chatted quietly as she spooned. "I'm so sorry thet yer down. I didn't hear of it 'til today. Jedd should have let us know, an' we could've been over to help sooner.

"Nice thet ya got those two fine girls to be helpin'. When I came, Nandry was washing up the dishes an' Clae sweepin' the floor. Must be a great comfort to ya—them girls."

Mrs. Larson's eyes took on a bit more life, and she nodded slightly. Marty knew how she loved her girls.

"Must be a real tryin' time fer ya. A woman jest hates to git down—hates to not be carin' fer her family. Makes one feel awful useless like, but God, He knows all 'bout how ya feel—why yer sick. There's always a reason fer His 'llowin', though we can't always see it right off like. I'm sure there's a good reason fer this, too. Someday, maybe we'll know why."

The broth was almost gone, but Mrs. Larson feebly waved the remainder aside. Marty didn't know if she was full or just tired. Then Mrs. Larson spoke. Slowly at first, but gradually her words poured one over the other, tumbling out in quick succession in a need to be said. She breathed heavily, and the effort of speaking cost her dearly, but she seemed determined to get it out.

"My girls," she said, "my girls never had nothin', nothin'—thet's not what I want fer my girls. Their pa, he's a good man, but he don't understand 'bout girls. I been prayin'—prayin' thet somehow God would give 'em a chance. Jest a chance, thet's all I ask fer. Me—I don't matter now. I lived my life. Yet I ain't sayin' I'm wantin' to die—I'm scared to die. I ain't been a good woman, Marty. I got no business askin' God fer nothin', but I ain't askin' it fer me—only my girls. Do ya think God hears my prayers, Marty? I wouldn't 'ave even dared to pray, but my girls, they need—" She finally broke off with a sob.

Marty caressed the thin hand grasping the blanket.

"'Course He hears," she said with deep conviction.

Mrs. Larson looked as though a great weight was being lifted from her.

"Could He show love to young'uns of a sinful woman?" Her eyes pleaded that the answer be reassuring.

"Yes," Marty said slowly. "He loves the girls, an' He will help 'em. I'm sure He will. But, Mrs. Larson, He loves you, too, an' He wants to help you. He loves ya, He truly does. I know thet yer a sinner, but we all are no different. The Book says thet we all be sinnin' an' hangin' on to our sin like it's somethin' worthwhile keepin', but it's not. We gotta let go of it, and God will take it from us an' put it there in thet big pile of sin thet Jesus took on himself the day He died. It isn't our goodness thet makes us fittin' to share heaven with Him. It's our faith in Jesus. We jest—well, we jest say 'thank ya, Lord, fer dyin', an' clean me up on the inside so's I'll be fittin' fer yer heaven'—an' He will. He takes this earth-soiled soul of ours an' He cleans and polishes it fer heaven. Thet's what He does, an' all—jest in answer to our prayer of askin'." Marty smoothed the tangled hair back from the feverish brow. "Do ya want to pray, Mrs. Larson?"

The woman looked surprised. "I've never prayed. Not fer myself—jest fer my girls. I wouldn't know what to say to Him."

"Ya said it to me," Marty reminded her gently. "Jest tell Him thet yer done hangin' on to yer sins—thet ya don't want to carry 'em anymore, an' would He please git rid of 'em fer ya. Then thank Him, too—fer His love an' His cleanin'."

Mrs. Larson looked hesitant but then began her short prayer. The faltering words gradually gathered strength and assurance. When Marty opened her tear-dimmed eyes, she was met by a weak yet confident smile and equally teary eyes.

"He did!" Mrs. Larson exclaimed in a hoarse whisper. "He did!"

Marty squeezed Mrs. Larson's hand and wiped the tears from her own cheeks.

"'Course He did," she affirmed. "An' He'll answer yer other prayer, too. I don't know how He'll manage it, but I'm sure thet He will."

She stood up. The sun was quickly moving to the west, and she knew she must be on her way home. "Mrs. Larson, I gotta go soon. I promised Clark I'd not be late, but there's somethin' I want ya to know. Iffen anythin' happens to ya—an' I'm hopin' ya'll soon be on yer feet again—but iffen anythin' does happen, I'll do my best to see thet yer girls git thet chance."

Mrs. Larson was silent. She seemed to be holding her breath, and then Marty realized she was too deeply moved to speak—save to her newly found God.

Again the woman's eyes filled with tears. "Thank ya, oh, thank ya!" she finally managed to say, over and over.

Marty touched her hand lightly and turned to go. She had to hurry home so there would be enough time for Clark to get back to the Larson homestead with a load of firewood and warm quilts.

FIVE

Exciting News

Marty finished patching a pair of Clare's overalls and laid them aside. It was too early to begin supper. She picked up another item of mending and let her mind slide over some of the events of the past few months.

She had gone several times to visit Mrs. Larson. Ma Graham and other neighbor women helped out often, as well, nursing the woman and caring for the needs of the family. Though Mrs. Larson rested contentedly in her newfound inner peace, she continued to weaken, and though none of them expressed it in words, Marty knew they were fighting a losing battle. The doc had been called, too, and he silently shook his head and encouraged them to keep her as comfortable as possible.

The children's laughter about something or other as they played near the warm stove pulled Marty's thoughts away from Mrs. Larson's illness to more cheerful things.

Spring would soon be upon them, and with its coming two new babies would be welcomed to their neighborhood—in April. Marty was very happy for the new mothers-to-be and prayed that all would go well.

The first to arrive would be Wanda's. She, who had already lost three children and wanted a child so badly, deserved to have this happiness.

Now with a doctor available, Wanda had been given the confidence to hope this time would go well.

"Please, God, let it be all right for Wanda," Marty prayed many times a day.

The second baby was Sally Anne's. This first grandchild for Ben and Ma would be very special. Sally Anne, too, had hoped to be a mother earlier but had not carried her first baby to full term. Now the days of her delivery were very near at hand and things seemed to be going well this time. Marty knew that Sally Anne wasn't the only one counting the days.

As Marty mulled over the promise of new young lives that the month ahead would bring, her eyes turned to her own small ones as they played contentedly near by.

Missie was dressing a kitten in doll clothes. After much arguing and persuading on Missie's part, Marty had finally agreed to allow one small barn cat in the house. It was named Miss Puss by Missie and treated like a baby. Never had a kitten had more love and fondling than Miss Puss. Marty wondered if Miss Puss might have welcomed a few moments of peace.

Clare was piling blocks in an effort to construct a barn. The blocks would periodically fall on the unfortunate pieces of broom straw that were his farm animals, and then he would need to start over again.

Arnie, who could now sit alone, watched Clare intently, looking particularly fascinated by the noise created when the blocks came tumbling down. This would bring gurgles of delight, and his round little body would rock back and forth with excitement.

Clare dutifully explained to young Arnie which straws were the horses, which the cows, the calves, and the hogs. Arnie listened wide-eyed and squealed in response.

At the sound of Ole Bob, the room came alive. Clark had returned from town. Marty hadn't expected him for another hour. She got up quickly and checked the clock to see if she had misread the time. No, it was indeed early.

Clare jumped up from his spot on the rug. "Pa's home!" he shouted, letting his building blocks fall where they may, unmindful of the damage done to the straw horses and cows.

Marty started to call him back to pick up the toys, then changed her mind. He could pick them up when he came in for supper. It was important to him—and to Clark—that he now greet his pa.

Missie, too, holding carefully the blanketed kitten, headed for the door.

"Boy, I'll bet Arnie's sad!" Clare yelled as he ran through the kitchen.

"Whatcha meanin'?" Marty had to call after him to be heard.

"He can't run," the fleeing boy flung back over his shoulder and was gone, the door slamming behind him.

Marty smiled and went for Arnie, now deserted on the rug.

"Are ya sad?" she asked the baby as she lifted him up.

Arnie didn't look sad—maybe a bit puzzled at all the sudden bustling about, but otherwise content. A happy smile spread over his face. Marty kissed his cheek and walked to the kitchen window.

She had expected to see Clare and Missie hitching a ride with Clark to the barn, so she was surprised when all three were coming up the path to the house together. The youngsters were skipping along beside their father, chattering noisily.

Clark, too, seemed excited. Marty walked toward the door to meet the group.

"Good news!" he fairly shouted, taking hold of her waist and whirling both her and the baby around the kitchen. Marty held on tightly to Arnie, who was enjoying the whole thing immensely.

"'Sakes alive, Clark!" she said when she had caught her breath. "What's happened?"

Clark laughed and pulled her close. Young Arnie grabbed a handful of his father's shirt.

"Got great news," Clark said. "We got us a teacher."

"A teacher!"

"Yep—come fall thet there little school's goin' to be bustlin' with book learnin' and bell ringin'. Hear thet, Missie?" He stopped to lift the little girl up and swing her around.

"We got us a teacher," he repeated. "Come fall, ya can start off to school, jest like a grand lady."

"Grand ladies don't go off to school," Marty argued with a laugh.

Then, nearly ready to explode with curiosity, she caught hold of her husband's arm. "Oh, Clark, do stop all the silliness and tell us all 'bout it. Oh, it's such wonderful news. Jest think, Missie, a teacher fer yer school. Ain't thet jest the best news? Who is it, Clark, an' where does she come from?"

"He—it's a he. Mr. Wilbur Whittle is his name, an' he comes from some fancy city back east—can't recall jest now which one—but he's jest full of learnin'. Been teachin' fer eight years already, but he wanted to see the West fer himself."

Missie came to life then. "Goodie! Goodie!" she shouted, clapping her hands, obviously just catching on to all the excitement. "I git to go to school. I'll read an' draw pictures an' everythin'.'"

"Me too," said Clare.

"Not you, Clare," Missie insisted in big-sister fashion. "Yer too little."

"Am not," Clare countered. "I'm 'most as big as you."

Marty wasn't sure where the argument would have ended had not Clark intervened.

"Hey," he said, sweeping up Clare, "ya'll sure 'nough go to school all right, but not yet. I need ya to help with the milkin' an' chorin' yet awhile. In a couple of years maybe I'll be able to spare ya when Arnie gits a little bigger an' can help his pa."

Clare was satisfied. Let Missie go to school. He'd sacrifice for a while. He was needed at home.

The commotion that the news stirred up was hard to control, but finally Marty placed Arnie in his chair with a piece of bread crust to chew on. Clare went with Clark to care for the horses and do the chores. Missie unbundled her kitten, explaining gravely that she would no longer be able to play as much. She was grown-up now and would be going off to school. Then she proceeded to lay out her best frock, clean stockings, and her Sunday boots—only about five and a half months prematurely.

Marty smiled at Missie's earnest preparations and went about the supper preparations with a song in her heart. This fall they would have their new school. Missie would get the long-coveted education. Would Nandry and Clae be as fortunate? Marty promised herself again that she would do all in her power to see it happen.

SIX

Wanda's New Baby

Warm April sun shone down on the earth, melting away the winter snow and bringing forth crocuses and dandelions. Marty rejoiced in the springtime sun, thinking ahead to the days spent planting her garden and tending her summer flowers.

The children, too, were delighted to now spend time outside in the sunshine. Clare tagged along with Clark whenever it was possible, and Missie enjoyed bundling up Little Arnie and taking him out to play. Clark had made a small wooden cart with wheels, and she carted the toddler all around the yard. When she—and Arnie—finally tired of that, she would return him to Marty and scamper outside to dig around in a protected area of soil near the house she had dubbed "my garden." Marty had given her a few seeds, and already some shoots of green showed where a turnip or some lettuce was making an appearance. Missie found it difficult to leave them alone and often was admonished for digging them up to see how they were doing. Her "garden" would have been much further along but for its periodic setbacks from its overly solicitous gardener.

Marty was about ready to ask Clark if he would turn the soil in the big garden for her, but then she cautioned herself not to get into too big a rush. The nights were still cool, and early plants might yet be damaged by frost. Still, she found it nearly as hard to be patient as Missie did.

In the meantime Marty put every available minute into knitting two baby shawls. One was for Wanda's new baby and one for Sally Anne's. Missie loved to watch the shawls take shape and begged to add a few stitches of her own. When Marty had to quietly undo the extra stitches, she set the child up with wool and needles for her own small project. Missie announced it would be a sweater for her kitty.

One evening as Marty sat waiting for the potatoes to boil for supper, using the time to add a few more stitches to the final shawl, Ole Bob started up with an awful racket outside. Marty had never heard him so fussed over something before. She looked out the window to see an approaching rider, and she understood why the dog was wrought up. Never had she seen such agitation and determination exhibited in a horseback rider. He was leaning well over the animal, using the end of the rein as a whip and pumping with his legs as though to produce more speed from the animal. The horse, already lathered, was breathing hard and obviously pushing forward with every muscle.

As the rider swung through the gate and straightened up, Marty could see it was Cameron Marshall.

Clark appeared from somewhere and caught a rein as the man threw them from him and slid to the ground. He could barely stand and supported himself on the rail fence. Marty's thoughts jumped to Wanda and immediate concern filled her. She rushed out of the house and met Clark and Cam coming in.

She looked to Clark with her unasked question, and he must have understood, answering her quickly to allay her fears. "Wanda's fine," he told her. "She is in labor, and Doc is there—but she is uneasy like, an' she wants you. I'll hitch the team, an' you can take Cam home. I'll bring his horse over later. The animal needs a rest now. She's already been to town an' back for the doc, an' now here."

Marty glanced at the foam-flecked, rather worn-out looking creature. So this was Cam Marshall's prize horse. She didn't look very promising at the moment, but maybe Clark would be able to coax some life back into her with feed and a good rubdown.

"I'll be right back with the team," Clark said, leading the limping, tired animal away.

"Come inside," Marty spoke to the man, who was still trying to catch his breath. "I'll jest take a minute to gather a few things."

He followed, though she wondered if he was really aware of his surroundings.

"Sit down there," Marty directed. She pushed the boiling potatoes toward the back of the stove. The meat in the oven was smelling delicious and made her feel hungry. At least supper would be ready for her family. She poured a cup of coffee and handed it to Cameron.

"Do ya take cream or sweetenin'?" she asked.

He shook his head.

"You drink this while I get me ready," Marty said, wondering if he actually was accustomed to drinking it black or just couldn't be bothered to think about it.

She left him sipping from the cup while she hurried to the bedroom and began to put a few things in a bag. She'd have to take Arnie with her in case the hours dragged past his feeding time. The other two tykes she'd leave in the care of their pa.

By the time she had put together what she needed and bundled up their small son, Clark was in the kitchen talking to Cameron. Marty noticed that Cam had downed the coffee. Maybe that would keep him on his feet at least.

Clark helped her to the wagon, where she deposited Arnie into a small box filled with hay. They kept it in a corner of the wagon for the express purpose of bedding down the little ones. She then took her place on the seat, and Clark handed her the reins.

Cameron did not object to Marty driving the team. She was relieved, knowing instinctively that in Cam's present state of worry, Clark would be concerned about the team being pushed unnecessarily hard. Doc was already there, so Marty could drive sensibly. Even with this knowledge, though, she urged the team forward and kept them traveling at a fairly fast pace. Wanda had asked for her. She planned to be there as soon as she could.

By the time they reached the Marshalls' one-room cabin, Cameron had settled down and seemed again to be in control of himself.

He helped Marty from the wagon, handed Arnie to her, and placed her bag of belongings on the ground, promising to bring it in for her upon his return from settling the team.

Marty hurried into the house, placing Arnie on the floor on her coat while reminding herself to later see to having the box with its hay mattress brought from the wagon for him.

She crossed to the bed at the far end of the one room. Doc paid little heed to her approach, for Wanda was getting his full attention.

"May I talk to her?" Marty whispered.

"Go ahead," he answered. "Quiet her if you can."

Marty nodded. She found a place at the head of the bed and looked down at Wanda's pale face.

"I'm here," Marty told her friend softly.

Wanda tried for a smile. "You came," she said in a weak voice. "I'm so glad. I'm scared, Marty. What if—"

But Marty didn't let her finish. "Everythin' is goin' jest fine," she comforted. "Doc is here. Shouldn't be long now 'til ya have thet fine son—or pretty daughter—thet ya been wantin'. Jest ya take it easy an' listen careful to what Doc tells ya to do. He knows all 'bout birthin' babies."

Wanda looked unconvinced but said, "I'll try."

"Good! Now I'm gonna git yer man an' the doc some supper. 'Member, I'm right here iffen ya need me."

Wanda gave a slight nod, then closed her eyes again.

Marty squeezed her hand and left her to see what she could find to go along with the meat and loaf of bread she had brought for their supper. She was thankful that Arnie slept contentedly on. Cameron came in from the barn, but he seemed to want to stay as far as possible from his wife and the doctor at the other end of the room.

Supper was prepared, and Cam didn't even make the attempt to eat something. But Doc took a moment from his vigil to gulp a cup of coffee and eat a cold meat sandwich. Marty could read a bit of uncertainty in his face. It unnerved her and made her feel awkward and fumbling as she cleared the table and washed up the dishes.

The single room seemed overcrowded with people and anxiety. Cameron left to pace back and forth beneath the stars. Marty found a moment to whisper an inquiry to the doc.

"She should have delivered by now," he answered honestly. "I don't like it. The baby is small and sure doesn't need that added struggle to get into the world. I'm afraid the extra time will weaken it. I'm thinking of sending for Mrs. Graham. I hope I'm wrong, but I'm afraid that once that baby's here, it's going to take all we've got to keep it with us."

Marty prayed a silent prayer, the tears flooding her eyes.

"I'll send Cam," she whispered to the doctor.

She carefully removed all traces of her tears. There was no need to alarm Cameron further. She went out into the cool night and found him sitting, head in hands, on the chopping block.

"Cam," Marty said. He looked up rather frantically.

"Doc says he'd like to have Ma Graham here, jest as an extra pair of hands like, so's one can sorta look to Wanda an' the other care for the baby when it comes. Doctors like to work with assistants, an' me, I know nothin' 'bout deliverin' babies. Ya can take the team. Doc says there's lots of time." She tried to keep her tone as matter-of-fact as possible.

Cameron got to his feet, looking relieved there was something he could do.

Marty returned to the house and listened for the team to leave the yard.

Good, she thought, *he's drivin' sensibly,* as she went to feed Little Arnie.

When Cameron and Ma arrived, Ma was able to relieve the doctor while he had a cup of coffee and then took a stretch around the farmyard.

Marty made more coffee, consoled Wanda, and put Arnie down for the night. She looked at him tucked into his hay-filled box and envied him. There was no place for anyone else to lie down.

After a long night of waiting and just after the new day had poured its dawn over the eastern horizon, the new baby made his appearance. Marty had gone to the woodpile to replenish the fire, and upon her return she heard the weak cry of a newborn.

Wanda, too, heard the cry and a murmur came from her pale lips.

"It's a boy," the doctor announced in the triumphant tone a doctor uses on such occasions. But Marty carefully watched his face to read his expression. She saw him go over to Cameron, and though he kept his voice low, she heard him tell the father that the baby was not very strong, but he'd do all in his power to save him. Cam simply nodded dumbly and sank back down on his chair.

Doc nodded to Ma to take over with Wanda, and he carried the fragile bundle to the table.

Marty was instructed to push the table nearer the stove and spread the small blankets to receive the little one, and there, with his satchel opened beside him, the doc waged a battle for life that would last many hours.

Marty instinctively knew he was calling on every bit of his training and available medication to assist him in the fight against the Grim Reaper. He quietly told her later that twice he thought he'd surely lost, but somehow a spark of life was again coaxed into the tiny body.

And so it was that twenty-eight hours later, when Marty and the doctor left for their homes, Wanda still had her baby boy, and Cameron's eyes spoke volumes about his thankfulness and appreciation. He even promised Doc his horse in payment for his services.

Ma remained to spend some days with Wanda until she was able to be on her feet again. Cameron took a couple of blankets to the hayloft for himself and spread a feather tick on the cabin floor for Ma.

Cameron seemed to have recovered from the ordeal and was already making boasts about the boy his son would become and the great things they would accomplish together.

Marty returned home so weary she could hardly guide the horses. Good old Dan and Charlie, given their head, found their own way at their own pace. And Arnie cheerfully enjoyed the ride from his convenient perch in the box behind his mother.

Clark strode quickly over to welcome Marty when she drove into the yard, as did two excited children and a dog half wild with excitement. Marty felt herself fairly drop into Clark's arms.

"It's a boy," she murmured, "an' he's livin'. Doc says he should make it now."

Marty reached her bed with Little Arnie. She held him close as she nursed him. He had been such a good baby through the whole difficult time. She kissed his soft head and then sleep claimed her. She never heard Clark enter the bedroom a little later to find the contented baby playing with bare toes and jabbering to himself and the tired mother sound asleep.

SEVEN

Mrs. Larson

The month of April brought new life into the neighborhood, but sadly, it claimed life, as well. Word came to Clark and Marty on a rainy Wednesday afternoon that Mrs. Larson had quietly slipped away in her sleep.

Marty was deeply concerned over the fact that Clae had been the one to find her. It seemed like the poor girl should have been spared that much at least, but her father, Jedd Larson, had not been home at the time.

The funeral was to take place the following day. The women in the community carefully bathed and prepared the body for burial, and the neighbor men built the plain wooden box in which it was laid. Marty took one of her own dresses over for Tina Larson to rest in, and Mrs. Stern was able to spare a blanket to drape the inside of the coffin.

The continuing rain made the digging of the grave a miserable task, but all was in readiness by the appointed time.

At two in the afternoon the farm wagons slowly made their way to a sheltered corner of Jedd's land where a short service of committal was held. Clark and Ben Graham were in charge.

Marty's heart ached and she wept for the two young girls standing huddled together in the rain as they watched their only source of love and comfort lowered into the ground. After a whispered conference with Clark following the service, she plucked up her courage and dared to approach Jedd with a suggestion that the girls come home with her for a few days "until things are sorted out."

"Be no need," he informed her. "There's plenty at home to keep their minds an' hands busy."

Marty felt anger rise sharply within her and turned away quickly to keep from expressing it. She wouldn't forget her promise to Tina Larson and would plan and work as long as she could to fulfill it—yet how was it ever to be accomplished? School would be starting in the fall, and somehow those two girls must be there. She'd pray more, and she knew Clark would join her in the petition. God had mysterious ways of answering prayer, beyond a person's imagination.

Marty bit her lip to stop its quivering, wiped the tears mingling with the rain on her cheeks, and went to join Clark, who was waiting in the wagon.

⸎

The death of Mrs. Larson hung heavy on Marty's mind during the next days and weeks. She could not rid herself of a deep burden for the girls now left without a mother and saddled with a father who didn't know how to cope with life in the best of times. She knew the poor little things were facing a loss too big even for an adult.

She visited the girls several times in the days following the funeral, taking fresh baked goods, vegetables, and cold meat. Still her heart ached within her each time she thought about them. She decided that a visit to Ma Graham was what she needed. Ma could help her think this thing through and come up with something that would help her persuade the stubborn Jedd to allow the girls their rightful and needful education.

Marty had come to know the girls much better during the days of Mrs. Larson's illness. Nandry, the older of the two, was quiet and withdrawn. Marty feared that even now it might be too late to help Nandry come out of herself and her recent sorrow to develop into a young lady capable of self-expression and self-worth. Younger Clae was like a small flower that had been kept out of the sunshine. Given a chance, Marty felt confident that Clae could burst forth into full bloom. Gradually she had lost her shyness with Marty, and Marty noticed that even though she was the younger, Clae was the one who often took the lead in conversations.

Marty set her chin determinedly. Somehow she must get that promised chance for those girls. At breakfast she approached Clark with her plan.

"It bein' sech a fine day, I thought I'd give the young'uns some air an' pay a visit to Ma."

"Good idea," he responded immediately. "Ground's not dry enough fer seedin' today. Ya can take the team. I'm gonna spend me the day cleanin' more seed grain jest in case it dries enough to plant the lower field later this spring. I'll bring ya the team whenever yer ready."

"Should be all set in 'bout an hour's time," Marty answered. "It'll be right good to have a chat with Ma. She hasn't been home that long from tendin' to Wanda and her baby. I'll be able to hear all 'bout how thet new boy's doin'."

"An' . . ." Clark prompted, looking intently into her face.

"An' . . . I'll maybe give her a chance to talk 'bout thet comin' baby of Sally Anne's. 'Magine she's gittin' right anxious waitin' on thet one, it already bein' on the late side."

"An' . . ." Clark prompted again.

Marty looked at him. All right—so he knew neither of those reasons was the real purpose for her calling on Ma. She sighed. "I wanna talk to her 'bout the Larson girls," she answered forthrightly. "Clark, somethin's jest got to be done 'bout 'em, but I'm not smart enough to figure out what."

Clark pushed aside his empty porridge bowl and rose to get the coffeepot. He rested a hand on her shoulder as he poured Marty a second cup, then refilled his own and returned the pot to the stove.

So that's it, his eyes seemed to say, but he sipped the coffee silently.

Finally he spoke. "Jedd Larson be a mite bullheaded. Seems unless he decides thet his young'uns need thet edjecation, there's not much hope of anyone changin' his mind."

"I know thet," Marty mourned. "Oh, I wish I had me some way of persuadin' 'im. Do ya think you as a man talkin' to 'im might help?"

Clark shook his head. "Jedd never did listen much to my say-so."

"It's so selfish and mean," Marty stormed, "jest plain mean."

"Don't fergit thet those girls be gittin' his meals an' washin' his clothes."

"It's still not fair."

Clark's eyes twinkled. "Maybe ya'll have to pray the Lord to send along a new Mrs. Larson."

Marty didn't think it was funny. "I wouldn't pray thet on any woman—no matter how ill I thought of her," she shot back with eyes flashing.

Clark just smiled and rose to his feet. "Don't know of any other way out," he said. "I'll have the team waitin'. C'mon, Clare, let's go git the horses ready. You too, Arnie, c'mon with yer pa."

The boys both responded joyfully to the offer—Clare with a bound toward the door and Arnie holding up his arms to be carried.

Marty hastened to clear the table and do up the dishes. Missie decided it was her turn to wash and thus slowed down the procedure, but Marty knew it was worth the extra time to encourage the little girl's helpfulness.

When they drew up to the Graham home, Ma was obviously glad to see them. She hurried them into the house, where her children welcomed the Davis youngsters and took them off to play. Nellie volunteered to entertain young Arnie, and Marty accepted her offer gratefully.

Ma and Marty sat down to a cup of coffee, warm nut bread, and a long-awaited chat.

"How's thet new boy of Wanda's?" Marty wondered.

"Tiny—but he's a spunky little'un. He's got a lot of fight in 'im fer sure."

"What did they finally name 'im?" Marty smiled, remembering the long list of names from which Cam and Wanda were trying to choose.

"Everett Cameron DeWinton John."

"Quite a handle fer sech a small bundle."

"Seems so, but maybe someday he'll fit it."

"I'm so glad he's doin' fine," Marty said with feeling. "It would have crushed poor Wanda iffen she'd lost another baby."

Ma nodded solemnly.

"How's Sally Anne?"

"She's fine, but she sure is tired of waitin'." Ma shook her head. "Ya know how it can seem ferever. I called over to see her yesterday. Even got the cradle thet Jason made all laid with blankets, an' she's jest achin' to fill thet little bed up. Still, I don't think the time's settin' as heavy on her as on her ma. I never dreamed I'd ever git so flustered like over the comin' of a young'un."

"Are ya gonna deliver her?"

"Land sakes, no! We're gittin' the doc fer sure fer thet one. Funny thing—me havin' delivered so many young'uns in my time, but jest thinkin' on thet 'un makes me feel as skitterish as a yearlin' first time in harness. We's all set to send Tommie off fer Doc at the first warnin'. I'll sure be glad like when it's all over."

Marty nodded. She'd be glad, too. She wondered what it would be like to see one's own daughter about to give birth. Must be a mite scary—knowing the pain but unable to share or relieve it. She reckoned that when it was Missie's turn, she'd be even more nervous than Ma. She pushed the thought from her and changed the subject.

"Ma, I really came 'bout somethin' else. Ya know I promised Tina Larson I'd do all I could to see thet Nandry and Clae had a chance fer their schoolin'. An' Jedd—well, I jest fear he won't be 'llowin' no sech thing. In jest a few months now thet schoolhouse will be openin' its door, an' Jedd Larson declares thet no daughter of his be needin' it."

Marty looked at Ma, the helplessness weighing her down. "What we gonna do to make 'im change his mind?"

"Reckon there ain't much of anythin' thet will make Jedd Larson change his mind, lessen he wants to. Me, I wouldn't know even where to begin to work on thet man. He ain't got 'im much of a mind, but what he has got sure can stay put."

"Yeah." Marty sighed and played with her coffee cup. There didn't seem to be much hope for her to keep her promise. What could she do? She had prayed and prayed, but Jedd did not seem to be softening in the slightest toward the idea of schooling for his girls. But she wasn't giving up yet. Maybe somehow the Lord could open the mind of that stubborn man.

As she helped Ma gather up the dishes, an excited Jason arrived at the door.

"Ma," he called, rushing in without a knock or a howdy. "Sally Anne thinks it's time."

"Tom's in the field by the barn," Ma told him quickly, all in a flurry. "Send 'im fer Doc and you come back with me." She grabbed a bag from a corner, threw her shawl about her shoulders, and left the house almost on a run.

Marty realized that the bag in the corner had been all packed and ready to go just for this eventuality.

Tom left the yard on a galloping horse, and Ma and Jason left at a not much slower pace in his wagon.

Marty gathered up her small family and headed for home. She was sure all would go well for Sally Anne and her baby. Still, she found herself praying as she traveled.

Later that afternoon Tom arrived with the glad news that Sally Anne was safely delivered of a small daughter and that Grandma and Grandpa were holding up fine.

"Jest think," he said proudly, "I'm Uncle Tom now. Guess I'll have to go out an' git me a cabin."

Marty smiled.

"What ya mean?" Missie queried. "Can't ya live at home when yer an uncle?"

Tom winked at Marty. "Yeah," he said, "guess I can. Guess they won't kick me out jest 'cause I'm an uncle. 'Specially when I'm an uncle who does most of the chorin'. Won't need me thet cabin fer a while. Anyway, I'm not in the mood fer batchin'." He paused, then said rather sheepishly, "I'll wait 'til I git me a cook 'fore I go movin' into a cabin of my own."

Marty suddenly realized that young Tommie was indeed growing up, and perhaps his jesting about a cabin of his own had more serious meaning than he pretended. How quickly they grew up and changed, these young ones.

Her mind checked the girls of the neighborhood. Would any of them be just right for young Tom Graham, who had so endeared himself to her when he had cheerfully done Clark's chores and spent his evenings reading to the young Missie? Now he stood before her on the threshold of manhood. Marty hoped when the time came for him to take a bride, he would find one worthy of him.

Tom sat bouncing Arnie on his foot and went back to the subject of his new niece.

"They still haven't decided fer sure on her name. Sally Anne wants to call her Laura, but Jason be holdin' out fer Elizabeth. Seems he read 'im a story 'bout an Elizabeth an' always wanted a daughter by thet name. Then he insists thet she should have Sally or Anne in her name, too. Elizabeth Sally sounds kinda funny. Me, I'm a favorin' Elizabeth Anne. What ya think?"

"I like it," Marty assured him. "I think it's a right pretty name."

"Me too," Missie joined in, anxious to share her opinion and make her presence known to her beloved Tom.

"Thet should settle it, then," he said. "I'll jest tell Sally Anne thet Missie says it should be Elizabeth Anne, so Elizabeth Anne it must be."

Missie grinned and clapped her hands with glee.

Tom placed Little Arnie on the floor and prepared to take his leave.

"I best be gittin'. Nellie will be mad iffen I'm late fer supper, an' there's still the chorin' to do. Don't s'pose I'll git much help from 'ole Grandpa' tonight." He enjoyed his teasing, but he said it with love and respect in his voice.

Marty smiled. "Tell 'Grandpa' thet we send our love," she told him.

With a nod and a wave of his hand, he was off.

"I like 'im," Missie whispered. "I think when I grow up I'll marry Tommie."

"My land, child!" Marty exclaimed. "Yer not yet six an' talkin' of marryin'. Let's not rush things quite so much, if that's all right with you."

"I didn't mean *now*," Missie explained firmly. "I said when I grow up. First, I gotta go to school."

EIGHT

A Strange Answer

The garden produced its welcome crops, and the warm summer sun began to be almost too warm to bear. Marty was glad for the cool breezes that blew off the nearby hills, and she chose the early morning hours for any necessary weeding and preparing for the harvest to come. Missie loved sun-ripened tomatoes and would eat her fill right off the plants when they were ready to pick.

But like the spring, soon summer, too, would be gone, and fall would be upon them. With the fall would come preparations for school. Correspondence with Mr. Wilbur Whittle assured them he had not changed his mind and would be arriving in late August to acquaint himself with the people and the area and to prepare the schoolhouse for the commencement of classes.

Arrangements had been made for the unmarried Mr. Whittle to board at the Watleys, and Mrs. Watley had her two grown-up daughters polishing themselves as well as the family silver.

Missie was counting the days. Her whole life was now filled with thinking of the new school year. What she would wear, what she would learn, and who she would play with were all very important in her daily planning and in her regular reports to anyone who would listen.

Missie had two deep regrets. One was that Miss Puss would need to put in long days alone in her absence, and the second was that Tom Graham had declared himself to be too old to attend school with all the neighborhood youngsters. She'd miss Tommie. She wanted very much to have him there. She would be so proud to stand and recite a well-studied lesson if Tommie were listening. She would work extra hard at her reading and sums if he were there to observe her skills. But Tom was not to be there, and Missie, though still excited about the prospect of school, was definitely disappointed.

Marty, too, was disappointed—not over Tom but over the Larson girls. The school term was only a few weeks away, and there had been no change in Jedd Larson's attitude. Marty was about to conclude that her prayers had all been in vain.

At their usual pre-breakfast prayer time, Marty was mulling over these thoughts in her mind as Clark read the morning Scripture: "'Ask, an' it shall be given you; seek—'"

I been askin', Lord, an' nothin's been happenin', she admonished her Lord and immediately felt guilt and remorse.

I'm sorry, Father, she prayed silently. *I guess I'm 'bout the most faithless an' impatient child ya got. Help me to be content like an' to keep on havin' faith.*

Clark seemed to sense her mood and in his morning prayer included this petition: "An', Lord, ya know thet 'fore long now our school will be startin', an' ya know how Marty promised Mrs. Larson to try an' see thet the girls got their schoolin'. Only you can work in Jedd's heart to let her keep thet promise, Lord. We leave it to you to work out in yer own good way and time."

Marty was deeply grateful for Clark's understanding and silently thanked him for his caring. Maybe now God would be free to act. He often did when Clark prayed. She immediately reprimanded herself. True, Clark seemed blessed with answered prayers, but she was God's child, too. And the Bible said that God did not regard one of His children above the other. If Clark's prayers were answered more frequently, it was because Clark had a stronger faith. She determined to exercise her own faith more.

Later in the day Ole Bob announced an approaching team. To Marty's surprise, it was Jedd Larson. It had been some months since Jedd had been over, and Marty could not contain a surge of excitement that this visit might be an answer to prayer.

Clark met Jedd outside and Marty could see them talking in a neighborly fashion while Jedd tied the horses to the rail fence.

Marty quickly put on the coffeepot and cut pieces of gingerbread. *I wonder jest how he'll say it without havin' to back down none,* she wondered.

Jedd and Clark were soon in and seated, and Marty fairly held her breath waiting for Jedd to spill the good news. He'd brought news all right—news that made him grin from ear to ear—but hardly what Marty had been expecting.

"Sold me my farm yesterday."

Clark looked up in surprise.

"Ya did? Someone local?"

"Nope—new guy jest come in. He was with thet wagon train goin' through—had planned to go further west, but his missus took sick. Decided to stay on here. I showed 'im my farm, and he offered me cash—outright. Good price, too."

Jedd stopped and looked back and forth between them, no doubt waiting to let his good fortune take proper effect on his hearers. Then he went on. "The train's restin' fer a couple of days 'fore goin' on. I'm thinkin' o' takin' his spot with the train. Al'ays did want to see what was further on. Never can tell—might find me gold or sumpin'."

Marty finally drew a shaky breath.

"What 'bout the girls?" she asked, trying to keep her tone even.

She knew it was a foolish question. All hope now of keeping her promise seemed to be vanishing. If Jedd was moving away, there would be no chance of the girls ever getting any schooling.

Jedd answered, "What 'bout the girls? Wagon trainin' won't hurt 'em none. Do 'em good to see more o' the country."

"But . . . but they're so young. . . ." Marty stopped. Something within her warned her to be silent, but she suddenly felt sick to her stomach as all her hopes and prayers came crashing down about her.

Jedd looked at her evenly but said nothing. He then reached for another piece of gingerbread and went on as though Marty had never spoken.

"This new man—name's Zeke LaHaye. Seemed to like the looks of my land real good—paid me a first-rate price fer it. He's got 'im three young'uns—a near-growed girl an' two young boys."

"Thet right?" Clark responded. "Guess I should pay me a call on 'em. Might want to send his young'uns to school."

Jedd snorted. "Don't know why he'd do a fool thing like thet. Both of those boys are big enough to git some work out of. Must be around twelve an' eight, I'd say. An' thet daughter's almost of an age to take on a home of her own. I been thinkin' myself thet she might be right handy to have along goin' west."

His meaningful grin made Marty feel further sickened.

"I s'pose," Clark said slowly, "thet a young, good-lookin' buck like you be takin' another bride 'fore ya know it."

He winked at Jedd, and Marty felt anger rise against him. *What is he thinking of, Clark humoring the despicable man this way?* she thought hotly.

Clark looked thoughtful, then broke the silence. "Ya know, I'm thinkin' thet when it comes to marryin' agin, a young woman might think twice 'bout takin' on two near-growed girls. 'Course an older, more sensible-like woman might not mind. Ya could always do thet, ya know—take ya an older, settled one 'stead of some flighty, pretty young thing. Might not be as much fun, but . . ."

Clark fell silent, and it was obvious by the look on Jedd's face that he was thinking on the words.

"Ya could leave the girls here, I s'pose, so's they wouldn't slow ya down none, either in yer travel or any other way." Clark gave Jedd a playful jab with his elbow. Jedd grinned.

"Hadn't thought of thet," he deliberated, "but those new folk gonna move into my house—hafta have everythin' all cleared out tomorra. Don't s'pose they'd want the girls hangin' on."

"Thet's tough," said Clark and appeared to really be working on Jedd's problem. "Kinda puts a man at a disadvantage like, don't it?"

Jedd looked worried. Marty wished she could excuse herself and go be sick. Never had Clark made her so angry—or so puzzled. To sit there feeding the ego, the very worst impulses, of this—this disgusting person, and disposing of his two daughters as though they were unwanted baggage—she was so upset she feared any moment she might lose her temper with both of them.

Then Clark seemed to suddenly think of something.

"S'pose ya could put 'em up here fer a while," he said nonchalantly. "We do have us an extry bedroom. Might jest be able to make room."

So that's where he's goin' with all this. Marty's climbing temper began to recede. Clark was using Jedd's self-image as a male of desirable qualities to try to fight for the girls. He was offering to keep them—take them off the man's hands, so to speak. Marty wondered why she hadn't realized immediately what Clark was doing. She sent Clark a quick imploring glance to show him she now understood and for him to please, please continue.

Jedd rubbed his grizzly chin. "Thet right?"

"I think we could manage—'til ya got kinda settled like." Clark grinned and jabbed with his elbow again.

Jedd appeared to be thinking carefully.

"'Course," Clark continued, a somewhat doubtful note now in his voice, "Marty has the say of the house an' how crowded in she wants us. Sorta up to her, I guess."

Marty wanted to cry out, "Oh, please, please, Jedd," but instead she took her cue from Clark and even surprised herself at her casual, matter-of-fact voice.

"S'pose we could . . . fer a while . . . iffen it'll help ya out some."

"Might do," Jedd finally said. "Yeah, might do."

Marty didn't dare look up. The hot tears in her eyes threatened to run down her cheeks and into her coffee cup. She quickly left the table on the pretense of tending to the fire. When she had herself somewhat under control, she poured the men another cup of coffee and then went to the bedroom where she leaned against the window ledge and prayed for God to please forgive her lack of faith and to please help Clark in the battle in which he was presently engaged.

A few moments later Clark came in, gave her shoulder a quick squeeze, rummaged in a drawer, then was gone.

Marty heard the men leave the house, and she went into the sitting room a short time later to watch Jedd's team on its way out of the yard.

Marty heard Clark come into the house and walk over to stand behind her at the window. As Jedd's wagon disappeared over the hill, Clark gently turned Marty to face him. Her tear-filled eyes looked into his and she hardly dared voice the question.

"Did he—?"

"Did he agree? Yeah, he agreed."

Her tears started again.

"Oh, Clark, thank ya," she said when she was able to speak. "I never, ever thought thet I'd be able to have the girls right here." She wiped at her eyes and sniffed, and Clark pulled out his handkerchief. "Thank ya," she said again.

Her face buried in his man-sized handkerchief, she then sputtered, "At first I was so mad, you talkin' thet way to thet . . . thet conceited . . ." She floundered to a stop, knowing she should not voice the words she had been thinking.

She began over again. "I couldn't imagine why ya'd say sech things 'til . . . 'til I began to see. An' he believed it all, didn't he? Believed thet a woman—a young woman—in her right mind would take to him."

She was getting angry again at the very thought of it all, so she decided to change the subject before she worked herself up.

"An' he said thet we could take the girls?" she asked.

"Yep."

"To keep?" She couldn't help the pleading in her voice.

"Well, he didn't exactly say fer how long, but I'll be one surprised farmer iffen Jedd Larson ever wants his girls back. He'll git hisself all tied up in this or thet, an' his girls won't enter much into his thinkin'."

Marty had a sudden question she knew she shouldn't ask, yet she felt she needed an answer.

"Ya didn't make 'im pay fer their keep, did ya?"

Clark grinned. "Well . . . not exactly," he said slowly.

"Meanin'?"

"Jedd said thet we could keep the girls iffen we gave 'im ten dollars apiece fer 'em."

Marty pulled back. "Well, I never!" she retorted. "I never thought I'd live to see the day thet one had to pay fer the privilege of feedin' an' clothin' another man's young'uns."

Clark pulled her back against him and smoothed the long brown hair. Maybe he thought by so doing he could smooth her overwrought nerves. But when he spoke there was humor in his voice. "Now, now," he said, as though to an angry child, "ya wanted yer prayers answered, didn't ya? Who are we to quibble as to how it's done?"

Marty relaxed in his arms. He was right, of course. She should be feeling thankfulness, not frustration.

"The girls will be here tomorrow," he continued. "It's gonna be strange fer us all at first an' will take some gittin' used to. Seems thet all of our energy should be goin' into makin' the adjustment of livin' one with the other."

He lifted her chin and looked into her eyes.

"You've got yerself a big job, Marty. Already ya have yer hands full with yer own young'uns. Addin' two more ain't gonna lessen yer load none. I hope ya ain't takin' on too much. Yer tender heart may jest break yer back, I'm thinkin'."

She shook her head. "He answered our prayer, Clark. Iffen He thinks this right, what we're doin', then He'll give the strength an' the wisdom thet we need, too, won't He?"

Clark nodded. "I reckon He will" was all he said.

NINE

Nandry an' Clae

As he had agreed, Jedd arrived the next day with the two girls. Their few belongings were carried in a box and deposited in the bedroom that would be theirs. Marty wondered if the parting would be difficult, particularly so soon after the loss of their mother. But she could not detect any show of emotion from either side.

Jedd was obviously anxious to be off. He had his possessions packed in his wagon, and with the money from the sale of the farm laying heavy in his pocket, he was hard-pressed to hold back, even for a cup of coffee. He did fill up on fresh bread and jam, however, and with the food barely swallowed announced that he must be on his way. He seemed to be fully recovered from his wife's death. He gave Marty and his two daughters a quick nod, which Marty supposed was to suffice for thank you, good-bye, and God bless you, and went out the door. He was full of the coming trip west and all the good fortune he was sure it would hold. Jedd always had regarded good fortune more highly than hard work.

Thus it was that with no further fanfare, Nandry and Clae were established as members of the Davis household.

Marty decided to give the girls a few days of "settlin' in" before establishing routine and expectations.

She looked at their sorry wardrobes and decided that a trip to town would be necessary if they were to be suitably dressed for the soon-to-commence school.

Marty seldom went to town, sending instead a carefully prepared list with Clark, but she felt this time she should go herself. Clark would find the selecting of dress materials and other articles difficult and time consuming.

Marty had been saving egg-and-cream money over the months and felt that now was the time to dip into her savings. It wasn't fair to lay all the expenses on Clark. He'd already had to pay Jedd for the privilege of raising his daughters. Marty felt her hackles rise again at the mere thought.

Well, that was all past and done—so be it. From here on the two youngsters were hers to care for, and to the best of her ability and with God's help—and some from Clark, too—she planned to do it right.

Nandry seemed her usual withdrawn self, neither expecting nor finding life to be interesting. But Clae clearly was observing everything around her and even dared at times to delight in what she discovered.

Both girls were surprisingly helpful—for which Marty was grateful. Nandry preferred to spend time with young Arnie rather than the other members of the family. Marty did not mind, for help in keeping up with the adventuresome and often mischievous little boy was always welcomed.

Marty planned her journey to town for the following Saturday. She would go in with Clark and thus save an extra trip.

On Friday after breakfast was over, she called the girls to her. It was time, she decided, that they work a few things out.

They sat down silently, their hands nervously twisting in their laps. Marty smiled at them in an effort to relieve their tension.

"I thought thet it be time we have a chat," she began.

They did not move nor speak.

"Is yer room to yer likin'?"

Clae nodded enthusiastically and Nandry more quietly followed suit. The additional bedrooms Clark and their neighbors had put on the cabin really came in especially handy now that the two girls were with them. Marty had made sure the bed was soft with warm, nice-smelling blankets, and she had put colorful rag rugs over the floor, printed curtains with ruffles at the window, and two framed pictures on the wall. A neat row of pegs was on the wall behind the door and a wooden chest stood beneath the window. There was even a small bench with cushions all of its own.

Clae nodded again and said with a sparkle in her eyes, "I never knew anything could be so fine. . . ." But she stopped when her sister gave her a long look.

Marty continued to smile.

"I thought maybe we should be sortin' out our work," she said. "Missie washes the dishes two mornin's a week, an' she cleans her room—makes her bed and hangs up her clothes each day—an' she helps some with Arnie, too. Now then, what ya be thinkin' thet you'd like to be doin' fer yer share?"

No response, although it looked like Clae might have something in mind.

"I know ya already been makin' yer bed. Thet's good; an' ya do a nice job of it, too. But is there anythin' ya 'specially like to do? Better than other things, I mean."

Still no answer.

Marty felt stymied, and just when she was wondering whether to simply make assignments as she saw fit, assistance came from her own Missie, who had come over to join the proceedings.

"Mama says I wash dishes good," Missie announced from her place leaning against her mother, "but I'll share. Do ya want to wash dishes sometimes, Nandry?"

Nandry nodded.

"An' do you, too, Clae?"

Clae nodded.

"Well," said Missie, very grown-up, "then why don't we take turns?"

It was settled.

Missie added, "We all need to make our own beds, but Clare is too little yet to make his bed, an' Arnie can't make a bed at all! Ya have to git 'im up an' dress 'im every day. Who wants to make Clare's bed an' who wants to dress Arnie?"

"I'll care fer Arnie," Nandry was quick to say.

"Then I'll make Clare's bed," Clae said cheerfully.

"An' sometimes there's special jobs," went on Missie, "like gittin' more wood or hangin' out clothes or peelin' the vege'bles."

"I'd rather feed the chickens," Nandry said slowly. "An' gather eggs," she added as an afterthought.

"She likes chickens," Clae informed the group. "She was always wishin' thet she had some. Chickens an' babies—thet's what she likes."

"Fine," said Marty to Nandry, "you can feed the chickens and gather the eggs iffen ya like thet. What 'bout you, Clae? What else would you be likin'?"

Clae looked suddenly shy. Finally she blurted out, "I'd like to learn to make things." She looked carefully into Marty's face as if to determine if she was going to get into trouble for her request. Finding no resistance, she added, "Pretty dresses an' aprons an' knitted things."

"Stop it, Clae," Nandry scolded her. "Ya know ya can't do all thet. Ya'd wreck the machine fer sure."

So now it was out. Marty had noticed the younger girl eyeing her machine hungrily. So she wished to be creative. Well, she would be given instruction and opportunity.

"The machine doesn't break so easy," she said, carefully choosing her words. "Ya must both learn to sew, an' then you'll be able to make whatever ya want. Perhaps we could start on somethin' simple, an' then when ya practice a bit ya can do somethin' more fancy. I learned to sew when I was quite young, an' I've always been glad I did. Sewin' somethin' pretty always makes me feel good inside."

Clae's eyes shone with a mixture of delight and disbelief.

Marty said, "Now, tomorra you're goin' to have yer first big job. I'm goin' into town with my husband to buy the things you'll be needin' fer school, an' I will be leavin' ya here on yer own." She looked over the faces arrayed before her and secretly wondered if she would be brave enough to leave them when the time came, or would she bundle them all up and take them along. No, that would never do. Five youngsters underfoot and hanging on her skirts and begging for this or that while she tried to hurry through a great deal of shopping just wouldn't work at all. Besides, the girls really did need the opportunity to prove themselves. They were quite old enough to be caring for younger ones, and she must give them the chance to show it.

Her announcement caused no change of expression on the faces before her.

"Do ya think, Nandry, thet ya can care fer young Arnie an' help fix some dinner fer ya all?"

Nandry nodded her head in agreement.

"An', Clae, you an' Missie will need to help with the dishes an' the dinner an' keep an' eye on Clare. Can ya do thet?"

The two girls exchanged glances, then nodded vigorously. Missie was obviously very pleased to be included with the older girls in this responsibility.

"Good," said Marty, "then it's decided. Now, we have lots thet must be done today. First, I want ya all to slip off yer shoes so I can get a tracin' of yer feet fer new boots fer school."

Marty's face flushed as soon as she realized the two Larson girls were not wearing shoes.

"Our shoes are all worn out," Clae explained matter-of-factly. "They won't stay on no more."

Marty carefully traced and labeled the feet on her pieces of brown paper. She would cut them out later so they could be slipped into a shoe for fitting.

"Now then," she told the girls, "Clae an' Missie are to do up the dishes. Missie, you show Clae where the pans an' towels are kept. Nandry, you come with me an' I'll show ya how to be carin' fer the chickens. Then we'll gather an' clean the eggs so I can add 'em to the ones I've set aside to take to town."

"Can I bring Arnie?" Nandry asked, uncharacteristically animated. "He likes chickens, too."

Marty consented, knowing Arnie did love the chickens, though Marty was convinced that what he liked the most was their delightful squawking and flapping when he chased them around the pen.

They left the house together. The two younger girls were already at work on the dishes.

Maybe things would fall into place after all. The girls seemed almost eager to get to their new tasks. Marty breathed a relieved sigh and led the way to the grain bin, Nandry and Arnie in tow.

TEN

A Trip to Town

Marty still had some nagging misgivings the following morning as she tied on her bonnet and gathered the eggs, butter, and cream for the trip to town. Should she actually leave them all on their own, or should she at least take Arnie with her? No, she told herself, she needed to establish a sense of trust and responsibility with Nandry and Clae. After all, their father had made them shoulder grown-up responsibilities for years. She couldn't require that they go back to being treated as children. So she again went over all the instructions with them, and they assured her they understood and would abide by her wishes.

But it was with reluctant steps she left to join Clark in the wagon. She waved good-bye once more and put on a brave smile.

"Bring us some yummies," Clare called to her.

"An' some new hair ribbons fer school," added Missie.

"Thet girl," laughed Clark, "she thinks far too much 'bout how she looks."

Marty coaxed forth a smile.

"Clark," she said as they left the gate, "do ya think it's good to leave 'em like thet—with jest the girls an'—"

"Why not?" Clark interrupted. "They been cookin' an' cleanin' fer years already."

"But they haven't had young'uns to care fer."

"No, thet's right, but carin' fer young'uns seems to be the one thing thet pleasures Nandry."

"I noticed thet, too," Marty responded. "She really seems to enjoy Arnie. An' he likes her, too. Oh, I hope it will be all right, but I won't feel easy like until we git home agin. I sure hope this is a fast trip."

"Yer frettin' too much, I'm thinkin', but we'll try to hurry it a bit. Won't take me long to take care o' the things I be needin'. How 'bout you?"

"Shouldn't take long. I need school things fer the girls an' the usual groceries."

"Ya need money, then."

"I have my egg savin's."

"No need to spend all yer savin's on outfittin' the girls. I'm ready to share in the carin' of 'em."

Clark tucked the reins between his knees and pulled out his wallet. He extracted a couple of bills.

"Think this is enough?"

"Thet'll be fine," she answered. "I 'preciate it. It's gonna take a bit to git 'em off to school proper like. They really own nothin' now thet's fittin' to wear."

Clark nodded. "Well, we knew when we took 'em thet they'd cost somethin'. No problem there."

They drove into town to find the streets filled with commotion. A wagon train was getting ready to move on. Dogs barked, horses stomped, and children ran yelling through the street. Men argued prices and women scurried about, running to the store for a last-minute purchase or looking for children who had been told to stay put but hadn't. Marty shook her head and decided she had picked a poor day to come to town—surely her shopping would be slowed down considerably.

She entered McDonald's General Store with some trepidation. She always dreaded facing the proprietor's scrutinizing eyes and sharp tongue.

"I declare," Marty had said to Clark on one occasion, "thet woman's tongue has no sense of propriety."

Missie had overheard the word and latched on to it, henceforth declaring of all things—particularly to young Clare—"You've no sense of pa'piety," which seemed to mean, "Yer jest plain dumb."

Marty had decided after that she'd better guard her tongue more carefully in Missie's presence.

Marty now straightened her shoulders to help her brace up before opening the McDonalds' door. To her relief, Mrs. McDonald was busy with three women from the train. She glanced at Marty and opened her mouth to call out something, but must have changed her mind to give full attention to her customers. Marty smiled briefly and crossed to the bolts of dress goods. What relief to be left on her own for making the selections. Mentally she calculated as she lifted bolt after bolt. The new dresses had to be serviceable, but, oh, how she'd like to have them pretty, too, and the prettier material added the cost up so quickly. The dark blue would wear half of forever, but how would one ever make it look attractive for a young girl? The soft pink voile was beautiful but looked like you could sip tea through it without even changing the taste. Hardly appropriate for a farm girl.

Mrs. McDonald was now enjoying the bits of gossip the travelers could supply, prying rather transparently for the whys of their coming or going. Marty weighed her decisions with care. She picked neither the dark blue nor the pink. *No use takin' material thet'll wear too long,* she reasoned. *They'll outgrow it 'fore ya know it anyway. But ya never know—maybe Nandry's can go to Clae, then to Missie. . . .* Eventually she selected a length of medium blue, a pearly gray color that she would make up with white collar and cuffs, some warm brown, and a couple of prints, one with a green background and the other red. She then chose materials for underclothes, nighties, and bonnets and moved on to choose stockings, boots, and some heavier material for coats. Until the colder weather arrived the girls could get by with capes she could make out of material she already had on hand.

As she added bolt after bolt to the stack on the counter to be measured off, she realized what an enormous sewing job she had ahead of her. She was thankful she already had worked on Missie's school clothes.

Missie! She had asked for new hair ribbons. Marty moved quickly to choose some for Nandry and Clae, too.

Her shopping was going well, thanks to the wagon-train ladies keeping Mrs. McDonald busy. She laid the last dry goods items on the counter and rechecked her list. Even with the money that Clark had given her, most of her egg-and-cream money would go. Well, she couldn't help that. She had promised Tina Larson she would give the girls a chance, and she planned on doing just that.

She went on to her grocery list, placing items on the counter as she selected them. Before she had finished, Clark entered the store. His eyebrows moved up at the great heap on the counter, but he made no comment.

"Most done," Marty offered. "Did ya git the things ya be needin'?"

"All but a piece fer the plow. The smithie had to order it in, but I expected thet. Thet's why I sent now 'stead of waitin' fer later." He grinned in anticipation. "There be jest a chance thet it'll make it fer spring plowin'."

The other women gathered their bundles and left the store, and Mrs. McDonald scurried toward Clark and Marty.

"Well, well, how are the Davises?" she began but left no time for a reply. "I hear thet ya took on them two Larson girls." Her eyes dared them to deny it, at the same instant declaring them out of their minds for so doing.

She now waited just a moment, but neither Clark nor Marty commented.

"I have my purchases laid out here, Mrs. McDonald," Marty said evenly. "I believe thet's all I be needin' today."

Mrs. McDonald went to work adding up the groceries, but her snapping eyes promised Marty she wasn't finished with her yet. When the woman had the total figured, Clark stepped forward to pay that bill, then began gathering up the purchases.

"I'll take the groceries on out to the wagon," he informed Marty, "then be back to help with them other things."

"I can manage 'em," Marty assured him. "Jest wait in the wagon fer me. Where is the team?"

"Jest across the street."

"Fine. I'll be there quick like."

Marty walked to the door with him and opened it as he went out, both arms loaded. She picked up the box she had left by the entrance, placing it on the counter.

"My eggs, butter, and cream fer today. I'd like 'em to go toward these things, please," she said to Mrs. McDonald, motioning toward the stack on the counter.

When she had figured the worth of the farm produce, Marty began to push bolts of material forward, naming the yardage she desired from each one. In between snips of the scissors, Mrs. McDonald managed to pry for tidbits that Marty was sure she would later be able to pass on to her next customers.

"Jedd said ya was most keen on keepin' the girls."

Marty nodded.

"People here figurin' as to why. Some say thet with yer own three young'uns, ya figured to need the help pretty bad. I said, 'Now, Mrs. Davis wouldn't stoop to usin' mere children like,' but . . ." She stopped and shrugged her shoulders to indicate she could be wrong.

"'Seemed to me thet it makes more sense to keep 'em fer their board,' says I. 'Girls thet age ain't much fer workin', but with Jedd jinglin' all thet hard cash, no reason the Davises shouldn't git in on some of it.'"

Marty could feel her cheeks flushing with anger. How this woman could goad her!

"Anyway, I says to folks thet, knowin' ya like, I'm right sure Miz Davis won't overwork those two, an' a bit of good hard work might be the best thing fer 'em. Never did care much fer those two—real shifty eyes. Grow up useless like their pa. I'll bet ya won't git much work outta those two, but iffen ya got a fair cash exchange—"

Marty could take no more.

"Mrs. McDonald," she said, trying hard not to let her anger show through her words, though she knew she probably wasn't succeeding, "we took the girls 'cause their ma wanted 'em to have a chance, an' I made a promise 'fore she died. I aim to keep thet promise iffen I can—an' there was no money, Mrs. McDonald. Fact is, my husband paid Jedd Larson to be 'llowed to keep his daughters."

"I see . . ." But Mrs. McDonald quickly recovered. "Thet's what I wanted to know. Why didn't ya say so without all the fuss? Some people are so closed like with information."

Then she added, "Thet's jest what I been figurin'. Thought me thet folks were wrong in their speculatin'."

Mrs. McDonald had scored again. *Why does she always get what she wants from me?* Marty fumed. She had told no one else of her promise to Tina except Ma, and Ma guarded secrets carefully. Now the whole county would know, and the story would change as it was passed from mouth to mouth.

She fought for composure, paid for the purchases, and quickly gathered her parcels. They made quite a load, and she wished she had accepted Clark's offer to return to help her.

"All them fancy things ain't fer those girls, are they? Seems to me stuck way out there on yer farm, ya could jest as leave patch up their old things."

"The girls will be goin' to school come September." Marty said the words firmly. And she recognized just a trace of pride in her voice. Well, so be it. Before Mrs. McDonald could say anything further, Marty resolutely headed for the door with quick steps.

As she entered the street the commotion from the wagon train was even more intense. The teams were lined up now, ready to leave within a few minutes. Horses still stomped, dogs still barked, and children still yelled, but the bartering of the men was over and the final purchases of the women had been made. People stood in clusters by the wagons saying farewells and giving last-minute messages to be passed on to someone at the other end of the journey.

The third wagon back must be simply a passenger wagon, Marty decided, for a miscellaneous group of people seemed to be aboard it. The canvas, for the present, was down, and several plank seats had been placed across the wagon box. Most of the passengers appeared to be making a journey of short duration, perhaps to a nearby larger center, for they obviously traveled light. Maybe men on business or women going out to shop or visit. Some of them had young children with them, and their faces showed anticipation at the prospect of the trip.

In the midst of the clamor and excitement sat a white-faced, somber-eyed lady with three small children. One child cried, another clung to his mother fearfully, and the third and oldest, a boy, sat hollow cheeked and drawn, simply staring ahead silently.

"Thet's Miz Talbot from the other side of town," said a voice at Marty's shoulder, and she turned slightly to see that Mrs. McDonald had come out from the store, no doubt to get in on all the excitement. "Never should've come west," she stated. "Not made of the right stuff. She's leavin'. Goin' back." Her words were clipped and sounded rather biting.

Marty looked at the poor young woman and wished with all her heart she'd had a chance to speak with her.

Suddenly a young man pushed through the crowd almost at a run. The oldest child jumped to his feet, arms open wide, and shouted with delight. The woman looked alarmed. Marty could not hear the words, but she sensed the man was arguing and pleading for the woman to stay. However, the woman just set her lips tightly and shook her head. Finally she turned her back on him completely, her shoulders held stiff and stubborn.

The order of "move out" was given, and with a creak and a grind, the cumbersome wagons began to move forward. The man had to disentangle himself from the arms of the crying child and gently push him back into the wagon. The child screamed and shouted after him, and Marty thought for one terrifying moment that he was going to jump.

All his life he'll wish he'd left those two little arms around his neck and kept thet young boy with him, Marty mourned.

The wagon moved on past her. She could not see the woman's face, but she noticed her shoulders had lost their defiance and were now shaking convulsively.

Oh, you stubborn thing, Marty's heart cried, *come back—come back,* but the wagon moved on.

Marty turned to see the man, hands over his face, leaning against a hitching rail for support, the sobs wrenching his body.

A sickness filled her whole being. It was wrong, it was wicked, it was so cruel to tear a family apart like that.

"Good riddance, says I," said the voice beside her, and Marty turned quickly away and stumbled across the street to the waiting wagon.

Clark placed her bundles in the wagon box and helped her up. Then the team, at his command, moved out of town.

They traveled some distance in silence. The warm summer sun shone down upon late flowers waving at the sides of the road, and birds dipped back and forth in the path of the team. Marty's anger and hurt had begun to subside, but her confused thoughts still fought to sort it all out.

Suddenly she felt her hand gripped tightly and looked up into Clark's probing eyes.

"So ya saw it, too, huh?" he questioned.

She nodded dumbly, her eyes filling with tears.

He squeezed her hand again.

"Oh, Clark," she said when she finally felt enough control to speak. "It was so wrong, so awful, an' . . . an' . . . it could have been *me*," she finished in a rush of emotion.

"But it wasn't," he answered firmly. "It wasn't, an' somehow . . . somehow, I really don't think it ever could've been."

Marty looked up in surprise to meet his even gaze. Their unspoken communication assured her.

"No," she finally said with similar conviction, "no, maybe it never could've."

Clark was right for her—so right. Their love was strong and good. The good Lord had prepared them for each other—even when Marty didn't know Him and even had loathed the thought of staying on with Clark. Yes, their love had promise—enduring promise.

ELEVEN

Family and Teacher

Marty and Clark's return to the farm found everything in order, and Marty couldn't help but breathe a sigh of relief. Arnie was very glad to see his mother, but he quickly forgot she had been gone and went on with his play.

Besides her usual daily chores and the garden, Marty had only a few weeks to complete the sewing she planned to do for the Larson girls. Nandry seemed to accept the new items as inconsequential, but Clae's eyes took on a shine as they laid it all out and distributed the various things to each. Marty began her sewing lessons with Clae almost immediately and discovered her to be a good student. This pleased them both, and Clae soon was actually able to be a help and do more and more. Nandry also was shown how to sew, but though she went through the motions and did well enough at it, she never seemed to be too interested. She was much more involved in caring for Arnie and entertaining Clare. Nandry's contribution to the household was much appreciated. With the two small boys out from underfoot, Marty's and Clae's sewing progressed without too many interruptions, as did the other tasks that needed to be done.

Clark looked at the finished garments and smiled his approval. "My girls will all look jest fine a-sittin' in thet new schoolroom," he declared. Nandry flushed and Clae beamed at being included as one of "my girls."

Marty began to notice little things and wondered if indeed Nandry was a bit too taken with her benefactor. Clark's appearance was the only thing that ever brought a change of expression to Nandry's face, and Marty often caught her watching Clark as he went about the yard. She noticed as Nandry set the table that Clark's plate and cutlery were arranged with special care.

I think I'll be plum glad to git thet girl off to school, she thought with a sigh, then immediately reprimanded herself. *Ya silly goose,* she scolded inwardly, coloring in spite of herself. *Here ya are havin' jealous pangs over a mere child.*

It surprised her somewhat to discover this feeling. She had never been in a situation to feel threatened before, never having had to share Clark with anyone but her children.

"God, fergive me," she prayed, "an' help me not to be selfish with the man I love. Nandry is growin' up, perhaps too quickly, but it's by no choice of her own. She didn't have much to look up to in her own pa, an' now seein' a man, thoughtful an' carin', hardworkin' an' with humor in his eyes, no wonder she admires 'im like. Anyway, Lord, help me to be wise an' to be just. Help me to love Nandry an' to help her through these painful years of growin' up. Help Clark, too. Give 'im wisdom in his carin'."

Marty made no mention of her observations to Clark. There was no use drawing his attention to something of which he seemed to be completely unaware. It could accomplish no good and perhaps would only serve to put an unnatural restraint between the man and the girl, and Nandry so much needed to be able to reach out, to love and be loved. Secretly Marty hoped Clark would never realize the young girl was nursing a youthful infatuation.

For the most part, Clark was away in the fields, and though Nandry took care of the chickens and the little ones in comparative silence, Marty observed her looking off in the direction that Clark was working and the flush on her face when he entered the house. Clark never did seem to notice and teased each of *his girls* equally.

Missie, being only "goin' on six," could still climb on her pa's knee, insist on combing his hair, or curl up beside him under the shelter of his arm.

Clare was his "helper" and followed his father wherever his young steps were able. It often meant a piggyback return, for the little boy played out quickly.

Arnie's toddler's steps determined to follow Pa, also, and Marty, looking out of the window, often shook her head at the patient Clark trying to complete his chores with two small boys "assisting" him, making his tasks most difficult. Yet she knew, all in all, Clark also found it enjoyable.

Though patient and loving with his family, Clark was very firm, and Marty at times had to bite her tongue when she felt Clark was expecting a bit too much for their tender years. She would have coddled them, but Clark would not, for he had a strong conviction that what was learned through discipline in early years would not have to be relearned through more painful lessons later on.

Clae seemed almost to have forgotten that she had ever lived elsewhere but with the Davises; and though neither of the girls called them Pa and Ma, Marty felt Clae truly looked on them as such. She openly admired Clark and enjoyed his teasing, even teasing back in return, her eyes sparkling with amusement.

So they adjusted to one another and began to feel like a family. Morning worship at the breakfast table was a special time. The two oldest girls listened carefully to things they had never heard before, while Missie and Clare coaxed for their favorite Bible stories.

Eventually enough of the sewing was done so the girls at least could start school dressed appropriately. Marty would finish the rest as she found the time.

Missie's excitement grew with each day that passed. Every morning she wanted to know how many days were left before school started. Marty felt the child was on the verge of hysteria and tried to slow her down. Clark just laughed and advised Marty to let Missie enjoy the anticipation. Daily, Missie changed her mind about what she would wear on her first day, going from plaid, to gray, to blue, to plaid again—over and over. Finally she settled on the blue because she liked her blue hair ribbons the best. Her only remaining sadness was that Tommie would not be there.

"I'm gonna marry Tommie," she informed Clae.

"Yer only five," Clae responded.

"Almost six, an' I'll grow," Missie retorted.

"But Tommie's 'most twenty."

"So!" said Missie with a mighty shrug of her shoulders, and that settled it.

It would indeed be good for Missie to have more contact with other children. Marty would be right glad when school was finally in session.

The Saturday before school was to begin was a day of high anticipation in the Davis household. The whole community was invited to a meeting at the schoolhouse, a chance for the parents and children to meet Mr. Wilbur Whittle and for him to be introduced to his pupils. Marty supposed there wasn't a home in the whole area that wasn't touched by the excitement.

The meeting was scheduled for two o'clock, and the neighborhood women had decided to serve coffee and cake at its closing. "Eatin' together always breaks the ice, so to speak," observed Mrs. Stern sagely.

At the Davis house the noon meal was a rather hurried affair, and the dishes were done in short order, in spite of Missie's constant chatter telling Clae all the things she was going to see and do come Monday morning. Marty gave careful attention to the grooming of each family member. Nandry and Clae had never looked better. Nandry still seemed rather noncommittal about her upcoming chance at an education, though Marty did see her glance at Clark for his appraisal of her appearance. Clae, on the other hand, shone with excitement about this opportunity, running back and forth between Marty and the mirror to check on how she looked. With her flushed cheeks and the new ribbon tying back her hair, she looked downright pretty. The fact that Clae had helped to sew the dress she wore filled her with honest pride. Marty complimented her, making her rosy cheeks turn even brighter.

Marty commented on Nandry's dress, as well, and the girl's eyes lit momentarily, but she didn't allow herself any further response.

Missie pranced around the house, singing and dancing. She had Clare and Little Arnie doing somersaults and jigs with her. Marty shook her head in exasperation as she tried to fasten a ribbon in her curls. Finally Clark and Marty were able to usher their brood out the door in some semblance of order.

It was a beautiful day for this welcome meeting of neighbors, and everyone seemed to have turned out for the important event. The wagons and teams were tethered at the far end of the school yard, with the folk gathered around outside and inside the schoolhouse, there not being enough room for them to all go in at once.

Neighbor greeted neighbor, with good-natured talk flowing all around. The two spring babies were there to be shown around and admired. Little Elizabeth Anne was radiant with smiles and coos. She insisted on being held upright so she wouldn't miss a thing, and even tried to sit on her own. A "bundle of wigglin' energy," her proud grandma Graham called her. Marty took a turn holding her and had to agree with the assessment, biased or not.

Wanda and Cam were there with their new son, Everett Cameron DeWinton John. Marty had thought it a rather long name for a small boy but was surprised to learn that his father, after all his grand ideas for his son, had cut it down to plain "Rett." Baby Rett had gained rapidly after his somewhat difficult birth. He was already a big boy for his age.

"Look at thet, huh," his father announced. "Look at thet fer a boy, an' 'im not yet five months. Gonna be a big fella, thet 'un." He grinned broadly, and Wanda smiled quietly beside him.

Marty agreed and took the baby. She held Rett for some time, walking around the yard with him. Finally she had to acknowledge the little warning signals that shivered up her arms and to her heart. The baby did not move as an infant should. When she raised him to her shoulder, there wasn't the proper lift of his head. *Something is wrong with this baby,* her heart cried. She looked at his beaming mother, his proud pa, and prayed that her eyes hadn't betrayed her thoughts, that she would be proved wrong. But she could not shake a heavy feeling from her heart.

At ten past two the Watley family wagon finally pulled in with the new teacher sitting in front beside Mr. Watley. All eyes were on the man. Marty wasn't sure what any of the neighbors might have expected, but she was nearly positive none had pictured the man before them. They were accustomed to seeing strong, muscular farmers out here on the frontier, and this gentleman looked somewhat out of place. Not only was he short but very slight of build. What he lacked in size he seemed to compensate for with an enormous mustache. Though carefully tended and waxed on the ends, it nearly hid the lower half of his face.

His vest was a bright plaid material, and he wore white spats, most unusual this far west. Marty had to quickly hush Missie's loud whisper about "What's he got on his feet?" A bowler hat topped his small head, and he often reached for it, dusting it and then replacing it again.

Marty was relieved to note his expression held both friendliness and curiosity.

Clark had been asked to get the meeting going, and he gave his welcome to Mr. Wilbur Whittle in most courteous fashion and introduced him by name to the audience. They responded with smiles and applause, even the folks listening from outside. Clark then announced the name of each neighborhood family, having them stand together so they could be properly introduced and recognized. Mr. Whittle nodded and smiled at them in turn.

After all had been presented, the new teacher was given the floor. Marty expected to hear a small voice to suit the small man, but she was surprised when a deep bass voice emerged.

Why, he must've practiced fer years to be able to do thet, she thought in amazement.

But Mr. Whittle's voice was not loud, and his audience had to listen carefully to hear his words. He expressed his pleasure at being selected to be the instructor in their school.

Ya were all we could git, Marty answered silently.

He told them he was charmed with the fine boarding place they had so thoughtfully provided.

She was the only one with room, Marty added mentally.

He was gratified to behold the fine facilities and careful selection of instructional aids.

Marty wasn't quite sure what he was referring to, so she let that comment pass.

He was looking forward to an amicable relationship with each one in the community, adult and child alike. He would look forward to making their further acquaintance, for he knew it would be both stimulating and intellectually rewarding.

Well, yes, sir! Marty felt like saying along with a salute, but of course she didn't.

Classes would begin on the following Monday at nine o'clock sharp, the bell employed at five minutes of the hour. Each child was to be seated and ready to commence the opening exercises on the hour. No tardiness would be accepted. Two recess breaks of fifteen minutes each would be given during the day, and an hour at midday to allow for the partaking of the noon meal and a time of physical stimulation for the students. Classes would end at three o'clock each day.

The children would get the benefit of his undivided attention and unsurpassed education, having been trained in one of the country's foremost institutions, recognized universally for its top-quality professors and its comprehensive and exhaustive courses.

He continued on in like vein for a few minutes more, but Marty's attention was diverted by Mrs. Vickers when she leaned toward Mrs. Stern and whispered rather loudly, "I hope he means he still is plannin' to teach."

Mrs. Stern vigorously nodded her assurance that he so intended.

The meeting finally ended with the community crowd giving the teacher a rousing round of applause, and he beamed on the group and withdrew.

Marty and the other women served the coffee and cake, and the animated visiting among the neighbors resumed. When she was finished, Clark sought out Marty to introduce her to the new neighbors on the Larson place.

The LaHayes seemed to be a nice couple. Mrs. LaHaye still looked thin and drawn but assured Marty she was feeling much better and was sure she'd soon be back to full strength. After an unspoken exchange between Marty and Clark, the LaHayes were invited to join the Davises for Sunday dinner the following day.

Mr. LaHaye said he was disappointed his journey west had been cut shorter than he had planned, but he was farmer enough to see the possibilities in Jedd Larson's good farmland. He had plans for building a new farmhouse and outbuildings, and he had already undertaken some much-needed repairs until he could replace them.

Tessie, their only daughter, was a bit plain but pleasant. Marty took to her immediately. Nathan, the older boy, appeared to feel smugly confident about his own wit and ability. The younger boy, Willie, had an endearing sparkle in his brown eyes. At the same time a hint of mischief alerted Marty there was no tellin' what this youngster would think to try next.

"How old are ya, Willie?" Marty asked.

"Nine," he responded good-naturedly. "I been in school before. Took three grades already."

Marty wondered if he thought that put him in a class by himself, for it was a well-known fact that none of the children in the area had as yet had any formal education.

"Guess ya'll be able to help the other young'uns here quite a bit, then," Marty said and watched carefully for Willie's reaction.

"Some of 'em," he said nonchalantly. "If I want to. Some . . ." He hesitated. "I might help *her*," he said with a grin, pointing a finger.

Marty followed the direction he pointed and noted with a bit of alarm that the "her" on the other end was none other than Missie.

"Don't expect she'll need more help than the teacher can give," Marty said firmly. "She's startin' first grade, an' she already knows her letters and numbers."

Willie shrugged again and continued to grin. "Might help her anyway," he said. Then he was off on a run to join the other children.

The LaHayes were leaving early. He had much to do, he told the Davises. Shouldn't really have taken the time off, but his wife fussed about gettin' the boys in school. Well, they'd better git on home. He had a pasture to fence to supply his cattle with better grazin'. Glad to make acquaintance. They'd look forward to Sunday dinner. He shouted for his brood—and then they were gone.

TWELVE

School Days

Instead of being bright and sunny as had been ordered, Monday dawned overcast and showery. Missie couldn't hold back a wail of despair as she looked out of the window.

"My new blue dress will get all wet," she cried. "An' so will my brand-new hair ribbons."

Clark came to the rescue by offering to hitch up the team to drive the girls to school. This idea met with unanimous approval, and Missie's cheerful disposition returned even if the sun did not.

Marty carefully packed lunches and supervised the combing of hair and cleaning of fingernails. She wasn't sure who was most excited, but it no doubt was a close race between Missie and herself.

Clark decided that Clare and Arnie could go along for the ride in spite of the drizzly day.

"They won't melt," he assured Marty, "an' it will be good fer 'em to feel a part of the action."

The breakfast prayer that morning included the three new scholars—that they would study well, show their teacher respect, and use what they would learn for the bettering of self and everyone they would meet, now and in the future.

After the meal was over, the excited group left the house, and Clark covered the girls in the wagon to keep the rain off their new clothes. Clare and Arnie, feeling proud and important, took their places beside Clark on the wagon seat. Marty felt a tightness in her throat as she watched the eager faces, taking particular note of Missie's shining eyes. And then they were off.

"First school, then courtin' and marriage, an' gone fer good," she said softly. "'Fore we know it, they'll all be gone—one by one."

She blinked her eyes quickly and turned back to the dishes. Soon Clark would return with Clare and Arnie, and all the work of their care and nurture would fall on her now that the girls were away much of each day. She must hurry through her tasks to be ready to spend much of this rainy day indoors amusing two restless little boys.

When Clark brought the boys back to the house, Marty changed them into dry clothes and made suggestions as to what they might like to do. She had thought she was prepared for what was in store but found it was even more difficult than she had imagined.

Arnie fussed and refused to be distracted with toys. Clare whined and pouted, insisting that he should be able to go to school, too. When he failed to convince his mother, he plagued her to let him go out to play. She pointed out the window at the wet landscape, but Clare only complained the more, seeming to imply that Marty could do something about the weather if she would just put her mind to it.

Marty finally gave them each a cookie. Arnie shared his with Miss Puss, then immediately undid all his generosity by deliberately pulling the kitten's tail. She responded with a well-deserved scratch to his hand. Arnie's howls brought Clare on the run. He chased the cat behind the kitchen stove and proceeded to poke at her with the broom handle. Marty sent Clare to sit on a chair while she washed the scratches on Arnie's hand.

By midmorning the clouds cleared away and the sun returned. Marty was glad to send Clare outside. She imagined him staying out only long enough to get thoroughly wet, but even that would give her some measure of respite.

As she suspected, the puddles drew Clare like a bee to flowers, but he played in them only long enough to become soaked and muddy. He stood at the door grumping that there was nothing to do. Marty despaired as she cleaned him up. Whatever would she do with them through this long, long day? And what if it rained tomorrow . . . ?

With noon's arrival Clark came in for lunch. The boys squealed with delight, and Marty breathed a sigh of relief. He could talk and play with them for a bit, and after the meal she could tuck them in for a nap.

But the usual naptime didn't go well, either. Arnie fussed and fretted, trying to climb out of his crib, and Clare never did go to sleep. So then they were cranky when she finally got them up.

The seemingly endless day finally righted itself when the three girls came home. Arnie ran to Nandry with a glad cry, and Clare began a list of questions for Missie to see if she really had learned anything. Clae stood by smiling demurely.

Marty had to raise her voice to be heard above all the chattering. "How'd it go?" she asked.

"Oh, Mama," cried Missie, "it's jest so great! Guess what I learned—jest guess. Here, I'll show ya."

"I want to see," Marty told her, "an' I can hardly wait. But first how 'bout ya all change yer school dresses an' hang 'em up nice." The girls quickly went to comply, anxious to be able to tell their news.

The time until supper was spent telling of the day's many activities. Only Nandry had nothing to offer. Missie jabbered on about the teacher, the other kids, the new work, her desk, and the poor fire in the potbellied stove.

"Know what? I don't think Mr. Whittle ever built a fire b'fore. From now on, Silas Stern is gonna build it. It smoked somethin' awful."

She stopped a moment to pet the cat. "I like Mary Lou Coffins. She's my favorite friend—'cept fer Faith Graham."

The Coffins were new to the area, Marty knew.

Missie continued, a twinkle in her eye. "Guess what?" she said in a whisper. "Nathan LaHaye likes Clae."

Clae blushed and protested but not too vociferously.

"He does, too," declared Missie. "He pulled her braids an' everythin'."

Marty had no idea what the "everythin'" might be.

Then Missie's expression took on fire. "But I hate thet Willie LaHaye. He's a show-off."

"Missie—shame on ya," admonished Marty. "We are not to hate anyone."

"Bet God didn't know 'bout Willie LaHaye when He made thet rule," Missie declared. "*Nobody* could love him."

"What did he do thet was so terrible?"

"He reads—he reads real loud, an' he reads everythin'—even the *eighth primer*. He thinks he's smart. An' he teases, too. He said thet I'm too cute to be dumb. He said he'd help me. I said, 'No, you won't,' an' he jest laughed an' said, 'Wait an' see.' Boy, he thinks he's smart. I wish Tommie was in school with me."

Missie tossed her head in a grown-up fashion, and Marty wondered where her little girl was, so suddenly replaced by this rather dismissive young lady.

Please, prayed Marty, *don't let school change her thet much—thet fast.* But the next moment the little girl was back again.

"Can I lick thet dish, Mama? I got so hungry today, an' guess what, Mama? Mary Lou has a shiny red pail to carry her lunch in. Could I have one, too, Mama? It has a handle on it to carry it by, and the letters on it are white."

"What kinda pail is it?"

"I don't know yet. I don't know the words, but it's so pretty, isn't it, Clae?"

Clae agreed that it was.

"Could I git one, Mama, please?" begged Missie.

"I don't know, dear—we'll have to see."

"I don't like carryin' my lunch in thet old thing," pouted Missie. "Mary Lou's is lots nicer."

"We'll see" was as far as Marty would go.

The subject of school was dropped for the moment, but Missie picked it up again after supper when she had her father's attention.

"An' Mary Lou has a shiny red pail fer her lunch—with white letters an' a handle. Can I have one, too, Pa, please?"

"Are shiny red lunch pails necessary fer learnin'?" Clark asked.

"Not fer learnin'—fer lookin' nice," Missie answered, her voice determined.

At least she's honest, thought Marty wryly.

"We'll see," said her pa.

"Thet's what Mama said," Missie objected.

"Ya have a wise mama," Clark told her with a grin.

Missie wrinkled her nose but said no more, no doubt figuring she'd best not press it further—for the moment.

⁓⁓

The days fell into a routine. Gradually the two little boys accepted the fact of the girls' absence and adjusted their play to include each other.

The girls settled into a pattern of learning. Missie, quick and eager, was soon leading her class, even without the help of Willie LaHaye, she was proud to note to her mother. Clae, too, had taken to school and surprised and delighted both the teacher and the Davises with her ability. She loved books and would have spent all her time with her nose buried in one or another of them had she been allowed to do so. Only Nandry seemed to drag her feet each morning at the thought of another day spent in school. Marty noticed it and wished there was some way she could help the girl. She knew most of the beginners in the school were much younger than Nandry and this in itself would be a discouragement to her. Marty endeavored to encourage without nagging at her.

Missie was the little busybody who furnished the household with all the news. One day she came home giggling, and Clae joined in.

"Guess what?" Missie announced. "When Mr. Whittle wants to yell loud, his voice goes from way down deep to a funny squeak." Missie demonstrated as she said the words.

Marty hid her smile, attempting to support an attitude of teacher respect.

"The big boys like to make 'im yell so it happens," Missie continued. "It sounds so funny, Mama, an' then he gits real red like an' growls real low—like this." Missie's six-year-old growl was rather comical.

"I hope ya don't laugh at yer teacher," Marty cautioned as solemnly as she could.

Missie looked sheepish, but then she raised her head to say, "Bet you'd laugh, too, but I jest laughed a little bit."

Missie also had frequent reports on "thet Willie LaHaye."

Willie LaHaye had dipped her hair ribbon in an inkwell.

Willie LaHaye had chased her with a dead mouse.

Willie LaHaye had put a grasshopper in her lunch box.

An' Willie LaHaye had carved her initials with his on a tree by the crik an' she'd scratched 'em out.

An' furthermore, she hated thet Willie LaHaye, an' she bet God didn't even care.

Thet dumb ole Willie LaHaye.

THIRTEEN

Somethin' New

When Clark made his next Saturday trip to town, Marty was glad there was no good reason for her to go along. She might have enjoyed the outing, being sure now that the girls were quite capable of watching over the others while she was gone. But going to town meant having to meet up with Mrs. McDonald. The woman never failed to get Marty in an emotional corner. Marty declared she'd rather face a bear or an Indian.

Actually, Marty had come across very few Indians since she had come west. Those she had seen or met in town or along the road seemed friendly enough. Most of the Indians in their area had moved on up into the hill country or had settled on a reserve set apart for them. Some wondered how they managed to survive, but most of the community told each other "an Indian is an Indian," and the prevailing opinion was that Indians were able to survive on very little. As long as the Indians were no threat to their well-being, the settlers were content to let them ride the hills hunting for meat and tanning necessary hides. On the other hand, they felt neither responsibility for nor obligation to the welfare of the Indians in the area. Marty was a bit uncomfortable with the general attitude but didn't quite know what to do about it.

As for the bear—Marty was glad she had never had reason to concern herself with one of those. Like the Indian, the animals were content to remain in their native hills, away from the smell and the guns of the settlers. Occasionally a neighbor lad felt he must venture into the hills and return with a bearskin to place on the cabin floor or hang above the fireplace. This was a symbol of the conquering hunter rather than a necessity.

Even when gazing at a huge fur hide in a neighboring home, the head still carrying the fierce beady eyes and the long yellow teeth, Marty was sure the bear was preferable to facing Mrs. McDonald. So Marty avoided town when she could, somewhat ashamed of herself for doing so, yet content in her weakness.

Since school had begun, Marty always looked forward to Saturdays. It gave her a chance to catch up on many extra jobs because the girls kept the little boys out from under her feet.

And this time she had particular tasks because tomorrow would be a special Sunday. The new schoolteacher was coming to share the Sunday dinner with them. Marty was both anticipating the visit and dismayed by it. What was this odd-looking man really like? Missie brought home both positive and negative reports—one moment praising him, the next critical of some unusual conduct, and the next breaking into uncontrollable giggles over what she considered silly deportment.

Marty had set her freshly baked pies on the shelf to cool and was carefully cleaning two young roosters when Clark drove into the yard.

As usual, his return brought the children running to meet him. Marty, watching from the window, saw Clark climb slowly and carefully down from the wagon. At first Marty was concerned, wondering if Clark had somehow been injured or was not feeling well, but he straightened up and walked normally as he headed for the house, the youngsters in tow. Marty noticed that he carried something inside his jacket—there was a bulge there and he seemed to be carefully guarding it as he walked. The children had spied it, too, and they clamored to see what he was carrying, but Clark just grinned and motioned them on to the house.

Now, what's he up to? mused Marty, shaking her head as she watched the little parade come in the door.

"What is it, Pa?"

269

"Whatcha got, huh?"

"Show us, Pa!"

Clark finally pulled back his jacket, and a tawny curly head poked out. Sharp little eyes blinked at the sudden light, and the commotion around him brought a joyful wiggle to the little body. Shrieks filled the air, and each of the children pleaded to be the first to hold the little cocker spaniel.

"We start with the littlest first," said Clark, handing the squirming bundle to Arnie. Arnie giggled as he held the puppy close. It was the first time Arnie ever had a face-wash from a puppy's warm tongue. He laughed out loud.

Little boys and puppies belong together, thought Marty. Arnie must have thought so, too, for he was most reluctant to pass the puppy on to Clare.

As the children enthused over the new pup, Marty found opportunity to speak to Clark.

"Where'd ya git 'im?"

"The smithie's dog had a litter. Jest big enough now to wean. This one looks like the pick o' the pack to me."

"Sure is a bright one."

"Yeah, an' look at the eyes, the head—looks like a smart 'un."

The children finally agreed to put the puppy down so they could watch it waddle and prance across the kitchen floor.

"Look at 'im! Look at 'im!" they cried, giggling and clapping at his silly antics.

"Well," said Clark, "let's take 'im out an' see what Ole Bob thinks of 'im."

Ole Bob was truly becoming *old*. His legs were stiff and unaccommodating, his eyes were getting dim and his movements slow. Clark and Marty had realized that Bob's days were numbered, but perhaps with care, he could be with them for a while yet.

The family followed Clare carrying the puppy out to the doghouse. Bob came out slowly, stretching his stiff muscles, and wagged a greeting to them all.

As the puppy was placed on the ground, Bob lowered his head slowly and sniffed. He didn't seem impressed, but he wasn't put off by the new arrival, either. The puppy, upon catching sight of one of his kind, went wild with excitement, bouncing and bobbing around on unsteady feet like a funny wind-up toy whose spring would not run down. Ole Bob put up with this ridiculous display for a few moments, then walked away and lay down. The puppy toddled after him and began to tug at his long, fluffy tail. Bob chose to ignore him as the children shrieked their delight.

Eventually the puppy was left with Ole Bob. Clark and the boys went to put away the team and unload the wagon. The girls, after filling the puppy's little tummy with warm milk, returned to the chores they had been assigned. The family needed to decide on a name for the new dog. This would be discussed and settled at the supper table.

Marty went in to finish washing the chickens and wipe off the cupboard top so Clark and the boys could place the groceries there for her to put away.

As she went through the bags and boxes, she suddenly stopped, a pail marked LARD hanging from her hand. "What's this?" she asked. "I didn't have lard on my list, did I? And you got three pails of it. I got lard stacked up high from our last butcherin'."

Perplexed, Marty picked up her list and glanced over it to see what she might have ordered that Clark had read as "lard."

"No," he answered evenly, "ya didn't have lard on the list."

"Then why . . . ?" Marty left the question hanging.

Clark was looking a mite sheepish. "They're red, ain't they—an' shiny—an' they have a handle—an' white letters?"

Then it dawned. *Missie's pail. Red and shiny with white letters—LARD.*

"Now, I ain't sayin' thet Missie should have thet jest 'cause she asked fer it," Clark hurried to explain. "No reason fer her to be thinkin' thet she'll always git what she's wantin' jest by askin', but iffen ya think it won't hurt none fer her to have it—like this once, then it'll be there. An'—well, I could hardly git her one an' not the other two—now, could I?"

"No, I s'pose not."

Clark turned to leave the kitchen. "Ya can decide," he said again as he left.

Marty turned back to the three red, shiny pails. Three pails of lard, and she already with more lard than they could use, and another fall butchering coming up soon. What would she ever do with it all?

"Ya ole softy," she murmured, but she was forced to swallow over the lump in her throat. The thought of the happy faces and Missie's glowing eyes when she passed them their lunches on Monday morning made it difficult to wait.

The chores had been done and the Saturday-night bathwater put on the stove to heat in the big copper boiler when the family gathered around for the evening meal.

"I thought iffen somethin' happens to Ole Bob, it'll make it less painful like iffen they have a new pup to fill their minds," Clark confided in Marty as she dished up the potatoes. She nodded.

Clark moved on to the table and saw to the seating of his family.

"Know what, Ma?" said Clare. "I stopped to see the puppy, an' it's all curled up sleepin' with Ole Bob. Does Ole Bob think he's the puppy's mama?"

Marty smiled. "No, I doubt Ole Bob is thet dumb, but as long as the puppy doesn't torment 'im too much chewin' an' chasin', Ole Bob'll be content to let 'im share his bed."

"He's so nice," enthused Missie. "I wish he could share my bed."

"Oh no," said Marty firmly. "Animals belong outside, not in."

"Miss Puss—" Missie began. Marty's eyebrows went up as she waited for Missie to confess that the kitty occasionally did climb into bed with her. But Missie must have thought better of it.

"Well," said Clark, "thought of any good names yet?"

"I think we should call 'im Cougar," said Clare.

"Cougar, fer a dog?" Missie sounded unimpressed.

"Thet's the color he is," argued Clare.

"I like King or Prince or somethin' like thet," said Missie.

"Fer a little puppy?" Clare was just as incredulous.

"He'll grow," Missie said defiantly.

"What about you, sport?" Clark asked Arnie. Arnie pushed in a big spoonful of potatoes and gravy with the help of his free hand. He shifted them around, swallowed some of the bite, and then answered, "Ole Bob."

"But what ya want to call the new puppy?"

"Ole Bob."

"But Ole Bob is the name of—Ole Bob," Clark finished lamely.

"I know," said Arnie. "I like it."

"Ya want Ole Bob an' Ole Bob," repeated Clare, obviously thinking only he was really capable of understanding and interpreting young Arnie's desires.

"Yeah," said Arnie, nodding his head. "Now we got . . ." Two rather potatoey fingers struggled to stand upright with the rest remaining tucked in. "Now we got two Ole Bobs."

The family laughed, but they all finally agreed that the new puppy would carry the name of Ole Bob, as well.

"He'll grow," said Missie sagely.

"Yeah, an' he'll git old someday, too," said Clare. "'Sides, when we call 'em, we'll jest hafta say one name an' they'll both come."

Clark smiled. "Save ourselves a heap o' time and trouble thet way, won't we?"

Arnie grinned. "Now we gots a little Ole Bob an' a big Ole Bob."

As it happened, big Ole Bob did not remain with them for long. As Clark had hoped, the loss of the old dog was much easier for the children to accept with the growing young pup running and nipping at their heels.

FOURTEEN

Tommie's Friend

Before it seemed possible, the school year was coming to a close and it was time for the summer break. Some of the older boys had left school early in order to help with spring planting. The rest stayed in class until June. Missie celebrated completion of first grade by bringing home bouquets of flowers and red ripe strawberries in the beloved red pail that had, over the winter months, lost a little of its shine.

Summer was full of work in the garden and enjoyment of its produce. Marty often looked around her as she and the children gathered its bounty and thanked the Lord for His blessings. Missie, Clae, and Nandry now used their pails when picking beans and corn and tomatoes. And summer, of course, was expecially busy for Clark as he and neighbors helped one another with their harvests.

Then it was fall again, with the excitement of school preparations. Poor Clare was still a year short of school age and grumbled about having to "stay home with the little kids." Marty wasn't exactly sure who all he was referring to, since there was just Arnie, but at least he didn't complain about it for very long.

Clae and Missie both were anxious to return to class. Clae had spent the summer poring over books that Mr. Whittle had supplied and was closing the gap to where she should have been. Mr. Whittle was pleased and told her so.

Missie delighted in learning, and she loved to read to Arnie and Clare whenever she could get them to sit still for a bit.

Only Nandry remained out of sorts about the whole idea of schooling. She didn't say much on the subject until school opening was just days away.

"I'm not goin' back," she declared, her tone boding no argument, "—not with all those little kids."

Clark and Marty discussed it privately and finally decided that, as much as they were reluctant to do so, they would allow her to drop out.

"We'll jest have to concentrate on the homemaking an' the baby carin'," said Marty. "Nandry has the makin's of a good wife an' mother. Maybe thet's plenty. An' at least now she can read and write some. And I can work more with her on the schoolin' here at home."

Clark nodded in agreement. At fifteen, Nandry seemed quite capable of caring for a home. Some area young man was bound to welcome her eventually as his helpmate.

It was easier this time to watch Missie heading out the door that Monday morning. And actually it was easier to manage the boys because Nandry was there to provide supervision. Marty was very pleased to see the rather withdrawn young girl beginning to blossom in an atmosphere of love and nurture.

Marty also welcomed Nandry's extra pair of hands because of the fact that in only two months the Davis family would increase again. With little direction, Nandry assumed the lion's share of the youngsters' care, taking them with her to feed the chickens, putting Arnie down for his naps—Clare having declared himself too big for such "baby stuff"—and in general assisting with the household duties. Marty greatly appreciated her help and often told her so.

Marty was sitting in the coolness of the cabin with a pile of mending one afternoon when she heard an approaching horse. She laid aside the sock she was darning and went to the window.

"Why, it's Tommie," she said over her shoulder to Nandry, who was rolling out a piecrust. "I wonder what's bringin' him out our way." She moved quickly to the door.

"Tommie," Marty called to him, "do come in. We haven't seen ya fer jest ages."

He came into the kitchen and nodded toward Nandry, who flushed and dropped her eyes back to her work.

"How're yer folks?" Marty wanted to know.

"Fine, we all are fine. Thet little Lizzie be growin' like a weed."

"Isn't she a sweetheart?" Marty said. The last time she had seen little Elizabeth Anne, she was practicing her newly learned skill of walking. The tottering steps were awarded with lots of praise, hugs, and kisses by doting grandparents and her young aunts and uncles.

Marty recalled with a pang that little Rett Marshall still was unable to sit properly alone. She took a long breath and turned her attention back to Tommie. "I hear ya got yer own land."

"Yep," he said proudly. "Even got a small cabin on it. Not very big, but it should make do fer a while."

"Farmed it yet?"

"Nope. I take over come spring."

Could young Tom be showing interest in their Nandry? Her thoughts were interrupted by Tom's voice.

"Mind taking a little turn outside? It's a first-rate day an' kind of a shame to waste it."

Marty quickly determined he was talking to her, not Nandry, and she reached for her shawl.

"Be glad to," she said. "Been wantin' to take a little look at the spring afore freeze-up. Nandry, you'll keep an eye on the boys?"

At the girl's quick nod, Marty led the way outside. Their conversation as they walked continued with news of weather, crops, and family. They reached the spring, and Tom sat down on the cool grass, his back against a tree trunk. Marty watched him, realizing from his expression that something was bothering him. Still Tom said nothing. She watched him pick up a piece of bark and break it with his fingers.

"It's 'bout a girl, right?"

He looked up quickly. "How'd ya know?" he asked.

"It shows," Marty said with a smile.

"Yeah, guess maybe it does."

He waited a moment, then said, "She's special, Marty . . . really wonderful. I . . . I had to talk to someone. Ma wouldn't understand . . . I'm sure she wouldn't."

Marty was perplexed. What did he mean?

"Maybe yer selling yer ma short," she wondered.

"No, I don't think so. Iffen she'd give herself a chance to git to know her . . . then she'd understand. But I'm afraid at first . . . thet's why I came to you, Marty. Ya know Ma. Could ya . . . could ya talk to her like, an' . . . ?"

"Is she . . . is the girl from around here?"

"Not really. She's . . . she's from back in the hills. She lives there with her grandfather."

"An' her name?"

"It's Owahteeka."

"O-wah-tee-ka . . . why, thet sounds like an—" Marty broke off her sentence as she realized what Tommie was telling her. "She's . . . she's an Indian girl," she finished quietly.

Tom just nodded.

"Yes, Tommie, I see," Marty finally said. Looking at the anguished face of the young man, she did not know what else to say.

She walked away a few steps as she tried to get things to fall into some perspective, but somehow she couldn't think through her muddled thoughts and emotions.

Dear Father, she prayed silently but fervently, *please help us work this out.*

When she returned to Tom, she chose a stump near him and lowered herself onto it.

"All right," she said, "I would like to hear about her. Where did you meet Owahteeka?" she asked, saying the unfamiliar name carefully.

Tom took a deep breath. "I met her last fall," he began. "The first time I saw her I was out looking fer a couple o' stray cows. They'd crawled the fence and gone off into the hill country, an' I went after 'em on horseback. I didn't find 'em thet day, but on my way home I found this here saskatoon patch, great big juicy ones, an' I stopped an' et a few. An' then I decided to take some to Ma fer a pie, so I took off my hat an' started fillin' it with berries.

"While I was pickin' I suddenly could feel eyes lookin' at me, an' I looked up, half expectin' to see a black bear or a cougar, an' there stood this girl—her eyes and her hair were black as a crow's wing. She was dressed in buckskin with beads, but what really hit me, she was laughin' at me. Oh, she was tryin' not to, but she was, all the same. Her eyes jest . . . jest lit up like, an' she hid her mouth behind her hand.

"When I asked her what was so funny, she understood my English an' said she'd never seen a brave pickin' berries like a squaw afore. Thet made me kinda mad, an' I told her maybe her braves weren't smart 'nough to know how good a saskatoon pie tasted.

"She stopped laughin' an' I cooled off some. We talked a bit. She told me her name—Owahteeka, meanin' Little Flower. Either way, it sounded pretty.

"Well, anyways, we met agin—many times. In the winter months I used to leave her venison or other game. She lives alone with her elderly grandfather. He couldn't stand the government reserve so moved back alone to the hills. Owahteeka jest shakes her head when I ask if I can go to her home ta meet 'im. He's old—very old. Actually, he is her great-grandfather, an' when he's gone, she won't have nary a person left. She says she'll go back to the reserve—thet someone will take her in or some brave will make her his wife. But I don't want thet."

He looked directly at Marty now. "Marty, I want to marry her. I love her. I . . ." He groaned. "How am I gonna tell Pa and Ma?"

Marty shook her head. Poor Tommie. Poor Ma. And what would Ben . . . ?

Marty stood up and pulled her shawl about her, feeling a sudden chill in the air.

"Oh, Tommie!" she said, shaking her head. "I don't know . . . I jest don't know."

Tommie, too, got to his feet.

"But ya'll talk to 'em? You'll try—won't ya, Marty?"

"I'll try," she promised. "But Tommie, ya know . . . ya know it's not gonna be easy . . . not fer yer folks . . . not fer her grandfather, either."

"I know." He swallowed hard. "I know, but I've thought it all out. I've got my own land, my own cabin. It isn't much, but she's lived the winter in a tent of skins. A cabin should seem good after thet. We won't have to mix much with folks. Our land is sort of off by itself like. We won't bother no one. She'll be close to the hill country—she loves the hills. And she can see her people some—"

"Yer not thinkin' ahead, Tommie," Marty interrupted. "Yer not thinkin' straight. Babies—family—what about that? Ya can't jest hide the young'uns away from yer families. Think about yer ma—how much she loves you, how much she loves her grandbabies."

Tommie's face dropped into his hands. "Thet's the only answer I don't have," he said, his voice so low she could hardly hear the words. "The only one. But . . . we'll . . . we'll work thet out when the time comes," he said, lifting his face to look into hers.

Marty didn't know what to say.

"Please, Marty," Tom begged. "Please try to talk to Ma. Iffen Ma can see it, she'll convince Pa. Please . . ."

Marty sighed. "I'll try," she promised, but tears filled her eyes. "I'll honestly try, but I'm not sure how good I'll be at it."

Tommie stepped forward and gave her an impulsive hug.

"Thanks, Marty," he whispered. "Thet's all I ask. An' . . . an' . . . someday I'll take ya with me to meet Owahteeka. When you see her, you'll know why . . . why I feel like I do. Now I gotta run."

He turned to go.

"God, please bless Tommie," Marty whispered as she watched him walk away. "And Owahteeka. . . ."

FIFTEEN

Search for a Preacher

A meeting of the community was called for on a Saturday afternoon in early October after the fall harvesting had been completed. All the neighbors were invited to attend and very few declined the opportunity to get together once again.

Zeke LaHaye sent word that though the meeting no doubt was a worthwhile one, he was hard put to keep up with his farm work and just couldn't spare the time.

The neighbors already had discovered Zeke LaHaye could spare no time from his farming duties—not to honor the Lord's Day, not to help a neighbor, not for any reason. Clark, who rarely made comment on a neighbor's conduct, confided to Marty, "Thet poor farm sure must be confused like—first owner Jebb Larson contents himself to let everythin' stay at rest; next owner nigh drives everythin' to death. Makes me stop short like an' look within. I hope I never git so land hungry and money crazy thet I have no time fer God, family, or friends."

Marty silently nodded a fervent agreement.

They gathered at the schoolhouse on the specified Saturday. Ben

Graham would be in charge of the meeting. When the noise of visiting had subsided to a lull, he rose to his feet.

"Friends and neighbors," Ben began, "I'm sure ya all know why this meeting has been called. Fer some time now our area has been without a parson. Twice a year we've had the good fortune of a visitin' preacher passin' through our neighborhood an' stoppin' long enough to preach us a sermon and marry our young men and women.

"We're concerned thet this ain't enough to give our young'uns the proper-like trainin' in the truths of Scripture. And us older folk need to be taught the Word of the Lord, too, and reminded what's important in life.

"A few of us met a while back and talked it over, an' we feel it's time to take some action. We has us a schoolhouse now. This here fine buildin' is a tribute to what we can do when we work together. Now's the time fer us to go to work together agin."

Some people began to applaud and others cheered. Ben seemed somewhat flustered by it all, but he soon recovered, cleared his throat, and went on.

"What we need to do at this point is to choose us two or three men to form a committee to look into the gittin' of a preacher. One thet will stay right here fer regular-like services, fer the buryin' an' the marryin' anytime of the year. For the preachin' of the Word."

Again people applauded. Ben looked to Ma for support. He must have been encouraged by what he saw in her expression, for he raised his hand for silence in order to continue.

"We're gonna take names now as to who ya would like on the committee. It can be two men—or three iffen ya like. Any more then thet makes it a bit cumbersome."

A man near the back stood and called for Clark Davis to be on the committee. Marty heard several ayes for the nominee.

Todd Stern named Ben Graham, and again people voiced approval and heads nodded.

Mr. Coffins then stood and in a loud voice announced Mr. Wilbur Whittle for the committee. Awkward silence followed. Marty guessed no one in the room knew what particular religious bent the new teacher might have. Finally feet began to shuffle, throats to clear.

Ben stepped forward. "Ya all have heard Mr. Coffins's choice. Mr. Whittle, are ya willin' to let yer name stand to help in the selectin' of a new preacher?"

Mr. Whittle rose to his feet rather grandly. "I believe I have many connections in the East that could indeed be of great assistance to the men on the committee," he offered in his carefully modulated voice.

"An' yer willin' to serve?" asked Ben.

"Certainly, certainly," agreed Mr. Whittle. "I believe that a resident minister will be a great asset in our community."

"Thank ya, Mr. Whittle." Ben looked around at the group. "Ya all have heard the three names given: Clark Davis, myself, and Mr. Whittle. What is yer pleasure?"

"So let it be," called a voice from the back of the room.

"We will vote," declared Ben. "Those in favor say aye, those agin, nay." There were no nays.

After the meeting, Mr. Whittle sought out Clark and Ben, nodding courteously to Ma Graham and Marty as they chatted nearby.

"Now, gentlemen," he began rather formally, "I am personally acquainted with many seminarians whom I have no doubt could fill our need quite adequately. Do you wish me to act as correspondent on behalf of the committee?"

Ben looked uncertain, but Clark answered, "I reckon you could do the letter writin' iffen ya wish. First, though, we'd like to know a bit 'bout these here fellas you'll be writin' to."

"Most certainly," said Mr. Whittle. "I shall draw up a résumé of each candidate for presentation, and you can select the ones whom you would want me to contact."

"This, ah, re-su-may," said Ben, "would thet be like an acquaintant-ship?"

"Acquaintantship?" inquired Mr. Whittle. Then, nodding rather vigorously, "Precisely—precisely."

"You go ahead an' do thet, Mr. Whittle," said Clark, "an' then Ben and me will go over thet list with ya."

"Fine, gentlemen, fine," said Mr. Whittle and strutted away looking quite pleased with himself.

The new teacher had heard so much back east about westerners not letting the easterner into the inner circle to become part of their frontier life. Yet here he was, out only a year and now serving on an important committee—a very important committee. After his contribution here, his place would be secure, he was sure.

He would go to his rooming house where he stayed at the Watleys, to his bedroom, close the door, and comb his memory for the best possible candidates he could recall. Scholars—he knew lots of scholars and some who would even be willing, just as he himself had been, to venture west to sample the excitement of opening a new frontier.

The West had its drawbacks, he was willing to admit, but there were compensations. One of them, in his case, being Miss Tessie LaHaye. Back east the young ladies had the less-than-cordial habit of turning away when they saw him approaching. Tessie entertained no such coyness. True, she was barely eighteen and he thirty-two, but in the West people seemed to quibble less over such social niceties. He was willing to accept her as a very pleasant young lady, and she seemed equally willing to accept him as an eligible man. In fact, he felt that she was rather impressed with his bowler hat and white spats. He planned to make a call on Miss Tessie—he hoped very soon, for he was anxious to discover just where he stood. And this meeting and his membership on the committee to find a preacher had given him the added confidence he needed. He no doubt would have to tread carefully, since Mrs. Watley clearly had her eye on him for her oldest daughter, but he surely would keep himself out of that quagmire, he assured himself as he sat down at his desk to begin his list.

SIXTEEN

Marty Talks to Ma

Marty put off the visit to see Ma as long as she could, but eventually she knew she must make the difficult call. Tommie was counting on her, and she had given her promise. Soon winter with its cold and snow again would make such a trip much more difficult to manage, and then she would be exhausted physically as well as emotionally.

What can I use as a reason to call on Ma? she asked herself but could come up with nothing. Finally she just decided to go.

Clark was heading for town for his usual Saturday trip, so Marty said, "Thought I'd trail along iffen it not be upsettin' anythin'."

He looked pleased. "My pleasure," he said. "Isn't often enough I git to show off my wife in town."

"Oh, I'll not be goin' on into town," she quickly told him. "I'm plannin' on stoppin' off to chat with Ma while ya be doin' yer errands."

His smile of pleasure faded a bit but not altogether. "Well, at least I'll have me yer company fer a spell," he said.

Marty informed the girls of her plans. Nandry seemed more than content to be in charge of the children and have the place to herself.

Marty put on her coat and tied on her bonnet. Her coat wouldn't button properly over her expanding waistline, so she had to be content with just pulling it about her.

Clark eyed her as she struggled up into the wagon, clumsy in spite of his helping hands.

"Ya sure this be the proper time to be takin' a bumpy wagon ride?" he asked.

"Won't hurt me none," Marty assured him.

She did notice that he drove more slowly than usual.

Ma's surprise at opening the door to Marty was quickly replaced by pleasure.

"I'm so glad ya came whilst ya still could," she said. Marty was relieved that Ma assumed her reason for coming was simply a social call and that this would be her last opportunity for a while.

They talked of this and that over cups of coffee, both women doing handwork as they chatted. Marty kept one eye on the clock, knowing she mustn't put her purpose for coming off too long. Finally she took a deep breath and began, "Tommie came to see me a while back."

Ma looked up, no doubt more at the tone of Marty's voice than the words themselves.

"He needed to talk," Marty explained.

Silence.

"A girl, huh?"

"Yeah. Ya knew about her?"

"I thought as much—it shows, ya know. He's got all the signs, but I can't figure it. He ain't said nothin' at all 'bout her. I've tried to lead in thet direction a few times, but he shies away."

Silence again.

"Somethin' not right about it? Is thet it, Marty?"

Marty swallowed hard. "No, not thet, really. Jest . . . well, jest different . . . yeah, different."

"Different how?"

Marty nearly choked as she took another swallow of her coffee to delay the inevitable. "Well, this here girl thet Tommie loves . . ." She paused a moment, then rushed on, "An' he truly does love her, Ma . . .

I saw thet by the way he talked . . . the way he looked. Well, this here girl . . . her name is . . . is Owahteeka."

Marty looked quickly at Ma, and she could tell immediately that she caught the significance. Her needles ceased clicking, her face looked pale, and her eyes held pain.

"Tommie?" she whispered.

"Yeah, well . . . ya see . . ." Marty now felt the need to hurry with an explanation. "Tommie wasn't lookin' for this to happen. Ya see, he was jest lookin' fer stray cows, out in the hill country, an' he stopped at a berry patch to pick some berries fer pie. An' . . . an' this girl was there, too, pickin' berries, an' they started talkin' . . . she does speak English . . . an' then they got to know each other better over the months like. An' . . . well . . . Tommie loves her. An' it sounds like she loves Tommie."

Ma laid aside her knitting and rose to her feet.

"But he can't, Marty, they can't. Don't ya see thet? It jest doesn't work. It always means sadness, sorrows—always."

"I see," Marty said slowly, "but Tommie doesn't."

"What did he say? Don't the girl's people care?"

"She doesn't have people—thet is, no one but an old man—a grandfather. They haven't told 'im yet. Owahteeka thinks . . . thinks it better to wait," Marty finished lamely.

"To wait, huh?" repeated Ma. "Then thet'll stop 'im from doin' somethin' foolish. Maybe there's somethin' more thet we'll know then?"

"I don't know," said Marty, trying to carefully feel her way along. "The way Tommie talked, I don't think the grandfather will be around long. An' . . . an' . . . I don't think she plans to tell him. Jest wait 'til he's gone—an' then go ahead. Thet's what I think," she finished in a rush.

"Oh, dear God," Ma prayed, nearly weeping, "whatever are we gonna do?"

Marty sighed and leaned back in her chair. Who was she to try to give advice to a woman like Ma Graham?

"Well, seems to me," she finally said, weighing every word, "ya have only a couple choices. Ya can fight it an' probably lose Tommie, or ya can come to terms with it and welcome an Indian daughter-in-law."

Marty tried to read Ma's expression as she paced the floor between the table and the stove. Suddenly Ma stopped and straightened her shoulders.

"Marty," she said, "I jest thought me of a third choice. I won't fight it an' I won't encourage it, but I sure am goin' to do some prayin'.'"

"Prayin'? How?"

"Prayin'—how do ya think?" The words tumbled out from Ma. "It jest won't work, Marty. An' I won't have my Tom hurt. Grandchildren thet ain't anybody's grandchildren 'cause they're neither white nor brown. It ain't to happen, Marty."

"Iffen ya pray like thet, Ma," Marty spoke quietly, slowly, "will ya be askin' fer help? For both of 'em? Or jest givin' orders?"

Ma's shoulders slumped and tears slid down her cheeks. She did not bother to wipe them away. Finally the battle within her seemed to subside. She sat down heavily in the chair across from Marty.

"Yer right—course ya are. I'd like to pray thet God would jest quickly put an end to all this. It scares me, Marty. Truly, it does. I jest feel thet no good can come out of it—no matter what. I'll pray—I'll pray lots, an' I'll try hard to say, 'Thy will be done' an' truly mean it. But I'll tell ya now, Marty, it don't seem ta me thet God's wantin' folks of different races to be marryin' an' raisin' young'uns thet turn out ta not belong nowhere. God ain't fer bringin' confusion of ideas or skins, far as I can tell—nor hurt an' pain of bein' shut out, put down. How can thet be of Him, Marty?"

Ma didn't seem to expect an answer and stopped her discourse. She sat rubbing her work-worn hands together in agitation.

"Me an' Ben gotta have a long talk on this," she finally said. "Then the two of us will try an' talk some sense into Tommie. He's a good boy, Marty, and he's got a good head on his shoulders. He'll realize thet this can't be good—won't be good for him or for her, either."

She wished that Ma had left just a wee small crack in the door instead of closing it so firmly, but Marty only nodded. She felt she had not done what she had come to accomplish, had nearly promised Tommie she would do. Maybe Ma was right. Who was she, Marty, to know the proper way to handle such a situation? And surely as Ma spent time in prayer, if she were wrong it would be revealed to her. But it might take time.

Poor Tommie. Marty's heart ached for him. Somehow she felt that no matter how things went, there was heartache in store for the boy. If only there were some way to spare him the sorrow. She hoped Clark was well on his way back from town. She was feeling like it would be awkward for both Ma and her if she stayed much longer for this visit. And she was anxious to lay it all out for him on the quiet ride home.

SEVENTEEN

A Call on Wanda

Marty was busy at the kitchen table making Clark's favorite dessert. Clare came in from outside, pulled up a stool, and stood on it to watch her work.

"Are ya mad at Pa?" came his voice at her elbow.

Marty stopped rolling the dough and looked at the boy. "Whatcha meanin'?"

"Thet's his favorite," explained Clare. "Ya always make his favorite when ya been mad."

He jumped down and was gone before Marty could even answer. He had laid the words out very matter-of-factly, as though they bore no consequence and needed no explaining. Marty frowned. It was a while before the rolling pin again went to work on the dough.

Do I really do thet? she asked herself. *An' iffen I do, does it show thet much?*

The fact was, she hadn't had a fuss with Clark at all. She was simply softening him up a bit to ask him for the team so she could pay an afternoon call on Wanda. Certainly Clark was not one to keep his woman restricted to home, but he did have some rather stubborn notions when it was nearing her confinement time. Marty easily could envision Clark wanting her to stay put for the present. Maybe his favorite dessert would put him in a more pliable mood, she had reasoned, and then this smart young Clare had come along. If he could see through her so easily, it was quite likely Clark would, too.

Marty shrugged and couldn't help but smile wryly as she put the dessert in the oven. Her menfolk maybe knew her just a bit too well. It possibly was foolish to think of venturing out right now, but she really felt she should have a talk with Wanda.

Gradually the news was making its way from neighbor to neighbor that something seemed to be wrong with the Marshall child, and Marty held her breath lest word of the rumors get back to Cam and Wanda. She knew there was not much she could do, but she hoped she could just learn if Wanda was aware that her small son was—different. Marty felt that Wanda's acceptance of the fact would be her own protective wall—the only thing that could shield her from the hurt if the neighbors' questions and comments did get back to her.

The dessert baked to perfection, and Clark must have picked up the aroma even before he stepped through the kitchen door.

"Umm," he called ahead, "apple turnovers. Makes a man's mouth water."

Marty smiled but still felt unsure about how she should proceed with her request. Nandry led Arnie in and washed him up at the hand basin, and they joined the rest of the family at the table.

The meal was pleasant but a bit on the rushed side. Clark had pressing work to which he wanted to return as soon as possible. Marty knew she must not waste a moment before getting down to business.

"Ya be needin' the team this afternoon?" she began.

Clark gave her a long look. "Ya plannin' on pickin' rocks?"

Marty felt warmth rise into her cheeks, but she bit back a quick retort and instead spoke quietly, her voice controlled. "I thought as how I'd like to take me a quick trip to see Wanda."

"It could be a mite quicker than you'd planned for."

Marty got his implication with no difficulty.

"Oh, Clark," she said with some impatience, "I been through this before. Now, don't ya think if my time was close I'd be knowin' it?"

Clark looked unconvinced. "As *sudden* travail cometh upon a woman," he said, looking at her with meaning in his gaze.

Marty was sure she had lost the argument.

Clark finished his coffee in silence and rose to go.

"Tell ya what," he said, stopping as he put on his coat, "iffen yer so set on seein' Wanda, I'll drive ya on over."

"But yer work—"

"It'll keep."

"But it's not at all necessary," Marty told him. "I'll be jest fine on my own. Honest, Clark, there's no need—"

"It's my drivin' ya or not at all—take yer pick," Clark said, his voice telling her the discussion was over.

Marty swallowed a lump of anger. *Yer so stubborn. Most as bad as Jedd Larson,* she shot back, though silently.

"All right," she said finally, her anger still churning her insides. "I'd be much obliged iffen ya'd drive me over."

"I'll be ready in fifteen minutes," Clark said and went for the team.

Marty turned to the table and vented some of her anger on the dirty dishes.

"Ya gonna make another apple dessert, Ma?" asked Clare.

Marty felt like swatting him.

"An' you, boy," she said instead, "you go out an' haul in some firewood. Fill up the woodbox—right to the top—an' be quick 'bout it, too."

Clare went. Marty knew she had been unfair. Clare was used to hauling wood, and goodness knew it wouldn't hurt him any, but she hadn't needed to take out her frustrations on him.

The ride to the Marshalls' was a fairly silent one. Marty still felt peevish, and Clark did not make any attempt to draw her out. When they arrived, Clark went on to the barn, where Cam was working on harnesses, and Marty went in to see Wanda. Little Rett lay on the floor on a blanket.

Wanda's eyes shone as she spoke of him. "He can sit up real good now," she told Marty and went over to demonstrate.

But, Wanda, Marty wanted to protest, *he's a year and a half old. He should be walkin'—no, runnin'. He should be runnin' after his pa and sayin' words. And here you are gloryin' in the fact that he can finally sit.*

But of course Marty did not say it. She merely smiled her approval at Rett's achievement as he teetered back and forth, trying to maintain a sitting position with his mother catching him when he was about to topple over. Wanda talked on enthusiastically, and soon the men joined them.

They were seated at the crowded little table when Marty felt the first labor pain. It caught her by surprise, and she stiffened and tried to breathe slowly and regularly. She soon felt normal again and hoped no one had noticed the episode. When the next one came a few minutes later, she felt Clark's eyes upon her and looked up to see him watching her closely. She knew he was aware.

Clark refused a second cup of coffee and said they really must be getting home.

Cam, still bragging about his boy, pushed back from the table and went with Clark for his team.

Marty smiled bravely as she bid Wanda farewell, and prayed that Clark would please hurry.

In short order the team was at the door, and Clark jumped down to help Marty into the wagon. They traveled home at a much brisker pace than they had made the journey to the Marshalls'.

"Are ya gonna make it?" Clark asked at one point, and Marty nodded, holding her hands tightly in front of her as another spasm swept over her. "I sent Cam for the doc."

Marty felt thankfulness flow through her. Her previous impatience with her husband's concern for her welfare now seemed petty and shortsighted.

The tiny baby girl arrived safely, in Doc's presence and in her mother's bed, at precisely five-twenty that afternoon.

Missie, Clare, and Arnie were all impressed with the little bundle. Clae and Nandry, too, gave an enthusiastic welcome to the new addition to the Davis family.

"Can we call her Elvira, Ma?" Missie asked.

"Iffen ya like," said Marty.

"Good. I read a story about an Elvira in a book of Mr. Whittle's. I think it's a nice name."

This was the first time Ma was not present at the birthing of one of Marty's babies. But in the days immediately following, Nandry took over the running of the household. Marty couldn't believe the young girl's efficiency.

"Nandry," she said as she rocked the baby after a feeding, "I jest don't know how we ever managed without ya."

Nandry gave a brief small smile and went back to her supper preparations.

EIGHTEEN

The New Preacher

Teacher Whittle took his new responsibility very seriously. He had drawn up careful descriptions of each likely pastoral candidate, including background, disposition, and education, and presented it to Clark and Ben.

From the eight names under consideration, the committee chose three they felt might be possibilities. Mr. Whittle, as the contact man, was commissioned to write the necessary letters. He did so with great flourish, describing in detail the community, the great pioneer fervor of its settlers, and their depth of religious conviction. The letters were sent off in due course, and the committee awaited the answers with a great deal of expectancy and some trepidation.

A letter finally arrived. The candidate appreciated their interest in him, and the position sounded indeed worthy, but after much prayer, he "did not feel the Lord leading" in their direction. Ben wondered if this meant the promised salary was not enough.

Then they heard from Candidate Number Two. He, too, found it difficult to resist such a splendid opportunity, but he was getting married in a month's time, and as his wife-to-be was a very delicate little thing, he felt he could not ask her to move so far away.

"Kinda likes his soft chair and slippers," mused Ben.

Candidate Three was finally heard from. He had considered the proposal with great care, had taken much time to think about it, and perhaps in the future he would be able to consider it, but for the present he was unable to give them an answer.

"So he's hopin' fer somethin' bigger," murmured Ben and struck the name from the list.

The other five were reconsidered. To Clark and Ben they didn't seem like the kind of men who would fit their needs, but the schoolteacher was sure of their capabilities.

"Take the Reverend Knutson here," he said with enthusiasm. "He has just graduated from seven years of study for the ministry. He would be a splendid minister."

Clark and Ben couldn't help but wonder what had taken him so long, but they finally consented to allow Mr. Whittle to contact Reverend Knutson, as well as a Reverend Thomas, whose name was also on the original list.

After some time, the Reverend Knutson wrote back to declare he was most eager to take the gospel to the people of the sin-darkened western territory.

With the prospect of a minister willing to come, a meeting of the community was called to make final plans and preparations.

The group decided to approve the selection and agreed that the pastor, too, would board at the Watleys'. Their boarder's room was a large one and could accommodate another single bed and an extra desk. Mr. Whittle was delighted with this arrangement. He could renew acquaintance with the good reverend, and it would be such a boost to his own morale to have stimulating conversation with someone of his own educational status. Really, there was a great lack of intellectuals in this community. Then, too, his calling on Tessie had been received with favor, and he was most anxious to have someone with whom he could discuss this new and exciting part of his life.

The Sunday meetings would be held in the schoolhouse. It would be cramped, but they could squeeze in, so long as there was no need to move about.

Everyone was full of excitement at the prospect of their very own minister. It would be so wonderful, so comforting, to have someone there permanently. In times of birth, death, or marriage, that's when a minister was needed—not just once or twice a year as he made his itinerate pass through the area.

Secretly, the teacher hoped it would not be too long before he personally would be standing before Pastor Knutson with his bride, Tessie, at his side.

True, he had a few things to work out yet—like where to live with a wife. He could hardly move her in with him at the Watleys', though the idea had occurred to him before it was planned that the minister would lodge there. However, he was confident these things would work themselves out.

Arrangements were made to bring the new parson out, and the people eagerly looked forward to the first church meeting. March fifteenth was the date set, and the winter months seemed to pass more quickly in anticipation of this important event in the life of the community.

⁂

Shortly after Baby Ellie had arrived, Ma Graham came to call. Marty was awfully glad to see her, not just to show off the new baby girl, but also to have a chance for a nice long visit. Chats with Ma were always full of news. Her face now was flushed with it.

"I declare, Marty," she beamed as they settled to cups of coffee, "I'm gonna have me another son-in-law."

Marty looked up in surprise.

"Really?" She caught some of the excitement from Ma. "Nellie?"

"Yeah, Nellie."

"I didn't know—"

"Not many did. Don't know much about it myself. Nellie doesn't say much, an' the young man—well, I'm still marvelin' thet he finally got it said, him being as tight-lipped as he is."

"Who—?"

"Shem Vickers."

"No! Really?" Marty laughed with Ma as she nodded in confirmation.

"Can ya 'magine thet!" Ma was still marveling about it all. "Never even really got to know the boy 'til the last few weeks. He's right nice—even if he don't have much to say."

Marty chuckled. "Don't s'pose the poor fellow ever had much of a chance to develop his talkin'. He sure oughta have first-rate ears, though—iffen they're not already worn out."

Ma smiled her understanding. "Yeah, Mrs. Vickers can talk 'nough fer a crowd."

"When's the weddin' to be?"

"Most as soon as thet new parson gits here. Prob'ly April."

Marty smiled and nodded. "Well, thet's really nice. I'm so happy fer 'em both."

Ma agreed. "Nellie been a right fine girl. I'm gonna miss her, but she's all excited like with the plans fer a place of her own."

"She'll make Shem a fine little wife, I'm sure of thet."

Marty passed Ma the cookies and then asked carefully, "Ma, have Ben and you talked over 'bout Tommie yet?"

Ma nodded, the smile fading some from her face. "Yeah, we talked 'bout it. Then we talked to Tom, too. Ben, he don't seem too upset 'bout it. Oh, he was at first, but then he sorta jest seemed to think—what'll be, will be. But I sure don't want Tommie hurt—nor the girl, either, fer thet matter. Oh, I wisht it were all jest a dream an' I'd wake up and it'd all be over."

Ma sat shaking her head, her eyes downcast.

"I'm sure thet it will work out," said Marty, trying to sound confident. "Tommie's a smart boy. Iffen it's not gonna work, he'll know it."

"Tommie is too far gone to see anything," Ma replied. "Never saw a young man so dew struck. Tommie wants to bring her to the house to meet Ben and me."

"Why shouldn't he?" Marty blurted out, then wondered if Ma would take offense.

"I don't know, Marty," Ma answered slowly. "Seems iffen we say he can, we sorta be puttin' our blessin' on . . . on the other, too. An' the other young'uns—sure thing they wouldn't be able to keep it quiet like, either—babble it 'round the school an' all. The whole area would know 'bout it. It's jest not a good idea—not good at all."

Marty ached for Ma in her uncertainties, but she also felt deep concern for Tommie. There just didn't seem to be any way through the situation without someone getting hurt—and maybe more than one.

"Ma, I think I'd like to have a chat with Tom again," Marty finally said. "Could ya send him on over when he's got a minute?"

"Sure—guess chattin' won't hurt nothin'—might even help some."

"Tell ya what," said Marty. "I'll send along a note with ya. Fer Tom. Thet be okay?"

Ma looked surprised but quickly agreed.

"It'll jest take a minute," said Marty, pouring Ma another cup of coffee as she spoke. "Ya jest enjoy yer coffee an' I'll be right back."

She went to the bedroom and found a sheet of paper and a pencil.

"Dear Tom," she wrote. "I think it would be good if you could bring Owahteeka to see me. Come next Wednesday, if you can. Your friend, Marty."

Carefully she folded the sheet and returned to the kitchen. Ma tucked the note into a pocket and made no comment. Marty knew the short letter would be handed over to Tom.

NINETEEN

School and Visits

The afternoon sun seemed weak as it shone listlessly on the winter snow. A biting wind had arisen, and Marty fretted over Missie and Clae tramping home from school in the cold.

She kept glancing nervously out the window for the two figures to appear, worried with a mother's heart that the cold might somehow detain them or return them home with frostbite.

When the two girls finally came into view, they looked cheerful and nonchalant, chattering together and not seeming to be in much of a hurry to get in out of the weather.

Marty met them at the door. "Aren't ya near froze?" she asked.

Missie looked at her with surprise, glanced around, then nodded with, "Sure is cold out."

"I know. I was worried."

"'Bout what?"

"'Bout you—an' Clae—comin' home in the wind."

"We're all right, Mama."

She shrugged out of her coat and had to be reminded to hang it on its peg.

"Here," Marty said, "I've heated some milk. Best warm yerselves up a bit."

The girls accepted the warm milk and the slice of cake that went with it.

"It was cold in school today, too," offered Clae.

"Yeah," teased Missie, "Nathan gave Clae his sweater to keep warm."

Clae flushed. "Oh yeah—well, Willie loves you."

"Does not," Missie responded heatedly. "I hate thet Willie LaHaye."

"Well, he don't hate you."

"Does too. We hate each other—him and me," Missie declared with some finality but sounding rather too comfortable with "him and me" in spite of her words.

"I don't think we should talk about *hating* each other," Marty murmured. Neither girl responded, and she decided another time was better for pursuing that lesson.

Next it appeared that Clae was changing the subject, but to Marty's dismay it turned out to be the same old one.

"Know what?" Clae announced. "Today we had honor time fer the two—boy an' girl—who got the best marks in sums and in spellin'. An' guess who got honored—had to go up front an' stand?" Marty noticed that Missie was shooting daggers at Clae with her eyes, but Clae ignored her and went on, "Had to stand right up there while everybody clapped. Guess who? Missie and Willie."

She gleefully clapped her hands together in demonstration and repeated, "Missie and Willie."

"I'm proud, Missie, thet ya got top marks," Marty interrupted, hoping to divert the conversation.

"Missie and Willie," Clae said again. "Bet ya get married when ya grow up."

"We will not." Missie bounded off her chair, spilling the remainder of her milk. "I'm gonna marry Tommie, Clae Larson, an' don't ya fergit it." She was in tears now, and as a final vent to her anger she reached for a handful of Clae's hair and yanked hard before she ran off to her room.

Now of course Clae was angry, but Marty's intervention was too late to stop the girl's initial indignant outburst. She tried to calm Clae, at the same time admonishing her not to tease Missie so much, reminding Clae that as the elder it was her responsibility to keep quarrels from starting but assuring her that Missie was wrong to pull her hair. Marty wiped up the spilled milk and went to talk to her daughter.

Missie was hard to convince that the hair pulling was not in order—a just dessert for Clae's teasing. Marty firmly informed her that it was not to happen again. The most difficult part of the talk came when Marty explained, as gently as she knew how, that Tommie was a man full grown and he might have other ideas as to whom he wished to marry. This was hard for Missie to comprehend. Tommie had always been her "best friend," she said, her voice trembling.

"I know," said Marty, "but best friends don't always grow up and git married. 'Specially when one is a grown man already and the other a little girl."

"Then I'll never, ever marry anyone," Missie vowed, "not iffen I can't marry Tommie."

Marty smoothed her hair and said she supposed that would be fine—but if Missie ever changed her mind, that was all right, too.

Missie finally wiped away the last of her tears and at her mother's bidding went to offer her apology to Clae. Within minutes the two were chattering away again as if nothing had happened.

❧

When Wednesday arrived Tom appeared at Marty's door. At her invitation to come in, Tom asked, "Would ya mind comin' out," he asked, "back to the spring? We'd rather see ya private like."

Clark was away, Ellie sound asleep, and Nandry had Clare and Arnie occupied, so Marty bundled up against the cold and followed Tom outside. The air was crisp but still, so the cold was not penetrating.

Marty and Tom moved along the path to the spring without speaking. Marty wondered just what to expect. What would the girl at the other end of the trail be like?

As she approached the appointed spot, a slender figure clad in beaded buckskins turned to meet her, a long, shining black braid over one shoulder. *She's beautiful,* was Marty's first thought as she looked from the dark eyes to the sensitive face. The girl's lips were slightly parted, and she stood there silently, no doubt taking Marty's measure even as Marty tried in a moment's time to measure her.

"Owahteeka," said Marty softly. It was not difficult to smile and reach out a hand. "I'm right glad to meet ya."

"And I," the Indian lass spoke carefully, "I am happy to meet you . . . Marty. Tom has told me much about you."

Marty's eyes widened in surprise.

"Ya speak English—very well."

"I went to a mission school when my mother still lived," she explained, showing little emotion about the matter.

"An' yer father—?"

"Is gone. I now live only with my grandfather. He did not wish me to continue in the mission school."

"I see."

Tom had moved over beside Owahteeka. His face shone with love and with some relief.

"Has Tommie met yer grandfather?"

"Oh no," she said quickly. "He must not."

"I'd like to," Tom interjected. "I'd like to talk to the old man, tell 'im—"

"He does not speak nor understand the white man's tongue," Owahteeka broke in.

"Well, then," said Tom, "at least I could shake his hand—could smile. And you could interpret—"

"No." Owahteeka shook her head firmly. "You must not. My grandfather—he would not wish to meet you."

"But Marty has met you. She's white an'—"

Owahteeka's dark eyes flashed. "The white lady did not lose her sons and grandsons to Indian arrows as my grandfather lost his to the white man's bullets."

Marty stepped forward and placed her hand on the young girl's arm. "We understand," she said softly. "I'm sure Tom will not try to see yer grandfather—not now, anyway. But can . . . can you *always* hide your love?" She waved a hand to include the two young people. "Can ya hide it from yer grandfather?"

"My grandfather is very old," said Owahteeka softly. "He is very old and weak. He will soon go to his fathers—he will not notice. There is no need to tell him."

"I see." As silence followed, Marty fumbled for the right words and finally just blurted it out. "An' you, Owahteeka, do you wish to . . . to marry Tommie?"

"Oh yes." The dark eyes softened as Owahteeka looked at the young man beside her. Tommie's arm encircled her waist. Who could deny the love that passed between them?

Marty swallowed a lump in her throat and turned to walk away a few paces. She came back slowly again. Her heart ached for the young people before her—of different culture, of different heritage, of different religions, of different skin color. Why had this happened? Why did they make it so difficult for themselves? What could she say or do?

She finally found her voice. "Owahteeka, I think I understand why you and Tommie love each other. You're a lovely, sensitive girl, an' ya probably know what I think about Tommie." She looked away a moment. "I . . . I wish I could feel thet . . . thet life will treat ya both kindly iffen ya marry. I don't know. I really don't know."

Marty looked again into the perceptive eyes of the girl before her. "But this I want ya to always know. Ya can count on me fer a friend."

"Thank you," whispered Owahteeka. Marty stepped forward and embraced the girl, looked deep into Tommie's eyes, and turned back toward the path to the house.

Tears fell down her cheeks as she walked. Her mind and heart swirled with contrasting emotions. She cared deeply about Tommy and now Owahteeka.

But if it hadn't been for Ma Graham with her staunch faith and her wealth of life experience from which to draw, would she herself have made it? Was it her responsibility now to offer consolation and counsel to the older woman? She didn't know if it was her place to interfere. But before she reached the house, she had decided. She wouldn't try to persuade Ma that this marriage was the right thing, but she would try to make Ma see that Tommie's mind was not going to be changed either by trying to talk him out of it or by resisting it.

TWENTY

Bits 'n Pieces

When Clark went to town the following Saturday, he returned with the sobering news that Mrs. McDonald was gravely ill. The doc, who had been faithfully attending her, reported her problem as a severe stroke. One side was paralyzed, her speech was gone, and she was confined to her bed in serious condition. Hope for her recovery was slim.

Mrs. Nettles and Widow Gray, from town, took turns with Mr. McDonald in round-the-clock nursing. The store was put up for sale.

Marty felt sick at heart upon hearing the news. She had never particularly liked Mrs. McDonald, and the news of her illness filled her with feelings of guilt and self-reproach.

Maybe iffen I'd really tried, she told herself, *maybe I could have found a lovable woman behind the pryin' eyes and probin' tongue.*

But there was little inward relief to her in the "maybes."

"God," she prayed when she had a quiet moment, "please forgive me. I've been wrong. Help me in the future to see good in all people. To mine it out iffen it seems buried deep. An' help me to love even ones where I can't discover some good."

She sent a roast and a pie along with her condolences to Mr. McDonald.

That was about all she could do, though it certainly wouldn't make amends for the past.

⊂✦⊃

Nellie's wedding plans were progressing favorably. Shem Vickers had found his tongue and was talking more than probably he had done in all his previous years. He seemed to take great pleasure in spreading the word that he was soon to be a groom.

Mr. Wilbur Whittle was also making progress with his courtship, but he had given up his hope of being the first one to escort his bride to the altar when the new preacher arrived. He still hadn't solved the problem of where to live, therefore had withheld asking the fateful question. Tessie, not understanding what was holding him back, was becoming rather impatient.

Mr. Whittle finally dared to approach the committee that served as the school board, requesting that a residence be built at the school site. He supplied them with a list of the reasons why such a move would be advantageous.

He would be there to watch the fire in the winter.

He would be available should a student require his services apart from school hours.

It would mean less time spent on the road, and he was able to list several other worthy grounds for his request.

None of the reasons he gave was the real one, but the board, after some consideration, decided that a resident teacher would not be a bad idea and voted to take out logs over the next winter to construct a modest but adequate teacherage come the spring.

It was a step in the right direction, but it seemed rather far in the future. Mr. Whittle had hoped for action a bit sooner. He deemed it wise, for the time, to hold his tongue as far as his intention toward Miss Tessie LaHaye.

And so the matter lay. Tessie didn't exactly give up—but she did do a considerable amount of complaining to her poor mother.

⊂✦⊃

Marty bundled Ellie against the spring wind and set off for the Grahams'. She felt the time had come to have her discussion with Ma.

With Missie and Clae off to school, Nandry would be keeping Clare and Arnie at home. *She should get out more*, Marty worried to herself. *She's getting to be a real loner.* But the company of the two small children seemed to be enough for the withdrawn young woman.

With a large family usually swarming through the Graham house, it seemed awfully quiet today. The youngsters were off to school and Tom was out working around the farm buildings, so only Nellie was left to keep Ma company during the day. Ma quickly laid aside the towels she was hand-stitching and came to take wee Ellie from Marty and unwrap her, exclaiming over her "darlin' little face, that soft-as-cream skin."

Ma looked up from Ellie to ask, "Did ya know thet Sally Anne be expectin' another—not till fall. This time Jason is hopin' fer a boy, though he sure wouldn't trade thet Elizabeth Anne fer an army of boys."

Marty smiled at the good news of an addition to the family. "How's Sally Anne keepin'?" she asked.

"Fine. She's busy as can be carin' fer Jason and thet girl of theirs."

Nellie had taken little Ellie as soon as her mother would give her up. After a bit she laid the baby in a cradle kept for little visitors—one small granddaughter in particular—and went to put on the coffee.

Marty oohed and aahed over all the household items Nellie already had prepared for her new home. Ma was piecing another quilt. Marty asked Ma who was anticipating the coming wedding the most—Nellie or her mother. They both laughed; enough of an answer, Marty felt.

The coffee was ready, and each of the three took up her sewing and prepared to visit.

They shared news from the neighborhood, expressed their concern for the McDonalds, and discussed in detail Nellie's coming wedding.

When there was a pause in the conversation, Marty brought up the subject she had really come to discuss. "Tommie came last week—like I asked him to."

Ma nodded. "Yeah, he said he'd seen ya."

"Did he also say he'd brought a friend?"

306

"No, he did not." Ma had stopped her sewing and was watching Marty.

"He brought . . . he brought Owahteeka with him."

Ma went even more still, and Nellie's needle also stopped.

"I asked 'im to," Marty hurried on. "I felt thet somebody should meet her an' get to know jest what kind of a girl she is. I knew it was awkward like fer her to come here, but it wouldn't be a problem jest comin' to my place."

Ma's eyes were asking Marty to quickly continue—to tell her what the girl who had captured Tom's heart was like.

Nellie said the words. "What's she like?"

"She's beautiful—lovely in every way. It's no wonder Tom has fallen so hard. She's tiny and straight as a willow. She's slim and brown, with big black eyes an' long black braids. She's educated, too—speaks English real good. She's polite . . . an' . . ."

"Oh, dear God!" whispered Ma, laying aside her sewing and bowing her head. "What are we gonna do?"

Marty stopped at the interruption and the three sat in silence.

Finally Marty said softly, "But she's sorrowin', too. She loves Tommie— I'm sure of thet. But I think . . . I think maybe Tom's the only white man she could love or trust. Her grandfather—he . . . he hates the whites and with good cause, maybe. He took Owahteeka out of the mission school after her parents were gone. Fer Tommie's sake, I think she tried to accept me, but the doubtin' was still in her eyes."

Marty waited, then said, "Still, she did try . . . fer Tommie. An' maybe . . . in time. . . . I jest don't know."

Ma had not lifted her head. She passed a careworn hand over her face. "Iffen I only knew what to do. Iffen I only knew," she murmured.

Nellie quickly said, "Don't seem no problem to me. Iffen they love each other, why shouldn't they marry?"

Ma looked up. "Indeed, young Nell," she said pointedly, "all yer seein' right now is love. Me—I see beyond—to heartache an' even shunnin' an' a family neither white nor brown."

Ellie fussed from the cradle, and Marty rose to get her. Had she said the right things? she wondered. Should she argue further for the young

307

couple? No, she didn't have the right, nor the wisdom, to know if it was proper. She had told them how she saw the Indian girl—Owahteeka's strength, her love, her doubts. Now Ma—and her Lord—would have to take it from there.

Lord, you know I've been talkin' to you 'bout this nearly every day, she prayed silently as she lifted Ellie from the cradle. *Please make your way clear to everyone—to Tom and Owahteeka, to Ma and Ben, to their families. An' yes, Lord, bless her old grandfather. Help him find you 'fore he dies. . . .*

TWENTY-ONE

Reverend Knutson

Ben took a team and wagon to the train stop in the neighboring town to pick up the new preacher and bring him back. Reverend Knutson would spend two days at the small hotel getting rested after his long trip, and then he would arrive at the Watleys', where he would make his home. Belle Watley was all in a dither. Imagine! Not only did she have the distinguished honor of housing the schoolteacher but now the new preacher, as well. Belle, however, did not believe in allowing her excitement to mean overexerting herself. Though her chatter and color were at their peak, she was still content to let her daughters do the bustling about in preparation for the pastor's arrival.

Word quickly spread through the town and countryside that they had indeed gotten "their man." The reverend was resting as planned in the hotel and would be picked up by the Watleys for residence at their farmstead the following Friday. This would give him a day to settle in and prepare himself for the Lord's Day and the first meeting with his new congregation.

The whole neighborhood felt the excitement, and early on Sunday morning the teams and wagons began to stream into the school yard. Even the less faithful members of the flock turned out, except for Zeke

LaHaye, though he allowed his wife and family a few hours off so they, too, could meet the preacher. There would not be sitting room for everyone, that was for sure. Fortunately the weather allowed for setting up some makeshift benches outside.

Marty was mentally prepared to see another rather small man like the teacher, thinking perhaps that was the way "they made 'em out east." The sight of the still-young Reverend Knutson provided quite a shock to all. He was tall, but that was not his outstanding feature. It was his size! And it was not the weight itself the reverend carried that was remarkable but how—or where—he carried it. He was hard put trying to cover his girth with his suit coat. His face was round and full, like a small replica of what was behind his straining coat buttons.

Seeing a round face raised the expectation that it should appear jolly—but not so the Reverend Knutson. There were no laugh lines there, no crinkles at the corners of the eyes.

Maybe he's still weary, Marty told herself. *By next Sunday he'll likely be more himself.*

The good reverend possessed a booming voice, both in word and song, and in spite of some of the hymns he chose being unfamiliar to the rest of them, the singing went well. His prayer, too, was very meaningful to Marty. It sounded as though he was on good speaking terms with the Almighty. Marty felt her soul moved and her spirit warmed as the congregation worshiped together under the leadership of Reverend Knutson.

The sermon left Marty somewhat puzzled, though. The reverend had a voice that was easy enough to listen to, but some of the words and ideas were unfamiliar and difficult for Marty to grasp. Just when she felt perhaps she knew what he was saying, she would get lost again. She chided herself for her ignorance and determined to check with Clark on the way home.

There was general visiting and introductions as the people filed out of the schoolhouse. Marty heard several comments of "Good sermon, Parson," and was more convinced than ever that she was terribly dull.

On the way home she put it to Clark. "Reverend Knutson's jest fine, ain't he?"

"Seems so."

"Got a nice voice that carries even to the outside, hasn't he?"

"'Deed he has."

"Sings real good, too."

"Fine singer."

"Clark—what *was* he talkin' 'bout?"

Clark started to laugh.

"Be hanged iffen I know," he finally managed through his mirth.

"Ya don't know, either?"

"Haven't a notion," said Clark. "Don't s'pose there be a soul there who did."

"Thought it was jest me thet's dumb," admitted Marty, and Clark laughed again.

"Well," he said, getting himself under control, "I think the good parson was sayin' somethin' about man bein' a special creature, designed fer a special purpose, but I never did get rightly sorted out what thet purpose was. 'Fulfillment of man's higher purpose' or some such thing seems to have come up more than once. Not sure what he's meanin'."

Marty sat quietly.

"Maybe next Sunday he'll explain," she said thoughtfully. She decided right then and there that she'd be praying for Reverend Knutson as he fit himself into the community and their needs. She truly wanted their children—all the children, actually—to receive further spiritual nurture and training now that they had a regular pastor.

Marty was clearing away the supper dishes when she heard a lone horse approaching. Tommie swung down from the saddle, appearing to be in a great hurry. Marty prayed that nothing was wrong as she rushed to the door to meet him.

His face was white and drawn and there was a determined set to his chin.

"Can I see ya?" he asked, his tone as tense as his expression.

"Of course, Tommie," she said, drawing him inside, then asking quickly, "Tommie, what's wrong?"

311

"I'm leavin'."

"Leaving! Fer where? Why?"

"I'm goin' west."

"But why?"

"I got a note this afternoon from Owahteeka. We were to meet as usual, but she wasn't there. I waited an' waited an' I got worried, an' then jest as I was gonna go find her—grandfather or no—I spotted these stones piled up—an' in 'em a letter."

He shoved the crumpled paper toward Marty, and she took it with trembling fingers.

Dear Tommie,

Grandfather must have learned of us. He is taking me back to the reservation. Please don't try to follow. It would mean danger. I am promised to Running Deer as his wife.

Owahteeka

"Oh, Tommie!" Marty whispered. "I'm so sorry." She now understood the anguish in the young man's face.

Tom shuffled around, and Marty realized he was fighting for control of his emotions.

"But why . . . why go away?" she finally asked him.

"I won't stay here." There was bitterness in his voice. "This is jest what Ma wanted. She should be happy now."

Marty laid a hand on his arm, feeling the muscles tense with his anger and grief.

"Tommie, no mother is ever happy when their young'uns are in pain. Can't ya see thet? Oh, I know Ma was worried, worried 'bout you an' Owahteeka. She didn't feel it was right. But yer hurtin', Tommie—an' yer sorrow will never make her happy. She's gonna be in terrible pain, too, Tommie—truly she is."

Tommie wiped the back of his hand across his face and half turned from Marty.

"I still gotta go," he said eventually, his voice hoarse. "I jest can't stay here—thet's all. Every day I'll think I see Ma lookin' through me, sortin' me out, wishin' me to find another girl. . . ."

"I see," Marty answered gently.

"I left 'em a note. Didn't say much. You tell 'em, will ya, Marty? Try to tell 'em why I had to go."

Marty couldn't speak over the lump in her throat but agreed with a nod of her head. "Be careful, Tommie, ya hear," she whispered, "an' write a note now and then, will ya?"

He nodded but said nothing further. He turned and was gone. Marty was left standing in the doorway, watching him go, while tears streamed down her cheeks.

TWENTY-TWO

Life Moves On

Tom's departure was very hard on the young Missie. His family and friends were left with deep inward sorrow because of it, but along with the pain in Missie's heart was deep confusion. It was simply beyond her comprehension that Tommie would choose to leave everyone—to leave her. Marty tried to explain, but her efforts were in vain.

Ma's aching heart was hidden by the attention and activities required for Nellie's wedding. Marty watched her bustling about, organizing everything that needed to be done, but she knew beneath Ma's smile and her instructions to everyone within sight and sound was a mother's heart broken for her grief-stricken son.

When March was torn from the general store calendar and discarded, April promised new growth, new life, new vigor. Nellie plunged into the last-minute preparations with flushed cheeks and a beaming face.

"Do folks always smile when they gonna marry?" Clare wondered after a Sunday morning service in which he had spent more time watching those around him than listening to the reverend.

Marty chuckled. "Mostly," she said, "mostly they do."

Clare shrugged and let it go at that. The "why" of the whole matter quite escaped him.

Reverend Knutson had by now presented five sermons to his congregation, and Marty had long since given up on any reasonable explanation of his meaning. Others seemed to have given up, also, and a few of the less ardent families had ceased to attend. The schoolroom was still overcrowded, however, and the worship service wasn't always as worshipful as many wished it to be.

Marty did wish the reverend weren't quite so educated, so formal. She longed so much for spiritual nourishment, similar to what she found during the daily Bible reading with Clark and their family. Sunday by Sunday she went home feeling uncertain and agitated. She was sure she was hearing truth in those fancy phrases, but she did wish that truth could be presented in a way she could take home with her and apply to her life.

The Davis family had invited Reverend Knutson to join them for a Sunday dinner. Never had she seen a man tuck away as much fried chicken or mashed turnips. She of course said nothing and continued to pass the serving bowls his way, but when she saw Clare watching him in wide-eyed disbelief, she suppressed a giggle and quickly diverted Clare's attention lest he blurt out some embarrassing remark.

Marty and Clark talked about the situation over those early weeks. They decided to accept their new minister—accept him for who he was, for whom he represented, for what he had come to do. He had come a very long way to teach them from the Bible, and certainly they could open their hearts to the Word of God and trust Him for the rest.

When school began again that fall, along with the girls trudged small Clare, self-confident and assured. His only concern was how Clark would manage the farm without him. But when Clark told him he supposed he could make do—he had Arnie now—Clare nodded reluctant agreement.

He was full of tales of school, often about some lark or humorous playground happening or classroom mishap. Missie occasionally accused him of being a downright tattletale, but that did not dampen Clare's enthusiasm for a good story.

One day Marty sat in the quietness of the house knitting a new pair of mittens before winter set in. Nandry was off picking blueberries in the far pasture, Arnie was "helping" his dad, the three school children were at school, and Baby Ellie was having her nap.

Marty's thoughts turned to Wanda. By now the whole community was aware that little Rett was not progressing normally—everyone, it seemed, but Wanda and Cam. Marty's heart felt heavy as she thought of the boy. Though finally walking on his own, he still did not attempt to speak, and it was evident he would never be like other children.

Cam still boasted about his son. "See how big and strong he is?" he would ask anyone within earshot. How would he take it, Marty wondered, when he finally realized the truth?

Marty was surprised to look up from her thoughts to see Wanda herself driving into the yard. She had brought Rett with her, and he sat upright beside her on the wagon seat, delightedly holding the end of the reins beyond where she grasped them.

Wanda tied the team and lifted the big boy down. He shuffled about the yard and became excited at the sight of Ole Bob. The boy and the dog soon became acquainted.

Then Wanda took the boy's hand and led him toward the house. He did not protest, but he did not show any eagerness, either.

Wanda wasted no time with small talk. "I had to see you, Marty," she began. Marty noticed her quivering chin.

"I know the neighbors are all talking about Rett being different," she said, her voice shaking. "I know they are. I know, too, that they think . . . they think Cam and I aren't aware. We know, Marty, we know. I guess I've known from the time Rett was a tiny baby. Oh, I hoped and prayed that I'd be wrong . . . but I knew. For a while I wondered . . . I wondered about Cam. I wondered when he'd learn the truth . . . how he'd feel when he did. And then . . . one night . . . well, he just spilled it all out. He'd known, too."

Wanda stopped and her hand went to her lips. She took a deep breath, then went on, "Marty, have you . . . have you ever seen a grown man cry? I mean really cry? It's awful . . . just awful."

Wanda wiped away her tears, took a breath, and continued, her voice stronger now. "I felt I just had to share with someone . . . someone who would understand. It was hard at first . . . really hard. But, Marty, I want you to know I wouldn't change it, not really. He has brought us so much joy. You see"—she looked at Marty, the tears glistening in her eyes—"I asked God so many times for a baby. And . . . and He's given me one—a boy that will, in some respects, never grow up. Now, can I fault God for answering my prayer? I don't suppose, Marty, that Rett will ever leave me, not even for school. I have . . . I have my baby . . . for always."

"Oh, Wanda." Marty went to put her arms around her friend, and they wept together. When their tears had washed through the grief, they were able to talk of other things.

Rett played contentedly with the building blocks, pushing them back and forth on the kitchen floor, for he couldn't seem to succeed in stacking them.

TWENTY-THREE

Church and Family

The small log teacherage was built the following spring, and Mr. Wilbur Whittle and his bride moved into their new little home. The community had long since realized the true reason for Mr. Whittle's insistence on a home of his own near the schoolhouse, for immediately after receiving assurances it would indeed be built, he asked for the hand of Miss Tessie. The community smiled its approval, and as the finishing touches were put on the teacherage, Reverend Knutson did the honors of pronouncing the couple husband and wife.

Among the members of the community, though, was a growing dissatisfaction with the Sunday morning worship service. Rather than laying the fault on the "learned man" and his lofty sermons, the people instead felt the problem was related to the place of meeting. The school was crowded, the seating was inadequate, and there was no place to take fussing children. That the situation was not conducive to worship was the thrust of neighborhood discussions.

In between the planting of crops and the haying season, a meeting was organized to discuss the matter. The turnout was strong, and many expressed their feeling that the community was in dire need of a proper church. Then followed a lengthy discussion as to where this building should be located. Several generously offered land, but the group finally decided the most central location would be a corner of the Watley farm. Come fall, a group of volunteers would pace off and fence the area. Another group would take up the task of log count. Then throughout the winter months, men and horses would strain and sweat getting the lumber transformed from tall standing timber in the hills to stripped logs in ever-increasing piles at the building site. Clark would oversee the job of sorting the logs to make sure the number snaked in would be adequate for the building.

Wooden benches would satisfy the seating of those full-grown men who had, Sunday by Sunday, been forced to squeeze their tall frames into desks created for fifth graders. An altar would provide a place where those with spiritual needs could bow in prayer, and the Word of God would be proclaimed from a specially fashioned pulpit.

All of the plans drew great excitement from the group, and all went home from the meeting with spirits lifted. Now they were finally getting somewhere. Their worship time surely would have a better chance of meeting their needs with an appropriate gathering place. The church would be much larger than the schoolhouse. It would have two side rooms, one where the children could be taught in a Sunday school class and a smaller one where crying babies would not disturb the rest of the congregation.

The reverend seemed to agree with the plans, though he did not show any particular enthusiasm. He was quick to inform the group of the great number of hours needed in his study for the purpose of preparing himself for his Sunday sermon. The clear message was that it was fine with him as long as he was not called upon for some such task as log cutting.

So be it, the planners concluded. After the crops had been harvested and the fall work completed, the menfolk took to the wooded hills. Their family's wood supply had to be secured first, and they were in a hurry to complete the task so they could start tallying up the logs for the new church.

As the winter wore on, each day that was fit for man and beast to be out carried the sharp sound of axes and the crashing of large timbers.

Gradually the piles of logs at the site grew, and Clark, who was keeping the tally and overseeing the peeling, reported to Marty the steady progress they were making.

With the spring thaw, large piles of naked, steaming logs lay in the warm spring sun. A day in May was set aside for the church raising. Because it was special and larger than most of the buildings they had erected, the men knew the church would take more than one day to see completion, but the first day would give them a sense of direction, the raw outline with which to work.

The community met on the appointed day, and the men set to work, grouping rather naturally into teams for the various endeavors required to put up their meetinghouse. The women chatted and cooked and chased hungry children out of the food set aside for dinner. By evening as the farmers headed for home to their waiting chores, the walls of the church stood stout and strong. Those who could take the time agreed to come the next day to work again on the building. The important things now were to get the roof on, the windows in, and the door hung. The finishing on the inside would be done throughout the spring and summer as men could spare the time.

By fall their church stood tall, even bearing a spire pointing one and all to heaven. "Only a bell is lacking," noted some who remembered such traditions back east.

To the east of the church a cemetery was carefully staked out. As she watched the men plotting the area, Marty wondered if any others carried the same question in their hearts: *Who would be the first to be laid to rest there?*

She tried to brush it aside, but in spite of herself her eyes traveled over her neighbors. She loved them. She did not want to lose any of them. Then she caught sight of her own family, and she found herself choking up a bit.

I'm bein' silly, she scolded herself. *Our lives are all in God's hands. He'll do the choosin'.*

She went to join Clark, who was attempting to hold a squirming Ellie as she tried to get down to run with the rest of the small fry. *Yes, Lord,* Marty prayed silently as she watched the toddler go after a ball that came her way, *we're all in your care. We'll do our best to be careful and wise, but you are the one who's watchin' over us all.*

The dedication of the new church would take place on the first Sunday in October. They all decided they'd make a real celebration of it and bring in a potluck meal.

When the great day arrived, the wind was blowing and the sky was overcast, making the day less favorable than desired, but Marty was thankful that at least there was no rain falling.

She packed with care the food she had prepared and made sure her family was warmly clothed against the weather. As usual, Arnie was hard to corner long enough to be sure he was properly buttoned with cap firmly on his head. "I ain't cold," he muttered as they went to the wagon for the trip to the church.

A larger-than-usual crowd poured into the churchyard, full of great expectation. They now had a church in which to worship.

The congregation enjoyed singing the familiar hymns. By now they also knew some of the new songs the reverend had brought with him.

The prayer was long and elaborate. Marty found herself praying her own more simple one that met the need of her own heart.

Then began the dedication service for the new building. Clark, Ben, and Mr. Watley each had a part. Marty thought it was beautiful, and her heart swelled with pride as she watched Clark participate.

Now ya watch yer pa, her expression said to their youngsters sitting on either side. *See how straight he stands—how steady his voice—how proud he is to be a part of God's people. Watch yer pa.* They seemed to catch her meaning, and even little Ellie sat silent on her mother's lap, earnest eyes fastened on Clark's face.

Oh, dear God, make it special. Make it a time for feedin' our souls, Marty prayed when the sermon began. But the dear reverend hadn't gone far into the message before she realized she was going to again be disappointed. She settled back to hear out the sermon with at least attentiveness if not with understanding.

The reverend must have felt the sermon on such a splendid occasion also should be special, so he had prepared an extra long one.

Children were beginning to fidget, and Marty couldn't help but feel that some fathers probably felt a bit envious of the mothers who got to take them into the new crying room.

At last the sermon ended, and the congregation stood for the closing hymn. The people filed from the building—the men to gather in small clusters, the children to stretch muscles cramped from so long a time unused, and the women to put out the noonday meal.

In spite of the long service and the unfriendly weather, it turned out to be a very pleasant time spent together. As true among friends, there was frequent good-natured banter, babies were passed around and exclaimed over, news from town and community was exchanged. It was a good day.

A short note had arrived from Tommie. It was the third time the Davises had heard from him. With each letter Marty breathed a prayer of thanks that he was still safe. This letter told them he was doing fine. He planned to stay where he was for the winter—working in a lumber mill. Thought he would push on farther west come spring. Maybe even to the coast. Hadn't had himself a look at the ocean yet. He sent his love.

The envelope showed no return address, and even the postage stamp was blurred, so they were none the wiser as to his whereabouts. Marty had hoped to respond in writing, letting him know they wished him well and hoped he would soon be returning home.

Marty read the letter aloud at mealtime with their family around the table. Clark had already read it previously, but she could tell he was listening carefully as she read it again. She could see his relief and his care for the young lad in his expression.

The long months since Tom had left had erased much of the sorrow from young Missie's heart. She now seemed to think little about the young man who was suddenly gone from her life—the one she had childishly pledged herself to marry.

Marty looked with interest about the table at each of them. Actually, they all had changed during the time since Tom had left. She supposed he had changed, too.

Nandry, now a young lady, was still quiet, though always industrious.

Marty had eventually given up attempts to get close to the reserved girl and accepted her as she was. *Bless her heart,* thought Marty, *in her own way she's fit into our family.* A small smile touched her lips as she silently noted, *She's been worth her keep an' thet ten dollars over and over again.*

Marty was well aware that Nandry would likely be moving along into adulthood and her own home before long. At least two of the neighborhood boys were busy studying the girl, Marty had seen. And, Marty observed, Nandry's cheeks flushed and an unusual twinkle sparkled in her eye at the attention.

Clae, too, was almost a young lady. She was nearing the completion of her education in the one-room school but not anywhere near the end of her hunger for knowledge. Marty and Clark had lain in bed nights quietly discussing her future. Her burning desire was to become a teacher, and Clark felt that even though many dollars would be involved, Clae should be given the opportunity. She would have to go away to continue her education and get her teaching certificate. As much as Marty yearned for Clae's happiness, she dreaded the thought of her leaving them.

Missie was eleven now—still a bundle of energy that was one minute a little girl and the next minute stretching toward womanhood. She loved school; in fact, Missie welcomed each new venture whether at home, on the farm, or in the classroom. She still did not like Willie LaHaye, she announced occasionally.

Clare, at nine, was a bright boy who still preferred *doing* to learning, though there was nothing wrong with his ability in either area. He still mimicked Clark and watched carefully to see how his pa handled situations.

So it's been more'n nine years, Marty continued her musings, *since Clark rescued me at the side of a broken-down wagon and a fresh-dug grave.* . . . But she didn't linger long with those memories. She could feel Clark's eyes watching her, and she turned to look at him and share a smile across the table. He still insisted "if there was any rescuin' to be doin', it was Missie and me that needed it."

Marty now turned back quickly to snatch Arnie's cup of milk from the edge of disaster. At almost six, he was their outgoing and very busy little boy, and scrapes of various kinds seemed to follow him around. He was going to be allowed to attend school this fall, which Marty was anticipating with mixed emotions.

Three-year-old Ellie was a small bundle of brightness in everybody's life. Happy and playful, she darted among them like a small butterfly, enriching the lives of all she touched.

In the family cradle rested new Baby Luke. More than once Marty had sincerely thanked God for Nandry's help since the arrival of little Luke, for unlike her others, this baby was a fussy one, demanding attention just at the time when a mother was the busiest. Nandry did her best to comfort the cranky infant.

My family, thought Marty, once more looking round the table. *My strange, wonderful family.* Lest she become teary-eyed with emotion just thinking of each one, she herded her thoughts back to safer ground and went on with her meal.

"Saw Cam today," Clark said between mouthfuls of food.

"Did ya?"

"He had Rett with 'im. Do ya know thet thet boy can already handle a team? Should've seen Cam. Proud as punch. Says Rett's gonna be the best horseman in these here parts. Might just be, too. Seems to be a natural with animals."

"Isn't thet somethin'." Marty marveled at the good news.

"Cam says he wouldn't be none surprised to see thet lad take 'im on the tamin' of even a bear. Never says a word, but he seems to make the animals understand 'im.

"Mr. Cassidy at the store says Cam never comes to town but he brings Rett either on the wagon beside 'im or up in front of 'im in the saddle."

Clark seemed to be deep in thought for a moment. "Funny thing," he then said, "Cam's changed. Watchin' 'im move about town with his son, I noticed a thoughtfulness 'bout 'im. He ain't thinkin' jest on Cam Marshall no more. I think others note it, too. Seem to have new respect fer 'im someway. Thought as I watched 'im leavin' town with thet boy up there beside 'im handlin' the reins, 'There goes a real man.'"

Marty nodded, her eyes misting over a bit, but mostly her thoughts were of Wanda and the happiness she would feel in having given Cam a son he could love and proudly bring with him to town in spite of his difficulties.

"Did ya happen to see Mr. McDonald when you were in town?" she asked. Mrs. McDonald had passed away two years previously, having never recovered from her stroke. Mr. McDonald had decided after her funeral to sell the store to Mr. Cassidy and return east, but time had brought him back to the area.

"Yeah. Saw 'im sittin' on the bench out in front of the store with Ole Tom and Jake Feidler. Didn't talk to 'im much more'n a howdy."

"How'd he seem?"

"Pretty good. I think he be right glad to be back. He jest didn't feel to home there," Clark went on to explain. Mr. McDonald had taken a room at Mrs. Keller's boardinghouse and now spent his days chatting, whittling, and spitting tobacco juice out in front of his old store. Mr. Cassidy didn't seem to mind, though Mrs. Cassidy was probably tired of scrubbing the steps.

Marty fleetingly wondered what it would be like to return east after having been away so long. Her own pa was gone now, and her ma lived alone. They kept in touch, though mail delivery meant the letters they exchanged were sometimes far between. Marty did try to keep her posted on each new grandchild and to send her greetings at Christmastime.

No, she was sure she wouldn't feel at home back east anymore, either.

She gently but firmly moved Arnie's fingers away from the butter and gave him a piece of buttered bread. The years had brought so many changes—most of them good ones, she decided.

Young Josh Coffins was the first to show serious intentions toward Nandry. Marty knew it was bound to come, and she welcomed it and despaired over it at the same time. She knew Nandry longed for a home and family of her own, yet the Davis family would have a large hole in it without her. Marty and Ma Graham had some long chats about these kinds of changes in a family and how to set one's heart and mind on the good.

Josh approached Clark after church one Sunday to ask permission to call.

"Sure thing, Josh," Clark said, clapping the young man on the shoulder, "I'd be most happy to have ya drop by to see me. Reckon we could have us a quiet talk—maybe out in the barn where we'd not be interrupted by small fry and women." Clark did enjoy his teasing.

Josh reddened and stammered as he tried to explain that wasn't really what he had in mind. Clark laughed and once more good-naturedly slapped him on the back, and Josh realized that he'd been "had."

Josh laughed at the joke on himself, and he appeared to feel good that this respected man of the community would take time to joke around with him.

"Yer welcome to come," Clark said more seriously, "an' I promise not to be holdin' ya at the barn."

Josh grinned, muttered his thanks, and walked away. Marty lingered nearby, furtively watching his approach to Nandry. He came up to her as she sat on the church steps, several youngsters around her. Baby Luke was on her lap, pointing out horses and wagons with his usual "Wha' dat?"

Josh leaned over the handrail. Nandry looked up, and the color of her face deepened.

"Been talkin' to Clark," Marty could hear him say. It had always been "Mr. Davis" till now, but the way had been cleared for a new relationship.

Nandry's eyes widened at his words.

"He says it's fine with 'im if I come callin'."

Nandry's color deepened still more, but she said nothing.

"Is it all right with you?" There, the question was out. The ball was now handed to Nandry. There was no way she could pretend not to understand his meaning. She flushed a deep red and studied the child on her lap. Minutes ticked by. It no doubt seemed an eternity to Josh, who stood waiting, heart pounding and hands sweating. Marty certainly hadn't intended to eavesdrop, but now she could not move away without drawing attention to herself. She held her breath. What would Nandry say?

"I reckon" finally came the soft answer, and Josh's face broke into a relieved grin.

"Thanks," he said to Nandry, sounding surprisingly calm. "Thanks. Next Wednesday, then. I'll be lookin' forward to it," and then he was gone, probably suppressing the urge to run and leap over the nearby pump.

Nandry buried her blushing face against the small Luke. Later that day she was surprisingly forthcoming with Marty, and she said she'd been hoping it would be Josh. She had noticed Willis Aitkins looking at her, too, but she really favored Josh.

"He isn't even waitin' for Saturday," she noted to Marty with wonder in her voice. Usually when young folks started to keep company, the calls were made on Saturday night. Only the very serious called on *both* Saturday and Wednesday.

Nandry was watching Marty's face very carefully, her eyes begging for Marty's approval.

Marty put her arms around the young woman, noting with a pang that they were now the same height. "Oh, Nandry," she said, "I am happy for you, and I'm sad for me."

Nandry hugged her back with genuine warmth, then turned quickly away in embarrassment to swing small Luke up in her arms and hold him so closely he squirmed in protest.

"Oh, Lukey." Marty knew Nandry called him that only when she felt especially affectionate. "How can one feel so happy, an' sad, an' excited, an' scared all at one time?"

Luke didn't understand the question, but he reached out his little hand to touch the tear that lay glistening on her cheek.

TWENTY-FOUR

Christmas

As Marty made preparations for the coming Christmas, she felt this would be a very special celebration. As much as she appreciated this time of year, never before had Marty felt such anticipation.

Baby Luke, a happy child, scurried about, having outgrown his early colicky fussiness. Ellie was still their bright butterfly, but now small bits of her boundless energy were being channeled into productive and helpful activities. Arnie, Clare, and Missie would enjoy the holiday from school and were already making plans for sliding on the creek's frozen surface and sledding down its banks. But the most important item adding to the extra excitement was that Clae would be home—Clae, their young teacher-in-the-making. Marty could hardly wait till she arrived, and she could tell that Nandry also was anticipating seeing her sister again.

Clae's letters from normal school were filled with excitement about what she was learning, who she was meeting, but most important, how much she was missing them all.

Marty fussed over all Clae's favorite dishes, made sure Nandry had their shared room prepared, and encouraged the younger children to feel the same excitement she felt. There would be a new face at their Christmas table, as well. Josh Coffins, Nandry's promised, would be joining them. Marty shared in the joy of the young couple along with dismay at the thought of losing her Nandry.

A spring wedding was planned, and as soon as the rush of Christmas was behind them, Nandry and Marty would get down to the serious business of preparing the bridal dowry.

Nandry looked very happy, and Marty had for some months been giving her the egg money so she would have something with which to buy the little extras for her first home of her own.

But first Marty would feast upon Christmas.

Clark chose the tree and some evergreen boughs that would form their traditional wreaths.

Nandry had added a half-dozen turkeys to her chicken pens, so one of them would grace the table. She selected a fine young gobbler, and it was getting extra daily care and attention.

Pies, tarts, and cookies, along with loaf cakes, lined the shelves in the pantry.

Marty had been to town for her shopping, and gifts lay wrapped beside her chest of drawers and hidden beneath her bed to supply the socks hung above the mantel for Christmas morning.

On the day Clae was to arrive, both Nandry and Marty were almost too excited to work. Eventually Marty decided she was glad she had so much to do to help the time go faster. Still it seemed the clock would never get around to four o'clock, when Clark and the team were expected back from the train station.

At last Marty heard Ole Bob's sharp bark and the happy shouts of children.

Missie burst into the house. "Guess who we found?" she teased.

They all came tramping in, Clark carrying Clae's suitcase and a large bag.

Marty pulled the girl into her arms.

"Oh, Clae, jest look at ya. Why, ya've gone and plumb growed up on us since ya been away."

Clae hugged her in return, laughing as she pointed out it had only been three months. "But oh, it's so good to be home. I could hardly wait," she added.

Clae went from Marty to her sister and then to Ellie and Luke, hugging each one in turn and exclaiming over how the youngsters had all grown. Nandry's cheeks flushed with Clae's teasing about her Josh, but she looked pleased.

"I'm thinkin'," said Clark over the joyful commotion, setting down the suitcase and the bundle, "thet we're in need of a bigger house."

Marty just smiled. They were hard put for space at times, she knew. She was once again having to put up with a crib in their bedroom, and the three girls who shared one room barely had room to turn around.

They were crowded, but they were happy. The lively conversation did not lessen as the evening wore on. There were so many things for Clae to tell, to describe. There were so many questions for the others to ask.

After the young ones had been put to bed with the promise of full Christmas socks in the morning, Marty, Nandry, and Clae still talked on, Clark nearby adding an occasional comment or question.

"When is the day for your wedding?" Clae asked Nandry, and Marty noticed Clae's careful speech.

"The last of May. We wanted to wait 'til ya'd be home. You're to be my maid o' honor, ya know."

"I hoped I would. Where are you going to live?"

"There's a small cabin on the Coffins' farm. The people who used ta own the farm lived in it. The Coffins built a bigger one when they came. We'll use the little'un fer now."

"You must be excited."

"I am," said Nandry, and her smile confirmed it. "It's a funny feelin'. I want so much fer time to go quickly, yet I don't want it to at the same time."

"Meanin'?" Clae forgot herself for the moment, using the familiar expression.

"This house—the little'uns—I really hate to leave the kids."

Marty marveled at the more frequent glimpses they had been getting of Nandry's heart.

"You won't be too far away," said Clae. She shook her head and sighed. "No one will ever know how homesick I was at first. I thought I'd just die if I didn't get home. I thought I'd never make it—but I did.

I reminded myself of the money being paid for my schooling—the faith that people have in me . . . and . . . and I remembered our ma, too, Nandry. Sometimes I think about Ma, about how proud she'd be, how happy that we're getting a chance."

Yes, Marty was sure Mrs. Larson would be proud of her two daughters.

"She'd be happy for both of us," Clae went on "—for me being a teacher, for you marrying Josh. It sort of gives it extra meaning, remembering Ma."

It was the first time the girls had ever talked about their mother in Marty's presence.

"Yer ma would be very proud." Marty spoke softly. "She wanted so much thet ya both make good, an' ya have, both of ya, an' I'm proud, too."

Clae put her arms around Marty's neck and gave her an affectionate squeeze.

"And we know why," she said. "We haven't said much maybe—not as much as we should, but we know why we've made good. Thank you—thank you so much. I do love you, and I'll never forget . . . never."

Nandry nodded her head in agreement, her expression saying more than words.

⁂

The household was awakened early by Arnie's squeals of delight. Clare's voice soon joined his and then the general commotion followed. Marty pulled herself out of bed and slipped into her house socks and robe. Clark was already on his feet, tucking his shirt into his trousers. They entered the sitting room at the same time Nandry came in carrying Luke, barely awake. Ellie danced, 'round the room waving her arms, so caught up in Arnie and Clare's excitement at their bulging stockings she had not even thought to check out what her own might hold.

Luke quickly rubbed the sleep out of his eyes and stood transfixed, gazing at the tree in the corner that had sprung up from somewhere during the night.

Missie finally emerged, yawning and complaining about the noise.

"It's not even five o'clock," she said in disbelief. "Ya used ta make me wait a lot longer than this when I was little."

"They'd've waited, too, iffen I'd had anything to do with it," responded Clark, but Marty noticed that he seemed to be enjoying the whole pleasant uproar.

Eventually the fire was kindled in the kitchen stove and the kettle put on to boil. Clark replenished the fireplace and coaxed it to flame. Calm again reigned in the Davis household.

The older ones took advantage of the near quiet to exchange their gifts. Clae had somehow managed to bring a small gift for each of them. Marty knew she did not have much extra spending money and appreciated her gift the more for it. What Clae had lacked in dollars she had supplied with creativity, and her sewing skills had come to the fore. Luke hugged a stuffed teddy bear. Ellie wore a pint-sized apron complete with a pocket. Arnie and Clare eyed their checkered man-sized handkerchiefs, pleased that the squares matched their pa's. For Missie there was a lace-trimmed bonnet, and Nandry opened a carefully embroidered pair of pillowcases for her hope chest. Marty unwrapped the most beautiful lace handkerchief she had ever seen, but the note that accompanied the gift was what made Marty cry, for it bore the simple words *To Mother, with love, Clae*. None of her children had ever called her anything but Ma, and it seemed very meaningful for this special girl to use the more formal title.

Clark's gift handkerchief carried sentiment, too, and he slipped the card that accompanied it into Marty's hand. The card read, *Thanks for being a true pa. Love, Clae.*

Marty tried to blink away the bittersweet tears in her eyes as she thought of the one who had not been "a true pa" to his daughters. What a privilege for Clark and her to fill in as mother and father to them.

Nandry, too, had surprises for them. She had made picture books for all the younger children, gluing newspaper and calendar pictures she had gathered onto pieces of cloth. Missie received new hair ribbons, which still delighted her feminine senses. Marty got a little wooden box to hold her many and varied recipes that were forever overflowing the drawer where she kept them. Clark received a handmade cover for the well-worn family Bible.

Marty and Clark then passed out their presents for each of their family members and watched with pleasure the shining eyes of the recipients.

The clutter was cleared away, the cherished gifts put carefully in their new owners' places, and the day's celebrations proceeded.

After breakfast Clare and Arnie went out to try the new sled Clark had made them. Ellie, apron-clad to Clae's delight, was playing with her tiny set of new dishes, and Luke was put back to bed to catch up on some sleep.

Missie, feeling quite grown-up, joined the women in the kitchen, where she helped prepare the Christmas dinner.

Josh just didn't seem to be able to stay away and arrived earlier than expected. He shyly offered Nandry his gift, a new lamp to be used in their home. Marty told him she had never seen a prettier one. A soft cluster of roses was painted on the bowl in reds and pinks, and the chimney was generously trimmed with gold. Whatever it was Nandry presented to Josh the family was not allowed to see, but Marty had her suspicions that it was a mustache cup. Josh was carefully nurturing a mustache that he hoped to have full and well groomed by his wedding day, making him look more manly.

They roasted chestnuts at the fire and sniffed hungrily at the inviting fragrances coming from the kitchen. Just before the meal was set on the table, the family gathered for the reading of the Christmas story. Even Luke, from his spot on Nandry's knee, appeared to listen. Marty looked around the room at all the faces intent on Clark as he read, and her heart filled with praise to God. She slipped her hand into Clark's during his prayer, and he pressed her fingers firmly in his own.

Just as the chairs were being placed around the table, Ole Bob began to bark. It was unusual to have unexpected guests on Christmas Day, and Marty felt her heart flutter. She hoped nothing was wrong. She followed Clark to the door, almost afraid to look out.

She could hear footsteps approaching the door, and with barely a knock the door pushed open.

"Tommie," was all she could say.

"Tommie," echoed Clark, sounding equally incredulous. "Good to see ya, boy," he said, welcoming the young man with a bear hug.

Then it was Marty's turn—followed by greetings all round, excitedly and with great enthusiasm.

"Jest a minute," Tommie said, holding up his hand. "I got somethin' to show ya."

He was gone but soon back with his arm around a small young woman, her brown curls captured under a blue bonnet.

"My wife," he said with pride. "My wife, Fran."

"Oh, Tommie," exclaimed Marty. "Tommie, when did ya marry? Why didn't ya write?"

Tommie laughed. "Five months ago now. I wanted to surprise ya. Isn't she somethin'?" He looked at her again and his arm tightened. Fran smiled shyly.

"I'm pleased to meet ya all," she finally said, putting out one small hand to Clark and then Marty.

Marty stepped forward to give her a warm embrace.

"An' we are jest so glad to meet you. Won't ya come in? Take off yer coats. We are jest sittin' down, an' we are so pleased to have ya join us."

"No, no," said Tom, "we haven't been home yet. Since we were comin' right by here, I wanted ya to meet her. But we must move along. Ma might forgive me for stoppin' here on the way, but she'd never fergive me iffen I stopped here to eat Christmas dinner."

"Oh, it's gonna be so hard to let ya go now. I've so many questions—"

"They'll keep," Tommie interjected. "We'll be around. I decided I'd take up thet piece of land o' mine. See iffen I can make a farm outta it. Fran's ma and pa owned a store out west. Now there's a switch, huh?" he winked. "'Long comes a guy, marries their daughter, an' takes her *east*."

"Oh, Tommie! I know the both of you'll be so happy."

"Thet we already are," Tommie assured her, and his eyes said it was true.

They bid their good-byes and promised to be back soon for a nice long visit.

"Well, this has truly been some day." Marty expressed the feelings of them all as the family returned to their Christmas dinner.

They bowed their heads and Clark's deep voice spoke reverently to their Father, thanking Him for the many blessings that life held, and especially for Tommie, a son come home and the joy that this would bring to the Graham household.

Marty wondered briefly about the pretty Owahteeka. Had she found happiness with her Running Deer? Marty prayed that she had.

TWENTY-FIVE

One More Time

Finally the people of the community reluctantly admitted to themselves and to one another that the highly trained Reverend Knutson simply was not fitting in, nor was he meeting the needs of the congregation.

Once they had admitted this fact, they wondered why it had taken them so long to put it on the table. What to do about the problem became the next question, and it certainly did not seem to have an easy answer.

A committee again was picked in due course, and much to Marty's chagrin, Clark was named to be the chairman. The committee asked for a meeting with the pastor, at which time the men hoped to discuss quite openly with Reverend Knutson how the people felt.

Reverend Knutson showed no surprise or concern at being asked to meet with the men, but the meeting itself had its touchy moments. The reverend seemed to think the meeting had been arranged to offer him commendations, and perhaps to even suggest an increase in his rather modest salary, modest by his standards at any rate.

He was noticeably taken aback when the meeting took a different turn.

The reverend was not only well educated himself, he informed the little group, but he was also dipping into the writings of other highly trained theologians. His sermon material came directly from the greatest minds of Christendom. He could show them chapter and page.

The good reverend found it hard to fathom that anyone would not highly favor his intellectually charged sermons. He'd had no idea when he accepted their call that the people of the area were so bereft of learning and so insensitive to spiritual enlightenment. But he was sure he could do better. He knew of a great scholar whose books had just been made available, and though they were full of exceptional material, they were written in the "easy language of the layman." He'd send for a couple of those books. He was sure the congregation would find encouragement and religious sustenance in the works of this great man.

It was with great difficulty that the committee, Clark in particular, was able to convince the reverend that they wished him to end his service to them as their minister.

Clark explained it thus: "Reverend, we realize thet ya are a very learned man, an' we realize thet we are a mite slow. We wouldn't want to hold ya back from preachin' to those who could understand and appreciate yer great skills, so we are releasin' ya to go back to wherever ya wish to go, an' at such time as ya are first able to make the arrangement."

The reverend, red-faced, sputtered around, trying to formulate his response. "Are you saying, gentlemen," he finally choked out, "are you saying that my service has been terminated?"

"Shucks, no," put in the elder Coffins, another committee member, "not terminated, jest excused."

So they excused the parson, gave him a going-away purse, wished him well, and got on with the job of selecting a new minister. This time the schoolteacher, Mr. Wilbur Whittle, was not asked to serve as correspondent.

⁂

As yet the cemetery beside the little church stood empty of markers. They all knew it could not remain so, and the unasked question often hung in the air—*who?* Who would be the person whose passing would cause the ground first to be broken that they might be laid to rest?

Without conscious thought, various ones observed their neighbors.

Grandpa Stern was well on in years and seemed to be failing. Mrs. LaHaye had never truly recovered her full health. One of the Coffin girls seemed very delicate and was always down with one sickness or another. Her parents didn't even allow her to go to school. Mrs. Vickers showed signs of high nervousness, and some feared she'd talk herself right into an early grave.

But when it happened it was none of these, and the whole community was shaken by the suddenness and the sadness of it all.

It was their own Tessie, who recently had married Mr. Whittle. She had always seemed like such a strong, healthy girl, and the community folk were pleased when it was known she was going to make her school-teacher husband a father. As for Mr. Whittle himself, his bowler hat had never been dusted more frequently, his giant mustache been trimmed with more care, nor his spats whitened with such vigor. He was well pleased with himself and his new wife. To have a young and attractive woman adore him was a wonder in itself, and to be about to become a father was beyond belief. Mr. Whittle was on cloud nine. The big boys joked among themselves that his voice was now always squeaking with excitement, but Mr. Whittle did not seem to notice or care.

The great day came and the doctor was quickly sent for. With tired eyes and a heavy heart, he left the next morning. Both Tessie and her baby boy had died during the night. The news shook the whole community. The neighbors responded with deep care and sympathy, and several gathered to dig the grave in the new cemetery. A pine box was built and carefully draped, and the two bodies, one so tiny, were prepared for burial. Through it all Mr. Wilbur Whittle moved in silent shock. It was beyond his comprehension, this great loss. In the absence of a parson, Mr. Whittle did have presence of mind to ask Clark if he'd read the Scripture and say the words of interment. Clark, with a heavy heart, agreed.

⚜

The day of the funeral was cold and dreary. Marty, wiping her eyes, thought the weather matched the occasion. The pine box was lowered, the earth heaped upon it.

338

She stood gazing at the fresh grave that held a young mother with a baby boy in her arms. *It's no longer virgin—this cemetery. From now on it will be grave added to grave,* she thought numbly. Time and again the earth would be opened up to receive a new burden.

Oh, Tessie, Marty cried inwardly, *who would've thought it would be you! Life is full of the unexpected.* And once more her thoughts went back over the years to another gravesite and her own loss. She lifted Ellie into her arms and held her tight, thanking the Lord for His goodness to her and to Clark in spite of the tragedies of life.

Classes were canceled until further notice, but Mr. Whittle was never able to resume his teaching, so school for that year ended in April. Toward the end of May, when the roses were beginning to bloom and the birds were rebuilding their nests, Mr. Whittle gathered a bouquet of wild flowers and placed it on the new mound of earth. Then dusting his bowler hat, he picked up his suitcases and returned to the East.

TWENTY-SIX

Josh and Nandry

The parson's departure left two members of the congregation particularly concerned. Josh and Nandry were worried about what this would do to their wedding plans. Clark picked up on what they must be thinking and did some investigating on his own.

He discovered there was a parson two towns away, and he visited the man and made arrangements for him to be at their community church on the day set for the wedding.

When he felt quite confident that nothing would happen to put a hitch in the plans, he opened the subject to Josh and Nandry one day when the two were sitting at the kitchen table with rather concerned expressions.

"This here weddin' ya been plannin'—ya changed yer minds 'bout it?"

"Oh no," Nandry said, looking to Josh for support.

"Gonna be a bit tricky without yerself a preacher."

Josh agreed, looking down at his hands folded in front of him. Nandry seemed about to cry, a thing she had never been known to do.

"Jest so happened," Clark went on in a rush, the teasing now gone from his voice, "thet I heard of a man within ridin' distance who also happens to be a church-recognized parson."

The two faces turned as one to focus intently on his.

"Where?" asked Josh. "Do ya think we could go to 'im?"

"Reckon there ain't much need fer thet," Clark said calmly. "He said he'd be happy to come on over here."

Nandry sat silently, her eyes wide, then rose with sudden comprehension and an exclamation of joy.

"Are ya sayin' thet ya found us a parson?" she cried, her hands clasped tightly together.

Clark grinned. "Thet's 'bout it, I guess."

"Oh, bless ya!" Nandry squealed. She looked about ready to throw her arms around Clark, then turned quickly to embrace Josh instead. Josh didn't mind.

Marty smiled from her place at the cupboard, remembering Nandry's early crush on Clark and so glad to see her genuine love for Josh.

Her attention was drawn back to the happy couple and the grinning Clark.

"When?" begged Nandry. "When can he come?"

"Well, I thought as how you'd set yer mind on May twenty-eighth."

"We did—we have. Ya mean we can have the weddin' jest as we planned—in the church—with our friends?"

"Yup—jest as planned."

"Oh, thank the Lord!" said Nandry. "He does answer."

The two young people left for a walk down by the creek, no doubt to share this moment of happiness and to finalize their plans.

"Well," said Marty, her own happiness filling her heart, "how did ya ever manage this bit of happy cunning?"

"Didn't take no cunning," Clark answered. "Jest money." They couldn't help but laugh together.

The much-planned-for wedding came off as scheduled. The hired parson did a commendable job of reading the vows and instructing the bride and groom.

Nandry was glowing and even lovely in her special gown she and Marty had carefully stitched for the occasion, and Clae looked almost as pretty as she stood beside her sister.

Josh's younger brother, Joe, stood with him. It was a beautiful wedding ceremony full of meaning and promise, and when the guests turned from the service to the bridal supper, there was much laughter and good-natured banter.

"Here ya are," Todd Stern joked to Clark, "hardly dry behind the ears yet, an' already givin' a girl away."

Clark looked over at his young Missie, who was growing up all too quickly.

"An' 'fore I know it," he said quietly, "I'll be losin' thet one, too."

Clark's mood turned sober as he thought about it.

"Seems like yesterday I had 'em all stumblin' round under my feet," he said to Todd, "an' here I am on the edge of bein' a grandpa. Sometimes I wish thet time had a tail, so's we could grab ahold an' slow it down some."

Throughout the summer months the church remained without a pastor, but it did not alarm Clark and Marty or their neighbors to be left with a vacant pulpit. They were sure that in God's good time He would bring someone to them. They did continue to meet to sing, pray, and read the Scriptures together.

The school, too, had no teacher. A meeting of its governing board resulted in Clae being asked to take the position come fall. Clae could hardly believe her good fortune. Here she was, newly returned from her teacher training and already a school was promised to her—her beloved home school at that.

Marty couldn't help but be excited, too, about Clae's new job.

"It will be so good to have ya home agin. We missed ya so," she told Clae with a hug.

"You spoil me," said Clae slowly. "In a lot of ways I would love to live at home . . . but . . . well . . . I've a notion that I sort of want to be on my own. I really want to set up housekeeping in the teacherage. There are still dishes and everything there, and Mrs. LaHaye told me I could just move in and make use of them if I'd like. I'd really love to. You wouldn't mind, would you, Ma?" She looked a moment into Marty's face. "Besides," she hurried on, "I'm doing some studies by mail, and I'll truly need the quiet if I am to complete the course in the time allowed."

Marty was disappointed, but she hid her feelings from Clae, simply saying she and Clark would talk it over. After a long discussion with Clark, she reluctantly gave in. It wasn't like Clae would be off on her own, after all, Clark said. She would be just down the road and over the hill.

It was decided that Clae would move back in with Missie for the summer months to fill in some of the emptiness left by Nandry's departure. Then before the fall classes began, she would move her belongings into the teacherage and set up housekeeping on her own.

A few leads came in concerning a possible pastor. These were followed up, and one or two seemed to fit the bill. But eventually those doors closed. Not that the search committee was hard to please, but the few available for the post wanted more salary than the little community could provide.

It was getting on toward fall when Ben heard about a young man from Mr. Cassidy.

"He's from my former hometown," said the store manager. "Young fella—not too much book learnin'—did get some trainin' but hasn't been on to seminary in the East like he's aimin' to do. Got lots of zeal, an' sure does study out of the Good Book—honest an' hardworkin', but green."

"We don't mind greenness none," Ben offered. "We's all pretty green ourselves—maybe we could learn together."

A two-man delegation left on horseback to see if they could track down the young man in question. It was eight days before they were home again, but they returned with good news.

They had located the man, and he was eager to begin pastoring. He still hoped to advance his education, but if they'd take him as he was, he'd do his best to serve them. They had agreed.

Pastor Joseph Berwick arrived on the fifth of September, the same day

Miss Clae Larson began teaching her first classes in the country school. He would not be giving his first sermon until the following Sunday, but in the interim he began to call on his parishioners.

He would be boarding with the Watleys, as had his predecessor, and when Mrs. Watley laid eyes on the tall, handsome young man, she turned to her two daughters with a twinkle in her eyes. She nodded the parson into the parlor, where tea was served. "Surely this time," she said, sighing.

Parson Berwick was not content very long to sit and sip tea, and before the dust of his last horseback ride had had a chance to settle, he was off again to meet more of the inhabitants of the area whom he saw as members of his flock.

He was not above lending a helping hand, either, and he spent some time cutting wood for Widow Rider, helped pound a fence post that Jason Stern was placing, and forked hay along with the Graham boys.

Gradually he worked his way through the community toward the schoolhouse, and on Thursday around four o'clock he rode into the school yard for a call on the local teacher.

Clae, down on her knees in the neglected flower bed, was not prepared for visitors. Hair hastily pulled back with a ribbon, she was busy cleaning out the weeds that had been left to grow where they wished over the summer, and her hands were deep in the soil.

She looked up in surprise at the approaching stranger, involuntarily leaving a streak of dirt across her cheek as she tucked a loose strand of hair back.

"I'm Parson Berwick," the man said politely as he dismounted. "Is your father at home?"

Clae shook her head dumbly, trying to sort out who he might mean by her father and where she should tell him that he could be located.

"Your mother?"

"No . . . no one . . . I'm . . ." She took a breath and changed course. "You're meaning the Davises," she asked, "or the Larsons?"

It was the parson's turn to look confused. "I'm meaning the teacher," he said, "whoever he is. I haven't yet heard his name."

"There is no *he*."

"I beg your pardon."

"The teacher . . . he's . . . he's gone," Clae stumbled along, trying to explain. "He doesn't live here anymore."

"I'm sorry," said the parson. "I understood the children are at school, having classes."

"They are—we are," Clae quickly amended.

"And you are one of the pupils?"

Clae stood up to her full height, which probably didn't make much of an impression alongside the parson's tall frame.

"*I*," she said with emphasis, "am the teacher."

"The teacher!" he stammered, his face turning red. "Oh, my goodness!" he exclaimed. "Then I guess I must be wanting to see you instead of your father. I mean—I didn't really come to see him. I came to see the teacher."

After a pause, he chuckled with some embarrassment. "Let's start all over, shall we?"

He stepped back, then forward again with a boyish smile.

"Hello there," he said, holding out his hand. "I'm Pastor Berwick, new to your area, and I'm endeavoring to call on each of my parishioners. I understand you are the new schoolteacher hereabouts."

Clae looked down at her dirt-soiled hand, but the pastor did not hesitate. He reached for it, and Clae felt her hand held in a firm handshake.

"I'm sorry," she stammered. "My hands are dirty—"

"You've got dirt on your face, too," he said with a smile.

"Oh my!" said Clae, further flustered. She reached up to rub at the suspected spot, only to make it worse.

He laughed, and pulling out a clean handkerchief, he stepped forward with "May I?" and wiped the smudge from her face.

Clae held her breath. Her throat felt tight and her heart pounded. She wondered if Mr. Berwick could hear it.

"As I said, I'm calling on my parishioners," he said, stepping back and putting his handkerchief in his pocket. "Can I expect to see you in church on Sunday?"

"Oh yes," whispered Clae, feeling her cheeks grow hot at her foolishness.

"And you really are the schoolteacher?"

She nodded.

"Sure didn't have teachers like you when I went to school."

She caught the twinkle in his eye, and her color deepened.

"I'll see you Sunday."

She nodded.

He mounted his horse and was about to move on, then stopped and turned to her.

"You didn't give me your name."

"Clae—Clae Larson."

"*Miss* Clae Larson?"

"Miss Clae Larson."

"How do you spell that? Clae. I've never heard that name before."

Clae spelled it. She was so nervous she hoped she'd said the right letters.

"Clae," he repeated. "That's unusual. I'll see you on Sunday, Miss Larson."

She watched him ride away with a wave of his hat.

So it was that Clae met the new preacher, and so it was that she had problems concentrating. Right from the very first she had trouble keeping her attention on the sermon rather than the one who delivered it—but she never missed a Sunday.

TWENTY-SEVEN

A New Parson, a New House

Soon known as Parson Joe, their pastor quickly established his place in the community. His willingness to lend a hand certainly endeared him to the men.

"Not 'fraid to dirty his hands, thet one," commented a farmer.

"No—nor to bend his back" was the immediate agreement.

But the real reason for their nods of approval was the Sunday services. Parson Joe made a list of all the hymns the congregation knew by heart, and these were the ones from which he selected their Sunday songs. Occasional new ones were added and learned by writing the words on a chalkboard borrowed from the school. Parson Joe had a nice tenor, and the congregation joined him heartily.

His prayers were not just words but were filled with sincerity, and his sermons were the highlight of the whole service. Simple, straightforward messages, developed from a text or passage in the Bible, gave them all a real sense of being spiritually nourished.

Even the younger ones began to take notice and listen, and eventually young Clint Graham surprised his folks by announcing that he felt the call to go into the ministry.

Only Mrs. Watley felt any disappointment in the new parson—and it had nothing whatever to do with his Sunday sermons. She was beside herself to discover how to make him pay more attention to one of her daughters—which one he chose, she didn't care, but the man seemed oblivious to both of them.

The congregation continued to grow both numerically and spiritually. Young Willie LaHaye never missed a Sunday, and even his father, Zeke LaHaye, put aside work for an occasional Sunday morning of worship. The loss of his daughter Tessie no doubt had softened the man. Marty noticed on more than one occasion his eyes on the silent mound across the churchyard. A carefully crafted cross had appeared at the gravesite bearing the words *Tessie LaHaye Whittle and Baby Boy. May their rest be peaceful and never alone.*

Parson Joe called on his flock more than for Sunday dinner, and wherever he went he was welcomed.

Claude Graham was overheard remarking to his twin brother, Lem, "The reason he fits here so well is thet he don't know nothin' from them books neither."

To which Lem replied, "Don't let him fool ya. He's got a lot more of a load up there than he's throwin' out each Sunday. No use forkin' a whole haystack to growin' calves."

As for Clae, she felt rather befuddled about the whole state of affairs. To get her mind off her confusion, she worked every spare minute on her mail-order education. The study course that normally should have taken until the next summer was completed by Christmas.

The parson was always friendly to her, but no more so than with each member of his congregation. Still, Clae couldn't stop the ridiculous skipping of her heart, the hoping that perhaps, just perhaps, he had noticed her and he was maybe just a bit more attentive to her than to some of the other young women. At times she despaired; at other times she dreamed . . . if only . . . if only.

And then on Easter Sunday morning following a wonderfully inspirational service, the young parson held her hand just a bit longer as she left the church. She was the last one to leave, having stopped to pick up her chalkboard for its return to the school.

"Good morning, Miss Larson." He smiled, and then he whispered, "I do wish you didn't live alone. How in the world is a gentleman to call?"

Clae caught her breath.

Allowing what she hoped was a decent amount of time, Clae moved back home with the Davises.

~~~

Clark and Marty sat after breakfast enjoying a second cup of coffee. It seemed as though they rarely had the opportunity anymore for a long chat.

"Looks like we got us a real growin' church," Clark commented.

"Yeah, it's so good to see folks comin' out, giving themselves—"

"Thet isn't what I'm meanin'."

"Then what?"

"I noticed Nandry an' Tommie's Fran are both in the family way."

Marty smiled. She had noticed it, too, and Nandry already had shyly shared her happiness with Marty.

"Speakin' of growin'," Clark said after a moment, "I'm thinkin' thet we've put it off fer too long."

"Meanin'?"

"This house—it's way too small. Shoulda built another ages ago."

"Seems a strange thing to be thinkin' on now. Notice who's around here much, at least during daylight hours—jest you an' me an' little Luke. Soon he'll be off to school, too."

"Yeah," said Clark, "but they start out here every mornin' and come home agin every night, an' they don't usually come alone—iffen you've noticed."

Marty thought of Missie and Clare each showing up with a friend after school during the last few weeks. Arnie was a big boy like his pa, and he and Clark seemed to fill up any room they were in at the same time. Ellie, their little social butterfly, no doubt would also be inviting her friends home, too, during the coming years. Marty also thought about Nandry and Josh and their baby who was on the way. Then her thoughts moved to Clae and the young parson. And Missie was quickly maturing into a young woman; before long she would be entertaining her young men callers.

"Maybe yer right," she said, "maybe we do need a bigger house. It's jest thet it seems so quiet like when they're all off to school. This little house has been a cozy home for us, Clark." She reached across the table for his hand. "Thank ya again for—"

"It's me doin' the thankin', Marty," Clark said, squeezing her hand. "This was jest a roof over our heads till you came and made us a home."

Marty's eyes misted and her smile was a little wobbly at the corners. Then she said, "Yeah, we do need us more room. What're ya thinkin'?"

"I think I'll spend me the winter hauling logs," he answered. "This here new house—I been thinkin' on it a lot. Not gonna be a log one. Gonna be boards—nice boards."

"Thet'll cost a fortune."

"Not really. There's a mill over 'cross the crik now. I can trade my logs in on lumber. Been thinkin' on the style, too. How ya feel 'bout an upstairs—not a loft but a real upstairs? With steps goin' up—not a ladder. Like them fancy houses back east."

Marty caught her breath. "Seems to me ya got pretty big dreams," she said carefully, not wanting to dash them.

"Maybe—maybe I have, but I want you to do a little dreamin', too. I want this house to have what yer wantin'. More windows, closets fer clothes 'stead of pegs—whatever yer wantin'. Ya do some dreamin' an' write yer plans down on paper. We'll see iffen we can't make some dreams come true."

"When, Clark?" Marty finally asked, feeling nearly overwhelmed with the possibility but also worried that it was too much.

"Not next year—I don't s'pose," he answered. "Gonna take a long while to git all those logs, but the year after—should be able to do it by then fer sure."

"Sounds . . . sounds . . . like a fairy tale," Marty said in wonder, finally accepting the fact that it really could happen.

Clark grinned and stood up. He reached out and touched her hair.

"Did I ever tell ya that I love ya, Mrs. Davis?"

"I've heard it afore," said Marty, wrinkling up her nose, "but it bears repeatin' now an' then." She caught his hand and held it to her cheek.

He tipped her face up to his, then leaned to plant a kiss on her forehead.

"By the way," he said, "thet's mighty good coffee."

TWENTY-EIGHT

Livin' and Learnin'

Missie had arrived at her last year in the local school under the supervision of Clae, and as her school days came to an end, Luke's would begin. Clae had promised the school one more term, and then it was hoped Missie would take over, for she, too, had decided to pursue teachers' training.

Clae, living again in the Davis home, clearly was not committed to a life in education, though she certainly made a fine teacher and her students loved her. Marty was sure that Clae would make a fine parson's wife. Though the Davis household got the lion's share of the young parson's calls, he did not neglect the rest of his parishioners. Only Mrs. Watley had any real difficulty with the frequency of his calls at the Davis household.

Marty could hardly bear the thought of Missie going away for further education. Somehow it seemed more difficult to face than when Clae left. Missie was a bit younger than Clae had been when she left, having started school at not quite six—Clae had been older when she began her schooling. But Marty knew she had to get herself mentally and emotionally prepared for the inevitable.

Clark spent the winter months hauling logs to the mill across the creek. He was well pleased with the progress he was making and could see no problem with scheduling and building the new house during the next year.

Nandry's baby girl arrived, and they named her Tina Martha after her *two* maternal grandmothers, Nandry said. Marty felt very honored.

"Well, *Grandpa,*" she said to Clark as she held the soft little one, "we've got our feet in two worlds—parents and grandparents both." The family laughed and joked about it all, and Luke wondered what he should now call his ma and pa.

Fran and Tommie's baby arrived about the same time—a solid, healthy boy whom they named Ben and who immediately was Little Ben.

Sally Anne gave birth to her third child, but Little Emily lived only three days, and a tiny fresh mound was sorrowfully dug in the cemetery by the church.

Rett Marshall was now handling a team of horses almost as well as a grown man. He loved creatures, tame or wild, and even had a young jackrabbit for a pet. A strange boy, people occasionally noted, but there was admiration in their voices. Several farmers had hired his services when they needed a pair of strong arms and a way with animals.

Marty remembered an overheard conversation from long ago between a neighbor and the doctor. "I often wonder, Doctor," the woman had said, "do ya ever wish thet maybe ya hadn't . . . well . . . hadn't fought quite so hard like at the birthing of the Marshall boy?"

The doctor had looked at her a moment, then said evenly, "Of course not." He then went on to say, "I didn't make that life—the Creator did. And when He made it, I expect He had good reasons for doing as He did—and whatever that reason is, it is in His hands."

Marty thought of this each time she watched the boy whistle a bird down or make friends with a prairie dog. She thought of it, too, when she saw the love in Wanda's eyes and Cam's pride in his son.

The LaHaye farmstead no longer resembled anything that had ever belonged to Jedd Larson. Zeke LaHaye was a good farmer who knew land well. Under his care the fields produced and the farm prospered. New buildings and a new well grouped nicely under the trees. Neat rows of fencing encircled the holding. But for all the prosperity of the homestead, Mrs. LaHaye remained in poor health. Their son Nathan married a girl from town and moved her into the big house with the family. She was a pleasant girl and was able to take over much of the running of the household. This was a great source of comfort to the senior Mrs. LaHaye.

Marty sat in her rocker with another pair of Luke's torn overalls on her lap and thought about all the changes that were happening. New neighbors moved in. Very little farmland in the area now was not in use. New buildings sprang up in town, almost overnight it seemed, as new businesses were added. The town had built a church of its own and had brought in a pastor to care for the people. There was even a sheriff's office and a bank. A daily stage now ran between the local towns. All these developments made their small community feel no longer like they lived on the frontier. Why, they were nearly self-sufficient.

They had their church, they had their school, they had a doctor they could call on. Marty certainly didn't consider herself a pioneer woman anymore.

The next summer saw Clae and the young parson joined together in marriage. Instead of asking the town's parson to do the honors, the young couple went back east to his hometown. Parson Joe was anxious to introduce Clae to his family and also eager to have his former pastor and dear friend perform the ceremony. The Davises of course were sorry to miss the event, but they made plans for a community potluck supper to honor the couple upon their return.

The school board agreed to rent the teacherage to the pastor and his wife for a modest amount, and this was fine with Missie, since she preferred to live at home upon commencing her duties. She no doubt had realized the restrictions on her social life if she were to live alone.

In spite of a bad accident with an axe, Clark met his log quota the following winter.

He had been cutting logs alone on the hillside when the axe blade glazed off a knot and spun sideways, slicing deeply into his foot. He had bound his foot as best as he could, packing moss against it and tying it tightly with a strip of his shirt. He was trying to make it home on one of his new workhorses, Prince, when Tom Graham crossed paths with him.

Prince was not used to being ridden, and Clark'd had his hands full trying to handle the excited horse in his weakened condition. He had lost a lot of blood and was quite content to be helped from the skittish horse to Tom's wagon box, where he could lie down.

Tom pressed the horses forward in an effort to get Clark home as quickly as possible. He threw the harnesses on the fence, helped Clark into the house, and jumped on his own horse to go for the doc.

Marty nearly fainted at the sight of Clark. He tried to assure her that he would be fine, but his face was so white and his hands so shaky she wasn't convinced. Marty got him to bed, where she fussed and fretted over him, hardly knowing what should be done.

"If ya see no fresh blood," Tom had admonished over his shoulder as he left, "best ya leave thet foot alone 'til the doc gits here."

Marty studied the foot for signs of fresh blood, but thankfully none seemed to appear.

"Could ya eat a little broth iffen I fixed it? You're gonna need strength, ya know." Being a woman, her thoughts went to nourishment.

At first it didn't seem to appeal much to Clark, but he nodded his head in the affirmative, then cautioned, "Not too hot—jest warm."

Marty complied. The time until the doctor got there seemed endless, but at last Marty heard a horse approaching. She stayed out of the room while the doctor cleaned and sutured the cut. A couple of times she heard Clark groan, and her knees nearly buckled beneath her.

"And you," the doctor caught her by surprise as she tried to busy herself in the kitchen, "you're almost as white as he is. You best sit you down and have a cup of hot weak tea with some honey in it." He sat her on a chair and found the items for the tea.

Doc handed her the cup. "It's going to take him a while, but he'll be fine. He's young and tough. He'll make it. Your big job will be to keep him off the foot until it has a chance to heal properly. I've a notion your job won't be an easy one. Can't you put him to mending or piecing a quilt?"

There was humor in the doctor's eyes, and Marty couldn't help but laugh. The thought of Clark sitting contentedly with a little needle in his big working hand, matching dainty pieces for quilting, was just too much. Doc patted her shoulder and laughed, too.

In spite of the deepness of the cut and the loss of blood, the foot healed neatly and quickly. Clare and Arnie very capably took over the chores, reporting it all to their pa when they came in to supper.

As predicted, Marty's biggest problem was to keep Clark down as the doctor had ordered. He grumbled and fussed at not being able to be up and busy as he was used to being.

Their new son-in-law, Parson Joe, came as often as he could for a game of checkers. He usually brought Clae along. Other neighbors dropped in now and then. They informed Clark that the logs already felled would be hauled to the mill before spring thaw, just as he had planned. Clark accepted their kindness with deep appreciation. And they, of course, remembered all the times he had put his shoulder to their plows when they were in difficult straits.

Missie brought books from the school for him to read, which helped him pass many hours.

Finally the long ordeal was over and Doc declared the foot healed enough to be stepped on again. Clark hobbled, but at least he was again on his feet—a fact that each member of the household was truly thankful for. Marty noticed that on some days his limp seemed to be a bit worse than others. *It must still bother 'im,* she said to herself. But when she asked him about it, he brushed off her concerns as of no consequence.

During the day the house was left to just Marty and Clark. First with Missie's semester away at teacher's training and now with Luke in school, rites of passage had been marked in the Davis family.

As soon as Clark was able, he was back at the logging again. The neighbor men, true to their word, had indeed hauled out all the logs he previously had cut, but according to his calculations, he still needed another four wagonloads.

Marty watched him leave every morning with a feeling of anxiety and breathed a silent prayer of thanks when he returned safely at the end of the day.

Marty was thinking about spring and the start on the promised new house. Having the actual construction begun would take on special meaning, for once it was started, it would mark the end of Clark's daily and solitary trek to the woodlands.

⁂

Marty watched as the new clapboard house took shape. It was even bigger than she had dreamed. There were windows in every room. A fieldstone fireplace graced not only the family living room and the parlor but their bedroom, as well.

Clark had obtained the services of two men from town to assist with the building, so that even when he was busy in the fields the work went on. Marty measured the windows and bought material for the curtains so they would be ready to hang when the house was completed.

The house would not quite be ready by fall, but they planned to celebrate their next Christmas in their new home. Nandry and Josh with little Tina, and a second new family member by then, as well as Parson Joe and Clae, would all be home to share the Christmas turkey with them. They could even stay the night if they wished, and no one would be tripping over anybody in unexpected places.

It was something grand to look forward to, and Marty spent many hours planning, sewing, and dreaming.

TWENTY-NINE

Missie's Callers

Missie closed the exercise book she had been marking and heaved a contented sigh. It was hard to believe she was already into her second year of teaching. She loved it. True, she had some rascals in her classroom, including her own young brother Luke, but all in all she was glad she had chosen to be a teacher.

She piled the books neatly together and got up to clean the chalkboard. Her back to the door, she screamed in alarm when a pair of hands suddenly circled around to cover her eyes.

"Hey, hey, it's okay," a voice said. "I didn't mean to frighten ya, only surprise ya like."

Missie turned to look into the face of Willie LaHaye. Through her mind flashed the dead mouse, the grasshopper, and other nasty pranks Willie had played in the past. Her fright turned to anger and she swung away in disgust.

"Willie LaHaye!" she exploded. "When are you ever going to grow up?"

She immediately wanted to bite her tongue, for her eyes assured her that Willie LaHaye had indeed grown up—at least on the outside.

Broad shoulders topped strong muscled arms showing inside his shirt sleeves; bushy sideburns indicated what his beard would be were he not clean-shaven, and Missie had to look up a good way in order to signal her wrath.

Willie only grinned, the same maddening, boyish grin.

Missie again spun around on her heel.

"Well, now that you've had your fun, you can just take yourself right on out the door. I'm busy."

"But I came to see the new schoolmarm," he said, seemingly not at all perturbed by her anger. "I think thet I could use a little help on my ABC's." He moved around to get in front of her.

"*A* is for apple, *B* is for bait," he recited. "*C* is for coyness—*E* is for Eve, and thet's about as far as I can git."

"You're not funny—besides, you missed *D*."

"*D*," said Willie, "*D*—hmm. 'Bout the only thing I remember thet starts with *D* is—dear."

Missie was so angry she considered throwing the chalk brush she discovered was still in her hand.

"Willie LaHaye!" she started in sternly.

"I know, I know," said Willie comfortably, "I'm not funny. Actually I stopped by to give ya some good news."

"Such as—?" prompted Missie.

"Such as, I'm leavin'."

"Yer what?"

"I'm leavin'. I'm goin' on further west." Willie suddenly had turned very serious.

"To where?"

"Not sure. Ya know when Pa settled here, he'd been planning on goin' on further. Hadn't been fer Ma gettin' sick we would have gone on. Well, I always was a mite disappointed. I'd sorta like to see what's over the next hill. Pa's all settled in here now, and Nathan's married and settled in, too, an' I suddenly got to thinkin' they don't need me around a'tall."

Missie had cooled down some and was willing to talk if Willie would be sensible.

"What does your pa think?"

"Haven't told 'im yet."

"When would you go?"

Willie shrugged. "Don' know—that depends on a few things."

"Like—?"

"Like Ma—she's still not well, ya know, an' other things. Thought maybe next summer—maybe."

"Not soon, then?"

"Depends."

Missie turned back to her boards and finished erasing the day's lessons.

"How's the teachin' goin'?" Willie asked.

"Good," said Missie "—only I had to send Luke to a corner today."

"What'd he do?"

"He dipped Elizabeth Anne's ribbons in an inkwell."

"Spoilsport."

Missie remembered her own ribbons being dipped in an inkwell. And who had done it.

"It's not funny," she said, angry again. "Hair ribbons cost money."

"Reckon they do. I never thought about that."

"Well, I told Luke he had to save his pennies to buy new ribbons for Elizabeth Anne."

"You're a smart teacher."

"Not smart—just—"

"Pretty?"

"Of course not. Look, if you're not going to be sensible, I refuse to talk to you."

Missie walked over to close the open window. It was stuck—as usual.

"Here, let me help."

Willie stood directly behind her and reached out toward the window. Missie was imprisoned between his arms. Her face flushed. She dared not turn around or she would be face to face with him.

Willie didn't seem in any hurry to lower the window, though looking at the muscular arms, Missie knew the problem wasn't his lack of strength.

"Can't you get it, either?" she asked, her voice surprisingly controlled.

"It's stuck, all right."

"Willie LaHaye!" she stormed, "you're a liar."

"Yeah," he said, grinning as the window came effortlessly into place. And there was Missie standing within the circle of Willie's outstretched arms.

Before Willie could make a further move, Missie ducked down under his arms, then stepped back a pace, her eyes flashing fire. Then she swung on her heel and grabbed her coat.

"Please see that the door is closed when you leave!" she threw over her shoulder and was gone.

That fall Missie had her first caller. She sure didn't count Willie's visit to the schoolhouse as one. Marty knew this time in their daughter's life was bound to come, and soon. But even so, she was unprepared for it when it happened.

Missie had been the youngest member of her small class at the normal school for teachers. Though Missie never said so, she was a popular student, as well. Occasionally since returning home, Missie would refer to this fellow student or that fellow student, but Marty had not had any reason to feel that one was more special than the other. Then one day at the Davis door appeared a tall sandy-haired young man, well groomed and properly mannered. A large, beautiful horse, appearing to have some racing blood, stood tethered at the hitching rail.

"How do you do?" he began. "My name is Grant Thomas. Would Miss Melissa Davis be in please?" His voice was most respectful.

Marty stammered, "Why . . . why, yes . . . she's in." She finally found her tongue and her own manners. "Won't ya come in please?"

"Thank you. And are you Melissa's mother? She spoke of you often."

Marty was still flustered. "Thet's right . . . please step in. I'll call Missie . . . um . . . Melissa right away."

Missie seemed pleased to see the young man. Marty watched carefully for signs of more than just gladness at seeing an old school chum.

Grant stayed to share supper with them and proved to be a quiet, intelligent young man. Clark seemed to quite enjoy him, and Marty attempted to send Clark silent warnings that he shouldn't encourage him too much.

The two young people visited and laughed over the supper table, seeming to thoroughly enjoy each other's company, which made Marty feel funny little shivers of fear run through her. Missie was so young— only seventeen. *Please, please, Lord, I'm not ready to give our Missie up yet*, she implored.

Grant told them he planned to ride back into town before nightfall, and Missie saddled Lady and rode part of the way with him.

When she returned, Marty saw her go to the pasture gate to turn Lady loose, brushing and fussing over her before she sent her on her way. When Missie stopped outside at the basin to wash her hands, she looked quite normal enough. She paused on the porch to admire Ellie's cushion top that the younger girl was making before coming into the kitchen, humming to herself as she often did.

Marty had quickly picked up her knitting and was trying to look and sound normal herself. "This here Grant," she began, "don't recall ya sayin' much 'bout 'im."

"Not much to say. Let's see . . ."

Marty could already see Missie's ploy coming: *Throw Ma off with some facts, nonessential facts, but facts, nonetheless.*

"He's three years older than me," Missie hurried on, "an only child; his ma leads the Ladies' Aid and his pa's a doctor. His folks live in a big stone house on Maple Street, I believe it is, only about seven blocks from the normal school. They like to entertain, so they have Grant's friends—which includes almost everyone—over for tea, or tennis, or whatever." She finished with a noncommittal smile.

Marty wasn't to be sidetracked so easily. "What I want to know is, are you one of Grant's friends?"

"Guess so."

"Special like?"

"Oh, Ma," Missie groaned, sinking to a chair nearby, "how do you make a fella understand that you like him fine—but it ends there?"

"Did ya tell 'im?"

"I thought I had done that before."

"An' this time?"

"I hope he understands."

Missie rose with a shrug of her shoulders and moved on to her room. Marty kept her knitting needles clicking. She must remember to speak to the boys and inform them that she wanted to hear no teasing about the young man who had called. She hoped the fellow truly did understand. Poor Grant. But she couldn't help but feel relieved.

Marty was not to be at peace for long, for Lou Graham asked Clark for permission to call. Marty had no problem with Lou himself, but she still had difficulty accepting the fact that Missie was growing up. Nandry and Clae had both been older when they received their callers and married, and Marty had half hoped Missie would follow their example. Perhaps Missie would have, but several young men seemed to have other ideas.

Lou sat in their parlor now, he and Missie playing checkers. Marty noticed Missie deliberately attempting to lose. Missie was good at checkers and would never, without intention, be caught in the situation she was in now. Lou's mind didn't seem to be on the game, however, and he was not taking advantage of the opportunities she was presenting.

Clare, Arnie, and Luke found it most difficult to understand why Lou did not choose to join them in pitching horseshoes as he always had in the past. The three boys were finally sent to bed, still puzzling over the situation.

After checkers, Missie fixed cocoa and sliced some loaf cake. The adults were invited to join the young people at the kitchen table, and they found no difficulty in chatting with young Lou, whom they had known nearly all his life.

Missie walked with Lou to the end of the path from the road and waited as he untied his horse and left for home.

"Will he be back?" Clark asked Missie when she returned to the kitchen.

"I expect so."

Marty thought her voice lacked enthusiasm.

"Nice boy," she commented.

"Uh-hum. All the Grahams are nice."

"Do ya remember when ya were gonna marry Tommie?" Marty asked.

Missie giggled. "Poor Tommie. He must have been embarrassed. I told everybody that—but he never said a word."

"Well, thet's all long in the past," continued Marty. "Tom has his Fran now."

"And me?"

Marty looked up in surprise.

"That's what you're thinking, isn't it, Ma? What about me?"

"All right," Marty conceded, "what about you?"

"I don't know," said Missie, shaking her head. "I think I need lots of time to sort that all out."

"Nobody's gonna rush ya," Clark said, expressing both his and Marty's feelings.

Lou continued calling. Missie was friendly and a good companion, but Marty noticed she didn't show the bloom of a girl in love. Which was just fine by her.

THIRTY

Missie's Discovery

Missie was about to close up the school building when the door opened and Willie once more came in.

"Should I have knocked?" he asked.

"Wouldn't have hurt."

"Sorry," said Willie. "Next time I'll knock."

Missie continued to button her coat.

"Come to think of it—guess there won't be a next time."

Missie looked up then.

"I really came to sorta say good-bye."

"You're leaving?"

"Yeah."

"When?"

"Day after tomorra."

"You said you weren't going until summer."

"I said thet it depended on some things, remember?"

"I . . . I . . . guess so. Is your mother better, then?"

Willie shook his head. "'Fraid not. I don't think Ma will ever be better." There was sadness in his voice.

"I'm sorry," Missie said softly, then, "How are you going?"

"I'm takin' the stage out to meet the railroad. Then I'll go by rail as far as I can. Iffen I want to go on, I'll buy me a horse or a team."

"What are you planning to do once you get there—pan for gold?"

Missie's slightly mocking tone was probably not missed by Willie, but he chose to ignore it.

"Kinda have my heart set on some good cattle country. Like to git me a good spread and start a herd. I think I'd rather raise cattle than plant crops."

"Well, good luck." Missie was surprised that she really meant it, and she was also surprised by how much she meant it.

"Thanks," said Willie. He paused a moment, then said, "By the way, I have somethin' fer ya. Sort of an old debt like."

He put his hand in his pocket and came out with some red hair ribbons.

"Iffen I remember correctly, they were a little redder than these, but these were the reddest red thet I could find."

"Oh, Willie," whispered Missie, suddenly wanting to cry. "It didn't matter. I . . . I don't even wear these kinds of ribbons anymore."

"Then save 'em fer yer little girl. Iffen she looks like her mama, she'll be drivin' little boys daffy, an' like as not she'll have lots of ribbons dipped in an inkwell."

He turned to go. "Bye, Missie," he whispered hoarsely. "The best of everythin' to ya."

"Bye, Willie—thank you—and God take care of you."

Missie wondered later if she had really heard the soft words, "I love ya," or had only imagined them.

Missie tossed and turned on her pillow that night. She couldn't understand her own crazy heart. One thing she knew. She'd have to face up to Lou—tell him honestly and finally that she wanted him as a friend but nothing more. But even with that settled, her whirling thoughts and emotions would not let her sleep. She reached beneath her pillow to again finger the red hair ribbons. Crazy Willie LaHaye! Why did he have to trouble her so, and why did the thought of his leaving in two days bring such sorrow to her heart? Was it possible that after all these years of fighting and storming against him, she had somehow fallen in love? Absurd!

But Missie was not able to convince her aching heart.

The news came with the Coffin children at school the next day. Mrs. LaHaye had died during the night. Somehow Missie made it through her teaching duties. Her heart ached for Willie. He had dearly loved his mother. What would he do now? Certainly he would not be able to leave on the stagecoach on the morrow.

If only she had a chance to talk to him, to express her sorrow, and to take back some of the dismissive and sometimes downright unkind things she had said down through the years.

The school day finally drew to a close. Missie announced that due to the bereavement in the community, classes would be canceled for the following day.

That evening Lou came to call. It didn't seem quite right to Missie that a young man should go courting on the eve of a neighborhood funeral, and her agitation made it easier for her to follow through on her intention of putting a halt to the whole thing. Lou walked to his horse looking rather dejected.

The next day another mound was added to the cemetery by the church. Missie stood with the other mourners, the wind whipping her long coat around her.

When the others went in to be warmed by hot coffee, Missie left the group and walked toward a grove of trees at the far end of the yard.

She was standing there silently, leaning against a tree trunk, when a hand was placed on her elbow. She did not even jump. Perhaps she had been expecting, hoping for him to come.

"Missie?"

She turned. "I'm sorry, Willie—truly sorry about your ma." Tears slid down her cheeks.

Willie lowered his head to hide his own tears, then brushed them roughly away. "Thank ya," he said, "but I'm glad—sort of glad—thet I was still here. It could have happened after I'd gone, an' then—then I'd always have been sorry."

"Are you still going?"

Willie looked surprised at her question.

"Well, you said it depended on your mother, and I didn't know how you meant—"

"I didn't say thet—entirely. I said it depended on other things, too."

"On what?" The question was asked before Missie could check herself.

For a moment there was silence; then Willie said with difficulty, "On you, Missie—on you an' Lou. Guess ya know how I've always felt 'bout ya. An' now thet you an' Lou are . . . well . . . friends, there's nothin' much fer me to hang 'round here fer."

"But Lou and I aren't . . . aren't . . ."

"He's been callin' regular like."

"But it's over. There was never much to it—only friendship, and last night I . . . I asked Lou not to call again."

"Really? Really, Missie?"

"Really."

Another silence. Willie swallowed hard. "Would there be a chance . . . any chance thet I could . . . thet I could call?"

"You're crazy, Willie LaHaye," said Missie, laughing and cying as she reached up and put her arms around his neck. "Are you ever going to grow up?"

Willie looked deeply into her eyes, and he must have seen there the love he had hardly dared to hope for. He pulled her close in a tender embrace. Willie LaHaye grew up in a hurry.

THIRTY-ONE

Christmas Surprises

True to Clark's promise, the new house was ready before Christmas. The moving in was a big job, and on one of her many trips between the new and the old house, Marty told Clark she sure didn't want to do this again anytime soon. But once all the furnishings had been moved over and set in place, the new curtains hung, and everyone settled in their own rooms, Marty was well satisfied. Marty and Clark sat at the breakfast table with the first cups of coffee in their new place and thanked the Lord for His blessing on them and their family over the years.

"Well, the coffee is as good as ever. Sure relieved 'bout thet." Clark joked as he rose to go out to the barn.

Willie LaHaye was a frequent guest at the Davises' new home, and Marty and Clark both appreciated him. If they had to give up their Missie, they were glad it looked like it would be to such a fine young man.

But on Christmas Eve, Willie unintentionally broke into their sense of comfort and acceptance of the courtship. It was during a casual conversation with the men of the house. Nandry's Josh had been telling of his plans to get a better grade animal for his pig lot, and Willie stated this was the direction he wished to go—starting with a few really good cattle and gradually building his herd. But first he'd have to choose just the right land for the project. He hoped in the spring of the new year to leave on a scouting trip and take plenty of time in picking his homestead. After he had secured it, he would return for Missie.

Clark went very still and Marty's head swung around.

"Yer not plannin' on farmin' 'round here?" Clark finally asked.

"I'm not plannin' on farmin' at all," Willie answered. "Got me a real hankerin' to do some ranchin' instead."

"How far . . . how far away ya think ya have to go to find good ranch land at an affordable price?" Marty asked hesitantly.

"Few hundred miles, anyway."

Marty felt weakness go all through her. Willie was heading farther west. Willie was also planning to marry her Missie. *Oh, dear God,* she mourned inwardly. *He's plannin' on takin' Missie out west.*

She slipped quietly out to the kitchen, hoping no one had noticed her leave. She walked into the coolness of the pantry and leaned her head against a cupboard door.

"Oh, dear Lord," she prayed again, mouthing the words through lips that trembled. "Please help 'im git this silly notion out of his head." Her head came up at a sudden thought. *I wonder, does Missie even know 'bout it?*

But Missie had followed her into the pantry. "Mama," she said, laying a hand on Marty's arm. "Mama, are you feeling all right?"

"I'm fine—fine," Marty assured her, straightening up.

"Is it . . . what Willie said?"

"Well, I will admit it was some kind of shock. I had no notion he had such plans."

"I should have told you sooner—"

"Then ya knew?"

"Of course. Willie talked about it even before . . . before we made any plans."

"I see."

"I should have told you," Missie said again. "I suppose Willie thought I had."

"It's all right, Missie."

"It's . . . it's kind of hard for you, isn't it, Mama?"

"Yeah . . . yeah, I guess it is." Marty tried to keep her voice from shaking.

"I suppose," said Missie carefully, "that you feel kinda like your own mama felt when you planned to leave with Clem."

Now, ya listen here, Marty wanted to admonish, *you're bein' unfair, throwin' thet up to me.* But after a moment she said instead, "Yes, I guess it is."

For the first time, Marty thought about her own mother's feelings and recognized why it had been so difficult for her own family to accept her leaving.

"Yeah," she said again, "I guess this is how she felt."

"But you loved Clem," prompted Missie, "and you knew you had to go."

"Yes. I loved him."

Missie put her arms around Marty and gave her a squeeze. "Oh, Mama, I love Willie so much. We've prayed about this together. We can go on farther west. We can open up a new land together. We can build a school, a church, can make a community prosper and grow. Don't you see it, Mama?"

Marty held her little girl close. "'Course I see it. 'Course. It's jest gonna take some gittin' used to, thet's all. You go on back, now. Me, I'm gonna catch me a little air."

Missie looked a bit reluctant, but she turned back to the laughter coming from the family sitting room.

Marty wrapped a warm shawl closely about her shoulders and stepped out into the crisp night air.

The sky was clear and the cold emphasized the brightness of the stars above her. Marty turned her face heavenward.

"God," she said aloud, "she's yer child. We have long since given her back to you, Clark and me. Ya know how I feel 'bout her leavin', but iffen it's in yer plan, help me, Father . . . help me to accept it an' to let her go. Lead her, God, an' take care of her . . . take care of our little girl."

❧

The Davises saw much of Willie LaHaye in the next few months. It seemed to Marty that he might just as well move in his bedroll. They liked Willie and approved of the relationship between him and Missie, but Marty knew their remaining time with Missie in their home would be far too short. After she and Willie were married . . . Marty tried to not even think that far ahead. But with Missie at school all day, it was difficult to be required to share her with Willie almost every evening.

Missie and Willie were full of plans and dreams. Willie spent much of his time talking to men who had been farther west, inquiring about good range land. He was advised by most to travel toward the mountains and then follow the range southward. The winter snows were not as deep there, was the consensus of opinion, and the range land was excellent. Willie was cautioned to make sure he chose carefully with a year-round source of water supply in mind.

One evening Missie returned from bidding Willie good night, but this time her eyes sparked and her cheeks were flushed with anger. She took a quick swipe at her cheek with the back of her hand in an effort to hide her tears.

Clark and Marty both looked at her in surprise but said nothing.

"That—that—Willie LaHaye!" Missie muttered and headed upstairs to her bedroom.

She did not tell them what the quarrel had been about, but two evenings later it appeared to be well patched up, forgiven, and forgotten.

On the tenth of May, Willie would be leaving to seek his new land.

Missie bade him farewell in private. His excitement carried over to her, filling her heart and imagination. She did want him to go find their land to fulfill their dreams, but, oh, she would miss him. And there was always the slight chance he wouldn't be coming back. She had heard tales of other men who had gone and, because of sickness or accident, never returned. He assured her, over and over, that he would return. She wanted to believe him and tried to shut out the black thoughts, but they refused to be thoroughly banished.

She knew that Willie, too, had wrestled with doubts. They had discussed many times the reality that the West was calling to him, but sometimes he wondered if maybe he was doing this all wrong. Maybe they should marry first and go together; then there would be no need for a separation. But then again it might be awfully hard on Missie—

trailing him around looking for a place that could be theirs. Land was not as easy to come by now as it had once been—at least not good land. It would mean perhaps living in a covered wagon for many months. No, he had concluded, making her go through all that was selfish. He'd go alone first, then come back for her. Perhaps the months would pass quickly for both of them. He prayed that they would.

Willie also had talked frankly with Missie about the fact there were other neighborhood young men around—Lou Graham, for one—and Missie was a very pretty and appealing girl. Could a lonely girl, left for months on her own, hold on to the flame for him? Wait for him to return for her? She assured him, over and over, that she could.

Missie, who now walked beside him, her hand in his one more time before he left, put into words the thoughts of both of them. "It's going to seem an awfully long time, I'm afraid."

Willie stopped walking, turned her to him, and looked deeply into her eyes.

"For me, too." He swallowed hard. "I hope an' pray thet the days and weeks go quickly."

"Oh, Willie," cried Missie, "I'll pray for you every night . . . that . . . that God will keep you and . . . and speed your way."

"An' I fer you." Willie traced a finger along Missie's cheek, and she buried her face against his shoulder and let the tears flow freely. He held her close, and she could feel him stroking her long brown hair. A man wasn't supposed to cry, but she knew he was and loved him all the more for it.

It was time for Willie to go. He kissed her several times, whispered his promises to her again and again, then put her gently from him. He did not look back at her once he started for his horse.

"He'll be back," Missie promised herself aloud. "Willie will be back." And she lifted her face to the stars and whispered, "Please take care of him, Father."

⁂

Willie's good-byes were not yet over. Zeke LaHaye accompanied his son into town and puttered around at last-minute fixings and unnecessary purchases. When the time finally came for the group heading west to be off, Zeke stepped forward and gave his son a hearty handshake and some last-minute cautionary advice.

"Be careful now, son. Like yer ma woulda told ya iffen she still be here, be courteous to those ya meet, but don't allow yerself to be stepped on. Take care of yerself an' yer equipment. It'll only be of use to you iffen ya look after it. Keep away from the seamy side of things—I not be needin' to spell thet out none. Take care, ya hear?"

Willie nodded, thanked his pa, and was about to turn and go when Zeke LaHaye suddenly cast aside his usual reserve and stepped forward to engulf his boy in a warm embrace. Willie returned the hug, acknowledging how good it felt to be locked in the arms of his father. The last thing Willie saw as he left was his pa, big and weathered Zeke LaHaye, brushing a tear from his sun-darkened face.

THIRTY-TWO

One More Surprise

It was a Saturday, and Marty was in the kitchen turning out a batch of bread when Luke skipped in.

Missie sat hemming a tablecloth and didn't even lift her head toward her young brother until he announced in a teasing, sing-songy voice, "Willie's comin'."

"Oh, Luke, stop it," said Marty. Missie was lonely and miserable enough without someone playing with her emotions. It had been nearly a year since Willie had left, and letters between them had been far too few. Not that either of them didn't want to write, but postal delivery to someone on horseback was difficult at best.

"He is *too* comin'—jest see fer yerself," Luke argued and pointed down the road.

Missie ran to the window. "He *is*, Ma!" she nearly screamed in her excitement and was out the door on the run.

"Well, I'll be." Marty stood at the window and watched Willie's galloping horse slide to a stop and the young man leap to the ground, all in one motion.

"I'll be," said Marty again. "The boy's been all the way west and back and then risks his neck in my yard." She smiled as she watched the young couple embrace, obviously caring not at all whether they had an audience.

Marty turned back to her bread. After he first had gone, she had secretly looked forward to having extra time with Missie all to themselves. But the look in Missie's eyes and the evidence of sleepless nights soon made Marty realize that she, too, would gladly welcome Willie's return.

There was a lot of joy at the table that evening. Missie and Willie spent more time feasting their eyes on each other than eating. Marty couldn't help but hope maybe Willie's quest had been in vain and that he would settle for a farm in the area.

Finally Clark posed the question. "Did ya find what you're lookin' for out west?"

"Sure did."

Marty's heart sank, but she held on to her calm and kept a smile on her face.

"What's it like?" she made herself ask, surprised her voice sounded normal.

"Well, ma'am," Willie said, his eyes shining as he talked, "it's 'bout the nicest thing—landwise," he quickly amended with a grin toward Missie, "thet a man ever set eyes on." He turned back to the family as he continued, and Marty rose to replenish the bowl of potatoes.

"There's no tall timber in that area—only scrub brush in the draws. The hills are low and rolling with lots of grass. Toward one end is a valley—like a picture—with a perfect spot fer home buildin'. It's sheltered an' green, with a spring-fed crik runnin' down below. Lotsa water on the place, too. Three springs thet I know of—maybe more thet I didn't spot out yet."

The enthusiasm in Willie's face was contagious.

"Almost makes me wish I wasn't old an' crippled, son," Clark quipped.

Marty reached over his shoulder with the refilled bowl, then stood behind his chair and touched his hair affectionately. "I most surely am not married to anybody old and crippled, Clark Davis," she told him. "Who on earth are ya' talkin' about?" The family laughed with her.

"Were ya able to make the deal?" Clark was a practical man. Searching out good land did not mean ownership.

"Thet's what took the time." Willie nodded. "Man, ya jest wouldn't believe the hassle—goin' here, goin' there, seein' this man, lookin' up thet 'un, sendin' fer government papers. I began to wonder iffen I'd ever git through it all."

He grinned and nodded again. "Finally did, though. The papers I hold declare it all to be mine. An' it's a lot closer to here than I'd expected it to be." Marty could tell he was stating this mostly for her benefit. "Won't take too long at all to travel on out," Willie told them. "There's a couple of wagon trains travelin' through thet way every summer. Takin' supplies mostly to the towns down south, but they have no objection to travelers followin' along with 'im. Thet way ya git there safe an' sound with all yer supplies at hand."

So it would be by covered wagon after all that Missie traveled. Marty remembered her own trip west by wagon and its tragic end not far from here. She had secretly hoped that if Missie really had to go, it could have been by train. She crossed to the fire and began adding wood where none was needed but soon checked herself. She'd be driving everyone from her kitchen with the heat.

No use trying to pretend anymore. Their beloved Missie would be leaving, going west, and in a very short time. Marty had not spoken out against it, but somehow she had pushed the idea aside, hoping that things would change—that the young couple would decide not to go. Now here was the excited young man, in possession of papers that declared him a landowner out west, and an equally excited Missie hanging on his every word as though she could hardly wait to get started. There was no stopping it now.

Marty decided to slip quietly out for a little walk to the spring.

As the wedding day drew nearer, the house was caught in the flurry of preparations. Besides the wedding itself, careful consideration needed to be given to each item Missie was collecting in preparation for her frontier home, for each one must be essential, must fit into the wagon, and would need to withstand the long trip.

Marty had gone to her old trunk and produced a lace tablecloth that had been made by the hands of her own dear grandmother for her wedding gift. Most of the things Marty had brought with her from the East she had long ago put to use, but this was special. Also in the trunk was a spread that Marty's mother had made. This would be saved for Ellie.

Besides sewing the linens and the various other household needs, Missie was busy preparing her wardrobe. There was no way she wanted to be caught short no matter how long they should be on the trail. Her dresses had to be light for the hot summer ahead and yet wear well during the rugged travel.

Missie sewed with enthusiasm. She enjoyed sewing, and with a purpose as exciting as this, the job was a pleasure rather than a chore. Bright bonnets and colorful aprons took shape. She crafted calico gowns, then bundled and packed them into stout wooden boxes that Clark had made. Marty kept thinking of things Missie would need. Things that she herself had not had the foresight to pack when she herself came west. Pans, utensils, kettles, crockery, medical supplies, jars, containers for food—the list seemed endless and often left Missie laughing with an "Oh, Ma."

Marty's anxious mind refused to find rest but continued to go over the same worn-out path again and again—no doctor, no preacher, no schools, maybe no near neighbors—which meant no Ma Graham. Oh, how much she did not want to see Missie go.

But Missie sang as she worked and packed. The girl fairly danced through the house in her happiness.

⁓

At the sound of an approaching horse, Missie stood quickly from the machine, where she had been busy finishing a gingham dress.

"There's Willie. He promised me that he'd help me pick enough strawberries for supper. We won't be long, Ma."

Marty sighed and put aside her own quilting that also would be going into one of the boxes. She would make some shortcake to go with the berries.

The young people set off, arm in arm, for the far pasture, Missie's old red lunch pail swinging at Willie's side.

On the way to the kitchen Marty stopped and looked at Missie's sewing. She had become a good seamstress. Marty was proud of her.

She stood fingering the garment, and then her hand lovingly traveled over the machine. All through the years since she had become Missie's mama, this machine had sewn the garments for each of her children. Clothing was mended, new towels hemmed, household items for three brides had been made here, young hands had learned the art of sewing. It was a good machine. It had never let her down. True, it didn't have the same shine that it had when it was first carried through her door, but it had borne the years well.

Marty was deep in thought, and eventually her tears began to fall unattended. Then Clark was there beside her, and he reached out and took her hand. She looked up at him and shook herself free from her reverie. It was a moment before she felt in control enough to speak.

"Clark, I been thinkin'. I'd like to give the machine—Ellen's machine—to Missie. Ya mind?"

It was silent for a time and then Clark answered. "It's yours to give. Iffen thet's what ya want, then it's fine with me."

"I'd like to—she'll be needin' it in the years ahead. And Ellen *was* her mama."

"An' so are you." His arm circled her waist, and she leaned against him.

"An' what will you do?" Clark finally asked.

"I can go back to hand sewin'. I was used to thet, but Missie—she's always used the machine. She'd be lost without it. 'Sides, I think thet it be fittin' like."

She brushed away the last trace of the tears, then reached out a hand to run it again over the smooth metal and polished wood of the well-loved machine.

"Will ya be good enough, Clark, to make it a nice strong crate, an' then I'll wrap an old blanket around it so's it won't get scratched."

Clark nodded his head. "I'll git right to it tomorra."

"Thank ya," Marty said and went to prepare the shortcake.

THIRTY-THREE

A Special Day

When Missie's wedding day dawned clear and bright, Marty felt it just suited the girl—their happy, excited, and pretty young daughter.

Marty paused a moment before leaving her bed to send heavenward a quick but fervent petition. *Oh, God. Please, please take care of our little girl . . . an' . . . an' make today a day thet she can look back on with joy and good memories.* She looked over at Clark still snoring softly and quietly slipped from under the covers.

There was much to be done. Marty knew she mustn't dawdle in sentiment or emotion. She dressed quickly and went to the kitchen. Clark soon joined her and built a lively fire in the old cook stove. When they had moved into the new house, Clark had told her she could have a new cook stove, something more up-to-date—but Marty had refused.

"Why, I'd feel disloyal," she had explained, "castin' out a faithful ole friend like thet. Thet old stove and I have boiled coffee fer friends, baked bread fer family, an' . . . an' . . . even cooked pancakes," she finished with a knowing smile, remembering her long-ago menu limitations.

So the old stove had moved with her. She checked the wood in it now and pushed the kettle forward.

Missie had decided to be married at home.

"I want to come down those stairs there on Pa's arm. Really, Ma, if you open up all of the rooms, it's most as big as the church anyway."

Clark and Marty had been happy to agree.

The morning hours flew by too rapidly. There were last-minute preparations of food for the afternoon meal. Fresh flowers needed to be brought in and arranged. Children needed to be checked to see that they had done their assigned chores. Marty felt as though she was on the run most of the morning.

The wedding was set for three o'clock in the afternoon. It was after two before Marty was able to hurry from the kitchen, do a last-minute check on the rooms, and run to her bedroom for a quick bath. Arnie had filled the tub for her. She then slipped into her new dress. Her long hair tumbled about her shoulders, and as she pinned it up, she noticed her fingers trembled. After a last quick check on her appearance, she went to Missie's room.

Marty thought Missie had never looked prettier than at that moment. Standing there in her wedding gown, her cheeks flushed, her eyes bright with tenderness, she looked so happy Marty's throat caught in a lump.

"Oh, Ma," Missie whispered.

"Yer beautiful, Missie," Marty whispered back. "Jest beautiful." She pulled the girl close to her.

"Oh, Ma," sighed Missie. "Ma, I want to tell you something. I've never said it before, but I want to thank you—to thank you for coming into our lives, for making us so happy—me and Pa."

Marty held her breath. If she tried to speak she'd cry, she knew, so she said nothing, only pulled her little girl closer and kissed the brown curly head.

Clark came in then and put his arms around both of them. His voice sounded tight with emotion as he spoke. "God bless," he said. "God bless ya both." He placed a kiss on the cheek of each of them, and then he placed his hand gently on Missie's head, tried to clear the hoarseness from his throat, and prayed in a low voice, "The Lord bless ya an' keep ya, the Lord make His face to shine upon ya and be gracious unto ya; the Lord lift up His countenance upon ya and give ya peace—now an' always, Missie. Amen."

Missie blinked away her tears and moved out into the hall to hear last-minute instructions from Parson Joe.

Clark reached for Marty. At first he said nothing, only looked deeply into her eyes.

"It hurts a mite, doesn't it?" he whispered.

Marty nodded. "Isn't she beautiful—our Missie?"

Clark's eyes darkened with emotion. "Yeah, she's beautiful."

"Oh, Clark—I love her so."

"I know ya do." He pulled her close and his hand stroked her back. "Thet's why yer lettin' her go."

Down below, the waiting neighbors were beginning a hymn. Marty knew it was time for her to take her place downstairs. Soon Clark would be coming down, too, with the radiant Missie on his arm.

She looked at Clark, silently accepting with deep appreciation the strength he offered. Then she slipped away.

She would not cry anymore—not today, Missie's wedding day. There would be many times ahead for that. Today she would smile—would face her neighbors as the happy mother of the bride—would welcome, with love, another son.

She stopped at the top of the stairs, breathed a quick prayer, took a deep breath, and descended smiling.

LOVE'S LONG JOURNEY

This book is dedicated to you,
the readers of *Love Comes Softly*
and *Love's Enduring Promise,*
with thanks for your kind words
of encouragement.

Prologue

Let's imagine for a moment a family separation back in the days of the pioneers. Grown children have announced to their parents that the West is calling them.

For weeks and months the entire family is in a fever-pitch of excitement and activity, making plans, sewing clothing and bedding, purchasing and packing crates and crocks with supplies sufficient for many months—or even years. All the food, from coffee to flour, lard to honey, molasses to salt—and other items pickled, salted, dried, canned—is collected and prepared for the long journey. Lamps and fuel are needed, grease for the wagons, repair parts for the harnesses, as well as guns and gunpowder, tools, nails, rope, crocks, kettles, pots and pans, dishes, medicines, seeds, and material to make more clothing when what they wore would become threadbare. Any furniture or equipment that the family can afford and find room for is packed in the wagons—stove, sewing machine, bed, table, and chairs all have to be taken along.

Breakables are carefully packed in sawdust and crated in handmade boxes. Everything needs to be protected against possible water damage, for there will be rivers to ford and rains to endure. At the journey's end, the crates will be unpacked and disassembled, every board hoarded for some future building project—a window frame, a stool, a baby's crib. The sawdust will be sparingly used to feed a fire, sprinkled lightly over smoking buffalo chips.

The crocks and jars containing food will be used for other storage when their original purpose is complete.

Yes, it is a monumental task. The preparation for such a move will tax minds, bodies, and emotions to the limit. But when the sorting and packing is finished, the wagons are loaded and the teams hitched and ready to move out—what then?

Mothers and fathers will bid their offspring farewell with the knowledge they might be seeing them for the last time. Communication by letter across country will take many months, if such letters arrive at all. So parents in the East will know next to nothing of their children's and grandchildren's whereabouts or their well-being. Those who stay behind no doubt hope that no news is good news—for only bad news is of sufficient import to be delivered across the empty miles.

Wife follows husband, convinced that her rightful place is by his side regardless of the strong tug toward the home she has known and loved. Danger, loneliness, and possible disaster await them in the new world toward which they are heading, but she goes nonetheless.

I often think about those pioneer women. What it must have cost many of them to follow their husband's dream! To venture forth, leaving behind the things that represented safety and security; to birth their babies unattended; to nurse sick children with no medicines or doctors; to be mother, teacher, minister, physician, tailor, and grocer to a growing family; to support their men without complaint through floods, blizzards, sandstorms, and droughts; to walk tall when there was little to wear, little to work with, and even less to eat.

God bless them all—the women who courageously went forth with their men. And bless those who stood with tear-filled eyes and aching hearts and let their loved ones go. And grant to us a measure of the faith, strength, courage, love, and determination that prompted them to do what they did.

Janette Oke

ONE

The Journey Begins

Missie experimentally pushed back her bonnet and let the rays of the afternoon sun fall directly on her head. She wasn't sure if that was preferable, since the loss of protection from the sun with the shade from its wide brim also kept the slight breeze from her face. It certainly was hot! She comforted herself with the thought that the worst of the day's heat was already past—surely it would begin to cool before long as the sun moved lower in the western sky.

Her first day on the trail seemed extremely long and tiring. The excitement of the morning's early departure already felt as if it were weeks behind her. But no, time insisted it truly had been only at the dawning of this very day when they had exchanged painful good-byes with her beloved family.

As she recalled the tears and sadness of the morning, Missie also felt a tingle of excitement go through her. She and Willie were really heading west! After all the planning and dreaming, they were actually on the way. From her perch on the seat at the front of the wagon, the dream, though still a long way off, was now anchored in reality.

Missie's weary, aching body verified that they were indeed on the way, and she shifted on the hard wooden boards to try for a more comfortable position. Willie turned to her, though she knew his hands expertly holding the reins were still aware of every movement of the plodding team.

"Ya tirin'?" he asked. His eyes searched her hot face.

Missie smiled in spite of her distress and pushed back some strands of damp hair. "A bit. About time for me to stretch my legs again, I reckon."

Willie nodded and turned back to the horses he was driving. "I miss ya when yer not here beside me," he told her, "but I sure won't deny ya none any relief ya might be gettin' from a walk now an' then. Ya wantin' down now?"

"In a few minutes." Missie fell silent, then commented, "Sure's one bustling, dusty way to travel, this going by wagon train." She could feel Willie's sideways glance at her as she continued, "Harness creaking, horses stomping, people shouting—hadn't realized it would be so noisy."

"I 'spect it'll quieten some as we all get used to it." Willie's tone sounded a bit anxious.

"Yeah, I reckon so," Missie assured him quickly. He had enough to worry about without wondering if she was all right.

She reached out to tuck a hand under Willie's arm. She could feel his muscles tighten as he pulled her hand against his body in silent communication. She could see the strength in his arms as they gave firm guidance to the team. His coarse cotton shirt was damp in many places, and Missie noticed he had undone a couple of buttons at the neck.

"Guess we just brought our noise and bustle along with us," she said wryly.

"Meanin'?"

"Well, you know what it's been like at home for all these weeks we've been planning, packing, crating, loading—it seemed it would never end. And the noise was really something—everybody talking at once, hammers pounding, and barrels and pans banging. It was like a madhouse, that's what it was."

Willie laughed. "Was kinda, wasn't it?"

Silence again.

Missie could feel Willie steal a glance her way. She made no further comment, and finally Willie spoke cautiously. "Ya seem to be thinkin' awful deep like."

Missie allowed a quiet sigh to escape from her lips and tightened her grip on Willie's arm. "Not deep . . . just thinking of home. It must seem awfully quiet there now. Awfully quiet. After all the days and months of getting ready. . . ." Missie was so taken up with her reverie she didn't finish her sentence, and Willie did not interrupt.

Missie thought of their two wagons crammed full. Never had she dreamed it possible to get so much into two wagons. Everything they would be needing in the months ahead had been loaded into those wagons—and a fair number of things they could very well have lived without if they'd had to, Missie realized with some chagrin. She thought particularly of the fancy dishes her ma had purchased with some of her own egg money and insisted on packing in sawdust herself. "Someday you'll be glad thet ya made the room," Marty had assured her. And Missie knew in her heart that she would indeed look at the dishes with the bittersweet joy and memories they brought to her soul.

A sense of sadness overtook her, and she had no desire to have Willie read her mind. The thoughts of home and loved ones brought a sharp pain deep inside of her. If she weren't careful, she'd be in tears. She swallowed hard and forced a smile as she turned to him.

"Maybe I should get in a little more walking now," she said briskly.

"I'll pull over right up there ahead at thet widenin' in the road," he promised.

Missie nodded.

"Have you noticed we're already beyond the farms we know?" Willie asked.

"I've noticed."

"Makes it seem more real. Like we really are goin' west." The genuine jubilance in his voice made her smile. She did share his joy and excitement, but at the same instant that now-familiar pain twisted within her. She was going west with Willie—but she was leaving behind all the others she knew and loved. When would she see them again? *Would* she see them again . . . ever? Tears pressed against her eyes.

Willie pulled the team over for a quick stop so she could climb down over the wagon wheel. The dust whirled up as he moved on without her, and Missie stepped away a few paces and turned her back. She pulled her bonnet up to keep the dust from settling on her hair. She waited until both their wagons had passed, giving a brief nod to the young fellow they had hired to drive their second team, then looked around for someone she might have already met among the other walkers who followed the teams. She didn't recognize anyone right off, so Missie smiled at those closest to her and, without a word, took a position in that group.

As she walked the dusty, rutted road, her body, though young and healthy, hurt all over. She wondered how the older women were able to keep going. She glanced about her at two women walking slightly to her right. *They look 'bout Ma's age,* she mused. *She is well and strong and can often outwork me. But, still, I wouldn't want to see her have to put in such a day.*

The women did look tired, and Missie's heart went out to them. Then she remembered the wagon master, Mr. Blake, giving the whole group their instructions that morning. At the time it had seemed foolish to Missie to even consider having a short day the first few days on the trail. Now she understood the wisdom in Mr. Blake's announcement. The sun was gradually moving toward the horizon, and they would be stopping soon, she was sure. She moved over to the two ladies and introduced herself. A bit of a chat would help them all get their minds off their aching bodies.

When their conversation had tapered off, Missie's thoughts turned to Willie. She wondered if he would welcome the early camp tonight, or if his eagerness to reach their destination would make him want to push on.

Missie was proud of Willie, proud of his good looks. He had a dark head of slightly curling hair, deep brown eyes, a strong chin with an indentation akin to a dimple (though Willie would never allow her to call it such), a well-shaped nose that had narrowly spared perfection by his fall from a tree when he was nine years old—these descriptions were her Willie. So were the broad shoulders, the tall frame, the strong arms.

But when Missie thought of Willie, she pictured not only the man whom others saw but his character she had come to know so well. Willie, who was as manly as any but who seemed to read her thoughts, who considered others first, who was flexible when dealing with others but steadfast when dealing with himself. This was a man who was strong and purposeful in his decisions—a mite stubborn, some felt, but Missie preferred to describe him as having "strength of determination." Well, maybe a *little* stubborn, she conceded, if being stubborn was hanging on to a dream—his dream of raising cattle, of working with fine horses, of owning his own ranch, of going further west.

When Willie, two years previously, had made the trip west to seek out the spread of his dreams, he had persevered through seemingly endless searching and red tape until he actually held in his hand the title deed for the land. After he and Missie were married and when their actual going had been delayed in order to set aside the money needed for the venture, Willie had chafed at the delay, but his dream had not died. He had worked hard at the mill, laying aside every penny they could spare until he felt sure they had saved enough. Missie had been proud to add whatever she could from her teacher's salary to make the sum grow more quickly. It gave her a sense of having a part in Willie's dream. It was now becoming her dream, too.

Missie's glance lifted to the sky to figure out the time by the sun. She calculated it was somewhere between three and four o'clock.

Back home the time of day was easily distinguished by the activity in evidence. Right now her ma would be taking a break from heavier tasks, spending some time in her favorite chair with mending or knitting. Her pa would still be in the field. They, too, had been awfully generous in adding to Willie's little nest egg. She then thought of the final moments with her parents. Though it had happened just this morning, time and distance were no longer the only measurements. That was her other life, and she was now heading to a new life, the one she had chosen with Willie.

Pa and Ma had been so brave as they had bid her good-bye. Clark had gathered them all close around him and led them in family prayer. Marty had tried desperately not to cry. At Missie's "It's all right, Mama . . . go ahead and cry if you want to," the tears did come—for both of them.

The two held each other close and wept, and afterward Missie could tell her ma felt a similar measure of relief and comfort as she did.

Missie now brushed away unbidden tears and glanced about to see if she had been observed. Deliberately she pushed the thoughts of loneliness from her. If she weren't careful, she'd work herself into a real state and arrive in camp with red-rimmed eyes and blotchy cheeks. Besides, she had Willie—she need never be *truly* lonesome. And her pa's prayer that morning was a reminder that "the Lord was goin' a'fore and behind" them on their way.

Missie trudged on, placing one tired foot before the other. Even in sturdy walking shoes, her feet looked small, and she knew the plain brown cotton frock did not hide her youthfulness. She had overheard two fellow travelers commenting on "thet wisp of a thing ain't gonna last a week—why, she can't possibly be more'n fifteen!" She couldn't decide whether to laugh or cry about the whole exchange, so she decided to do neither. They probably wouldn't believe she had a normal-school teaching certificate and two years of teaching behind her. But she certainly intended to prove them wrong and pull her weight with the rest of this little traveling community.

Missie now raised a hand to push away some hair that had come untucked and insisted upon wisping about her face. Strands of it clung to the dampness of her moist forehead. She knew her normally fair cheeks were flushed from the heat of the day. In spite of homesickness, weariness, and the hot sun overhead, she couldn't help feeling Willie's enthusiasm and excitement as she looked forward to their new life in their own place.

Missie's attention was drawn back to her traveling companions. Some of the women were now gathering dry sticks and twigs as they followed the wagons. A number of children also were running here and there, picking up suitable fuel, as well. *They must be anticipating stopping soon,* Missie thought, so she, too, began to look about as she walked, gathering fuel for her own fire.

A commotion ahead brought Missie's attention back to the wagons. The drivers were breaking line and maneuvering into a circle as they had been instructed that morning. Missie's steps quickened. It wouldn't be long now until she would be resting in some shade. How wonderful it would be just to sit down for a spell and let the afternoon breeze cool her warm face and body! She was looking forward, also, to chatting with Willie and learning how he had fared in the short time they had been apart.

Missie wondered, with a fluttering of her pulse, if tonight by their campfire would be the time to whisper to Willie about her growing conviction that *perhaps* they were to become parents. She was quite sure now, though she still had not mentioned it to him. *Don't want to raise false hopes—or cause concern for no reason,* she had told herself.

Would Willie be pleased? She knew how he loved youngsters, and she knew his eagerness to have a son of his own. But she could also guess his concern for her in their current circumstances. He had hoped to make the trip west and be settled in their own home *before* starting a family. A long wagon trip could be very difficult for an expectant mother. Yes, Willie might just feel the baby could have selected a more appropriate and convenient time.

Missie had no such misgivings. She was young and healthy, and besides, they would reach Willie's land long before the baby was due. Still, she had to admit to herself that she had put off telling Willie her suspicions until they were actually on the trail. She had been somewhat anxious that if he knew, he would suggest postponing their journey until after the birth, and to Missie's thinking, he had experienced enough delay already.

So she had kept her precious secret. She hadn't dared even share it with her mother, though her whole being ached to do so. *She'll fret,* Missie had told herself. *She'll never rest easy for one night while we're on the trail.*

In the distance Missie spotted their wagons side by side in the big circle. Willie was unhitching the team from their first wagon, and Henry Klein, their hired driver, was working with the second team. When they had begun to load weeks before, it became evident one wagon was not going to be sufficient to provide both living quarters on the way plus transportation for all their supplies and household needs. Missie's father, Clark, had suggested the second wagon and had even helped in locating a driver. Many other members of the wagon train also had more than one wagon, but most of them were fortunate enough to have another family member who could drive the teams. Willie wouldn't have considered for one minute Missie's serving in such a capacity.

As Missie neared their wagons, the twenty-seventh one creaked into position, the driver sweating and shouting to his horses as they completed the circle for the train's overnight stop.

Missie approached Willie now and responded to his grin with a smile of her own.

"Been a long day. Yer lookin' tired," he said, concern in his eyes.

"I am a bit. The sun's been so hot it sure takes the starch out of me."

"It's time fer a good rest. Bit of that shade should revive ya some. Ya wantin' me to bring ya a stool or a blanket from the wagon to sit on?"

"I'll do it. You have the team to care for."

"Mr. Blake says there's a stream jest beyond thet stand of timber there. We're gonna take all the stock down fer a drink an' then tether them in the draw. Blake says there's plenty a' grass there."

"What time are you wanting supper?" Missie asked.

"Not fer a couple hours anyway. Ya got lotsa time fer a rest."

"I'll need more firewood. I didn't start gathering soon enough. That little bit I brought in won't last any time."

"No rush fer a fire, either. I'll bring some wood back with me. Henry won't mind bringin' some, too. Ya jest git a little time outta thet hot sun fer a while—ya look awfully tuckered out." Willie's voice continued to sound anxious.

"It's just the excitement and strangeness of it all, I expect. I'll get used to it. But right now I think I'll take a bit of rest in the shade of those trees. I'll be as good as new when I can get off my feet some."

Willie left with the horses and the two milk cows that had been tied behind the wagons. Missie went for a blanket to place on the ground in the shade of the trees.

She felt a bit guilty as she lowered herself onto the blanket. All the other women were busy with something. Well, she'd just rest a short while and then she would begin their supper preparations, as well. For the moment it felt good just to sit.

Missie leaned back comfortably against the trunk of a tree and closed her eyes, turning her head slightly so she could take full advantage of the gentle breeze. It teased at the loose strands of her hair and fanned her flushed face. All her bones cried out for a warm, relaxing soak in a tub. If she were home . . . but Missie quickly put that thought away from her. Her folks' big white house with its homey kitchen and wide stairway was no longer *her* home. The upstairs room with its cheerful rugs and frilly curtains was no longer *her* room. She was totally Willie's responsibility now, and Willie was hers. She prayed a short prayer that she would be worthy of such a man as her Willie—that God would help her make a home for him filled with happiness and love. And then, her eyes still closed, she felt the achiness weighing her whole body down on the blanket.

Ignore it, she commanded herself. *Ignore it, and it will go away.*

TWO

Day's End

When Missie opened her eyes again, she was surprised at the changes that had taken place around her. It was much cooler now, and the sun that had shone down with such intense heat during the day was hanging, friendly and placid, low in the western sky.

The smell of woodsmoke was heavy in the air—a sharp, pleasant smell—and the odors of cooking food and boiling coffee made her insides twinge with hunger. Now fully awake, she looked around in embarrassment at the supper preparations. Surely every woman in the whole train had been busy and about while she slept. What must they think of her? Willie would soon be back from caring for the animals and not even find a fire started!

Missie hurried toward her wagons, swishing out her skirts and smoothing back her hair.

It took a moment for her to realize that the fire that burned directly in front of their wagons was *her* fire, and that the delicious smell of stew and coffee came from *her* own cooking pots. She was trying to sort it all out when Willie poked his head out of the wagon. His face still showed concern when he looked at her but changed quickly to an expression of relief. "Yer lookin' better. How ya feelin'?"

Missie stammered some, "I'm fine . . . truly, just fine." Then she added in a lowered voice, "But shamed nigh to death."

"Shamed?" Willie's voice sounded unnecessarily loud to Missie. "'Bout what?"

"Well . . . me sitting there sleeping in the middle of the day, and you . . . you making the fire, and the coffee and . . . my goodness, what must they all think of me . . . that my husband has to do his work and mine, too?"

"Iffen thet's all thet's troublin' ya," Willie responded, "I reckon we can learn to live with it. 'Sides, I didn't make the fire. Henry did. He was mighty anxious fer his supper. Boy, can thet fella eat! We're liable to have to butcher both of those cows jest to feed 'im, long before we reach where we're goin'."

"Henry's eaten?"

"Sure has. I think he even left us a little bit. Seemed in a big hurry to be off. There jest happens to be a couple a' young girls travelin' with this train. Think maybe Henry went to get acquainted like." Willie winked.

"Aren't you coming out?" Missie asked when Willie made no move to leave the wagon.

"I'm lookin' fer the bread. Can't find a thing in all these crocks, cans, an' boxes. Where'd ya put it, anyway? Henry wolfed down his food without it, but I'd sorta like a bit of bread to go with my supper."

Missie laughed. "Really!" she said, shaking her head. "Bet you almost took a bite of it. It's right there, practically under your nose." She clambered into the wagon. "Here, let me get it. Mama sent some of her special tarts for our first night out, too."

As Missie lifted the bread and tarts from the crock in which they had been stored, another tug pulled at her from somewhere deep inside. She could envision Marty's flushed face as she bent over her oven, removing the special baking for the young couple she loved so dearly.

Willie seemed to sense Missie's mood; his arms went round her and he pulled her close. "She'll be missin' you, too, long 'bout now," he said softly against her hair.

Missie swallowed hard. "I reckon she will," she whispered.

"Missie?" Willie hesitated. "Are ya sure? It's still not too late to turn back, ya know. Iffen yer in doubt . . . ? Iffen ya feel—"

"My goodness, no," Missie said emphatically. "There's not a doubt in my mind at all. I'm looking forward to seeing your land and building a home. You know that! Sure, I'll miss Mama and Pa and the family—especially at first. But I just have to grow up, that's all. Everyone has to grow up *sometime*." How could Willie think she was so selfish as to deny him his dream?

"Yer sure?"

"I'm sure."

"It won't be an easy trip—you know thet."

"I know."

"An' it won't be easy even after we git there. There's no house yet, no neighbors, no church. You'll miss it all, Missie."

"I'll have you."

Willie pulled her back into his arms. "I'm afraid I'm not much to make up fer all thet you're losin'. But I love ya, Missie—I love ya so much."

"Then that's all I need," whispered Missie. "Love is the one thing I reckon I just couldn't do without, so—" she reached up and kissed him on his chin—"as long as you love me, I should make out just fine."

Missie drew back gently from Willie's arms. "We'd better be eating that supper you cooked. I'm powerful hungry."

Willie nodded. "But you might change yer mind once you've tasted my cookin'." They both laughed.

After they had finished their meal together and Missie had washed up the few dishes, Willie brought out their Bible. It was carefully wrapped in oiled paper with an inner wrap of soft doeskin.

"Been thinkin'," he said. "Our mornin's are goin' to be short and rushed. It might be easier fer us to have our readin' time at night."

Missie nodded and settled down beside him. It was still light enough to see, but the light would not last for long. Willie found his place and began in an even voice.

"Fear thou not; for I am with thee: be not dismayed; for I am thy God: I will strengthen thee; yea, I will help thee; yea, I will uphold thee with the right hand of my righteousness."*

*Isaiah 41:10 KJV.

He closed the Bible slowly.

"Yer pa underlined thet for us. When he handed me the Bible this morning, he read it to me and marked it with this red ribbon. He said fer us to claim thet verse fer our own and to read it every day, if need be, until we felt it real and meaningful in our hearts."

"It's a good verse," Missie said, her voice tremulous. If she closed her eyes, she was sure she would be able to see her pa sitting at the kitchen table with the family Bible open before him and all of the family gathered round. She could even hear his voice as he led them in the morning prayer time. Her pa—the spiritual leader of the home. No . . . not anymore. Willie was the head of her home now; he was her spiritual leader. Now she would look to him for strength and direction to get her through each day—whether happy or difficult. She was not Clark's little girl anymore; she was a woman—a woman and a wife. Clark had handed her into the care and keeping of Willie. And though Missie was sure that her father's love and prayers would always reach out to her, she also knew Clark was content in his knowledge that she had taken her rightful place in life . . . by Willie's side.

Missie reached for Willie's hand and clung to it as they prayed together. Willie thanked God for being with them through the day and for the love of those left behind. He prayed for God to comfort their hearts at this difficult time as he and Missie learned to live without their families near. He asked for safety as they traveled and for special strength for Missie in the long days ahead, his voice tight again with concern. Missie determined that tonight was not the time to share her secret. There was no need to trouble Willie. She'd wait until she had gotten used to the bumping and the walking and had toughened to the pace of the trail. Besides, she told herself, there was still a chance she could be wrong.

If she was right—and deep down inside, Missie admitted that indeed she must be—she was bound to gain new vigor and strength with each passing day. In fact, the fresh air and exercise would be good for her. She'd wait. She'd wait until Willie could see for himself that she was healthy and strong and then she'd tell her secret. Then he would be as excited over the coming event as she was.

Oh, if only she could have told her ma and pa. She would have looked into their faces and exclaimed with joy, "I think you're going to be Grandma and you Grandpa—now, what do you think of that?" They would have hugged and laughed and cried together in one grand tangle of happiness. It would have been so much fun to announce her good news. But that wasn't to be . . . and it wasn't the right time to announce it to Willie, either. She'd wait.

THREE

Another Day

Missie stirred herself with difficulty, testing her back, legs, and arms to see just how much pain the movement brought to her. How she ached! Her mind scrambled around for the reason. As sleep left her, it all came back, a mixture of excitement and misgivings. Willie and she were on the trail. They were headed west, and she had been jostled until she could stand it no more and then had walked behind the wagons until her body protested with every step. And now, after sleeping on the hard, confining bed in their new living quarters, she ached even more.

Willie must hurt, too, she thought. She reached for him, but her hand touched only his empty pillow. Willie had already quietly left the cramped canvas-covered wagon that was to be their home for many weeks.

Missie quickly pulled herself from her bed, suppressing a groan as she did so. "I suppose I've gone and done it again," she muttered. "Willie likely had to cook his own breakfast, too."

But after Missie quickly dressed and climbed stiffly down from the wagon, she was relieved to find the sun just casting its first rays of golden light over the eastern horizon. Very few people were stirring

403

about the camp. Willie had started a fire and left it burning for her. Missie added a few more sticks and watched as the flames accepted them with crackling eagerness.

"Land sakes!" Missie exclaimed under her breath. "I wonder if I'll ever get my tied-up muscles all unwound." She began to pace back and forth, flinging and flexing her arms to limber them up. *Me, a farm girl, and so pampered that one good day's walking bothers me! Guess Mama didn't work me hard enough.* She shook her head ruefully.

As Missie stepped briskly back and forth she came across another good reason for keeping on the move. In the coolness of the morning, the mosquitoes were out in droves, and they all seemed to be hungry. After a quick visit to the nearby woods, Missie decided to return to the wagon for a long-sleeved sweater to protect her arms.

She poured a generous amount of river water from the bucket into the washbasin sitting on the shelf outside the wagon and began her morning wash. The water was cold, and Missie was relieved to reach for a rough towel to rub the warmth back into her face and hands. But she did feel refreshed and ready to begin her day. She draped the towel over its peg and started the breakfast preparations. The coffee was bubbling and the bacon and eggs sending out their early-morning "all's well" signals when their driver, Henry, made his appearance.

Missie thought of Henry as no more than a boy but smiled to herself as she realized he was at least as old as her Willie. *Still,* she thought, *he doesn't have the same grown-up manner Willie has.*

"Mornin', Henry."

"Mornin', ma'am."

The "ma'am" brought another smile to Missie's lips.

"Hungry?"

Henry grinned. "Sure am."

"Did you sleep well?"

"Pesky mosquitoes don't let nothin' sleep. Bet the horses had to swish and stomp all night."

"The mosquitoes didn't bother me until I got up this morning. Maybe we didn't have any in our wagon."

"Willie said they were botherin' him."

Missie looked up from turning the bacon. "That so? I guess I was just sleeping too soundly to notice. Do you know where he is?"

"We checked out the horses and the cows, an' then he went over to have a chat with Mr. Blake."

"Everything all right?" Her brow furrowed as she looked up from the frying pan.

"Right as rain. Willie jest wanted to chat a spell, I reckon—to see how far we're goin' today."

"Oh." Missie didn't have to worry. She began to set out the tin plates for the morning meal.

It wasn't long before she heard Willie's familiar whistle. Her heart gave its usual flutter. She loved to hear that tuneful sound. It was a sure sign that her world was all in proper order. Willie rounded the wagon and his whistling stopped.

"Well, I'll be. Ya sure are up bright an' early this mornin'," he joked. "Thought maybe Henry an' me . . ." But he stopped after a look at Missie's expression. "Mosquitoes drive ya out?"

Missie smiled. "Truth is, I didn't even notice them. My aching joints were the first to tell me it was time to do a little stretching. Are you feeling a bit stiff, too?"

"Reckon I'd be fibbin' iffen I didn't own up to feelin' a little sore here an' there," Willie said with a grin. "An' thet's all yer gonna git me to confess. Full-grown able-bodied man shouldn't be admittin' to even thet. Folks will be thinkin' I never worked a day in my life."

Missie glanced at her husband's well-muscled body. "If they do," she said, "they sure have got their eyes in the wrong place."

"Boy, do I ever hurt," Henry put in. "Never realized how sore one's arms could git from drivin' horses or how much work it is to just sit on thet bumpin' ole wagon seat."

"We'll git used to it," Willie assured him, rolling a log over to sit on it. "In a few days' time, we'll wonder why we ever felt it in the first place."

Willie asked God's blessing on the food and on the day ahead, then Missie served up their breakfast.

After they had eaten, Henry left to check the other wagon. As Missie washed up and packed away their supplies, Willie carefully inspected his wagon and harness. The others in the train were also moving about now. Amid the sounds of running and yelling children, barking dogs, and calling mothers, Missie heard a baby cry.

"Didn't know we had a baby along," she commented, watching Willie out of the corner of her eye.

"It's the Collins'," Willie answered. "Only 'bout seven months old, the father tol' me."

"Quite a venture for one so young."

"An' fer her young mama."

"This is her first?"

"No. She's got another one, too. Jest past two, I'm thinkin'."

Missie paused for a moment, then said, "She'll have her hands full. Maybe the rest of us women can give her a hand now and then."

"I'm sure she'd 'preciate thet," Willie said. "There's another woman with the train who might need a hand now an' then, as well."

Missie turned to face him. "Someone not well?"

"Oh, I hope she's well enough—not fer me to know or say—but she's expectin' a young'un."

"Oh."

Missie could feel herself flush and hoped Willie didn't notice.

"It jest could be thet it'll arrive somewhere along the trail," Willie continued. "I talked to the wagon master and he says not to worry. Claims lots of young'uns are born on the way west. We have a midwife along, a Mrs. Kosensky. I hear tell she's delivered a number of babies. Still, iffen it were *my* wife . . ."

When he didn't finish his comment, Missie prompted, "If it were *your* wife . . . ?"

"Iffen it were my wife, I'd prefer thet she had a home to do the birthin' in—and a doc on hand, jest in case. In spite of Blake's bold words, I still got the feelin' thet he was jest a mite edgy 'bout it all, an' would much prefer to have thet young mother safely into a town and under some doc's responsibility when her time is come."

"He can't be too worried," Missie argued, "or he wouldn't have taken her on."

"From what I understand, the fact of the comin' baby wasn't told to Blake till all the arrangements were made—an' then he sure didn't want to turn them down. They'd already sold their farm back east."

"Then Mr. Blake can't really be faulted, him not knowing."

"Her man knew."

Missie turned away and busied herself with packing the coffeepot and frying pan. "I'm sure she'll be fine. I'll look her up today. What's her name, by the way?"

"Her man's name is Clay. I think it's John Clay, but I'm not right sure 'bout thet."

"Have you seen her?"

"Jest offhand like. Their wagon is one of the first in line. I saw them last night when I was takin' the horses down for water. He was helpin' her down from the wagon. I don't think she was out much yesterday."

"She'll get the feel of it," Missie said quickly, but she really wasn't as sure as she sounded. "Maybe she'll walk some today and I'll get a chance to meet her."

One of the trail guides was riding toward them on a rangy big roan with wild-looking eyes. Missie stared at the big-boned horse, thinking he looked as if he could handle anything, but she sure would not want to ride him.

The guide was calling out to each driver as he toured the circle, "Let's git those wagons hitched. Time to hit the trail."

The men moved almost as one toward the tethered horses. The women hurried with their tasks of repacking each item into the wagons, putting out the fires, and gathering their families together. Missie's preparations were already done, so she stood beside her wagon and observed the bustling scene before her.

Again she heard the crying baby. She loved babies and had lots of experience with them, growing up as she did in the Davis family. Still, she wasn't sure how wise or easy it would be to be heading west with one. She would offer the young mother a hand, maybe get some helpful hints on mothering for when her own baby arrived.

Her thoughts then turned to the other woman, the mother-to-be, hoping that today she would be able to meet her. She also hoped with all her heart that all would go well for the young woman. But Willie's expressed concern tangled itself about her like a confining garment. *I'll just have a chat with Mrs. Kosensky,* she thought. *She's had experience birthing babies, and she'll know what to do.*

Missie shook off her concerns and pushed away the nagging bit of guilt about not alerting Willie before they left. *I wasn't sure then,* she told herself again. *There was no point in putting another delay in front of poor Willie.* She climbed up on the wagon bench beside him and gave him a confident smile.

FOUR

Traveling Neighbors

That day Missie made a special effort to get acquainted with more of her traveling companions. Mrs. Collins was not hard to find. Missie simply followed the sound of the crying baby. She located the family a few wagons behind her own during the noon-hour break. Mrs. Collins was trying to prepare a midday meal for her hungry family with a small boy tugging at her skirt and the wailing infant being jostled on the young mother's hip.

Missie smiled and introduced herself. "We've already finished eating," she said, "and I was wondering if I could help with the baby while you prepare your meal."

"Oh, would ya?" Mrs. Collins said with great relief in her voice. "I'd sure appreciate it. Meggie's cryin' most drives me to distraction." She pushed the small boy from her. "Joey, please be patient. Mama will git yer dinner right away. Jest you sit down an' wait."

The boy plopped down on his bottom and also began to cry, his voice loud and demanding.

Missie reached for the baby, whose wails seemed to gain volume along with those of her brother, and walked back toward her own wagon. The poor mother would somehow have to cope with the howling Joey.

Missie walked back and forth beside their wagon, gently bouncing the baby and singing softly to her. The crying subsided until only an occasional hiccough shook her tiny frame. Missie continued to rock and pace. When finally she checked little Meggie in her arms, she discovered the infant was sound asleep.

Missie returned to the mother, who was now busy clearing away the dishes and pots after having fed her husband and son. *I hope she took time to properly feed herself,* Missie thought.

Joey was sitting on a blanket, no longer crying, although the smudge of tears and trail dust still marked his cheeks. He looked very sleepy, and Missie wondered how long it would be until tears might overtake him again.

"Thank ya . . . I thank ya so much," Mrs. Collins said as she looked up from her tasks. "Ya can jest lay her down on the bed in the wagon."

Missie did so, having to move several items in order to find room for the tiny baby on the bed. She noticed that the Collins' living area was even smaller than the cramped quarters she and Willie shared—and there were four in their family.

Missie ducked out through the flap in the canvas. "Looks like Joey should get in a nap, too," she commented matter-of-factly.

"He's so tired," sighed the mother. Missie noted silently that she looked in need of a bed, also.

"I'll tuck him in," offered Missie, wondering if Joey would allow himself to be put to bed by a stranger.

To her surprise, he did not protest as she took his hand and helped him up. She started to lift him into the wagon but stopped long enough to dip a corner of her apron in water and wash the tear-streaked face. His face was warm and flushed, and Joey seemed to welcome the temporary coolness of the damp wash.

Missie laid Joey on the bed, trying to keep him far enough away from Meggie that he wouldn't waken her. Even before Missie left the wagon, Joey's long eyelashes were fluttering in an attempt to fight off sleep. She was sure sleep would soon win and the boy would get the rest that would improve his disposition. She hoped that when he awakened, his young mother would have an easier time of it.

Missie left the wagon just as Mrs. Collins was stowing the last of her utensils. The wagons were about ready to move out for the afternoon's travel.

"Why don't you crawl in an' catch a bit of rest with the children?" Missie advised.

Mrs. Collins sighed deeply. "I think I will," she said, then turned to Missie. "I jest don't know how to thank ya." She blinked away tears. "Truth is, I was 'bout ready to give up."

"It'll get better," Missie promised, hoping sincerely that she was speaking the truth.

"Oh, I hope so . . . I truly hope so."

"We'll help."

"Thank ya." The young mother spoke with bowed head and trembling voice. "Yer very kind."

The call to "move out" came, and Missie stepped aside. "Best you get yourself settled," she encouraged. "I'll watch for you later."

Mrs. Collins nodded, trying valiantly to smile her gratitude. She climbed wearily into her wagon. Missie knew it was hot inside in the full heat of the day, but it was the most comfortable rest the overburdened mother would be able to find.

That afternoon Missie walked and rode in turn. When she was walking, she chatted with the other women and children who happened to be near. She met Mrs. Standard, a kind-looking woman with a sturdy frame and graying hair. She had a family of eight—five girls and three boys. It was the second marriage for Mr. Standard, Missie learned, and the woman was a bride of seven months—and a mother for only the same period of time. So the adjustment of suddenly caring for a brood of eight was indeed daunting. She had always wanted a family, but to acquire eight all at once—of various sizes, ages, and temperaments—was an awesome undertaking. Missie admired the woman for her enthusiasm and good humor as she faced all the changes in her life. Mrs. Standard had been a "town girl," so her marriage to the widower included facing the challenge of frontier life. He was convinced the rainbow's end must rest somewhere in the West, so Mrs. Standard had packed up his eight children and the few things of her own she could find room for and joined him on the long trek.

Mrs. Standard's usual walking companion was Mrs. Schmidt, a small, wiry woman who walked with a slight limp. She had three children—two nearly grown sons and a girl of eight.

Neither of the two women talked much as they walked. Missie assumed that just giving instructions to her large family was enough talking for Mrs. Standard, and Mrs. Schmidt didn't seem to have the need for much conversation. She was always busy *doing,* not talking. She gathered more firewood than she could ever manage to burn herself during the evening camping hours.

The women travelers included Mrs. Larkin, dark and unhappy looking, and Mrs. Page, who talked even faster than she walked—and she walked briskly. Whoever would care to listen—and some who didn't— had already been informed of every item Mrs. Page possessed, as well as the cost to purchase it, and how it had been obtained. Missie could endure only short sessions near the woman, then would drift farther away, thankful for the excuse of picking up firewood.

Mrs. Thorne, a tall, sandy-haired woman, walked stiff and upright, striding ahead in a rather manly way. Her three children walked just like their mother, their arms swinging freely at their sides, their steps long and brisk. Missie was sure Mrs. Thorne would have no difficulty taking on the West.

A young woman who had waved to Missie on her first day on the trail she now discovered to be Kathy Weiss, who was traveling west with her widowed father. She had a sunny smile and an easygoing disposition. She seemed a bit dreamy, and at times Missie wondered if she realized where this journey was taking her or if she just felt herself to be on an afternoon adventure in the woods that had simply gotten extended a bit.

Already Kathy had made friends with the young Mrs. Crane, a dainty porcelain-doll type of woman who appeared to be in a perpetual state of shock over what was happening to her. She was the train's fashion piece, refusing to dress herself in common yet practical cotton—the sensible thing to be wearing for this mode of travel and living. She wore instead stylish dresses and bonnets and impractical smart shoes. Her grooming every morning took far more time than her breakfast preparations. Missie smiled at such vanity, but her heart went out to the girl, who seemed so ill equipped for the journey and its unfamiliar end.

Missie sought out Mrs. Kosensky, the midwife, and she liked the stout motherly woman immediately. Her kind face and ready smile made Missie wish she could somehow ease the miles for the older woman, who had difficulties both with riding in the lurching wagon and walking alongside over the rutted trail.

Missie saw other small groups of women and children here and there, changing and interchanging with one another as the day wore on. She promised herself she would make an effort to get to know each one of them as quickly as possible, so she might take full advantage of friendships on the trail. Since they all had a common purpose and destination, it seemed to Missie that they should somehow be more similar, but she was amazed at the differences in personality, age, and variety of backgrounds that existed among them.

Missie watched carefully for the expectant mother Willie had mentioned. She was eager to meet the young Mrs. Clay, feeling a kinship with her, though her own secret would have to be guarded for a time. Missie sought the other woman each time she walked for a spell, but she still had not spotted her when the teams were again called to an early halt. As she had the day before, Missie almost stumbled into camp, so weary was she from the day's long trek. She deposited her few sticks of firewood beside the wagon and went to speak with Willie.

As Willie's hands moved to unharness the team, Missie caught sight of swelling blisters where the reins had irritated the skin on his fingers. She mentioned them, but Willie shrugged it off.

"They'll soon toughen up," he said without concern. "Only takes a few days. How're you?"

"Tired . . . and sore. But I think I'm faring better than some of them. I noticed poor Mrs. Crane was really limping when she climbed into her wagon back a piece."

"Is she the young peacock in the fancy feathers?"

Missie smiled. "Don't be too hard on her, Willie. She appreciates nice things."

"Well, she'd be a lot wiser to pack 'em away fer a while an' wear somethin' sensible."

"Maybe so, but she'll probably have to come to her own decision on that."

"Well, I'm jest glad you don't have sech notions," he said as he looked at her with a grin. "You'd best git some rest," Willie said, watching her closely as he prepared to move off with the horses. "Yer lookin' all done-in agin."

Missie did rest, though this time she determined not to fall asleep. With no trees of any size in the area this time, she settled herself against the wagon wheel and worked on some knitting. She noticed other women and children had found shade by the wagons and were finding some rest time, as well. In fact, the only one bustling about was Mrs. Schmidt, who was throwing more wood onto her already abundant pile.

The sounds of soft snoring drifted across from the direction of the next wagon. Missie looked over to see Mrs. Thorne stretched out full-length on the grass beside her wagon, one arm tucked beneath her head.

This in spite of some commotion around the Standard wagons. Mrs. Standard was busy tending the stubbed and bleeding toe of one of her stepchildren. He wailed as she washed the injured foot but soon quieted after he realized what a fine conversation piece that neat white bandage made. He hobbled off in search of someone who would appreciate his badge of courage.

Another Standard youngster rolled on the ground with the family dog. Mrs. Standard moved away from the yipping dog and laughing boy to lower herself to the ground with a heavy sigh. She removed her walking shoes and sat rubbing her feet. With her own feet suffering in empathy, Missie could imagine how they ached.

It seemed to her that the precious rest time moved as quickly as the sun dropped toward the horizon. Gradually things in the camp began to stir. Mrs. Schmidt was the first to have a fire going. But then she was going to need an early start if she was to burn up all that wood, Missie noted with a little smile as she stirred herself and laid aside her knitting. Smoke began to waft upward on the cooler evening air as supper plans began.

By the time Willie arrived, the fire was burning and the stew pot simmering. There was no need for Missie to make biscuits. Her mother's bread supply would last for a number of days yet, even though it would soon lose its freshness. Tonight, though, it was still soft and tasty. Missie savored each bite.

Henry ate with a hearty appetite, and Missie noticed that Willie wasn't far behind him in the amount of supper that he devoured.

"I've been thinking," said Missie, "we should have brought along one cow that was milking, instead of two that are months away from calving."

"Ya hankerin' fer some milk?" Willie wondered.

"Coffee and tea suit me fine, but just look at all of the youngsters around. They sure could do with some milk." Secretly, Missie realized that milk wouldn't be a bad idea for herself, as well, but she mentioned nothing about that fact.

Willie glanced around the campsite. "Yer right," he responded. "Seems to be young'uns aplenty. Seen any more of Mrs. Collins since noon?"

"No. She must ride in the wagon most of the time. Who could walk with two babies to carry? I was thinking maybe I'd slip over after we eat and see if she has some washing that has to be done."

Willie frowned slightly. "Don't mind ya bein' neighborly, Missie, but are ya sure ya aren't pushin' a bit hard? Ya still look a bit peaked an' weary to me."

"Speakin' of bein' neighborly," Henry suddenly chimed as he laid his empty plate aside, "think I'll do a little visitin' myself." He rose to his feet with sudden enthusiasm, obviously suppressing a grin as he sauntered off.

"Oh, I'm fine," Missie quickly assured Willie. "A couple more days on the trail, and I don't expect it'll bother me much at all."

Willie nodded a response of "I hope so," but the concern did not leave his eyes.

"I still didn't see Mrs. Clay," Missie said. "I watched for her all day."

"I think she stayed pretty close to the wagon. I saw John—that *is* his name—when I watered the horses. He says the sun has been a bit hard fer her to take."

"Do you suppose after we finish here we could walk over and see how they're doing?"

"Sure. Don't guess thet would be intrudin'." Willie reached for the Bible he had placed nearby and again turned to the passage in Isaiah that Clark had marked.

"'Fear thou not, for I am with thee,'" he read, then paused for a moment, staring at the page in front of him. "What does thet mean to you, Missie?"

Missie gazed off into the distance at the sun's warm glow still lingering in the west. She thought about the words, so familiar in one way but taking on new meaning as she and Willie were now on their own, heading away from home and family.

"I guess . . ." she said slowly, deliberately. "I guess it means that God is right here with us by our campfire. Oh, Willie!" she exclaimed. "We need Him so much. Not just for the physical journey . . . but for the inner self and strength and . . . I would be so lost without the Lord. It's hard enough leaving Pa and Mama and the family . . . but, Willie, if I'd had to leave God behind, too . . . I just couldn't go. I'm so glad He's coming with us. So glad."

Willie's arm went around Missie's shoulder and drew her close.

"Ya said what I'm feelin', too," he spoke quietly, his voice full of emotion. And when he was able to speak with control again, he led in a grateful prayer, including a petition for God's care and protection on Mrs. Clay and her coming baby.

FIVE

Rebecca Clay

Missie cleared away the meal while Willie carried water from the little stream to refill their water barrel. The couple then set out arm in arm to make the acquaintance of the Clays. It was a leisurely walk, and many times they paused to talk with fellow travelers. Missie introduced Willie to the women and children that she had met, and he in turn presented her to the men he already knew.

When they passed the Collins' wagon, Missie stopped to ask if she could help with any laundry. Mrs. Collins assured her they were quite all right for at least another day. Missie was secretly relieved and hoped it didn't show. She would gladly have helped the young woman if the need had been there, but her own body was still sore and weary from her two days on the trail. Maybe by the morrow she would begin to feel more like herself.

When eventually they came to the Clay wagon, Willie greeted John and proudly introduced Missie. John, in turn, called for Rebecca, who was inside the wagon. When she thought about it later, Missie wasn't sure what she had expected, but she was unprepared for her first glimpse of Rebecca as she pushed back the flap of the canvas and slowly stepped down, reaching for her husband's hand to assist her descent. Her face looked tired and so very young, but an easy smile brightened her countenance as she saw Missie. The long auburn-brown hair was swept back from a pale face and held fast with a dark green ribbon. Her eyes held glints of the same green. Rebecca was attractive, but her appeal was definitely more than that. Missie immediately found herself wanting to know her and become her friend.

As soon as Rebecca's feet were securely on the ground, she held out her hand to Missie.

"I'm Rebecca Clay." She spoke softly, controlled. "I'm so glad to meet you."

"And I'm Melissa LaHaye," Missie responded. She wasn't sure why she had said her given name, but somehow she felt Rebecca should know who she *really* was. "Folks all just call me Missie," she quickly added.

"And they call me Becky."

"That suits you," Missie said with a warm smile. She turned to Willie. "My husband, Willie—he's met your John."

"Yes, John told me. I've been anxious to meet you both, but I've been a bit of a baby for the past two days. I hope I'll soon be able to walk some with the rest of you. I'm sure your company would be much more enjoyable than my own." She extended her hand. "Please, won't you sit down. We have no chairs to offer, but those smooth rocks John rolled over aren't bad."

Missie joined in with Becky's chuckle as the four seated themselves on the rocks and settled in to talk. John replenished the fire. "Hope I can keep away some of those pesky mosquitoes," he said over his shoulder as he went for more kindling.

"An' jest where are you folks headin'?" Willie asked the first question on all lips of those traveling west. Missie found herself hoping the answer would bring good news of future neighbors.

"We travel with this train to Tettsford Junction, then rest for a few days before joining a group going northwest," John answered. "My brother went out last year and sent word home that you never did see such good wheat land. He can hardly wait for us to get there so he can show it off. Says you don't even have to clear the land—just put the plow to it."

Missie found that hard to believe, but she had heard others tell the same story. She couldn't help but feel disappointment as she realized that the Clays would not be their neighbors after all.

"And you?" John Clay asked.

"We catch the supply train headin' south when we git to Tettsford. I've got me some ranch land in the southern hills."

"Ya like thet country?"

"It's pretty as a dream." Willie's eyes lit up as he got on his favorite subject for an audience who hadn't heard it all many times over. "All hills an' sky an' grassy draws. Not much fer trees in the area. The little valley where I'm plannin' to build has a few trees, but nothin' like we have where we come from."

"Understand there's no trees at all where we're heading," John noted.

"I can't imagine country without trees," Becky said slowly. Becky's voice sounded so wistful, Missie knew immediately that this deficiency would be a trial for the young woman.

Missie loved forests also and felt a sympathetic stirring inside, but she pushed it aside with a quick, "We'll get used to it."

Becky smiled. "I guess we will. Anyway, I suppose I'll be too busy to notice much."

The men had moved away to inspect John's harness. One section of the shoulder strap seemed to be rubbing a sore on his big black's right shoulder, John had explained, and he was anxious to find some way to correct the problem. As the men talked it over, Missie and Becky were left on their own.

"Did you leave a family behind?" Missie asked, thinking of her own parents.

"Only my father," answered Becky. "My mother died when I was fifteen."

"You don't look much more than fifteen now," Missie smiled.

Becky laughed. "Everyone thinks I'm still a youngster. Guess I just look like one. I wager I'm every day as old as you—I'll be nineteen next October."

Missie was surprised. "Why you *are* almost as old as me. When is your baby due?"

"In about two months. We're hoping all goes well so we'll be in Tettsford Junction by then. They have a doctor there, you know."

"They do?" said Missie. "I didn't know the town was that big."

"Oh, it's quite an important place, really. Almost all the wagon trains pass through it and then branch off in different directions."

"I sure find myself wishing that you were coming down our way," Missie said with sincerity.

Becky looked at her frankly. "I feel the same way. It wouldn't be half so scary if I knew I'd have you for a neighbor, even if you were nearly a day's ride away."

Both young women were silent for a few minutes. Missie toyed with the hem of her shawl while Becky poked without purpose at the fire.

"Missie," Becky spoke softly, "are you ever scared?"

Missie did not raise her eyes.

"About moving west?"

"Yes."

"I didn't *think* I was." Missie hesitated. "Willie was so excited, and I honestly thought I wanted to go, too. And I do, really I do. But I didn't know . . . that I'd . . . well, that I'd have such a hard time of it, that it'd hurt so much to leave Mama and Pa. I didn't think that I'd feel so . . . so empty." She stumbled over the words and finally raised her head and said deliberately, "Well, yes. Now I'm beginning to feel scared."

"Thanks for telling me, Missie. I'm glad I'm not the only one, because I feel like such a child about it all. I've never told anyone, not even John. I want so much for him to have his dream, but . . . sometimes . . . sometimes I fear I won't be able to make it come true for him, that my homesickness will keep him from being really happy."

Missie felt her eyes widen in surprise. "You feel homesick?"

"Oh yes."

"Even without leaving a mother behind?"

"Maybe even more so. My pa loved my mama so much it was awfully hard on him when he lost her. I was all he had, and when John came along, I . . . well, I fell so in love I couldn't think of anyone else." She stopped to take a deep breath. "So now I've . . . I've left Pa all alone," she finished in a rush.

Becky's eyes filled with tears. She brushed them away and continued, "If only he still had Mama, I wouldn't have this worry about him. I miss him . . . so very much. He's such a good man, Missie, so strong—big, muscular, tough. But inside, deep inside, Pa is so tender, so . . ." She took another breath. "Do you understand what I'm trying to say?"

Now it was Missie's eyes that filled with tears. She nodded. "Yes, indeed I do. I know just such a man, and I wouldn't be one bit surprised that he's crying silent tears for me just as often as I'm weeping for him. At least he has Mama and the other youngsters who are still at home."

"So you are lonesome, too?"

A quiet nod was Missie's answer.

"I expect it gets better."

"I hope so. I truly hope so," Missie said fervently. "I'm counting on God to make it so."

"You know . . . you talk to God?"

"Oh yes, without Him—"

"I'm so glad!" Becky exclaimed. "It's He who gives me daily courage, too. I'm not very brave . . . even *with* Him. But *without* Him, I'd be a downright coward."

Missie sniffed away her tears, and the two shared a laugh at Becky's confession.

"I'm glad I've got Willie," Missie said. "He has enough courage for both of us."

"So does John. He can see nothing but good in our future. Oh, I do hope that I won't let him down."

Missie reached over and squeezed the girl's hand. "You won't," she encouraged firmly. "You've got more than you allow yourself, or you wouldn't be here."

"Oh, Missie, I hope so."

"Are you afraid . . . about the baby?"

"A little. But I try not to think about things like that. Mostly I'm tired and a little sick from the sun and the motion of the wagon. I'll be so glad when I'm feeling well enough to walk."

"You must be careful not to walk too long at first."

"John thinks that walking will do me a lot of good. He says fresh air and good exercise is what I need. His ma had nine babies and never missed a day's work with any of them."

Well, good for John's ma, Missie wanted to say, but she held her tongue. Instead she said, "There's a midwife here. She's delivered lots of babies. She'll tell you if you should be pushing yourself and walking some."

"John told me about her, but I haven't met her yet."

"You'll like her, I'm sure. I met her today. She's just the kind of woman one would like to help with a birthing. I'll bring her around to meet you, if you'd like."

"Would you, Missie? I haven't felt up to seeking her out, and I do have a lot of questions. If my mama . . ." Becky did not finish but blinked quickly.

"I'll bring her by tomorrow, if I can," Missie assured her gently. Then she said, "When we left—Willie an' me—my pa gave us a special verse. We have sort of claimed it as ours, but no one really has any *special* claim on God. His promises are for all of His children. I'd like to share our verse with you. I hope it will be as special to you as it is to Willie and me. It comes from Isaiah." She paused, then quoted from memory, "'Fear thou not; for I am with thee: be not dismayed; for I am thy God: I will strengthen thee; yea, I will help thee; yea, I will uphold thee with the right hand of my righteousness.' That's an awful lot of promise for one verse to offer, but I feel sure that God really means it. He can—and will—be with us, in life or in death. I know He is with us through *everything*."

"Thank you, Missie, I really needed that truth. When you drop by on the morrow, would you do something for me? It's too dark to see right now, but I'd like you to show me where that verse is so I can read it for myself. Would you do that?"

"I'd be glad to."

The menfolk had gone on down to check the horses and rub some of Willie's ointment on the black's sore shoulder. The silence that followed Missie's words was broken only by the crackling of the fire. Missie found herself wishing she could tell Becky her own good news, but she held it back. Willie must be the first one to know. She must tell Willie—soon.

It wasn't right to keep it from him. If only he wouldn't be worried. If she could just conquer her tiredness and perk up a bit. How thankful she was that she hadn't been troubled with bouts of morning sickness.

Becky interrupted her thoughts. "I'm afraid I have to confess to a lie, Missie. I'm not just a little afraid—I *am* scared—about the baby, about maybe not having a doctor, about the way I've been feeling. I don't know one thing about babies, Missie—not about their birthing or their care. The thought of maybe having that baby on this trip west nigh scares me to death, but John says . . ." She shook her head slowly and let the words hang.

Missie spoke quickly. "An' John's right. That baby will probably be born in Tettsford in a pretty bedroom with a doc there to fuss over him. But if . . . if the little one does decide to hurry it up a bit, then we have Mrs. Kosensky—about as good a woman as you'd find anywhere. Just you wait till you get to know her. She'll put your mind at ease. I'll fetch her around, first chance I get."

Becky summoned a smile. "Thanks, Missie. You must think me a real crybaby, carrying on so over an ordinary circumstance like a baby's coming. I'd like to meet Mrs. Ko . . . Ko . . . what's her name? Maybe she can even get me feeling better so I can do some walking with you. I feel like every bone in my body is turned to mush by the jarring, bouncing wagon." She smiled and rose. "The men should be coming back soon. Do you think they'd like some coffee?"

On Saturday night after supper, Trailmaster Blake called for a gathering of the wagon-train members.

"Life on a trek west can be a tad dull," he stated matter-of-factly, "so iffen any of ya can play anything thet makes a squeak, we'd 'preciate it iffen you'd bring it out."

Henry produced a guitar and Mr. Weiss a rather worn-looking fiddle. A time of singing around the fire was arranged, and folks joined in heartily, humming the tunes when they did not know the words. Some of the children jumped or skipped or swayed to the music in their own version of a folk dance.

What Mr. Weiss could accomplish on his well-used fiddle was quite remarkable, and Henry was rather adept at keeping up with him. Henry was also blessed with a pleasant singing voice, and he led the group in one song after another, some of them camp choruses and others favorite hymns. Missie loved every minute of it, and the singing brought back memories of their little congregation back home worshiping together. She decided Henry's healthy appetite was well worth feeding, and she determined to always be ready with generous second helpings.

Far too soon for Missie, Mr. Blake stood and waved his hand for attention.

"Thank ya, men . . . thank ya. You've done a fine job. Now it's gittin' late and time to be turnin' in. 'Sides, the mosquitoes are 'bout as hungry as I've ever seen 'em." He waved a few away from his face.

"Tomorrow, bein' Sunday, the train will stay to camp. Me, I'm not a religious man, but a day of rest jest plain makes sense—both fer the animals an' fer us people. Now, iffen you who are religious are han-kerin' fer some kind of church service, I'm leavin' ya on yer own to do the plannin'. I'm no good at sech things. Fact is, I plan on spendin' tomorrow down at yonder crik, seein' iffen I can catch me some fish." He looked around the group. "Now, then, are there any of you who'd be wantin' church?"

Quite a few hands were raised.

"Fine . . . fine," Mr. Blake said. "Klein, ya figurin' thet you can take charge?"

Henry looked a little nonplussed but nodded his assent, and the meeting was dismissed.

Henry then spent some time calling upon his wagon neighbors in preparation for the morning service. A few did not wish to take part, but most were eager to worship together on the Lord's Day.

Willie was appointed to read the Scripture, and Henry himself took charge of the singing. Mr. Weiss could play hymns on his old violin with even more feeling than he played the lively dance tunes and folk songs, and everything was set.

Sunday dawned clear and warm. The service had been set for nine so it would be over before the sun was too high and hot in the sky. The people gathered in a grove of trees near the stream and settled themselves beneath the protective branches on logs that Willie and Henry had cut and placed there for that purpose.

They began with a hearty hymn-sing, Henry leading out in his clear baritone voice. Kathy Weiss taught the group a new song—simple and short but with a catchy tune. Many hands clapped in accompaniment when they were not occupied with slapping mosquitoes.

After the final triumphant stanza of "Amazing Grace," Henry indicated the singing had concluded and asked Mr. Weiss to lead the group in prayer. He did so with such fervor that Missie was reminded of home.

Anyone who wished was invited to tell of finding God's presence on the trail. One by one, several stood to express their thanks to God for His leading, for strength, for assurance in spite of fears, for incidents of protection along the way. Missie and Becky exchanged glances and meaningful smiles.

After the last voluntary testimony had been shared, Willie read the Scripture. He had chosen the passage about Jesus feeding the multitudes with only a small boy's lunch. Missie was sure that others caught the special significance of trusting God to provide for them and to protect them in their travels together. The group listened carefully as Willie's voice presented the words from the Bible and his confidence in the promises of God. When he closed the Book there were many nods and "amens."

Though their wilderness setting gave no hint of a church building, the time of worship had been just as meaningful as if they'd had a roof over their heads and a church bell tolling. As the group scattered to their own campsites, they shook Henry's hand and thanked him for a job well done. Some suggested another hymn-sing around the fire that night, and so it was arranged.

The Sunday service and Sunday night hymn-sing became even more popular with the wagon-train members than the Saturday night gathering. As the weeks went by, some of those who had not been interested in joining the Sunday crowd for their worship time found themselves washing their faces, putting on clean clothes, brushing the trail dust off their boots, and heading for whatever spot had been set aside for that week's service. Missie and Willie were thrilled to see the interest grow. The folks appeared to yearn for that restful time of worship and sharing on Sunday.

Mr. Blake, on the other hand, was left to his own choice of Sunday activity, whether it was hunting, fishing, or just lying in the shade. Missie noticed him on one particular Sunday morning, though, when he had chosen to simply hang around camp. It looked suspiciously as if he were listening.

SIX

Tedious Journey

Day after long day rolled and bounced by in mostly tiresome predict-ability. Even the weather seemed monotonous. The sun blazed down upon them with only an occasional shower to bring temporary relief.

But gradually the travelers adjusted to the journey. Bodies still ached at the end of the day, but not with the same intense painfulness. Blisters now had been replaced by calluses. Occasionally a horse would become lame, and their drivers watched with great care and concern for any serious signs of injury to their animals.

One family, the Wilburs, had been forced to pull aside and retire from the train due to an injured horse that simply could not continue. Mr. Blake thoughtfully detoured the train about two miles out of its way in order to drop the young couple off at a small army outpost. The sergeant in charge promised he'd send a few of his men back with Mr. Wilbur to retrieve his stranded wagon and lead the horses to the safety of the fort. At the earliest future date, the Wilburs would be escorted to the nearest town. Missie could have wept when she saw their expres-sions of intense disappointment as the train moved on without them.

Some minor mishaps during the journey reminded them all of the need for care and caution. One of the Page children had been burned when playing too near a cooking fire. Mr. Weiss, the train's blacksmith, had been kicked by a horse he was attempting to shoe, but fortunately nothing was broken. Mrs. Crane's ankle had twisted badly as she attempted to scale a steep hill in her fashionable shoes, and she was confined to the family wagon far longer than she would have liked. A few of the young children were plagued with infected mosquito bites, and occasional colds made one or the other miserable for a time. But, all in all, everyone was adjusting quite well to life on the trail.

As the group slowly made its way westward, the countryside began changing. Missie tried to determine what made it seem so different—so foreign to her from the farming community she had left. The trees were smaller and unlike most of the trees she had been used to. The hills appeared different, too. Perhaps it was the abundance of short undergrowth that clung to their slopes. Whatever the differences, Missie also realized she was getting farther and farther away from her home and those she loved. The now-familiar feeling of lonesomeness still gnawed and twisted within her. Once in a while she was forced to bite her lip to keep the tears from overflowing onto her cheeks. She must try harder, pray more. And as she walked or worked she repeated over and over to herself the blessed promise of Isaiah. Her greatest ally was busyness, and she tried hard to keep her hands and her mind occupied.

Missie visited Becky often, and she had kept her promise to introduce her to the midwife, Mrs. Kosensky. The capable woman had dismissed husband John's advice that Becky walk more and cautioned her to be careful about the amount of activity she involved herself in each day. Now that she was feeling better, Becky wasn't sure she liked the restrictions but obeyed the new instructions, nonetheless.

Missie found plenty of opportunity to help Mrs. Collins with the care of her two young children. She often took the baby girl to visit Becky so she might have some experience in the care and handling of a baby.

Try as she might to keep her thoughts on the future and the adventure ahead, Missie found herself continually recalling the events of the day as they would be taking place "back home." *Today Mama will be hanging out the wash, all white and shimmering in the sun,* or *today Pa will be making his weekly trip into town.* Or on Sunday, *the whole family is in the buggy and heading for the little log church. They're going to meet and worship with the neighbors—people I've known all my life—and Parson Joe.* She could almost hear his voice as he would preach the sermon and the "amens" accompanying his presentation of truth from Scripture. And she could close her eyes and see her dear sister Clae's smile as she gazed with love and pride at her husband behind the simple pulpit.

And so Missie went through each day. Her weary but gradually strengthening body traveled with the other pilgrims of the wagon train, but her spirit soared "back home," where she shared the days' activities with those she had left behind.

She realized with surprise as she prepared their evening meal that they had been on the trail for almost four weeks. In some ways it had seemed forever; in others, it seemed not so long at all. But after this amount of time, why was she still feeling that inner homesickness and loneliness? Time, she had thought, would lessen the pain, ease the burden of loneliness. How long would it require for her to be at peace with her circumstances?

As Missie's body ached less by each day's end, it seemed that her spirit ached more. How she missed them—her family and friends. How good it would be to feel her mama's warm embrace or her pa's hand upon her shoulder. How she would welcome the teasing of Clare and Arnie, enjoy watching the growing up of her younger sister, Ellie. And Luke in his soft lovableness—how she ached to hug his little body. Would she even recognize him when she saw him again—whenever that time might come? *Oh, dear God,* she prayed over and over, *please make me able to bear it.*

With all her might, Missie fought to hide her suffering from Willie. But in so doing, she didn't realize how much of her true self she was withholding from him. She often felt Willie's eyes upon her, studying her face. He fretted over her weariness and continually checked to be sure she was feeling all right, was not overworking, was eating properly.

The truth was, Missie was not feeling well. Apart from her deep homesickness, she also was suffering with nausea and general tiredness. But she hid it from Willie. *It's not the right time yet. Willie would just worry,* she kept telling herself. But she sensed—and did not like—the strain that was present between them.

Each day followed the last one in very similar fashion. The LaHayes always rose early. Missie prepared breakfast for Willie and Henry while they checked and watered the animals and prepared them for the new day's travel. They ate, packed up, and moved out. At noon they took a short break, and Missie again prepared a quick meal.

When they stopped at the end of the day, there was the fire to start, the supper to be cooked, and the cleaning up to be done. Very little fresh food now remained, so Missie had to resort to dried and home-canned foods. She was fast wearying of the limited menu. She wondered if it was as distasteful to Willie and Henry as it was to her. What wouldn't she give to be able to sit down to one of her mother's appetizing meals with garden produce and fresh-baked bread? She shook her head quickly and determined to put her mind on other things.

♲

The amount of walking Missie included in each day's travel depended on the terrain and the intensity of the heat. Becky Clay did not attempt to walk very much at all. John refrained from prodding her to do more than she felt comfortable doing after Mrs. Kosensky had told him that all women were not as hardy as his mother. Becky did welcome her short episodes with the other women, though she had to be careful not to overdo.

The travelers began to know one another as individuals, not just faces. For some, this was good. Mrs. Standard and Mrs. Schmidt seemed to accept and enjoy each other more every day. They hoped to be close neighbors when the journey ended.

Kathy Weiss and Tillie Crane also became close friends. Kathy spent many hours with Anna, as well, the oldest of the five Standard girls. But Anna and Tillie shared no common interest and seemed to have no desire to spend time in each other's company. In turn, Mrs. Standard appeared to enjoy Kathy and embraced her right along with her own recently acquired brood of eight. Missie imagined that Mrs. Standard would have been willing to take almost anybody into the family circle.

Henry, too, was a welcome visitor around the Standard campfire. Missie often wondered if the attraction for him was one of the young girls or the motherly Mrs. Standard. Henry, whose mother had died when he was young, no doubt yearned for the care and nurturing he had missed growing up.

As well as fast friendships among the travelers, there were also a few frictions. Mrs. Thorne still carried herself stiff and straight, never making an effort to seek out anyone's company. Neither by word nor action did she invite anyone to share time or conversation with her. There were no neighborly visits over a coffee cup around the Thornes' fire.

Most of the travelers tried to avoid the chattering Mrs. Page, but she had a way of popping up out of nowhere and making it virtually impossible for one to escape without being downright rude. It seemed she would have cozied up to a cactus if she had thought it had ears. Yet even Mrs. Page was not willing to share her goodwill with everyone.

Missie never did know what had started it in the first place, but for some reason a deep animosity had grown between Mrs. Page and Mrs. Tuttle. Mrs. Tuttle was a widow, traveling west with her brother. Unlike Mrs. Page, she had very little to say, but what she did say was often acidic and painful. So she, too, was avoided but for the opposite reason from the voluble Mrs. Page.

The woman simply did not know when to stop her running commentary on this and that. Her elaborations on any subject included expounding on the reason Mrs. Tuttle was going west. According to Mrs. Page, a trapper was waiting at the other end of the trail, having made a proposal of sorts by mail. Mrs. Page announced she was sure the trapper was "trapped," that if he'd been able to get any kind of look at Mrs. Tuttle's stern face, he would have preferred solitude. So the war waged on.

Most of the battles between the two women were carried on through messengers. "You tell Jessie Tuttle thet iffen she doesn't learn how to crack the ice on thet face of hern, she'll lose thet trapper as soon as she finds 'im."

"You tell Mrs. Page"—Jessie Tuttle would not allow herself to use Mrs. Page's first name, Alice—"thet when she cracked the ice off'n her own face, she did a poor job of it. Now the button fer her mouth don't hold it shut none."

Of course, the emissaries never did deliver the messages, but it wasn't necessary for them to do so. The insults were always spoken loudly within earshot of the opposing party. The running battle provided no real alarm and even a small measure of amusement for the other members of the wagon train. There was little enough to smile at, so even a neighborly squabble was welcome.

Occasional meetings of all adult members of the train provided opportunity for the wagon master to give reports on progress, or to issue a new order, or to explain some new situation. Even such a meeting was looked upon as a pleasant diversion from the mundane and the usual.

Mr. Blake now told the travelers he was pleased with their progress and that they were right on schedule. His concern was the large river they were approaching. They would reach the ford in four days' time at the current rate of travel. He was sure the river would be down, making the crossing an easy one. High water from heavy rains was the only possible obstacle that could hamper the crossing, Mr. Blake said, and they had been particularly blessed with sunny, clear days. Once across the Big River, as it was called by the local Indians, they were well on their way to their final destination.

Everyone seemed to rejoice at Mr. Blake's news, but deep down, Missie knew she did not. Within her was a secret wish that the river would not be fordable and that Willie would decide to turn around and go back home.

Willie obviously did not share her yearnings to return. At the wagon master's encouraging announcement, he had cheered as loudly as any of the travelers. Missie did notice there were a few other women who had remained silent—Becky, Sissie Collins, and Tillie Crane among them.

Missie was quiet on their way back to the wagon, but at first Willie was too energized to notice.

"Jest think," he enthused, "only four more days an' we cross the Big River, an' then . . . then we'll *really* start to roll!"

Missie nodded and tried to work up a smile for Willie's sake.

"Are ya still worryin' 'bout Becky?" Willie queried, trying to look into her face and no doubt hoping for some reasonable explanation for Missie's restraint.

"Yeah, kind of," Missie responded, feeling the answer was both safe and, to a measure, truthful.

"But there's something else . . . isn't there? I've been feelin' it fer a long time. Aren't ya feelin' well, Missie?"

It was asked with such genuine concern that Missie knew somehow she must attempt to put Willie's mind at ease. This wasn't the way she would have planned to break the news to Willie. She had pictured the intimacy of their own fireside of an evening, or the closeness of their shared bed in the privacy of their covered wagon. But here they were walking over a rutted dusty path with people before, behind, and beside them. There seemed almost no way for her to speak low enough so she wouldn't be heard by others. Yet she knew she must tell him.

"I've been wanting to tell you, but the time never seemed right," she said quietly. She took a long breath. "Willie . . . we're going to have a baby, too."

Willie stopped walking and reached for Missie, his face very sober. "Ya aren't joshin'?"

"No, Willie."

"An' yer sure?"

"Quite sure."

Willie stood silently for a moment, then shook his head. "I'm not sure thet wagon trains an' babies go together."

For a brief moment Missie hoped maybe this would give Willie a reason to head for home, but she quickly pushed the selfish thought from her and managed a smile. "Oh, Willie, don't fuss. We'll be in our own place long before our baby ever arrives."

"Ya sure?"

"Of course. How long you think we're going to be on this trail, anyway?"

The expression on Willie's face suddenly changed and he let out a shout. Missie reached out to hush him before he'd announced his news to the whole wagon train. Willie stopped whooping and hugged Missie tightly. Relief flooded over her. He was truly excited about it—there was no doubting it.

Suddenly Missie wanted to cry. She wasn't sure why, but she felt such a joy at telling her news to Willie, seeing his exuberance, and feeling his strong arms about her. She had been wrong to withhold it from him. A great wave of love for Willie washed over her. She would go to the ends of the earth with him if he wanted her to.

They laughed and cried together as Willie held her in his arms and kissed her forehead and her hair. Their fellow travelers had passed on by and left them alone for the moment.

"So this is why ya haven't been yerself," Willie murmured into her hair. "We gotta take better care of ya. Ya need more rest an' a better diet. I'll have to git fresh meat oftener. Ya shouldn't be doin' so much. Ya'll overdo. I was so scared, Missie, thet maybe you'd changed yer mind, thet ya didn't want to go out west . . . or thet maybe ya didn't even love me anymore . . . or thet ya had some bad sickness . . . or . . . oh, I was scared. I jest prayed an' prayed an' here . . . here . . ." She could hear the emotion in his voice.

Missie had not realized before what her long days of listlessness and homesickness had meant for Willie. She must not hold back from him again.

"I'm sorry, Willie," she whispered, "I didn't know that you were feeling . . . were thinking all those things. I'm sorry."

"Not yer fault. Not yer fault at all. I'm jest so relieved, thet's all. Still sorry thet yer not feelin' well—but we'll take care of ya. After all, it's fer a *very* good reason!"

"I'm glad that you're happy—"

But Missie didn't get a chance to finish her sentence. Willie stopped her as he drew her close. "Everything is gonna be fine now, Missie. Ya should be feelin' better soon. We'll have a chat with Mrs. Kosensky. We'll make sure thet ya git lots of rest. An' 'fore ya know it, you'll be fine, jest fine."

"Willie? Willie, there's something else, too. True, I've been feeling a mite down. But I think the true reason for me . . . my . . . ah . . . well, the way I feel is just lonesomeness, Willie. Just lonesomeness for Mama and Pa and . . ." Missie could not continue. The tears ran freely.

Willie held her close against him. He stroked her hair and gently wiped the tears from her cheek.

"Why didn't ya tell me, Missie?" he said at last. "I woulda understood. I've been missing those left behind, too. Maybe I couldn't have eased yer sorrow none, Missie, but I'da shared it with ya." He tipped her face and gently kissed her. "I love ya, Missie."

Why had she been so foolish? Why had she hugged her hurt to herself, thinking that Willie would not understand or care? She should have told him long ago and accepted the comfort of his arms. Missie clung to him now and cried until her tears were all spent. Surely there was some healing in shared heartache, in cleansing tears. At length she was able to look up at Willie and smile again.

Willie kissed her on the nose and gave her another squeeze.

"Hey," he said suddenly, "we gotta git this little mama off to bed. No more late nights fer you, missus. An' not quite so much walkin' an' doin', either."

"Oh, Willie," protested Missie, "the walking is a heap easier for me than that bumpy old wagon."

"Ya reckon so?"

"I reckon so. It's not exactly a high-springed buggy, you know."

Willie chuckled as he led Missie carefully across the clearing to their wagon.

"Mind yer step, now," he said earnestly as he boosted her up. "Mustn't overdo it."

"Oh, Willie," Missie laughed in exasperation. But she knew she was in for a lot of babying in the future. Well, maybe it wouldn't be so bad if he just wouldn't overdo it. She smiled to herself and ducked to enter their canvas doorway.

SEVEN

Rain

The next morning Missie could tell Willie was still in a state of bliss as he climbed out of the wagon to begin a new day.

She had watched him pull the gray wool shirt over his head with all those buttons from waist to neck, then tuck it quickly into the coarse denim pants that made up his trail clothing. He had glanced over at her and, seeing she was awake, gave her a delighted grin, then quickly sobered as he told her to stay in bed for a bit longer. She'd need extra rest. She smiled sleepily, then suggested that if the day got too hot, he'd probably want to change the shirt for a cotton one. He nodded, raised his suspenders, and snapped them into place. At the entrance to the wagon he stopped to pull on his calf-high leather boots. He shrugged his way out of the canvas doorway and headed out to get the team ready for the day's journey. He went with an even jauntier step and cheerier whistle than usual. Missie knew he was pleased about the coming baby. She also knew he was thinking, *Four more days to the Big River!*

To Missie, it meant four more days to the point of no return. She tried to shake off her melancholy for Willie's sake and went about her morning chores with a determined cheerfulness. Today, if she had the opportunity, she *might* reveal the good news of her coming baby to Becky. They could plan together.

Willie stopped the team often that morning to give Missie opportunities for walking—and then to check that she hadn't already walked far enough. She humored him by walking for a while and then welcoming a ride when he suggested it. She actually could have traveled by foot most of the morning. The walking had bothered her less each day, but there was no use worrying Willie.

In the afternoon a chill came with the wind, and dark storm clouds gathered on the horizon. The whole wagon train seemed to be holding its breath in unison. It was soon apparent to all that this storm would not pass over with just a shower. Still, the team drivers and their apprehensive womenfolk entertained the hope that the rain would not last for long. The animals seemed to sense the approaching storm, too, and by the time the thunder and lightning commenced, they were already nervous and skittish.

The rain came lightly at first. The women and children scrambled for the cover of the wagons, while the men wrapped themselves in canvas slickers and drove on through the storm.

But rather than decreasing in intensity, the storm with its dark clouds swirling above seemed angry and vindictive as the waters poured down. Soon the teams were straining to pull the heavy high-wheeled wagons through the deepening mud. Those fortunate enough to have extra horses or oxen hitched them to their wagons, also.

The guides ranged back and forth, watching for trouble along the trail. It came all too soon. One of the lead wagons slid while going down a slippery steep slope, bouncing a wheel against a large rock. The wooden spokes snapped with a sickening crack. The wagon lurched and heaved, though fortunately it did not tip over. Mr. Calley somehow kept the startled horses from bolting.

The teams following had to maneuver around the crippled wagon, slipping and sliding their way down the rocky hill and onto even ground. As soon as the last wagon was safely down the badly rutted hillside, Mr. Blake ordered a halt. They should have had many more miles of traveling for the day behind them, but it was useless to try to go on. The Big River would have to wait.

The sodden wagons gathered into their familiar circular formation, and the teams, with steam rising from their heaving sides, were unhitched. Some of the men went back up the hill to help the unfortunate Calley family. Their wagon could not be moved until the broken wheel was mended. The men labored in the pouring rain, attempting to raise the corner of the wagon by piling rocks and pieces of timber underneath. The Calleys would have to spend the night at a little distance from the rest of the camp.

While Willie and Henry were gone, Missie wrapped a heavy shawl about her and went in search of firewood. The other women and children were seeking material for their fires, as well, and the rain meant there was very little to be found. Missie felt wet and muddy and cross as she scrambled for bits and pieces of anything she thought might burn. At one point she heard a commotion and then a voice shouting, "You tell Jessie Tuttle thet once a body is headin' fer a stick of firewood, thet body is entitled to it." Missie smiled in spite of herself. The two were at it again!

Only the forward-thinking Mrs. Schmidt did not have to join the others in the dispiriting search. Her ever-abundant supply of dry wood was unloaded from under the wagon seat. Missie wondered why she hadn't had the presence of mind to plan ahead, as well.

Missie finally had gathered what she hoped would be enough to cook a hot meal, then slogged her way back through the mud to her wagon. The fire was reluctant, at best, but Missie finally coaxed a flame to life. It sputtered and spit and threatened to go out, but Missie encouraged it on. The coffee never did boil, but the reheated stew was at least warm, and the near-hot coffee was welcome to shivering bodies.

Missie cleaned up in a halfhearted manner, and they crawled into their canvas home on wheels to get out of their wet clothing and into something warm and dry. It was far too early to go to bed, even though the day had been a strenuous one. Willie lit a lamp and settled down beside it to bring his journal up-to-date. Missie picked up her knitting, but her fingers were still too cold to work effectively. At length she gave up and pulled a blanket around herself for warmth. Willie lifted his head to look at her and started fretting again.

"Ya chilled? Ya'd best git right into thet bed—don't want ya pickin' up a cold. Here, let me help ya. I'll go see what I can find for a warm stone fer yer feet." He tucked the blanket more closely around Missie, right to the chin, and started to reach for his coat.

"Don't go back out in the rain—please, Willie," Missie begged. "My feet aren't that cold. They'll be warm in no time. I'll just slip on a pair of your woolen socks." And Missie did so immediately so Willie could see she meant what she had said.

It was too early to go to sleep, Missie knew. She also knew it was unwise to protest being tucked in, so she snuggled under the blanket, and gradually the chill began to leave her bones. She even began to feel drowsy.

Willie finished his journal entries and picked up a leather-covered edition of *Pilgrim's Progress* that had been a wedding gift from Missie's schoolchildren. Missie murmured, "If you don't mind, would you read it aloud?"

Willie read, his voice and the familiar story lulling her toward a sense of well-being, and the long evening somehow passed.

The rain continued to fall, splattering against the canvas of the wagon. Before lying down to sleep beside Missie, Willie checked carefully all around the inside of their small enclosure to make sure there were no leaks. Then in a very few minutes Missie knew by his breathing that he slept. She wished she could fall asleep as easily, but instead she lay and listened to the rain. Again her thoughts turned to home.

She used to love to listen to the rain pattering on the window as she snuggled down beneath the warm quilt her mama had made. The rain had always seemed friendly then, but somehow tonight it did not seem to be a friend at all. She shivered and moved closer to Willie. She was thankful for his nearness and his warmth. And his confidence.

⁂

When Missie awakened the next morning, the rain was still falling. Puddles of water lay everywhere, and the shrubbery and wagons dripped steady little streams in the damp morning air. Willie arrived just as Missie was about to crawl down from the wagon, wondering what in the world she would ever do about a fire. Instructing her to stay where she was, he managed to get a fire going and make some coffee and pancakes. He served Missie in the covered wagon, ignoring her protests.

"No use us both gittin' wet and cold," he reasoned. "'Sides, Mr. Blake hasn't decided yet whether we move on or jest sit tight."

But they all knew of Mr. Blake's concern about reaching the Big River before the waters were swollen with the rain. So in spite of the mud, he ordered them to pack up and move out as usual.

Willie was already soaking wet as he climbed up onto the wagon seat and urged the balking horses out. He told Missie to make as comfortable a place for herself as she could and to stay under the canvas.

It was tough going. The wagons slipped and twisted through the mire. Wheels clogged up and had to be freed from their burdens of mud. Teams and drivers were worn out in only a few hours' time. When one poor horse finally fell and needed a great deal of assistance to regain his footing, Mr. Blake called a halt. It was useless to try to travel farther under such conditions.

Missie didn't know whether to feel relief or dismay when their wagon creaked to a stop. The rain had slackened a bit, so she wrapped her shawl closely about her and went on the inevitable search for firewood. But when Willie returned some time later, Missie still had not succeeded in getting a fire going. She was close to tears and felt like a complete failure. The wood just would not burn. Willie took charge, talking Missie into changing out of her wet clothes. He dared to beg some hot water from Mrs. Schmidt, whose fire was burning cheerily—as if it were sticking its tongue out at the whole camp. Mrs. Schmidt seemed pleased—though possibly a bit smug—to share her hot water. Missie made tea in the confines of the wagon, and she, Willie, and Henry enjoyed the hot refreshment, along with their biscuits from yesterday.

Still the rain continued. Missie went back to her knitting while Willie mended a piece of harness. When that was done, he pulled out his journal, but this source of activity was soon exhausted, as well. He picked up the John Bunyan volume again and attempted to read, but eventually restlessness drove him from the wagon and out into the rain, muttering an excuse about checking on the teams and the cows.

With Willie gone, the afternoon dragged even more for Missie. She was on the verge of venturing forth herself when she heard Willie return. At his call from the back of the wagon, Missie raised the tent flap. He handed her a bundle, the Collins' baby.

"Their wagon is leakin'," he explained. "There ain't a dry place to lay the young'uns. I'll be right back with the boy."

Missie busied herself with unwrapping the baby. True to his word, Willie was soon there at the canvas opening with little Joey in tow. When baby Meggie fussed, Missie cheerfully spent the time hushing her, rocking her back and forth and coaxing her to settle into a comfortable position. Willie entertained Joey, helping him make a tiny cabin with small sticks. Then he read to him out of *Pilgrim's Progress,* and even though the young boy could not possibly understand much of the story, he listened intently. Missie finally managed to get the baby to sleep. She joined Willie and Joey, now involved in a little-boy game with sticks and stones.

Sissie Collins came by later to check on her children and nurse the baby. Willie made the rounds of the camp to see if there was anyone else needing a helping hand.

When the long day came to an end, they drank the remains of the now-cold tea and ate some cold meat with the remaining biscuits.

Willie moved into the other wagon with Henry so Sissie and her two little ones could stay with Missie in drier surroundings.

As Missie went to sleep again with the sound of the rain on the canvas, she wondered if it would ever stop. How could they possibly endure another day such as this?

But they did. At times the rain slackened to a mere drizzle, and at other times it poured. Each time the rain slowed, Missie pulled on her shawl and left the confines of the wagon. But actually there was little place to walk around and stretch her cramped legs. The ground around the site looked like a lake with only a few high spots still showing through. At first Missie tried to stay to the high ground, then giving up with a shrug, she sloshed about through the water.

Finally even Mrs. Schmidt ran out of firewood, so the men made a concerted effort to find something farther out that would burn.

Eventually it was decreed that one fire, built under a stretched-out canvas, would be shared by the whole camp. The women took turns, three or four at a time, hastily preparing something hot for their families.

The Collins family wasn't the only one having problems with leaking canvas. Other wagons, too, were wet—inside and out. Families were doubling up and sharing quarters wherever possible.

The rain heightened the tension between the two female antagonists. But the howls of outrage from Mrs. Page and the biting retorts of Mrs. Tuttle were often the very thing that kept the rest of the company sane. It was a nice diversion to be able to chuckle—even at one another.

On the fifth day the sky began to clear, and the sun broke through on the dripping and miserable wagon train.

The travelers, too, came out, quickly stringing lines and hanging clothing and blankets to dry. The ground remained wet, and it could be days before the stands of water disappeared and even a longer time before the ground would be dry enough to allow the wagons to roll ahead once again.

Missie felt somewhat like Noah as she descended from her wagon. There was water everywhere. How good it would be to see the dry land appear and the horses kick up dust. Oh, to be on the move again!

Mr. Blake clearly felt impatient, too, but his many years of experience on the trail no doubt told him it would be useless to try to travel on in the mud. No, they'd have to wait, he told them, explaining that with the rains of the past few days, the Big River would be impossible to cross very soon anyway. They'd been delayed, but they'd just take the problems one day at a time. "We'll be there a'fore ya know it." He finished his announcement with a tip of his hat to the glum faces before him.

Missie wondered how much time "a'fore ya know it" actually meant. But her first duty was to collect firewood, wet though it might be, and lay it out to dry for future use. She would not be caught short again if she could at all help it.

EIGHT

The Big River

For six days Mr. Blake kept the wagons in their camp circle. He no doubt would have held them longer, foreseeing the unwelcome surprise that probably awaited them at the Big River, but the growing impatience to be rolling again made the group restless. The ground in the immediate vicinity was dry enough to travel, and the risk of tempers flaring from tense nerves and idle hands overcame his reluctance to face a swollen river. On day seven he called for the travelers to break camp.

But those six days had not been lost in inactivity. Harnesses had been repaired, wagons reinforced, canvases carefully patched and oiled where the relentless rain had found a way inside. Clothes had been washed and mended, blankets aired, and bodies scrubbed. A hunting party returned to camp with two deer, and the venison fed the whole camp. The fresh meat was a welcome change from their dried and canned diet.

The scent of frying steak wafted over the camp that last evening, bringing a light spirit and unusually intent interest in supper preparations. Some women had found a berry patch and in short order stripped it clean. The tangy fruit made that special meal seem like a banquet. All were refreshed and looking forward to beginning the journey again.

It took the train three days to reach the Big River. When they finally arrived, Mr. Blake found exactly what he had been afraid they would face—a current far too strong and swift to allow safe wagon passage. He again called a meeting and explained the situation to the entire group. Another camp would have to be made beside the river until the waters subsided. The determined but weary travelers were all disappointed, but even the most impatient agreed with the decision.

So camp was set up, and the families again tried to establish some sort of daily routine to keep boredom from overtaking them. The men formed regular hunting parties, and the women and older children again ranged out in search of berries. Missie spent a part of each day gathering wood, as did the other women who did not have children to assign to the task. As she gleaned her daily supply, she also added to her stack of surplus piled under her wagon. If the rains should come again, Mrs. Schmidt would not be the only one who was prepared, she told herself firmly.

Some of the older ladies began to suspect Missie was "in the family way." Although no comments were made, Missie often noticed the motherly glances of interest and concern that came her way. The birth of her baby was almost five months away by Missie's reckoning, and that seemed like a long, long time into the future. Far longer than anyone should worry about, she silently told herself.

Missie found herself searching out the company of Becky Clay. There was no doubt in anyone's mind as to Rebecca's condition, and the other women found many little ways to make the young woman's work load lighter. Dry sticks were tossed onto her pile as the women walked by with their load of wood, extra food was presented at her campfire, and her pail went along to the stream for water with someone who had a free hand.

For Becky's sake, Missie felt extra concern over the travel delay. She was hoping along with Becky that they would reach Tettsford Junction and the doctor in time. Each day Missie prayed and hoped that by some miracle the swollen waters would be down and the train could be on its way. But just when the river appeared to be receding, somewhere along its banks another storm would raise the waters again. Rafting the wagons to the other side was out of the question in this deep, swift river, and day after day passed with the wagons still unable to cross.

On the fifteenth day by the Big River, the whole camp came to life as news of another wagon train's appearance passed quickly around the circle. Soon they could see it slowly wending its way down a distant hill. Many went out to meet it. Those who remained behind waited in feverish eagerness for any news the newcomers might bring.

When the smaller train finally arrived and made camp near the Blake group, Missie and Willie soon discovered the second train had begun its journey far south of their own area, and they had to be satisfied with only general news. The wagon master turned out to be a good deal more impatient than their Mr. Blake. After sitting downriver for only two days, he decided that the water had receded enough for him to get his wagons across. Mr. Blake tried to dissuade him, but the man laughed it off, roughly declaring Blake to be as skitterish as an old woman. He had taken wagons across when the water had been even higher, he stoutly and loudly maintained. He then turned to the waiting wagons and ordered the first one into the water.

Women and children joined the men on the bank to watch the wagons cross. Murmured complaints about Mr. Blake passed among the observers. "Here we been sittin' when we coulda been days away from here" was muttered around the group.

Mr. Blake did not choose to watch. With a look of disgust and a few well-chosen words directed at the other wagon master, he spun on his heel and marched off.

It seemed for a time that all would go well with the wagon. Then, to the horror of all those on the bank, it suddenly hit the deeper water and the current lifted it up and swirled it about. The horses plunged and fought in their effort to swim for the distant shore, but the churning waters were too strong for them. When the driver realized his predicament, he threw himself into the murky deep, trying desperately to fight his way to the shore. The wagon, weaving and swaying, was swept downstream as the frantic horses neighed and struggled in their fright. The pitching canvas cover gave one last sickening heave and then toppled over on its side. The sinking wagon and team were carried downstream and out of sight around a bend in the river.

Meantime, the driver was fighting to keep his head above water. At one point he managed to grab a floating tree that was also being carried along by the muddy current. A cheer went up from the shore, but the next instant a groan passed through the entire group—the tree struck something under the surface and flipped in midstream, jarring the man loose and leaving him to struggle on his own again.

The riverbank became alive with activity as men scrambled for their horses in an effort to reach near enough to at least throw him a rope. The observers watched the bobbing spot of his dark head as the water swirled him around the river bend. A young woman in the group from the other train collapsed in a heap, and some of the women who traveled with her bent over her to give her assistance.

"Poor woman," Missie gasped. "It must be her man!" She covered her face with her hands and wept.

The body was pulled from the river about a half mile downstream. All attempts to force some life back into the man were futile. The horses and wagon were never seen again.

The following day the travelers from both wagon trains met together. The grave had been dug and a service was held for the drowned man. His widow had to be helped away from the heaped-up mound that held the body of her young husband. A feeling of helplessness and grief settled over both camps. Respect for Mr. Blake mounted, and most of the group averted their eyes when the other wagon master, looking rather subdued, passed by.

A new determination passed through the Blake train. They would wait. They would wait if it took all summer! Horse and wagon were no match for the angry waters.

After breakfast one day a week later, someone in the camp drew their attention to a hill across the river. On ponies, their faces painted and headdress feathers waving in the wind, sat several Indian braves. The almost-naked bodies glistened in the morning sun. In silence they gazed across the river at the ring of wagons. Then at a signal from their leader, they moved on and out of sight over the hill. Missie shivered as she wondered what could have happened if the churning water had not been between them. Maybe this was a fulfillment of the Scripture promise she and Willie had been given by her father before they left home, "Yea, I will help thee. . . ."

After another week of patient and not-so-patient waiting, the river finally did recede. Mr. Blake, who had been carefully watching it each day, crossed it on his horse before he allowed any wagon to put a wheel into the water. When he felt satisfied, the order was given to move out.

It took the whole day to make the crossing. The women and children were guided across on horseback to await the coming of their menfolk and the canvas-covered homes. Some of the wagons needed two teams in order to pull them across. Many outriders traveled beside each wagon, steadying it with the many ropes that Mr. Blake insisted upon; thus no wagon got caught in midstream by a current that tried to take it sideways rather than forward. Missie couldn't help but remember the tragic death in the other group. If the other wagon master had used such precautions . . . Mr. Blake was a careful and experienced wagon master—another of God's provisions.

Once the group was gathered on the river's western shore, Willie offered a prayer of thanks to God for all the travelers. The weary men and animals were glad to make camp once more for a good night's rest before taking to the trail. The next day they would resume their journey after their month-and-a-half delay.

Missie was becoming increasingly concerned about Becky. They still had many days on the trail before reaching Tettsford Junction. Would Mrs. Kosensky's midwifery services be required after all?

⌒⁄◯

Early the next morning the camp was a bustle of activity. The travelers could hardly wait for the word to move out. Even the horses stamped in their impatience. Missie was surprised at the feelings that clamored for attention within her. During their previous weeks on the trail, she had dreaded the crossing of the Big River, for it seemed to mark the point of no return. But now that it was finally behind them, she was as restless as the teams. She felt like starting out to walk on her own. If she had known the trail and the direction she was to take, she might have done just that.

Finally the wagons were lined up and the order shouted. The creak of the harnesses and grind of wheels sounded like music to Missie's ears. At last! They were on their way again! All were alive and accounted for. They had crossed the Big River; surely only lesser obstacles lay in their pathway. Since turning back was no longer possible, she was anxious to forge ahead.

Missie could sense Willie's excitement as he carefully guided the team to follow the wagon ahead of him. It was hard for him to restrain himself from urging them on at a faster speed, but no one in the long line of teams was allowed to change the pace set by the wagon master.

The day passed uneventfully. The travelers quickly fell into their familiar routines. But their aching muscles reminded them that they had been idle for too long and must again break in to the rigors of the trail. Missie walked and rode in turn, gathering sticks as she walked, and when she climbed up again to ride, she stashed her bundle under the wagon seat.

At day's end everyone was weary, but tensions were gone. They were moving again, and that was what mattered.

⁂

As they progressed, the land about them continued its gradual change. There were fewer trees now, and those that did grow were smaller than the ones left behind. The women found very little wood for their fires as they followed the train. They began to carry buckets, which they filled with buffalo chips. Missie had preferred the wood, which made a much more pleasant fire. Besides, the cumbersome buckets soon had one's arms and back aching.

Occasionally herds of buffalo or deer were seen off in the distance. Twice, Indians were sighted, but though the hearts of the travelers beat more rapidly for a time, these Indians did not approach the train.

The widow of the drowned man, Mrs. Emory, had asked Mr. Blake for permission to join his train. Mr. Blake had found it impossible to refuse her. Arrangements were made for her to share Mr. Weiss's wagon with his daughter, Kathy. Mr. Weiss moved in with Henry, and the train moved on.

The unfortunate woman had lost everything in the river—her husband of six months, her home, and her belongings. The women of similar size dug into their trunks and showered her with enough garments to outfit her for the remainder of the trip to Tettsford Junction. Though some of the clothes didn't fit very well and weren't particularly fashionable, Mrs. Emory was very grateful for their kindness.

She proved to be a worthy member of the train. Even in her deep sorrow, she was aware of those about her who could use her helping hand. Her quiet manner and helpful acts won her a secure place in the group.

And so they journeyed on. Each day found them a little nearer to their respective destinations, and talk around the fire at night was filled with shared hopes and plans and dreams. The new land held many promises. It seemed to hold out open arms, ready to embrace a stranger—any stranger with hope in his heart and a strong back willing to bend itself to the work.

NINE

Town

Mr. Blake seemed to have a great aversion to towns. In every possible instance, he skirted far around them, no matter how small the settlement. When he could not avoid one, he ordered the wagons to keep on moving. No one was allowed to stop for any dallying. Each family made a list of needed supplies, and either Mr. Blake or one of his scouts rode into the town and made the purchases.

The wagon master said his job was to get the wagons, and the folks in them, to Tettsford Junction, and he planned to do just that. Further, he said the most deadly enemy of the westbound settler was a town. Blake had lost no one to swollen rivers, prairie fires, or Indians on his many trains west. But he had lost people to *towns,* he grumbled. And since he did not like having his good record smudged, he considered towns the enemy.

Everyone was surprised, therefore, when Mr. Blake called a meeting and announced, "Tomorrow we reach Lipton. Ain't much of a town, but we'll be stopping there fer a day. Our campsite is to the right of the town within easy walking distance. No teams—no horses a'tall, no wagons—are to go into the town. Those of you thet have more purchases to make than can be carried will be glad to know the Lipton General Store will make deliveries. The place carries a fair line of essentials." He stopped a moment to look around the circle.

"The train will move on again at the usual hour on Wednesday mornin'. I suggest ya all be ready to go."

A general uproar of excitement followed his announcement. To see a town again! To be able to more than just drive by, only imagining the opportunity of browsing through shops, going to the barber, selecting food delicacies . . .

How large was the town? Did it have a blacksmith? A hairdresser? A butcher? Maybe even a doctor? Questions flew furiously, but Blake was the only one with answers—and he had somehow disappeared after his announcement.

Missie couldn't help smiling as she and Willie walked back to their wagon. Her mind was busy calculating just what she wanted most and whether they would be able to spare any of their hard-earned cash in order to purchase it.

It was difficult to break from their fire that night and get to bed. Missie delved into a trunk to pull out a favorite dress. Shaking out the wrinkles as best she could, she hung the blue-flowered frock up in hopes it would be smooth by morning. She had noticed some wives adding another patch to their husband's already worn overalls. Whole families pored over lists, adding, changing, dreaming, wishing—and reluctantly deleting.

Missie thought even the dogs of the camp had seemed to catch the fever. They ran back and forth, yapping and tussling and making general nuisances of themselves.

The next morning everyone was ready to roll long before the call was given—even the often tardy Standards. The sooner they began the journey, the sooner Lipton would be reached—and the longer the time available for shopping.

The wagons lumbered out, set for another dusty day on the trail, everyone hoping that it wouldn't be too late when they made camp to be off to the town.

To everyone's amazement and delight, the town lay before them as they topped the first hill. They had camped only a few miles from it the night before! They all laughed at themselves and at their wagon master, but Mr. Blake's face remained as impassive as ever.

They quickly reached the new campsite and formed their customary circle. The men set about the task of caring for the animals while the women scurried around, building fires to heat water for sponge baths within the confines of their wagons. By the time they and their children were ready to head into town, the sun had climbed high into the clear sky for another extremely warm day.

They departed in little groups, eager and expectant. Henry accompanied some of the younger people. The Collinses walked together, Sissie with Meggie in her arms and Tom with Joey hoisted on his shoulders. Mrs. Thorne strode off, her offspring matching her long strides. Her husband grumbled that he would have none of the foolishness and elected to stay behind and mend the harness. Mrs. Page, after voicing a parting barb at Jessie Tuttle, hurried down the trail without even waiting for a reply. Tillie Crane went along, too impatient to wait even for her young husband. At last she could have *something* done to her hair! Mrs. Schmidt threw a bundle of hastily gathered sticks under the protection of her wagon, shook out her apron, and started off with her family members. They quickly overtook and passed the slow-moving Mrs. Kosensky.

Missie and Willie walked with John and Becky. They chose a much slower pace for Becky's sake.

As they passed the Weiss' wagon, they saw Mrs. Emory fastening the tent flap down before leaving for town. Her sad face lit up with a smile when she saw the young couples. Without a word, Willie stepped over to lend her a hand.

"Eager to git into town?" She directed her question to the women.

"Oh yes," Becky enthused. "It seems like forever since I've walked on a boardwalk or looked in a shop."

Mrs. Emory just smiled.

She is so attractive when she smiles like that, thought Missie, *and so very young. I reckon she's not much older than I am. What would I do if something happened to my Willie? How would I ever get home again? Would I just be stranded somewhere out here in the West?* Just the thought of such a thing made Missie's stomach churn. *Dear God,* she prayed inwardly, *I don't think I could stand it.*

Then she thought of her own mother. A new awareness of what Marty had been through those long years before filled her being, and tears threatened to fill her eyes. She hurriedly blinked them away before anyone could notice them.

"Are you going shopping, too?" she asked Mrs. Emory.

The woman's face sobered, and she shook her head. "Not exactly," she replied slowly.

Missie realized the woman would probably have nothing to go shopping with, even though her needs were great.

There was silence for a minute. The young woman seemed to be debating whether she should say anything further about her plans for the day. Finally she spoke, her voice soft and even. "I . . . I'm really goin' to look for a church. I . . . have this need for a place of prayer."

Willie reached for the woman's hand. He just looked into her face and patted the small hand with his other one. Missie blinked back more tears. The woman nodded, withdrew her hand, and turned away with tears glistening on her cheeks.

Missie then reached for Willie's hand. He was so much like her pa, her Willie. He felt so deeply what others were feeling. Homesickness for her father and a surge of love for Willie swept through Missie in one wave.

They followed the Clays, who were already walking slowly down the path toward town.

"Willie," Missie whispered, "we should try to draw her out more. She's such a sweet thing, the poor soul. I can't imagine anyone suffering so much—so young."

"Yer ma an' pa did," Willie reminded her gently. His hand tightened on hers.

Missie was silent, too deeply moved to try to speak. Yes, her ma and pa had suffered, but she had been too young to be aware of it. She only remembered them as laughing, loving parents. Would Mrs. Emory someday be able to laugh and love again, too? Missie prayed that the town would indeed have a fine little church where she could commune with God.

⁖

The town wasn't much, as towns go, but to the travelers it would suffice. There were sidewalks for Becky to walk on, although there were loose, broken, and even missing boards. The shoppers soon learned to keep an eye on their next step.

After a quick general look at the town, the various couples separated. The women went to yearn over threads, yarn, yard goods, and other "luxuries." The men found themselves around the livery stable to check on more "practical" supplies, such as a new harness or new shoes for the horses.

Becky and Missie spent a long part of their morning surveying soft yarns and materials, planning and dreaming of what they would make for their coming babies. Becky already had most of her necessities, her baby having been expected before she left home, but she was eager to add some special things to the baby's wardrobe. Missie would wait for her main preparation until she reached Willie's land and was settled— but it would be so much fun to select a few pieces to work on during the journey.

There was a hotel of sorts in Lipton, and Becky's and Missie's husbands had promised to take their wives there for a meal. The four looked forward to it eagerly. It would be so good to have food that didn't taste of woodsmoke, to drink real store-bought tea, to eat meat that wasn't wild, and maybe even have some fresh bread. And vegetables! How long it had been since they had tasted fresh vegetables!

Promptly at noon the men returned and made an elaborate display of escorting Missie and Becky to the dining room. The room was already crowded, and they had to wait for a table.

The two couples deliberated long over the menu, and finally, sensing the impatience of the waitress, placed their orders. Missie was surprised at how flat things tasted without the tang of the smoke. The bread turned out not to be fresh, but it *was* bread. The meat was mild enough, but more than a little tough, and the vegetables were definitely overcooked.

They enjoyed it immensely, however, and pretended to one another that it was the finest they had ever eaten. They even ordered pie and lingered over it, savoring each bite as they slowly sipped their cups of tea.

In the afternoon they continued their inspection of the stores. They knew wise decisions had to be made, and each purchase had to be carefully considered. It was a difficult task to make up one's mind after not having shopped for such a long time.

Their lists were consulted and changed before the goods were finally ordered. Necessary foods were restocked, and a few fresh vegetables were purchased. Missie did pick out a few soft flannels and cottons to make into baby clothes and also bought additional wool for heavy socks. They began their walk back, weary and a little poorer, but refreshed by their day spent back in civilization. They clutched in their arms a few of their most cherished purchases, eagerly awaiting the rest to be delivered that evening.

Missie and Willie left John and Becky at their wagon and walked on to their own. Becky was looking tired after her exciting and busy day—this in spite of the fact that Missie had insisted she sit and rest for a spell every so often throughout the time spent in town. Missie invited them to share the evening meal with them so Becky might get some much-needed rest. Becky was happy to accept.

Upon reaching the wagon, Missie stowed away her purchases and set to work building the fire and preparing the meal. Willie changed back into his old overalls and went to take care of the cows and horses.

It had been a good day. Missie hummed as she worked. She could hear Willie's whistle moving down the path toward the draw where the animals were staked out to graze.

TEN

Breaking Camp

The town, as Mr. Blake feared, had produced some casualties. Tillie Crane had found her hairdresser. She had also found a job in a shop, and she adamantly refused to move one more step into that "God-forsaken land" of wind, sun, and rain. Her husband had spent the night badgering and pleading by turn, but nothing would make Tillie change her mind. A heartbroken Jason Crane finally came to inform Mr. Blake that their wagon would be withdrawing. There was no way he would travel on without his wife. He'd see what he could do for a job in Lipton. Surely there was work somewhere for a man who was willing.

The Cranes weren't the only ones with problems. A number of the men from the train had been "out on the town." Most of them staggered in, sometime during the night, in various stages of disrepair. Mrs. Kosensky had taken care of her husband—a cold bucket of water for the outside of him and several cups of hot coffee for his insides. The next morning he was bleary-eyed and a bit belligerent but ready for travel.

Jessie Tuttle handled her driver-brother, J.M. Dooley, by simply stuffing him into the wagon and hitching the team herself.

Mrs. Thorne had the most trouble. Her husband failed to reappear at all. After waiting tight-lipped, she set off for town in search of her errant man, striding back to camp empty-handed after two hours of searching. It was Mr. Blake's turn. Maybe he was more familiar with where to look; at any rate, after about three-quarters of an hour, he returned. The livery wagon followed, delivering a very sodden Mr. Thorne. His wife said nothing, simply nodding to the men where Mr. Thorne was to be placed and picking up the reins of her team.

After a three-hour delay, the teams finally moved out. By then the sun was already hot, the children cranky, and the adults out of sorts.

Mrs. Thorne did not so much as give her neighbors a nod or a suggestion of apology. She smacked her team smartly with a rein and maneuvered into position, her face stern and her eyes straight ahead.

Missie watched as the woman drove up in her wagon. It had been said that Mrs. Thorne had known all along her husband wouldn't remain in the camp mending harnesses and that she knew exactly what he would do once he got to town. It had happened many times in the past and would likely happen often in the future.

Missie was sure the invincible Mrs. Thorne would be able to cope. Nothing seemed to shake that woman from solid-rock indifference.

Mrs. Thorne smacked her team again and passed on by, her hands steady, her eyes unblinking against the glare of the midmorning sun. Missie almost missed it, but there it was—and what she saw made her stop short and catch her breath. Unmistakably running down Mrs. Thorne's coarse, tanned cheeks was a steady stream of tears.

When Missie could breathe again she whispered, "You poor soul. Here you are suffering inside, and nobody knows . . . nobody even suspects, so no one reaches out to you in understanding. Oh . . . God forgive me. Forgive me for not seeing past her stiff jaw to the hurts and needs. Help me to help her, Lord—to show her kindness and love. She needs me. She needs *you,* Lord."

Thereafter, Missie took every opportunity she could find to greet the woman with a smile, to show little acts of kindness. The older woman did not really melt, but she did begin to show a little softness around the firm, hard edges of her soul.

They had been on the trail four days since leaving Lipton, and the wagon train seemed to be making good progress. The men who had visited the tavern had sobered up and were now back to their hard tasks. But it was strongly suspected J. M. Dooley had somehow managed to smuggle some whiskey along in his wagon against Mr. Blake's explicit orders. It was a true source of contention between J. M. and Jessie Tuttle. And, of course, anything involving Jessie, Mrs. Page considered her right to become involved in, as well. So a three-way war was now raging.

Folks smiled at the ridiculousness of it all, but finally Mr. Blake decided it was time to step in. J. M.'s booze was discovered and discarded. Mrs. Page and her wagon were assigned a new position at the end of the line far from Jessie Tuttle. Things seemed to settle down again.

When they made camp the fourth night, a message carried by Mrs. Kosensky's daughter, Nell, arrived for Missie as she cleaned up after the evening meal.

"Ma says, could ya come to Mrs. Clay? She's been in labor most of the afternoon an' wants to see ya."

Missie was stunned at the news. She had missed Becky that day but had supposed she just didn't feel up to taking in her customary short walks alongside the train. Missie called over to Henry to tell Willie where she would be and quickly grabbed a shawl. In her haste she almost ran to get to Becky but held herself back lest others watching would be unduly concerned.

As she approached the Clay wagon she could hear Becky's soft moaning. She ran the last few steps and was met by a very worried-looking Mrs. Kosensky. Instead of inviting Missie up, the other woman climbed down and drew Missie aside.

"Ain't good, ma'am, ain't good," she said in a hoarse whisper. "Me . . . I deliver babies. Yes, lotsa babies . . . but this kind, no. He small . . . he twisted . . . and he early." She shook her head, and Missie noticed tears in her eyes. "Ain't good. She need a doctor . . . bad."

"May I see her?" Missie begged, longing to be a source of comfort and aid to Becky.

"Yes . . . yes, do."

Missie scrambled up into the wagon. Becky was flushed and damp with perspiration. Missie looked at her pale, anguished face in alarm. She reached for Becky's hand and then began to smooth back her long, loose hair. She spoke softly, not really aware of what she said to Becky, but it seemed to comfort the distraught girl.

Missie stayed with Becky for most of the night, but the situation did not improve. Occasionally, Becky seemed to drift off into a troubled sleep, but she was soon reawakened by her discomfort. Willie, who had come to wait outside by the fire with John, suggested that Missie should get some rest or she would be in danger, too. Mrs. Kosensky agreed.

The next morning the LaHayes crawled wearily from their bed and began the preparations for another day on the trail. Missie sent Willie over to ask about Becky. He returned with the news that nothing had changed. Missie's heart felt heavy as she went through the motions of preparing their breakfast.

While she was hurrying to pack up their belongings, one of the trail scouts came by on his horse. He stopped at each wagon with the same message.

"Mr. Blake says we stay put today. He's not breakin' camp till thet baby's arrived."

Missie was greatly relieved and would have willingly hugged the grisly wagon master. She could not imagine what it would be like for Becky if she had to bounce around in a moving wagon in her condition.

A rider had been sent back to Lipton the night before to see if a doctor could be found and brought to the camp. Everyone who knew how, and even some who didn't, prayed that there might be a doctor and that he would arrive soon.

The women tried to keep busy with a little cleaning and straightening up of their wagon homes, and men checked harnesses and wheels. Neighbors used the long hours as an excuse to sit and discuss anything that came to mind. Still the time only crawled, and by the time the day was coming to an end, everyone's nerves were on edge. Becky and her unborn baby were a heavy concern on everyone's mind.

With no more valid reason to stay up, they finally extinguished their campfires and went to bed, hoping that the good news of the baby's birth would reach them during the night.

It did not happen.

As they stirred about the camp the next morning, the news spread quickly that the child had not yet been born. Another long day began. With no harnesses to mend and no further wagon cleaning to be done, time lay heavy on hands and minds. Yet hope remained alive. Surely with the additional delay, the doctor from Lipton would have plenty of time to make it. But the rider finally returned, tired and dusty and with a weary, limping horse. There was no doctor to be found in Lipton.

It was almost one-thirty in the afternoon when Mrs. Kosensky climbed down from the Clay wagon. Willie, Missie, and several other neighbors had been waiting outside. No cry of a newborn baby followed her. Mrs. Kosensky's shoulders sagged and tears coursed down her plump cheeks. To the waiting friends she shook her head.

"No," she said brokenly. "No . . . he did not make it, the little one."

"Oh, Becky!" cried Missie. "Poor Becky. She'll be heartbroken."

"No," said Mrs. Kosensky, again shaking her head. "No. The little mama . . . she did not make it, either."

For a moment Missie chose not to understand, not to believe. But she knew, as she looked at the older woman, that the news was indeed true. Then, from the depths of the covered wagon, came muffled sobs of a man.

"Oh, dear God," Missie whispered with her hands to her face. She didn't know if her legs could hold her upright. Willie was by her side in a moment, and she turned to bury her face against his shoulder. He held her close for a time and let her weep. When her spasm of tears had subsided, he gently held her away and looked into her face.

"I must go in to John," he said. "Can you make it to the wagon alone?"

Missie nodded, but it was Henry who led her away, easing her over the rough terrain and opening the canvas flap so she could stumble into the wagon.

She lay down in the stuffy heat and once more felt overcome with the sorrow and confusion in her soul.

The funeral service was held the next morning. John stood in bewildered silence as the young mother and her infant son were laid together in a blanket. Shock and grief no doubt had numbed his mind, and he didn't seem to comprehend the event.

After the service was over, the wagons were quietly ordered to move out. The men guided their animals into line silently, thoughtfully. Willie had suggested that John ride with them for a while, but he preferred to be alone. Missie rode beside Willie, but they had not gone far before she asked if he would stop a moment so she could climb down and walk for a while.

She stood quietly for a time, letting the wagons roll past her, turning her back to the dust swirling from their wheels. When the last one had gone by, Missie looked back the way they had come. In the valley below was the circle where they had camped. The evidence of a recent train was still there—the trampled grass, the campfire ashes, the wheel marks—and there, just to the left, was the little mound of bare earth marking the spot where they had left Becky. And Becky's baby. For a moment Missie wanted to run back, but she knew it was pointless. Becky was gone from them now. Missie felt a certain measure of comfort in the thought that Becky and her baby were not alone. They had each other.

"Good-bye, Becky," Missie whispered. "Good-bye, Rebecca Clay. You were a dear, sweet friend. May you—and your little one—find great pleasure and comfort in the house of God."

Missie turned to go, tears streaming down her face. But just then a lone rider emerged from the bushes in the valley and stopped beside the soft mound. Missie recognized the form of Mr. Blake. The man dismounted from his horse and approached the new grave. He removed his hat and stood momentarily with bowed head. Then he bent down and placed a small cluster of prairie flowers on the fresh earth. As he turned and mounted his horse, Missie felt a fresh stream of tears slide down her cheeks.

That was a lovely thing to do, she thought.

But it was much later that Missie learned that many years before, the same man had stood beside another mound—one that held his own wife and infant son. At that time, too, he had been forced to ride away and leave them to lie alone beside a prairie trail.

ELEVEN

A Tough Decision

Missie found a measure of comfort in the fact that Tettsford Junction was getting nearer and nearer, but the days always seemed long. She kept herself occupied as much as she could. She carefully looked after her own responsibilities, as well as devoting much time to helping others—especially Mrs. Collins. The two Collins youngsters kept quite healthy, in spite of the rigors of the trail. But they were young enough to still require a lot of time and attention.

Missie and Willie had not yet been able to talk about Becky's death. Missie wept often. If Willie was there when she cried, he held her close, stroking her hair and listening to her sorrow with his heart. They each realized that sometime—and sometime soon—they must discuss it. Probably only then could their hearts begin the true healing process.

John Clay's name was always mentioned in Willie's evening prayer. But though Missie ached for John and his loss, she also realized she felt a twinge of resentment toward him. Her emotions swung between grief and anger.

One night, after they had retired, Willie gently broached the subject they had been avoiding.

"It easin' some—'bout Becky?" His arm tightened around Missie as he asked the question. She could tell he wanted her to know that he understood, that he suffered with her.

"I guess . . . some," Missie was able to answer, holding back the tears.

"I think maybe it's gittin' harder for John," Willie commented after a few moments of silence.

"How so?"

"Well, at first I don't think it . . . it was real to John. Now it is. He's over the shock. An' he's missin' Becky . . . knowin' thet she won't be back, won't be his . . . ever again."

Missie pondered Willie's words. That small feeling of anger toward John stirred within her. She decided to express it.

"John was too sure of himself, too cocky about Becky and that baby. Just because his mother . . . Things can go wrong . . . they can. He should have known that." Now Missie could no longer hold back her tears.

"I was feelin' those same thoughts," Willie said quietly, "but maybe we're bein' too hard on John. Sure, he was cocky. But . . . but maybe it was just a cover-up, to sorta make things happen the way he wanted them to. I don't know. All I know is thet he loved Becky . . . very much . . . an' he wanted thet son . . . very much. An' now he has neither of them . . . an' he's truly sorrowin', Missie. Maybe . . . maybe we're *all* guilty of holdin' too lightly those we love."

Missie's sobs quieted as she thought over Willie's words. He was right, of course. John did love Becky, and he had wanted the baby. It was no fault of John's that things had gone wrong. If it hadn't been for the long delay at the Big River, they would have reached Tettsford Junction and the doctor in time—even with Becky's baby arriving early.

A feeling of great sorrow for John swept over Missie. *The poor man . . . to lose so much.* She must pray for him more, she decided.

Willie interrupted her thoughts. "Missie . . ."

When he didn't continue, she turned toward him, but it was too dark in the wagon to read his face.

"I been thinkin'," he finally said, his voice low but determined. "When we git to Tettsford Junction, there's a doc there."

"I know."

"I want ya to have a doc, Missie."

"But our baby is almost three months away," she said.

"I know."

Missie thought about it. "I suppose we could," she finally stated, "get back to Tettsford Junction in time. How far is our land from Tettsford Junction?"

"Good week's travel by wagon."

"A week? I suppose if we left early enough—"

"That's not what I had in mind, Missie," Willie said too quickly.

"What *did* you have in mind?"

Willie swallowed. "Well, I figured thet maybe ya should stay at Tettsford until after the baby is safely delivered."

"But you're in a great hurry to get to the land—to put up some corrals, fix a house, and get yourself some cattle before winter."

"Yeah, yer right, Missie, but—"

"That'd make you late and rushed. By the time I'm ready to travel and we make the trip, you'd hardly have time—"

Willie interrupted. "I'd go on as planned, Missie, an' see to all those things."

"An' leave me behind?" Missie could scarcely believe her ears.

"It's the only way, Missie . . . far as I can see."

"But I don't want—"

Willie's arm tightened again, but his voice was firm. "I don't want it, either, Missie, but it's the only way. I'm not takin' any chances like John took. I will not—"

But Missie quickly stopped him. "It's not the same . . . can't you see? Becky was sick from the beginning. Me . . . I've been fine all along."

Missie felt Willie's hand grip her shoulder.

"It *could happen* thet ya need a doctor. There are no doctors where we're goin'. There aren't even neighbors who could be midwives. There's no one to help ya, Missie. No one! Can't ya see? I can't take ya there. Not after what's happened here!"

A sob caught in Missie's throat, but she tried one more time. "Then we'll just have to go back to Tettsford when the time comes. I don't want to stay there without you, Willie. We'll just have to go back."

"An' iffen the baby comes early—like Becky's? How will we know when it's time? Something could go wrong *anytime*. Already I'm prayin' every night thet you'll be fine fer the next day's travel, fine till we reach Tettsford. Iffen I take ya on from there, down to the ranch with the idea of bringin' ya back—what iffen we're caught on the trail? What then?"

Missie knew she had lost, for the moment. She didn't bother to argue anymore but buried her face against Willie's shoulder and wept. To be without Willie for three long months or more, in a strange town, waiting all alone for their first baby . . . how could she ever bear it?

She felt a tear drop onto her forehead. Willie was weeping, too.

"It's gonna be so hard," he finally managed to say, his voice husky. "So awful hard . . . but we'll make it. Remember our verse—'Fear thou not; for I am with thee: be not dismayed; for I am thy God: I will strengthen thee; yea, I will help thee; yea, I will uphold thee with the right hand of my righteousness'!"

Fear thou not echoed over and over through Missie's mind. How could she *not* be afraid?

The wagon train made its final camp just outside Tettsford Junction. The town proved to be a larger settlement than anyone on the train had anticipated. Missie looked around at the bleakness of the countryside and wondered what sustained it. The land about didn't appear able to produce any more than a bit of sagebrush. *Who could possibly endure such barrenness?* Missie thought with a shiver. She turned her back on the wind that seemed to be constantly blowing.

The traveling companions from the many weeks shared mixed emotions. John still felt empty and alone. He had difficulty deciding what he should do, whether to continue on his way and join his brother as planned or look for some kind of work in the town. The bright promises that the land had held for him seemed empty now that Becky was gone.

The Pages made up their minds to stay in town, as did a couple of other families that Missie didn't know very well. Jessie Tuttle would continue on, so Mrs. Page saved a few choice sentences for a parting shot. Jessie ignored the needling, much to Mrs. Page's annoyance and everyone else's amusement.

Mrs. Emory, the young widow, knew she had very few options open to her. She would stay in the town. The kindness of the members of the wagon train had gotten her to Tettsford Junction. Now it was up to her to take care of herself. She had blossomed and matured during her days on the trail, and though she still obviously felt the loss of her husband, she seemed prepared to face life again.

Mr. Weiss and Kathy also decided to remain in Tettsford. Her father declared with certainty that such a busy town would be able to use another smithy. Missie wondered if that was the real reason—or if he had developed a secret attachment to the young widow and was willing to bide his time. She rather hoped not. Melinda Emory was scarcely older than Mr. Weiss's daughter, Kathy. But it was their business, Missie decided, and Mr. Weiss certainly was a very kind man.

Most of the other travelers would be leaving in a few days' time with other trains, traveling northwest to the "prairies." Missie couldn't see how any place could be more *prairie* than where they were at present, and how anyone would actually *choose* to live here. But she did not voice her opinions.

Willie asked Missie if she wanted to go in and see the town as soon as camp was made and the necessary tasks performed. But she was remembering her last visit to town in the company of Becky and was thinking ahead to her own dreaded stay in this one.

She declined and excused herself to the wagon to be alone.

If only Willie would change his mind! Did he expect her to spend three miserable months cooped up in this horribly cramped wagon? In this dreary town, with the sun beating relentlessly on the treeless landscape and the wind howling constantly about the canvas flaps? If only she had known ahead of time that Willie wouldn't be taking her on to his land, to help build a home and establish his ranch. She might as well have stayed at home with her own folks who loved her and would have provided for her. *Why trek halfway across the world and suffer all of the heat, the rain, the mosquitoes, the blistered and aching feet—just to be dumped off here?* Her thoughts raged round and round in her mind. It just wasn't fair of Willie. It wasn't fair at all.

The hot tears coursed down her face, and Missie finally fell into an exhausted sleep.

Willie started calling to Missie even before he entered the wagon. "I've found a place!" she heard him call, obviously elated. Missie quickly sat up.

"A place for *what*?" she demanded when his head poked through the canvas flap.

"For you," he declared, looking surprised at her question. "For you—while yer waitin'."

She stared at him. So Willie hadn't ever planned for her to spend these months waiting in the wagon.

Missie stubbornly didn't tell him she didn't intend to *wait*. She intended to *go*. But deep inside she knew it was useless to fight it.

"It's only one room—but it's a nice fair size. An' it's with fine folks. I'm sure you'll like 'em, an' they even said I can stay there, too, till the supply train is ready to leave."

"That's right good of them," Missie said with some spark, "seeing how you *are* my husband."

Willie ignored the remark. "Mr. Taylorson runs a general store, an' his wife teaches a bit of piano. Says ya might even learn to play the piano while yer waitin'."

"Oh, Willie!" Missie said in exasperation. "What in heaven's name would I want to learn piano for? What good would that do me where—"

"It would help fill in the long hours," Willie interposed. "It might help a heap, iffen ya choose to let it." His tone was mild, but he gave her a searching look.

Missie wanted to stomp away, but there was no place to go—neighbors' eyes were watching all around. So she turned her back on Willie and began to trim the wick of the lantern that usually sat on the outside shelf, making sure she seemed at ease and composed.

Willie continued, "The doc lives only three houses down from the Taylorsons, so he'll be right handy when—"

"If he's not off somewhere setting a broken leg or treating a bullet wound," Missie muttered.

"Guess thet could happen even back home," Willie said calmly. "But there are two midwives in town—in case he should be away. I inquired."

"Midwife didn't help Becky none."

Missie grimaced at her own unreasonableness. She was being unfair to Willie. She knew that. He was doing what he believed was right. She blinked back her tears and steadied her voice.

"An' when does the supply train go?" she asked, deliberately changing the course of the conversation.

"'Bout a week—maybe a little less."

"And you'll be ready?"

"Plan to be. Think I'll do like yer pa suggested. I'll pick me up another wagon with the rails fer the corrals an' other supplies. That way, I won't be held up none once I git to our land."

"And where would this treeless town ever get rails for a corral?" Missie couldn't keep her dislike for the place from her voice.

"They haul 'em in. Lots of folks need 'em. Guess there's lumber a lot closer than it looks—some of those hills to the west are treed."

Missie nodded bleakly.

"Well, I'd best see to the stock," Willie said and turned to go, then turned back again. "Henry said to let ya know he won't be here fer supper."

"What's he planning?"

"He's eatin' with the Weisses. But what he's *plannin'*—who knows?"

Missie smiled in spite of herself. So it was Kathy Weiss that Henry was setting his cap for. He had kept her guessing the whole trip, seeming to give equal attention to more than one girl. Well, at least Kathy also would be staying on in Tettsford—Missie would be assured of some company.

As she began work on the evening meal, she regretted her refusal to go into town. She could have been cooking something special and fresh for supper instead of the same old fare—if she hadn't chosen to remain at the wagon feeling mistreated and sorry for herself.

She was bored with the food, she was bored with the wagon, she was even bored with her neighbors. Tomorrow she *would* go into town. She might even let Willie introduce her to the Taylorsons. It wasn't their fault she would be stuck here in the town until the baby arrived. Not their fault at all.

TWELVE

The Taylorsons

Missie awoke refreshed and ready to venture into Tettsford Junction. She determined to make the best of the day. She washed carefully and chose one of her favorite dresses. Loose and full, with a sash that tied in the back, the small print was cheerful and becoming. Missie was relieved it would be usable throughout her confinement—though it wouldn't be as stylish as when it showed off her slim waist. The loose shirtwaists and expandable skirts she and her mama had prepared for "some future day" when Missie would be needing them were suitable for everyday wear. But Missie was not too taken with the plain, simple dark skirts and was thankful she had a nice assortment of colorful aprons to wear over them. She combed her hair with particular care and began to prepare breakfast for the men.

Henry was the first to appear. He seemed to approve of how Missie looked.

"See yer not wearin' yer hikin' shoes today," he joked.

Missie looked down at her trim feet carefully encased in smart black boots. She smiled.

"I just may *never* wear them again," she answered in kind.

"Now, now," Henry replied, "ya sure wouldn't want thet part of yer edjication to jest go to waste, would ya?"

"Seems every *other* part of my education has gone to waste," Missie responded. There was a little quiver in her voice as she thought of the classroom of eager children back home.

"Not so," Henry was quick to say. "Don't fergit thet you'll soon be 'teacher' agin."

Missie glanced down at her blossoming figure and felt her cheeks grow warm.

Henry quickly changed the subject. "See'd the town yet?"

"Not yet—but Willie has. I didn't feel much like going in yesterday. I'm more ready today."

Henry nodded. "Big place really—but not too fancy."

"Where do you think they got the name?"

"Man named Tettsford first set up a store there to catch the trade of the wagons goin' through."

"Is he still there?"

"Naw. He made his money, then cleared out. Went back east—to spend it, I guess."

"Smart man," Missie murmured under her breath.

"Ya know what I'm gonna miss most 'bout wagon trainin'?" Henry asked.

His abrupt change of subject surprised Missie, but she soon recovered and answered with a teasing voice, "Now, I *wonder*."

Henry turned red. "Naw," he said, "nothin' like thet. I'm gonna miss the Sunday gatherin's."

Missie quickly turned serious. "I guess I will, too," she said. "They weren't anything like home, but they were special in their own way, weren't they? And you did a first-rate job, Henry. A very good job. Did you ever think of being a preacher?"

Henry's color deepened. "I thought on it . . . sorta. But I ain't got what it takes to be a preacher. Very little book learnin' and not much civilizin', either."

"That's not true, Henry," Missie remonstrated with him. "You're a born leader. Didn't you notice how the people followed you, accepted you, expected you to take the lead?"

Henry sat silently. "They did, some," he agreed. "But thet was a wagon train, not a settlement church. There's a heap of difference there. I did decide one thing, though. . . ." He hesitated.

"And that is?" Missie prompted.

"Well, I jest told the Lord thet iffen He had a place fer me—wherever it was—I'd be happy to do whatever I could. I don't expect it to be in a church, Missie, but there's lots of folks who need God who never come lookin' fer Him in a church."

"I'm glad, Henry," Missie said softly. "I'm glad you feel that way. And you're right. God needs lots of us—everywhere—to touch other people's hearts."

Missie turned back to finish up the breakfast preparations, and Henry settled himself on a low stool. It wasn't long until Missie heard a cheery whistle and knew Willie would soon join them.

Willie's whistle changed abruptly when he saw Missie, and he paused to look at her carefully. Then he grinned.

"Yer lookin' right smart this mornin', Mrs. LaHaye."

"Oh, Willie, stop teasing. You've been seeing me in plain dresses and walking shoes for so long you've forgotten what I really look like."

"Then I hope ya remind me often. Looks good, don't she, Henry?" Willie said with a wink.

"I already told her so."

"Oh, ho," Willie laughed. "Now thet young Miss Weiss has favored yer presence, ya think ya can pass out compliments to all of the womenfolk, do ya?"

"Nope," said Henry. "Jest the *special* ones."

Willie laughed again. "Well, she's special, all right."

He kissed Missie on the cheek. Missie leaned primly away. "Really, Willie," she reprimanded. "We don't need to put on a show for all to see." She busied herself with serving the breakfast.

After they had eaten, then read a portion of Scripture—which Willie ended as he had throughout the journey with the special passage given to them by Missie's father—they had prayer together.

"Will ya be needin' me today?" Henry asked Willie as Missie began clearing up.

Willie thought a moment. "No, I can manage carin' fer the stock. Go ahead. Make any plans ya want to."

"Thanks. I reckon I'll give the Weisses a hand at gettin' settled in town. They did manage to find a house—such as it is."

"Is Mrs. Emory gonna stay with 'em?"

"No, and she needs some settlin', too. She found a small room over the general store, but there's not much furniture there to speak of. She's already signed up to teach school come fall, but until then she's gonna work in the hotel kitchen."

"The kitchen? Seems rather heavy, burdensome work for such a genteel little woman," Missie commented doubtfully.

"Thet's what I thought. But the job is there—an' she insists."

Missie detected genuine concern in Henry's voice.

He put on his hat. "Well, iffen yer sure I'm not needed, I'll git on over there an' give 'em a hand."

"He's got it right bad, hasn't he?" Willie remarked with an arched brow after Henry had walked away. "Well, Mrs. LaHaye, may I escort ya into town? I take it ya didn't git all prettied up jest to sit out in the sun."

"I think, sir, that I might consent to that," Missie replied playfully.

Missie found the town much as she had expected. There seemed to be very little that was green. A few small gardens looked parched under the sun-drenched sky. The vegetables fighting for an existence were dwarfed and scraggly. Here and there some brave grass put in an appearance—under a dripping pump or close to a watering trough. As far as Missie could see, there had been no attempt to plant trees or shrubbery. Puffs of dust scattered whenever the wind stirred.

The buildings, too, were bleak. No bright paint or fancy signs. Square, bold letters spelled SALOON over a gray, wind-worn building. Another sign announced HOTEL. Missie winced to think of Melinda Emory working in a hot, stuffy kitchen making meals for the guests. Several other weathered buildings lined the dusty streets. There were sidewalks, fairly new, but they, too, were layered with dust except where women's skirts had whisked them clean.

More than one saloon lined the main street. In fact, Missie counted five. *What does such a town need with five saloons?* she wondered. It certainly was not nearly as blessed with churches, but Missie did spy a small spire reaching up from among the buildings huddled over to her left.

There were blacksmith shops—at least three—but maybe, as Mr. Weiss had said, a town this size could use another.

A bank, a sheriff's office, a printshop, a telegraph office, liveries, a stagecoach landing, and an assortment of stores and other buildings that Missie had not yet identified filled out the downtown area. Missie smiled as she read the notice, *Overland Stagecoaches,* and wondered where on earth they took passengers way out in the middle of nowhere.

The fact was, the town didn't interest her much at this point. She still dreaded the fact that she had to stay in it for three months without Willie. She didn't want this town. She wanted Willie's land, the place where she intended to make a home. It would be so different there. The cool valley, the green grass, and Willie's beloved hills, rolling away to the mountains. Missie could hardly wait for a glimpse of those mountains.

"The Taylorsons live jest down here," Willie announced, interrupting her thoughts. He made a right-hand turn, and soon they were walking down a street lined with houses. There were no sidewalks, but the street was smooth, though as dusty as the rest of the area.

"Thet there is where the doc lives. He has a couple a' rooms for his office in the sheriff's, but he also has one room there at the front of his house fer off-hour treatin'."

Missie let her glance slide over the doctor's residence. The house was unpretentious.

"An' here we are," Willie said cheerfully and opened a gate. Missie stared at the house. It was of unpainted lumber, big and sturdy looking, but as barren as the rest of the town. The two passed by a bit of a garden that seemed to be struggling valiantly for existence. Missie remembered Marty's full, healthy vegetable garden at home.

"My, things are awfully dry!" she ventured.

"They git a little short on water here 'bouts."

Willie rapped on the door and a plump, pleasant-faced woman opened it.

"Oh," she said with a smile, "ya brought yer little wife." Her gaze traveled over Missie. "She is in the family way, all right."

Missie felt the color rush to her face.

"This is Mrs. Taylorson, Missie," Willie said carefully, obviously attempting to ease over the situation. "An' this is my wife—Mrs. LaHaye."

Missie was glad Willie had introduced her as *Mrs. LaHaye.* Somehow it made her feel more grown-up and less like an awkward schoolgirl.

"Come on in," Mrs. Taylorson said, "an' I'll show ya yer room."

She turned and tramped up the stairs to the left of the hall, puffing as she climbed. At the top of the stairs she again took a left turn and pushed open a door. The room was stifling hot, the only window shut tight. It was a plain room, but it was clean. The bed looked old but rather comfortable. Mrs. Taylorson seemed like a no-nonsense person.

"Yer husband said ya had yer own things," said Mrs. Taylorson, "so I jest took out the beddin' an' such."

"Yes, I do," Missie answered, wondering why the faded curtains at the window had escaped Mrs. Taylorson's clean sweep. "It will be just fine."

"I don't usually keep boarders," she said, "but yer husband seemed in a real need like. An' he said thet ya were clean—an' sensible. So I says, 'Okay, I'll give it a try.'" She looked Missie over once more.

"One must have rules, though, when one has boarders," she continued, "so I've made 'em up an' posted 'em here. Don't expect this third one will bother ya much, ya bein' the way ya are, but one never knows—an' one needs rules. I'll leave ya now to look over things an' decide what ya want to be bringin' in. I'll go put on some tea."

She stepped out of the room, and they were alone.

Missie wanted to cry, but she fought against it. She must keep herself well in hand.

Willie went over to the window and threw it wide open. Missie turned to the posted list, headed "Twelve Rules of This House."

"Uh-oh," she said, "you just broke rule number one."

Willie quickly was at her side.

"'Number one,'" Missie read. "'Do not leave window open; the dust blows in!'"

"'Number two: No loud talking or laughing,'" Willie said, picking up with the next one.

"Number three: 'No having men to your room or going out with them, excepting your husband.'" Missie turned to Willie. "I guess you're legal."

They continued down the list, alternating the reading.

"'All water must be used *at least twice* before it is thrown out. We're powerful short, you know.'"

"'Mealtimes are eight, twelve-thirty, and six, and must be strictly kept. It bothers Mr. T's ulcer to be kept waiting.'"

"'Bedtime is ten.'"

"'Borders'—look at the spelling of that. Makes me feel like a bunch of petunias," Missie commented. "'Borders are expected to attend church on Sundays.'"

"'Rent must be paid in advance.'" Then Willie added, "I'll take care of it."

"'No borrowing money or property.'"

"'Border must care for her own personal needs and clothes.'"

"'Hair can be washed at back-door basin—once a week.'"

"'Number twelve'—I guess she ran out of ideas," Missie said. "There's nothing listed here for number twelve."

"Good," Willie said. "Then I won't be breakin' a rule when I kiss ya." He pulled Missie into his arms.

Missie struggled against her tears as Willie held her close. She was glad he did not release her right away. It gave her time to regain her composure. At last she stepped back and smiled.

"I'll bet if she'd thought of it, that would have been on the list," she said. Willie grinned and kissed her again.

Willie and Missie went downstairs and promptly settled the account. Missie could have cried as she watched him pay for three long months. How could she ever bear it? She would die of loneliness. She turned her back and bit her lips in an effort to keep herself under control.

Mrs. Taylorson tucked the money into the bosom of her dress and smiled warmly at the couple.

Mrs. Taylorson insisted that Missie move in right away. The day would be spent in sorting out what Missie would need and getting her settled. There was no rule about sewing machines, but just to be safe, Missie asked. She was pleased Mrs. Taylorson did not object to having hers in the room. Missie would appreciate her machine, which would help fill the hours while she sewed for her coming baby.

Mrs. Taylorson informed them they would be expected for the evening meal at six o'clock sharp. She would see them then. If they needed assistance in the meantime, they could feel free to knock on the kitchen door.

Willie drove their wagon back up the street in front of the Taylorsons' home, and the sorting began. It was hard to decide what should go and what should stay. Missie tended to want to send everything, and Willie kept thinking of things she might need or long for. At last they reached a compromise, and Missie was soon settled into the small upstairs room. Willie, too, moved in his few needs for the one week he would share the room with Missie. He then returned the wagon to the outskirts of the town, where it was left in Henry's care.

Promptly at six the LaHayes descended the steps toward the hall. Finding the dining room was not difficult with the aroma of home-cooked food guiding them. They entered the room and found the table set for four.

A gentleman was already seated, fork in hand, but he did have the courtesy to lay down his fork and rise to his feet as the couple entered. It wasn't exactly a smile that crossed his face to welcome them, but neither was it a frown.

"Howdya do," he said officiously, extending a hand to Willie. "I'm J. B. Taylorson."

Missie wondered what the *J. B.* was for.

"I'm William LaHaye—an' this is my wife, Melissa," Willie responded. Missie didn't dare look at "William," or she would have started giggling.

Mr. Taylorson nodded to the chairs, "Won't ya sit down." It was plain he wanted to get on with the business of eating.

Willie seated Missie and took the chair beside her just as Mrs. Taylorson entered from the kitchen with a bowl of food in each hand.

"Here ya are," she said. "I told Ben thet I told ya six sharp."

So the *B* was for Ben. That still left the *J*.

Mrs. Taylorson settled herself, and Mr. Taylorson blessed the food in a rather perfunctory manner—the same way he said his "howdy." Once the formality was over, his full attention was given to the meal. The beans, potatoes, and meat were simply prepared, yet tasty, and very welcome after the monotonous trail fare.

Mrs. Taylorson allowed no slack in the conversation. Her questions followed so closely on the heels of the previous one that there was scarcely time for a civil reply. She offered many suggestions as to what a mother-to-be should be eating and doing, and most of them made a lot of sense.

After the meal was over, Mr. Taylorson slid back his chair and pulled a pipe from his pocket.

"Now, Ben," Mrs. Taylorson chided, "smoke's not good fer a woman in Mrs. LaHaye's condition. Why don't ya take thet on out to the porch?"

Missie felt embarrassed. "That's fine, Mrs. Taylorson. We don't want to drive your husband from his own home. Willie and I were thinking of a walk, anyway."

But Mr. Taylorson had already risen. "I'd rather smoke on the porch enyhow—git out of this insufferable heat." He gathered his pipe and tobacco and headed for the door. "You smoke?" he asked Willie.

"No, sir."

"Ya can join me enyway iffen you'd like."

Willie followed him out, and Missie began to help Mrs. Taylorson clear the table.

"Now, now," Mrs. Taylorson said in alarm. "Yer room-and-board payment doesn't say enything 'bout deductions fer yer help."

Missie stammered, "I . . . I wasn't thinking of deductions. I just thought I could give you a hand."

"Fine, fine, iffen ya wish to, but it ain't called fer—an' it won't change a thing."

Missie helped carry the leftover food and the dishes to the kitchen. It really was unbearably hot. She finally excused herself and went to find Willie. She really did want a walk.

The first thing Willie said when they were alone was that he felt greatly relieved to know Missie would be well cared for. She wanted to answer that she would just as soon take care of herself, thank you just the same. But she held her tongue. She knew this arrangement and separation was very hard for Willie, too, and he was doing it only because of necessity. Doing it for her. Missie decided she would work at making these last days together peaceful and cheerful.

THIRTEEN

News

Amid the busyness of getting ready to leave with the southbound supply train at the end of the week, Willie burst through the bedroom door. Missie looked up at him from her sewing machine.

"Guess what?" he exclaimed.

"Whatever it is, it must really be something," Missie answered with puzzled surprise.

"It is! It really is! I went in to thet telegraph place uptown and I found out thet fer only a few cents we can send a telegram back home."

"Back home?"

"Yep! Right to yer folks. The office in town there will git the message to 'em. So I figured as how we should do jest that."

"What would we say?"

"Jest let 'em know thet we made it safe an' sound . . . an' . . . maybe tell 'em about the baby."

"Oh, Willie," Missie cried, "could we?"

"Grab whatever ya need an' let's go."

Missie quickly smoothed her hair, then picked up a light cotton bonnet. Just in time she remembered the window and gently closed it just in case Mrs. Taylorson should check her room while she was gone.

"Slow down some," Willie cautioned with a chuckle. "It ain't gonna go away." Then he continued, "The man says thet ya have ten words."

"Oh, dear," Missie sighed, "how are we going to say everything we want to tell them in ten words?"

They reached the office, and Willie opened the door for Missie. She couldn't have said if her breathlessness was due to their brisk walk or her excitement.

They labored together over the wording, composing and changing, recomposing and changing again. Finally they felt they had done the best they could. Willie handed the message and the money to the man behind the desk.

"ISAIAH 41:10," the message read. "MISSIE REMAINS TETTS-FORD STOP GRANDCHILD DUE OCTOBER STOP INFORM PA."

Missie felt her heart constrict with emotion as she envisioned her parents' excitement and relief at receiving the telegram, then passing the news on to Willie's pa.

"Oh, Willie," Missie asked, "do you think Pa LaHaye will mind getting the message secondhand?"

"Iffen I know my pa," Willie said, "he'd think me a squanderin' ignoramus iffen I sent two of 'em to the same town."

"When will it get there?"

"Fella says if no lines are down and there's no other trouble, they should have it in a couple a' days." He took her arm and turned her toward the door of the telegraph office. "Now I'll walk ya on back to the Taylorsons' and then git back to the figurin' an' loadin' of my supplies."

"No need to go with me. I'll find my way back and just take my time. Where's Henry?"

"He's over at the smithy's. He's been a powerful help to me. I don't know what I'da done without 'im."

"Has he been callin' again?"

"Iffen ya mean has he been to town, yes. I haven't asked him his doin's."

Missie smiled. "It's not really that hard to figure out, is it?"

"Poor Henry," said Willie, "he has my sympathy. Once one of you pretty little things gits yer fingers all twisted up in a fella's heart, he's a goner. Well, I'll see ya at six."

Missie turned to walk back to the Taylorsons' lighthearted in spite of the oppressive heat at this small but satisfying link to the family back home.

She tried again to picture her pa and ma when they received the telegram. It wasn't hard to imagine it. They'd stop whatever they were doing and thank God for His care for their children, and they would pray for the new baby. Missie felt both joy and sadness together.

When she reached her room she was no longer in the mood for sewing. She opened her window wide and lay down on the bed.

In a very few days the supply train would be going south, with Willie following. How she wished she could go, as well. The absurd notion of trying to stow away crossed her mind. Once he discovered her, Willie would simply turn around and bring her back. No, there seemed no way out. Willie would go, and she would have to stay.

"God," she prayed, "that help you're promising . . . I'm really needing it right now." The tears were again pushing behind her eyelids when Missie heard heavy steps on the stairs. She quickly went to the window and closed it.

"Ya got visitors," Mrs. Taylorson called. "Seein' as how they're ladies, I gave 'em the privilege of the parlor."

Missie hurried down. To her joy she found Kathy Weiss and Melinda Emory.

She greeted them eagerly, exchanging a quick hug with each young woman in turn.

"Henry told us where to find ya," Kathy explained.

"Oh, I'm so glad you came," Missie said. "I was up in my room lying down, and I confess I was beginning to feel sorry for myself."

Melinda Emory took her hand with great empathy. "And you have reason to. If I were you, I'd be feeling the same way."

"Would you?" Missie swallowed a lump in her throat as she looked into the face of the newly widowed woman. Her separation from Willie, difficult though it was, had a reunion time at the end of it.

Melinda was nodding her head in answer to Missie's question, and tears gathered in her eyes. "I would. In fact, I'm not sure I would stand for it at all."

"Oh, I tried to argue, but Willie just wouldn't hear of it," Missie said, shaking her head. "He's downright unreasonable about things . . . well, since Becky . . ."

"I can understand how Willie feels," Kathy said. "An' as hard as it is, I think he might be right."

"Of course he is," Melinda said. "Men *usually* are in this kind of situation. It's just very difficult for us women, that's all. We're too sentimental to be practical."

Missie nodded. "I guess that's so," she said, "and I'm afraid I have made it rather hard for Willie."

"I don't suppose he expected you to stay without *some* resistance," Kathy comforted.

Melinda then asked, "Are you all settled?"

"Yes . . . I guess so," Missie responded, glad for the change of subject. "I kept as few things as I could so it wouldn't mean too much trouble later. I did keep my sewing machine. Willie thought it would help me to be busy—and I do need to do the sewing for the baby. Anyway, I love to sew."

"So do I," Melinda said with fervor. "I had a machine. . . ." Her voice drifted to a halt, and there was an awkward pause among the three at another reminder of Melinda's tragic loss.

Missie then spoke up. "Oh, if you'd like to use my machine—anytime. I would be so pleased to have your company."

"Could I?"

"Please do! The little bit of sewing I have to do will never keep me busy for the whole three months."

Melinda smiled. "Thank you so much, Mrs. LaHaye. I would so appreciate that."

"Please, call me Missie."

"And my name is Melinda. You can even shorten it if you like."

"Melinda suits you. I like it."

Melinda smiled.

"I heard you found employment," Missie continued.

"Yes, of a sort."

"It must be awfully tiring."

"It is that, but at least I'm paying my own way, and it won't be long until school starts. With my salary from the hotel—an' your sewing machine—perhaps I can start school in style." She gave a small chuckle.

"I was a schoolteacher, too—before I married Willie."

"Really? And a good one, I'm sure."

"I hope so. At any rate, I loved it. Some days I miss it."

"I wish I had some trainin' like thet," Kathy remarked. "I'd love to git a position to help Pa out fer a while. But the only work thet is available fer a girl here, iffen she doesn't have special trainin' . . . well, Pa won't hear tell of it."

"Your pa will make out just fine, I'm sure," Melinda comforted. "In no time at all he'll have all the business he can handle."

Kathy smiled hopefully. "Yeah, I reckon he will. Still, I'd like to do more than just keep house."

"Do you like to sew?" asked Missie.

"I've never learned, so I really don't know."

"Well, why don't I teach you? Between Melinda and you and me, we'll really keep my machine humming."

They all laughed.

"Could ya? I mean, would ya mind?"

"Of course not. I'd love to."

"Then I'd love it, too."

Mrs. Taylorson bustled through the door.

"I brung you girls some tea," she said, carrying a tray of cups. "Company don't come to my house an' not git served—even iffen it ain't my company."

"Oh, Mrs. Taylorson, how kind!" Missie exclaimed, pleased that her landlady was so thoughtful. She introduced her friends and explained to Mrs. Taylorson that she might see them often. Mrs. Taylorson seemed to enjoy the idea. It occurred to Missie that the woman might not have much company of her own and was welcoming the idea of some female companionship.

The women continued their visit over their tea and cookies, including Mrs. Taylorson in their conversation.

At length the two visitors rose to leave. They requested that Missie visit them, which she promised to do.

Mrs. Taylorson eagerly invited them to return "jest anytime."

Missie climbed the stairs to her room feeling much better. It had been a good day. God had given the help He'd promised. The telegram home, the visit with friends—a reminder that she would not really be alone when Willie left—these were gentle kindnesses given from the hand of a loving Father. With all these blessings, Missie felt a warm glow inside.

But as she closed the door to her room, the thought of Willie's impending departure hit her once more. How was she ever going to manage three long months without him?

She moved over to the window and stared out over the rather bleak scene below her, trying to recapture the truth of her heavenly Father's care and presence. She turned at a noise from the stairway to find Willie entering the room to deposit a strange heap on the floor.

"What's that?" she asked, pointing at what looked like a bundle of canvas.

"The gear I'll be needin'."

"Gear?"

"Fer ridin', once I'm at the ranch."

"You're going to ride in *that*?"

"Sure am. It might look a bit strange, but it's a cowboy's best friend out on the range."

"What is it?" Missie asked skeptically. "And how do you use it?"

Willie lifted the canvas. "It's chaps," he explained. "Ya jest pull 'em on over yer trousers, like so. The heavy canvas sheds the rain, takes the spines of the cactus, and keeps all manner of weather and injury from a rider. Ya really ought to have some yerself."

Missie laughed and then pointed to a square of red material. "And what's that?" she asked again.

"A bandanna. Ya wear it round yer neck—tied loosely like this." Willie demonstrated. "When ya get drivin' them little doggies an' the dust flies so ya can hardly breathe, ya just pull it up over yer mouth an' nose—like this!"

Missie giggled. "I thought that's what you use when you're holding up a bank."

"Guess a few have used it fer thet, as well." Willie smiled with her. "I'll remember thet, should I ever think of holdin' up a bank."

Missie laughed again and then turned for a good look at the strange apparel. It was going to take some getting used to—seeing Willie decked out in these strange canvas pants. She tried to imagine herself in them and smiled softly.

"Reckon for now," she said, "I'll just plan to fight the cactus and the rain without the help of those."

FOURTEEN

Sunday

On Sunday morning Willie and Missie prepared themselves and headed for the church spire they had seen. The building looked bare and drab on the outside, but inside the clean-swept wooden floor and carefully dusted benches showed that someone did indeed care for this simple house of worship in this frontier town. Henry, Mr. Weiss and Kathy, Melinda Emory, and the LaHayes added considerably to the small congregation, and they were welcomed from the platform at the beginning of the service.

The pastor, getting on in years, seemed rather weary, Missie thought. But when he rose to preach, fire was in his voice, and his face came alive with passion for the truth he was presenting. Missie was overjoyed to be in a real church service and hear a true sermon once again. She had appreciated the Sunday services of the wagon train, but she had missed having a pastor speak from the Word of God.

The reverend greeted each one kindly at the door and personally invited the newcomers to return. Willie explained that he would not be around for another Sunday, but he was sure Missie would be there faithfully.

"We shall welcome you," the old gentleman said with warmth. "And if you should ever need a friend, my wife and I would be happy to have you to our home, as well."

Missie thanked him for his generosity and stepped out into the shining day.

"Anything you'd be carin' to do today?" Willie asked as they walked through the dust and heat back to the Taylorsons' and their rented room.

"Oh yes," said Missie with a sigh, "I'd like to go for a long walk among some cool trees, or picnic beside a stream, or maybe just lie beside a spring and watch the water gurgle."

"Missie"—Willie shook his head—"don't, *please* don't say things like that. . . ."

"I'm sorry," Missie whispered quickly. She tried hard to think of something that could actually be done and enjoyed in the heat of this drab town.

"We could call on the Weisses," she finally suggested.

"All right," Willie agreed enthusiastically, no doubt relieved she had thought of something. "I sure do hope Henry won't think I'm spyin' on 'im." He caught her hand in his with a chuckle.

That afternoon at the Weisses, they received such a hearty welcome Missie's spirits lifted even without green grass or a stream. Henry was there, also, though he didn't seem one bit put out to have his boss appear. Melinda Emory was there, too, so the six of them settled in for a good visit. Kathy served them all cold tea, declaring the day far too warm for hot tea or coffee.

Missie was surprised at the time when Kathy asked if they could all stay for supper.

"Oh, I don't think we can," Missie said. "We didn't say anything to Mrs. Taylorson, and supper is served at six."

She and Willie exchanged smiles.

"How 'bout I run over an' inform yer good landlady?" Henry asked.

"Oh, but—"

"Please stay," Kathy begged. "The men will be gone by next Sunday."

"Well, I'm not sure what she'll think," Missie said uncertainly, "but . . . well . . . all right. She probably hasn't started to actually prepare it, so she shouldn't mind, should she?"

It turned out that both Henry and Willie walked back together while the girls went to the kitchen to give Kathy a hand.

Mrs. Taylorson did not object. In fact, Willie got the impression she was relieved at not having to fuss about in a hot kitchen on such a warm evening.

Kathy's meal of fried chicken, hot biscuits, and gravy was served with love and laughter, and everyone enjoyed the time spent together.

"I know," Kathy suggested after the dishes had been washed, "let's have a time of singing, for old times' sake."

The rest agreed. Henry went for his guitar while Mr. Weiss tuned up his violin.

They sang all the songs they had enjoyed together from their trip west—folk songs, love songs, dance tunes, and hymns. When they were finished, they sang their favorite ones all over again.

It was late when Willie and Missie walked back to the Taylorsons' hand in hand.

"I'm afraid we've broken rule number six," Missie said.

"An' what is thet?"

"Bedtime is at ten o'clock," Missie replied in a mock stern voice. She broke into giggles, then quickly checked herself and added, "We'd better be careful or we'll break number two, as well."

"An' thet is . . ."

"No loud talking or laughing," Missie said, effecting a gruff, deep voice again.

"Ya little goose," Willie said, putting his arm around her waist and drawing her close. "Do ya have 'em all memorized by number?"

"I think so. I've read them often enough."

"Speakin' of readin'," Willie said, "ya really should have somethin' on hand to read. I'll talk to the preacher. He may have a good idea of what books can be had. He may even have some—"

"Oh, Willie, stop fretting about me. I've got all that sewing to do, and all that yarn to be knitted up, a piano to learn to play, and sewing lessons to give. Surely it will keep me busy."

"Well, we want to be sure," said Willie, giving her hand a little squeeze.

When Willie returned to their room on Wednesday evening, he quietly told Missie that the supply train was all loaded up and would be pulling out early the next morning. Missie knew he was keeping his voice even and matter-of-fact for her sake, but she had to bite her lip all evening to keep the tears from overflowing during supper with the Taylorsons. She hoped Willie didn't notice, but of course he did. They retired to their room soon after the meal was finished so Willie could get his belongings packed up. It didn't take long. Time suddenly seemed to be heavy on their hands.

"It's strange," Missie said as she stood and gazed out the window, "our time is so short and precious, and yet one doesn't really know how to spend it."

"Have ya everything ya need?" asked Willie for the umpteenth time, coming over to stand beside her.

"I'm sure I will be fine."

"Well, I'll leave ya some money, jest in case."

"Really, Willie, I don't think I'll be needing—"

"Ya never know. Maybe somethin' will turn up thet ya be needin' or wantin'—an' you'll need some fer the church offerin'."

Missie only nodded.

Willie led her over to the one chair in the room and sat near her on the bed. "I'm sure glad thet Kathy an' Melinda will be around."

"Me too."

"I hope ya see 'em real often."

"Melinda will be working—but she promised to come over of an evening to sew."

"An' Kathy is free to come anytime—right?"

Missie nodded again. "The first thing she wants to sew is curtains for her kitchen window."

"An' ya can visit 'em at their places, too," continued Willie.

Missie agreed.

"Ya might pay a call on the preacher an' his wife, too. They seem like real nice folks. Jest don't stay out after dark—please, Missie?"

"I won't. Promise."

"One can't be too careful."

"*You're* the one that needs to be careful, Willie! Here I am, all tucked away safe in a town, where the worst that can happen to me is to get dust in my eyes—and you're telling *me* to be careful. It's you that's going to have to take care, Willie." Missie swallowed hard over the lump in her throat as Willie smoothed her hair.

"Won't much happen to me," he assured her. "I'm travelin' south with a whole passel of supply wagons, an' Henry'll be with me once we reach our spread. No need to worry none 'bout me."

"I s'pose so," Missie admitted. "I just won't be able to keep from it, though."

"I'll worry, too," Willie said, his voice husky. "It doesn't pleasure me none to leave ya, Missie. If only there was some other way—"

"I'll be fine," Missie quickly assured him, trying for his sake to say the words as though she really meant them.

"Missie . . ." Willie hesitated, reaching over to hold her close. "Missie, the wagons are to pull out real early in the mornin'. I don't intend to wake ya up when I leave, so my good-bye will be tonight. I love ya. I've loved ya ever since ya were a little schoolgirl."

"And you showed it," she whispered, smiling around her tears, "by dunking my hair ribbons in an inkwell."

"An' carvin' our initials—"

"And putting a grasshopper in my lunch pail."

"An' tellin' young Todd Culver thet I'd knock out his teeth iffen he didn't leave my girl alone. An' closin' yer classroom window when it got stuck. An' prayin' fer ya every single day—thet iffen God willed, ya'd learn to love me."

"You did that?" Missie leaned away to look into his face.

"I did."

"Oh, Willie," Missie cried, pressing her face against his shoulder. "I'll miss you so. I can't tell you how much."

When Missie sat up in bed the next morning, she was alone, and Willie's things were gone from the room. An emptiness filled her that she could not have put into words. She turned back into her pillow and sobbed. How would she ever cope? She missed him so dreadfully already. She had secretly promised herself the night before that she would be sure to waken so she might feel the comfort of Willie's arms once more. She was annoyed at herself for failing to rouse, yet finally she had to admit it would not have made it any easier to say good-bye again.

If only I was at home with Mama and Pa to console me. . . . They would understand about pain and separation.

Her parents had personally known grief—far more devastating and final than her own sorrow now. They had lived through it. And she could, too. After all, Willie *would* be coming back. The wait wouldn't be so long—not really.

She forced herself to crawl out of bed, then bathed her face at the basin. She caught herself wondering if this was wash number one or two for this water, and if she could now throw it out and get some fresh. Her eyes moved to Mrs. Taylorson's list. The empty space for number twelve now had some writing beside it. Had Mrs. Taylorson come up with another rule? Missie crossed the room for a better look and read number twelve aloud: "Always remember that I love you—both of you."

"Oh, Willie, ya silly goose!" she cried as fresh tears streamed down her newly washed cheeks. She was going to have to wash her face again before going down for breakfast. That, for sure, would entitle her to some more water.

FIFTEEN

Surprises

Missie put her mind to settling in alone for the long stay. First she decided to list all the "must-do's" on a piece of paper. Then she listed all the "want-to-do's." Neither list seemed very long. How would those tasks and activities ever keep her occupied until she was free to leave this town? She laid the lists aside with a sigh and went to her sewing material.

She spread out all the fabric she had purchased and mentally planned just what she would sew from each piece. She then checked her yarn and noted the articles she would knit or crochet. She took a fresh sheet of paper for her weekly visitation list—one call per week on Kathy and Melinda and at least one call *from* them in return to use Missie's machine.

She sketched out a complete week on a piece of paper with a space for each hour of the day, and then she filled in her proposed activities: sewing, sewing lessons, knitting, laundry, reading, visits, shopping (she didn't know what for, but it filled a space and the walk would do her good). She even included time at the piano in her hopes for learning to play a bit. Her week still had many vacant hours, and she didn't see how she could stretch out her plans to fill them.

She juggled, rearranged, and stretched all she could and finally filled in all the extra spots with the words "free time" and tried to convince herself that somehow "free time" should be looked forward to as a special liberty. Maybe Willie was right after all about checking with the pastor and his wife for some reading materials.

She had scheduled sewing for her first morning, so she began on a small blanket. As simple as the project was, she just couldn't keep her mind on it, so she laid it aside. She picked up her Bible once more and opened the pages at random. She tried to concentrate on the words, but the words blurred in her mind.

"It's just no use," she muttered, grabbing up some knitting. "I just can't think clearly!"

She had added only a few stitches to the sock she was making when Mrs. Taylorson called up the stairs, "Ya have a caller, miss."

Missie so wished Mrs. Taylorson wouldn't call her "miss," as though she were still a young girl instead of a grown married woman. She smoothed her hair back and made her way down the steps.

Kathy Weiss was waiting for her in the parlor. Missie almost cried with relief at seeing her friend so soon after the men had left.

"Did you come to sew the curtains?" she asked after greeting Kathy.

"Goodness, no! I don't think I could concentrate on sewin' anything today. I jest had to go out fer a while, an' I thought maybe you'd be needin' it, as well."

"You're absolutely right," Missie said emphatically. "Just let me get my bonnet."

The two young women strolled through the streets of the dusty town, chatting as they browsed along the storefronts. Occasionally they wandered inside to peruse the merchandise. Neither of them purchased a thing, but Missie returned home in better spirits, and Kathy promised to return that very evening for her first sewing lesson.

That afternoon Missie sat down and made herself a calendar, one page for each of the three months ahead of her. She marked each day's date in big numbers, wrote Willie's name beside the first one—August second—then circled October twenty-fifth. It was as close as she could figure the baby's arrival date to be. In between the two dates stretched many weeks and days and hours. But Missie intended to strike them off, one by one, in hopes they would move quickly to the next one.

It was awfully warm in the room, and Missie was feeling emotionally and physically exhausted, so she took off her shoes and stretched out on the bed to rest.

"It all will be worth it," she told herself aloud. "By the time Willie comes for me and the baby, he'll have our house ready. I'll be able to move right in, instead of living cramped in that old wagon. Just think—our own home! I'll hang up the curtains Mama helped me sew, spread out the cozy rugs, make up the bed with all those warm quilts. I'll put my dishes in the cupboards, set up the sewing machine, put all the crocks and barrels in my pantry—all those things I'll be needing in my very own home."

She let the happy thoughts drive away the loneliness and drifted off to sleep.

Kathy came that evening as promised. Having never used a sewing machine before, she had a bit of difficulty in catching on to the rhythm of the foot treadle, but eventually she had a good start on her curtains.

Day one was finally over. With relief Missie crossed it off her new calendar and knelt beside her bed. Somewhere out there, in the dark, distant night, she knew Willie would be remembering her in prayer, as well. It helped to ease her loneliness.

At the end of each slow-moving day, Missie struck the numbers from the calendar in the manner of a general triumphant after battle. She had survived her first Sunday alone, her first hair washing, and her first washday. She was working on her third day at the piano when Mrs. Taylorson called, "Miss, ya have a feller here with a telygram."

Missie fairly flew to the door. What news could be so important that it needed to reach her by telegram? Her heart thumped wildly within her, every beat crying, "Willie! Willie!" She quickly took the telegram with a shaking hand and scanned the small sheet.

"RECEIVED MESSAGE STOP PRAISE GOD STOP HAPPY AND CONCERNED ABOUT BABY STOP ISAIAH," she read.

"Mama and Pa!" she exclaimed. To the waiting Mrs. Taylorson, she said, "It's from my folks—they've just acknowledged our message." The woman smiled and nodded in an understanding way, and Missie smiled back and hurried up the stairs to her room. Once inside, with the door closed behind her, she crushed the blessed message to her breast and fell to her knees beside her bed, tears falling unchecked.

"Oh, Mama . . . Pa . . . I miss you both so much, and I love you so. Oh . . . if only . . ."

Missie posted the telegram beneath Willie's rule number twelve. Many times a day she would read it and think of the dear ones who had sent it to her.

As the days were gradually crossed off on Missie's calendar, her pile of sewn articles and knitted things increased. Kathy had come often, and soon she had progressed to sewing dresses when the curtains and some aprons were finished.

Melinda also had spent evenings with Missie. Her job in the hotel kitchen had taxed her limited strength, so she never dared to stay very late. But eventually she had managed with her small income to buy yard goods for three attractive dresses and sew them up for use in the schoolroom. When September came, her days as restaurant cook and dishwasher were over at last, and she was happily employed as the town's new schoolmarm.

Missie twice had called on the preacher and his wife. She not only found their company delightfully refreshing, but they loaned her several books from their own library. They also returned each call, and Mrs. Taylorson was quite beside herself to have a real parson in her parlor.

⁂

After Missie had put on her nightgown and brushed her hair before bed one night, she stood studying her calendar. It was now September eighth.

"September eighth is a long way from August second," she whispered to herself. "Not halfway yet, but almost . . . almost." She made a long black mark through the number and went to kneel beside her bed. As she was praying, she heard a gentle rap on her door. Missie looked up in surprise. She hadn't heard any footsteps on the stairs.

Then the door opened, and there stood Willie. Paralyzed with shock, Missie remained on her knees and just stared.

Not one to wait for her bidding, he quickly was at her side and whisked her to her feet.

"It's really you!" Missie gasped. "It's really you!" And then she was in his arms, clinging to him, sobbing into his jacket while he showered kisses on her face, stroked her hair, and rocked her gently back and forth.

"I jest couldn't stand it anymore," he said huskily.

"You came for me?"

"Oh no," Willie corrected hurriedly. "Just to *see* you, thet's all. I was jest so lonesome thet Henry finally said, 'Why don't ya make yerself a little trip? Ya ain't rightly of much use here anyway.' So I did."

"Where's Henry?"

"I left him workin' on the corrals."

Missie laughed. "Don't know how you ever got away without Henry. Why, he must be near as lonesome as you."

"He did send a couple of letters with me—*three*, in fact. He sent you one, too."

Missie laughed again. "Dear old Henry—and he sent *two* others?"

"Yep. One to the Weisses and one to Melinda."

"He's just writing to *all* his friends."

"But I want to hear 'bout *you*," Willie said firmly, swinging her around. "How ya been?"

"Lonesome!" Missie said fervently.

"Me too," Willie replied. "Me too." And he kissed her again.

"How long can you stay?"

"Just till day after tomorrow."

"Only one day?" Missie's lips started to tremble.

Willie nodded. "I gotta git back, Missie. I shouldn'ta come, really. We've got so much to do 'fore winter sets in, but . . . well, I jest couldn't stay away. I've *gotta* leave mornin' after next."

"Do you have a place to live out there?"

"A temporary one—that's the way most folks do. Then they build later—as they can."

"And the cattle?"

"Only a few head. We can't really take on too many until we're ready for 'em, an' then ya need men to care for 'em, too. After that ya need a bunkhouse to bed the men."

"How many men?"

"Four or five at first."

"Ya mean I'm going to be cooking for six or seven men?" Missie's shock caused her to step back.

"No, silly," Willie said as he pulled her back against him. "The cook does thet in the cook shack."

"You must have a cook shack, too?"

"Yeah, an' we hafta git all thet ready this fall."

Missie took his hand, and they sat down on the edge of the bed.

"Didn't realize it took that many men to run a ranch," she said thoughtfully.

"Should rightly have more than thet, but I'm gonna try to make do fer the time bein'."

"What on earth do they all do?"

"Need shifts, fer one thing. Always should be some of 'em out there ridin' herd on things—watchin' the cattle an' keepin' an eye out fer trouble."

"Trouble—you mean like wild animals and things?"

"I s'pose wild animals enter into it, but they're not the greatest danger."

"What then?"

Willie grinned. "Accordin' to what I hear, a rancher's biggest threat comes from *tame* animals."

"What do you mean?"

"Rustlers."

"Rustlers?"

"Yep. More than one rancher has been driven from the land—forced to give up an' move on out—because of rustlers."

"That's horrible!" Missie exclaimed. "Do they carry guns?"

"Reckon they do," Willie said calmly.

"But what do we do?" Missie could not let the matter drop. "Will you order your men to carry guns?"

"My men won't need those orders. They'll be used to havin' a gun hangin' from their saddle."

"But . . . but, would they *kill* someone?" Missie could hardly force the word out.

"My men will have orders never to shoot to kill another human bein'," Willie said firmly, "even iffen it means losin' the whole herd."

"Might they do that—the rustlers, I mean? Might they take the whole herd?"

"Not usually. They normally just drive off a few at a time. Pickin' on stragglers, gradually workin' at a herd—especially one that isn't carefully watched. Sometimes their need—or their greed—drives 'em to make a bold move and try fer the entire lot."

"Oh, Willie, what will we do if—"

"Now, let's not borrow trouble," Willie said soothingly. "We'll hire the men we can and protect the herd the best we can. Thet's all we can do."

"But how can you afford to pay all those men?"

"'Fraid a cowboy don't make all thet much. Works out nice fer the ranchers, but not so great fer the cowboys. They do git their bed and board and enough money to buy the tobacco and few supplies they be needin'. Some even manage to lay a little aside. As to the payin' of 'em, I figured thet cost into my accounts when I was workin' out what we'd be needin'. When we start sellin' cattle of our own, their wages will come from the sales."

Missie was relieved to know Willie had things well under control.

"What else do they do?" she asked, getting back to the cowboys.

"Break horses, build and fix fences, watch fer sickness an' snakes an' varmints. They care for the critters during bad storms an' keep an eye on the pasture and water holes to make sure the cows are well cared for. Their main job, though, is to keep the cows grazin' well together so thet there ain't a lot of stragglers scattered through the hills—easy victims of prowlin' animals an' them rustlers."

"Sounds like a big job to me."

"Yup, it's a big job. But most cowboys wouldn't trade it fer any other job in the world."

"Let's forget cowboys, cook shacks, and bunkhouses," Missie interrupted. "Let's think 'bout us for a while."

Willie agreed as his arm tightened around her. "Yer lookin' good. Feelin' okay?"

"Oh, Willie!" Missie suddenly burst out. "I forgot to show you. Look!" She jumped up and pointed to the telegram on her wall. "Mama and Pa got our message," she reported enthusiastically, "and they sent one of their own!"

Willie grinned as he stood to read the telegram. "Makes 'em seem a lot closer like, don't it?"

Missie nodded.

"This trip made you seem closer, too," said Willie. "Took six days to make it down there by wagon—but I made it back in 'bout half the time on horseback."

"You did? Then it's really not so *awfully* far, is it?" Missie was comforted.

Willie climbed on his horse as the sun edged over the horizon. He had spent two nights and a day with Missie. She had wondered if she could face the dreadful agonies of parting again—but it was not as difficult as she had feared. She struck two more days from her calendar as she went to bed that night. She had completely forgotten it during Willie's visit.

Missie felt awfully restless. The book she was attempting to read now lay discarded on her pillow. Her sewing projects had all been completed days ago. She wasn't about to buy more fabric for things she really could do without. She had run out of yarn but had no wish to make a trip to the store for more—though that was one item she was certain she could put to good use. Willie always needed a new pair of socks. But, no, she'd wait till she had another reason to shop. Maybe a visit to Kathy's . . . no, her heart just wasn't in it.

Listless, edgy, and out of sorts, she paced her room—back and forth. Maybe she was just tired. When it was twelve-thirty, *sharp*—and time for the noon meal—she knew she wasn't hungry. She called downstairs to Mrs. Taylorson that she didn't feel like eating—could she please be excused? She'd just lie down awhile.

She hadn't been on her bed for long when a sudden contraction tightened her abdomen. To her relief, it soon subsided. Missie closed her eyes and tried to sleep, but before she could drop off, another one shuddered through her.

When this passed, Missie sat up and squinted at her homemade calendar on the wall. "It can't be," she exclaimed aloud, her emotions swinging between delight and dismay. "This is only October tenth. You can't come yet, baby. It just isn't time! It *can't* be!" But Missie soon realized that it was indeed time.

She climbed out of bed and paced for a while, then lay down, only to get up and pace some more.

What will Willie think? she asked herself. *I told him October twenty-fifth—and he said he'd be here on the twenty-second, just to be sure. Maybe I'm just imagining things, or maybe it's a false alarm.*

But it was not a false alarm. Missie's landlady came up the stairs to check on her, and Mrs. Taylorson soon recognized it for what it really was, even though she had never had children of her own. She suggested sending immediately for the doctor, but Missie insisted on waiting. She wanted to be absolutely sure the baby was indeed on its way. At last Mrs. Taylorson could stand the wait no more. She sent poor Mr. Taylorson over for the doctor before the good man could even enjoy his after-supper pipe. To Missie's relief, the doctor was not off tending a gunshot wound or setting a broken bone as she had earlier predicted to Willie, and the doctor came almost at once.

That night, about ten o'clock, a son was born to Missie—two weeks early by her calculations. He was not very big, but he was healthy and strong. His young mother, who had been repeating over and over throughout the delivery, "Fear thou not; for I am with thee," cried tears of joy at her first sight of him.

After the doctor had gone and Missie and the baby were bedded for the night, Mrs. Taylorson still scurried about the room, clucking and fussing like a mother hen.

"He's a dandy little wee'un, ain't he? Whatcha gonna call 'im?"

"I don't know," Missie replied sleepily. "I tried to talk about names with Willie—but he said he'd be here when the baby arrived and we'd pick a name then. After we'd seen the baby."

"But he ain't comin' fer two weeks yet," said the practical Mrs. Taylorson. "Don't seem fittin' thet a child should go fer two whole weeks without a name."

"I know," Missie said, smiling at her son, who lay snuggled up against her. "I guess I'll have to name him."

"Ya got a name picked?"

"One I like. I just *happened* to marry a man with the same middle name as my pa. Now, doesn't it seem fitting that our son should bear that name?"

"'Deed it do!" Mrs. Taylorson exclaimed, clapping her hands. "Yer Willie could hardly fault ya on thet choice. What's the name?"

"Nathan," said Missie. "Nathan." She said it again, savoring the sound of it.

"Nathan?" Mrs. Taylorson repeated and nodded thoughtfully. "Rather nice. I like it. I think it even suits the wee package. Nathan . . . jest Nathan?"

"No, Nathan *Isaiah*."

"Isaiah?" Mrs. Taylorson looked a bit doubtful on this one, but she made no further comment except to ask, "Is Isaiah somethin' special, too?"

"It certainly is," Missie said with a catch in her voice. "Very special."

Missie pulled the covers about herself and her small son. She was so happy—and so tired. She kissed the fuzzy top of Nathan's head and let her body relax. She had nearly dozed off when a sudden idea hit her.

"Mrs. Taylorson," she asked sleepily, "would you be so kind as to have a telegram sent to my folks tomorrow?"

"Certainly, miss," the woman replied. "What would ya be wantin' it to say?" She took a paper and pencil from the desk and handed it to Missie. "Better write it down, in case I forget."

Missie thought for a few moments, then began to write slowly: "Nathan Isaiah arrived safely October 10 Stop Love from Missie and Baby." She handed the sheet to Mrs. Taylorson.

"It would pleasure me to be the bearer of such good news," she said with a warm pat on Missie's shoulder.

Missie smiled ruefully at the small bundle snuggled beside her. "If only there was some way to let his pa know. I'm going to have an awfully hard time waiting for the twenty-second. Why, Willie's son will be nigh grown-up by the time his pa gets to hold him!"

Mrs. Taylorson looked down at the tiny bundle on Missie's arm. "Seems to me," she smiled, "a little growin' time ain't gonna hurt the wee fella much. I don't reckon he's gonna outgrow thet little nightie he's a swimmin' in, in jest two weeks' time."

Missie smiled contentedly and let sleep claim her.

<hr />

Willie drove into Tettsford Junction with the wagon on October twentieth, prepared for as many days of waiting as was necessary before welcoming his child. Mrs. Taylorson let him in the front door and managed, as promised, not to reveal the household's wonderful news. Willie went on up to Missie's room.

Missie was standing at her window looking wistfully out over the back garden at the distant hills. She was restless again, now that she was on her feet. Nathan, at this stage, seemed content to eat and sleep—and grow—daily, though he hadn't managed yet to fill out his nightie, just as Mrs. Taylorson had predicted. So Missie often felt at loose ends with time on her hands.

At the sound of the door, Missie did not even turn around. She had become accustomed to Mrs. Taylorson using any and every excuse to come in and out of the room. If she wasn't bringing Missie tea with lots of milk, she came just to check on the baby.

At Willie's alarmed "What's happened?" Missie whirled around.

"Willie!" she squealed.

He seemed paralyzed. "What's happened?" he repeated, fear in his voice. "What do you mean, what's *happened*?"

Willie gestured speechlessly at Missie's trim figure, and she then realized why his face had gone white.

A smile spread over her face, and she rushed to fall into his arms.

"You're a pa! That's what's happened."

"Already?"

"He fooled us, didn't he?"

"*He?*"

"Look!"

Missie grasped Willie's hand and led him to the foot of the bed, where the small bundle lay peacefully sleeping in a simple cradle made by Mr. Weiss. One fist curled gently beside Nathan's full cheeks.

"Ours?" Willie whispered in awe.

"Ours," Missie said. "Isn't he wonderful?"

"Can we . . . can we git 'im out of there?" Willie asked. She could see him swallowing hard and blinking back tears. Missie nodded. Willie bent down and carefully picked up his son.

"Isn't he somethin' wonderful?" he repeated.

Missie could hardly hold all the joy she felt. Willie was here. Willie was pleased with his son—her gift to him. She reached up and kissed her husband's cheek, then leaned against his shoulder.

"I think he looks like his pa," she whispered, stroking the soft little cheek. "Look, he's going to have dark hair. Oh, I know he'll likely lose all the baby fuzz, but I think when it comes in again, it'll be dark like yours. And wait until he opens his eyes. They're blue now, but a dark, hazy blue. I'm thinking that before long they're going to be as brown as his pa's." Willie turned his head and bent to kiss Missie once more.

"But just look at this." Missie's voice held a hint of amazement and joy. She gently touched young Nathan on his soft chin. "A dimple! A dimple just like yours."

She expected a protest, but instead Willie looked at the small chin and grinned.

"Aw, c'mon," he said, but he wasn't expecting an argument.

The two sat down on the bed, the baby still in Willie's arms.

"When did he arrive?"

"October the tenth."

"The *tenth*? That's way early."

"He's almost two weeks old already—and ready to travel."

"Yer sure?"

504

"Doc says if we take it easy, we should be able to go most anytime."
Willie seemed too moved to answer.

"It won't take long, will it—to be ready to go?" Missie asked.

Willie shook his head and found his voice. "No . . . no, not long. I'll
git right on it. Henry came with me this time. We brought two teams
so's we'd have plenty of room fer supplies and not have to crowd ya
none." He laughed. "Henry's gonna be a heap disappointed. We were
all set fer a month-long stay."

Missie laughed quietly. "Oh, Willie, I can hardly wait. I'm so tired
of being on my own in this town. I've been so lonesome."

The baby stirred, and Willie adjusted him in his arms.

"Hey," Willie said suddenly. "Has he got a name?"

"He has," Missie assured him, "and a good one, too. He's Nathan—
Nathan Isaiah."

"Nathan Isaiah," Willie repeated. "I like it. I like it a lot." Lifting his
small son up so he could plant a kiss on his downy head, he whispered,
"Nathan Isaiah, I love you." The baby answered by wrinkling up his
little face and letting out a lusty cry. His parents both laughed, and then
Missie took him in hand to feed him.

⁂

After four days, the LaHayes were ready to leave. Mrs. Taylorson
could hardly bear to see them go. She cooed and cuddled the baby
and insisted upon holding him until the very last moment. Even Mr.
Taylorson took time off from his store to come and see them off. He
reminded them three times to consider their home as their own, should
they be back in town.

Kathy and Melinda were both tearful, and they both brought going-
away gifts for Baby Nathan. The kind old preacher offered a parting
prayer, and his wife insisted they have some of her fresh-baked bread
for the trail.

Henry fussed over Missie's bed in the wagon, determined that no
wind or rain should be allowed to cause discomfort for her or the baby.
It was not so hot for traveling now. In fact, Missie had to bundle up
both herself and the baby against a cool breeze.

At last they were on the trail, and Missie mentally ticked off the *new* calendar she carried in her head. In just six days they would be *home*. Finally she would see the land Willie had learned to love. Her excitement grew within her until she could hardly contain it. At last she would be free of the drab, barren, dusty town. She would move into her own home like a nesting bird and make their dreams come true. She cradled her son close to her. "And you—you little rascal," she crooned to him, "you weren't even in those dreams. But I think you're going to fit in just fine."

SIXTEEN

The Ranch

"We're almost there now," Willie announced, excitement in his voice. "Jest over thet next hill."

They had already traveled six days. For fear of tiring Missie or the baby, Willie had stopped each evening a little earlier than would have been normal. Now it was noon of the seventh day.

Missie swallowed hard. Their very own homestead, their dream—Willie's and hers—was "just over the next hill." But the countryside they had been traveling through was even bleaker than that around Tettsford Junction. Until she saw some improvement in the landscape with her own eyes, Missie was finding it impossible to believe there would be any significant change. Hills and more colorless hills, covered only with coarse, dry-looking grass. Tumbleweeds somersaulted along in the wind, rolling and bouncing forever and ever. Occasional cactus plants or an outcropping of rocks were the only variations in the scenery. But maybe by some miracle . . . She so wanted to share Willie's enthusiasm.

Far in the distance was a line of dark mountains. Missie had expected—had hoped—that the mountains would become her friends. But they remained aloof, offering only a dim outline, shadowing themselves in a gloomy haze.

"Sometimes they're purple—sometimes blue—sometimes almost pink," Willie had explained, "dependin' on how the sun hits 'em. An' then in the winter, with the snow on their peaks, they're a dazzle of white."

"Can we see the mountains from our place?" Missie had asked, fervently hoping it might be so. She was eager to enjoy Willie's mountains in each of their changing moods.

"Not from our valley," Willie had responded. "In order to see the mountains ya'd have to build up on a hill—an' ya wouldn't want thet. Too much wind, no protection."

"Too much wind," Missie murmured softly now, thinking back on Willie's words. "Way too much wind." She wrapped her heavy shawl more tightly about her against its steady blowing.

So they couldn't see the mountains from their house. Then what *could* they see? She had asked Willie that, too.

"Lookin' to the east, down the draw," Willie had told her, "ya can look right out on the range. Mile after mile of low hills, with nothin' to git in the way of yer lookin'." Willie seemed to feel those empty miles to gaze upon were a great asset. What Missie pictured in her mind's eye made her shiver.

They now topped the hill, and Willie reined in the team. Missie shut her eyes, wishing she didn't have to open them just yet.

"Well," Willie announced triumphantly, "there it is. Ain't it somethin'?"

Missie opened her eyes slowly.

Tucked in a small valley, just as Willie had said, were a few small scattered structures and what seemed like miles and miles of corral fence.

"You said it was *green*," Missie said through stiff lips, immediately regretting the remark.

"It is in the springtime. This is late fall. Nothin's green now." Willie remained unshaken. "Well, what d'ya think of it?"

Missie had been dreading that question. How could she answer it? She couldn't let Willie down—yet she couldn't lie.

"It's . . . it's . . . really something," she managed, thankful she had remembered Willie's own words.

"Sure is," Willie agreed, obviously interpreting her answer with his own optimism.

He pointed a finger toward the valley and leaned toward her.

"The corrals for the horses and cows all lay over there."

Missie fleetingly wondered how he ever thought she or anyone else could miss them. They seemed to fill up the whole valley.

Willie continued, "Thet there buildin' is the barn. We'll build an even bigger one later. Thet there's the bunkhouse right in there, an' the cook shack is there beside it."

"Where's the house?" asked Missie.

"The *temporary* one? Right there."

Missie's eyes followed his finger. The *temporary* house, like the bunkhouse, cook shack, and barn, looked to her like a giant heap of dried grass.

"They're made of sod," Willie informed her matter-of-factly.

"Sod?"

"Yeah. Ya cut blocks of sod from the ground an' pile 'em up. Makes a real snug place to live in fer the winter."

Missie swallowed, eyes staring and heart pounding. "Sod," she whispered. Her lips trembled as she fought to control her emotions, and she turned her face away.

Willie spoke to the team and the wagon rumbled on. Missie closed her eyes again. No miracle had taken place "over the next hill." There was no fairyland awaiting her. But she needed a miracle now—to help her through the ordeal she knew lay ahead.

The sod house at a distance had been shock enough, but Missie's close-up view of it was even more difficult. As the wagon creaked to a stop before the small, low structure, Missie caught her lip between her teeth to keep a sob from escaping.

Henry had arrived earlier and started a fire to warm the house for the baby. He emerged now, grinning eagerly from ear to ear.

The smoke poured from the little pipe of a chimney and dissipated into the wind. Missie recognized the pungent odor of buffalo chips. They had been forced many times on the trail to use them when wood supplies had been scarce, but Missie had never really accepted or appreciated this type of fuel. As she sat on the wagon seat, she looked around and realized that there would be no wood. There were few trees in sight.

Willie helped her down and she stood a moment to steady her legs and her mind, bracing herself for whatever she found behind the dwarfed door that guarded the entrance to her new home.

Willie led the way, and Missie ducked her head to follow him into the dark interior of the little sod house.

It was high noon, and still the room was so dark Missie's eyes took several moments to adjust. When she finally could see, she gazed around the one small room. In the corner was their bed, but not the neat, spread-covered version she had pictured. It was an oversized platform with a quilt hastily thrown over some kind of lumpy bedding—definitely made up by a man.

A small black stove hovered beneath the smoke-spewing chimney. Close beside it were a small wooden table and two stools pushed beneath it. A cluttered shelf stretched along the wall, with crocks and tins randomly stacked across it.

The two tiny windows were hardly large enough to look out of—and one had to stoop to do so. The small panes of dirty glass were held snugly in place by the sod stacked firmly around them. Missie, her thoughts swirling around like leaves in a wind, promised herself she would give them a good washing at her first opportunity. She jerked her thoughts away from the windows, amazed that at such a traumatic moment she could even notice the dirt on the tiny panes.

Her gaze traveled up to the ceiling. It, too, was sod held precariously in place by strips of board, twine, and wire. It looked as if it periodically gave up parts of itself. Would it come tumbling down—on her, on her baby?

She quickly lowered her eyes lest they give her away—and immediately noticed the floor. It was dirt! Hard-packed, uneven dirt. Missie sucked in a ragged breath, but Willie was talking cheerily.

"It ain't much, but it's warm an' snug. Come next year we'll build a *real* house—of either rock or wood—ya can have yer choice."

"Coffee's ready," Henry called. Willie stepped forward to take Nathan from Missie. She was reluctant to let him go but gradually released her grip, and Willie put him down on the bed. Her eyes surveyed the roof above the bed to be sure a clump of turf was not about to fall.

"Sit right here," Henry invited, and Missie numbly did as she was told.

The hot coffee revived her somewhat, and Missie soon discovered that her hands and feet could move again. She felt Henry's eyes upon her and knew she must respond in some way.

"Well," she said, forcing a chuckle past the lump in her throat, "sure won't be much to keeping house." She saw Henry's face relax.

Willie reached for her hand. "I know it won't be easy, Missie—this first year—but jest you wait. Next year, I promise, we'll build ya jest what ya want."

Missie took another swallow of coffee. Henry had brewed it strong and dark. Oh, how she needed its strength right now.

"Where are all the crates and boxes of my things?" she asked softly. She was surprised she had said the word *my*, but she couldn't have avoided it.

"We stored 'em in the back shed by the barn until ya got here. We didn't rightly know jest which stuff you'd want. I can git 'em fer ya right away, iffen you'd like."

Missie looked around her at the already crowded room.

"I think you'd best leave them where they are for now. There doesn't seem to be much room for extras here. And, Willie, put my sewing machine with them, too, will you please?"

Willie started to argue, but then his eyes also surveyed the room.

"Does seem a mite crowded like," he said. "Funny, it seemed plumb empty when you were gone."

"Yer team is still standin' out there," Henry broke in, placing his cup on the table. "I think thet I'd best go on out an' take care of 'em. Where d'ya want the wagon left?"

"Jest pull it up beside the house. We still have to move in all the things fer this young'un."

Henry nodded and left.

"Where's Henry stayin'?" Missie asked, toying with her cup.

"In the bunkhouse."

"Alone?"

"No, we have three others there now. Two hands an' the cook."

"Must be crowded."

"They don't have much gear."

"You've got more cattle, then?"

"A nice start."

"And horses?"

"A fairly good string."

"You're about fixed, then, I imagine."

Willie nodded slowly, pushed his cup back, and rubbed his hands over his weary-looking face. He stood and walked to the window, bending his head to look out at whatever lay beyond.

"Missie," he said without turning around, "this was a mistake. Don't know why I didn't see it before. Jest too plumb lonesome to think straight, I guess. I never shoulda brought ya here. I shoulda left ya there at Tettsford till I had a decent house built. This ain't no fittin' place fer a woman . . . an' a baby."

Missie went silently to him, terribly sorry her feelings had been so transparent. It must have hurt Willie to see her disappointment.

"Oh, Willie," she said reaching her arms around his neck and pulling his head down toward her. "It's all right. Truly it is. I admit, it did catch me off guard, but I'll get used to it. Really. Really I will. I'd have never stayed there in Tettsford—not without you. I was so lonesome for you I nearly died of it every day. I'd as soon be here—no, *sooner*—I'd *sooner* be here with you than back there in that bedroom all alone."

Willie pulled her tight. "Missie, I'm sorry . . . sorry," he whispered, "but it won't always be this way. I promise. I'll make it up to ya someday. Jest as soon as I can. Ya'll have jest as fine a place as yer own home was . . . as ya deserve to have."

My home! Missie thought, closing her eyes. *Oh, if only I were at home!* Wasn't that where she really belonged? Why hadn't Willie been content with it, too?

She looked across at the sleeping baby and the tears stung her eyes. Willie was kissing the top of her head. If she could keep from looking up at him, she could recover her composure. Nathan began to fuss, and Missie turned gently from Willie without lifting her face.

Taking a breath to steady her voice, she said, "He's hungry. Guess I'd better care for him before I do anything else."

"I'll bring in his things," Willie said and reached for his hat. "Missie." He stopped at the door and turned to her. "I love you."

She looked at him, nodded, and forced a smile before he went out the door.

I'd sooner be here with you than back there in that bedroom all alone, she repeated over and over again.

SEVENTEEN

Winter and Christmas

Missie lifted the already heavy buckets and trudged forward a few paces. She dropped them with a thump and stooped again to gather buffalo chips from the near-frozen ground. The driving wind whipped her shawl, and she made an effort to wrap it more securely about her. Her fingers tingled from the cold. She chided herself for not having worn mittens.

At length the second pail was full. She hoisted her load and hiked slowly back to her sod house, the buckets thumping against her legs. She would need two more pails to complete the day's supply. She dreaded the thought of going out once more. Her arms and back were aching, and she was now having to range farther and farther from the house in order to fill the pails.

As she neared the soddy she could hear little Nathan crying. She hurried her steps. Poor little fellow! How long had he been asking for his dinner?

Missie set down her load, then scrubbed her hands thoroughly at the basin in the corner. The cold water increased the tingling feeling, and she rubbed them vigorously with the rough towel in an effort to restore the proper circulation. At last there was feeling in her fingers again. Casting her shawl aside, she hurried to her baby, crooning words of love to him even before she reached his bed.

Somehow she had managed two long weeks of living in the crowded soddy. Nathan was a big part of the reason she was able to function at all. The wee baby brought life and meaning to Missie's world, such as it was.

The air was growing colder now and the wind more harsh. Willie's eyes, full of concern, often watched the sky. A winter storm of sleet and snow could sweep in upon them long before he and his farmhands were ready for it. Missie worried about her dwindling fuel supply, but she said nothing to Willie. No need to give him further worries. Surely a woman should be able to shoulder the task of keeping the fire going. Still, she didn't know how she would manage it once the snow covered the ground. Frets about that and other matters related to simply surviving nagged constantly in the back of her mind.

She changed Nathan, fed him, and held him close for several minutes before returning him to his bed.

Missie checked the coffeepot on her small stove. The full-sized stove she had brought from "back home" at her mama's insistence remained packed in its crate. It was too big for the little sod house. Missie pushed the kettle toward the center so the water would boil. Willie might soon be in, and he would be chilled to the bone. But it was Henry's voice Missie heard first, just outside the door.

"Still think thet we can't put it off any longer—no matter what else needs to be done. Snow could come anytime."

"Yeah," Willie agreed, "yer right. Shouldn'ta let it go this long. We'll plan on first thing in the mornin'. We'll use two wagons an' all the hands."

"Ya think they'll mind?"

"I'm boss, ain't I?"

"Sure ya are."

Missie could sense the grin in Henry's voice.

"But I reckon they might think they was hired on to punch cows—not pick up chips."

"We'll see," Willie said as the two men ducked through the door.

Oh, Missie thought, *if only this means what I hope it means.*

The next morning, soon after breakfast, two wagons and five men set out to gather chips for the winter fires. All day long they shuttled back and forth. They heaped the cook's supply beside the cook shack but favored Missie with more consideration. Her pile was stored in a sod shed just behind the house. This would save her the struggle of breaking frozen chips out of the snow.

Missie nearly cried with relief as she watched the shed fill up. Gathering chips would have been an increasingly difficult task with the coming of the winter snows. *Thank you, God,* her heart whispered. "And thank you, Willie—and all of you," she would say to each of them as she was able. Missie felt light with her gratefulness. She groped for a way to express her deep appreciation. At the same time she reached for her large coffeepot and filled it to the brim. She'd at least have steaming coffee waiting to warm the men on their next trip in.

The next day the men continued hauling, and even the next—piling the overflow beside the shed. To Missie it looked like the supply would last forever. It did to some of the hands, also, if their mutters and scowls were any indication. But Willie declared he wanted to be absolutely sure his wife had plenty on hand for warm fires throughout the coming winter.

Missie's days became easier after the chips had been gathered. But her time was also more difficult to fill with activity. The little room needed very little attention. Missie made attempts at sweeping the floor, made up the bed, prepared the meals, and washed the dishes. Of course, she often had to make a trip to the spring when she ran out of water, which Willie hauled for her before leaving for his daily duties. Beyond that, there wasn't much to fill her hours.

She decided to knit socks for Henry—then continued to knit a pair for each of the ranch hands. She would have them ready for Christmas. After the socks were finished and Missie's idle hands lay useless in her lap once again, she decided to make each of the men heavy woolen mittens for the winter days ahead. She hesitated—not sure if cowboys would scorn such things as woolen mittens, but eventually she proceeded anyway.

Missie did not know the men well. The tall, lean, hard-faced one with the large nose was Clem. The shorter tobacco-spitting one was Sandy. Missie was a bit more familiar with Cookie—the cook, of course. He was a quiet but pleasant man whose sharp eyes seemingly missed nothing. His face was plain until lit with a smile—which occurred whenever he saw Missie or her small son. Cookie suffered with a bad limp, the reason he was content to cook rather than ride the range with the other men. A bad fall while breaking a horse was his explanation for the faulty hip and leg. Missie was glad he was around, for though they rarely conversed, his occasional nod and grin brightened her day a bit.

The baby's laundry was Missie's most trying task. The water had to be hauled from the spring below the house. Though Willie filled the two available pails before he left in the morning, it wasn't nearly enough for Missie to do the job. The little stove was too small to hold a tub or a boiler, so Missie had to heat the water kettle by kettle. By the time she had the next kettleful hot, the first one had cooled. Having been raised to wash clothes in *hot* water, she found her patience sorely tested.

<hr />

The first winter storm attacked with fury. Driving wind whipped the cutting sleet, smashing it against the small windows, swirling it around each corner of the sod house. The snow stacked in drifts and buried any obstacle in its pathway. Missie prayed that their little soddy would be able to withstand the storm's anger.

Willie insisted on being out with the men and animals, and Missie felt it was only sensible for him to be *in*. All hands rode throughout the day to insure that the three hundred cattle now wearing the *Hanging W* brand were not lost in the storm.

They returned late in the afternoon, having hazed the cattle into a box-canyon, which they hoped would offer some protection from the worst of the weather.

Still, Willie fretted and paced, ducking down to watch the driving snow through the small pane of window glass.

The storm had lost some of its fury by the next afternoon, and Henry and Sandy rode out to check the stock. They were able to report back that all were accounted for. Willie relaxed again.

The snow did not melt away, and Missie realized that winter was not about to retreat. The spring soon froze, and Missie was forced to melt snow for their water supply. It was a tedious task, particularly on washdays. She didn't care for the taste of snow water, either, but gradually adjusted to it.

Missie found her life to be uneventful, repetitious, boring. The deep drifts all about the little sod house blocked her view of even those empty frost-painted hills. The tasks of bringing in fuel for her fire and melting enough snow to keep water in the house provided Missie with nothing except *work*.

How glad Missie was for Nathan. As he became aware of what was happening around him and his smile greeted Missie when she looked over at him in his bed, her days took on some meaning and purpose. She talked to him constantly. Without him, the dark walls of the tiny soddy would have been a prison during those long, empty wintry days.

"Thank you, Father," Missie prayed often. "Thank you for our son. And help me to be cheerful and patient and to make a happy home for Willie," she added.

⟨⟨⟩⟩

As Missie hung the baby's laundry from the lines strung across their one room, she suddenly realized that only a few days remained until Christmas.

She ducked under a line of hanging diapers and made her way to another homemade calendar clipped on the wall. It was true. There were only four days until Christmas.

She looked about her. Christmas? Here? She shook her head quickly to blink away threatening tears and scolded herself. But the aching feeling within her was not to be shaken off so easily. What could she possibly do to make this soddy ready for Christmas?

That evening as she and Willie sat at their small table to eat their stew and biscuits, Missie brought up the subject.

"Did you realize that in just four days it's Christmas?"

"Christmas?" Willie said, looking surprised. "Christmas already? Boy, how time does fly!"

Missie felt a sharp retort forming on her tongue, but she refused to voice it.

"Christmas!" Willie repeated. "I can hardly believe it."

He finished the biscuit. "Guess I can't provide ya with a turkey. Will a roast of venison do?"

"I think so. Maybe Cookie can tell me how to fix it."

"Be kinda hard havin' Christmas alone, won't it?" Willie's eyes searched her face carefully.

"I've been thinking about it," Missie said. "Why don't we have the hands in?"

"In *here*?"

"Why not?"

Willie stared at the lines of hanging baby things. "Not much room."

"I know, but we could make do."

"They could come two at a time, I guess."

"That wouldn't be *Christmas*."

"How'll ya do it, then?"

"I'll set the food out on the table and the stove, and we'll just help ourselves and sit wherever we fit—on the stools, on the bed—wherever. I think there's one more stool in the bunkhouse—and Cookie has one in the cook shack."

Willie laughed. "You've got yer heart set on it, ain't ya?"

Missie lowered her head but made no comment.

"Okay," said Willie, "invite the men."

"Would you invite them, please, Willie? I . . . I don't see them much."

"Sure, I'll invite 'em. Fer what time?"

"Let's make it one o'clock."

Willie nodded. "An' I'll git ya thet venison roast."

"Maybe Cookie could do the roast in his stove. Then I can have mine free for other things."

Willie nodded again. "I'll talk to 'im."

⸎

Cookie agreed to do the roast, and when the day arrived, Missie got busy on the remainder of the meal. She didn't have much to work with, but what she lacked in ingredients, she made up for with ingenuity. She had been hoarding some of her mother's preserves for just such a time as this. She opened them now and used some of the fruit to fill tart shells. She prepared some of the last canned carrots and beans from home to go with the roast venison. The only potatoes left were a few precious ones that she had kept, hoping to plant them in the spring. They looked sorry and neglected, but Missie still prayed they might have the germ of life left in them. She refused to use any of them now, although the thought of potatoes with the meal made her mouth water. Instead, she baked a big batch of fluffy biscuits and set out her last jar of honey to go with them.

When the men arrived, Cookie proudly carrying his roast of venison, Missie was ready for them.

"Before we eat," Willie said, "I've somethin' else to bring in. We don't have much room, iffen ya noticed"—this brought a guffaw from the men—"so I left it in the other shed."

He soon returned carrying a scrub bush, held upright in a small pail. On its tiny branches hung little bows made from Missie's scraps of yarn.

"Didn't rightly seem like Christmas without a tree," he said apologetically. The men whooped, and Missie wept.

When the commotion had died down, Willie moved with some difficulty to the middle of the room and led them in prayer: "Father, we have much to thank you fer. Fer the good-smellin' food of which we are about to partake. Fer the warmth of this little room in which we are to share it. Fer friends who are here with us an' those who are far away. Fer the memories of other Christmases spent with those we love. Fer Nathan Isaiah, our healthy son. And most of all, dear God, fer my wife, who has blessed us all by givin' us this Christmas. We are reminded thet all of these blessin's are extras. Yer special gift to us on this day was yer Son. We accept thet gift with our thanks. Amen."

As the menfolk devoured the tasty and plentiful food, Missie sat quietly. She tried to keep her thoughts from wandering to her parents' home. What would it be like if she could be there right now? In a house big enough to serve a whole family in comfort, with fresh butter, mashed potatoes, turkey, baked squash, and apple pie topped with whipped cream.

She looked at her plate filled with sliced venison and gravy, canned carrots with no garnish, canned yellow beans, and a biscuit with no butter. But she reminded herself that many days during the last year she had partaken of even simpler fare. This was a rather sumptuous feast by comparison. The men obviously felt it was such. And when it came time for the tarts and coffee, they licked their lips in anticipation. Missie picked her way across the room to check on Nathan. One could barely move without tripping over feet, but the close proximity just made it easier for laughing together.

"Son," she whispered to the baby, "you're not going to remember one thing about this, but I want you to get in on it anyway. Your very first Christmas, and I don't even have anything to give you—but a kiss and laughter with friends." She took him in her arms.

After the meal Missie summoned all her courage and presented each of the men with a pair of socks and woolen mittens. She was unprepared for their deep appreciation. She soon realized that it may have been their first Christmas gift since they were small boys at home.

Cookie shifted his position to "git outta the smoke from the blasted fire—it's makin' my eyes water."

Clem swallowed over and over, his Adam's apple lurching up and down.

Missie prayed that none of them would feel embarrassed at having nothing to give in return.

After the men had expressed their thanks as best as they could, Missie began timidly, "Now I want to say thank you for your gift to me."

Five pairs of eyes—six, counting Nathan's—swung to her face.

"I want to thank you," she said shyly, "for working so faithfully for my husband, for making his load—and thus mine—easier, for not demanding things that we can't provide." She hesitated, then added, smiling, "But most of all, I want to thank you for the good supply of chips you didn't fuss about hauling. I've been thankful over and over for those chips."

Missie couldn't suppress a giggle. Though the expressions of the men acknowledged her sincere thankfulness, they also saw the humor in it and gladly chuckled with her.

Though unaware of it at that moment, Missie had just made some friends for life. Not one of those men sitting round her tiny soddy would have denied her anything that was in their power to provide. There she sat, just a little scrap of a girl-woman, youthful and pretty, her cheeks glowing with health, her eyes sparkling near tears, her trim figure clothed attractively in a bright calico, the tiny fair-skinned, chubby-cheeked Nathan contentedly in her arms studying her face.

That picture was their Christmas gift, one they would remember all their lives.

Later Henry brought in his guitar, and they sang Christmas carols together. Cookie just sat and listened. Sandy whistled a few lines now and then. But Clem, to Missie's surprise, seemed to know most of the traditional carols by heart.

It was hard to break up the little gathering. Several times Missie added more chips to her fire. Little Nathan made the rounds from one pair of arms to another. Even the tough-looking Clem took a turn holding the baby.

At last Missie put the coffeepot back on and boiled a fresh pot. She was glad she had made enough tarts for each of them to have another one with their coffee.

The men lingered over their tarts and coffee but finally took their leave, tramping their way through the snow back to the bunkhouse.

Missie hummed softly as she washed the dishes. There had been no point trying to find room to wash them earlier. Willie put on his hat and coat and left for the barn to check the horses, Missie assumed.

Missie had finished the dishes and was feeding Nathan when Willie returned, bearing a box. Missie was astonished, and he answered her unasked question.

"I did my Christmas shopping 'fore we left Tettsford." He set his box on the table and began to unpack it.

"'Fraid my gift don't seem too fittin' like in these surroundin's. I was sorta seein' it in our *real* house when I bought it, I guess. Anyway, I

thought thet I'd show it to ya, an' then we can sorta pack it off again."
Willie lifted from the box the most beautiful fruit bowl Missie had
ever seen.

She gasped, "Willie! It's beautiful."

Willie looked very relieved when he saw the bowl had brought her
pleasure. He set it gently on the table.

"I'll let ya git a better look at it when yer done with Nathan. Then
I'll pack it on back—out of yer way."

"Oh no," Missie protested. "Just leave it here. Please."

She laid the baby on the bed and went to the table to pick up the
bowl. "It's lovely," she said, her fingers caressing it. "Thank you, Willie."

She reached up to kiss him. "And I don't want you to pack it away. It'll
be a reminder . . . and a promise. I . . . I need it here. Don't you see?"

Willie held her close. "I see."

After a moment of silence, Willie spoke softly. "Missie, I wonder . . . I
wonder iffen you'll ever know jest how happy ya made five people today?"

"Five?"

"Those four cowpokes . . . an' *me*."

Missie's heart was full, and she smiled.

"Then make it *six*, Willie . . . because in doing what I could, the
pleasure all poured right back on me. And I got the biggest helping of
happiness myself!"

EIGHTEEN

Missie's New Home

After the anticipation and preparation for Christmas and the joyful celebration it turned out to be, the winter days fell back into their previous monotony. At times Missie felt she could endure no more, confined as she was in the cramped, stuffy soddy. Her only company for most of her days was Baby Nathan. She wondered if she might spoil him with all the attention he received. It was a good thing he fussed very little, for Missie used every little cry or murmur as an excuse to pamper and cuddle him. He responded with toothless smiles and waving fists.

When he slept, Missie tried her best to find other things to keep herself busy. If there was laundry to do, that could take most of a morning, leaving dripping clothing hanging around the already crowded room. But it was satisfying to have clean garments ready to wear. Of course clean diapers for Nathan were a daily chore. Occasionally there was wild game that one of the men had brought in, and after it had been butchered and dressed, she would prepare her and Willie's portion in stews or panfry it. But most days' meals meant very simple fare and did not require much time to make.

She no longer had to make those daily treks to the fuel shack—ever since Christmas, a good supply of chips appeared beside her door every day before she had even climbed out of bed. Missie never discovered which one of the men delivered them.

She had no room for books except the Bible she and Willie read from each morning after breakfast. Her hands had long since run out of materials for crafts and activities to occupy them, and the walls of the room seemed to press ever more closely about her.

Baby Nathan gained weight, gurgled and cooed, and tried to chew everything his small hands could get to his mouth. It became more and more difficult to find a safe place to leave the wee child, who could now scoot to the edge of the bed. She couldn't put him on the dirt floor to roll around, and she had to watch him carefully when she put him on the bed for his playtimes.

Though time with his son was limited by the demands of the ranch, Willie also doted on little Nathan. Missie sometimes teased that if it had not been for the baby, Willie would have been content to live out with his precious cows! When Nathan began to squeal at the sight of his daddy and laugh at their roughhouse play, Willie found it more difficult to say good-bye and leave the house to go back to the men and the stock.

Missie was gazing out the tiny window with glimmers of hope that the worst of the winter was over when a sudden angry-sounding wind swept in from the north. It caught the crew off guard, and before the men could even saddle up to go look after the cows, the snow came— swishing, blinding clouds of it seemed set on devouring everything in its path. Willie realized it was foolhardy to send men out in such a storm. He would just have to leave the animals on their own and hope they could find some shelter.

The storm moved on after two days. By then the drifts of snow had piled high all around. The soddy's door was almost buried by the whiteness. Willie had to wait for the ranch hands to dig him out.

All were finally able to leave their quarters, and the men quickly saddled up to go out looking for the range cattle in the hills. After combing the area for three days, the reports were heartbreaking. At least seventy-five head of cattle had been lost in the storm. Missie wept. Willie tried to assure her they'd make out fine, that temporary setbacks were to be expected. But she could see a troubled look in his eyes. They both turned again to their Isaiah passage for comfort and strength.

At the end of February one of the milk cows calved, and Missie felt as though she had been handed an unimaginable treasure. Even the loss of the cattle the week before was put from her mind. With milk on hand, what wonderful possibilities she could imagine for improving their diet!

"What I couldn't do now if I just had some eggs," she told Willie. She promised herself that as soon as possible she'd do something about that.

⁓

Spring eventually did come—slowly, almost imperceptibly, until one morning Missie was confident there was a faint warmth in the air. The drifts of snow began to shrink, and gradually dark spots of earth appeared. The spring started to trickle again and the stubby bushes beside it dressed themselves in a shy green.

Missie secretly mourned for the sight of budding trees, of blossoming shrubs, but only empty hills stretched away from her gaze. To her great joy, a few wild flowers timidly made their appearance. Missie couldn't resist picking some to grace her table. In the dimness of the little sod house, one had to bend over the tin cup that held the flowers in order to fully appreciate the tiny bits of color. But just knowing they were there helped to lift her spirits.

As the snow receded, the men spent much more time out on the range, watching the cattle vigilantly. Spring calves were arriving daily. They would not totter about many days before the *Hanging W,* Willie's brand, would show on their flanks.

Missie wasn't particularly happy about the name attached to Willie's ranch, not in favor of "hanging" even a W. But Willie laughed at her squeamishness. All of their stock bore the brand.

Willie told her that the hard range riding of spring roundup was beginning. Day after day the men would ride, gathering the scattered stock and their calves. They would all be driven to the wide box-canyon where they had been protected during the first winter storm, he explained before kissing his son and Missie good-bye for a few days.

When the roundup was completed, the men counted one hundred ninety-eight head of cattle and one hundred six calves.

"Even with the last storm," Willie maintained, "thet's a few more'n we started with."

The wagons were moved out to the canyon to serve as bunkhouses during the spring branding. Cookie slept in the chow wagon, as well as using it for kitchen, supply shack, and blacksmith shop.

The men were divided into shifts for the night hours, and Willie and Sandy took the first watch.

It wasn't long until the cattle adjusted to their more confined surroundings. The lowing and milling subsided, and they bedded down for the night.

After midnight Henry and Clem took over the night-watch duties. Sandy and Willie gladly unsaddled their mounts and cozied up to Cookie's open fire. They drank mugs of hot coffee to warm their bones before trying to get a few hours of sleep. The early morning sun would soon summon them to another busy day with the branding irons.

Shortly before daybreak a commotion among the herd got Henry's and Clem's attention, but they could not quickly pinpoint the source of the sudden restlessness and shifting of the herd.

By the time they realized the cause, a band of rustlers was driving off a large portion of the herd. Henry and Clem rode hard, but in spite of their best efforts they were able to cut back only the stragglers from the stampeding cattle. No shots had been fired, but Henry and Clem had counted, in spite of the darkness and confusion, at least five rustlers. By the time the sleeping men in the wagons heard the ruckus and recognized what it was, it was too late for them to assist.

The next morning the discouraged men ranged out farther, gathering the few head that had somehow eluded the rustlers. After all the cattle in their possession had been gathered and counted, Willie found that his herd now numbered only fifty-four head of full-grown cattle and thirty-two calves.

After the final count, Willie turned away in defeat. He had known all along that he would suffer some losses to weather and rustlers, but he had dared to hope that the numbers would be few and over a longer period of time. *Why,* he asked himself, *why did I think we would be spared when so many other ranchers have been completely wiped out? I should feel lucky to have any cattle left—any at all.*

Willie swallowed the hard lump in his throat and lifted his broad-brimmed hat to wipe the dust from his brow. The sick feeling in the pit of his stomach refused to leave. Could he get back on his feet? How long would it take? If he had been more patient and had worked for another year before coming out to his ranch, he could have laid aside enough cash to cover such a tragic setback.

Now the only cash he had on hand was the money for Missie's house. How could he ever tell her? Even now he could picture those frank blue eyes, intense with hurt and fright and disappointment from the news.

Though he wished with every ounce of his being he could do so, he knew it would be useless and untruthful to try to keep it from her. She deserved to know the facts—even to know the seriousness of their situation. But Willie determined that in every way possible he would try to shield her from the pain and fear that came with the knowing.

When Willie presented Missie with the facts, she could tell he was explaining the situation as honestly and simply as he knew how. He talked as though this was inevitable—the loss of some cattle. But deep down, Missie knew better. She ached for him. If only there was some way she could help him.

Then within her breast arose a tiny surge of hope. Maybe now he would be satisfied to have tried his dream and be content to go back home. But very soon she knew Willie had no such intention. Instead, to Missie's surprise, he told his men that as soon as the work could be started, they would begin building the permanent ranch house.

Missie said nothing until they were alone that night. She began very carefully, "I overheard you discussing with the hands your plans for building."

"Yeah, iffen it's gonna be ready as planned, we need to get started."

"But, Willie," Missie protested softly. "Can we manage it now? Can we afford it?"

"What're ya meanin'?"

"Well, with the cattle losses and all."

"Thet changes nothin'. The money for the house has been set aside."

"But what about rebuilding the herd?"

"Thet'll jest have to wait."

"But can it? I mean, if we don't have a herd, there won't be cattle to sell, and if—"

"There'll be some . . . eventually. And I promised ya a house. We can't do both, Missie . . . an' the house comes first."

"Willie, listen." Missie was afraid she might later regret what she was about to say. But she had to say it. "Willie, I know about your promise. I know you want to keep it . . . and you will. But it could be postponed, Willie, for just a bit . . . until . . . until we have the cattle to sell. If we stay in this house, just for now, and use the put-aside money to help rebuild the herd, then next year . . . well, we could build our house then."

Missie saw Willie's jaw muscles tighten as if he was fighting for control.

"Please, Willie," she coaxed. "The cattle are important to *me*, too, you know."

"But ya couldn't keep on livin' here, not fer another whole year . . . another winter."

"Yes, I could," she hurried on with as much conviction as she could muster. "I'm getting used to it now. It's not very big, but it's warm. And now that spring is here, Nathan and I can go outside more. By fall he'll be walking. We'll manage. Honest!"

Silence followed. For a time Missie wondered if she had been refused. She didn't know whether to feel relieved or sorry. The house was small and difficult. Yet she knew if Willie was intending to stay here and ranch—and it seemed that indeed he was—then he needed to rebuild that herd. Without it their future was very insecure.

Her love for Willie drove her to decide for his happiness. She knew now he'd never be content to simply admit defeat, to leave his beloved hills and valleys, and return back east.

Oh, God, she prayed silently, *help me support Willie in spite of what I want. Keep your promise to uphold me now.*

Missie felt peace go through her being. The next thing she knew, Willie was pulling her close. She understood Willie was accepting her gift of postponement on the house in order to rebuild his herd. She reached her hand up to touch his cheeks and felt the tears. Her Willie was crying. She cried, too, but their shared emotions drew them even closer to each other.

NINETEEN

Missie's Garden

With the smell of spring in the air, Missie found herself even more restless as she anxiously waited for the final disappearance of snow. Nathan, increasingly active now, needed room in which to explore, and that would require the outdoors. Missie dared not leave him in the small sod house longer than a dash out back for more chips or to scoop up a pail of snow for her water supply.

She had tired of the melted snow for her water supply, but she did not feel it was any longer safe for her to make the trek to the trickling spring and leave the baby alone in the house, and she certainly could not carry him and a bucket of water, too. But logic did not keep her from *wanting* to go to the spring. Just the sight of its running water would be confirmation to her that spring was truly here.

She desperately needed to escape the four tight walls. She also needed a change of activity. Her fingers felt heavy and numb from hours of knitting and sewing. She was just plain bored—fed up with nearly everything that could be done in one small room.

Missie looked out on the sparkling day and, as many times in the past, wished with all her heart that she had some excuse to be out in the sunshine. If only she could saddle a horse and go out onto the prairies like the menfolk did. But with no one to leave small Nathan with, the idea was not workable.

Or is it?

Missie suddenly recalled a nostalgic item she had slipped into one of the boxes when packing. Before they left on their long trip west, she had found it tucked in the back of a drawer at home, and with tear-filled eyes, she had smuggled it in among some blankets. To another's eyes it would just have seemed like some kind of strange contraption, but to Missie it was *love* wrapped up in one simple, practical piece of equipment. Though Missie had no recollection of being carried in the backpack, her mama had long ago showed it to her and explained how her pa had lovingly fashioned it in order to carry her with him after she, just a tiny girl, had lost her first mother. He had never left her at home alone while he plowed his fields and did his choring until Marty joined the little family. Missie ran to the storage shed in her eagerness. With the backpack, she would be able to take that horseback ride, and the baby would be able to join her!

Once she had located the backpack and shown it to Willie, he selected a gentle mare and made her available to Missie whenever she wished to ride. Now she had something to look forward to when the weather cooperated. Even with the backpack, though, she could not ride far before Baby Nathan became too heavy, and Missie would reluctantly return to the little soddy. But she also used it to take him with her to the spring for fresh water.

Missie was bored with the sameness of the food she had to prepare every day. Nothing tasted good anymore—nothing was fresh. "Canned, dried, and bland" described everything. Her precious herbs and spices were carefully parceled out, since she didn't know when they could be replaced. She wondered if Willie found the meals as unpalatable as she did. But, of course, Willie was too much of a gentleman to comment in any way but positively.

It seemed to Missie's worn, restless spirit that planting a garden would revive her again—and so she paced back and forth, willing the snow to go away. When fresh flurries sent scattered flakes whirling through the still crisp air, Missie wiped tears of disappointment on her apron.

Finally the snow flurries changed to rain showers, and Missie's hopes grew.

The snow melted reluctantly—especially where it had drifted by the spring. And that was the very location Missie wanted for her garden. She felt sorely tempted to go out with a shovel but checked herself from such foolish use of time and energy. The snow gradually lost the battle, and one day when Missie went to check she was surprised and thrilled to find all traces of the winter's cold and ice gone. She began hinting to Willie that he put a plow to the sod. Willie showed more patience than Missie.

"It's a bit early yet," he insisted. "The ground hasn't had a fair chance to warm. An' remember, this ain't the East. We're right close to the mountains here, an' frosts still come on the early spring nights."

But Missie could not bear the thought of being detained. Willie, realizing what it meant to her, relented and plowed the spot, though he shook his head at rushing the season like this.

Missie felt released from captivity as she sorted her seeds and set off for planting. She took a blanket on which to deposit Nathan, and set to work. She was sure the baby would be as joyful as she at finally being free from the four walls of the soddy, but he looked about in a perplexed manner and began to fuss. Missie tried to amuse him, but he continued to wail. She then turned him over onto his tummy and patted him gently until he fell asleep. At least the fresh air would do him good.

"You're missing so much by sleeping right now, my boy," she whispered. "The clear blue sky, the feel of the spring air, the smell of the soil. I do hope that someday you appreciate it all. But for now, your mama will just enjoy it for you."

Missie went to her planting. She was so glad she had plenty of seed. She was hungry in both body and soul for green growing things. Her impatience mounted with each seed she dropped into the ground. She could almost smell the vegetables cooking on her stove in the days ahead. The imagined taste and tang of them was pungent in her imagination.

Her job ended too soon, and the little garden was planted. Nathan still slept, so Missie sat down beside him on the blanket and listened to the soft gurgle of the spring only a few paces away. It was so good to feel alive again. She thanked God that life was not always winter, that spring always came at last—to chase away the cold and heaviness, and to release one to warmth and movement again.

Nathan awoke and Missie reached for him. She talked to him, encouraging him to behold and enjoy what she saw, to feel the things that she felt, to breathe as deeply as she breathed. But all the baby seemed aware of was the face and arms of the mother who held him close and cooed words of love to him. At length Missie gathered everything together, bundled up her baby, and headed back to her sod house. Nathan was hungry, she knew, and would soon be demanding his own dinner. She would nurse him before preparing their noon meal.

That very night it snowed. When Missie looked out the next morning, hoping to see another fair and sunny day, she saw instead a thin layer of white over the entire world. Willie saw her face and heard her sharp gasp. He joined her at the window, ducking his head so he could look out.

"Moisture!" he said quickly. "Be mighty good fer those seeds of yers. Soon's the sun's up to work on it, it'll soak in real good."

Missie changed her mind about crying and gave Willie a rueful smile instead. She didn't know if Willie was right, but she wanted him to know that she loved him for his concern for her and her disappointment.

The sun did melt the snow, almost as soon as its warm fingers began to reach out over the brown earth, sending up to heaven little shimmering mists, like dancing vapors.

There were other mornings when Missie awoke to scattered snow or frost on the ground. On such mornings she prayed that none of her brave little plants had as yet lifted their heads from the protective soil bed. Though Missie knew her seedlings were safe as long as they were not exposed, she still longed for their appearance. Daily she watched for signs of life in her garden. Eventually it came—a green blade here and there, a suggestion of a green spray down a row, a pair of tiny leaves breaking forth, gradually joined by others until a row could be defined. At length Missie was able to recognize onions, radishes, beans, peas, and carrots. Her garden was growing.

And then one night—the dreaded frost. Some of the hardier vegetables were seemingly untouched, but the more tender things wilted and curled up tightly against the ground.

"Still plenty of time fer replantin'," Willie assured her. "Ya want me to turn those rows with the spade?"

Missie shook her head. "The exercise will be good for me—and I know how busy you are."

She replanted and again watched for new growth. It came—but it seemed oh so slow this time.

One day as Missie checked on her garden, she was surprised to find an onion plant that looked as if it might be close to being ready. It wasn't that big, really, but when she pulled it up, it truly did smell like an onion. She pulled off its outer skin and popped it into her mouth. Oh, it tasted good! She had almost forgotten how good an onion tasted. Or anything *fresh,* for that matter. She reached for another and devoured it, too. Down the row she went, searching, pulling, and eating, until at length she turned and looked at the trail of discarded tops she had left behind. She was shocked at how many she had eaten. As she bent to pick up the top nearest to her, she felt the results of a lunch of onions. Missie burped—then giggled. "Oh my," she said to herself. "If Willie could see what a pig I've been!"

Guiltily Missie retraced her steps, picking up onion tops so that her gluttony would not be so obvious. She pulled a few more onions to season a stew, then, gathering Nathan up, returned to the house.

The onions did not sit well, and Missie felt an uneasiness in her stomach for the remainder of the day. By the time Willie came for his supper, she wished she didn't have to join him at the table. Even the savory smell of the onions in the stew could not tempt her.

Willie must have observed her white face and instantly showed concern. "Ya sick?"

"Just off my food a little."

"Yer sure?"

"Yeah—I'm sure."

"Ya'd best lie down—I'll look after myself." He led her to their bed. "Where's the problem? Ya got a pain somewhere?"

"Just a little."

"Where?"

"My stomach's a mite upset."

"Taken any of yer ma's medicine? There's stuff there fer—"

"It'll pass."

Willie looked unconvinced. Missie was beginning to *feel* unconvinced, as well. She lay down on the bed, almost groaning as she did so. Willie covered her gently. Then he lifted the box of medical supplies onto the table, sorting through bottles and tins, carefully reading each label.

"Describe what yer feelin'," he said, "an' I'll know better what to look fer."

Missie answered with a loud belch and then a helpless giggle. Willie wheeled around, probably wondering if the loneliness of the western prairies had finally gotten to her, or if maybe she had somehow gotten into some of Cookie's "painkiller." Missie couldn't help herself—she was laughing, not hysterical laughter but controlled mirth.

"I doubt if you'll be finding anything," she said between embarrassed chuckles, "to counteract onions!"

"Onions?"

"*My* onions. They're big enough to eat . . . and I just went right at them and made a pig of myself." She finished her confession with a weak grin.

"Oh, Willie, they tasted so good . . . at first. But," she added seriously, "they're getting so they don't taste nearly so good now."

"Ya mean . . . ya ate onions until . . . ?" Willie asked incredulously.

Missie nodded—and burped again.

The concern was now gone from Willie's face. He lowered himself onto a stool and howled with his own laughter. "Ya little goose," he finally said when he could speak, and they laughed together. He came over to her bed, reached down to kiss her, then backed away.

"Ma'am, you *did* eat onions," he said, wrinkling his nose.

"Put away the medicines. I'll be fine in the morning."

Willie still insisted that she take something for indigestion, then tucked Missie in so she could sleep.

Missie *was* fine again the next morning—but poor Baby Nathan was not. He fussed and fretted all day. Missie scolded herself over and over for not considering him before she attacked the onion patch. But when Missie's stomach had remedied itself and Baby Nathan again slept quietly, Missie smiled to herself. Every mouthful of the fresh, crisp onions had been worth it. They had tasted *that good*—like spring itself.

TWENTY

Summer

Summer was well established, and Missie's garden was daily supplying their table with a variety of tasty fresh produce. Willie had purchased cattle to bolster his herd, and he had decided that his next task would be to hire more riders before the cattle were brought to the Hanging W. This would insure proper protection day and night, once they were wearing his brand. He and Henry spent several days constructing another sod bunkhouse so the hired men would have a place to bed down. After the new dwelling was completed, Willie prepared for a trip to Tettsford Junction to pick up the necessary supplies and also scout out some new ranch hands. He and Henry would each drive a wagon. They left on a Thursday.

Missie looked at her homemade calendar and mentally prepared herself for Willie's three weeks' absence. Oh, how she wished she could have gone, too. She longed so much for a chat with a woman, for a browse through a shop, for tea and cake. But she knew the journey would be long and the weather hot, so she had forced herself to keep from asking Willie if she could go, too. Even if she could have borne the discomfort, she didn't think Nathan would do too well on such a trip.

She wrote notes for Willie to deliver—to Melinda, Kathy, and the preacher and his wife. She then wrote a longer letter to Mrs. Taylorson, bringing her up-to-date on all the things Nathan could now do—or was attempting to do.

She and Willie worked carefully on the supply list. Missie tried to think of all the things she might need over the next year. And could afford.

It was difficult for Missie to predict everything her growing child would need. Nathan had developed and changed so much already that it was hard to keep up with him even day by day. How could she possibly know what Nathan would need in a year's time? He would be walking and playing outside—needing shoes and shirts and pants. How did one shop for the needs of a fast-growing son? Missie decided that Willie would need some help. She composed a separate list that Willie was to give to Melinda. It was for yarns, sewing fabrics, and two special gifts for Willie—one for his fast-approaching birthday and one for Christmas. She also asked Melinda to choose a small toy for Nathan's first birthday.

Willie tucked away Missie's list for Melinda, then checked and re-checked their supply sheet. He finally turned to Missie.

"Is there anythin' *special* thet ya be wantin'?"

Missie did not hesitate. "Some chickens," she said. "About a dozen hens and a couple of roosters."

Willie's mouth dropped open. "Chickens?"

"Yeah, chickens. Do you realize what it would mean for us to have chickens? We could have eggs—fried, boiled, and scrambled—and roast chicken, fried chicken, chicken and dumplings—"

"Whoa," Willie said. "I'm not doubtin' none the merits of chickens—but *here*?"

"And why not?"

"We don't have the feed."

"They can scrounge for themselves."

"They'd starve!"

"Then we'll just have to buy feed."

"An' they'd need a hen house."

"They could live in a sod hut just as well as I can," said Missie, lifting her chin stubbornly.

Willie must have seen that her mind was made up. "Okay," he laughed. "I'll see what I can do 'bout chickens—but I won't make any promises."

"That's all I'm askin'," Missie said, satisfied that Willie would indeed try.

⸙

If Missie had been bored and lonely before, she was doubly so now with Willie gone. Each day she took Nathan out for a short walk or horseback ride. She did not dare go far and could only go out in the morning before the sun got too hot. While Nathan slept she often went to the spring or to her garden. She was pleased her garden was doing well. Each time she went down there she took the time to pull some weeds and pour water on her thirsty plants.

Once in a while she stopped to chat briefly with Cookie. With Willie gone, he seemed to feel responsible for her. Missie was touched by his trips to the spring on her behalf, hobbling along with her buckets of water.

She was careful to stay inside her small hut during the heat of the day and was often surprised that the cozy little soddy of the winter was also cool in the summer. It got awfully still, though, and Missie often yearned for a fresh, cooling breath of summer air, such as she had enjoyed beneath the tall shade trees back home.

The days managed to progress forward, one by one. Soon Missie was down to day eighteen. Her eyes kept searching the distant hills. She hoped that by some miracle Willie would complete his tasks in less time than anticipated and be home early.

One afternoon as Missie's eyes again swept over the hills visible through her window, she was surprised to see a lone rider heading directly toward the house.

Who could that be? she puzzled. *It's sure not Clem or Sandy.* As the rider neared the house, Missie couldn't hold back a gasp of unbelief.

"It's a woman!" she exclaimed aloud, bursting through the door and unexpectedly waking small Nathan with her sharp cry and rush of activity. Tears filled Missie's eyes as she ran toward the rider. She hadn't realized just how starved she was for the company of a woman. Oh, to talk, to laugh, to visit, to sip tea—oh, the joy of it!

Missie brushed away the tears and forced herself to a walk as the woman dismounted—the visitor might be frightened away, thinking she was crazy. They stood and gazed at each other, a smile spreading over their faces. Missie wondered if she detected loneliness in the woman's eyes.

Missie's visitor was hardly more than a girl, with dusky skin, long, loose-flowing dark hair, and black eyes. Her full lips suggested that they liked to laugh. Missie felt drawn to her new friend immediately.

"Oh," she cried, "I'm so glad to see you." She moved forward and threw her arms around the girl, laughing and crying at the same time. The stranger responded, and Missie received a warm hug in return.

They stepped back and studied each other.

"Where did you come from?" Missie asked. To her amazement the girl answered with words she could not comprehend.

Missie frowned.

"I'm sorry," she said, "I don't understand you. You'll have to speak English."

A smooth flow of words followed, but again they meant nothing to Missie.

"You mean, you don't speak English?"

The girl just shrugged. Missie wanted to cry but checked herself and took the girl's arm.

"Well, come in anyway," she said. "At least we can have some tea."

She led the young woman to her tiny sod house and pointed to a stool. She then began to build a fire in her little stove for tea. Upon hearing an exclamation of joy, Missie turned to see the girl bending over Nathan. He had gotten over his fright with Missie's startled exclamation and was lying on the bed playing with his fingers. She looked back at Missie and spoke. From the look in her eyes, Missie took the question to be concerning Nathan and she nodded her head in approval.

The young woman gathered the baby to her, her face full of pleasure. She crooned to him and spoke softly. Nathan could not have understood the words, but he seemed to grasp the meaning, smiling and cooing in return.

The fire caught quickly, and Missie pushed the kettle to the center, then joined the girl.

"Nathan," she said, indicating the baby.

"Na-tan," the girl repeated.

Missie pointed to herself.

"Missie," she said.

"Mis-see." The girl smiled, then added, "Maria," pointing to herself.

"Maria."

There was so much Missie wanted to talk about, so much she wanted to ask. But all they could do was play with Nathan, smile at each other, and sip tea.

At last Maria indicated that she must go. Missie could hardly bear the thought of losing her. She needed her so much—the friendship of another woman. It made her think of her home, of her mother—and the thoughts of her mama made her think of all the precious times they had shared together.

"Wait," she said, "before you go, would it be all right for us to . . . to pray together?"

Maria shrugged, obviously not comprehending.

"Pray," Missie said, pointing to herself and to Maria and then folding her hands for prayer.

"Sí," said Maria, her face lighting up. "Sí." She knelt down beside her stool on the hard-packed earth of the soddy floor. Missie, too, knelt down.

"Dear God," Missie began, "thank you so much for sending Maria to me. Thank you that even though I can't talk with her, I can feel a friendship and warmth. May she be able to come again—soon—and may I be able to learn some of her words so that I can tell her how glad I am to have her. Thank you that we can pray together, and bless her now as she goes home—wherever home is for her. Amen."

Missie prepared to rise, but Maria's soft voice stopped her. Missie opened her eyes and saw her new friend with face upturned in prayer. Her folded hands grasped the beads that hung from her neck.

Maria's voice rose and fell, much like the gentle waters of the creek that ran by Missie's old home. Missie caught "Mis-see" and "Na-tan" in the flow of words and also recognized the "amen."

They rose together and smiled at each other. Missie's cheeks were wet. She had never shared prayer with someone of another language before, of another faith tradition. She only knew that this young woman, Maria, seemed to know Missie's God, and that by sharing these moments together in prayer, their spirits were uplifted and refreshed. Surely God himself had sent Maria. Missie stepped forward and gave her another warm embrace.

TWENTY-ONE

Willie's Return

Missie had struck off the twenty-first day of Willie's trip on her calendar, but still he had not come. There was no sight of dust or wagon on the northern hills, no sound of grinding wagon wheels. She kept his supper hot on the back of the stove, but the fresh biscuits cooled in spite of her efforts. She lit the lamp and tried to read. Her thoughts returned to the verse she had for so many months been clinging to with all her might. She turned in the Bible to read it again. She would not have had to look it up—she knew it by heart. But right then she needed the assurance she could find on the printed page. *Fear thou not; for I am with thee: be not dismayed; for I am thy God: I will strengthen thee; yea, I will help thee; yea, I will uphold thee with the right hand of my righteousness.*

Missie read the verse several times. Eventually she felt quiet enough in her spirit to blow out the lamp and go to bed.

As soon as she got out of bed the next day, she searched the distant hills for small dots that might mean riders, or small clouds that could mean dust from churning wheels and tramping hoofs. But only the glare of the rising sun met her anxious eyes. When dusk came, she was once more forced to give up her vigil. Again that night she read by lamplight and embraced the words of Isaiah 41:10. At length she crawled into bed beside her small son, softly repeating the words to herself in an effort to drive the disquiet from her heart.

The third day dawned, and Missie paced back and forth, scanning the hills for anything that moved. She prepared a third supper for an absent husband and tried to push away the uneasiness within her. *What if Willie doesn't come back?* The question finally demanded her attention, and her thoughts once more went to her mother and the ordeal she had faced when her Clem did not return.

Who was she to think such a thing could not happen to her? Her heart seemed to flutter and then stand still, flutter again and remain silent. Missie threw herself on the bed.

"Oh, God," she wept as she spoke the words aloud, "you know I've been reading and clinging to your Word, but I guess I haven't been believing it, God . . . not really, not down deep in my heart. Help me, Lord. Help me to believe it, to really believe, that no matter . . . no matter what happens, it's in your hands and for my *good*. God, I turn it all over to you . . . my life . . . my Willie . . . everything, dear Father. Help me to trust you with all that is mine."

Missie continued to sob softly until finally a deep sense of peace stole into her heart and gently stilled its wild beating.

She awakened much later to the thumping of hooves in the yard. She pulled herself up quickly and rushed to the window, expecting to see Willie's wagons. Instead, it was several strange horsemen milling about in the bright moonlight. Cookie was approaching them.

"It's happened," Missie whispered, her heart feeling as though it were being squeezed. "Something's happened to Willie." Her weak knees buckled beneath her and she sank onto a stool. "Oh, God, help me now . . . help me to trust you."

She laid her head on her arms on the table and steeled herself for the news that Cookie would bring. No tears came—only a dull, empty feeling.

It was Cookie's footsteps at her door. He called softly and she just as softly bid him enter. He stepped inside, with the moonlight washing over him. Missie knew he could not see her where she sat in the darkness.

"Mrs. LaHaye?"

"Yes."

"Jest thought ya might hear and wonder 'bout all the ruckus in the yard. The new hands thet yer husband hired have jest arrived. The wagons will be in tomorra."

Missie's pounding heart caught in her throat. The new hands! The wagons were a short distance behind them! Willie would be home tomorrow!

It took a moment for it all to sink in. She wanted to shout. She wanted to laugh. She wanted to throw herself on her bed and cry in pure thankfulness. Instead she said in a choked voice, "Thank you, Cookie. I *was* wondering."

When the door was closed and Cookie was gone, she put her head back down on her arms and sobbed out her pent-up feelings in great bursts of joy. "Thank you, God, thank you. Oh, thank you."

⁂

Missie never told Willie of her anxious days of waiting or of her traumatic nighttime experience. She was sure he would not understand. When the wagons pulled into the yard in the heat and the dust the following day, a calm and smiling Missie greeted her man. He had brought supplies, letters, news that could hardly keep.

Willie turned from Missie to give orders to the ranch hands, then followed her into their small house.

He held her close. "Oh, I've missed ya. I thought thet trail would *never* end. It jest seemed forever." He kissed her. "Did ya miss me—a little bit?" he teased.

"A little bit," Missie said, smiling to herself. "Yeah, a *little* bit," she repeated and returned his kiss.

Willie produced the letters, but even before Missie could read them, Willie had some news.

The preacher's wife had fallen and was laid up with a broken hip. Missie's heart went out to the poor woman.

Kathy Weiss had found herself a young man.

"Poor Henry!" cried Missie.

Willie smiled. "Poor Henry, nothin'. Do ya know, thet young rascal

Henry had us all fooled? He wasn't ever after Kathy—not a'tall. It was Melinda Emory, the young widow, right from the start. Only Henry had to wait fer a proper length of time before lettin' her know his feelin's."

"You're not fooling!" Missie spoke incredulously. "Melinda? Well, I'll be!"

"And," Willie went on, "Henry has gone so far as to get some land of his own right next to ours—and in a short while, we'll have neighbors."

Missie could hardly contain herself for joy. Melinda for a neighbor! Another woman she could see often and enjoy her company. She could scarcely wait.

But Willie also had some other big news. "And guess what? They're gonna build a railroad. An' they have it figured to put the main cattle-shippin' station jest eighteen or twenty miles southwest of us . . . maybe even a little closer . . . who knows fer sure? Ya know what thet means? A railroad, a town, people movin' in, connection with the East . . . before we know it, we'll have so many neighbors we'll be trippin' over each other."

Missie exclaimed, "Oh . . . oh," over and over, while amazement and happiness filled her eyes with tears. "Willie, when? When?"

Willie spoke calmly. "Well, I'm sure it won't be tomorra like. But they're workin' on the railroad fer sure . . . from the other end. It should git here within a couple years . . . maybe even next year, some say. An' as soon as the line is in, the people will follow for certain. Always happens thet way. Jest think! A railroad an' shipping station. What thet will mean to the ranchers! No more long cattle drives with heavy losses. Every beef thet gits safely to market means a lot of dollars in a cattleman's pocket." He picked her up and swung her around the room while Nathan watched from his bed, hoping to get in on the excitement, whatever it was.

"We've come at jest the right time, Missie," he said, putting her down after bumping into the table and bed. "Things have never looked better. From now on, every available parcel of land will be snapped up at a big price, an' the price of cattle is bound to go up, too.

"Silly little soddy," he said. "We're gonna git us thet house just as soon as we sell some of the herd next spring. Place ain't fit to live in."

"Oh, Willie," Missie chided—though secretly and silently she agreed with Willie's statement—"it's a home. We can eat, sleep, and keep dry here. That's not bad for starters."

Willie laughed as he hugged her, then went over to swing Nathan up in his arms. "How's the boy?"

"He's been good."

"No more onions?"

"Only a little now and then to flavor a meal."

Willie gazed at his son in his arms. "Look at 'im," he said softly. "He's gone an' growed by inches."

Willie cuddled him close and kissed the soft head of hair while Nathan squirmed. Missie blinked away happy tears.

"Got somethin' fer ya, boy," Willie said to his son. "An' it weren't near the trouble of yer mama's confounded chickens."

"My chickens!" Missie squealed. "Where are they?"

"Well, I hope by now the boys have 'em corralled inside thet wire fence. What a squawkin', complainin' lot they turned out to be!"

"How many?" Missie could barely control her excitement.

"Couple roosters an' eleven hens—an' I had me one awful time to gather up thet many. Folks out here seem to know better than to bother with chickens."

Missie accepted the teasing and hurried out to see her flock. Willie followed behind her with Nathan.

The men had just finished tacking up the wire mesh to poles they had pounded into the ground. As Henry finished hanging the gate that had quickly been built for the enclosure, the other two men turned and left shrugging their shoulders. Let someone else do the fussing with the blamed chickens—they had done more than their share in building the pen.

Willie passed Nathan to Missie and went to lift down the large crate. The chickens squawked and flapped as they were released, not appearing the least bit grateful to be set free. They were a sorry-looking lot, not at all like Marty's proud-strutting chickens back home. Missie wondered if she would ever be able to coax them to produce eggs for her family. One of the hens did not leave the crate. She had succumbed to the heat of the trail or the lice that inflicted her or perhaps some other malady. Willie said he would bury it later so it wouldn't draw any flies.

"Seems to me," he observed, "another good dose of louse powder might not hurt 'em any. I think we'll jest leave 'em outside—shut 'em out of their coop until I treat 'em again. I gave 'em all one good dustin' 'fore I loaded 'em. Left a trail of dead lice from Tettsford Junction to home."

Missie laughed but agreed. They did look like they could stand another good treatment of *something*.

"I'll do the dustin'," Willie said, "but from then on, they're all yers. Never was overfond of chickens, I must say."

Poor Willie. To bring the chickens had been a real ordeal, Missie realized. She looked at him and love filled her heart. Before she could stop herself, the feeling burst forth into words. "Willie," she said, "I love you . . . so much."

Willie dropped a chicken and turned to her, his expression full of his own feelings. "In thet case, Mrs. LaHaye, yer welcome to yer chickens."

⁓

Willie's surprise for his young son was a smart-looking half-grown pup. Nathan seemed to instinctively know it was for him, and his chubby hands reached for the fur while the dog licked his face.

"He'll be a big fella when he's full-grown, an' I thought him a good idea," Willie said as he held Nathan in a standing position by the dog. "He'll help to keep the coyotes away from yer chickens. An' ya never know," he said with a grin, "with thet railroad comin an' all those folks pourin' in, ya never know jest who might come callin'. I'd feel safer iffen ya had a good watchdog." He let Nathan sit down beside the puppy and stood to his feet.

Missie looked at the empty miles stretching before her and smiled at Willie's prediction of the crowded countryside. Suddenly she remembered she had not told Willie about her own news.

"Willie, I had a visitor—honest! A real live *woman*—though sometimes I feel I must have dreamed it. Oh, I wish she'd come back. We had the best visit, and we prayed together—"

"Where was she from?"

"I don't know."

"Ya didn't ask?"

Missie laughed. "I asked her lots of things that she didn't answer—or maybe *did* answer—I don't know . . . and then we just gave up and enjoyed each other."

Willie looked perplexed.

"She couldn't understand English . . . an' I couldn't understand whatever it was that she spoke," Missie tried to explain.

"Yet ya had ya a good visit?"

"Oh yes."

"And ya prayed together?"

Missie nodded in agreement.

"But ya couldn't understand a word the other spoke?"

"Not the words . . . but we could understand the *meaning*. She was really nice, Willie. And young, too. And, oh, I wish so often that she'd come back . . . that we could have tea, and play with Nathan, and laugh and pray together again."

Willie put a hand under her chin and gently lifted her face until he could look into her eyes.

"I didn't know ya were so lonesome," he said huskily. "Here I've been so busy an' so taken up with the spread an' the cows an' all. I never noticed or gave thought to jest how lonesome it'd be fer a woman all alone, without another female nowhere near.

"I shoulda taken ya into town with me, Missie. Given ya a chance to see the outside world again, to visit an' chat. I missed yer need, Missie, an' . . . an' ya never complain . . . jest let me go on makin' dumb mistakes right an' left. A sorry-looking bunch of cowpokes, a work-crazy husband, an' a baby who can't say more than 'goo' ain't much fer company. Yet ya never, never say a thing 'bout it. I love you, too, Missie . . . so very much." They stood for a long moment, arms entwined, until Nathan started to crawl through the dirt after his new playmate.

TWENTY-TWO

Afternoon Tea

While Nathan slept Missie left the house early the next morning to fetch water from the spring for her chickens. She was determined to have eggs for the breakfast table as soon as possible. Already it felt as if it would be a hot day, and she thought of the staleness of the air in their small house on such a day. Perhaps she should take Nathan to the shade bushes near the spring for the most oppressive part of the early afternoon.

She felt lighthearted and hummed as she walked, swinging the empty pail to and fro. Willie was home, she had heard news from dear friends, her strange new world was being enhanced—first with fresh milk, then with her bountiful garden, and now with chickens. It would soon be easy to prepare good meals. She and her family would be able to enjoy many of the things they had been accustomed to back east.

As Missie walked she reviewed parts of the letters she had received. She again felt a pang of sympathy for the misfortune of the preacher's wife. And Mrs. Taylorson! What a kind friend she had turned out to be. She had even sent a pair of tiny shoes to Nathan for when he began to walk—which wouldn't be long at the rate he was growing. Kathy's letter had been full of news of her young man. Seemed he was Samson,

Solomon, and the apostle John all rolled into one. Missie smiled. But the letter she had read and reread was the one from Melinda. Knowing that Melinda would one day—*soon,* she hoped—be near enough to be called a neighbor, was very special for Missie. Oh, how she wished Melinda were already here. Another winter in the soddy would be far more bearable with such a friend nearby.

Melinda had written much about the town of Tettsford and her activities with the school and the church. She described the lessening of her pain since the death of her husband, even though his memory still brought tears oftentimes. She also spoke of Henry, of his thoughtfulness, his manliness, and his faith.

Yes, Missie thought, *Henry truly is worthy of a woman like Melinda. They will make such delightful neighbors.*

Missie returned from the spring with the water for her chickens. She talked to them as she poured it into the trough and then portioned out the feed.

"And you better start laying very quickly," she threatened, "or you might find yourselves smothered in dumplings." The chickens fought for rights at the watering trough, paying no mind to Missie's speech.

"You're a motley-looking bunch," Missie said, laughing as she looked at the rather skinny, droopy birds, "but just you wait a week or two. We'll get some meat on those bones and get those feathers smoothed out and back where they belong. Right now you look like you're wearing half of them upside down."

She picked up her pail to hurry back to the house before Nathan would awaken and miss her.

As she rounded the corner of the cook shack, she found Willie and his new hands gathered for a get-acquainted session. The men lounged around in various positions. Some leaned against the sod walls; others squatted on the ground or lay propped up on an elbow. Apparently Willie had let the men know this was a time for "at ease." Cookie sat on his bench near his cook-shack door and was the first to notice Missie. Missie paused a moment to listen.

". . . an' as we'll all be livin' an' workin' together," Willie was saying, "I hope we'll feel free an' easy with one another. By now I'm sure you've all met Scottie, our foreman. Scottie knows all thet there is to know 'bout ranchin'. He'll be takin' over the matters connected with the herd. You'll take all orders from him, an' he'll be responsible to me. You are his concern, an' any requests or complaints thet ya might have are directed to him. If he can't take care of it, he'll see thet I hear 'bout it. He'll assign the shifts an' the jobs, accordin' as he sees fit. Cookie, here, will feed ya. He'll have yer chow waitin' fer ya at the same time each day. There'll always be fresh coffee on, fer those comin' an' goin'—even for those on the night shift."

Willie must have noticed Cookie's grin and turned to see Missie standing hesitantly. His eyes lit up.

"An' now fer the bright spot on this here ranch," he said, holding out his hand to her. "I want ya to meet my wife, Mrs. LaHaye."

Missie stepped forward shyly.

"Missie," Willie said, "here are the new riders. Scottie—the foreman." Missie looked into two very kind blue eyes, a twinkle just barely daring to show itself. Scottie looked as weathered and western as the hills that stood behind him. His bowlegged stance spoke of many years in the saddle. Missie felt confidence in Willie's choice of his second-in-command. Scottie, she felt sure, was one to be trusted.

He nodded slightly in acknowledgment of the introduction, his expression conveying, "If you need me, I'm here."

Missie's brief smile was a silent *Thank you.*

Willie moved on. "This here is Rusty." Missie's eyes traveled over a freckled face and a mop of unruly red hair. A wide grin greeted her.

He's no more than a kid, Missie thought. Her motherly heart wondered about this boy's mama and if she was somewhere worrying and praying for her son. She offered a warm smile.

"An' Smith," Willie continued. Missie turned to look into fierce black eyes in a sun-darkened face. His nod was barely perceptible, and his gaze dropped quickly to the ground. *I wonder,* Missie thought, *what happened to put all that bitterness into your soul.*

"An' Brady," Willie said. Missie looked into another pair of eyes. These were cold and calculating. They seemed too bold and even cruel, making her blush beneath the stare. She nodded quickly, then gave

Willie an imploring glance to move on. She could still feel those un-nerving eyes upon her.

"An' over here," Willie said, turning to the man who had risen from the ground to acknowledge the introduction, "is Lane."

Lane looked as if he would gladly have willed the earth to open up and swallow him. He started to look at Missie, changed his mind, and looked at the toes of his boots instead, a dark flush spreading steadily over his face. His hands sought something to do or somewhere to go but ended up only rubbing against his sides.

Missie smiled gently, hoping to put him at ease. Never had she seen a man so shy.

Turning from him to the group, she said, "Glad to have you all here at the Hanging W," addressing herself to Scottie in particular. "I know that I won't really be seeing that much of you—you having your work to do and me having mine. But should there ever be a need that my husband and I can help with, we'd be most happy to oblige." She shyly nodded to them all, a small smile crossing her lips. "Now I'd best get back to my baby," she said and turned to the house.

Scottie took over the meeting, and Willie walked to the soddy with Missie.

"Think I found out 'bout yer mysterious neighbor."

"Maria?"

"Yeah."

"How did you find out?"

"Scottie's already been out scoutin' the range. Says they're 'bout seven miles to the south of us. They're Mexican."

"Mexican?"

"Yep. The man speaks some English—but mostly Spanish. Prob'ly had him his own reasons fer strikin' out so far north."

"It couldn't be too serious a reason—it couldn't. I just know Maria would not marry a man who was trying to escape the law or—"

"'Course."

"Maybe they just wanted to be on their own—to make their own way. Lots of people feel that way, all hemmed in by . . ." Missie decided to let it drop. "And only seven miles?"

"Yep."

"That's not so far, is it, Willie? Just think! Our first neighbors—and so close. Why, I could even ride over and see her—if I knew the way," she finished lamely.

Willie laughed. "Yeah—iffen ya knew the way. An' iffen ya didn't have to ford a river to get there. An' iffen ya knew some Spanish. *Then* ya could make a visit. But I shouldn't joke. I promise I'll do my best to take you over to our new neighbors. In the meantime, why don't ya learn a little Spanish? It would be a real nice surprise for Maria."

"But how can I?"

"Cookie. Cookie knows 'bout everything there is to say in the Spanish tongue. He worked fer a Spanish family when he was little more'n a kid. I got the feelin' when I heard him talk 'bout 'em he kinda wishes thet he'd stayed with 'em—but at the time he was young an' had the wander bug. He's 'bout crossed the whole continent on horseback since, it seems, workin' on spreads as he's traveled."

"Oh," said Missie, alarmed. "I do hope he won't decide to leave us. I—"

"Not much chance of thet. He's not as young as he used to be, nor as adventurous, either. An' I'm thinkin' thet he don't sit a horse near as comfortable since he had his fall."

"And he knows Spanish?"

"He sure does. Mind ya, though," Willie teased some more, "thet he doesn't teach ya *all* the words he knows. Some of 'em ain't very ladylike."

"Do you think he would—*teach* me, I mean?"

"I'm sure he'd be glad for an excuse to git off his bad leg occasionally."

⁂

So Missie timidly approached Cookie about the possibility of Spanish lessons. He was delighted to help out, and they began with their first lesson down by the spring that very day. She had only advanced as far as *buenos días* and *adiós* when Maria arrived again.

Maria cuddled Nathan, all the time directing a steady stream of flowing Spanish, first to the baby and then to Missie. When Missie smiled and nodded, Maria's Spanish flowed even more rapidly. At length Missie could bear it no longer.

"Wait," she said to Maria, gesturing with her hands. "Don't go away—I'll be right back. You just sit right down and hug my baby. I'm going to get us both some help."

Missie hurried out the door, realizing as she ran to the cook shack that Maria, like herself, had not understood one word of the exchange.

"Cookie," Missie panted out, her voice pleading, "would you mind, please . . . please, would you have tea . . . with two ladies?"

Cookie's eyes grew round with dismay.

"Oh, please," Missie begged. "Maria has come again, and I can't understand her Spanish—not one word except 'buenos días.' And she can't understand me. And we're just dying to say something to each other. Please, could you just this once . . . please? I'll make you coffee if you prefer," Missie quickly promised.

Cookie's good-natured face crinkled into a begrudging smile. He wiped his hands on his greasy apron, which he removed and cast aside.

"Iffen it means thet much," he agreed.

"Oh, it does, it does."

"Fer a few minutes," Cookie amended. "Gotta git back to the steak I'm poundin'. But I can spare a few minutes. An' I reckon I can pass up the coffee an' drink yer tea—long as it ain't in one a' them fancy little cups."

Missie hurried with him to the sod house.

"Maria," she called triumphantly as they approached. "Here's Cookie! He knows Spanish!" When Cookie turned to Maria with a fluent welcome in her own tongue, Maria clasped her hands with a merry laugh, and silvery-sounding Spanish arced between them.

Cookie turned to Missie and shrugged. "She says this is gonna be more fun than a fiesta," he said, but the look in his own eyes still indicated doubt. Missie poured his tea into a big mug and passed him some fresh bread and butter.

Cookie fell into the spirit of the visit and soon seemed to be enjoying his time at the tea party almost as much as the two young women. Missie was careful to keep his mug of tea replenished and to make sure the bread was within his reach. He didn't seem to mind even their female talk, which he had to translate back and forth.

When Maria prepared to go, the two truly did feel like *neighbors*. Missie gave her promise, through Cookie, that Willie would bring her over sometime soon.

"Cookie *también*?" Maria teased, and Missie needed no translation. They both laughed as Cookie muttered and grinned.

"I know you're busy, Cookie," Missie said as he bounced little Nathan on his knee, "and I thank you so much for taking the time. It's all right. We'll let you go now."

Cookie put Nathan down and declared he had to get back to supper fixings. But Missie noticed he took his time about leaving.

"*Muchas gracias,*" Maria added her thanks, and Cookie shuffled off to return to his cook shack.

Maria's next comment came with actions rather than words, and Missie enthusiastically nodded her agreement to pray together.

Again the two young women—of different races, different cultures, different religious backgrounds—knelt together in the small kitchen and poured out their hearts to the one true God who could hear in any language. Missie could tell that Maria's need and longing for fellowship in the faith was as real and deep as her own.

Missie prayed, "Please, dear God, may I quickly learn enough of Maria's Spanish to be able to share with her about matters of faith, about the life I have received through the death and life of your Son. I long so much to talk about you, your love and forgiveness, and to study the Bible together. Help me, God, to learn Spanish soon." Missie added one more thought, "And dear God, help Cookie to know the right words to teach me."

TWENTY-THREE

Another Winter Ahead

Missie and Willie made plans for the promised trip to their new neighbors, Maria and Juan, two weeks after Maria's last visit. Missie tried to cajole Cookie into accompanying them, but Scottie, who could also speak a little Spanish, went with them instead. When the day came for the trip, Missie felt far more inclined to ride her horse than travel in a bumpy wagon. Little Nathan was lifted up to share his father's saddle, and the four started off, Scottie setting a leisurely pace in spite of Missie's impatience to reach their destination.

The fording of the river gave Missie some inner butterflies, and she saw again in her mind's eye the Emorys' bobbing, tilting wagon and the plunging terror-stricken horses. But once her horse was in and swimming strongly, Missie realized the current was not that swift.

They found Juan and Maria in a sprawling stone house that was cool and comfortable. Missie decided right away that she would prefer stone to any other available material. Juan was pleased to show Willie around and explain the process of building such a home. It wasn't the style of house Missie had been used to, but it was cool against the heat of the day and seemed so spacious after their small soddy. Juan promised his help when the day arrived for Willie to begin the building.

The four took their leave well before dark. Mountain rains had swollen the river waters, and Scottie declared them to be higher than normal for the time of year. And even though it was not considered dangerous, he wanted to ford the river in full daylight.

Maria and Missie told each other there was great comfort in knowing another woman lived within visiting distance.

When they reached home, Willie took Missie's horse and passed Nathan to her. Missie lingered outside, enjoying the cool of the late afternoon.

Willie turned and called back to her, "Hold supper a bit, will ya? I'm gonna ride on up to the upper spring an' see iffen it's still flowin' enough fer the cattle over thet way. I should be back in an hour or two."

Missie agreed, glad for the extra time before lighting the fire in the stove. She placed Nathan on the ground, guiding his tottering steps toward their small home. How shabby and tiny it looked compared to Maria's. Missie would be so thankful to have more room, a floor for rugs, and windows big enough from which to hang curtains. She heard Willie's horse leave the yard as she laid Nathan down for a much-needed nap. He was sound asleep before Missie had completed a row on the sock she was knitting.

She looked up in surprise at a knock on the door. Maybe Henry had found time for a chat. She hadn't seen him since their Sunday "church" time. She stepped to the door and opened it, fully expecting Henry—or Cookie. But it was Brady. Missie fidgeted beneath the smile he tried on her and the intensity of his eyes.

"Oh . . ." she began, but he moved past her and entered the room. Missie felt the air tighten around her.

"'Scuse me fer intrudin', ma'am," he said, but there was no apology in his voice. "I thought maybe you bein' a woman thet ya could help me out some."

Missie remembered her lightly spoken promise of help if there was a need. A strange fluttery feeling made her wish she hadn't been so quick to speak. She did not move from the door.

"I seem to have picked up a sliver in my finger here, an' do ya know, there's not one of those mangy ol' cowpokes thet has 'em a needle."

"Oh," Missie said again, and then life returned to her limbs. "Oh yes . . . I have needles. Of course." Missie moved from the open door to her sewing basket and heard the door close behind her.

She fumbled with a package of needles and finally disengaged one she thought was the proper size. As she rummaged, her mind whirled. *What is Brady doing here? At this hour of the day all hands are normally busy checking cattle, mending fences, fixing gear—something. I haven't even noticed Cookie about—oh yes, I did. As we rode up, Cookie was heading for the spring with two water pails.*

She turned with the needle to find Brady standing close behind her.

"Here you are," she said, trying to keep her voice steady. But he didn't take the needle extended to him.

"I'm afraid, ma'am, thet I'll have to ask you to be kind enough to work thet little bit of a tool fer me. My hands never were any good with anything thet size."

"Me?" Missie asked dumbly, thinking there was no way she was going to bend her head and work over this man's hand as she held it in her own. She could almost feel his breath upon her now in the closeness of the small room.

"I'm sorry," she said evenly. "You'll have to do it yourself—or else ask Cookie to help you."

"Now, ma'am," the cowboy murmured, inching closer. Even in the dimness of the soddy, Missie could see his eyes seem to darken. "Don't tell me yer man-shy?"

He reached a hand out to touch her arm and Missie stepped backward, feeling the side of the bed as she bumped up against it. She wanted to scream, but her throat tightened in a dryness that she had never felt before. She thought her knees were going to give way beneath her. A short but fervent prayer welled up within her. *Oh, God, strengthen me, help me, uphold me as you promised.*

Then the door swung open. "Mrs. LaHaye?" There had been no knock, but there stood Scottie. "The boss home?"

You know he's not, Missie responded to herself. *You heard him say he was going to the upper spring.*

Instead, she said nothing. She shut her eyes to muster enough strength to remain on her feet.

"Brady?" said the foreman as though surprised. "Got those fences checked already?"

Brady twisted around, his face full of anger. Without a word he slammed out through the door. Scottie pulled out a stool for Missie. She accepted it without speaking. Then he walked to the pail and handed her a small dipper of water. She was surprised to find she could still swallow.

"Brady had himself a problem, ma'am?" Scottie asked lightly, but Missie noted that his voice was edged with steel.

"A sliver . . . in his hand."

"You fix it?"

She looked down at the needle she still held in her trembling hand and shook her head. "I told him he'd have to do it himself . . . or get Cookie."

"Did he bother you?"

"No," Missie replied shakily, "no, but something about him frightens me. I only know . . ." She swallowed again. "Here," she said, holding out the needle, "would you give it to him?"

"That's all right, ma'am. Keep yer needle. I'll look after Brady." Then he was gone, gently closing the door behind him.

Missie sat for some time before she felt her legs strong enough to stand. At length she was able to stir herself. She went over to lay a trembling hand on her sleeping son and whisper, "Thank you, Lord, for protecting us." She turned to build a fire for preparing Willie's supper.

She said nothing to Willie that night—not yet. But she vowed to keep an eye out for Brady. She'd put some kind of lock on the inside of the door if she had to. There was no way that man would enter her house again.

The next morning as she left the house to go to the spring for water, she glanced about furtively. *How dreadful not to feel safe in one's own yard,* she thought. Then she heard voices coming from the side of the bunkhouse. One was Willie's voice, and with the words came renewed courage for Missie.

"Henry says thet Brady drew his pay."

"Yep," Scottie replied.

"Not happy ridin' fer me?"

"He didn't say nothin' 'bout bein' unhappy."

"But he quit?"

"Nope." And after a pause, "I fired 'im."

"Thought he was known to be *good* with cattle." Willie's voice seemed to suggest a shrug of his shoulders as though he couldn't quite understand the situation, but Scottie was in charge where the cowhands were concerned.

"Reckon he was." Scottie was noncommittal.

"Reckon you had yer reasons," Willie said.

"Yeah," Scottie said softly, "reckon I did."

Missie continued on her way to the spring. Her world suddenly belonged to her again—her garden, her chickens, her house. She could count on Willie's men to care not only for his cattle but to care for her and Nathan, as well. And with Willie's men and her heavenly Father, she really had no need to worry. None at all.

⁂

Missie placed a chair in the shade of the sod house and continued her work on a pair of trousers for Nathan. His dog lay nearby, already grown almost to full size. The black mongrel showed some intelligence, and he was ever so gentle with young Nathan. For the gentleness, Missie allowed him her devotion.

It was cool in the evenings now, and Missie was thankful for the relief from the intense summer heat. For many days she had been busy canning the produce from her garden. As she watched it stack up around her, she began to wonder where she would keep it from freezing over the long winter. Unless she could persuade Willie to dig a root cellar, they would have to bury the food in the hay in the barn. Missie wished again for a new bigger house, but she held her tongue. She knew it would be hers as soon as Willie was able.

She looked up from her work and saw Henry approaching. "Hi, stranger," she teased. "I'd begun to wonder if you were still riding for this outfit. I haven't seen you for so long."

"It's this boss I got," Henry responded. "Don't know nothin' but work, work, work!"

Missie laughed.

"But then," Henry added, "guess he can't be all bad. He's promised me two weeks off."

"Really? You're going to make a trip?"

Henry flushed. "I sure am," he offered. "Jest as fast as ol' Flint can carry me. Seems like downright years since I last saw—"

"I'm so happy for you and Melinda," Missie said. "She must be missing you, too, something awful."

"I sure hope so," Henry said. "Iffen she misses me half as much . . ." He let the sentence hang.

"Have you set a date?" Missie asked. "Or am I being nosy?"

"Don't mind yer interest none. An' no, not yet. Sure wish thet we could, but it depends."

"On what?"

"On how soon I can build me a house."

"With a little help, you can have a house up in a few days."

"I mean a *house*, Missie, not a soddy."

Missie was surprised at the intensity of Henry's reply.

"I agree," she said carefully, "that there's not much inviting about a soddy, but it can be a home—be it ever so simple and confining."

"I'd never ask Melinda to live in such conditions—never," Henry said heatedly. "Don't you think thet I saw the look in yer eyes when ya spotted the dirt floor, the dingy windows, the crowded—"

"Henry," Missie interrupted softly but steadily, "answer me honestly. Do you still see that look there now? That look of surprise, of hurt, of disappointment? Is it still there?"

Henry paused to look into her face, then shook his head. "No," he said, "I guess not. You've done well, Missie. Really great . . . an' I've admired ya fer it. A girl like you . . . leavin' what ya had, an' comin' way out here to this. I've truly admired ya. But, beggin' yer pardon . . . I won't ask thet of Melinda."

"An' I respect you for your thoughtfulness concerning her, Henry. But you should know something." Missie stopped to choose her words.

"Henry, I want you to know that I'd far sooner share this little one-room dirt dwelling with Willie than to live in the world's fanciest big white house without him. And I mean that, Henry."

Henry chuckled softly, but his expression held wonder.

"You women are strange creatures indeed," he said. "It's a marvel we men ever succeed in understandin' ya a'tall. But I do thank the good Lord fer makin' ya the way ya are." He paused to look again into her face. "Ya really do mean thet, don't ya?"

"I really do," Missie said. And deep in her heart she marveled at just how much she meant it. The glory of that truth somehow unshackled her spirit from the small, shabby little dwelling, to soar far above it in the strength of her love for Willie. Somehow, the long, unwelcome winter ahead did not look so frightening now, even though she still faced being shut away inside the one confining room. She and Willie and Nathan might be crowded together, but they were bundled comfortably in the blanket of love.

TWENTY-FOUR

Sundays

When Henry returned from visiting his Melinda, Missie sensed about him a new depth of loneliness. She wondered if he was silently realizing that perhaps love could have seen them through a winter in a little sod house, but Henry never admitted as much. He missed Melinda—that was very evident. He often found excuses to drop by the soddy and chat or play with Nathan to help fill the lonely hours in between work.

Missie noticed that Henry and the young Rusty seemed to enjoy each other's company and often rode out together. Missie knew Scottie wisely tried to team up the men who worked well together. In the evenings in the bunkhouse, Henry was teaching Rusty to strum his guitar. The two young cowboys spent many hours singing range songs and old hymns.

One Sunday as Willie, Missie, and Henry sat talking after the three of them had their usual time of Bible reading, hymn singing, and prayer, they discussed the coming railroad, the people it would bring, future shops, schools, and even a doctor.

Then Willie said with deep feeling, "Ya know what I long fer most? A church. I jest ache sometimes to gather with a larger group of believers and sing an' pray an' read the Word. And hear a real sermon. It seems like so long . . . what I wouldn't give fer jest one Sunday back home."

Missie felt her eyes become misty. A Sunday back home meant Pa with his baritone voice expressing his praise, Ma in her quiet, confident manner joining in. It meant Clare and Arnie, Ellie and little Luke gathered around. It meant Nandry and Clae and their families. Missie wondered if there were more members to those families by now, how tall Clare was, if Arnie still teased Ellie, and if everyone outdid each other spoiling little Luke. She wondered if her mother Marty still looked west each night and breathed a prayer for her faraway little girl, and if Pa still lifted down the family Bible and read with a steady, assured voice the promises of God. *Are they all well . . . my family?* If only there was some way to span the miles, as Willie had put it, to spend a Sunday at home.

Missie blinked away her tears and came back to the reality of their small home.

"It would be so good to hear the Word with others," Willie was saying. "I'll be awful glad when we have enough neighbors to have our own little church and a preacher."

Then Willie was looking around the room, seeming to size it up. "Remember how we all managed to crowd in here fer Christmas?"

"Yeah, we were toe to toe—but we fit," Missie laughed.

"Well, we can fit again," Willie said. "Boy, have I been dumb!"

He reached for his hat. "I'm gonna go find the rest of our *congregation*," and he ducked quickly through the door.

And so it was that all the hands working on the Hanging W Ranch were invited to share Sunday services in the little sod house.

That next Sunday only Rusty came with Henry, but what a time they had singing the old hymns, accompanied by Henry's guitar, and reading the Scriptures together. The next Sunday it was Henry and Rusty again.

A couple of Sundays later, Cookie hobbled in, clearing his throat and looking a bit embarrassed. He'd been heard to say that "religion was fer the weak and fer women."

In spite of ridicule from the hardened Smith (who, whenever he was asked his full name snapped, "It's Smith—jest Smith," making Missie wonder if he truly had a claim to even that), the weeks passed with attendance gradually growing. By Christmas Sunday, Smith was the only holdout. He saddled his horse and rode away into the quietness of the snow-covered hills. Missie prayed that God might somehow reach his cold, unhappy heart.

After their service together, Missie managed to serve them a special Christmas dinner. She even had been tempted to sacrifice two of her chickens for the occasion but could not bring herself to do so. She was getting four or five eggs a day, and as she still hadn't determined who were the producers and who were the sluggards, she granted them all extended life, lest she slaughter the wrong ones.

With her milk, eggs, and a few hoarded raisins, she made some bread pudding. Even those who did not care for the chickens themselves did not scorn what the hens were able to produce. They smacked their lips in appreciation as they went back for seconds.

Nathan thoroughly enjoyed the whole crowded celebration. He shook his head sadly when the last figure left the small soddy. "Aw gone," he sighed, "Aw gone."

After having taken the plunge for Christmas Sunday, the last of the men who'd been reluctant about "religion" continued to join the regular Sunday services. Unless duty called them away, at the appointed time of two o'clock they all, except for Smith, entered the house, dusting the snow from their coats with their hats and stamping their boots. Then they quietly found places to sit for the short time of singing, Bible reading, and prayer.

Missie prayed for Rusty, the easygoing, openhearted young boy of the group. He eagerly sang the old hymns and listened attentively as the Scripture was read. She hoped his heart was being touched by the truth.

But it was the shy, backward Lane who knocked on their door one evening and mumbled in an embarrassed voice, "Is the boss in?"

Missie welcomed him in, and he stood facing Willie, nervously twisting his hat in his hand.

"I wondered, boss, iffen y'all wouldn't mind . . . iffen you'd . . ." He cleared his throat. "I don't have much understandin' 'bout the things of the Bible. Could ya . . . would ya sorta go over it again . . . slow like, iffen ya don't mind?"

So Lane was invited to sit down at the table, and by the light of the flickering lamp, with fresh cups of coffee before them, he and Willie again went over the words of the Book while Missie silently prayed.

"'If thou shalt confess with thy mouth the Lord Jesus,'" read Willie, "'and shalt believe in thine heart that God hath raised him from the dead, thou shalt be saved.'"

Missie was sitting off to the side, her hands finding jobs to do for which she needed little light. She was praying that God would bless His Word and open the understanding of the young man.

Her heart was full. God had been good to Willie and her. And He had given them their own unique, and very special, *congregation*.

⸎

Missie's second winter in the soddy was nearing its end.

The winds seemed to be abating, and she even dared to hope for an early thaw. Already she was mentally planning her garden, though she knew full well that it would be weeks before she could actually do the planting. This year, she promised herself, she would listen to Willie and not rush the season. But she wondered if her logic could hold her eagerness in check.

This spring she hoped to have some setting hens, as well. Though she still made use of her daily egg supply, she had been holding some back each day for the sittings. A spring calf was due to Ginger, one of their two milk cows. In no way could Willie's anticipation of the dozens of range calves expected compare to Missie's excitement for that one calf that would be born to the cow in the barn. Pansy was still milked daily, although her supply was running low. It would soon be time for her to take a rest from the daily production and wait for her calf that was yet some months away.

And then there was the promised house to look forward to! Missie had fretted about it, fearing that the money shouldn't be spent on one for an additional year. But Willie was determined that the start be made on their stone home as soon as possible. A good share of the outer material was almost free, he assured her, and the labor would be cheap.

With Scottie to oversee the activities of the ranch, Willie would be free to get on with the building. Juan also had promised him two helpers who had a great deal of experience with stone buildings. Willie sat at night at the small table, and he and Missie talked over plans for the house. The low rambling stone building would be built with the main living area in the middle, the kitchen and dining area located in the left wing and the bedrooms in the right. A shaded porch and small courtyard would provide a good spot for Missie to sit and do handwork while young Nathan enjoyed the out-of-doors. Willie sketched out the plans, then redrew them, over and over. Missie tried to restrain herself, not daring to let the hope become too real lest something happen to prevent it.

But she did her share of dreaming.

Oh, the fun she would have unpacking all their stored things—the proper-sized stove, the sewing machine, the rugs, the curtains, the fancy dishes. At times she thought she would burst in her eagerness.

Henry had decided that with the spring, he also would do some building. He had bought the land bordering Willie's and had plans to put his house just as close to the LaHayes' home as he could, so it would be convenient for the women to visit and do things together. Missie could scarcely wait for Melinda to arrive.

Willie agreed to sell Henry fifty head of cattle, with whatever calves were at heel, so Henry could get a start on his own spread. This would also give Willie some cash for the new house. If Scottie disapproved of a cattleman making sales of stock in the spring, he did not say so. He no doubt knew the transaction would assist both men in realizing their dreams.

Rusty decided to go to work on Henry's spread, so Scottie needed to find two more hands for the Hanging W. He assured Willie he would take his time and choose carefully.

Scottie reported that the outlying ranches were already planning a fall trail drive to move their cattle to the market. If Willie wanted to, he could send as many head of cattle as he wished, along with a designated number of riders. Willie decided he'd hold his herd that year unless unexpected expenses demanded more cash. Everyone was hopeful that before another fall rolled around, the railroad would have made its promised appearance. This would eliminate the costly, time-consuming, wearying trail drive.

This winter's losses seemed to be low, and the calf crop looked good. As each count came in, Missie's hopes for the new home mounted. She anticipated the summer before her, and even the thought of the approaching heat was not able to shrivel her spirits. She gazed across the endless hills. She and Willie had lived in the area such a short time and already they were seeing changes—and the future promised many more. Would they all come true—the dreams, the plans? Whatever the outcome, things were going well now. She was sure, for the first time, that if they really needed to, they could carry on indefinitely just as they had been living.

She decided that as soon as Nathan woke from his nap, she'd ride up to the top of the hill for a look at the distant mountains. She was wondering what color they would appear on this bright springlike morning.

Cookie appeared at the cook-shack door carrying a dishpan. He tossed the water carelessly to the side of the path and stopped to look up at the sky. Missie wondered if he also was willing spring to come.

TWENTY-FIVE

Nathan

Willie went to check the horses before retiring while Missie finished the dishes and prepared Nathan for bed.

"You are getting so big," she told the little boy. "Soon you aren't going to fit in that wee bed anymore. Your pa is going to have to make you a bigger one."

Nathan smiled. "Big boy."

Missie kissed his chubby cheeks. "Big boy, all right. You are Mama's big boy."

Nathan returned her kiss in his damply affectionate fashion.

"Now," Missie said, "let's say our prayers."

Missie prayed, stopping often to let Nathan try to repeat her words. He finished with a hearty "'men." As Missie tucked him into bed, she noticed his breathing sounded heavier than usual.

"I do hope you're not coming down with a cold," she told him. "Won't be long now until the days will be nice and sunny and warm, and you can go outside to play as much as you like."

"Doggie?"

"Sure, you can play with your doggie. You always think of 'doggie' when I talk about outside, don't you? Well, soon now you can be out with Max as much as you want to."

Nathan seemed to like the idea.

Missie pulled the blanket up under his chin and kissed him again, then began to refill the lamp with oil. Willie might wish to work on the house plans again.

Willie returned and, as Missie expected, pulled his stool up to the table. He still wasn't sure the entrance to the house was in the most convenient place. He tried various drawings, first shifting it one way and then the other. Missie watched and made suggestions while she darned a sock. Willie finally decided his first choice had been the right one.

The next day's branding was bound to be long and tiring, and they went to bed early.

Missie lay for a few moments listening to Nathan's breathing, then Willie's snoring drowned out the sound. She felt a tightness in her stomach as she turned over to try to go to sleep but couldn't decide just why.

Missie wasn't sure who awakened first, she or Willie. But she suddenly realized she was sitting upright in bed, a feeling of panic making the blood pound in her ears. Already Willie was springing from the bed.

"What is it?" Missie called in the darkness.

"It's Nathan! He's chokin' somethin' awful."

Missie heard it then—the rattling gasp for breath.

"Oh, dear God, no!" she cried and stumbled out of bed after Willie.

"Light the lamp," Willie ordered, already reaching for the small boy.

Missie hurried to fetch it, her bare feet feeling the coolness of the dirt floor.

"What is it? What's the matter with him, Willie?"

"Was he okay when ya put him to bed?"

"He was a little raspy sounding, but nothing like this. Oh, Lord, what can we do? What is it, Willie?" Missie cried, her heart tearing at each ragged breath of her baby.

No doctor! her mind screamed with each wild beat. No doctor! Not for miles and miles! No help anywhere near here!

"Have you ever seen this before in any of yer family?" Willie asked frantically.

"Never!" replied Missie, the tears overflowing. "Never! I've no idea what it might be. Unless—could it be pneumonia? He can't breathe." *Oh, dear God, we need you now,* her heart cried. *Little Nathan Isaiah needs you now. Please, dear God, show us what to do, or send us some help—someone who knows. Please, God.*

"Have ya some medicine?" implored Willie. "Some things from yer ma? Where do ya keep it, Missie?"

"All I ever brought in were the first-aid supplies. There's more still stored in the barn, though. I've never unpacked it—never needed it—"

"I'll git it—ya stay and keep 'im warm, Missie."

"No, Willie, you wouldn't know the box—it'll take you too long to find it. I'll go, I know just where it is."

Missie pulled on her boots and shoved her arms into the sleeves of Willie's coat, then quickly lit another lantern. She ran from the house, the mud and slush from the spring puddles splashing on her bare legs.

"Oh, heavenly Father," her prayers continued aloud as she gasped for breath, "please help us. We don't have a doctor. We don't even have a neighbor near. We don't know what to do. Please help us, God. I couldn't bear to lose him. I just couldn't, God." The tears poured down her cheeks.

She found the box of medicines quickly enough and ran with it back to the house, still pleading, "Oh, please, God, please save my baby."

As she neared the soddy she could see inside through the tiny window. Willie stood with the baby in his arms. He was praying. Missie saw his tears and the anguish on his face.

"Oh, dear God," she prayed, coming to a sudden stop. "It's Willie's *son,* his pride and joy, God. If you must take our baby . . . be with my Willie. Give him the strength to bear it, God. He loves his boy so much. Oh, dear God, please help us, please, please help us . . . if only someone knew. . . ." She tried to silence her sobs as she hurried into the house.

She placed the wooden box on the table. Without removing the heavy coat, she frantically clawed at the lid with a hammer from a peg near the door. The lid came loose with a loud squeak. She rummaged through the medicines, having no idea what she should be looking for.

Willie paced the floor, holding young Nathan upright in an effort to ease his troubled breathing. Suddenly there was a "hullo" outside the door, and without even waiting for a reply, Cookie walked in.

He did not ask questions. His eyes and ears must have already taken in the answers because he announced, "Croup!" in a loud voice.

"What?" Willie exclaimed.

"Croup."

"You know what it is?"

"Sure do. Thet breathin'—thet's croup."

"Can you . . . ?" Missie was afraid to ask.

"Can sure try. Git the fire goin'. Make it as hot as ya can and git some water boilin' fast."

Willie handed the struggling baby to Missie and hurried to comply. He filled the stove with cow chips and soaked them with fuel from the lamp. A brisk fire was soon blazing. Willie set the kettle directly over the flame, though it still seemed to take forever to boil.

Cookie placed a stool in the middle of the room.

"Git me a blanket."

Willie whipped a blanket from their bed.

"Now we need a basin fer the water."

Willie pulled the dishpan from its hook.

Cookie busily dug through the medicines Missie had strewn across the table. He carefully read the labels that had been placed on each one by Missie's mother.

"This oughta do," Cookie said. "Got a spoon?"

Willie handed him one and Cookie poured out a large helping of the ointment and dumped it into the basin. The water finally boiling, Cookie poured it into the pan and held out his arms for the baby. Missie was reluctant, but Cookie seemed to be their only hope. She passed over their beloved son.

"Put some more water on and keep thet fire goin'," Cookie ordered and sat down on the stool. "Now push thet basin over here, an' toss thet blanket over the both of us. We gotta have us a good steam bath."

They covered the two and then waited silently. Willie poked at the fire, and Missie paced the floor in the small space left to her, praying and listening painfully to Nathan's choking, rasping efforts to breathe.

The minutes ticked by. From beneath the heavy blanket came Cookie's voice, startling both Willie and Missie.

"Thet other water boilin' yet?"

It was.

"Pull out this here basin an' change the water. Put in another spoonful of the medicine, too."

It was done, and Willie pushed the steaming pan back under the blanket tent, being careful not to release the buildup of steam already trapped within.

Again Missie paced and prayed while Willie poked at the fire and prayed. He stuffed in another chip every time he could possibly make one fit. The room was becoming unbearably hot.

Nathan began to fuss. *Is he worse?* Further panic seized Missie.

"Good sign," Cookie called out. "Before, he was too busy fightin' fer breath to bother to fight the steam. His breathin' seems to be easin' some."

It has, Missie thought with wild joy. *He's not choking nearly as much.* Her tears began to fall as she repeated softly to herself, "'Fear thou not; for I am with thee: be not dismayed; for I am thy God: I will strengthen thee; yea, I will help thee . . .'" Missie could go no further. Sobs of thankfulness were crowding out all other thoughts. "Oh, dear God, thank you, thank you."

Willie made another change of water, passing it to Cookie beneath the blanket. Nathan stopped fussing and his breathing steadily improved.

"He's asleep now," Cookie announced in a loud whisper. "He seems able ta breathe without too much strugglin'."

Missie's arms ached to hold her baby, but Cookie kept him under the blanket.

The first streaks of dawn were reaching their golden fingers toward the eastern hills before Cookie ventured to lift the blanket from his head.

"Put on the coffeepot, would ya, missus?" was his only comment.

Willie reached to take away the blanket and move the basin.

Missie woodenly filled the coffeepot and put it on the stove. She then turned to Cookie, who was handing the sleeping baby to his father.

"Put him back to bed now," he said, then added slowly, "This might come again fer a night or two, but iffen yer watchin' fer it, ya should be able to ward it off. In a few nights' time he should be over it. Croup always hits like thet—in the dead of night, scarin' one half to death. The steamin' helps."

Missie looked at the little man. He spoke quietly, matter-of-factly, as though he were used to working miracles. His body appeared limp, his clothes soaked with steam and perspiration, his wispy hair clinging wetly against his scalp. His face was drained and white, and glistened with moisture in the early morning light. Yet Missie's heart cried out that he was truly the most beautiful person she had ever seen.

She crossed the room and reached out to gently touch his soft, stubbled face. "Cookie Adams," she said, tears and laughter in her voice, "you can't fool me—not for a minute. You're no grouchy, hard-riding ole cowpoke at all. You're a visiting *angel*."

TWENTY-SIX

Love Finds a Home

Missie finally planted her garden and set her hens. Green things soon appeared and so did soft, fluffy yellow chicks—eighteen of them. Missie rejoiced, thinking ahead to leafy vegetables and fried chicken. Even Willie admitted that her idea of raising chickens was not such a bad one after all. The cow calved, a fine young heifer. Missie's milk supply was assured for many months ahead.

Willie, with the instructions of Juan and his men to guide him, began the work on the house, just a few yards east of the soddy. Day after day Missie watched excitedly as it took shape.

Henry had left for his own nearby ranch. Missie missed him and the redheaded Rusty. She was always glad to welcome them back for a visit or a meal. Henry and Rusty still joined them for their gathering each Sunday, and Missie and Willie were glad to have them. She wasn't sure yet how Willie's two new hands felt about working on a spread where the boss had Sunday singsongs and Bible reading. So far, they had chosen to follow Smith's lead and stay away from such goings-on.

Willie took time from his house building to ride over to Juan's for a meeting of cattlemen. Missie itched to go along, but she knew that chatting women and a business meeting of the men might not mix too well.

She contented herself with plans for a visit on some future day, when she and Maria could enjoy each other's company without interruption. Maria's English was improving even faster than Missie's Spanish, and the two young women spent much of their infrequent visits laughing at each other's mistakes and celebrating new levels of communication.

When Willie returned from the meeting, he was bursting with news. A group of men had been in to stake out a site for the train station, he told Missie. Land already was sold for a general store. He was certain that other buildings would soon follow. And the best news was that the station would be only fifteen miles away! An easy trip in one day! No more two-week supply trips to Tettsford Junction. The first train was due to come chugging in during early spring of the following year.

The thought nearly took Missie's breath away. To have supplies come in so close, to be able to make a trip to town, to greet people and walk on sidewalks—it was all too overwhelming to comprehend.

"Sure, it'll take time—but it'll all come," Willie declared. "An' guess what else? Thet there train station is gonna be more'n jest a cattle-shippin' place. It's gonna have a post office, too. We'll be able to mail letters right here an' git answers back from our folks."

Missie caught her breath. Just to be able to write home to her mama and pa! To be able to tell them of Nathan's progress, of her new house, of Cookie—their faithful old ranch hand sent to them by God himself, though Cookie didn't realize that yet—of her chickens, her garden. Oh, how she wanted to tell them everything, to pour it all out on paper, letting them know and feel that she was doing just fine. And to get back an answer from them assuring her that they were all well. She tried to imagine their first letter. It might tell her that Luke was almost a man now, that Ellie had herself a beau, that Clare was getting set up to go farming on his own, and that Arnie was busy working the plow for Pa. She wanted to hear that the apple trees were in blossom, and the ever-bubbling spring had just been cleaned for the summer cooling, that soft green lay on the land, and the school bell was ringing clearly in the crisp morning air.

Missie's eyes softened with her musings.

"Oh, Willie," she said, "I'd never even thought of such a wonder."

"An' I been thinkin'," Willie said cautiously, probably in case it was a dream that would never be realized. "Been thinkin'—not a reason in the world thet I can see, why yer folks couldn't jest hop thet train someday an' make a trip out here."

"Oh, Willie," Missie cried, "could they really? Could people—it's not just for cows?"

Willie laughed. "'Course not. At the meetin' they said they 'spect lots of folks will be comin' out by train. Special car jest for folks to ride in—maybe even two cars iffen they be needin' 'em. Yer folks could come right on out, an' we could meet 'em at the station."

Missie caught hold of his sleeve. "It's too much—too much all at once. I feel I could simply burst if it doesn't stop."

"Don't ya go bustin'," Willie teased, pulling her to him. "We still got no doctor—an' I need ya. Who else is gonna look after Nathan an' me, an' git thet there house lookin' like a home 'stead of an empty, bare shell?" He chuckled as he held her close.

Missie was content to rest quietly in his arms.

"Speakin' of houses," Willie said against her hair, "iffen it's gonna be ready fer yer folks, I'd best git back to buildin' it. I decided today to send twenty or thirty steers along on thet cattle drive. No use doin' a thing by half measures. Soon as Scottie gits back with the money, I'll take one of the boys an' head fer Tettsford. An' this time, I'm takin' you, too, Missie. Iffen I don't git you away from this all-male company, you'll be losing all yer feminine charms!" But his eyes told her he didn't think that was likely.

Missie laughed, then retorted primly, "Why, yes, I believe I will be able to join you on your trip to Tettsford." But her dancing eyes gave her away, and she laughed again for sheer joy.

"We can git our winter supplies at the same time," Willie added.

"I need more preserving jars," Missie said. "Mercy! I planted more garden than either Cookie or I know what to do with."

Willie chuckled and released her.

"You be thinkin' on yer list," he said. "We'll be doin' our best to be fillin' it." He picked up his tools and started off for the new house. As he went he whistled, and the sound of it was pleasant to Missie's ears.

Around the corner of the cook shack limped Cookie, and close be-hind him trailed young Nathan, followed by his ever-present guardian, big Max.

Nathan chattered away and Cookie grunted in response. The dog was content to be the silent partner, giving an occasional wag of his tail.

Missie turned back to the little sod house. It was time to build a fire and begin preparing the evening meal. As she walked, she mentally composed her first letter home.

Dear Mama and Pa, she'd write.

God truly has kept His promise of Isaiah 41:10, just as you said He would. You should see our Nathan. He's about the greatest boy that ever was. He's quick, too, in learning and doing. You'd be real proud of your grandson. I think his nose and chin are like Willie's, but he has your eyes, Pa.

Truth is, we're expecting another baby. Not for several months yet, but we're excited about it. We haven't talked yet about what we'll do for the birthing and all, but maybe by then we'll have other folks around, and I won't have to go way back to Tettsford Junction. I pray that might be so.

Willie is building a stone house—our real house. The one that we've been living in, temporarily, is kind of small. It's been just fine, though, but now we're getting all set to move into the new one. We want to be in before winter comes again.

I have a nice big garden. It grows very well down by the spring. The soil is rich and easy to water there. I scarcely have to coax it along at all. Cookie, the cook, uses it for the ranch hands, as well.

I have chickens, too. This spring they gave us eighteen chicks, and we only lost two. I get seven or eight eggs a day. We're going to have chicken for Christmas dinner this year!

And we have neighbors! Maria is the closest one to the south. She is a very good friend, and we have enjoyed prayer times to-gether. Soon Melinda, a friend from the wagon train, will live to the north of us. You remember our Henry, the driver that you found

*for us, Pa? Well, he met Melinda on the trip out here, and as soon
as he finishes his house, they will be married. I can hardly wait.*

*We have a real good ranch foreman, Scottie, and several men
who work the spread. There is Cookie—I mentioned him before—
who is Nathan's favorite—mine, too; and Lane, Smith, Clem,
Sandy, and two new ones whom I still don't know very well. The
new ones haven't yet come to our Sunday Bible reading, but we're
still praying. Their names are Jake and Walt. Of course they all
have last names, too, except Smith, but we hardly ever use them
here. Pray for all of them. Lane has become a real believer, but
he takes a lot of ribbing from Smith. It would really help him if
Jake and Walt broke from Smith and started coming on Sunday,
too. Especially pray for Smith. He really needs God to thaw out
his heart.*

Missie pushed the kettle onto the heat and went outside for a new
supply of chips. Her eyes traveled over the miles of hills. They were not
just distant barren knolls now, but separate, individual, each with its
own characteristics. She remembered the coyote that appeared on that
closest one. She had gazed at the one to the northeast when she looked
for Willie's returning team. On the far ones she often saw the cattle
feeding. The ones close by were covered with beautiful spring flowers.
She'd transplanted some of them around the soddy door and watered
them faithfully with her dishwater, almost always remembering Mrs.
Taylorson's rule number four: All water must be used *at least twice.*

She turned her eyes toward the west. Even though she could not see
them from her valley, her memory brought to mind the mountains—
shadowy, misty, and golden by turn. "Like a woman," Willie teased,
"always changin' in mood and appearance."

She turned back to the hills. How pretty they looked. In the distance
were dots she knew were Willie's grazing cattle. A faster-moving black
figure appeared for a moment and then disappeared over a rise—one
of the hands checking on the herd. Another cowboy rode into the yard
down by the corrals. Missie heard the thud of the hoofbeats and saw
little smoky swirls of dust. She had missed her ride that morning. She

would be sure to take Nathan out on the morrow. The sting of the wind on her face and the smell of sage in the air always awakened her and sent her home, eager to begin her day of scrubbing clothes or canning vegetables.

You know, her letter would go on, *how Willie boasted of his land when he came back? Well, it's even prettier than that. I didn't see it that way at first, but I love it now. The air is so crisp and clean, you can almost serve it on a platter. And the distant mountains change their dress as regularly as a high-fashion city lady.*

Missie filled her pail, hoisted it up and started for the sod dwelling.

Willie brought wonderful news today, her mental letter continued. *He says the railroad, which is coming soon, will not only haul out cattle but will bring people, as well. He says that you'll be able to come right on out here for a visit. Can you imagine that? I could hardly believe it at first, and now I can hardly wait. I never dreamed when I left back east that I'd ever be able to show you my home.*

Missie's eyes filled with unbidden tears. "My home," she said softly, realizing she had never said the words about this place before. "My home! It truly is! I don't feel the awful tug back east anymore. This is truly *my home*—mine and Willie's." Joy and pride filled her heart.

I can hardly wait to show them. Her thoughts tumbled over one another. *They'll love it. It's so beautiful—the mountains, the hills, the spring—I wonder if an apple tree would grow down by the spring. I could have Pa bring out some cuttings—it wouldn't hurt any to try.*

Missie turned back to the temporary soddy that had been her home for two whole years.

"You know," she said aloud as she paused in front of the door, "I'll almost miss you, my little first home with Willie. I think I'll ask him to leave you sitting right here. You can be my quiet place, and I can come here sometimes and think and remember—the Christmas dinners when we crammed in here all together, Cookie sitting there on that stool nursing Nathan back to us, the planning that Willie did at that little table, the dreams, the tears, the fears that we've shared here. I've done a whole lot of growing since I entered this door—and there's still more to do, I reckon."

Missie looked about her. What else would she tell Mama and Pa? Maybe very little more. Maybe it was best for them to come and see for themselves. It was hard to put hopes and dreams on sheets of paper. Dreams of a church and a school for Nathan and his brothers and sisters. Dreams of white curtains and a sunlit sewing room. Dreams of Willie with a herd the size he had always planned. Dreams of neighbors and friends, laughter and shared recipes. Shared prayer times.

It would be hard to put her dreams down in neat rows of writing. It would be so much better when she could open her door and her arms to her mama and pa and say, "Welcome! Welcome to my home. There's love here. Love that started growing way back on the farm and traveled all the way here with us, growing and strengthening every mile of the way. *God's* love—just as He promised. *Your* love, for us as your children. And *our* love for one another and for our son. Love! That's what makes a home. So, welcome, Mama and Pa. Welcome to our love-filled home."

LOVE'S
ABIDING JOY

Dedicated with love
to my second sister, Jean Catherine Budd,
who left us for heaven in 1998,
with deep appreciation for the many times she
was my extra pair of hands
and for her open heart and open home
that always made me welcome;
and to Orville, the special guy
she brought home
to the family, who was reunited
with her in 2001.

ONE

Family

"Good mornin'."

The words came softly, and Marty opened sleep-heavy eyes to iden-tify their source. Clark was bending over her, smiling, she noted. Clark did not normally awaken her before his early morning trek to the barn. Marty stirred and stretched, attempting to come fully awake in an effort to understand why he was doing so now.

"Happy birthday."

Oh yes, today was her birthday, and Clark always wanted to be the first one to greet her on her special day. Marty snuggled the covers below her chin, planning to close her eyes again, but she couldn't resist answering his smile.

"An' you woke me jest to remind me thet I'm another year older?" she teased.

"Now, what's wrong with gettin' older? Seems to me it's jest fine—considerin' the alternative," Clark teased back.

Marty smiled again. She was fully awake now. No use trying to get to sleep again.

"Fact is," she said, pushing herself up and reaching to run her hand through Clark's graying hair, "I don't think I'm mindin' this birthday one little bit. I don't feel one speck more'n a day older than I did yesterday. A little short on sleep maybe," she added mischievously, "but not so much older."

Clark laughed. "I've heard tell of people gettin' crotchety and fussy as they age. . . ." He left the sentence hanging but leaned over and took any sting from the words with a kiss on Marty's nose. "Well, I'd best get me to the chorin'. Go ahead, catch yerself a little more shut-eye, iffen ya want to. I'll even git yer breakfast—jest this once."

"Not on yer life," interjected Marty hurriedly. "I'd hafta clean up yer mess in the kitchen." But her hand brushed his cheek, and the love and care between them would have been apparent to anyone who might have been watching.

Clark left, chuckling to himself, and Marty lay back and stretched to her full length beneath the warmth of her handmade quilt. She wouldn't hurry to get up, but Clark's breakfast would be waiting when he returned from the barn.

Today is my birthday, Marty's thoughts began. Though she wasn't actually feeling older, it seemed, suddenly, that there had been many birthdays. Forty-two, in fact. *Forty-two.* She silently repeated the number in an attempt to grasp the fact of it. *Funny, it really doesn't bother me a bit.* No, there was nothing disturbing about this birthday—not like thirty had been, or forty. My, how she had disliked turning forty! *It seems a body must be near worn out by the time one reaches forty,* she mused. Yet here she was, forty-two, and in all honesty she felt no older than she did when she had come to those previous monumental milestones.

Forty-two, she mulled over the number again but did not dwell on it for long. Instead she thought ahead to the plans for the day. Birthdays meant family. Oh, how she loved to have her family gathered about her! When the children had been little, she herself had been "the maker of birthdays." Now they were grown and old enough that it was her turn to have a special day celebration. Nandry had served the birthday dinner last year, Clae had reminded them at a recent Sunday dinner. Marty couldn't really remember. The years had a tendency to blur together, but, yes, she was sure Clae was right.

Today being Saturday, the birthday dinner would be held at the noon hour instead of in the evening. Marty liked it better that way. They had so much more time with one another, instead of trying to crowd in the celebration between the return of the schoolchildren and the milking of the cows and other farm chores. Today they would have the whole afternoon ahead of them for visiting and playing with the grandchildren.

Just thinking about the promise of this day filled Marty with anticipation. All thought of sleep now long gone, she threw back the covers, stretched on the edge of the bed, and moved to the window. She looked out upon a beautiful June morning. The world was clean and fresh from last night's rain shower. What a lovely time of year! There was still that lingering feeling of spring in the air, even though many plants had already grown enough to ensure that summer really had arrived. She loved June. Again she felt a stirring of thankfulness to her mother for birthing her in this delightful month.

Marty's thoughts turned to her own children. Nandry . . . Nandry and her little family. The oldest of the Davis brood now had four children of her own, and what a perfect young mother she made. Her husband, Josh, teased about their "baker's dozen," and Nandry did not even argue with his joking remarks. Yes, their beloved adopted Nandry would have made her natural mama proud. And then there was Nandry's sister, Clae, their second adopted daughter—Clae and her parson husband, Joe. Clae, too, loved children, but Marty felt—though Clae had not said so—that she secretly hoped the size of their family would not grow too quickly. They had one little girl, Esther Sue. Parson Joe still dreamed of getting more seminary training. Marty and Clark added little amounts to the canning jar, which was gradually accumulating funds to help pay for the much-wanted schooling. Marty hoped there would soon be enough for Joe to go, though the thought of their moving so far away was bittersweet.

Marty could feel the smile leave her face and her eyes cloud over as she thought of their next daughter, Missie. Oh, how she missed Missie! She had assumed it was gradually going to get easier over the years of separation, but it had not been so. With every part of her being Marty ached for Missie. *If only . . . if only,* she caught herself thinking again, *if only I could have one chat—if only I could see her again—if only I could hold her children in my arms—if only I could be sure that she is all right, is happy.* But the "if onlys" simply tormented her soul. Marty was here. Missie was many, many days' journey to the west. Yet how she longed for her sweet Missie. Though this daughter was not bone of her bone nor flesh of her flesh—Missie being the daughter of Clark and his first wife, Ellen—Marty felt that Missie was hers in every sense of the word. The tiny motherless baby girl with the pixie face who had stolen her heart and given life special meaning so many years ago was indeed *her* Missie. In fact, Missie had captured her love even before Clark had, she remembered. *Oh, how I miss you, little girl,* Marty whispered against the pane as a tear loosed itself and splashed down on the windowsill. *If only*—But Marty stopped herself with a shake of the head and a lift of her shoulders.

Across the yard she could see Clare and Arnie. Men now in size and years, they each still had much of the little boy in them. Some folks— those not aware of the death of Marty's first husband—were surprised by the differences in their appearance. Clare looked and acted more and more like his father, Clem—big, muscular, teasing, boyish. Arnie was taller, darker, with a sensitive nature and finer features like Clark. By turn they loved each other, teased each other, fought with each other, couldn't live without each other. They were laughing now as they came in for the milk pails, and Clare, who usually did most of the talking, was telling Arnie of some incident at last night's social event. Arnie didn't care much for neighborhood socials, but Clare never missed one. Arnie joined in his brother's laughter at Clare's description of the mishap, but Marty heard him exclaim over and over, "Poor ol' Lou! Poor ol' Lou. I woulda nigh died had it been me." Clare didn't seem to feel any sympathy for "poor ol' Lou," wholeheartedly enjoying the telling of the story. As the boys neared the door, Marty turned away from the window and dressed slowly. There was still lots of time to get the breakfast on. They were just now going to milk.

Marty brushed her long light brown hair and lifted it, heavy and full, to the back of her head. She had sometimes noted the thinning hair on many older women and secretly pitied them. Well, she didn't have any need to worry on that score yet. In fact, her hair had really not shown much gray, either. Not like Clark's. His hair was quite gray at the temples and was even generously sprinkled with gray throughout. *On him it looks good—rather distinguished and manly,* she thought.

Marty dawdled as she pinned up her hair, still examining her thoughts carefully one by one. A birthday was a good time to do some reminiscing. At length, her hair in place, she made up the bed and tidied the room.

As she left the bedroom, the smell of morning coffee wafted up the stairs to her. *Surely Clark didn't carry out his offer to make breakfast* was her first thought. No, she had just seen him down by the far granary. Marty sniffed again. Definitely it was coffee, and fresh-perked, too.

Her curiosity now fully roused, Marty picked up the fragrance of bacon frying and muffins baking. She hurried into the kitchen, her nose fairly twitching with curiosity and the inviting smells.

"Aw, Ma. It was s'posed to be a surprise!"

It was Ellie.

"My land, girl," said Marty, "it sure enough was a surprise, all right! I couldn't figure me out who in the world would be stirrin' 'bout my kitchen this early in the mornin'."

Ellie smiled. "Luke wanted ya to have it in bed. I knew we'd never git thet far without ya knowin', but I thought thet maybe I could have it ready by the time ya came down."

Marty looked at the table. It was covered with a fresh linen cloth and set with the company dishes. A small bowl of wild roses was placed in the center, and each plate and piece of cutlery had been carefully assigned to its place.

"It looks to me like ya are 'bout ready. An' it does look pretty, dear. Those roses look so good I think I could jest sit an' feast my eyes 'stead of my stomach an' not be mindin' it one little bit."

Ellie flushed her pleasure at the praise. "Luke found 'em way over at the other side of the pasture."

Marty buried her nose in the nearest rose, smelling deeply of its fragrance and loving it in a special way because it was given to her in love by a caring family.

"Where is your brother?" she asked when she straightened up.

"Don't think I'm to be tellin' thet," answered Ellie, "but Luke's not far away an' will be back in plenty of time fer breakfast. Ya like a cup of coffee while we're waitin' fer the rest to git here?"

"Thet'd be nice." Marty smiled. Instead of merely a birthday girl, she was beginning to feel like royalty.

Ellie brought Marty's coffee and then returned to the stove to keep an eye on the breakfast items. Marty sipped slowly, watching her younger daughter over the rim of the cup. Had she realized before just how grown-up Ellie was? Why, she was almost a woman! Any day now she might be taking a notion to cook at her own stove. The thought troubled Marty some. Could she stand to lose another of her girls? The last one? *How lonely to be the only woman in my kitchen!* Ellie had kept life sane and interesting in the years since Missie had left. What would Marty do when Ellie, too, was gone? Why, just the other day, Ma Graham had remarked about what an attractive young woman Ellie had become. Marty, too, had noticed it, but secretly she had been hoping no one else would—not for a while yet. Once people became aware of her little girl turning into a woman and began to whisper, there would be no turning back the clock. Soon their parlor would be buzzing with young gentleman callers, and one of them would be sure to win Ellie's heart. Marty was blinking back some tears when the men came in from the barn.

Clare was first. "Hey, Ma, you don't look so bad, considerin'," he joked, then laughed loudly at his own absurdity as though it were something truly hilarious.

Arnie looked embarrassed. "Aw, Clare, nothin' funny 'bout yer dumb—"

But Clare slapped him noisily on the back and declared with good humor, "Ma, ya forgot to have 'em give this kid of yers a funny bone when they made him up. Don't know how to laugh, this kid."

Clare then turned his attention to his sister. "Hey, it still smells all right. Haven't ya got it to the burnin' stage yet?"

Ellie laughed and tried to swipe a wet dishrag across his face, but he ducked away. She was used to Clare's teasing. Besides, she doted on her oldest brother, and he would have done anything in the world for her. Clare roughed her hair and went to wash for breakfast. Ellie tried to pat her hair back into its proper place, then dished up the scrambled eggs. Arnie, content to wait his turn at the washbasin, finally crossed to Marty. "Happy birthday, Ma," he said, laying his hand on her shoulder.

"Thank ya, son. It sure has had a promisin' start."

"An' soon we'll all be headin' for Clae's. Boy, those kids of Nandry's git noisier ever' time we see 'em. 'Uncle Arnie, give me a ride.' 'Uncle Arnie, lift me up.' 'Uncle Arnie, help me.' 'Uncle Arnie—'"

"An' you love every minute of it," cut in Ellie.

Arnie did not argue, only grinned. Marty nodded her agreement with Ellie. Arnie did indeed love the kids.

Clark came in, drying his hands on a towel, and glanced around the kitchen. "Well, it 'pears thet my family has 'bout gathered in. Everyone waitin' on me?"

"Yeah, thought you'd never git here, Pa," said Clare, taking the rough farm towel and winding it up to snap at Arnie.

"The boys jest now came in," Ellie informed her pa, "so I guess you haven't kept anyone waitin' any."

The men, finished with their washing and fooling around, took their places at the table. Marty moved her chair into position, and Ellie brought the platter of hot bacon from the stove. Marty looked at the empty place. "Luke," she said. "Luke isn't here yet."

"Still sleepin'?" asked Clare, knowing that Luke did enjoy a good sleep-in on occasion.

"He'll be here in a minute," said Ellie. "I think he'd like fer us to jest go ahead."

"But—" Marty protested, and just then the screen door banged and in came Luke, his hair disheveled by the wind and his face flushed from hurrying. Marty's heart gave a skip at the sight of her "baby." Luke was her gentle one, her peacemaker and dream-builder. Luke, fifteen, was smaller than the other boys and had serious and caring soft brown eyes. Marty felt she had never seen another person whose eyes looked as warm and compassionate as her little Luke's.

"Sorry," he said under his breath and slid into his place at the table.

Clark's love for the boy showed in his simple nod. "Would you like to wash?"

"I can wait until we pray; then the food won't be gittin' cold."

"Reckon the food will wait well enough. Go ahead."

Luke hurried from the table, inspecting his hands as he went. They were covered with red stains. He was soon back, and the family sat quietly as Clark read the morning Scripture portion and then led in prayer.

His prayer of the morning included a special thanks for the mother of the home and his helpmate over the years. Clark reminded the Lord that Marty was truly worthy of His special blessing. Marty remembered an earlier prayer, so long ago when she was a hurting, bewildered, and reluctant bride. Clark had asked the Father to bless her then, too. God had. She had felt Him with her through the years, and these dear children about her table were evidence of His blessing.

After the prayer ended and the food was passed, Clare looked over at Luke between bites of bacon and eggs. "So, little brother. What ya been up to so early in the mornin'?"

Luke squirmed a bit. "Well, I jest wanted Ma to have some strawberries fer her birthday breakfast, but boy—were they little and hard to find this year! Guess it ain't been warm enough yet." He held out a small cup of tiny strawberries.

Marty's throat constricted and her eyes filled again with tears. Her sleepyhead had crawled out early to get her some birthday strawberries. She remembered back to when Missie had first started the tradition of "strawberries for Ma's birthday breakfast." After Missie had left, the children had pooled their efforts for a few years. Then with the breaking of the pastureland that had housed the best strawberry patch, the tradition had drifted away. And now dear Luke had tried valiantly to revive it again.

Clare reached over and roughed his younger brother's hair. His eyes said, *You're all right, ya know that, kid,* but his mouth was too busy with Ellie's breakfast muffins.

"Ya should have told me," Arnie whispered. "I'da helped ya."

Marty looked around the kitchen at the four children still sharing their table, and her heart filled with joy and overflowed with love. The smile she shared with Clark needed no words of explanation.

TWO

Birthday Dinner

"Thet was a lovely dinner, Clae," Marty remarked, delicately catching the last traces of cake crumbs from her lips with the tip of her tongue. Clare's satisfied groan as he held his full stomach was eloquent. Nandry's Josh laughed.

As the plates were pushed back and another round of coffee poured, the pleasant clamor of visiting began. It seemed that everyone had something to say all at once, including the children. Clark held up his hands for silence and eventually drew the attention of even the youngest in the group.

"Hold it," he chuckled, "ain't nobody gonna hear nobody in all this racket. How 'bout a little organization here?"

Nandry's oldest, Tina, giggled. "Oh, Grandpa, how can one org'nize chatter?"

"Can I go now? Can I go play with Uncle Arnie?" Andrew interrupted, the only boy in Nandry and Josh's family.

"Just before we all leave the table and scatter who knows where, how about if we let Grandma open up her birthday gifts?" suggested Clae.

"Oh yes! Let's. Let's!" shouted the children, clapping their hands. Presents were always fun, even if they were for someone else.

Grandma Marty was given the chair of honor, and the gifts began to arrive, carried in and presented by various family members. The children shared scraps of artwork and pictures. Tina had even hemmed, by hand stitch, a new handkerchief. Nandry and Clae, presenting gifts from their families, laughed when they realized they had both sewn Marty new aprons. Clare and Arnie had gone together and purchased a brand-new teapot, declaring that now she could "git rid of thet ol' one with the broken spout." *Not too likely* was Marty's silent comment. *I'll plant spring flowers in it and put it in the kitchen window.* But aloud she admired the fancy new one.

Ellie's gift to her mother was a delicate cameo brooch, and Marty suspected that Clark had contributed largely to its purchase. Luke was last. His eyes showed both eagerness and embarrassment as he came slowly forward. It was clear he was just a bit uncertain as to how the others would view his gift.

"I'm afraid it didn't cost nothin'," he murmured.

"Thet isn't what gives a gift its value," Marty replied, both curious and concerned.

"I know you always said thet, but some folk . . . well . . . they think thet ya shouldn't give what cost ya nothin'."

"Ah," said Clark, seeming to realize what was bothering the boy, "but the cost is not always figured in dollars and cents. To give of yerself sometimes be far more costly than reachin' into one's pocket fer cash."

Luke smiled and looked more at ease as he pushed a clumsy package toward Marty.

"Ya said thet ya liked 'em, so . . ." He shrugged and backed away as his mother reached for the gift.

Heavy and bulky, it was wrapped in brown paper and tied at the top with store twine. Marty was trying to imagine what kind of a gift could come in such a package. She untied the twine with hurried fingers and let the brown paper fall stiffly to the floor. Before her eyes lay two small shrubs, complete with roots and part of the countryside in which they had grown. Marty recognized them at once as small bushes from the hill country. One summer when she and Clark had taken the youngsters into the hills for a family outing, she had exclaimed over them when in full bloom. How beautiful they had looked in their dress of scarlet blossoms. She caught her breath as she visualized the beautiful shrubs blooming in her own garden.

"Do you think they'll grow okay, Pa?" Luke's anxiety was clear in his voice. "I tried to be as careful as I could in diggin' 'em up. Tried to be sure to keep from hurtin' the roots an'—"

"We'll give 'em the best possible care an' try to match their home-growin' conditions as much as possible," Clark assured Luke, then continued under his breath, "—iffen I have to haul their native soil from them hills by the wagonload."

Marty couldn't stop the tears this time. It was so much like Luke. He had traveled many miles and had gone to a great deal of effort and care in order to present to her the shrubs he knew she loved. And yet he had stood in embarrassment before his family, his eyes begging them to please try to understand his gift and the reason for his giving it. She pulled him gently to her and hugged him close. Luke wasn't too fond of motherly kisses in public places, so Marty refrained from any further attention.

"Thank you, son," she said quietly. "I can hardly wait fer them to bloom."

Luke grinned and moved back into the family circle.

All eyes then turned to Clark. It had become a family tradition that the final gift to be given at such family gatherings was always from the head of the home. Clark cleared his throat now and stood to his feet.

"Well, my gift ain't as pretty as some thet sit here. It'll never bloom in years to come, either. But it does come with love, an' I hope it be somethin' thet truly gives ya pleasure. No fancy package—jest this here little envelope."

He handed the plain brown envelope to Marty. She turned it over in her hand, looking for some writing that would indicate what she was holding. There was nothing.

"Open it, Gram'ma," came a small voice, quickly echoed by many others.

Marty carefully tore off one corner, slit the envelope open, and let the contents fall into her lap—two pieces of paper and on them words in Clark's handwriting. Marty picked up the first. Aloud she read the message. "This is for the new things that you be needing. Just let me know when and where you want to do the shopping."

"Ya should have read the other one first," interjected Clark.

Marty picked up the second slip of paper and read, "Arrangements have been made for tickets on the train to Missie. We leave—"

Tickets to go to Missie! All Marty's recent thoughts and longings centering on their daughter so many miles away, all those "if onlys" crowded in around her. She was going to see Missie again. "Oh, Clark!" was all she could manage, and then she was in his arms sobbing for the wonder of it—the pure joy of the promise the tickets held.

When she finally could control herself, she stepped back from Clark's embrace. With a joyful heart but trembling lips, Marty said apologetically to her family, "I think I need me a little walkin' time, an' then we're gonna sit us down an' talk all 'bout this. . . ." She did well to get that far without more tears, and she left the cozy kitchen filled with the family she loved and walked out into the June sunshine.

Here at Clae's there was no place in particular to go, so she simply wandered aimlessly around the yard. The familiar trees and little spring behind her own house had been her refuge many times over the years when she had some thinking to do. Well, Clae's trees would suffice, she told herself. She tried to collect her scattered, excited thoughts. She was going to see Missie! She and Clark would travel those many miles on the train. No wagons—no slow days of wind and rain. Only padded seats and chugging engines eating up the distance between her little girl and herself. Oh, she could hardly wait! She held up the note she still clutched in her hand and read it aloud again. *"Arrangements have been made for tickets on the train to Missie. We leave as soon as you can be ready to go. Love, Clark."*

As soon as you can be ready to go. Oh my. There was so much to be done. So many things to prepare and take with them. There was her wardrobe. She would need new things for traveling. Why, her blue hat would never do to wear out among stylish people, and her best dress had a small snag near the hem that still showed even though she had mended it carefully. *Oh my.* How would she ever—? And then Marty remembered the second note. *This is for the new things that you be needing. Just let me know when and where you want to do the shopping.*

"Oh my," Marty said aloud. Clark had thought of everything, it appeared. "Oh my," she repeated and quickly changed direction back to Clae's kitchen. She must talk to the girls. They were far more aware of the present fashion trends, and they knew what stores carried the needed articles, and they knew where she should go to do her shopping and when the stages ran between the towns. "Oh my," she said again in a flurry, "I do have me so much to do. Oh my."

THREE

Planning

The days that followed were full of excited thinking and planning. Nandry and Clae went shopping with Marty for yard goods in their small town and then pored over design sketches that Clae made in an effort to achieve fashionable gowns. It was finally concluded that a trip to a larger center would be necessary if Marty was to be presentable to the outside world on a cross-country train trip. But when could she work that outing in to this busy time? Though her wardrobe consumed much of Marty's time and attention, there were other matters that weighed heavily on her mind, as well. One of them was the fact that Clare had wedding plans. As yet, a definite date for the marriage had not been set, but how could they go way off west not knowing? Marty held her tongue, but she did try to "plant the seed" in Clare's thinking that it would be most helpful if he and his young lady could finalize a date. Clare understood the subtle suggestion and told Marty he would see what he could do.

Marty was also anxious about the packing. It wasn't her own things that gave her worries, but every day she thought of something new that surely Missie and Willie and their young family might need. How much dare she accumulate before the railroad company—or Clark—would declare she had far too much baggage? She sighed as she tried to sort and select the most important items.

Clark occasionally tried to draw out an estimated day for departure from Marty. She knew a decision must be made. Clark had many responsibilities of his own that needed to be assigned to others. He couldn't properly sort them out until Marty had given him some idea as to when she would be ready to go. She didn't know whether to hope that Clare would set the wedding date for the immediate future or postpone it until they were sure to be back.

Then, of course, there were the other children. True, Ellie was capable of caring for the household, but it seemed like a big job to put on such young, slender shoulders. Marty conveniently forgot that at Ellie's age she had already been a married woman.

Yet Marty's heart was most concerned for Luke, her gentle youngest. How she wished they could take him with them. At the same time, she was afraid to suggest it, even to Clark. What if Luke did go, and what if he decided that he liked Missie's West, and what if he decided not to come back when Clark and Marty returned home? No, she'd best leave Luke safely where he was. She had no desire to have another child settled so far away from home.

So Marty spent her days musing and fretting. She tried not to let it show, but it must have. Nandry and Clae made arrangements for the care of their children and planned a trip to the city by local stagecoach for shopping. Ellie was invited to go along. With their loving but firm counsel, the necessary items were decided on, purchased, and prepared for travel. Marty was afraid she was spending an inappropriate amount of money, but she did rather enjoy this unusual extravagance. She also bought a few pretty things to take to Missie, as well. Who knew whether Missie had opportunity to shop since leaving her home?

Clare discussed marriage plans with his sweet Kate and, with the help of her mother, they were able to arrive at a suitable date. They wisely agreed that a hurried wedding would not be a good start for their marriage, so August 27 was chosen. Clark and Marty would have no problem being home by then. Clare and Kate planned to live in Clark's first little log home, so Clare would spend the intervening time preparing the place for occupancy, and Kate would spend her time on new curtains and floor rugs.

Ellie asked many questions and advice on the running of the home and the tending of the garden—questions to which she already knew the answers, but she probably knew it would help her mother depart with greater peace of mind if she explained it all again. Ellie assured Marty that she was looking forward to the experience, and Marty felt that it might truly be an adventure for the girl. Nandry and Clae promised to lend a hand if ever she needed assistance.

Luke took to making subtle observations about the coming separation. He suggested that it would be good for all of them to spend some time on their own and learn some independence. He pointed out to Marty that he would be spending most evenings studying for the entrance exams for college the coming fall, and he would have very little time for socializing even with family members. The additional quiet of the house during their absence would be very helpful in giving him extra study time, he said. Marty sensed he was trying to put her mind at ease about going off and leaving him, and she appreciated his concern.

Many times a day Marty went through the process of mentally sorting what she wished to take. She eyed her garden, her canned goods, her sewing materials, her chicken coop—she even eyed the milk cows. She shook her head. How in the world would she ever decide? At length, she knew she could never be sensible, so she asked for help from her family in the final decisions. Eventually it was narrowed down to a list over which Clark did not ruefully shake his head.

At length Clark was given the go-ahead. He could set a date for departure. It seemed that within a few more days, Marty could be ready to go.

"When are ya leavin'?" asked Ma Graham when they had a minute together after the church service.

Marty was relieved that she actually had a date. "Well, we take the stage out from town on Wednesday, and go on over to catch the train out of the city the next mornin'," she replied.

"Ain't ya excited?" Ma asked, but didn't need nor wait for an answer. "My, I miss thet girl of yourn so much myself thet I can jest imagine how yer feelin'. Give Missie a big kiss an' hug fer me. I have a little

604

somethin' here thet I want ya to take on out to her. I didn't dare send nothin' big—ya havin' so much of yer own stuff to tend to, so I jest made her a little lace doily fer her table."

Marty hugged Ma warmly, the tears in her eyes.

"Missie will 'preciate it so much," she whispered in a choked voice.

And so the packing of the crates, cases, and trunk was finished up, the clothes for travel carefully laid out, and the scattered items and thoughts collected. Many last-minute instructions, some necessary and some only for Marty's sake, were given to the three boys and Ellie. There was some measure of assurance in just reviewing them over and over.

Clare and Arnie had been farming right along with Clark for a number of years, so Clark had no doubts about their ability to take care of things. They each had a piece of their own land to farm now, too, but they could handle it all in Clark's absence. They had been instructed to get help if ever they needed it, and Luke was anxious to provide all the help his studying time would allow.

Without it actually being discussed, everyone understood that Luke probably would never be a farmer. He had a very keen mind and a sensitive spirit and was presently leaning toward the possibility of being a medical doctor. Clark and Marty felt he would be a great honor to them as a doctor, but Luke was not pressured for a commitment on his future.

And so the farming was left to the boys and the kitchen to Ellie. Marty knew she was quite able to care for the needs of the brothers, but still Marty fretted some as she thought of all the work ahead for the young girl.

The day of their departure dawned clear and bright, and the warm sunshine spilled through the bedroom window. Marty was up even before Clark and, in her excitement, flitted about working on last-minute things that really needed no attention. Her efforts were not totally without value, for it did give her something to do until it was time for them to load into the spring-seated wagon and head for town.

The four children from home accompanied them, and when they arrived—too early—at the stagecoach offices, Nandry and Josh and their family, and Clae and Joe and Esther Sue were already there.

The excitement was felt by everyone and resulted in too many talking at once, too much nervous activity, and too many near-wild children. Clark grinned around at the whole tension-filled bunch of them.

"Whoa," he finally called, lifting up his hand, his signal for quiet. "How 'bout we see iffen we can git a little order out of this confusion?" Everyone stopped midsentence and midstep and then began to laugh.

"I suggest," went on Clark, "thet we go on over to the hotel an' have us a cup of coffee an' a sandwich. Be a heap quieter, an' we still have lots of time to kill before this here stage is gonna be leavin'." Eventually they all fell into line and headed for the hotel and the promised coffee. Josh broke line, whispered to Nandry, and then fished in his pocket.

"Tina, yer ma says it be okay fer ya to take these here little ones over to the general store fer a candy treat. It being a special day, how 'bout ya all git *two* pieces of yer favorite kind."

Shouts of approval answered him, and he passed Tina the coins. She took Mary and Esther Sue by the hands and headed for the promised treat. Andrew disdained holding hands and marched off on his own. Baby Jane was content to be held in her mother's arms and to put up with the grown-ups while they visited over coffee cups.

When they finally were seated and had placed their orders, the talking did become a bit more orderly. They even waited for one another to finish their sentences before breaking in with a new thought or question. Marty knew her churning stomach had no interest in a sandwich. She ordered a cup of tea and sipped at it now and then between the talk and laughter. The men ordered sandwiches and even pieces of pie to go with them. Marty wondered fleetingly how they ever managed it, only a few hours since they had downed a big breakfast.

Departure time seemed to be in no hurry to come. The food had been eaten, the cups drained, replenished, and drained again, the same admonitions given and repeated, and the same assurances spoken over and over. Marty fidgeted in her seat. Clark at last said he supposed they could go on out and check on the progress of the stagecoach.

As they stood chatting before the stagecoach office, Zeke LaHaye, Willie's pa, joined them. He greeted them all with one nod and sweep of his hat, then reached to shake Clark's hand.

"Guess I needn't tell ya how I envy you. Sure would love to head on out with ya. Always had me a hankerin' to see the west country, an' with my boy out there it sure does git awfully hard to jest hold myself here at home sometimes."

"Well, now," said Clark, "ya oughta throw in yer bedroll an' come along."

Zeke answered with a smile. "Sure is temptin'. Did bring this here little parcel iffen ya think ya can find a little room fer it someplace. Hate to be botherin' ya like, but it jest ain't possible to let ya go without sendin' somethin' along fer the family."

"No trouble. No trouble a'tall," assured Clark and placed the parcel with the stack of their belongings.

Marty looked at the big pile of things going west. There were all of their own daily necessities, the many things they had packed to take to Willie and Missie, the added articles from Clae and Nandry, the gifts from Ma Graham, Wanda Marshall, Sally Anne, and even some from Missie's students during her teaching days. Yes, the pile had grown and grown and, indeed, each additional item meant "more trouble," but she would have no more denied Zeke LaHaye the pleasure of sending something to his family than she would have denied herself. She'd discard her new hatbox if necessary in order to make room.

The stage finally appeared, two minutes early, and all the baggage and crates were loaded. Zeke's package fit in, too, and Marty was able to tuck in the hatbox.

Over and over the words, "Ya tell Willie . . ." or "Give Missie . . ." or "Kiss them for me," were echoed from family members. Marty turned to each one with tears in her eyes and pounding heart. It was so exciting to finally be on their way. If only "good-byes" didn't need to come before one had the pleasure of "hellos." She kissed Luke one last time, gave Ellie one more hug, threw kisses to the many-times-kissed grandchildren, and hurried forward lest the stage driver get impatient with her.

The good-bye shouts followed them on down the road. Marty leaned from the window for one last wave before the coach turned the corner, and then she settled back against the already warm seat.

"I do declare," she remarked seriously to Clark, "I do believe thet travelin' be awful hard work. I feel all worn out like."

"We've barely started travelin', Marty," Clark laughed softly. "It's not the travelin' thet has ya all tuckered. It's the gettin' ready and the excitement. From now on, ya have nothin' to do but jest rest."

Marty smiled at Clark's calm assessment but felt rather doubtful. How could she ever rest when her whole body vibrated with excited energy? Well, she'd try. She'd try.

FOUR

The City

An awfully long, dusty, warm stagecoach trip faced Clark and Marty on the first leg of their journey. At least in their own farm wagon, they could catch the breezes and stop occasionally to stretch their legs. The morning sun moved up high in the sky, beating down unmercifully, and the open windows helped only a little. The other three passengers were men. Clark talked to them some, but Marty found little of interest in the conversation. Besides, her mind was on many other things. Had she brought the things that Missie really could use? How big was little Nathan now, the grandson they had never seen?

In spite of the warmth in the stagecoach, Marty knew that a stylish traveling lady did not remove her hat, even in the heat of the day, but how she longed to lift hers from her warm head and let it lie in her lap.

They stopped to change horses and to allow the passengers a few moments to walk around. Marty was enormously grateful for the bit of respite. Then on they went again, bumping over the rough tracks of the road. Marty had assumed the road would be fairly well traveled and smooth, but the stage wheels seemed to find every rut available.

At noon another rest stop was taken, and Marty climbed stiffly down with Clark's assistance and sought out the shade of some nearby trees.

The men scattered in various directions to walk, sit, or stretch out on the cool grass.

Marty took their little lunch bag and spread out a noonday meal of sandwiches and cool drink with tarts and cookies for dessert. Marty herself wasn't much interested, but she noted that the traveling was not adversely affecting Clark's appetite.

All too soon the stage was ready to move on again. They left the coolness of the trees and took their places on the hot, dusty leather seats. The minutes of the afternoon ticked away with the grinding and bumping of the wheels and the steady rhythm of the horses' hooves. Occasionally, a hoot or shout from the driver would call some new order to the teams.

In spite of the heat and discomfort, Marty found her head nodding. Probably the fact that she had been missing some sleep in recent days helped to make her drowsy. But it was hard to actually sleep in the jostling wagon. As soon as she would find herself slipping into relaxing slumber, another bump or shake would snap her awake. She found it to be worse than no sleep at all. She shifted position and fought to remain awake, catching glimpses of countryside through the stage windows.

A change of teams at another stagecoach station broke up the monotony of the afternoon. Marty's back and legs ached, and she was thankful for the stretch. She thought of Missie's long journey west by wagon train and more fully appreciated their courage through the discomfort of it all.

It was almost suppertime when the stagecoach pulled into the city station. Marty leaned forward eagerly to see all that she could as they traveled the busy, crowded streets, then realized she probably looked like a country bumpkin. She settled back against the seat and allowed only her eyes to move from side to side at a world very different from her own.

After alighting, Marty walked around, flexing her muscles and observing all of the strange sights and sounds as Clark collected their belongings and made the proper arrangements for everything to be on the morning's train west. All they took with them for the immediate were two cases and Marty's hatbox. Marty felt a bit panicky as she watched their luggage being carted away. Was the man truly dependable? Would he be *sure* to put them on the right train? Would everything arrive safely? Was it all properly labeled? What would they ever do if it did not make it?

But Clark seemed to have no such worries. Seemingly relieved and confident that he had all things arranged in good order, he took her arm.

"Well, Mrs. Davis," he teased, "here we are in the big city. What shall we be doin' with it?"

"Doin'?" asked Marty blankly.

"Well, they say a big city is full of all manner of excitin' an' forbidden things. Ya be wishin' to go lookin' fer some of 'em?"

Marty no doubt looked as shocked as she felt. "Me?"

Clark laughed. "No, not you. An' not me, either. I'm jest funnin' ya. I have heard they have some very good eatin' places, though. I could sure use me some good food. Somethin' about sandwiches thet don't stay with a man fer long. Though they sure enough hit the spot at the time, ya understand." He chuckled again as he looked into her face. "Ya interested?"

"I reckon," replied Marty, though secretly she found herself far more interested in what the people would be wearing than in what they ate.

"Well, let's jest find us a hotel room to git settled an' leave our belongin's, an' then we'll see what we be findin'."

They discovered a hotel quickly enough. It was the largest one Marty had ever seen. She looked around the lobby at the high ornate ceiling, the glistening hanging lights, and the elaborately paneled doors. *This is going to cost us nigh onto a fortune,* she thought, but she did not voice her opinion to Clark.

Clark was handed a key and given a few instructions, and then he gathered up their bags and took Marty's arm for the climb up the stairs—many of them. But she soon was distracted by the attractive paper on the walls and the colorful carpeting beneath their feet. At length, Clark stopped before a door and used the key. He pushed the door open and then stood to the side to allow Marty to enter. The room before them was the most elegant Marty had ever seen. She looked about her, studying carefully every detail. She wanted to be able to describe the room to her daughters.

The wallpaper was a richly patterned blue and the draperies were deep blue velvet with thick fringes. The bedspread, heavy and brocaded, had a cream background with some blue threads interwoven. The ornate chest appeared to have been hand-carved, and there was a special stool or small table on which one rested the travel cases. The imported carpet was a riot of rich purples, crimsons, blues, and golds, all blended together in an attractive overall pattern. The room even had its own bathroom. Marty took it all in and then turned to Clark.

"My," she said, then again, "my, I never know'd thet all of this grandness was possible."

"I jest hope thet this 'grandness' has a comfortable bed," he responded dryly, crossing over to the bed and testing it with his hand. "I'm thinkin' thet before mornin' I'll likely be pinin' fer the 'grandness' of our own four-poster."

Marty, too, felt the bed. "Feels fine to me," she stated, "though I admit to feelin' so tired thet a plank floor might even be welcome."

Clark laughed. "Before ya settle fer thet plank floor, let's go see what this here town has to offer an empty stomach." And, so saying, he attempted to lead her from the room.

"Whoa now," argued Marty. "Iffen I'm gonna dine out like a fine lady, I'm gonna need to freshen up first. Goodness sakes, the stage was so hot an' dusty, one feels in fair need of a bath an' hairwash."

As expected, it took Marty longer to prepare for going out than it did Clark. He waited fairly patiently while she primped and fussed and finally felt confident enough to venture forth. They descended the stairs slowly, and Clark made inquiry as to the location of a nice dining room. Assured that the one in the hotel was one of the finest the city had to offer, they proceeded into an immense room with elaborate columns and deep wine-colored draperies. Marty had never dined in such splendor. She could scarcely take her eyes from the room and its occupants long enough to properly select from the menu. Everything on the stiff card before her looked too fussy, too much, and too expensive. It was hard for her to make up her mind. She wished she could find something simple like fried chicken or roast beef. Clark asked for the house specialty and, without checking to see what it was, Marty echoed his order.

She tried not to stare, but the people moving about the room and sitting at the white-covered tables seemed to be from another world. She had to take herself consciously in hand and remember her manners. Still, she was relieved and pleased to note that she did not stand out in the crowd as "backwoods" or "frumpish." Her daughters had chosen her new clothing well. How thankful she was for their knowledge and encouragements.

When the waiters had brought their plates and settled the dishes in front of them, Clark took Marty's hand and bowed his head, thanking the Lord for His care on the journey and for the food before them. The meal was delicious, though they served far too large a portion in Marty's opinion. She, who was not in the habit of wasting anything, had a difficult time leaving the food on her plate and sending it back to the kitchen. She was concerned, too, that the cook might take offense and feel that the meal had not pleased her. After she had eaten all she possibly could and pushed back her plate, she still was not sure exactly what she had eaten. It had been very tasty—but not identifiable like her home-cooked farm suppers of roast beef, potatoes, and gravy. Everything about the city was different.

They ordered French pastries to go with their coffee and lingered over them, enjoying the taste, the atmosphere, and the pleasurable luxury of sitting with no responsibility to hasten them away from the table.

When they felt it would be impolite to remain any longer, they rose from the table and returned to the lobby. Clark purchased a local paper and tucked it under his arm as they again made their way up the stairs to their room. Marty held her skirt carefully as she climbed; it would never do to step clumsily on her skirt and damage such an expensive hemline.

"So how do you plan on spendin' this lazy evenin', with no mendin' or sewin' in yer hands?" Clark asked as he opened the door to their room.

"Isn't botherin' me none," responded Marty lightly. "As tired as I be feelin', I expect thet sleep sounds 'bout as good to me as anythin' I could be doin'."

Clark smiled. "Go on. Tuck yerself in then. Me, I'm jest gonna check the paper an' see what's goin' on in the world."

Marty prepared for bed and slipped between the cool, smooth sheets with a contented sigh. Oh, how tired she was! She longed for a good long sleep. She would be off before you could say . . . But it turned out she wasn't. Try as she might to relax in the big soft bed, her mind still kept whirling. She thought of Missie and her little family they were going to see. She thought of Ellie, Luke, Arnie, and Clare back home. Was there anything she had forgotten to tell them, any reminders she hadn't given, any instructions she had missed? Would their baggage really make it onto the train? What would it be like sharing the close proximity of a train car with strangers for days on end as they traveled? Marty's mind buzzed with questions.

Clark finished reading his paper, prepared for retiring, and climbed in beside her. Soon Marty heard his soft breathing and knew he slept in spite of the unfamiliar bed. Still sleep eluded her. She stirred restlessly and wished for morning. Once they were actually on that train and headed for Missie's, she was sure *then* she could relax.

In spite of her restless night, Marty roused herself early the next morning. Anticipation took charge, driving her from the bed. Clark stirred as Marty threw back the blankets.

"Rooster crow already?" he teased, then shut his eyes again and turned over.

Marty didn't let his joshing bother her but went about her morning preparations. She had already decided on the dress and hat she would wear for their first train ride and carefully worked out the wrinkles with the palms of her hands. She shook out the hat, fluffing up the feather, and stepped back to admire the plume. *My, this is some hat,* she thought. She felt a mite self-conscious about wearing it, but then assured herself that all the fashionable traveling ladies wore them.

Marty dressed carefully and then began packing her nightclothes and her gown of yesterday in her case. The gown smelled dusty and looked bedraggled from the stagecoach ride. *What a shame to pack it away in such a mess!* she fretted. She wished there were some way to freshen it first. She selected a few pages from Clark's newspaper and carefully wrapped the dress in it. Clark, still in bed, seemed not the least disturbed by the crackling newspaper.

Marty finished all her packing and preparation for their second day of travel, and Clark still hadn't stirred. She wasn't sure what she should do. She hated to waken him, but what if they were late and missed their train? She had no idea of the time. She crossed to where Clark's vest hung on the back of a chair and fumbled in his breast pocket for his pocket watch. *It isn't there!* Marty panicked and her mind immediately flashed to the terrible stories she had heard about the big city. They were true! Someone must have come into their room in the dead of night and stolen Clark's watch. If his watch was gone, what else had they taken? Marty hurried to her case. Was her cameo from Ellie still there? And what about the gold brooch that Clark had given her two Christmases ago?

Marty had packed them on the very bottom of the suitcase. Carefully now she lifted each item from the case, going down on her knees on the floor to lay things out all around her. When she remembered the hours she had spent carefully packing each item of her clothing, she could have cried. Would she ever get them so neatly arranged again? Many of the gowns she had folded in thin tissue wrap supplied by the dress shops in which she had made her purchases. And now, as she lifted them out, no matter how hard she tried to be careful, she disturbed the garments and wrinkled the tissue. Yet she *had* to know—were her few items of precious jewelry stolen along with Clark's watch? Clark would be so disappointed! His three sons had gone together to purchase the gift for his last birthday, and he had proudly worn the watch chain across his chest.

Marty stopped suddenly in the middle of her frantic search. Perhaps she shouldn't be wasting precious time now. Perhaps she should run down to the front desk and report the loss. Maybe there still was a chance to catch the thief. No, first she must know how many missing things to report. So Marty continued unpacking her case, item by item, laying each one around her in one of the neat piles on the deep blues, golds, wines, and scarlets of the carpeted floor.

Marty was almost to the last item when Clark roused from sleep and sat up in bed.

"Ya repackin'?" Clark asked mildly, though his expression looked rather dumbfounded.

"Oh, Clark!" Marty cried. "I'm so glad yer finally awake. We've had us thieves in the night." Marty's hands hurried on, emptying the last few items from her case.

"Thieves?"

"Yes, indeed."

"What ya meanin', *thieves*?"

But Marty interrupted him with a glad cry. "Oh, they're still here! Oh, I'm so glad, so glad."

Clark was out of bed by then, looking down at Marty, who clasped her precious jewelry to her bosom.

"Look!" she cried. "They didn't find 'em."

"Who find what? I'm not followin'—"

"The thieves—the thieves who stole yer watch. Oh, Clark, I'm so sorry. I know how much ya loved thet watch an'—"

"Ya meanin' this watch?" Clark asked, lifting it from the small table by the bed.

Marty gasped, "Ya found it!"

"Found it? I never lost it. I put it there by my bed so's I could check the time in the mornin'."

"Oh, Clark. I checked in yer pockets fer it, an' when I couldn't find it I thought thet someone had—"

But Clark had started to laugh. He pointed at Marty and at the empty case and the heaped-up clothing and laughed uproariously.

At first Marty felt chagrined by his outburst, since she was not yet over her concern and fear during the trying ordeal of the last several minutes. Then she looked about her at the clutter and then at the watch held dangling from its chain in Clark's hand, and the humor of the situation struck her also. She buried her face in her hands and laughed with Clark.

When she finally had control of herself again, she gasped out, "Well, if this isn't 'bout the dumbest thing I've ever done. Jest look at me! I think thet my sleepless nights have really addled my brain. Oh, Clark, jest look at the mess I got here!"

Then a new thought struck her. The repacking of the case was going to take some time if she was going to do it carefully. Perhaps she would need to stuff things into the case and run to catch the train. Nervously, she looked up, her hands quickly starting to return things to their proper places. "How much time we got 'fore—?"

Clark assured her they had far more time than she would ever need for the repacking, even though she was "as particular and fussy as Aunt Gertie." Marty had never come by any more information than that about Aunt Gertie, but when Clark wanted to make a point of someone's fussiness, he always brought up this aunt of his. The boys had taken up the phrase, too, though they knew nothing more than she did of the mysterious Aunt Gertie.

Marty, relieved that there was plenty of time, carefully set out to put everything back in its proper place while Clark shaved and dressed.

She was still laboring over the open case when Clark stood, hat in hand, ready to go.

"Be it time?" Marty inquired.

"Take yer time—we still got lots of it. Soon as yer ready, we'll go on down an' find us some breakfast. A man can't travel on an empty stomach. Then we'll come back on up an' pick up our things." Clark tipped up Marty's chin and looked into her face with a smile. "Guess we might as well do the rest of our waitin' at the train station. I have me a feelin' thet yer not gonna rest easy until yer sure thet yer gonna be on thet there train," he added.

Marty packed in the last few items and closed the case. She stood to her feet and nodded her head. There was no use denying what Clark had just said. He knew her far too well.

"I'm ready now," she said. "An', yes, I could be usin' some breakfast."

Clark offered his arm, checked his safe-in-hand watch, shook his head a bit, and chuckled again.

FIVE

The Real Journey Begins

At the train station, Marty was sure she had never seen so many people all in one place. Her eyes and ears were busy noting and storing up the new sights and sounds all around her. *What would Nandry, Clae, and Ellie think if they could see all this!*

Clark found a bench on which Marty could wait and went to make final arrangements for their journey. She sat and watched the array of marvelously colorful dresses, even on little girls. Why, the menfolk looked like they belonged on the pages of some storybook!

Even though there was still lots of time before the train was due to leave the station, Clark had been correct about her state of mind. Marty would not really rest easy until she was actually seated on the train and assured that its engine was pulling them westward. So in spite of her interest in the crowd, she fidgeted and was glad when she saw Clark moving back across the room toward her.

A rather confident looking woman with bright hair and a broad-brimmed scarlet-plumed hat sat across the room. To Marty's surprise, the woman also seemed to be watching Clark's approach. The woman looked out from under her hat brim, then she seemed to deliberately drop a glove at her own feet and pretended to go back to the book she held before her face. As Clark reached the "lost" glove, he bent, gentle-manlike, recovered it, and then glanced around to see who its owner might be. Marty saw the woman steal a very small peek, and then her long eyelashes began to flutter. Marty knew she was about to make her presence known to Clark in some clever little speech.

Marty stood quickly and spoke before the lady in the hat had time to open her mouth. "Everythin' set, Clark? Oh, a glove. Perhaps it belongs to you, ma'am," she said, reaching for it and turning to the woman with a smile. "It matches your hat perfectly."

The lady accepted her glove without comment. Marty moved away, taking Clark's arm and steering him to a seat nearer the exit door. *I can't imagine the brazenness of these city women,* she was fuming inwardly. *They'd try to steal a woman's husband right out from under her very nose. Why, that's even worse than taking a watch!* Clark seemed to remain unaware of the small hubbub as the two settled themselves on the bench together. Marty carefully avoided any eye contact with the woman across the station.

Someone finally called, "All aboard for points west," and Marty quickly stood, shook the wrinkles from her skirt, and straightened her hat. Clark gave her arm a reassuring squeeze and they moved with the crowd toward the waiting train.

Having never been on a train before, Marty was both excited and apprehensive. She found the high steps awkward to maneuver with her long skirt and was glad for Clark's helping hand as she climbed up.

Inside the train car, the rows and rows of seats were not as elegant as Marty had imagined they would be. The plush fabric was faded and even a little frayed in spots. Marty figured out that the fancier newer train cars would run between the large eastern cities.

They were jostled a bit as they sought a seat. Everyone seemed to be in a hurry to find a place, as though they were afraid the train might leave without them. Clark and Marty found a seat quickly enough. They settled themselves and tucked their carry-along luggage under the seat. Marty sighed deeply. They had made it. Now if she only could get a glimpse of the sun to make sure this train was pointed in the right direction.

Gradually the commotion around them began to subside as other passengers settled in, as well. Marty noticed that not very many women had boarded the train. The men around them appeared to be of every type and station in life—from businessmen to cattlemen, from miners to farmers like themselves, drifters and maybe even youngsters running away from home.

Marty shuddered as the scarlet plumes moved past them down the aisle and the woman from the station, with skirts and eyelashes fluttering, took a seat. She had selected a spot far from the other womenfolk in the car, among the men who had already pulled out a deck of cards and made themselves a makeshift table. Great drifts of cigar and cigarette smoke already blurred the air around them. Marty hoped there would be no smokers in her area, but it was in vain. Not being used to smoke at all, Marty found it particularly trying. Were they to endure this all the way to Missie's? Already she felt about ready to choke, and they hadn't even left the station yet.

The train gave a long low sound like an anguished groan, and the squeaking wheels began to revolve slowly. They were on the way at last. To Marty's vexation, she still couldn't tell if they were headed in the right direction.

Gradually the train began to pick up momentum. The rough-looking buildings on the back streets of the town flashed past them now. Marty watched carriages and horsemen pulled up on side streets waiting for the train to pass by. Children called and waved, and dogs barked. The train's whistle blew in response, but it steadily moved on.

They left the town behind and moved out into the open countryside. Marty could not draw her gaze away from the window. Trees swished by them, cattle lifted tails and ran off bawling, horses snorted and swung away, blowing angrily, tails and manes flying. Still the train pounded on, wheels clickity-clacking and smokestack spewing forth great billows streaming by their window.

It's a wonder, that's what it is, thought Marty. *Why, I bet we're going about as fast as a horse can gallop, and nobody needs to lift a finger for the doing of it.* Though she probably would have gotten a vigorous argument if she had expressed such thoughts to the train engineer or coal stoker.

Marty finally took her eyes from the passing countryside long enough to look at Clark, interested in his reaction to this captivating new experience. To her amazement, she found that Clark had settled himself comfortably and, with head leaning back against the makeshift package of their food bundle, he slept soundly as though sleep was the full purpose of a train ride.

"Well, I never," muttered Marty under her breath and then smiled. She should be sleeping, too. The recent days had been most difficult and busy, and the sleep she had gotten in the last few nights was limited indeed. Clark was wise. He, too, was tired. He needed the rest. She'd try, as well. But, in spite of her resolve, she could not as yet get her mind or body to relax. She'd just watch the scenery for a while. Maybe she could sleep later.

Marty must have slept, for she aroused at the sound of a crying baby. It took her a few moments to get her bearings, and then excitement again filled her as she recalled that they were on the way to Missie.

The baby continued to cry. Marty opened her eyes and turned toward Clark. But when she looked, he was not there. For a moment, she was unnerved. Where could one disappear to on a moving train? Remembering the "lost-watch" scare of the morning, she told herself that Clark would not be far away and not to get in a dither.

The coach was even more blue with smoke than it had been when she had dropped off to sleep. It was hot and stuffy, too, and Marty longed for some fresh air. She gazed about her at the crowded coach. The poker game was still going on at the far end of the car. The woman had removed her brilliant hat, and she no longer sat alone. A distinguished gentleman in a fancy suit and frilly shirt was sitting with her. They laughed as they talked.

The crying baby was in the seat across the aisle. The poor mother already looked tired out. She had two other little ones with her, as well. The man who accompanied her growled to her to "hush the brat 'fore we git throwed off the train," and the woman tried even more intently to quiet the infant. But the baby was not to be placated. The man got up and, angrily muttering to himself, left. This started another one of the children crying, and the young mother really had her hands full. Marty started to leave her seat and go to the woman's aid, but a matronly looking woman arrived on the scene first.

"Can I help you some?" she asked the mother, and, without waiting for a reply, she took the crying baby. "You care for your son, and I'll try to get the baby to sleep."

Marty's heart went out to the young mother, and she said a quick prayer of thanks for the kind motherly soul who was helping. She laid the baby in her lap and loosened the blanket. The baby soon was sleeping, and Marty wondered if perhaps the young mother had bundled the little one too tightly and the poor infant was nearly smothering in the discomfort of the sun-heated coach.

Marty laid aside her own hat and tried to fan her flushed face. *What I wouldn't give to be able to go for a walk*, she thought. *Sure would feel good to have a little wind on one's face.*

Clark returned, and Marty was relieved in spite of her little inner lecture earlier.

"Feelin' a little better?" Clark asked.

"I did sleep some, an' it sure didn't do me no harm. Would be nice to cool off a mite. This here coach is so stuffy an' so filled with smoke, I feel like I'm travelin' in a saloon 'stead of a—"

"Now, what you be knowin' 'bout a saloon?"

"I don't, it's jest—"

But Clark was laughing at her.

"Where ya been?" asked Marty to change the conversation.

"Jest stretchin' my legs some. Ain't much of a place to walk, thet's fer sure. Jest back an' forth, back an' forth. S'pose it helped a little."

"What I wouldn't give fer a walk 'bout now," said Marty.

"Ya want fer me to ask 'em to stop the train an' let ya off fer a spell?"

"Clark . . ." But she didn't finish, and Clark stopped his teasing.

"What time is it, anyway?" asked Marty finally.

Clark pulled out his pocket watch. "Well, it's almost noon. Quarter of twelve, in fact."

Marty sighed heavily. "Thought it would be at least late afternoon," she said. "Seems like we been travelin' fer half of forever already."

Clark smiled.

"How many days did ya say we'd be on the train?"

"Reckon they didn't say fer sure. They was rather offhand about arrivin' time. Said thet the trip usually took 'bout a week—dependin' on the weather, the track, an' such."

"A week! I'm thinkin' we'll have us enough of this train by the time *thet* week is over."

"Well, now, I didn't say *this* train, exactly. We'll be leavin' this train in three days' time. We transfer to another one. This one's usually on time to where it's goin'. It's the one further on thet's some changeable."

"I didn't know thet we would be gettin' on another train. What'll it be like?"

"I'm not rightly sure. Only thing I know, it seems a bit unpredictable. But it won't be so bad. By the time we board her, we'll already be in the West an' almost there."

Marty suddenly felt hungry. "Anythin' still fittin' to eat in thet there pillow of yours?"

Clark passed her the lunch. It hadn't suffered much. Ellie had packed it well.

Marty lifted out a box that held sandwiches. "Sure would be glad fer a nice hot cup of tea or coffee," she commented.

"I think thet I jest might be able to find us some," said Clark and left his seat, walked down the aisle and out the swinging door. He was soon back with two steaming mugs of hot coffee. It was too strong for Marty's liking, but it was coffee and it did wash the smoke taste from her throat.

They finished their lunch with a couple of tarts, and Marty carefully repacked the uneaten food.

"Ya know, ya could stretch yer legs a bit iffen ya like to," offered Clark. "Seed other women movin' 'bout some. An' the little room's down thet way," he motioned.

Marty smiled her thanks and stood up. She couldn't believe how rumpled her dress looked in just one morning. She tried to smooth the wrinkles out but they stubbornly remained, so she shrugged in resignation and moved out into the aisle.

Marty had been vaguely aware of the rock and sway of the train as she sat in her seat, but she had had no idea how decided it was until she took a step forward. The train suddenly seemed to lurch, throwing her off balance. She quickly put out a foot to rebalance herself when the train rolled the other way, leaving her startlingly off-balance again. Each place she went to put her foot was either too high or too low. At last she gave up trying to make it on her own and firmly grasped the seats as she moved forward. It seemed to be an awfully long walk to the "little room," and by the time Marty had made it back to Clark, she'd had enough of train-aisle walking for the time.

The train hooted and chugged, whined and rocked its way westward. Marty viewed more than one sunrise and sunset, happily content that the train was truly headed in the right direction.

They stopped at small towns to let off or take on passengers. Sometimes the train seemed to sit for a ridiculously long time while train cars were shuffled and shouting men hauled off or on some sort of cargo. At these times Clark and Marty would leave the train and walk, strolling around just to get the kinks out of their muscles. On occasion they visited a store to restock their little food supply. Often it was no cooler out on the station platform than it had been in the stuffy coach, but at least it was a bit of relief from the cramped position. Marty began to wonder if it really would have been much more difficult to cover the miles in a jolting covered wagon.

The landscape around them changed with each passing day. Trees were fewer in number, often forlornly clumped together by a meandering stream. The towns, sometimes no more than a few scattered houses, were now even farther apart than before. On the third day, they rolled into a town that Clark announced was the place where they would transfer to the other train. Marty was not reluctant to make the change. She had no ties to this present train, and she had found very little in common with their fellow travelers. Those few whom she had become acquainted with all seemed to have gotten off at earlier stops except for the one middle-aged lady in dove-gray gown and hat who had helped with the baby. Mrs. Swanson was heading west to live with her son, her husband having died recently. Marty thought it was awfully spunky of the woman to make such a life-changing move all alone.

Clark had visited with several of the men on the train, attempting to learn all he could about the West before arriving at his son-in-law's ranch. He did not wish to appear to the ranch hands as another "ignorant fella from the East," he told Marty.

When they arrived at their point of transfer and the train dismissed its passengers, Clark and Marty found their way across the rough platform. People milled about and called to one another, but as there was no one in this town they knew, they kept their attention on the task of finding their luggage and getting it stored in readiness for the next train in the morning. Then they made their way from the station into town to find suitable lodging.

The baggage attendant had informed them that a hotel was just down the street within easy walking distance. When Clark requested a room from the man at the reception desk, he was told that a room was available and named the price. Marty was shocked when she heard the amount. But Clark did not argue with him and counted out the bills from the small roll he carried in his pocket.

They climbed worn carpeted stairs and found their room number. Marty looked about her in shock at the sight that confronted them on opening the battered door. The room was almost bare, except for a good bit of dirt and dust, and the bed linens appeared to have been used by at least one other occupant—maybe more. Marty had little objection to sparse furnishings, but actual grime was another matter.

Marty could see Clark eyeing the muddy boot prints on the floor and the soiled pillows strewn on the bed. But he made no remark on the sad state of the room.

"I think I'll take me a little walk an' sorta check out the town. Ya wanta come along or jest rest a bit?" asked Clark.

A walk did sound appealing, yet from what Marty had so far seen of the town, she was not so sure she wanted to investigate it.

"I think I'll jest rest here fer a bit. I'll see the town when we go out to git our supper," she answered.

Clark took his hat and left.

Marty didn't know what to do with herself after Clark had gone.

She wished she had a broom, a pail of hot, soapy water, and a stiff scrub brush. The place looked as though it could use a good cleaning.

She crossed to the bed with the thought of lying down, but then eyed the soiled linen and changed her mind. She walked to the window, intending to pass some time by watching the action down on the street. The window looked out on nothing but the desolate countryside. She lifted her case from the only chair in the room, an overstuffed piece that certainly had seen better days, and tried to settle herself in it. It had a broken spring that made it impossible to sit comfortably. Marty decided her only choice was to pace the floor. Well, she could certainly do with the exercise after being confined to the swaying train for three days. She walked. Round and round she walked, wishing she had gone with Clark.

About the time she thought she would surely go crazy, Clark returned, carrying clean bed linens over his arm.

"The maid has arrived," he joked.

"Where'd ya git those?" Marty asked admiringly. "Ya been foragin' through hotel closets?" she teased.

"Not exactly. They weren't all thet easy to come by. I went out fer a walk, like I said. There's only one other hotel, of a sort, in this here town. It boasted 'bout bein' 'full up.' Couldn't find a decent roomin' house anywhere. So when I got back here, I jest asked the fella at the desk for some clean linens. I said it 'peared like the maid had somehow missed our room when she was makin' her rounds. He wasn't too happy to 'commodate me, but I jest stood right there, smilin' an' waitin'. He finally found me some."

Marty was happy to strip the bed and put on the clean sheets and cases.

"Not too much fer eatin' places, either," Clark continued as she worked. "Did see a small place down the street. Looks a little more like a saloon than a café, but it mightn't be too bad iffen we git there early an' leave as soon as we're done."

"We can go most anytime. I'll jest fix my hair some an' grab me a hat."

They left the hotel and walked out into the brisk wind. Marty held her hat with one hand and her skirt with the other.

"Fella I met says it blows like this most of the time here," remarked Clark as they leaned into the wind. Marty wondered what in the world the women did if they ever needed one of their hands free to carry something.

When they reached the unpretentious building where they were to get their evening meal, Clark held the door against the wind. They seated themselves at a small table, and Clark nodded for the waiter. They soon learned that the "house speciality" was stew and biscuits; or roast beef, gravy, and biscuits; or beans, bacon, and biscuits. They ordered the roast beef and settled in to wait for their meal.

Marty glanced around the room. The lighting, a lone flickering lamp on each table, was dim. The few windows seemed to be covered with some kind of dark paint. A blue haze from the smoking of the occupants further hindered visibility. Most of those who lounged around were not eating but drinking. Marty did spot three men in the far corner who were having a meal. The others just seemed to be talking or playing cards. Occasionally a loud laugh would break the otherwise comparative silence in the place. At least for now, Marty was the only woman in the place.

Marty hoped their order would come quickly so they might leave soon. If this was Missie's West, Marty wasn't sure she would be at home in it. She felt uneasy in her present surroundings. Having never traveled beyond her own small community since leaving her girlhood home, Marty was very unfamiliar with the present environment. She had seen and heard things on this trip that were entirely new to her. She was sure she was not in favor of a lot of what she saw—the brashness, the intemperate drinking, the gambling, the casual attitude toward life and morality.

Their meal arrived. The waiter asked gruffly, "Watcha drinkin'?" as he set the plates down, frowning when Marty asked for tea. She hastily changed her order to coffee before he had time to respond. He didn't fuss about the coffee, but when he set it before her it was so old and strong she wasn't sure if she'd be able to drink it.

The meat was a little tough and the gravy was greasy and lumpy, but Marty sopped her biscuits in it and ate like the men in the corner. She was unable to finish it all and was relieved when she felt she had eaten enough that she could leave the rest. Clark had a second cup of coffee, and then they were free to go.

Forgetting it was still daylight, Marty was unprepared for the bright sunshine when they stepped out the door. She took advantage of the fact to study the buildings of the town and look in the store windows. The things on display did not really seem all that different from what Mr. Emory carried at the general store back home. The fact both surprised and relieved her. Perhaps Missie was able to shop for needed items after all.

It was too early to retire, so Clark suggested a short walk. Marty didn't like the wind but, remembering her confining attempt to walk in the dismal little room, she agreed. They walked on past the remainder of the buildings on the street—the bank, the sheriff's office, the telegraph office, another store, on past the stagecoach office to the feedstore, the livery, and the blacksmith. Clark slowed his steps to better watch the action at the smithy's. Two burly men were shouting and shoving as they prodded a big roan-colored ox into the ox sling for shoeing. The ox had decided on his own that he didn't need new shoes. Marty heard some words she didn't think were intended for a lady's ears, so she hastened her steps. Clark lengthened his stride to catch up to her.

Having eventually left the board sidewalks behind, the roadway was dusty and rough, but it felt good to walk full stride. Marty let go of her skirt, allowing the hem to swish the ground as she walked. The wind wasn't as strong now, or maybe she was just getting used to it. There didn't seem to be anyone else around, so she took off her hat, carrying it carefully in her hand, and let the wind tease at her hair. It felt good, and she wished for a moment she could reach up and pull the hairpins from it, as well, and shake it loose to blow free.

They left the street and turned onto a well-worn path. It led them into a grove of small trees; and, after walking for about fifteen minutes, they were surprised to discover a tiny stream that flowed rather sluggishly along. It wasn't like Marty's spring-fed creek back home, but it was water, and its discovery brought rest and joy to Marty's heart. She stooped to pick a few of the small flowers that grew along its banks.

Clark seemed to enjoy it, too. He stood and breathed deeply. "I wonder jest where it comes from," he murmured, "an' where it goes. This little bit thet we see here before us don't tell us much 'bout it a'tall. It could have started high up in the mountains as a ragin' glacier-fed river and been givin' of itself all across the miles until all thet is left is what we see here. Or it could go 'most from ocean to ocean by joinin' up with cousin waters thet eventually make it a mighty river. Someday it could carry barges or sailin' ships. Rather interestin' to ponder on, ain't it?"

Marty nodded and looked at the small stream with a new respect.

They lingered awhile, and then walked much more slowly back into town. On the way they watched the western sun sink below the far horizon with a wonderful display of vibrant colors.

"Well," sighed Marty, "I sure do favor me Missie's sunsets."

The hotel room looked just as bleak and bare when they again reached it, but Marty felt much better about having a clean bed. And she was sure enough ready for it now. After two nights on a swaying train, it would be good to have a solid place to lie down. They prepared for bed, prayed together, and crawled between the sheets. Clark put out the light, and before many minutes had passed, Marty knew he was sleeping soundly. She lay for a while thinking of the family at home and feeling just a bit lonely. Then she thought of Missie and her family, and the lonely feeling slipped away as she, too, drifted off to sleep.

Sometime during the night Marty awoke. Something was wrong. Something had wakened her. Was it a noise of some sort? No, she didn't remember hearing anything out of the ordinary. Clark stirred. He seemed restless, too. Marty turned over and tried to go back to sleep. It didn't work. She turned again.

"You havin' problems, too?" asked Clark softly.

"Can't sleep," Marty complained. "Don't rightly know why, I jest—"

"Me too."

They tossed and turned as the minutes ticked slowly by.

"What time is it?" asked Marty. "Anywhere near mornin'? Might as well git up an' be done with it iffen it is."

Clark reached for his watch. He couldn't read the hands in the darkness.

"Mind iffen I light the lamp to git a look?"

"Go ahead. Lamplight ain't gonna make me any wider awake than I am already."

Clark struck a match and lit the lamp. As the soft glow spread over the bed, Marty gasped. Clark, who had moved the pocket watch into the light to get a look at the time, jerked his head up.

"Bedbugs!" exclaimed Marty.

Both of them were instantly on their feet, and many small insects darted for cover.

"Bedbugs! No wonder we couldn't sleep! Oh, Clark! We'll be scratchin' our way all across these prairies."

"Funny," said Clark, "I never felt 'em bitin' me."

"Thet's the way with bedbugs. Sometimes ya don't even feel 'em until the bite starts to swell up an' itch. You'll feel 'em fer sure tomorrow, I'm thinkin'."

Marty ran to check their cases and thankfully noted that they were tightly closed. Only their bodies and the clothing around the room to worry about.

"Clark, when we leave this here place, we gotta be awful sure we don't take none of them with us."

"An' how we gonna do thet?"

"I'm not rightly sure. One thing I do know—thet light stays on fer the rest of the night, an' I'm not crawlin' back into thet bed."

They washed carefully, then inspected each item of their clothing before they put it on. Marty brushed and brushed and brushed her hair in the hopes that if there were any of the little creatures in her hair, she would brush them out. None appeared. She didn't quite know whether that was a good sign or a bad one.

After checking and rechecking, they packed their belongings carefully and closed the cases tightly. Marty put the cases as close to the lamp as she could and stood vigil. It was still only four o'clock . . . hardly the hour of the morning to take to the street.

They managed to wait until the first rays of the dawn were showing on the eastern horizon, and then they left the hotel. The room had been paid for in advance, so Clark just tossed the key on the desk; the sleeping clerk stirred slightly, murmured something inaudible, and settled back to snoring. They walked through the unpainted doors and out into the street.

"Where are we gonna go?" questioned Marty. "Nothin' will be open yet."

"Well, there's a bench over there in front of the sheriff's office. How 'bout sittin' in the sun fer a spell?"

Marty nodded. It was a bit cool in the morning air; she could do with a little sun. She hoped that the warmth of the rays would reach them quickly.

It was a while before others were also stirring about the streets of the town. The livery hand arrived first and went about the duties of feeding the horses and a pair of mules. Roughly dressed men eventually swaggered out of the hotel, a few at a time; then the blacksmith began pounding on some metal in his shop. Shop owners began to open doors and rearrange window signs. The sheriff checked his office and then headed for the hotel and a cup of morning coffee. There was more movement toward the hotel, and soon Marty and Clark could smell cooking bacon and brewing coffee. Marty had not realized she was hungry until that moment.

Clark turned toward her. "Rather fun to watch a town wake up. I've never done thet before," he commented, and Marty nodded her head in agreement.

"It's not really so different from home as far as looks go—yet it *feels* strange," she answered. "Still, I haven't seen anything—" Her words were interrupted.

Four cowboys rode into view, their horses dusty and tired. They led four other horses behind them with some kind of bundles tied on their backs. The horses were spotted and wore no saddles, although two of them had colorful blankets tossed across their backs. The men rode past silently, their leather-encased feet swinging freely and their hair hanging past their shoulders in long black braids. Upon observing the braids, Marty snatched a second look. Why, those weren't cowboys. They were Indians! Now *that* was different. The riders looked neither to the left nor the right as they rode down the street and pulled their mounts to a stop before the general store. They swung down from their horses and began to untie the bundles from the backs of the pack animals.

"Looks like they've got 'em a pretty good catch of furs," observed Clark.

"Furs," said Marty. "I never thought of furs. What kind, ya supposin'?"

"I've no idea. Coyotes, badgers, maybe. Not close enough to the mountains fer bears or wildcats, I'm thinkin'. But then I'm not much fer knowin' jest what they do have hereabouts."

Marty turned only after they had all disappeared.

"Well," said Clark, "ya ready fer some breakfast?" He stood up and stretched his tall frame.

Marty stood, too, and picked up her lunch bundle and hatbox. Without thinking, she reached to scratch an itching spot on her rib cage, then checked herself; a lady did not go about scratching in public. At the same time, she realized that Clark was scratching his neck. Marty looked at the spot. "Oh my," she whispered.

Clark looked at her.

"Ya sure enough got yer share," stated Marty. "They're beginnin' to show up all along yer collar."

"Bedbugs?"

"Bedbugs. Well, not the bugs exactly—but where they been."

"Guess they liked me better'n they did you, huh?"

"'Fraid not," said Marty. "I got me four or five places thet I'd jest *love* to be scratchin'."

Clark laughed. "Well, maybe a cup of coffee an' a slice of ham will take our mind off 'em." He picked up the cases and motioned Marty toward the hotel's dining room they had passed up the night before in favor of the saloon place.

"Fella told me thet this ain't the fanciest place around; but it's the only one thet's open this time of the day, so I guess we'll give it a try. Surely nobody can make too much of a mess outta just boilin' coffee."

Maybe Marty was just hungry, or maybe the food actually wasn't so bad; at any rate, she ate heartily.

SIX

Arrival

The next three days on the train, a very slow-moving one, were even more difficult for Marty. For one thing, she was in a fever to reach Missie, and the many delays and the hesitant forward crawl irritated her. She also was tired from several nights without a good rest, and the train they rode was even more primitive and worn than the first. The wooden seats and cramped quarters made it difficult to sit comfortably, and the narrow aisles allowed little room for stretching or walking.

There were only two other women on the crowded train, and neither seemed inclined to make new friendships. The men, rough and rugged, appeared mostly to be gold seekers or opportunists. The constant smoking of cigars and cigarettes made Marty feel like choking. The temperature continued to climb, and the heat and stuffiness of the car almost overcame her. Discovering the bedbug bites from their previous hotel room did not help her frame of mind. Occasionally there was something of interest out the train window, like the small herd of buffalo that wandered aimlessly along beside the track. But usually there was nothing at all to see but barren hills and windswept prairie. Now and then herds of cattle or a squatter's makeshift buildings came into view. Marty counted only three *real* houses, each surrounded by many outbuildings. She guessed each of these to be someone's profitable ranch.

The small towns along the route, though few and far between, looked very busy. Marty wondered where the people came from. As much as she normally enjoyed watching people, she did not care for that activity now. She just wanted to get to the LaHaye ranch and Missie, and each time the train stopped and frittered away precious time, Marty chafed inside. What could they possibly be doing to take so long in such an insignificant place, anyway? Marty fussed, minding the heat, the cramped quarters, the smoke, the delay, and the itching bites.

But all her fretting did not get them one mile closer to Missie, she gradually came to realize. At length Marty willed herself to take a lesson from Clark and learn some patience. She settled herself in her corner and determined not to stew. She even decided to study the countryside and see what she could learn about it.

Early on the third morning, Clark returned from chatting with a fellow in a seat farther up the coach and informed Marty with a grin that the man had said Missie's small town was the next stop, and unless something unforeseen happened, they should be in by noon. Marty was wild with joy. Now it was even harder to sit still and not chafe about the slowpoke engine that took them forward at such a snail's pace.

The man was right. Just before the noon hour the train began to slow, and they all stirred themselves and started to gather their belongings.

Marty cast one final look around at her fellow passengers. She noticed a youth hoist up his small bundle and move toward the door. He looked tired and hungry, and there was a bit of uncertainty and loneliness in his eyes.

Why, he don't look any older than my Luke, Marty thought compassionately. *Supposin' he's come on out here all by himself an' don't know where he's goin' or what he'll find when he gits there?*

Marty was about to ask Clark if there was something they could do for the youth when the train stopped and the boy disappeared in the crowd.

They climbed down the steps from the train, looked around quickly, and moved toward the dusty new sidewalk. The boards had not fully weathered yet, and they obviously were newer than the town. Marty noticed the buildings were recently built, but many of them looked as though they had been constructed in a big hurry with the cheapest material available. Little attention was given to fanciness or even getting things straight.

Marty's eyes turned to the scores and scores of bawling cattle milling around in the corrals to the right of the tracks, kicking up dust and drowning out all other noises. Yes, this was a cattle town, to be sure.

But Marty really was not interested in buildings or cattle—only people. She was busy scanning the crowd for a glimpse of Missie.

Dust-covered cowboys—and equally dust-covered horses—moved back and forth on the main street, wide hats almost hiding their features. A number of women walked by, none of them in hats but wearing cheap and practical bonnets or nothing on their heads at all.

Marty was trying to stay close to Clark through the crushing passengers from the incoming train, all the while straining her eyes for the first sight of Missie, when a deep voice drawled beside them, "'Scuse me, sir, but are you folks the Davises?"

Marty looked up at the cowboy who stood beside them, hat in hand.

"Shore are," replied Clark.

"Right glad to meet ya, sir—ma'am. I'm Scottie, foreman for the LaHayes, an' I been sent to meet this here train." Marty felt her heart sink with disappointment. Missie was not here.

Clark set down a case so he could extend a hand. "Glad to meet ya, Mr. Scott."

"I'd be happy to take ya on over to the hotel, ma'am, and let ya freshen up some. It's gonna be a bit of a ride to the ranch. Then we'll collect yer things an' be off."

"I'd like thet," replied Marty as cheerfully as she could, and they followed Scottie down the street.

"Mrs. LaHaye is 'most bustin' with eagerness. She could hardly stand it thet she ain't here to meet ya herself. Never know when this here train is finally gonna pull in. This one was scheduled to be in here yesterday. 'Course, one day late ain't so bad. Sometimes it's been as much as five. A little hard fer her to stand around waitin' with two little ones in tow—ya know what I mean?"

But Scottie didn't wait for an answer.

"Boss, he came into town to check yesterday—brought the whole family, jest in case the train happened to be on time. Well, she warn't. He sent me on in today. He was gonna give it another try tomorra. Missus will be right glad thet it won't be necessary."

Marty was glad, too. *Mercy me,* she thought, *I'da never stood it if we'd been five days late—and neither would poor Missie!*

They entered the small hotel, and Scottie spoke to the man at the desk. Marty was shown to a room. It was not fancy, but it was clean. Marty was glad for a fresh supply of water for a good wash. The men left again to go pick up their baggage from the train station. Marty prayed that everything had arrived safely and intact.

She couldn't help but feel some disappointment at the further delay. She had thought when she arrived in this little town that her long wait to see Missie would be over. But of course Scottie was right. It would have been very foolish for Missie to make the long trip every day, not having any idea when the train might actually arrive.

The room seemed cool in spite of the warm weather, and after Marty's wash she lay down on the bed, promising herself that she'd just rest for a few minutes while she waited for Clark and Mr. Scottie to come.

The next thing she knew Clark was bending over her. He said Scottie was ready to take them for a little something to eat before they headed for the ranch.

Despite Marty's hunger, she begrudged even the time spent on the meal. They hurried with their dinner because Scottie, too, was anxious to get back to the ranch.

Marty sat in the wagon on a seat that had been especially fashioned for her by Willie and made as comfortable as possible. Clark sat up on the driver's bench with Scottie. Scottie was not a great talker, but he was generous in answering any questions. Marty paid no attention to the conversation. Nor did she particularly watch the passing scenery. Her mind was totally on Missie, wondering how much reserve the passing years might have put between mother and daughter. Would they still be able to share feelings and thoughts, or would the time and the experiences have closed some doors for them? Marty felt a little fear grip at her heart. And what about Missie's children, her grandchildren?

Would they see her as only a stranger they did not particularly welcome to their world? The questions and doubts persisted until her mind was whirling with anxieties as they rumbled along. Clark turned back to check on her now and then, and she managed to give him a shaky smile. She hoped he didn't notice her agitation.

And then they came over a hill, and Scottie pulled up the team. "There's the boss's spread, right down there," he said, pride coloring his voice. It was evident he felt a measure of ownership in the ranch, just by his association. Marty's heart skipped. Right down there! Right before her very eyes was their Missie's home. Marty saw a large, sprawling, gray stone home. Soft smoke curled up from the chimney. Off to one side, she could see a garden and a very small stream flowing away from a rocky embankment. She let her eyes seek out the pen with the chickens, the seeming miles of corrals, the bunkhouse and cook shack, and, yes, there on the other side was a straw-colored mound. *That must be Missie's soddy.* Marty's eyes filled with tears, and she had an impulse to jump from the wagon and run down the hill. Remarkably, she held herself in check. Scottie clucked to the team, and they moved forward.

Whether it was Scottie's driving or Marty's wishful thinking or the eagerness of the team to return to their stalls, Marty never knew for sure. But the remainder of the trip down the long winding hill went more quickly.

At the bottom of the hill, Scottie "whoaed" the horses and handed the reins to Clark. "I'll jest be gettin' on back to my duties," he said. "You'll be wantin' to make yer greetin's in private," he added as he stepped down from the wagon.

"And many thanks to ya fer yer welcome an' fer drivin' us this long way," Clark said warmly. Scottie tipped his hat to them and moved off toward the barn. Marty climbed up beside Clark for a better view of the house as the horses moved forward. A flash of red calico in a window, and then . . . there was Missie, her arms opened wide and her face shining with tears, running toward them calling their names. Marty ran to embrace her beloved daughter. They held each other close, crying and laughing and repeating over and over tender, senseless endearments.

At last, at last, sang Marty's heart. *At last I have my "if only."*

The hours that followed were wild with excited chatter and activity. The two grandsons had immediately captivated their newfound grandparents. Marty was so thankful that the boys moved forward without hesitation and even allowed hugging. Nathan beamed his pleasure. He was all ready to take charge of the entertainment of these two special people in his mother's life. "Mama said I could show ya my room," and "Mama said you'd go ridin' with me, Grandpa," and "Mama said you'd like to see my own pony," and "Mama said you'd read to me sometimes." Missie laughed, and Marty realized she had been carefully preparing her children for the adventure of meeting their grandparents.

Josiah was too young to be as active in the conversation, but he pulled at coattails and hands and insisted on "Up!" Marty was thrilled with how quickly the two little boys felt at ease with their grandparents. When Josiah did manage to steal a scene from Nathan, he was full of chatter of "See this" and "Do you like my . . . ?" and "Lookit, G'amma." For Clark and Marty, their hearts were captured at sight by the two small boys.

The whole house was filled with happy sounds as Missie proudly showed them from room to room. Marty exclaimed over the comfort, the coolness, and the attractiveness of the big stone house. They had entered through wide double doors into a large cool hall. The floor was of polished stone, and the inside walls were textured white stucco. Missie had used paintings with Spanish-Mexican influence to decorate the walls and had placed an old Spanish bench of white wrought iron against one wall. The bench had cushions of a flower-print material, and Missie had picked up the shade of green in them to highlight little finishing touches in the room, a pleasing and cool effect. The living room was large and airy with a mammoth stone fireplace and deep red and gold fabrics on the furnishings. The draperies, of matching material, were tied back with gold cords. It looked Spanish *and*—thought Marty—*very rich and inviting.* The floor was dark-stained wood, and the walls were, like the entry, textured stucco. Scattered across the polished wooden floors were deep-colored rugs—not the homemade variety but store bought. The pictures and lamps were Spanish—and elegant, with blacks, reds, and golds predominant. Marty viewed her surroundings in awe. Never had she seen such a grand living room, she told Missie.

On they moved to the dining area. "And," said Missie, with a wave of her hand and a laugh, "that's as far as we've been able to go with our grandness. From here on, it's common living. But it'll come together, little by little, with each cattle shipment."

Missie gestured toward a long homemade trestle table that easily seated eight. "Willie has promised me some dining room chairs and a *real* table this fall." Though the chairs looked comfortable enough, they were not matched or of particular quality. The white-stuccoed walls were quite bare, and inexpensive curtains hung at the windows. A simple cabinet against the far wall held the good dishes that Marty had insisted Missie take west. Somehow the simple, homey room put Marty's heart at ease. The differences now between them might not be so great after all.

"Oh, Missie, I'm so proud of you and so happy for you!" she exclaimed with a quick hug. Clark's approving grin echoed that sentiment.

The bedrooms were all big and roomy, but again, the furnishings here were simple and the curtains and spreads and the rugs on the floor were all homemade. Marty recognized many things she had helped to sew.

Missie led them to the other wing, the kitchen area of the house. Marty was surprised when Missie stopped at the door and gave a brief rap, then walked in. A wiry little Chinese man was busily engaged in preparations for the evening meal. Marty had not known that Missie had a cook.

"Wong," said Missie, "this is my pa, my mama."

The Chinese man favored them with a big grin and bobbed his head up and down as he acknowledged the introductions.

"How'do, how'do," he said over and over. "Wong pleased with pleasure. How'do, how'do."

Clark and Marty both answered with smiles and greetings.

"Wong is trying hard to learn our difficult English," Missie explained while Wong beamed at them. "He has done very well in a short time. He does not need to learn how to cook. He knew all about cooking when he came. Every rancher hereabouts envies us and hopes for an invitation often to eat his delicious food."

Wong bobbed his head again and led them around the large kitchen. Marty had never seen so much working room. The stove was big, too, and Wong proudly lifted the covers from several steaming kettles, all sending forth delicious fragrances.

Missie led her parents down a hall and toward a back door.

"I had me no idea thet ya had a cook. My, my," remarked Marty.

"Wong has not been with us for long," Missie answered. "At first, I thought Willie was being silly to suggest it, but I wonder now why I even tried to fight it. Wong is so much help. He helps with the laundry, too. It gives me more time for the children, and I still have plenty to keep me busy with this big house. I'm glad that we have him—and it gives him a job and a home, as well. Nathan and Josiah adore him. But it made Cookie terribly jealous at first," Missie continued. "He was so afraid that someone else would take his place with our boys. But the two rascals have managed to keep both of the men happy. Actually, the two cooks seem to really enjoy each other now. Most evenings they get together for a cup of coffee and a chat. In fact, Cookie is the one who volunteered to teach English to Wong."

Missie's long speech had brought them to the patio at the back of the house. The front, the bedroom wing on the one side, and the kitchen wing on the other surrounded this lovely area on three sides. The fourth side looked out toward the spring beyond Missie's flower beds. When Marty remarked on their beauty, Missie informed her that they were all flowers she had taken from the neighboring hills, except for the bed of roses. Scottie, a little red-faced with embarrassment, had presented her with the roses when he had returned from purchasing some choice livestock farther south.

The sheltered veranda between the patio and the house was shaded and cool in the late afternoon. Marty imagined what a pleasant place this would be to spend an afternoon sewing or reading to the children. She was very impressed with the home Willie had built for Missie. Marty was pleased with their good taste, and she admired Missie's choice of color and texture in the living room. Also, it all said to Marty that times were good, that Missie and Willie were making upward strides after their primitive start in the soddy. The homier simple furnishings in the remainder of the house also spoke to Marty. These told her that Missie and Willie were willing to wait, to build gradually, to not demand everything at once, showing maturity and good judgment. Marty *was* proud of them—both of them.

After the tour through the house, Willie invited Clark out to see the barns and stock, and Missie took Marty to show her the garden, the spring, her chickens, and then the little soddy.

Nathan, who clung to Grandma's hand, didn't like to leave her to go with the men, but he was most anxious to show off his pony. Josiah, who had been riding on Grandpa's shoulder, hated to climb down but did not want to get too far away from his mother. Besides, he absolutely adored the chickens! After some complaints from both of the children, the three "men" headed for the barn, and the women and the younger son took the path to the garden.

Marty was pleased at the sight of Missie's garden. True, it wasn't as far along as her own had been on the farm back east, but the plants looked healthy and productive, and Marty could see that many good meals would be coming from the little patch.

The water from the spring was not as ambitious as the spring back home, but the effect it had on the surrounding area outweighed the difference. All around were brown hills and windswept prairies, but near the spring crowded green growing things and small shivery-leafed trees—truly an "oasis."

Missie briskly led the way to the chicken pen. Forty or fifty hens squawked and squabbled in the enclosure. They looked healthy enough, and Missie assured her mother that they were very good egg producers.

Josiah immediately began hollering at the chickens, attempting to throw handfuls of grass and dirt at them through the wire. Since the wind was blowing from the wrong direction, most of it blew right back into Josiah's face, so Missie put a stop to the activity. Josiah was quick to obey, blinking dust from his eyes.

As they moved on toward the unassuming soddy, Marty noticed that Missie referred to it with love and even joy, a fact that Marty found very difficult to understand. Missie pushed open the rough wooden door and they entered the dim little sod shack. When Marty's eyes had adjusted, she could make out the bed in the corner, the black iron stove right where it had been, the small table, and the two stools.

Marty gazed all around her, from the simple furnishings to the sod roof and the packed-dirt floor.

This is the "home" that waited for you after that long, hard trip? And you actually lived here, Marty thought incredulously. *You actually lived in this little shack—and with a new baby! How could you ever do it? How could you stand to live in such a way? My, I . . .*

But Missie was speaking: "Willie wanted to tear it down, to get it out of here, but I wouldn't hear tell. I've got a lot of memories in this little place. We've had to resod the roof a couple of times. Roofs don't last too long with the winter storms, the wind and rain. And once they start to leak, they aren't good for anything."

Marty did not express her feelings about the soddy. Instead she expressed her feeling for her girl. "I'm so proud of you, Missie—so proud. I hoped to bring ya up to be able to make a happy home fer the one thet ya learned to love. An' ya did. Ya looked beyond these here dirt walls into the true heart of the home. Home ain't fancy dishes an' such, Missie. Home is love and carin'. Remember when I insisted on those fancy dishes, Missie? I said thet you'd be so glad fer them someday. So I fussed 'bout ya takin' 'em, even though ya really had no room fer 'em an' could've taken somethin' more sensible in the little space you had in the wagon. Well, I was wrong, Missie." Marty's hand touched her daughter's cheek. "I was wrong, an' you were right. Home ain't dishes, frills, an' such, Missie. Home is love an' carin'. You showed me thet ya could truly make a home, an' ya could do it with jest yer own hands an' yer own heart. I'm proud of ya. So very proud."

Missie's answering smile was understanding as Marty wiped the tears from her eyes. She looked around once more before leaving the small soddy. This time it did not look as bleak nor the floor as earthy. In those few short minutes, something had happened that changed the appearance of the little room.

SEVEN

Catching Up

After insisting on a story from both Grandma and Grandpa, the children were finally tucked into bed for the night. Clark and Willie moved into his office, a small room off the kitchen, to discuss the business of farming and ranching. Missie and Marty settled comfortably in the living room with coffee cups.

"It was useless to try to 'catch up' before this," said Missie, "but I think things are quiet enough now for us to talk—really talk. I have so many questions. I just want to know about everyone—everyone. I hardly know where to start, but you might as well start talking, because I just can't bear to let you go to bed until I find out all about those at home."

Marty drew a deep breath. "I've been jest 'bout dyin' to tell ya all 'bout the family. My, ya'd be surprised iffen ya could see yer brothers an' sisters now!"

"Is big Clare still the tease?"

"Worse . . . worse, seems to me. He's always funnin', and I sometimes wonder iffen he'll ever grow up. Yer pa says he will, once he marries an' settles down."

"And what is his Kate like? Clare wrote to me. Sounded in the letter as though she was nothing less than an angel sent from heaven. What's she really like?"

"Kate's a fine girl. We feel she's jest what Clare needs. She's quiet and steady, a little overly cautious at times, but they should balance each other real well. She's quite tall, with brown hair, large violet eyes . . . I think it was the violet eyes thet caught Clare's 'tention. Though she's not what ya'd call a beauty, she does have very pretty eyes."

"And you said they're going to marry this fall?"

"August twenty-seventh. Might have been a little sooner, but we wanted to be sure and have lots of time to get home again and git us ready fer the big event."

"Does Arnie have a girl?"

"He's been callin' on a little gal over in Donavan County. You remember Arnie—he's more the shy type. He takes things pretty slow like. Ellie says thet Hester will need to do the proposin' iffen it ever gits done!" Marty chuckled. "I think Arnie jest hasn't quite made up his mind yet. Wants to be good an' sure. She's a nice little girl, but her brothers are rather no-goods. Have a bad reputation in the area. Arnie ain't 'bout to let thet influence him, but he feels it's important when one marries to accept all the family members."

"Sometimes that just isn't possible," remarked Missie.

"Well, Arnie feels thet with Hester it has to be. She is very protective of her brothers. Would fight fer 'em if necessary. Arnie admires thet in her. But he wants to see the good in 'em that Hester sees. So far," Marty laughed softly, "I think he's been hard pressed to find some good, even though he's sure been lookin'."

"I hope he doesn't spend too many years *looking* and in the meantime let some girl with no such problems be snatched up by someone else."

Marty sighed. "Arnie deserves a good girl. He's so sensitive to the feelin's of others. He's got a lot of his father in him, thet boy."

"What about Ellie? Does she have a beau yet?"

"Not really. Not yet. Guess I was sorta hopin' ya wouldn't ask. I keep tryin' to pretend thet she ain't old enough yet—but I guess I know better, deep down. She's old enough. She's pretty enough, too. I guess she jest hasn't encouraged them much to this point. Ma Graham remarked 'bout her soon marryin' an' leavin' me. She's right. I've seen the boys tryin' to git her attention in a dozen ways. I always jest thought of it as schoolboy stuff. Not really. One of these days she'll notice 'em, too."

"Wish I could see her," Missie said, the yearning clear in her voice. "I suppose there would not be any chance she could come out and stay with us for a while?"

Marty felt a moment of panic. *Ellie come out here? The West is full of young men. Why, if she came to see her older sister, she might marry and never return home again!* Marty fought back her uncomfortable thoughts and responded in an even voice, "Maybe she could come on out on her honeymoon."

"But you said she didn't even have a beau—"

"She don't yet. But, my, thet can happen fast enough. I'm half scared she'll have her mind all made up 'bout some young fella by the time I git back home."

Missie laughed. "Now, I hardly think that's possible. Not for the short time you'll be away. Are you sure you can only stay for two weeks? Seems hardly worth coming all this way for such a short time."

"We couldn't possibly stay longer. Takes a week to come out an' a week to go home. By the time we git back, we'll have been gone a whole month. It's a busy time of the year, ya know. Pa left his boys completely on their own fer the summer hayin' an' all, an' Clare has to git his house ready. Luke is studyin' hard for his college exams an'—"

"Dear little Luke." Missie's voice was gentle. "How is he?"

A softness filled Marty's eyes. "He's not changed. Growed a little, I guess, but he's still got his same ways. Remember how he liked to cuddle up close in your lap when he was a young'un? Well, I git the feelin' sometimes he'd still like to do thet—iffen society wouldn't condemn it. He finds other ways to show love now. 'Member how you always used to pick me birthday strawberries? Well, yer pa broke up the pasture where the strawberries grew so well, so the last couple a' years the kids have jest forgot the strawberries. This year Luke decided thet I needed my birthday berries, so he went out real early an' went lookin' fer 'em. Had to really work hard, but he came back with a cupful. They was little and a mite on the green side, but I never tasted any better berries—ever."

"An' he's still doing well in school?"

"He's a good student, but he's through at the local school now. The teacher says she's given him everythin' she can give. He's read everythin' in sight an' still can't git enough."

"What will he do? He can't just quit."

"He plans to go on. Wants to go to the city fer college. I'm glad . . . an' scared . . . an' sad. All at the one time. I hate to see him go off alone like thet. Seems so young. He's only fifteen."

"Is he plannin' to be a teacher?"

Marty paused a moment before answering. "A doctor."

"A doctor?" Missie's tone was both surprised and admiring.

"He's had his heart set on it for a number of years now. He's talked to Doc Watkins 'bout it, too. Doc is pleased as a pappy. He doesn't have any children of his own, an' he's takin' great pleasure in nursin' Luke's ambitions."

"That would be nice to have a doctor in the family."

"Luke says he wants to help people. He's always wanted to help people, an' with so many towns not havin' a doctor—"

"What I wouldn't give to have a doctor here," Missie broke in, her tone wistful. "Young boy of our neighbor broke his arm last year. There was no one to set it properly. He'll always have a twisted, almost useless arm, just because . . ." Missie's words trailed off. "I keep thinking, what if it had been Nathan?"

Marty looked at her daughter and understood. She knew a mother's heart and the panic when a doctor is nowhere around when one is sorely needed. She, too, breathed a prayer that somehow this frontier settlement might soon have a doctor, but she also added silently, *Not Lukey. Please, not Luke.*

Missie interrupted her thoughts and her unspoken prayers. "How are Nandry's and Clae's families?"

Marty was happy to report on the two Larson girls who had joined the Davis family when Missie was just a youngster. Marty spoke lovingly of the grandchildren who brought such joy and delightful commotion to family gatherings. "Nathan and Josiah would have sech fun with all their cousins," she noted.

"Tell me about the neighbors," Missie said. "Do we still have the same people living round about?"

"Pretty much. The Coffins moved on back to the area where they came from. Mrs. Coffin never really did take to our community. Some said she jest couldn't stand bein' away from her twin sister. After they lost their little girl—remember the sickly little one?—well, after they lost her, Mrs. Coffin insisted they go on back to their home. Some new people on their land now. Called the Kentworths. Not friendly folk at all. All the neighbors have tried to git acquainted an' have been told not to bother. People say thet he's a lawbreaker an' jest doesn't want folks snoopin' round. Thet's what he calls it when anyone comes visitin'— snoopin' round. She's 'most as bitter and disagreeable as he is, so fer the time we jest have to sit tight an' pray fer 'em and watch fer a chance to show our carin'. Must be awful to live with such inner bitterness."

Missie nodded her head thoughtfully in agreement.

Marty went on, "Most of the other neighbors are the same as before, I guess. The Grahams are as dear friends as ever. Sally Anne has three girls, 'most growed up now.

"Tommie's Fran jest had a baby boy. He's six years younger than Tom, Junior, the boy who had been the baby fer a good while. Tom is thrilled with the new little fella."

"And the Marshalls? How are they doing?"

"It's sad," Marty answered, "sad to see the Marshalls an' their son, but it's beautiful, too. There is so much love there. Rett is a very loving child. He's a young man really, but he is still a child. Wanda and Cam really love 'im. He is so good with animals thet it's 'most uncanny. Wild or tame—they all seem to understand and trust Rett."

"And Wanda's happy?"

"Happy? Yah, she's happy. She needs to rely on her God daily, though. She has her hard times, but I'm sure she wouldn't be tradin' her boy fer all the boys in town."

Missie shook her head as she thought of the grief Wanda had carried. "She has suffered so much," she said softly.

"Yah," acknowledged Marty, "she has suffered—suffered and growed. Sometimes it seems to take the one to bring the other."

"When one does suffer, it is good to see that it hasn't been wasted—that the sufferer allows God to make it a blessing rather than a bitterness," Missie observed.

Marty nodded and then went on. "Wanda and Ma Graham both sent their love. They sent some small gifts to ya, too. We have some packages from them in the trunk. Pa and I decided the things we brought with us would jest wait until tomorra. No sense rushin' into everythin' tonight."

"Now that you've mentioned gifts, I'm not sure I can wait till morning," Missie laughed. "Kind of like teasing a body—"

"They'll keep," Marty assured her, thinking Missie was still curious and excited about things just like old times at home. "We didn't want to come rushin' in here handin' out goodies right an' left. You might have understood, but Nathan and Josiah might be thinkin' thet's all grandparents are fer."

Missie laughed. "I'm thinking my sons have you both sorted out already. They seem to know right off that you're here just to spoil them."

"We'll have to be careful, but it sure'd be easy to spoil a bit, all right. Clae's girl, Esther Sue, and Nandry's four shore think thet we are there jest to humor them. 'Course they like attention from their uncles, as well. Arnie does most of the fussin'. Arnie really loves young'uns. The others all love the little ones, too, but it is Arnie who never seems to tire of 'em, though he pretends he does."

"And Joe still hasn't gone off to seminary? Has he changed his mind?"

"Oh no. He's as set on it as ever. I'm hopin' he'll be able to go next year."

"Oh, it's so good to catch up a bit! Makes me feel closer to them somehow. I've missed them all so much."

Marty's eyes filled with tears. "An' we've missed you. Missie, you'll never know how many—" She shook her head and stopped short. "No, I won't say it. I'm here now with you. I see ya have a lovely home, two beautiful boys, thet you're happy. I've told the Lord so many times thet if He'd jest give me this special treat, I'd thank Him with great thankfulness. Now I'm here an' I'm gonna keep my promise. I *am* thankful, Missie—so very thankful." Tears finally spilled down Marty's face, and Missie went to kneel before her and put her arms around her.

"Oh, Mama," she said, tears shining in her own eyes, "I've longed for you so often. I promised the Lord that I'd be content with seeing you, too. And here I've already been upset because you can't stay longer. I'm ashamed of myself. We'll just make every minute we have together count. We'll fill our time with so much happiness that we'll have barrels of memories to keep us when the time comes that we need to part again."

Marty smoothed Missie's hair. "Thet sounds like a grand idea," she said. "I've tucked away a few of these precious memories already."

Missie stood up. "Well," she said, "let's just get on with another one. Willie has developed a real liking for popcorn before bed, so let's go pop some. He says there just isn't anything better than to have a close family chat over popcorn. It's warm, and homey, and filling." Missie laughed and led the way to the big kitchen. "I always feel like a little girl sneaking in where her mama doesn't want her when I do this. Wong is so fussy. But I always clean up very carefully." Mother and daughter laughed together.

The popcorn was soon ready, and Clark and Willie were called to join them in the living room. The visiting continued, as Willie and Missie asked all about the neighbors, the school, the church. Fighting emotion, Willie wanted to know how his pa, Zeke LaHaye, *really* was doing. The occasional letter somehow didn't seem to tell the whole story.

"I think a trip on out here would do him a world of good," Clark commented. "He needs to get a fresh outlook on things. Oh, he still loves his farm, but yer brother has 'most taken over now. Zeke loves his grandkids, too, but he still misses yer ma somethin' awful. He sent a little parcel along with us."

"All of this talk of parcels and presents from back home—and they plan to make us wait until morning!" Missie obviously could hold back her frustration no longer. "How can a body sleep tonight not knowing what's in the trunk?"

After some laughter and teasing, it was decided that the trunk and its contents would be brought in and distributed before retiring.

After the trunk was placed in the room and the straps removed, Missie dove in with a will, laying to one side those things intended for the children. She squealed and cried by turn, enjoying every item that had come with love from those "back home."

"We'll have Nandry's raspberry preserves for breakfast," she declared, holding up a sparkling jar.

The hour was late when they finally cleared up the clutter and said good-night with hugs all around.

Marty went to bed with an overflowing heart. Her prayers truly had been answered—and now she finally felt she could sleep for a solid week.

The next day even Marty was coaxed up on horseback in order to be given a tour of the ranch. She enjoyed the tiny flowers that nobly bloomed beside the trail, she thrilled to the sight of Willie's herds of cattle feeding on the hillsides, and she loved the placid mountains lined up against the sky in the distance. But she did *not* enjoy the wind sweeping across the prairie, pulling at her hair and skirt, nor the miles and miles of seeming emptiness. Marty watched Missie carefully as they rode together, and she could see in Missie's face that all she saw now was Willie's land as she had grown to love it.

Sunday arrived and with it some visitors to the LaHaye spread. At two o'clock in the afternoon, the opening hymn of their regular Sunday service was led by Henry Klein. Clark and Marty were happy to renew their acquaintance with the wagon driver who had come west with the LaHayes. Henry had changed much in those few short years. No longer a bashful, hesitant boy, he was now a sincere and confident man, presenting proudly an attractive wife and a two-year-old son, Caldwell.

As they sang the hymn, Marty glanced around her. Some of the LaHaye cowhands were there. She couldn't remember all the names, though she had been introduced. There was Cookie—she had no problem remembering Cookie—and Rusty and Lane. The other two names she could not recall. A neighborhood family had joined them for the service. Marty saw the small boy with the twisted arm, and her heart went out to him. These were the Newtons, a young couple with four young sons.

After the singing, Willie led the service and Clark was asked, as honored guest, to give the Bible lesson. The people were attentive, and Marty even heard an occasional quiet amen.

Juan and Maria and their baby girl and young son were not in attendance this time. Missie had told Marty about her friend and kept an eye on the road that twisted down the hill, no doubt hoping they would arrive, but when the service was over they still hadn't come. Missie was worried, she told her mother. It was the second Sunday in a row the de la Rosas had not showed up. They were not away from home, since Scottie had reported seeing them Friday. No one was ill, for they had all been in town together. Missie could not think of a reason for their absence, she explained, her voice low. She must call on them and see if there was some problem.

After the service ended, Missie served coffee and some of Wong's delicious doughnuts. They sat and visited, sharing their daily experiences, some joys and some difficulties. Marty and Clark were glad for the opportunity to get to know some of Missie and Willie's neighbors. They all seemed to feel that the service was a special time in their week.

The cowboys were the first to take their reluctant leave. It was time for their shift, and Scottie would be watching for them.

Next the Newtons also left. Mr. Newton as yet did not employ many hands on his spread and needed to get back in the saddle himself. He stated they hadn't been bothered much with rustlers lately, but one could never tell when they might decide to strike. The small, defenseless ranches were easy picking. The Newtons promised to be back again the next Sunday.

The Kleins stayed for supper. Marty could tell Wong was happy for the chance to show off his culinary skills. Nathan and Josiah, glad for a playmate, took Caldwell out to the patio to play with a delighted Max, who ran around in circles with excited yelps to remind them that for the last few days he had been getting very little attention.

Marty chatted with Melinda Klein while Missie fussed about the table, setting it with the good dishes and making sure everything looked its best. Marty soon came to feel very close to Melinda. Though some distance in age between them, they had shared similar experiences in their introduction to the West, both having lost a young husband in tragic accidents. Marty was glad that Melinda had Henry to help her over the hurt and confusion of losing the one she loved while so far away from friends and family. *And I'm glad I had Clark,* she thought with a quick glance at him across the room.

Henry, too, was anxious for news from the home area. Though Clark and Marty knew few of the people Henry would have claimed as neighbors, they were able to tell him some of the general news from the district.

Soon after the evening meal, the Kleins left for home and the boys were tucked in for the night. After their double portion of bedtime stories, they settled down, not to be heard from again till morning. Missie declared that the excitement of Sundays always tired them out.

Marty, too, felt tired, even though she was gradually catching up on the missed sleep. Willie informed her that it was the change in the altitude. Marty was willing to accept any excuse for her laziness. All she knew was that she was longing for her bed.

She hid a yawn and tried to get back into the conversation. Clark and Willie were making plans for the morning. It sounded as though wherever they were going, it would be a long ride. Willie was asking Missie if she wished to go. Marty was already stiff from her short ride of the day before. She wasn't sure she could handle another horseback ride, but Missie was answering, "I thought Mama and I should go on over to see Maria. I can't understand why they have missed two Sundays. If it's okay with Mama, we'll go and see what we can find out. I'm anxious for Mama and Maria to meet. You'll never believe Maria," Missie said, turning to Marty. "She speaks very good English now. Me—I hardly got a decent start on Spanish."

So it will be the saddle again tomorrow. Marty winced at the thought. Not only would she ride tomorrow, but from what she had understood, she would ride a long way. The de la Rosas were not *near* neighbors.

Marty nodded her head in agreement, hoping Missie did not read any hesitation.

Missie continued, "We should leave by nine. I think we'd better take the team so Mama won't need to ride so soon again, not being used to it. Besides, it's a fair ways and we'll need to take the boys. Could you have Scottie see that the team is ready for us, please?"

Willie nodded and Marty breathed in her relief. Everyone, now having settled on the plans for the morrow, decided that sleep would be needed to carry them through. They bade each other good-night and headed for their beds.

EIGHT

Marty Meets Maria

The sun rose over the distant hills the next morning and right from the sunrise seemed to pour forth intense heat.

After breakfast and the morning chores, Willie brought the team around, and Missie loaded her sons and canteens with plenty of water for the day. Marty placed her bonnet firmly on her head as protection from the sun and wished she had a cooler gown.

"My, it's warm!" she exclaimed, but Missie did not seem bothered by the heat.

"A breeze should come up and cool things off some," she responded, then clucked to the team and they were off.

They had not gone far before Marty could feel the breeze, though she might have preferred to call it a gale. It was not anything like the cooling breezes that swept over the valley at home. In fact, Marty thought the wind felt even hotter than the sun. It whipped at her cheeks, drying and scorching them. It tore at her skirts and made the brim of her bonnet flap. Marty did not care for wind, and she wished it would blow elsewhere.

"I guess I've gotten used to the wind," Missie remarked as Marty tried to hold her bonnet down with one hand and her skirts with the other.

Nathan and Josiah rode comfortably on the first part of the journey, then began the age-old question, "How much longer?" Missie dealt with it good-naturedly until Nathan began to tease his younger brother, for lack of something else to do, and then she stopped the horses and lifted the youngsters down to stretch their legs. She gave them each a drink from a canteen and a couple of cookies and instructed them to play in the shade of the wagon while Mama and Grandma took a short walk. There was no shade for walking, so there was no temptation to linger. In fact, Marty was glad to be back in the wagon and moving again.

When they came to the river, Marty glanced up and down its length for a bridge. There was none. Missie confidently headed the horses into the stream, explaining as she did so that it used to flow deeper at that point until the men of the area widened the riverbed and allowed the stream to spread out. "Now," said Missie, "it's safe to cross here almost any time of year."

Marty, most relieved to hear it was safe, still gripped the wagon seat with white knuckles and snatched anxious glances over her shoulder at her grandsons. Crossing the river was the most exciting part of the journey for the boys. Marty heard their squeals of delight as the swirling water foamed about the wagon wheels. Once across, though, they began to coax their mother to hurry the team and complained they were too crowded, too hot, and too hungry.

Missie eventually handed the reins to Marty and took Josiah on her lap. Without Josiah to torment, Nathan, too, settled down for the remainder of the trip.

It was almost noon before the de la Rosas' buildings came into view. Marty saw a large, low ranch house, built of the same stone as Missie's home, though not quite as spacious. It nestled among brown hills, and there was not even a spring to add some green to the area. Missie informed Marty that the de la Rosas were fortunate in having all the water they needed from the deep well they had dug. The well now was showing its worth as a windmill turned busily in the ever-present wind, causing a pump to send a constant stream of water from its spout into a large animal trough.

"Well, it's nice to know thet the wind is good fer somethin'," murmured Marty under her breath as Missie guided the team into the yard and directed them to the hitching rail.

A young woman came rushing from the house.

"Missie!" she cried. "Oh, I'm so glad you have come. I've been missing our visits!" She saw Marty and stopped with embarrassment. "Oh, please do excuse my bad manners. I did not know that Missie was not alone. You must be the mother. The one Missie has missed and cried and prayed for."

Marty nodded and smiled.

"And I am Maria—the mindless one," she quipped. "I run heedless when I see a friend."

Marty laughed and extended her hand, then changed her mind and hugged Maria close.

"Missie has told me of ya," Marty said carefully. "Yer such a special friend, and I am so glad to meet ya," she finished warmly.

"And I you," said Maria, giving Marty a warm embrace in return, "though I must say that seeing you makes me even more longing for the mama of my own. It has been so long. . . ."

Maria did not finish her sentence. Missie had lifted the boys down, and they were clamoring for some attention.

"Where's José?" asked Nathan.

"He's in the house, where we all should be out of this hot sun. Come, you must get in out of the heat. You are brave to come on such a day." And Maria quickly led them all into her home.

"José is in the kitchen bothering the cook," she told Nathan. "You may get him and you can play in his room. I don't think that even our patient Carlos could put up with *two* small boys in the kitchen."

Nathan went to find José, and the ladies walked into the coolness of the sitting room, Josiah in tow. Marty felt so much better out of the sun. She slipped off her bonnet and was glad to wipe the perspiration from her face with a handkerchief. *My, it was a hot trip!*

Maria seated them and went for cool drinks. Upon hearing the two older boys chattering as they came from the kitchen, Josiah decided to tag along with them to José's room.

The ladies were left to sip cold tea and visit. The talk was centered around the family, area news, and ranching. Marty was included, though some of the phrases the two young women used regarding ranching were new to her.

"You should have waited for a day more less hot," said Maria and then laughed at her mixed-up English. "How you say it?" she asked Missie.

"A cooler day."

"My goodness—cooler, no! There is nothing cool about this day. How can it be more cool than something that is not cool at all?"

Marty and Missie laughed at Maria's reasoning. They had no answer to her logic.

"Anyway," said Maria, "it is very warm in the sun. We are used to it here, but you, Mrs. Davis, must find it bad to you."

"It is warm," admitted Marty. "This tea is jest right."

"Well, I guess we should have waited," Missie said. "But who knows, it might get hotter instead of cooler, and I did want to see you, Maria."

"A special reason?" asked Maria seriously.

"Rather special. We've been missing you on Sundays, and I was afraid—well, I wondered—that is, I hoped nothing was wrong."

At the mention of the Sunday service, Maria's head drooped.

"I wanted to go. I missed it. But Juan—well, he is not so sure. Not sure that we do the right thing. At home we teach our boy one thing—one way to pray, one way to worship God—and at the meeting, you teach him another way. It puzzles him. You understand? Juan, he thinks that we should not confuse our son with more than one God."

"But, Maria," exclaimed Missie, "we've talked about that! It's the same God. We worship the same God, just in a little different way."

"I know, I know," said Maria, her hands fluttering expressively. "I know all that. And I think that Juan, he even understands that. But he is frightened—frightened that José will not understand and he will not wish to worship God at all. Do you not see?"

"Yes, I see," said Missie slowly, tears filling her eyes. "I see."

"Oh, I am so glad. So glad that you understand. I was afraid you would not be able to see how we felt. I did not want you to think ill of me."

"Maria, I would never think ill of you."

Maria turned to hide her own tears. For a moment she couldn't speak, and then she turned back to her guests and the tears were running down her cheeks.

"You must pray for us. Right now Juan has many doubts, many questions. He cannot leave the church of his past, but he has here no church of his own. He does not want his child to grow up without the proper church teaching, but he is no longer sure what he wants our boy to be taught. There were things about Juan's church—actually, my church, too—that he did not agree with, but we love our church. Juan has not forsaken it. He will never forsake it. In the services at your house we have heard new and strange things from the Bible. We did not know of them before. It takes much wisdom, much time, much searching of the heart to know the truth. Please be patient with us, Missie. And please pray for us that we may know the truth. One day we think, 'This is it,' and the next day we say, 'No, that is it.' It is hard—so very hard."

"I understand," said Missie slowly. "We will pray. We will pray that you will find the truth—not that you will believe as we believe, but that you will find the truth. We believe with all our heart that God has given His truth to us in His Son Jesus Christ, that He came to die for us and to forgive us our sins, and—" Missie stopped short. "But you believe that, too, Maria. You have told me that Jesus is the only way that one can come to God."

"Oh yes," said Maria. "That is the truth."

"Then all we really need to pray about is that God will show you and Juan if it's all right to worship with us."

"I . . . I think so. We have been taught one way—you another."

"We will continue to pray."

"It is so important to Juan to raise his children in the correct way. You see, his family—" But Maria stopped midsentence and hastened to her feet. "I must see if Carlos has our coffee and cakes ready. You will have cooled enough by now to be able to enjoy some of Carlos's coffee." She hurried away without waiting for a reply.

The talk over the coffee turned to lighter matters. They chatted about new material, dress patterns, and the gardens that were growing daily in spite of the heat. Missie finally announced that they must go, and

Maria sent José and Nathan to find Pedro, the yard hand, to bring the team and hitch up the wagon.

While the boys were running off to find the old man and give him the message, the women prepared to leave.

"Please," said Maria, "please could we have a prayer together? I have missed it so."

They knelt to pray. Missie prayed first, followed by Marty, and then it was Maria's turn. She began slowly, in carefully chosen English, and then she stopped and turned to the other two ladies. "Do you mind— will you excuse me—if I talk to God in my own language? I know He understands my heart in any language, but I think He understands *my* tongue better in the language of my birth." At their nods and smiles, Maria continued her prayer. Never had Marty heard a more fervent one. Maria poured out her soul to her God in honey-flowing Spanish. Though Marty could not understand a word of it, she understood the spirit of the prayer, and her heart prayed along with Maria. Surely God would answer this young woman's yearning for the truth.

NINE

The Rescue

Though still too warm for Marty's liking, the weather turned a bit more bearable. Missie and Marty kept close to the shelter of the house, but Clark rode with the men almost daily. Marty could tell his farmer's heart responded to the wide expanse of hillsides and roaming cattle, and he declared many times his love of the mountains.

Nathan clamored for his grandfather's attention. He was anxious to show off "his" part of the ranch to Clark. As yet, he was not allowed to roam freely on the open range. But there were well-worn trails closer to home that he claimed as his own. He had ridden them since he had been a baby carried on his mother's back. Now Josiah had replaced Nathan on Missie's horse, and Nathan was allowed the privilege of his own pony.

"Could ya ride with me today, Grandpa?" Nathan begged at the breakfast table.

"Well, I shore don't see why not," answered Clark. "I 'spect maybe yer pa will be able to git by without me fer this here one day."

Nathan took his grandfather's words seriously. "Ya can help him again tomorra," he assured Clark, causing laughter to ripple around the table.

"An' where're we ridin' today?"

"I'll show ya the west ridge."

"An' are there lots of excitin' things to see on the west ridge?"

Nathan nodded his head vigorously, since his mouth was too full of scrambled eggs to speak.

"Well, then," said Clark, "why don't we jest go on out fer a look-see?"

Nathan's eyes sparkled in anticipation. He hurried through his meal and bounced down from the table.

"What horse shall I tell Scottie to saddle for ya, Grandpa?" he asked with excitement.

"Nathan," said Willie quietly, indicating Nathan's empty chair.

Nathan crawled back up reluctantly and looked over at his mother, then back at his father. "May I be excused, sir?" he asked, subdued.

Willie nodded and Nathan swung down from the chair.

"What horse—" he began, but Clark stopped him with a laugh.

"I think Scottie's busy enough without worryin' none 'bout me. I'll saddle ol' Turk when I git down there."

Nathan spun around and was gone. "I'll get Spider," he called over his shoulder as he ran out the door, then followed it with, "Too bad Joey's too little."

"Joey?" questioned Marty.

Missie laughed. "I thought and thought of a name for my second son that wouldn't be all chopped up in a nickname. I thought I had one, too. Josiah. Surely no one could shorten that. But I wasn't counting on Nathan. He's called him Joey since the day he arrived."

"I think it's rather nice," Marty mused.

"Well, I guess it's all right—you know what I've decided? I've decided that almost any name is all right as long as it's spoken with love."

Marty smiled her agreement.

Clark finished his coffee and turned to Willie. "Well, cowboy, it looks like you'll jest have to do yer best wranglin' without me today. I've got me another pardner."

Willie grinned. "Wish I could come with ya, but I promised Hugh Caly thet I'd ride on over and take a look at some new stock he brought in. Yer lucky to be missin' thet ride. It's a long, hot one, an' to save some miles, we pass right through some bad cactus territory. Near scratches the clothes right off ya."

"Thet there west ridge sounds better 'n better to me." Clark smiled.

"Nothing much of danger on the west ridge. Thet's why we allow Nathan to ride there. Pretty lifeless over there. Ya'll be lucky to even spy a rattler slitherin' off."

"Well, iffen there be a rattler, I do hope it slithers off, all right," said Clark. "I haven't grown overfond of 'em."

"Jest don't surprise 'em," said Willie, "an' you'll be all right."

When Clark reached the barn, Scottie was unobtrusively giving Nathan a hand with the saddling of Spider. Clark went into the corral to bring out Turk. He still wasn't too handy with the rope, but he managed to get the horse on the second try.

They saddled up and left the yard, Missie calling to them as they rode out to make sure they both had full canteens.

"Ma always worries," confided Nathan in a loud whisper, to which Clark responded, "Thet's what mas are for."

They rode to the west, then turned toward the south and followed the ridge for a few miles. There really wasn't much new to see but an occasional glimpse of the mountain chain as it topped one of the nearer hills. Often they could look out to the east and see cattle, as Willie's herd fed its way across the prairie. Once or twice they spotted a cowboy as he hazed the cattle. The sun was high in the sky when Clark suggested they pull over in the shelter of some big rocks and eat the lunch Missie had sent along. Nathan seemed to like the idea. The eating time was the most important part of any trail ride. Nathan crawled down from Spider and ground-tied him. Clark did likewise with Turk, looking around cautiously to make sure there were no rattlers sharing the rocks with them. He noticed Nathan doing likewise.

"If rattlers are here, Grandpa, they'll be in the sun 'stead of on this shady side," he said. "But still Pa says ya always got to check to be sure."

Clark was pleased with the boy's knowledge of his environment and his carefulness.

"How much further we goin'?" asked Clark as they munched their sandwiches.

"Not much, I guess. Nothin' to see down there 'cept some ol' hills with holes in 'em."

"Ol' hills with holes?"

Nathan nodded.

"What kind of holes?"

"Pa says they used to mine it."

"Mine it?"

"Yeah."

"What kind of mine?"

"Dunno. Pa says fer me to stay away from the holes. He says they are dang'rous. Some stuff is gittin' rotten or somethin'."

"Best we stay away from 'em, then," agreed Clark, but he planned on asking Willie about the old mines when he got home.

They had just finished their lunch and were gathering things together when they heard an approaching horse. The rider was coming full gallop, and Clark stood up to see what the reason might be. One did not usually ride at such pace in the heat of the midday sun.

A young rider approached them, his legs beating at the sides of his horse and his unruly hair flying in the wind. Clark could hear him shout now and then, but he couldn't understand a word he was saying.

"Who's thet?" Clark asked the young Nathan.

For a moment Nathan just stood and stared without answering.

"Who is he? Ya know?" Clark asked again.

Nathan roused then, shaking his head.

The rider pounded closer, and Clark could plainly hear him sobbing now. Clark stepped forward to be ready to stop the horse when the boy drew near.

"You gotta come!" the frantic boy screamed even before he reached them. "You gotta come quick! Andy and Abe, they—"

He had reached them, and Clark hauled in the lathered horse.

"Whoa, there," he said, reaching up in one smooth movement both to pull the horse to a halt and to run a quieting hand over its neck.

"You gotta come—" The boy's voice was agitated and hoarse with emotion.

Clark moved a hand to the boy. "Jest take it easy. Take it easy. We'll come. Now ya calm down some 'n' tell—"

"Abe an' Andy!" cried the boy, tears making tracks down his dust-covered cheeks. "Abe an' Andy are in there."

"Take it easy," Clark said again. "Jest tell it slow like."

"We gotta hurry!" the boy barked impatiently.

"We'll hurry," said Clark. "But first we gotta know where to hurry to." Clark's purposeful calm seemed to have its effect, and the boy took a big breath before continuing.

"The mine. The ol' mine shaft—they're in there. It fell on 'em. They'll never git out."

"Where?"

"Over there. We were lookin' 'em over, an' the timbers broke an' the mine fell in—"

But Clark was already gathering the reins of his horse. "Nathan," he said, "can ya ride home alone? Does yer pa ever let ya do thet?"

"Sure," said Nathan, his eyes wide.

"Look, son," said Clark, pulling the boy close. "I want ya to ride on back to the ranch. Tell Scottie, or whoever is around, thet some boys are trapped in a mine. Tell 'em to bring shovels an' a wagon an' come on the double. Ya got thet?"

Nathan nodded his head in agreement, his eyes wide with the importance of his mission.

"Now ya ride on home. Take yer time—do ya hear? Don't try to go fast. Jest take yer time an' be careful. I'm gonna go with this here boy an' help those kids. All right?"

Clark boosted Nathan onto his pony and watched as the small boy headed back to the ranch on the familiar path. He was not concerned about the boy becoming lost. Nathan knew the way well. Clark was worried that panic might cause him to travel too fast and maybe end up in a spill. Nathan turned once to look back at his grandfather. "Remember. Go slow," Clark called to him, and the boy waved his hand.

The sobbing of the boy beside him brought Clark's head around.

"Okay, son. You lead the way. Take it easy. A fall with yer horse won't help yer friends none."

They started for the mine, the boy's spent horse wheezing for breath in choking gasps. Clark found that the mine was farther away than he had first thought.

The boy still wept sporadically. He pushed his horse as fast as the poor creature could go. When they finally reached an opening in the side of a hill, he threw himself off.

"They're in there!" he cried. "We gotta git 'em out."

Smoke-colored dust still lingered in the air, evidence of a recent cave-in.

"You know this mine?" he asked the boy.

"Some," the boy admitted with downcast eyes, and Clark could see that he knew it was forbidden territory.

Some boards that obviously had closed off the cave entrance had been pried off and discarded at the side of its open mouth.

"Tell me 'bout it," Clark said, and as the boy hesitated, Clark took his arm. "Yer friends are in there. Remember? Now, I don't know one thing about thet there cave. Tell me 'bout it. Does it have more than one branch? How far back were ya? Did the timbers collapse more'n once?"

The boy responded. "It has three main tunnels. The first one takes off real quick to the right. It's a short one. Don't think the miners found anything there, so they jest left it. The second one goes off to the right, too. But the fellas are in the left one. It's the biggest an' was used the most. The timbers're really bad in there. The shaft goes down deeper in the left one. Sometimes the steps are real steep an' slippery. We was climbin' up an' we kept slippin', so we grabbed hold of the side timbers to pull ourselves, an' thet's when it . . ." He couldn't continue but put his face in his hands and sobbed.

Clark stayed long enough to hold him for a moment. "It's okay. We'll git 'em. Are there any shovels?"

The boy shook his head. "We can use our hands," he snuffled.

"Yer not comin' back in," said Clark, seeing the terror in the boy's face.

"But I gotta," he said through sobs. "I gotta."

"No, yer needed here. They're gonna come from the ranch. Ya need to tell 'em where to go. They'll have shovels. Ya tell 'em, too, 'bout those rotten timbers. Ya hear?"

The boy nodded. Clark hoped the youth would be able to wait calmly without further panic.

Clark gently pushed him to a sitting position on a nearby rock. "Ya jest stay right there an' wait fer those men. Now, it might seem a long time till they come, but they'll be here. Ya jest keep watchin' fer 'em an' wave 'em on over here. Ya okay now?"

The boy nodded again, affirming that he was. His face was still white beneath the smears of dust and tears.

Clark turned and headed for the mine. The door was low, and he had to stoop to enter. Old beams above his head appeared as his eyes adjusted to the dimness. The supports looked fairly stable in some places and sagging and broken in others. Clark moved away from the light at the entrance and felt his way along the passage. He had not gone far when he found the first tunnel off to the right just as the boy had described. He continued on, feeling his way with his hands and his feet. A low-hanging beam caught him by surprise, and he banged his head against the knotted lumber. For a minute he felt dizzy with the pain, but he steadied himself until he had his bearings. From then on he went forward with one arm outstretched above his head.

Clark ducked his way past other obstructions. How he wished for a light. He figured the boys must have used some kind of torches or lanterns to find their way around. Clark discovered the second right-hand tunnel. *Only one more to go,* he told himself. The tunnel should soon swing to the left. After several yards of total darkness, Clark felt the tunnel veer sharply. The smell of dust was heavy in the air now. Clark was forced to stop and tie his handkerchief over his nose. He started down the left fork and soon came to one of the steep places the boy had described. Before he knew what was happening, his feet had slipped out from under him, and he felt himself sliding downward on his back. The rocks cut into him, scraping away shirt and skin. After he had come to a halt and felt cautiously about, Clark regained his feet and pressed slowly forward, testing carefully with his foot before he put his weight on it. Again and again the tunnel took a downward turn, but Clark was ready for them, most only a step or two. And then, just ahead of him, Clark thought he heard a groan. He fell to his hands and knees and felt his way forward.

"Hello," he called. "Hello. Do you hear me? Hello."

Another groan answered him, and Clark crawled on.

Soon he was in contact with a slight body. "Do you hear me?" he asked, reaching for the boy's wrist and the pulse. The boy stirred. Clark felt a faint pulse beat and breathed a prayer of thanks.

"Son," he asked anxiously, "son. Can you hear me? Are ya awake?"

In answer the boy began to cry. "Ya came," he sobbed. "Ya came."

"It's all right." Clark soothed him, brushing his hair back out of his face and feeling the dirt and debris falling off his head. "It's all right. Where are ya hurt? Can ya get up?"

"My ankle," sobbed the boy. "It's caught under thet beam."

"We'll git it out. We'll have it out in no time. Ya jest hang in there."

"Abe," said the boy. "Did ya git Abe yet?"

"Not yet," answered Clark.

Clark began to feel around in the darkness. He had to discover just what was holding the boy's leg. He found the beam, a big piece of timber, too thick and too long for him to tackle without some kind of tool.

He went on searching, feeling his way in search of the other boy. Carefully he made his way over the rubble and back again, the sharp stones cutting into the flesh of his palms. Nothing. He crawled on. He nearly missed it, but just as his hand slid over some rocky debris, he felt something smooth to the touch. It was a boot. Clark allowed his hand to search out the area. The boy was almost totally buried under the cave-in. Clark began to dig away at the rock and dirt, trying not to dislodge any more of the tunnel wall in his haste.

At length he could feel an arm. He dug on, frantically searching out the place where the head might be, eventually uncovering it. He longed for a light. If only he could see the condition of the boy. His hands traced over the temple, the face, the back of the head, and back again. They told him all that he needed to know. Clark crawled back to Andy.

"Andy," he said. "Andy. Ya still with me, boy?"

The boy groaned his answer.

"Andy, I've gotta try to git yer leg out. Now, I can't move thet there beam. It's too big an' heavy an' I don't have anything to cut it with. I'm gonna have to try to dig out from under yer leg and git it out thet way. It's gonna hurt, Andy. Can ya take it?"

Andy was crying again. "Yeah," he said. "We gotta git out. These timbers keep creakin' like they're gonna break again."

Clark crawled around, feeling for a sharp rock. He found one he thought would make a tool of sorts and began to dig around the boy's leg. At first he worked far enough away from the boy that the digging did not bother him, but as the rubble was gradually cleared away, the leg began to shift and the boy moaned in pain. This turned into a tortured scream, but Clark dug on, trying his hardest to be as gentle as he knew how. He must get him out, and quickly, for the boy was right. Clark, too, could hear the timbers snapping and creaking and feared at any time they might give way and pour forth more rocks and earth on top of them.

It seemed forever to Clark until he had a hole clawed away beneath Andy's foot deep enough to coax the boy's ankle out. He would have to slip off the boot in order to make the foot squeeze under. Pulling off the boot made Andy scream again in pain. Clark almost succumbed to the cries and stopped twisting, but he knew he would be signing the boy's life away if he did. He had dug away the earth to sheer rock. He could make the opening no bigger for the injured ankle to pass through. If Andy was to be freed, he must pull him loose now. Clark gritted his teeth, took the foot as gently as he could, and forced the leg out from under the beam. Mercifully, Andy fainted. Clark wiped dirt from the boy's face and loosened his collar. Then he picked him up gently and started carefully back up the tunnel.

Stumbling along in the darkness, feeling his way with an outstretched toe, bumping against rocks and beams that obstructed the path was treacherous going. The steep incline was the most difficult. One time he had to slide the boy up ahead of him, then claw his way up behind him and go on again. On and on he stumbled and fought until at least he could sense, more than see, the tunnel to his right. He breathed a thanksgiving prayer and hurried on. The tunnel floor was smoother now and walking was easier. Soon Clark passed the second tunnel, as well. If only the men from the ranch would be there with a light and some shovels.

And then, just ahead, Clark saw the opening of the mine. He hastened forward and burst out to fresh air and glaring sunshine. The boy was sitting in the shade on the same rock where Clark had seated him. He sprang to his feet when Clark made an appearance.

"Ya found Andy!" he cried. "Andy. Andy, ya okay?" He was crying again. "Is he dead, mister?"

"Naw," said Clark. "He's okay. He's got a busted ankle, but he'll be okay. Run over there to my saddle an' git thet there canteen. He needs a drink." The boy ran away in a flash.

Clark laid the boy gently on the ground in the shade. He stood to full height and looked off in the direction of the ranch. In the distance he could see whirls of dust. They were on their way. He couldn't wait. The timbers might give way at any moment and then the other boy, Abe, would be buried deep within the mine shaft.

He turned to the boy who was kneeling beside his friend Andy, trying to help him with a few swallows of water.

"Listen," he said. "They are on their way here now. See thet dust over there? It's gonna take 'em a while to git here. I want ya to take good care of Andy till they come, an' when they git here you just tell 'em to wait out here fer me. Ya understand? I know where Abe is, an' I'm gonna go git 'im."

The boy nodded his head and Clark turned and hurried back into the old mine. Traveling more quickly this time with a better idea of what was ahead of him, he still protected himself with a raised arm and a groping foot. But he moved with less caution because he knew that time was a major factor.

As he felt and slipped his way down the left tunnel, he prayed that he might get to Abe before the whole mine collapsed. The dust still hung heavily in the air, but Clark didn't think it was any worse than before. It appeared there had been no further cave-ins.

He came to the last steep slide and let himself down carefully, trying hard not to disturb any more of the rock around him. At the bottom, he dropped on all fours and felt his way forward to where he had left Abe. In the darkness he found the outstretched arm and the near-buried face, and he began to dig methodically, painstakingly, lifting away the debris from around him. It was slow work. Some of the rocks that buried the boy were boulder sized, and it took all of Clark's strength to move them to the side. He clawed and pushed, pulled and scratched, tore and pried until at last he had the boy freed from his prison.

He stopped for only a minute to catch his breath, and then he lifted the boy tenderly and once again began the climb to the outside world. Just as he pushed Abe ahead of him up the steep slope, there was a terrifying crack and a monstrous roar, and the ceiling of the cavern collapsed all around him. Pain seared through Clark as a heavy timber fell with sickening impact upon his leg, and then merciful blackness.

The men in the wagon had just pulled up and began to throw questions at the boy when the roar from within the cave burst upon them. Another cave-in! The boy crumpled to the ground with a cry of despair, and Andy, who lay on the ground shivering in shock, began to whimper.

"Someone look after thet boy," barked Scottie, and Lane moved forward to examine the youngster and ordered some blankets brought from the wagon.

Willie headed for the mine entrance and was stopped by Scottie's hands.

"I'm goin' in," Willie told his foreman.

"No, ya ain't. Nobody's goin' in there till we know thet it's finished fallin'."

Willie hesitated and stood listening to the rumbling inside the hillside.

The dust began to sift out of the entrance as they stood and stared, straining their ears. Willie turned to the sobbing boy.

"Did the man who came with ya go in there, boy?"

The boy nodded his head.

"Has he been out a'tall?"

"He brought Andy out."

"Where is he now?"

"He went back in fer Abe."

It was exactly as Willie knew it would be, yet he had dared to hope it might not be so.

The rumbling gradually stopped. Willie headed for the wagon and came back with a lantern and a rope. Again Scottie stepped forward and without a word took the lantern from him and lit it.

"Lane," Scottie instructed, "grab these shovels an' follow me."

Willie moved to fall in line.

"Mr. LaHaye," said Scottie, "you ain't goin' in there."

"What ya talkin'—" Willie began, but Scottie interrupted.

"I'm talkin' 'bout *you,*" said Scottie firmly. "You an' yer missus an' those two little boys."

"But—"

"No buts. Thet there mine might *give* again. Ya know thet, an' I know thet."

Scottie then turned to Lane. "I'm not askin' any man to take chances," he said. "You stay several feet behind me an' iffen ya hear a rumble, then run fer it. Now, boy, where do we find 'em?"

The youngster moved forward and was able to again intelligently give the men directions, and then Scottie and Lane moved through the mine opening.

Willie fidgeted at the entry. He wanted to go in and help with the search for Clark. He *would* go in. And then he thought of Missie. Of Missie and his two sons. If anything should happen to her father, she would need her husband even more.

Praying, he paced back and forth before the mouth of the mine and then went over to see if there was anything he could do for the young boy who lay groaning on the ground.

He turned to the one who leaned against the rock outcropping, staring at the gaping hole that had caused all this misery.

"Boy," he said, "do ya live 'round here?"

"In town," he answered.

"This yer brother?" asked Willie, indicating Andy on the ground.

"My friend. My brother—he's still in there."

"Yer folks be worryin'?"

"I reckon."

"Do ya think ya should ride on home an' tell 'em? Yer pa might want to git on over here an' help git yer brother out."

The boy looked surprised that he hadn't thought of that.

"Yeah," he said and headed for his grazing horse.

"An' git word to the folks of this here boy, too, will ya, son? They can come over and see what they can do to make 'im more comfortable."

The boy cast a backward glance at his friend and hurried off.

From then on, there was nothing for Willie to do except watch the entrance of the mine and pray there would be no more cave-ins. Occasionally he talked to the half-conscious boy or gave him sips of water. The broken ankle was painful, but as Willie examined it with his eyes, not wanting to move it, he thought it looked as though it might heal properly. He could see no protruding bones or broken skin.

There was nothing to speed up the minutes as Willie waited. Time after time he started down the mine tunnel, only to think of Scottie's words and turn back.

After what seemed like an eternity, another wagon pulled up. A man whom Willie had seen only once before jumped to the ground before the wagon even stopped rolling. He stopped briefly to touch the face of Andy and give a brief nod to Willie, and then he ran into the entrance of the mine. He did not even carry a lantern.

A woman approached more slowly. Already her face was tear-streaked and her eyes swollen from weeping.

"Is this yer son?" asked Willie with concern in his voice.

The woman knelt beside the boy and smoothed his hair with her hand and wiped the dust from his face with an edge of her simple gown.

"No," she said, her voice trembling. "It's my boy still in there."

"I'm sorry," said Willie.

"We've told 'em—over an' over we've warned 'em. 'Don't go near those mines,' we've said. 'They're not safe.' But bein' boys they jest gotta find out fer theirselves." She was sobbing softly, not bothering with the tears that ran down her cheeks.

"Somebody should do something 'bout those caves," the woman went on. "Ya never know whose child might be next."

Willie thought of his own two boys. "We'll git a permit to dynamite 'em, ma'am, jest as soon as we git these folks out."

The boy stirred and the woman spoke to him. "It's okay, Andy. Casey has gone fer yer ma an' pa. They should be here anytime now. They'll git ya on home an' look to thet ankle."

Andy, looking relieved in spite of his pain, closed his eyes again.

Willie scanned the hills once more and could see another wagon approaching in the distance. It was not long until Andy's folks arrived and the mother was running to him with shrieks and cries. Willie feared she was going to turn hysterical, but her husband calmed her. She fell on the ground beside her son and alternated between scoldings and endearments. The man knelt over the foot and began to prod the ankle. The boy cried out in pain, and the father grimaced and then went about preparing a makeshift splint. It was not a pleasant task. The boy screamed again and again as the foot was placed at the right angle and bound. Everyone present had broken into a cold sweat before the ordeal was over. At length the father's gruesome task was done, and he buried his face in his hands and sobbed. And still there was no sign of life from the mouth of the mine.

"How long they been in there?" asked one of the mothers.

"I've long since lost track of time," answered Willie. "Seems forever. At least there's been no more rumbles. Thet's a good sign."

He paced back and forth and again ventured into the cave a short distance. Then he heard the scraping and sliding of scuffling feet, and as he strained forward he could see the faint light of a lantern reflecting off the tunnel wall.

He pushed forward more anxiously and soon was face-to-face with Scottie. Scottie carried the front end of a makeshift stretcher made from broken timbers, and Lane stumbled along behind carrying the other end. On the stretcher lay Clark. His face was deathly white and blood smeared, and the arm that dangled at his side swung lifelessly back and forth.

"Oh, dear God," prayed Willie, and then to the men, "Is he dead?"

Scottie did not answer. Lane finally dared to voice a quiet "Not quite."

Willie took the lantern that swung from one corner of the stretcher and led the way. As he turned to check on the progress of the men behind him, he noticed the third man. It was the boy's father, and he, too, bore a burden. In his arms he carried his boy. Willie's eyes asked the question, and this time Scottie answered. "No" was all he said.

TEN

A Day of a Million Years

They took Clark to the ranch on a makeshift bed in the wagon. Even in his unconscious state, he groaned occasionally. They tried to drive as carefully as they could, but the jarring vehicle was distressful at best and a torment at worst.

Scottie guided the team, turning this way and that as he snaked a pathway home, trying his best to miss chuckholes and bumps. Willie sat with Clark, steadying him and bathing his face with water from the canteen. Except for the lump on his head from the falling beam and the badly injured leg, Clark seemed to have no other wounds. Willie dared to hope that the head injury would be a mild concussion, that Clark's mind would not suffer any serious effects from it.

The leg was another matter. As Willie looked at the severely broken leg with the bone splinter projecting from the skin, he shuddered. How could such a leg heal without the help of a doctor? "Oh, dear God," prayed Willie aloud, "please show us what to do."

As the wagon neared the ranch, an anxious Marty and Missie hurried out into the yard. Willie chided himself for not thinking to go ahead and prepare his womenfolk, and he jumped from the slow-moving wagon and asked Lane to watch Clark, and Scottie to drive as slowly as he knew how. Then Willie quickened his stride and reached the women slightly ahead of the wagon.

"Clark been hurt?" gasped Marty.

Willie nodded.

"Bad?" cried Missie.

"Pretty bad," answered Willie, "but not as bad as it will seem at first. He took a knock on the head, so he ain't conscious jest yet."

"Oh, dear God," whispered Marty, her hand fluttering to her throat, but Willie thought he saw relief showing in her eyes that at least Clark was alive.

"Did ya git the boys?"

"Yes," Willie nodded.

"Thank God," breathed Marty.

Just before the wagon rolled up, Willie placed an arm around each of the women. He wanted just another minute to prepare them.

"Yer pa also has a broken leg," he said to Missie. "We'll need to fix his bed right away. Then fetch some hot water and towels from the kitchen. We want to move him as gentle as we can. Will ya see to it? An', Ma, could ya check to see what we might have around in the way of disinfectant—he's got some scratches we should look after."

With a quick glance toward the now-stopped wagon, the two women ran toward the house to do Willie's bidding.

Willie moved forward.

"Quick," he said to Scottie. "I want him in there an' settled 'fore the women . . ." He did not finish. He did not need to. Scottie understood. Lane rushed out to help them, and with the three men manning the makeshift bed, they got Clark to the house. Missie had already turned down the bed in readiness, but just as Willie had hoped, neither of the women were in the room.

The men laid Clark on the bed and removed his shirt. Willie found some scissors and cut the pant leg from the broken limb. Scottie had removed the shoes and socks.

"We should bundle him warm against shock," said Lane, and Willie reached for a flannel nightshirt, which they struggled to slip over Clark's head.

"What we gonna do about thet leg?" It was a question they no doubt had all been asking themselves, but it was Lane who finally voiced it.

"For now we'll jest protect it all we can an' let the women see him fer a minute," Willie said.

Marty was the first one through the door. She cried out at the sight of Clark and went to kneel beside him, brushing at the dirt streaks and bloodstains on his pale face and running her fingers through his hair. Willie remained silent for a few minutes and then asked quietly, "Did ya find some disinfectant?"

Marty held up the forgotten bottle with trembling fingers.

Missie arrived with a basin of hot water and some towels. Willie took them from her and she rushed forward to kneel by her mother. She lifted one of Clark's limp hands and began to stroke it, as if willing it to become strong and independent again.

Willie remained silent for a moment and then passed Marty a small towel.

"Ya want to clean up his face some? Make sure the water isn't too hot. He won't be able to warn ya, and we don't want a burn."

Marty and Missie both came to life then.

"I'll go fetch a pitcher of cool water," said Missie and fled from the room. Marty turned to the business of cleaning Clark up. She inspected his dirty blood-caked hands, exclaiming over the bruised knuckles and the scratched and dirt-stained palms. His nails were broken and dirt filled from digging with his fingers.

"My, but they're a mess," said Marty, new calmness in her voice as she set about her task.

Willie sighed with relief and lifted the basin from the nearby chest so Missie could add the cold water she had just brought into the room.

The two women soaked and cleansed the damaged hands and then applied the disinfectant that Marty had produced. They wiped his face and found that, except for a couple of minor scratches, there were no open wounds there. Clark did not stir. Willie observed Marty slyly feeling for a pulse and looking relieved when she actually found one. After Willie was sure the women had spent enough time with Clark to reassure them, he turned to Missie. "I'm gonna have to ask ya fer a favor now. I know it'll be hard to leave yer pa, but I do need to ask ya to care fer a few things fer me."

Missie's eyes widened, but she nodded in agreement.

"Some of the boys were out there diggin' most of the afternoon. They're hungry an' Cookie's already cleared away from the last meal. Could you rustle up a bunch of sandwiches an' some hot coffee fer 'em?"

Missie, surprised, hesitated only a moment. She had never been asked to fix anything for the ranch hands before. Cookie always took care of their food needs no matter what time they came in. But she did not question Willie, only moved to obey.

"Do ya mind givin' her a hand?" Willie asked Marty.

Marty was about to protest and then rose to her feet. Surely this small request was not too much for Willie to ask.

"The boys have a shift change soon an' gotta git on out to the cattle," Willie went on quickly with his explanation.

He was relieved when Marty nodded and moved from the room. Willie immediately left the room and went to the boys' room. Josiah was napping and Nathan was playing quietly. Missie had asked him to go to his room before Clark was carried into the house so the small boy would not be unduly frightened by his grandfather's condition.

"Hi, fella," greeted Willie as cheerily as the occasion would allow him. "Would ya mind doin' a little chore fer yer pa?"

"Mama said thet I was to stay here till she came for me," answered Nathan. And then in deep seriousness, he went on, "Did Grandpa git the boys out, Pa?"

"He sure 'nough did," answered Willie, roughing the boy's hair. "But I need ya now. I'll tell yer ma thet I had a job fer ya. I want ya to run real quick an' tell Cookie an' Scottie thet I need 'em at the house. Tell 'em I need 'em *now*. Then come right back here to yer room. Okay?"

Nathan laid aside his book and ran as his pa bade him. Scottie and Cookie quickly arrived at Clark's room.

"Quick," said Willie. "I've got the ladies busy in the kitchen fixin' a lunch fer the hands."

"Lunch fer the hands?" repeated Cookie in disbelief.

"It was all I could think of to git 'em from the room. Now we gotta clean up thet leg, an' we gotta do it quick like."

The two men nodded and Willie threw back the blankets. The sight that met their gaze was not a pleasant one. For a moment, Willie wished he could just throw the blanket over the leg again and walk away.

Cookie forgot himself and swore under his breath. "'Bout the worst one I ever seed," he said. "Even worse shape than my hip was."

"Well, we gotta do what we can. Pass thet there basin." The three men worked over the wound, soaking and cleaning it and then pouring on the whole bottle of disinfectant. Willie tried to straighten the leg so that it didn't lie at such a bizarre angle, but they knew there was nothing they could do to set the bone. After the thorough cleansing, they fixed a loose makeshift splint and wrapped the damaged leg in it, more to conceal the injury than to do it any good. They were just finishing when Willie heard Missie's quick, light step.

"Thet lunch'll be ready soon," he whispered to the other two. "Ya go on out an' find someone—anyone—to eat it."

Cookie nodded and went out to round up some cowboys. Scottie, at a nod from his boss, also left the room. Willie heard him speak to Missie in the hall.

"I hear tell thet ya're gonna fix some sandwiches, ma'am. I'll jest wash some of the dirt off me at the cook shack an' I'll be right in. Mighty nice of ya, an' I sure am in need of a cup of coffee. Mighty obliged, ma'am."

Willie covered Clark carefully and picked up the basin with the dirty, bloody water. He held it up high so Missie couldn't see into it.

"Yer pa seems to be restin' a mite easier now," he said, backing out of the room with his rather gruesome-looking burden. "Thanks fer feedin' the men, Missie. Ya might tell yer ma thet if she wishes to sit with yer pa, the fellas can care fer themselves in the kitchen. An', Missie, I think thet Nathan might need a little reassurance. He must be wonderin' jest what's goin' on. I sent him on a little chore fer me, an' he was 'fraid you'd scold him fer leavin' his room unbidden. Ya might like to peek in and sorta calm him some. I gotta run. Gotta make a little trip. Won't be long."

Missie looked dumbfounded at Willie's announcement, but she nodded mutely and moved toward the boys' room. Willie ached to hold her for a minute, but his hands were occupied with the basin and dirty towels. He sensed that his wife was probably still in shock.

"Missie," he said softly and she turned back, "he's gonna be all right. He's tough. As soon as thet little bump on his head . . ." His voice trailed off. Then he went on. "Tell yer ma not to let him move. Iffen he wakes up an' thrashes 'round, call fer Scottie. We couldn't set thet there leg yet, an' he might hurt himself."

Again Missie nodded silent assent. Willie moved on by her with the basin.

"An', Missie. Try not to worry. I'll be back as soon as I can."

He passed through the door and headed for the bunkhouse and cook shack. He tossed the dirty water to the side of the path. When he reached the shack he found Cookie.

"Could only find three riders," said Cookie, "an' even they weren't hungry. Told 'em to eat or else."

"Lane an' Scottie should be hungry," said Willie. "They ain't had anythin' since—"

"This sort of thing takes one's appetite," answered Cookie. "But they'll eat. They'll eat all right, an' they'll drink the coffee. They need the coffee."

Willie passed Cookie the blood-soaked towels. "Think thet ya can clean 'em up some 'fore the womenfolk see 'em again?"

"Shore," said Cookie and tossed them in a corner.

"Tell Scottie I had to go into town. Tell 'im I want an eye kept on thet house. Iffen those women need help, I want someone to be there."

Cookie said nothing, but his eyes assured Willie that the order would be followed.

Willie strode on down to the corral, where he lifted a rope from a post and snaked out his saddle horse. In a few minutes' time the sound of pounding hoofbeats was echoing across the yard.

Marty had had a hard time concentrating on fixing a lunch for the men with Clark lying in the bedroom in his present condition. She couldn't remember how many scoops of coffee to put into the pot, nor could she remember where to find bread and butter. Missie's memory didn't seem much better, even if it was her own kitchen. Wong was down in the garden selecting vegetables for supper, and neither of the women thought to call him.

Numbly they went about searching out sandwich materials and spreading the bread. Neither talked, although both were aware of anxious thoughts that would not be stilled. They worked on in silence until Marty noticed Missie fighting back the tears. She went to her then and took her in her arms.

"He'll be all right. God won't let anythin' happen to 'im. He'll be fine." Oh, how Marty wanted to believe her own words! *They have to be true. They just have to. If anything happens to Clark . . .* Her arms tightened around Missie and she began to pray aloud.

"God, ya know how we need ya now. Ya know how we love Clark. Ya know how he has served you. He loves ya, Lord. An' now we're askin' thet ya lift him up. Thet ya give 'im back his mind an' body, iffen it be yer will, Lord. Amen."

Missie looked at Marty, her eyes wide and the tears streaming down her face. "Oh, Ma," she cried, "don't pray like that! *Of course* it is His will. Of course it is. He *must* heal him. He must."

Marty, too, was crying now. "Yer pa always prayed, 'Yer will be done.'"

"You can pray that way if you want to," said Missie insistently, "but I'm going to tell God exactly what I want. I want Pa. I want him well and strong again. What's wrong with telling God exactly what you want Him to do?"

"Yer pa always says thet we don't be orderin' God—we *ask*."

Missie pulled away, and Marty could feel frustration, even anger, in the slim body. Brushing at her tears, Missie went back to the sandwiches. Her whole person seemed shut away. Marty remained in silent prayer, for Clark and for Missie, as she began to slice beef and place it on the bread.

When the sandwiches and coffee were ready, Missie went to check on Nathan. She held the small boy close and let her tears fall. When she was sure she could speak coherently, she talked to him. "Grandpa got the boys out, Nathan. Grandpa is kind of a hero. He hurt himself saving others. Now he needs to be in bed and have a long rest. You and Josiah might have to be very quiet and especially good for the next few days. You can do that for Grandpa, can't you?"

She felt Nathan's head bobbing a yes up against her.

"We need to pray for Grandpa. God can make him all better again. Will you pray with Mama now, Nathan?"

Nathan agreed and the two of them knelt by his bed.

"God," said Nathan simply, "Grandpa got to be a hero an' is hurt an' needs you to help him. He needs me an' Josiah to be quiet an' not 'sturb him. Help us to not fight or yell. An' help Mama an' Grandma to nurse Grandpa good. Amen."

Missie wished to ask the young boy to pray again. She wanted to say, "Nathan, you didn't ask God to make your grandpa well. You didn't say it, Nathan." Instead she held him for a moment and told him if he'd like to go to the kitchen and share the lunch with the ranch hands, he could. Nathan bounded away, glad to be free of his room.

Missie returned to the kitchen, her heart heavy and her head spinning. How could God answer their prayers if they didn't pray them? Missie went to pour the coffee with a shaking hand.

When Missie had returned to the kitchen, Marty slipped quietly into Clark's room and knelt by his bed. She took one of his hands in hers and caressed it, careful not to bring further hurt to the already damaged hand. It did look better now that it had been cleaned up. She pressed it to her lips and let her tears wash it again.

"Oh, Clark," she whispered, "I couldn't bear it iffen somethin' should happen to you. Oh, God, I jest couldn't stand it. Please, dear God, make 'im better again. Please leave 'im with me. I need 'im so much." There, she was praying the very way she had warned Missie against. Well, she simply couldn't help it! She needed Clark so much. She loved him more than life itself. She couldn't bear to lose him. She just couldn't! "Oh, please, God—please, please, God," she pled.

She stayed beside his bed, crying and praying, until all her energy and her tears were spent. Clark still did not stir. Would he ever regain consciousness?

At length Marty was aware of a hand on her shoulder. "Mama," asked Missie, "do you want a cup of coffee?"

Marty shook her head.

"You should, you know. It might be a long night. Wong made supper for the boys. I didn't think anyone else would be hungry."

Marty looked up. "Yer right," she said wearily. "I couldn't eat a bite."

"Coffee, then," said Missie, holding out the cup.

Marty lifted herself to her feet and took it. She was surprised at how stiff she had become and she wondered how long she had been there beside Clark. Missie pushed a chair toward her and she sat down.

"The boys are already in bed," Missie ventured. "Willie still isn't back. Don't know why he—"

"Maybe he went fer a doctor. He said thet yer pa's leg—"

"I'm afraid there's no doctor anywhere around," Missie offered sadly. "He might have heard of someone good at setting breaks, though."

Marty sipped at the coffee and watched Missie's face.

"Didn't Willie say where he was goin'?"

"Just said he would be gone for a while and if we needed anything to call the men. He also said not to let Pa stir around none. Might hurt his leg."

Marty looked at the motionless Clark. "Looks like we needn't worry none 'bout thet. Wish he *would* stir some. It would make me feel some better iffen I could jest talk to him."

"Willie says that moving might injure his leg even more."

"Maybe it's a blessin' thet he has thet bump on his head. At least he doesn't suffer as much. By the time he comes to again, maybe the pain will be cared fer some."

Marty hadn't thought of the unconsciousness as a blessing, but perhaps it was. She just hoped it wouldn't last too long.

They sat together in silence. Scottie came for a few minutes and asked if there was anything he could do. They assured him they would call if there was any change.

⁓✍⁓

Cookie poked his head around the door, then hobbled in.

"Are you all right?" Missie asked him.

"Whatcha meanin'?" asked Cookie.

"You're lookin' sorta down."

Cookie shook his head. How could he tell her that seeing Clark's injury had reminded him of the injury in his past and the pain that had accompanied it? Clark was truly fortunate right now. He was unaware of pain. But if consciousness returned, would he be able to keep from screaming with the intensity of the agony he would feel? And how would those earth-rending screams affect the rest of the household?

"Guess it bothers me to see a good man hurt" was all Cookie said.

⁓✍⁓

The evening crawled on. The sun disappeared and the stars came out. Soon a silvery moon was shining down on a familiar world. The horses stomped and fought in the corrals, Max barked at some distant coyotes, the crickets chirped, and the night-winged insects beat against the windowpane in an effort to get to the light. Still Clark did not stir, and Willie did not come.

Marty and Missie sat together, talking in low tones and praying in turn. At length Missie stood and moved toward the door.

"I think I'll fix something to drink. Do you want tea or coffee?"

"Tea, I think," responded Marty wearily. She, too, stood and walked about the room. Missie left for the kitchen, and Marty moved to pick up Clark's ragged clothes from the floor. She looked at them. They were dirty and torn and the trousers were minus one leg. Clark's leg? She kept forgetting the broken leg in her anxiety over Clark's unconsciousness. But she was not overly concerned about the leg. Many people had suffered broken legs. Usually, with a little skill on the part of some attendant, the leg was soon whole and workable again.

Marty pulled back the bedcover and looked at the leg swathed in bulky bandages. *Actually, the men did a rather poor job of it,* she thought. She began to unwind the white material, determined to fix the bandage up a bit. To her surprise there was blood on the cloth. Broken legs did not bleed, unless of course the injury was more extensive. Marty unwound the bandage more hurriedly, and the little cry that escaped her lips was like the sound of a small wounded animal. Clark's leg was not just broken—it was destroyed! Marty felt a sickness sweeping all through her and rushed to the small basin on the stand in the corner. Her whole body shook as she retched. Faint and weak, she grasped the edge of the stand and fought to stand on her feet. At length she regained enough strength and presence of mind to be concerned for the evidence of her sickness before Missie returned. She gathered up the basin and the small pitcher Missie had used for the cold water and headed for the backyard, disposed of the basin's contents and washed it out, and then returned quickly to the room. The cool night air had helped to revive her some, and she hastily attempted to put things back in order. Hurriedly she rewrapped the broken limb, trying to copy the men's original bandaging as closely as she could. Then she chided herself. It was not a time for secrets. She knew Willie had tried to spare her—her and Missie—but the truth needed to be known.

She unwrapped the wound and began to methodically and carefully clean and bind it up, doing the best job possible for her to do. She finished just as Missie returned with the tea.

Marty was glad for the strong, hot tea. She sipped it slowly until she felt some of its strength gradually making its way through her body.

"I took a look at yer pa's leg," she stated as matter-of-factly as she could.

"The broken one?"

"The broken one."

"I hope you didn't move—"

"Yer father did not stir."

A minute of silence followed.

"It's bad, Missie, really bad."

"How bad?"

"A heavy timber or rock must have fallen on it."

"You mean—?"

"I mean it's crushed. It'll need a real doctor, one with special skills an' tools—"

"Then we'll find one. Willie probably went for one. That's what he did. He went to find a doctor."

"But ya said—"

"What do I know? Just bcause I don't know of a doc doesn't mean there isn't one. Willie hears far more—"

"I hope an' pray he knows of one."

"He will. He will. Just you wait and see. When he gets back here, he'll have—"

The sound of horses came faintly through the window. Missie ran to the door and looked out through the darkness into the yard. No, not horses—a horse. Willie was back, but Willie was alone.

"The doc must be following," Missie called over her shoulder to Marty. "Willie is home now."

Missie ran to meet him. When they returned to the house together, Missie's cheeks bore fresh tears. Marty guessed the meaning.

"Willie had them telegraph every town he knew. Nowhere around do they have a doctor," she confessed. Willie, standing with slumped shoulders and an ashen face, could not speak.

Marty crossed to him. "You've done all thet ya could," she comforted, putting her hand on his shoulder. "Thanks, Willie." She coaxed forth a smile that she did not feel. "We'll jest have to pray even harder," she said.

Three people now sat in silence or moved slowly about the room or spoke in hushed tones. Clark did not stir through the long night.

When dawn came, Willie insisted that Missie get some rest. The children would be needing her. Missie left to lie down for a brief time. Still no change in Clark. The day moved on, from forenoon to noonday, afternoon to evening. Marty left Clark's side only for a few minutes at a time. She was not interested in eating, could not think of sleeping. Her mind was totally focused on her husband lying silently in the bed.

Just as the long day ended and the sun was leaving the sky, Clark stirred and a groan came from his lips. Marty rushed to him. He opened his eyes, seemed to recognize her, and groaned again. He slipped back into unconsciousness, but to Marty it was a blessed sign. Just to see him move and look at her was something to be thankful for. She allowed the tears to stream down her face as she buried it against him.

ELEVEN

Struggles

Clark remained unconscious the entire next day. Marty stayed by his bed, longing to be able to talk with him. Missie came as often as her duties would allow. In the late afternoon Willie returned to the house and insisted that both of the women take a rest. After a bit of an argument, they went, realizing they could not carry on longer without some sleep. Willie had Wong bring him coffee, and he settled himself beside Clark's bedside. He had slept very little himself in the last two days. His eyelids felt heavy and his eyes scratchy. He rubbed a callused hand over his face.

Why did this have to happen? Why? The time they had looked forward to for so long—had dreamed of as a time of joyous reunion—had turned into a nightmare. *Why?* Surely God hadn't brought Clark and Marty way out here to take Clark's life and possibly damage Marty's faith. It was all an enormous puzzle to Willie.

And the boys? He worried about his sons. They had been so excited about meeting their grandparents. Missie had made it a great adventure for them. They had counted the weeks, the days. And then, when they had met their grandparents, they had loved them so quickly, so deeply— and now this tragedy. Poor little Nathan. Not only had his grandfather been taken from him in the last few days but even his grandmother and, thought Willie, his own ma, too. Missie's mind was far too unsettled and troubled by her father's condition to do more than respond to her children's basic needs.

Willie got up and moved to the boys' room. Josiah slept soundly, mostly unconscious of the burden the household was presently bearing, though he probably felt the emotional undercurrents. Nathan was not there; perhaps he was in the kitchen with Wong or visiting Cookie or playing with Max. The poor little fellow. He was trying so hard to be good.

Willie crossed to his own room and looked in on Missie. Though she was sleeping, her face was still pale and drawn. Willie's heart ached for her. He gently smoothed back her long hair and left her.

He looked in on Marty. She, too, slept soundly. She looked exhausted—as well she might. She had hardly left Clark's side since the accident.

Willie went back to Clark's room. He should check the leg. He pulled back the covers and looked at the neat, fresh bandage. This was not the bandage he had hurriedly wrapped. Someone else had been caring for Clark. Someone else knew of the leg's condition. Willie wiped his hand over his face again. Did the women know? If so, he hated the thought of their suffering this additional burden. At the same time, he felt some of the tension leave him. It would be far better if they did know. It would help prepare them for what likely was ahead.

Willie pulled the light cover up over Clark and sat down heavily in the chair. The house was quiet. Most of its occupants were asleep. Willie, too, dozed occasionally, only to waken to chide himself and determine not to let it happen again.

Josiah must have awakened from his nap and left his bed in search of another family member. Willie, hearing him in the hall, went to get him. He picked up the small boy and held him close, walking back and forth in the hallway and murmuring words of love to him. Josiah cuddled closely against his father, his pudgy hands around his neck and his fingers intertwined in Willie's thick hair. He liked to be held. He liked to be loved. As far as Josiah was concerned, the world had no sorrows.

At length, Willie held the little boy away and looked at him. "Are ya hungry?" he asked.

"Yeah. Where Mama?"

"Mama is restin'. She's very tired."

"Mama sleepin'?"

"Right. Do you want to go see Wong an' have him git ya some milk an' bread?"

"Yeah!" exclaimed Josiah in glee. He always enjoyed a visit with Wong.

Willie carried him to the kitchen. Wong looked up from the table where he and Nathan were cutting doughnuts.

"Aha," said Wong, "small boy is wake now."

"Awake an' hungry, Wong. Ya think ya might have somethin' fer him?"

Wong smiled. He enjoyed the children.

"Yes, yes. Wong find."

Nathan called to Josiah. "Hi, Joey. Ya all done with yer sleep? See what big brother is doin'. Look! I'm helpin' Wong make doughnuts. We're gonna have 'em fer supper."

"Maybe. Maybe not," said Wong. "Too slow. Maybe tomorrow."

"I'll hurry," said Nathan and began to slap down the cutter in rapid succession, making weird-shaped doughnuts with chopped-out sides as one cut overlaid another.

"Slow. Slow," called Wong. "We have some for supper. You make slow."

Nathan obliged with more careful cuts. Willie squeezed the boy's shoulder. "I can hardly wait," he said. "Those shore look like good doughnuts." Then he turned to Wong.

"Speakin' of supper, ya wanna jest feed the boys? The women are both havin' a rest, an' I plan to let 'em sleep as long as they can. The boys can play outside fer a while an' then they can eat. I'll jest have a bowl of soup or some stew in the bedroom."

Wong nodded.

Willie returned to the bedroom and took his place beside Clark. There was no change.

The hours crawled by slowly. Cookie came in and stayed with Clark while Willie washed up his sons and readied them for bed. He spent extra time with them, holding them and reading to them, and then he tucked them in and remained in their room until they both dropped off to sleep.

When he returned to the patient, he was surprised to hear Clark groaning. Cookie was bending over him, trying to restrain him from movement.

"He's comin' out of it," said Cookie. "Don't be surprised if there's some screamin'."

Clark moaned again and fought against his extreme pain, not aware enough to realize where the pain was coming from.

"Don't know how he's gonna stand it when he wakes up a bit more," Cookie muttered, and Willie had the impression Cookie knew firsthand what he was talking about.

Willie feared what Clark's cries might do to the sleeping household. "Isn't there anythin'—?"

"Ya watch 'im and try ta hold 'im down," said Cookie. "I'm gonna find Scottie."

Cookie hobbled out, and Scottie soon came noiselessly into the room, breathless from running. Willie watched as he pulled out a small package from his pocket and opened it. Willie did not see the contents of the package, nor did he ask any questions, but Scottie seemed to feel some information was in order.

"A little morphine. Cookie's. He needs it now an' then fer the pain thet still bothers 'im. Makes me keep it so he won't be tempted to take it oftener than he should."

Willie nodded.

Clark was thrashing and moaning, his brow covered with perspiration; his hands tried to clutch at the bedclothes as if to tear away the pain. Scottie leaned over him and spooned the drug into his mouth. It was a while before it took effect, and the men guarded and soothed Clark as they waited for the medicine to work. At last Clark became quieter and eventually fell into a deep sleep. Willie was thankful for the respite. But what would they do when Cookie's small supply of morphine ran out?

It was almost morning before Clark woke again. Willie had been dozing in the chair and was awakened by Clark's moaning. Clark's eyes were open when Willie looked up at him. Though the pain would have been considerable, Clark was rational.

He looked at Willie and, for the first time in three days, seemed aware of his situation.

Willie was relieved to recognize that Clark was alert. At least his mind had not been affected. "How ya doin'?" Willie asked softly, lifting some water to Clark's lips.

Clark sipped very little and then turned his head. A groan escaped him. "Pain" was all he said. "Pain."

"Where does it hurt the most?" persisted Willie. He had to know the extent of the head injury.

"Leg," said Clark.

Willie felt another wave of relief pass through him.

"How's yer head?"

"Hazy . . . little ache . . . all right."

"Good," Willie encouraged.

Clark rolled his head back and forth, the moans escaping from his throat.

"Where's Marty?" he finally asked.

"I made her go sleep fer a while."

This must have satisfied Clark. He lay clenching his jaw to keep the screams from coming. Willie knew he needed more medication and moved the lamp to the window, their prearranged signal.

"How long?" Clark gasped out.

"You've been here fer three nights. It happened the afternoon of the day before."

"The old mine . . . I remember."

It was a good sign. Willie breathed a thankful prayer.

"How're them boys?"

"Haven't heard much since we brought you out," said Willie and let it go at that.

"Did ya get Abe out?"

"His pa did."

"Good."

Clark closed his eyes, obviously trying to fight away the pain and maybe sleep again, but it didn't work. Scottie was soon there, and Clark took the medication without protest. This time he did not sleep as soundly. He dozed off and on. The pain was still with him, but he was able to bear it.

"Didn't give 'im as much," Scottie murmured to Willie. "We gotta ration this here stuff out."

Willie nodded.

The light from the dawn was gently coloring the morning sky. Clark slept, then spoke and slept again. Willie knew Marty was anxious for a word with her husband. Perhaps she had slept enough and needed to be called.

"Scottie, can ya stay a few minutes with 'im? I should wake Mrs. Davis. She'll want to see 'im." Scottie nodded agreement.

Willie woke Marty gently.

"He's awake now. Not too much awake, but he's able to talk some."

Marty threw back the quilt that covered her fully clothed body and scrambled from the bed.

Willie attempted to slow her down. He took her arm.

"He's in awful pain, Ma. It ain't easy to see 'im like thet."

Marty nodded dumbly, but her step did not slow.

When they reached Clark's room, Scottie stepped outside, and Marty threw herself at Clark's bedside and began to weep against him.

He reached out a trembling hand and soothed her hair. He no doubt knew her well enough to let her cry for a while. When her tears were spent, he spoke to her.

"I'm all right. Don't fret yerself." His voice sounded rough but surprisingly strong.

"Shore," she smiled weakly, blinking away tears. "Shore ya are."

"My leg's not too good, though. Ya knowin' thet?"

"I know." The way Marty said it confirmed to Willie that she truly did know. Marty must have been the one who had changed the bandages. Once again, Willie felt a surge of respect for this strong woman.

Clark ran a feeble hand through Marty's tangled hair.

"Yer not lookin' yer best, Mrs. Davis," Clark teased her.

"Thet's funny," said Marty, smiling and wiping away her tears, "ya ain't never looked better."

Willie quietly left them alone.

Scottie was there to portion out small amounts of the morphine as Clark needed it. Clark really could have used far more pain-killer than he was allowed, but once their supply was gone there would be no more.

Clark was able to talk a bit with his visitors. Nathan even was allowed a short visit with his grandpa. He was awed to see his strong grandfather lying pale and still on the bed. But when Clark teased him and rumpled his hair, Nathan looked reassured. Marty and Missie both spent most of their time trying to think of something they could do to ease Clark's pain or restore his body. Missie fussed in the kitchen over special dishes she hoped would encourage her father's appetite. He made a great effort to eat and please her, but even she could tell it was difficult with the dreadful pain always present throughout his whole body.

Word came from town concerning the boys who had been involved in the disaster. Andy seemed to be recovering. His broken ankle had not been crushed, and his parents felt that it would heal in time. They were deeply grateful to Clark for his courageous rescue and sent word that he was in their prayers.

Funeral services were held for Abe. Marty hardly knew how to tell Clark, but she felt he deserved to know. She approached the subject cautiously.

"They say thet Andy's ankle should be healin'."

"Thet's good," said Clark. "The way thet timber had 'im pinned, I was feared it might be bad broke."

"The other boy—Casey—he's fine. Jest some scrapes an' scratches an' his deep inner pain, I guess. The third boy, Abe, was his younger brother."

"He told me."

"Abe didn't make it, Clark."

"I know." Clark spoke very quietly.

694

"Ya know?"

"He was already dead when I first found him."

Marty was surprised and, for a moment, angry. "Ya *knew* he was dead when ya risked everythin' to go back on in there an'—"

Clark hushed her with a raised hand. "If it had been our boy, would ya have wanted him out?"

Marty was silent. Yes, if it had been her boy, she would have wanted to hold him one more time.

Marty was deeply relieved at the clarity of Clark's thinking. She was so glad the head injury had not caused permanent damage, but she could not shut from her mind the picture of Clark's leg and the condition it was in. Each time she entered the sickroom, the stench of the injured leg met her with increasing force. The leg was in bad shape. It might even claim Clark's life. Marty fought that thought with her entire being. They needed medicine. They needed a doctor. At times she was tempted to demand that Willie hurry them to the train so they could head for home. In more rational moments Marty knew he'd never survive such a long trip in his weakened condition.

And then Clark began to flush with fever. His eyes took on a glassy look, and his skin was hot and dry. *It's the poison,* admitted Marty to herself, *the poison from the wound.*

Marty could hardly bear this new dilemma. He had been doing well under the circumstances. He had been gaining back a little strength. He had been able to talk. And now this. They had no way to fight this. *Oh, dear God, what can we do?*

At first, they did not talk about Clark's condition, for to talk about it would be to admit it, and also to admit that they were defeated, for they had nothing with which to fight the dreaded infection.

At last Marty knew they could no longer try to pretend that the problem was not there.

"Bring me a pan of hot water," she said to Missie. "An' boil a good sharp pair of yer best scissors. We've gotta do somethin' 'bout yer father's leg."

Then Marty went to find Scottie. Willie and Scottie thought Marty had not noticed the drug ministrations to Clark, so Scottie was caught off guard when Marty walked up to where he was working on the cinch of a saddle and calmly announced, "Scottie, I don't know how much medicine ya still have left, but Clark needs a good-sized dose now. I've got to clean up thet leg the best I can or it's gonna kill 'im. The poison from thet gangrene is goin' all through his system, an' we don't have much time."

Scottie gazed into her face, wonder in his eyes. "Yer a better man than I am," he said, then must have caught his blunder. "Well, anyway, I'm thinkin' I'd not have the stomach to do what yer intendin' to do."

He went for the medicine and gave Clark a large dose. Marty waited until the morphine had taken effect, then gathered together all her limited supplies and every ounce of her courage and went to Clark's room. She threw the window wide open and lit a piece of rag in a tin can to help smoke out the odor, then threw back the light quilt and removed the bandages. It was even worse than she had feared. Never before had Marty faced such a sight and smell. She wanted to faint, to be sick. But she would allow herself neither. She soaked and snipped and cut away dead flesh, but even as she worked she knew she was fighting a losing battle. She finished her difficult task, knowing that what she had done would not be enough.

Gently she covered Clark, all but the damaged leg. She left it exposed to the air, thinking the fresh air might do it some good. Then she cleaned the scissors and knife she had used and put things away in their proper places and went to her own bed.

Down upon her knees, she cried out her anguish to God. She began by telling Him how much Clark meant to her and reminding God of how faithfully Clark had served Him over the years. She told God she had already suffered through the loss of one husband and couldn't possibly bear to lose another. She reminded the Lord of her family at home and of Missie and the grandchildren here. They, too, needed Clark. And then she pleaded and finally demanded that God heal her husband. Hadn't He promised to answer the prayers of His children when they prayed in faith, prayed believing?

Then she returned to Clark. Clark's breathing was just as shallow, his face just as flushed, his brow just as hot as before. But Marty determined that she would sit right beside him and wait for the Lord's miracle.

Missie came in. At the sight of her father's infected leg, she gave a little cry and, placing her hand over her mouth, ran from the room. Marty's heart ached for her. *What would she ever have done if she'd seen it before I cleaned it up?* thought Marty. Marty was thankful Missie had been spared at least that much.

The drug began to wear off, and Clark tossed and turned in his pain. Marty bathed his hot face and body in an attempt to get the fever down. It had little effect. Clark soon became delirious, and Marty had to call for help to hold him. Willie came and then Cookie, and the two men sent Marty from the room. Marty paced back and forth, back and forth, praying that God's miracle might soon come. Still Clark's screams and groans reached her ears.

Maria came. White-faced and wide-eyed, she stood in the hallway and talked to the tearful Missie. She did not stay long. Clark's agony and the distress of the entire household sent her crying from the home.

The hours crawled by. Marty went into the sickroom occasionally, but Clark's misery was more than she could bear. At last, she went to her room again . . . and again fell beside her bed. This time her prayer was different.

"Oh, God!" she wept from the bottom of her soul. "Ya know best. I can't stand to see 'im suffer so. I love 'im, God. I love 'im so. Iffen ya want to take 'im, then it's all right. I won't be blamin' ya, God. Ya know what's best. I don't want 'im to suffer, God. I leave 'im in yer hands. Yer will be done, whether it's healin' or takin', thet's up to you, God. An', God, whatever yer will, I know thet ya'll give me—an' all of us—the strength we need to bear it."

Marty eventually arose from her knees and went to find Missie. A strange peace filled Marty's being. She still shivered with each scream from Clark. It still pierced her to the quick to know he suffered so, but Marty knew that God was in control and that His divine will would be done.

She found Missie in the boys' room. The boys, however, were not there. Lane had taken them to the barn, where they wouldn't hear their grandfather's agonizing cries.

Missie clutched the small backpack Clark had used to carry her as an infant and that she in turn had used to carry her own sons. She was sobbing out her hurt and anguish.

"Missie," Marty said, taking the girl into her arms. "It's gonna be all right. I know it is."

Missie burst into fresh tears. "Oh, I want to believe that. I've been praying and praying for God to make him well."

"He may not," said Marty simply, looking into her daughter's face.

Missie looked at her mother in bewilderment.

"But ya said—"

"I said it will be all right. An' it will. Whatever God decides to do will be the best. He knows us. He knows our needs. He seeks our good. Whatever He wills—"

But Missie pushed her arms away.

"Oh, Missie, Missie," Marty began to sob. "I fought it, too. I fought it with all my bein'. I want yer pa. I want him here with me. But God knows thet. I don't even have to tell 'im. But, little girl, we've got to trust Him. We've gotta let God truly be God."

Missie rose and left the room, still sobbing. Marty heard her close the door to her own room, and she could hear the muffled sobs. There was nothing more that Marty could say. She could only pray.

Marty went to the kitchen to ask Wong for coffee for the men in the sickroom. They had given him the last of the medication, allowing him to sleep once more. Each one in the house felt the lingering question: *What then?*

As Marty carried the pot of coffee and cups to the room, she met Missie in the hall. Her face was still tear-streaked but more serene. "Mama," she said, "I just wanted you to know that it's all right. I've prayed it all through, and I'm . . . I'm willing to . . . to let God be God. He does know best. I knew it all along. It's just easy to forget sometimes when you want your own way so. . . ." She could go no further.

Marty managed a weak smile, and the tears flowed down her cheeks. She leaned over and kissed Missie on the cheek and then straightened to go on to Clark's room. She heard a knock sound on the front door and turned to watch Missie wipe her face with her apron and go answer it.

Missie opened the door, and there stood Maria, her shoulders square and her eyes shining with faith and pride. Just behind her stood Juan.

"Can we come in?" she asked. "My husband . . . is a doctor."

TWELVE

Juan

Juan de la Rosa walked purposefully into the sickroom and set his case on the bed. With a quick glance, he took in Clark's pallor and the flushed cheeks. His nose caught the stench of rotting flesh, and he turned to the leg.

He knew even before he looked just what he would find. The crushed limb was badly infected, and the gangrene was not only eating away the flesh of the leg but was also poisoning the man's body.

The leg would have to be removed.

Juan's thoughts went back to another time, one very much like this one. Another man lay before him with a leg in similar condition, and at that time, as well, Juan the doctor had needed to make a life-saving decision. He had decided then, as he was deciding now, that the leg must be sacrificed in order to save the life. All of his training and experience told him so. He had done what he needed to do. And the man had lived.

And then . . . Juan shuddered involuntarily as other memories crowded into his mind. The angry screams, the raging accusations, the shouts of betrayal, and finally the sound of a pistol shot. For a moment, Juan felt he must flee Clark's room—and all those memories. Then the groans of the sick man and the weeping of the women in the hall strengthened him. He straightened himself and looked at the two men in the room.

"I'm going to need lots of boiling water and a strong man to assist me," he said evenly, removing his jacket.

"I wish I could volunteer," said Willie. "I'd like to, but I'm afeared I'd cave in halfway through. I can see to the water, an' I'll find ya a man."

Willie told Marty and Missie about the need for boiling water. Maria, watching nearby, nodded quickly and led the other two women into the kitchen.

At the bunkhouse, Willie found Lane sitting in the doorway watching Nathan and Josiah playing with Max. He went into the bunkhouse, motioned Lane to follow him inside, and shut the door. He looked around at the cowboys in various stages of repose.

"We found us a doc," Willie said. At the surprise on everyone's faces, he explained, "Well, the Lord found us a doc. It's Juan. Juan has all the trainin' an' has even been in practice fer a few years. I know ya all have questions. So do I, but now ain't the time fer answers. We'll git 'em all in good time. Right now I need a man. I got a job thet won't be easy to do. The doc needs help. He's gonna take off thet there leg. Yer wonderin' why I don't offer, him bein' my father-in-law an' all. Well, I'll tell ya straight out. I'm not sure I could take it. I might fold up on the doc jest when he needs me most. Anyone here think he can do it?"

Willie's eyes scanned the bunkhouse. Some of the cowboys were out on the range taking their shift, but those who were in the room probably wished they were far away, as well, mending fence or herding cattle. Willie had asked a hard thing.

Jake, stretched out on his bunk, had been catching up on some sleep. He'd had the late shift the night before. Smith, the bitter, critical member of the crew, sat in the corner smoking a cigarette and staring at the cards in his hand. Browny was his partner in the game. Clyde, who sat on a stool near the window, shifted the lariat he was working on into the other hand and shot tobacco juice at the bean can on the floor. Lane went white and stared at his hands as though trying to determine whether they would be capable of such a job. The room was heavy with silence. At last, Lane cleared his throat and spoke softly. "I'll do it."

"Ya sure?"

Lane nodded agreement.

"It won't be easy."

Lane recognized that.

"Wish I could help ya . . . I can't promise. Yer sure ya can do it?"

Lane swallowed. "I know *I* can't," he said solemnly. "But I'm . . . I'm trustin' thet *He* can." He motioned upward with his hand.

The religion-hating Smith looked at the silent, shy Lane, a look of grudging respect on his face.

Willie and Lane went to the house, where the doctor was waiting. Willie led the group in prayer; then the men went to Clark's room and the women to the kitchen.

The hands on the clock seemed to drag their way around. The three women had boiled all the water they could find containers for and now sat at a small worktable, untouched coffee cups before them. They had prayed together off and on throughout the whole ordeal, weeping and praising and quoting Bible passages for comfort and encouragement.

"Juan always wanted to be a doctor," Maria began slowly during a pause in the conversation. The other two lifted red-rimmed eyes to her face as they listened to her story. "From the time he was a small boy, he dreamed and planned. At first his father said no. If he wanted to serve, he could be a priest and serve the church. But Juan argued and pleaded. Finally his father said, 'Yes, go ahead, but you will need to pay your own way. My money will not go for foolish dreams.' His father is very wealthy. In his own way, he loves his sons. He wanted both of his boys to stay and ranch with him. Juan went away to the city to school. It was hard. He had to work and he had to study. His father thought he would give up and come home again. But Juan did not. At last he was finished. He was a doctor and was given a good job in a city hospital. His father thought he should come home now. He could be a doctor to the gringos and make good money treating their families, but Juan said no, he must first know more, and then he would come home."

Maria stopped. It obviously was very difficult for her to continue.

"And then one day he was urgently called home. He must come right away. A man had been hurt. Juan went home and found the injured man.

He, too, had crushed his leg. A horse had fallen on him. The leg was too badly broken to fix. It might have been different if he had quickly had a doctor and been taken to a hospital soon. But by the time Juan got there, the leg was like this one. It was infected and stealing away the man's life."

Maria stopped again and took a deep breath.

"He had to take the man's leg. He had to. There was no other choice. Juan did the only thing he could do. The man lived and he again came awake. And then . . . then a dreadful thing happened. He discovered that his leg was gone. He was angry. He screamed at Juan. He wanted to kill him. He said Juan had always been jealous of him and had used his knife to make him less of a man. He screamed and screamed until the father came. He, too, was angry. He sent Juan from the room. And then . . . then there was a pistol shot. Juan ran back to the room. The man had shot himself. Juan's father had not stopped him. The father lay weeping across the body of the dead man. It was his son—Juan's brother."

Missie gasped her horror, and Marty shut her eyes against the tragedy of it.

"Juan left his father's home," Maria continued after a moment, "and said he would never, never be a doctor again. He hated what he had done to his family. He came to me. I loved him very much. We were planning to be married. Juan said he could not marry me, that he was going far away. That he would never again be a doctor. He threw his bag across the yard and wept as he told me. I said that I loved him. That I still wanted to marry him. That I would go away with him. At last he said I could come. I packed a few things and we went to the village priest, who married us. Juan did not know it, but I packed his medicine bag, as well. It has been hidden these many years.

"We came here and began to ranch. Juan knew ranching. He had been raised on one of the biggest ranches in Mexico. He had ridden and cared for cattle from the time he was a small niño. But still Juan was not happy. He could not forget the past. Nor could he hide the desire to be a doctor."

Maria toyed with the handle of the cup that held the now cold coffee.

"I said that Juan was troubled about coming to church, Missie. About what to teach our little ones. That is right. I did not lie. But Juan is also troubled about other things. He looks at the boy with the twisted arm and it turns a knife within him. He knows he could have set the arm properly and the boy would not have been crippled. He knows of the boy with the broken ankle in town. He knows that you all suffer here in this house with the good man, Clark. It makes my Juan suffer, too. He has not slept or eaten the last several days. He did not know what to do. He did not know that I had his bag and there was medicine in it."

Maria sighed.

"He will always ask himself, could he have saved the leg if he had come sooner?"

"No," Marty interjected. "He mustn't think that. The leg was crushed. It was a very bad break. I don't think anyone could have saved it. I pretended—but I didn't really believe it. Juan mustn't blame himself. He mustn't. He mustn't blame himself 'bout his brother, either. Juan did what had to be done. He couldn't have done anythin' else."

Maria smiled weakly. "I know that and you know that—and deep down I believe Juan knows that, too. But it still torments him. Only now . . . now I pray he can forget that deep hurt and go on to do what he was meant to do. He was always meant to be a healer, my Juan."

Willie walked into the kitchen, his face pale and his hands looking shaky.

"It's all over," he said, his voice low. "Doc says it went well. Now we jest have to wait an' see."

Marty rose and hurried in to Clark's bedside while Missie and Maria prayed together again.

During the next few days Clark was in and out of consciousness, mostly because of the medication. Dr. de la Rosa, as he was now known, stayed with him, Maria having returned home to their children. Marty found the time following Clark's surgery even more physically and emotionally taxing than her previous vigil, but Juan gave her encouraging reports daily. Clark's pulse was more normal and his color was improving. Juan was hopeful that the infection had been caught in time. Marty dreaded the moment when Clark would be aware of the fact his leg was missing. She worried about how he might respond to the shocking truth.

It happened on the third day following surgery. Clark awoke and seemed to be quite rational. He asked for Marty, who was having her lunch at the time. She went to him, and Dr. de la Rosa left the room.

"I'll be right here in the hall if you need me," Juan whispered softly as he left.

Marty crossed to Clark's bed.

"Hello there," she said softly. "It's nice to see ya awake. You've been sleepin' a powerful lot lately."

Clark managed a crooked grin. "I reckon," he admitted.

"Ya feelin' some better?"

"I think I'm feelin' lots better than even I know," said Clark.

"Meanin'?"

"Meanin' I've sorta lost track of time an' what's been goin' on. I need a few explanations, Marty. Seems I've been in an' out of a nightmare. Care to fill me in?"

Marty sighed heavily. "It's been a nightmare fer all of us—but I guess fer you, most of all."

Clark waited for her a moment and then prompted, "I think I need to know, Marty."

"Where do ya want to start?"

"How 'bout the beginnin'?"

"Ya remember the mine accident?"

"I remember."

"Ya know thet ya was hit on the head an' were out fer a few days?"

"I do."

"Do ya remember comin' round at all?"

"Yeah. It's sorta hazy. I was in an awful lot of pain. My leg was—"

Clark stopped for a moment, then went on, "My leg's not as bad now."

"We found a doctor. He's been carin' fer ya."

"A doctor! Since I woke up, Juan's been—"

"Juan is a doctor."

"Juan?"

"Right."

"Well, don't thet beat all?" Clark grinned. "How'd thet come 'bout?"

"It's a long story," said Marty. "Juan's been runnin' away from his past. One day I'll tell it all to ya."

"Well, don't thet beat all," Clark said again, shaking his head. "Juan a doctor. Folks hereabouts must be crazy-happy to learn—"

"They's excited 'bout it, all right. Soon's yer well enough to leave without his care, Juan is headin' fer a city to git what he needs to start up a proper-like practice. He's already set the ankle of thet boy in town who was in the mine. He thinks he might even be able to rebreak an' set the arm of the young Newton child. The parents are willin' fer 'im to try."

"Well, I'll be," said Clark and then, after a moment of silent thoughtfulness, he said, "Ya know, this here accident might be worth it if it got a doctor fer this town. Iffen it helped clear up Juan's problems so he could do his proper work again, it jest might be worth the price."

Marty cringed. Clark did not as yet know just how high the price had been.

"So Juan cared for me, huh?" Clark went on.

"He did," answered Marty, "right when we had 'bout given up."

"I was thet bad?"

"Thet bad."

"He had the proper medicine?"

"Enough fer it to do the job. Heard him fussin' thet he didn't have a certain somethin' else, but I guess what he *did* have worked."

"An' he fixed my leg."

"He saved yer life," said Marty.

"He fixed my leg an' saved my life."

Marty did not answer. She bit her lip and then realized Clark was waiting for her to go on.

"Clark," she said slowly, "yer leg was bad broke. It wasn't just a break, Clark. It was crushed. Then it got even worse. It got all infected with gangrene. The gangrene's poison nearly killed ya. It would have, too, if it hadn't been fer Dr. de la Rosa."

Clark's face had gone white as Marty said the words *gangrene* and *poison*.

"An' yer sayin'—?" His voice was husky with emotion.

"I'm sayin' thet Dr. de la Rosa fixed yer leg as best he could . . . in the only *way* he could. . . . He took it off, Clark. He took it off 'fore it killed ya."

Clark turned away his face. Marty saw a deep shiver vibrate all through him. She threw her arms around him and held him close. She waited for a moment until the reality of it had time to penetrate.

"Clark," she said, her tears falling freely, "I know thet isn't what ya wanted to hear. I know ya didn't want to lose a leg. I didn't want it, either, Clark. With my whole bein', I fought it. But it was yer leg or *you*. For a while, it looked as if it would be both. Oh, Clark, I'm jest so thankful to God thet He sent a doctor along in time to spare ya. I . . . I . . . I don't know how I'd ever make it without you, Clark. God spared ya, an' I'm so glad. So glad. We'll git by without the leg . . . I promise."

Clark smoothed her hair and held her close. His trembling eventually stopped. He could even speak. "Yer right. It'll be all right. Guess it jest takes some gettin' used to."

And then Marty just let herself go and cried out all of her pent-up worries and frustrations. "Oh, Clark," she sobbed. "I'm sorry. So sorry it had to happen to you like this. If I coulda jest taken yer place. . . . I know how important it is to a man to be whole—to be able to feed an' care fer his family. I could have done my carin' from a chair. It wouldn't have mattered near as much to me. Oh, Clark! I'm so sorry."

"Hush now, hush," said Clark. "Yer actin' like one a' those hysterical woman. This don't change things. I can still care fer my family. One leg ain't gonna make a lot of difference. Hush, now. Iffen the Lord hadn'ta figured I could do without my leg, He wouldn't've 'llowed this, now would He?"

At length, Clark got Marty comforted and in control. He pushed her gently away from him. "An' now," he said, "if ya don't mind, I'm feelin' in need of some rest. I'll talk to ya in the mornin'. Now you send thet there doc back in here, will ya?"

Marty left the room and sent in Juan. Juan entered the room, his pulse racing as he remembered the other incident when his brother had discovered his missing limb. He didn't blame any man for taking the news hard. He stood silently, looking at the big man lying still on the bed. Clark was the first to speak.

"I hear I owe ya my life."

Juan said nothing. Perhaps Clark did not yet know about his leg.

But Clark went on. "It must be a powerful hard decision fer a man to make—even a man trained in medicine—to take a man's limb an' spare the man's life, or let him die with both legs on. I'm glad I've never had to do the choosin'. I want to tell ya 'thank you' for bein' brave enough to make the choice fer me when I wasn't able to make it fer myself. I would have chosen to live, Juan—even without the leg—I would have chosen to live. Life is good—an' life is in the hands of almighty God. Now, I'm not sayin' I fancy learnin' to live without a leg. I'm not pretendin' to be some hero thet it won't bother none. But I am sayin' 'thank you' fer givin' me thet chance. With God's help, I'll make it. If He 'llowed it, then He must have a plan to git me through it, too. Fer He plans only fer my good."

Juan stood watching Clark—no angry cries, no cursing, no incriminations coming from the man. Clark knew of his handicap—he knew of his great loss—but he had accepted it and even thanked the doctor for giving him a chance to live. There was a difference here. A distinct difference between the way this man accepted his handicap and the way his own brother had. What made the difference? Juan determined to do some thinking on it when he could get off by himself and take the time. One thing he already knew—where his brother had cursed God, this man thanked God. Perhaps . . . perhaps it had something to do with that.

Clark interrupted his thoughts. "An' now, Doctor, I don't be pretendin' thet this here situation hasn't shook me up a bit. It's gonna take some gittin' used to the idea. I don't much feel up to thinkin' 'bout it at the moment. Ya happen to have somethin' to help a man git a little sleep instead? It might all be easier to handle come mornin'."

Dr. de la Rosa moved to prepare some medication.

Clark did not go to sleep immediately. He spent time thinking, even though he wished he could shove the whole problem off to the side and pretend it did not exist. He also did some praying—deep soul-searching conversation with the Almighty, asking for God's help in the hours, days, and weeks ahead of adjustment and growing. He even did some weeping—heartrending sobs that shook his large frame. When it was all over, he wiped the tears from his gaunt cheeks, set his chin, and reached for the unseen hand of God. It was a very long time before he discussed his feelings concerning his handicap again.

THIRTEEN

Adjustments

Marty thought Clark's recovery was slow indeed, but to Dr. de la Rosa, it was a daily miracle. Clark was doing much better than the doctor had dared to hope. When one considered what the man had been through, his convalescence was truly amazing, Doc often told her.

Willie had kept the family in the East informed throughout the whole ordeal by the means of telegrams. A great measure of relief accompanied the cable assuring them that Clark was well on the way to recovery. He stated that, at the present, he was still unable to give them a date for Clark's return home. The answer soon came by telegram: "PA DON'T HURRY STOP EVERYTHING FINE HERE STOP LETTER FOL-LOWING." Marty anxiously awaited the arrival of the letter.

As she sat one morning mending one of Nathan's small shirts, Marty was surprised to realize it was well past the time they had planned to return to their farm. How different the trip had turned out from what they had expected! It dawned on Marty that Clare's wedding was only days away. She and Clark would not—could not—possibly make it back in time. Deep disappointment flooded through her. How could she miss her son's wedding? But neither would she want the young couple to postpone it on their account. Then Marty thought of Luke's plans to go off to college. She should be home right now preparing his clothes and getting him ready. How she hated to miss that, too! A few tears slipped down her cheeks, and Marty wiped them away quickly before they could be observed. *But Luke is so young,* her heart cried. It was hard enough to let him go, but without her there to . . . She stopped herself. She'd be crying in earnest if she didn't get her imagination under control.

Marty laid aside the shirt and went to check on Clark. Missie was already there. In fact, it was not often that Missie was *not* with her father. She made up games to play with him, read to him, fluffed his pillows, sponged his face and hands, talked to him about her garden and children, discussed his meals, and told him of happenings in the district. Yes, Missie was often with her father. It was touching to see so much love between father and daughter. Marty smiled at the two of them.

"Do you know what he's saying?" said Missie in exasperation. "He's saying that he's going to get up."

Marty smiled again. "I think thet's a great idea."

"Great?" Missie exclaimed, shocked. "He's not ready for that yet! Juan said—"

"Juan said he should choose his own pace. Iffen yer father thinks he is—"

Clark stopped the two of them. "Hold it, hold it," he said, raising his hands in his customary way. "No use ya all gittin' into it. I will obey my doctor. I'll not git up till I'm good 'n' ready to git up. Iffen ya don't think the time is right, Missie, I'll wait."

Missie looked relieved and Marty slightly bewildered.

"I'll wait until right after lunch," Clark announced.

Missie sputtered, "Big wait—especially since it's now eleven-thirty." All three began to laugh.

After lunch Clark sat on the edge of the bed for a while. Later, with Marty on one side and Wong on the other, he moved to the porch to sit in a rocking chair. The day was hot, but Marty could tell the sun's rays felt good to this man who had been shut away in the house far too long. He took great breaths of the fresh air and sniffed deeply of the earth and growing things.

Nathan came to play by him, showing him all the tricks Max could do. Being a family dog rather than a show dog, Max had very few of them, so Nathan put him through the same ones over and over while Clark laughed appreciatively as though enjoying each trick.

Marty tried to keep herself from hovering over him, but she watched carefully for any signs he might be overdoing it.

Just then Scottie returned from town with the promised letter from the family back home.

Excitedly, Marty read it aloud.

"Dear Ma and Pa,

"We are so glad to hear that Pa is finally feeling better. We can't say how sorry we are for the accident that took Pa's leg, but we are so glad that he was spared. We have all been praying daily, I guess almost hourly, for you both.

"We don't want you to worry a bit about things here at home. Clare has decided to go ahead with his wedding. They had talked of waiting until you were back home again, but they thought that might pressure you into traveling before you are really ready. We want to be good and sure you are strong enough for the trip before you attempt it, Pa. So, for our sake, please don't come home until you are really well.

"Arnie is taking good care of the stock. That's been his job since you left, Pa. Of course he helps Clare in the field, too, but the stock is in his special care. He has not been seeing Hester lately. Her brothers just made it too miserable, and she says she doesn't want to marry anyone that her brothers can't drink with.

"There's a new girl in town, though. She is the new preacher's daughter, and Arnie has gotten pretty friendly with her. You would really like her, Ma. She's a very thoughtful person, and Arnie is beginning to think she's kind of cute.

"Luke's not going to college this fall. He's been spending a bit of time with Dr. Watkins lately. Dr. Watkins says he's still plenty young and another year of waiting won't hurt him any. Dr. Watkins is giving Luke the use of some of his medical books to read. He

is taking Luke with him on his Saturday calls, too, so Luke says he is learning more than he ever would in the first year of medical school. Dr. Watkins really seems to be enjoying Luke. He treats him as though he were his son. Guess Dr. Watkins maybe misses not having a family of his own. Anyway, Luke seems really happy with this arrangement.

"Everything is going well here. The canning is almost all done, Ma. The garden has done real good and the apples are coming on well. Ma Graham came over and helped me for one day. She sends her love. Everyone at church is remembering you in prayer.

"Nandry and Clae both say they will write now that we know a little better what to say. I will admit we were really scared for a while. God bless you both. We miss you to be sure, but we are doing fine on our own.

> *"In love,*
> *Ellie and the boys"*

The letter both relieved and saddened Marty. She missed them all so much, but it was good to hear they were all right and managing well in spite of the extended absence. She was glad Clare was going ahead with the wedding, and she was also glad Arnie had a nice girl for a friend. Marty was relieved to hear that her Luke would not be going off to college without his mother there to see him off. She quietly thanked God for working out these things and for allowing Dr. Watkins to shepherd the boy.

Clark turned from the letter with relief on his face. Marty had been unaware that, in spite of his ordeal, he also was concerned for the family at home.

"Well," he said, "seems as though they be makin' do jest fine without us. I'm proud of the young'uns you've raised, Mrs. Davis." He reached over from his chair for her hand.

Marty beamed. "An' so am I. 'Course you didn't have much of a hand in it at all."

"Maybe we can jest sort of take our time recuperatin' after all," sighed Clark. His grin was a little wobbly. "I think I'll jest get on back to my bed and catch me a nap."

Marty looked at him quickly and saw he was rather pale. Maybe Missie *had* been right . . . maybe Clark was pushing things too quickly. She and Wong got him settled back in his bed.

But Clark was content to take one day at a time. He attempted only what he thought he could manage. Very gradually, his strength was returning.

∽∅∽

The two couples from town whose boys had been involved in the mine accident came out to the LaHaye ranch for a visit. The two mothers, still unable to talk of the incident without weeping, thanked Clark over and over for going in after their sons. Mrs. Croft, whose Abe had been lost in the mishap, wiped away tears as she talked about how difficult the adjustment to life without Abe had been for his brother Casey and his parents. But she was so thankful they had been able to see Abe again and that his body had not been buried deep in the mine. They also were appreciative to Willie for taking charge of arrangements concerning the blasting of the mine opening so there would be no further danger to other children.

Though it was difficult for them to truly express what they were feeling, they did try to make Clark understand how sorry they were that he had lost his leg. Clark assured them that in every circumstance of his life—whether good or bad—he believed with all of his heart that God knew his situation and was more than able to help him through it. He told them he was aware that there would be adjustments and some of them would be difficult. But, when it came down to it, though *he* was human, *God* was sovereign. The visitors looked a trifle uneasy at Clark's forthrightness about his faith, and Marty, watching them with understanding, supposed it was as new to them as it had been to her when she had first joined Clark's household so many years before. Clark's face and voice held such confidence that in spite of their doubts, those in the room could not but be sure he believed every word.

Finally Mrs. Croft must have dared to speak some of what she was feeling. "It was hard fer me not to have a preacher man here fer my son's buryin'. Oh, I know I ain't rightly what you'd call a church person, but I believe in the Almighty. Can't say I'm on speakin' terms with 'im exactly . . . but . . . well, sometimes . . . 'specially in hard times like we jest been through . . . sometimes I jest wish I knew a little more 'bout 'im. . . ."

Willie spoke up then. "We have meetin's here together each Sunday. I know it ain't like being in a church, but we do read from the Word together an' sing a hymn or two. Ya all sure would be welcome to join us. Anyone is welcome anytime."

"Where ya meetin'?"

"Right here—in our home."

The woman's face expressed a new interest.

"What time ya meet?"

"Every Sunday at two o'clock."

"I dunno," interjected her husband. "It's a long way from town. By the time we got back home again, it'd be 'most dark."

The woman, disappointed, looked down at her lap and her clasped hands.

Clark suggested, "Maybe the service could be moved up a bit earlier and not 'llowed to go fer too long."

The woman raised her head again, her eyes hopeful.

"Well," said the man, probably sensing how much it meant to her, "we might give it a try fer a Sunday at the two-o'clock time an' see how it goes."

The slight smile flickering across the woman's face said it all.

Andy's parents had taken no part in the exchange about church. Willie turned to them. "We'd be most happy to have ya join us, too."

The man shook his head and shuffled his feet in an embarrassed fashion. What he mumbled was, "Don't think we be needin' thet. Our boy's jest fine now. Doc set his ankle and it's 'most as good as new."

Marty could tell that both Clark and Willie were biting their tongues to keep from jumping in with an answer.

Finally Clark said, "We spend a bit of time in our service thanking the Lord, as well. Perhaps you an' yer wife would like an opportunity to thank God thet He 'llowed yer boy to git out safely. Ya'd be welcome to join us anytime—fer any reason."

The man nodded silently.

Missie served them coffee and cake, and they went on their way. As she went out the door, Mrs. Croft whispered that she was already counting the days until Sunday.

Maria and Juan came often. Juan, like a new man, had been to the city to make arrangements for setting up a proper office for the practice of medicine. He had stocked a supply cupboard with the medicines and equipment he would need. The townsfolk had coaxed him to move into a building they would provide, but Juan wished to remain on his ranch. He did agree to be at a town office for two days of the week; the rest of the time he would work out of his own home. Glad that he had built a large house, he immediately converted one wing into an office and small examining room. He worried some, realizing that he had none of the conveniences of the city hospitals, but he could send some more serious cases out by train or stagecoach.

One night as they talked together, Clark noticed that the usually buoyant Juan was quiet. Maria tried to keep the conversation going, but it was easy to sense that something was troubling Juan. After asking about his new practice, the neighborhood, the ranch, and the children, and still getting very little response from Juan, the group grew quiet.

Clark eventually turned once more to Juan. "I'm a wonderin', Doc, if I might see ya in the privacy of my room fer a few minutes," asked Clark. Juan offered his arm and Clark managed the distance with short, awkward hops.

Clark sat on his bed and caught his breath. He needed some kind of a crutch. He must get busy fashioning one. Hopping was far too difficult and drained him of what little strength he had.

"Something troubling . . . ?" began Juan, concerned.

"Yah," said Clark easily, "I'm thinkin' there is."

The doctor automatically reached for the offending limb and began to unpin the pant leg, but Clark stopped him. "Leg's jest fine, Doc."

Juan was puzzled.

"Something else is bringing you pain?"

"Well, ya might say thet."

"And where is it hurting?"

"Well, I don't rightly know. Thet's what *I* was gonna ask."

Juan's puzzled frown deepened.

"Well," said Clark, watching Juan closely, "I kinda got the feelin' somethin' was hurtin' the doctor and he wasn't feelin' free to say anythin'."

Juan looked startled and moved away to the window, where he stood looking out on the soft night.

"It shows that much?"

"It shows."

"I am indeed sorry. I did not mean to bring my feelings to this home, to bring sadness to those I care for."

"Anythin' thet ya care to talk about . . . or thet I could do?" asked Clark.

Juan stood in silence for several minutes and finally turned with a deep sigh and troubled eyes.

"I think that you have heard my story—at least in part. You know that I became a doctor against my father's wishes. You know, too, that I was responsible for my own brother's death—"

But Clark's hand stopped him. "No," he said emphatically, "thet's not the way I heard the story. Yer brother had gangrene in a bad leg; you amputated, as you had to. Yer brother chose to take his own life."

Juan waved that aside. "My father does not see it that way. He told me to leave that night and forbade me to return to his home again."

"I'm sorry," said Clark. "It must be very hard for you."

"It is. It is very hard. Now that I am again going to practice medicine, I wish with all of my heart that I could do so with my father's blessing." Juan hesitated, then continued. "That sounds very foolish to you, I'm sure, but—"

"Not at all. I think I'd feel the same way."

"You would?"

"To be sure I would."

There was silence. Clark broke it. "What of yer mother? Is she still livin'?"

"I don't know. Perhaps that's what bothers me most. My mother never dared to say so, but I think she was proud that I had chosen to be a doctor. When my father sent me away, my mother, for the first time in her life, dared to protest. She fell on her knees before him and pleaded that he reconsider. In the name of Mary and all the saints, she asked him to allow me to stay. 'Must I lose both my sons on the same night?' she cried. I can see her yet, and the vision haunts me. If only I knew that my mother was all right."

"Why don't ya jest go on down an' find out?"

"Return home?"

"Sure."

"But my father has not asked me to come."

Clark shrugged his shoulders.

The minutes dragged by as Juan struggled with the thought. Then Clark asked softly, "Are ya afraid?"

"Of my own father?" Juan's shock showed the insult of such a question.

"Well, I don't know the man. Have no idea what he might do."

"My father would never harm me, if that's what you're thinking."

"I'm thinkin' nothin'," responded Clark simply. "You were doin' the thinkin'."

Juan nodded his head in reluctant agreement.

"So," said Clark, "since ya have nothin' to fear, why is it a problem to go back?"

"I have not been asked," said Juan with a great deal of dignity. "To go back so would be like a stray puppy crawling home for forgiveness and acceptance. Even my father would scorn such—"

"Ya mean it's a matter of pride?" Clark asked quietly.

Juan's head jerked up, his black eyes flashing fire.

"I understand," Clark nodded gravely. "A man does have his pride."

There was silence again. Juan began to pace the room. The air around them seemed to be heavy with unspoken ideas. Clark again dared to break the silence.

"'Course a man can, with God's help, swaller his pride an' do what he knows he should. If yer mother is livin', I'm sure she is hurtin', too.

She has no idea if you're alive or dead. An' if yer father is still livin' an' has maybe changed his feelin's some, how would he ever find ya to let ya know?"

Still Juan struggled with the issue.

"You do not know—" he began.

"No," agreed Clark, "I do not know. I admit to thet. But God does, an' I don't think *you're* admittin' to thet. Shore thing, I wasn't raised like you was, but things have been a bit tough fer me at times, too. Life can be pretty quick to take a swipe at a man. Sometimes we can't duck the blows. We jest gotta take 'em head-on. They smart a bit, to be sure. But . . ." Clark allowed his gaze to rest on his stub of a leg. "He knows all thet. He not only knows, but He cares. He doesn't ask from us thet we *understand* or even *like* what we face, but jest thet we face it like a man, an' do what we know to be right, even though it goes against us at times."

"And the right thing for me as you see it?"

"I can't tell ya thet. I know thet if yer troubled 'bout things as they are now, maybe ya should do somethin' to try to straighten 'em out. I know mothers can hurt somethin' awful, not knowing 'bout their sons. I know fathers can make mistakes thet they suffer fer, an' sometimes it's most difficult to be man enough to say they was wrong. Thet's all I know. Yes . . . I know another thing, as well. I know God can help us do the right thing—even though it seems impossible. But only you can decide what is the right thing fer you."

Juan weighed the words of the older man. At length he turned to him and extended his hand.

"I am not making any promises, except that I will think about what you have said. It is a very hard thing."

Clark took the hand and shook it firmly. "I'll be prayin' you make the right decision," he said.

They returned to the others. There were questions in many eyes, but none were asked. Maria and Juan soon declared that they must be on their way home.

Cookie came to visit Clark whenever his work would allow him a break. He usually waited until he saw Clark out on the veranda getting some fresh air or early-morning sun, and then he would hobble over to ease himself to a step or a nearby chair. He seemed to feel he and Clark had much in common. One day he even dared to talk about it.

"Leg bother ya much?"

"Not bad now. Gives me a bit of a jar if I happen to bump it."

"Any trouble with 'phantom pain'?"

"Some."

"Must be a peculiar feelin'. Somethin' hurtin' thet ain't even there."

"Yah, bothers me some, all right. Itches somethin' awful at times, an' ya ain't got nothin' to scratch." Clark chuckled ruefully.

"Well, at least I don't have them problems," said Cookie.

"Yer leg still bother ya a good deal?" asked Clark.

"Sometimes." There was a moment of silence while Cookie thought of the pain. "Not as bad lately, though. Was a time I near went wild with it."

Clark nodded his head in understanding. "How many years now?" he asked.

"I try to fergit. Guess it must be 'bout five already. No, six. Lotsa folks said as how I'da been better off to have it removed like you done."

"Well," Clark reminded him, "I wasn't able to do my own choosin'. Don't know's I'da really picked this way to do it, iffen I had."

"Yer leg was bad broke, Clark," Cookie assured him evenly. "I knew as soon as I seed it thet only a miracle could save it, an' seems to me we been a little short on miracles in my lifetime."

Clark smiled. "Well," he said firmly, "I ain't seen an overabundance of miracles myself, but I shore ain't doubtin' them none." Watching Cookie's expectant face carefully, Clark went on, "Guess one of the biggest miracles I know of is when God takes a no-good sinner and makes a saint fittin' fer heaven outta 'im. Now, thet's a real miracle, to my thinkin'. With some trainin' an' the right tools an' medicine, even an earthly fella like the doc can put a badly messed-up body together again. But only God, through His love an' grace, can take a crushed and broken soul and restore it again. Yes sir, *thet's* a miracle."

Cookie scuffed the dust with the toe of his boot.

"Take me now . . ." Clark said confidingly, "ya know what happened with me? When I first woke up to the fact thet I had only one leg, a part of me died inside. I started tellin' myself all kinds of stories 'bout bein' only half a man, an' how sad it was to be a cripple, an' how sorry I could be fer myself, an' even how God had let me down. Fer a minute, I almost had me convinced thet I had good reason to jest turn over to the wall and have a real good feelin'-sorry-fer-myself time. My body was broken . . . was bruised and hurtin' . . . an' my soul wanted to sympathize with it, see? My soul wanted to curl up an' hurt an' suffer an' become bitter an' ugly. Now, God didn't choose to do a miracle on this here leg." Clark tapped the stump lightly. "But He did a bigger an' more important miracle. He worked over the inner me—the soul of me. Thet's where I needed the miracle the most, so thet's where He applied His amazin' power. In here"—Clark pointed to his broad chest—"I don't hurt anymore."

Cookie's eyes hinted ever so slightly of unshed tears, and Clark wondered how many years Cookie had been in pain both inwardly and outwardly. He reached out a hand and gently squeezed the cowpoke's shoulder.

"We needn't fear." His voice was almost a whisper. "He's still doin' miracles."

FOURTEEN

Growing

In the fall Willie returned to the range and the business of ranching. Cattle needed to be rounded up and a few stray dogies branded. The steers for market required cutting and sorting from the herd and then would be driven to the train station for shipping. Sagging and broken fences were repaired and pastures checked out before the coming winter, including the all-important water holes for the cattle. And of course the dreaded rustlers mandated constant vigilance. The warm fall days were busy from dawn till dark at the LaHaye spread.

Missie still tried to spend most of her time with her father. Occasionally her own responsibilities suffered because of the attention she was showering on Clark—reading to him, though Marty thought that was one of the things he could do well on his own, making favorite dishes for him, and talking about this and that so his confinement would not seem too burdensome. But Missie's two little boys did not seem to fare too badly, because they also were usually hovering closely around their grandfather.

Soon, though, Marty was noticing that Willie, who came back at night exhausted from his day full of hard work and the pressures of running the spread, was getting little consideration from his wife. Missie was so busy fussing over Clark that she scarcely had time to notice. Marty hoped she was exaggerating things and tried to tuck her anxiety into the back of her mind. She attempted to take care of Clark so fully that Missie would not feel this was her duty, but this did not ease the situation. Missie still hovered close by.

Marty then turned some of her own attention toward Willie, hoping to at least make him aware that he was still loved and appreciated. She of course was fully aware that Willie needed the attention of his wife—not his mother-in-law. Even the boys did not run to meet Willie with the same exuberance at the end of the day, for they had spent the day with a grandfather who carved them tops and fashioned whistles and answered their every question with serious attention.

In spite of her determination to put the matter aside, Marty daily felt her concern grow. To her surprise, Clark, who was normally so sensitive to the feelings of others and aware of situations, did not seem to notice it. Perhaps he was just too close to it.

Marty put her worries into fervent prayers for the Lord to intervene as He saw fit.

❦

Henry came to see Clark. He obviously had something on his mind. After a simple greeting, he came directly to the point.

"Been doin' a great deal of thinkin' lately," Henry said. "We really need us a church."

Clark nodded his head in agreement and looked up from the crude crutch he was carving, having determined it was time he did something to aid in walking. "Good idea."

"Seems like now would be as good a time as any to be plannin' fer it," Henry went on. "I know thet now ain't a good time at all fer ranchers. Real busy time of the year, but things will be slowin' down again 'fore too long. But we shouldn't wait fer things to slow down 'fore we git started. Thet's sorta like puttin' God last. Been thinkin' thet we really are in need of some preachin'. We read the Bible together, an' thet's good, but some of these folks need someone to explain what it's meanin'. Take thet there new family thet's been comin'—the Crofts—

723

they need someone to tell them what the Word means, to show them how to accept the truth fer themselves."

"I was thinkin' thet when ya said 'church' ya was meanin' a buildin'," Clark noted.

"Well, I was, an' I wasn't," answered Henry. "Shore, we need a buildin', an' I think we could work on thet real soon, too. But I was also thinkin' of people an' of those who need to know the truth. I think it's time to give 'em more'n we been doin'."

"Sounds good to me," responded Clark. "Ya got some plans fer this?"

"Yah," said Henry, "been thinkin' on you."

"Me?" Clark couldn't keep the surprise from his voice.

"Shore. You." Henry did not waver.

"But I don't have any Bible trainin'."

"Ya been studyin' it fer years, haven't ya?"

"Yah, but—"

"An' you've heard lots of preachin'?"

"Shore nuff."

"An ya believe the Holy Spirit can teach the truth?"

"'Course I do."

Henry grinned. "An' ya ain't overly busy these days, are ya?"

Clark couldn't help but chuckle. "No," he said, "I ain't over busy. Been makin' a few tops an' whistles, an' tyin' a few knots, an' eatin', an' complainin', an' makin' folks run around waitin' on me. Come to think on it," he said, scratching his head with the blunt end of his knife, "seems I been powerful busy after all."

They laughed together.

"Well?" spoke Henry, turning serious.

"Well," responded Clark, "I need to do some thinkin' an' prayin' 'bout thet one."

"You do thet," encouraged Henry and straightened up. He looked quite confident about where Clark's thinking and praying would lead him.

"Gotta git," said Henry. "The fellas will be wonderin' where their boss has disappeared to. See ya come Sunday." And he swung up into the saddle and left the yard at a canter.

Clark continued the work on his crutch, but his thoughts were far away from the task at hand. He paused occasionally to wipe away a tear or two. Maybe God was indeed turning this whole tragic accident into something far beyond what any of them could have imagined.

The group that gathered on Sunday in the large living room of the LaHaye household had again increased. With the Crofts were two other women from town and their children. One was the mother of Andy, the boy Clark had rescued from the mine. The other woman, young and sad looking, had just buried an infant son.

Four of the LaHaye cowboys sauntered in and took inconspicuous seats toward the back of the room, clearing their throats and fingering their wide-brimmed hats self-consciously as they waited for the singing to begin. The simple service was just starting when Cookie hobbled in with a reluctant-looking Wong in tow. Cookie had privately told the family he was going to get Wong to come by telling him this would be a good opportunity to add some new English words to his vocabulary.

Henry led the singing with his guitar, and Willie read the Scripture. After a time for prayer and another song, Willie allowed anyone from the congregation to share a Scripture or a thought. Henry rose to his feet. Clearing his throat, he began slowly with great seriousness.

"Ya all know as how we been feelin' the need to git together like this Sunday by Sunday to hear the Word an' pray. Maybe ya all 'preciate it as much as I do, but ya still feel somethin' is missin'. Like we need to learn more 'bout the Bible. Thet's why churches have preachers—to explain the meanin' of God's Word. Well, we ain't had us a preacher. 'Course we do have the Holy Spirit as our teacher, an' I thank God fer thet.

"This here summer Missie an' Willie had the blessin' of Mr. and Mrs. Davis comin' fer a visit. It was jest to be a short one—a couple a' weeks. We all know the tragic circumstances thet bring 'em to still be here. I say 'tragic' 'cause thet's the way it seems to all of us. But I been thinkin'. Maybe God can bring good outta even this tragedy. The Word says thet all things can work together fer our good if we love God. Lately I've been thinkin' 'bout some good thet might come from this. I spoke to Mr. Davis 'bout it, an' he promised to pray on it. I've asked Mr. Davis if he won't be our preacher an' explain the Word to us

Sunday by Sunday. Now, he ain't a preacher, really. He's a farmer. But he knows the Word of God, an' he's heard lotsa preachin', an' I think he'd have lotsa good Bible teachin' to share with us."

Faces began to turn toward Clark, and it was apparent many people were waiting expectantly to see how he would answer. Clark looked around him at the strange little congregation. Missie and Willie, along with Henry and Melinda, had grown even more in their faith since coming west. Rough cowhands sat before him, probably knowing very little about the Bible but seeming to be open to learning more. The sad young woman from town was obviously longing for some kind of comfort. The Crofts also needed healing for their recent bereavement. The family with the son whose arm still needed to be straightened sat with the group, along with Andy beside his mother. The de la Rosas had joined them that day, and the pain and the questions still lingered in Juan's eyes. Clark's heart went out to them all. He felt a strange stirring within, and he knew that, with God's help, he must feed this flock. He stood up, his crutch held firmly in hand for support, and looked around at the faces before him.

"It honors me to be asked to open God's Word with ya here. With God's help, I will try to give to ya the meanin' of the Scripture read each Sunday. We can learn together."

He sat down, and enthusiastic nods and smiles swept around the room. Marty was so proud and happy she could have put her head against Clark's shoulder and wept tears of joy.

Henry stood again, his face beaming. "We got us a preacher!" he exulted. "Now, what we gonna do 'bout a church? We're gettin' to be too big a crowd to fit here anymore."

There were enthusiastic and spontaneous responses to the question. Many voices began to call that they would build their own church, and some made suggestions about where it should be located. Henry finally got things quieted enough to speak again.

"I've been thinkin'," he said, "thet since there's not a church in town yet, an' this is a powerful distance fer some to travel, we oughta try to even things up a bit an' put the church 'bout halfway fer everyone."

"I'm 'bout halfway!" exclaimed Mr. Newton, jumping to his feet. "I shore would be right proud to be givin' some of my land fer a church."

Others nodded, their faces full of enthusiasm and anticipation. It was agreed that the church building could be located on the Newton ranch. "We'll need us timber an' materials an' a buildin' plan," said Henry. "Lots of things to be decided."

"Then let's git us a committee," someone called.

Eventually the group concluded that Willie, Henry, and Mr. Newton would be the building committee. The rest of the congregation would wait for orders and do their bidding. Excitement ran so high that tongues could not slow down even when Missie served coffee and cookies. They were going to have their own church! A dream come true.

Marty wrote another long letter to send east. They would not be returning home to the farm and the rest of their family until the next spring. Though Clark was daily gaining strength and would now be able to tolerate the train trip, he was going to stay and help establish the new church, giving the people lessons from the Scriptures and encouraging them in their building project.

Marty was pleased to see the enthusiasm with which Clark greeted each new day. He spent hours poring over his already-well-used Bible, and as his heart discovered new truths, his lips shared them with others. He often could not wait for Sundays but spoke excitedly with anyone who was within listening distance.

Clark also was busy with other matters, thinking about little inventions that would help him in overcoming his handicap. Daily his independence was growing. He scarcely needed aid any longer. He even adapted a saddle so he could again ride horseback with the men or with Nathan. He moved about the ranch on his own, carrying buckets or saddles in the hand that wasn't occupied with the crutch. He went out to the garden and helped to dig the last of Missie's vegetables. He went with Nathan to gather eggs and prepared fryers for Sunday dinner. Marty marveled and rejoiced as she watched him move about with confidence and assurance.

Marty knew that Missie, too, was glad to see her father up and around again. But she still could not seem to keep from fussing overly much. Marty realized it was Missie's admiration for her father that was motivating her—trying to make him comfortable whenever she came near him, feeding him special treats from the kitchen, entertaining him with chats and games. But Marty could no longer ignore her concerns. Surely Willie could not help but miss the attention that rightly should have been his.

In her growing anxiety, Marty took a walk, hardly knowing where to begin in her thinking to address the problem. Certainly Clark was loved in Missie's home. Willie had great respect for him. Missie loved him deeply, and the boys doted on their grandfather. Still, Willie's immediate family needed their own father and husband, and he needed Missie and their sons.

Marty wondered just how to discuss the issue with Clark. Would he see her concern and understand? What could they do? They were committed now to staying for the winter. And it wasn't possible to live in Missie's home and shut one's self away from the rest of the family.

At last Marty decided she must at least talk it over with Clark. If he did not see it as anything to get concerned about, then Marty, too, would try to put it from her mind.

That night after they had retired, Marty hesitantly broached the subject. She hoped Clark wouldn't think she was just being foolish, making mountains out of molehills.

"I've been thinkin'," said Marty slowly from her side of the bed. "It must be rather difficult fer Willie with us here."

"Willie?"

"Well, it wouldn't be, normally. But now, with yer accident an' all."

"I try not to cut in on Willie's time," answered Clark. "I know he's a very busy man. I've even found a few little ways I've been able to help lately."

"Oh, Willie ain't feelin' at all thet yer a loafer, thet ya aren't doin' yer share," assured Marty quickly. "I know thet. He's always tellin' me jest how special it is for 'im to have ya here. An' he tells me, too, of how ya been organizin' the corrals an' fixin' up his barn."

"Yer talkin' 'bout his family, then?"

"Ya mean—"

"I've been thinkin' on it, too. Missie frets over me far too much. It's done in love, an' I 'preciate it, but it don't leave her much time fer payin' attention to her husband—to the boys, too. I love the little tykes very dearly. But they're gittin' so's they come to me when they scratch a knee or pound a finger."

"You've noticed!" exclaimed Marty, very relieved.

"I've noticed. An' now thet you've noticed, it won't be near so hard fer me to make the suggestion I been thinkin' on."

"Suggestion?"

"Well, we can't jest up an' pull out now. They do need us to git thet little church started. We can't leave 'em now, Marty."

Marty agreed with a nod.

"An' it don't seem too smart to be carryin' on here in the same household as Willie an' Missie. Two families in the same house for very long—especially when one of 'em is the grandparents—often don't work so good."

"So?" Marty queried.

"So I think it's 'bout time fer a move."

"A move? Now where could we move? Yer not thinkin' of goin' into thet wild town—"

Clark stopped her with a laugh. "No, no wild town."

"Then—"

"The soddy."

"The . . . the *soddy*?" Marty was incredulous.

"Why not? Willie and Missie lived in it fer two winters, an' they had Nathan at the time. Surely you an' me could make do fer one winter. Jest the two of us. I've been thinkin' it might even be kinda fun." He grinned and said, "Would be like the old days in our little cabin back when we . . ."

Marty's expression must have slowed him down for a bit, but then he went on, "I've been checkin' it over, an' the walls are sturdy, the windows in place. The roof looks real good. Guess Willie jest had a new one put on to humor Missie fer our comin' out here. No reason a'tall why we couldn't be nice an' comfy fer the winter there."

Marty's initial aversion to the idea began to soften. She laughed softly. "Well, I never dreamed I'd be livin' in a soddy. An' at my age!"

"Ya keep referrin' to yer age," said Clark. "I'm not about to consider myself married to an old woman, so ya jest better stop sayin' it."

Marty laughed again.

"Well," prompted Clark. "What 'bout the soddy? Ya willin'? It still has the furniture—such as it is."

"Why not?" said Marty, lifting her shoulders in a shrug. "Think of all the time I'll have jest to sit an' read or sew. Not much to keepin' a soddy up."

"Sounds like a woman of leisure," Clark commented. "But ya know I'll at least be expectin' as good care as I've got here—" But he couldn't finish the thought since Marty was throwing her pillow at him.

"Then it's settled," he said when they'd finished laughing. "We'll move in first thing tomorra."

"Don't ya think Missie might need some time to think on the idea?"

"She'll git used to it. Ya give her time an' she might jest think of all kinds'a reasons why we shouldn't."

"Maybe yer right," agreed Marty. "All right, we'll move tomorra, then."

She kissed Clark and turned over to go to sleep. In the darkness, a smile played around her lips. She and Clark were going to live in a soddy! Wouldn't her friends back home think that was something else? Well, she'd have her share of experiences to tell them, that was for sure. She could hardly wait to write the next letter back home to the children. Imagine that—she and Clark living in a soddy!

FIFTEEN

Moving

The next morning at the breakfast table, Nathan was busy shoving in Wong's muffins by the mouthful and making plans for himself and his grandfather for the day.

"An' we can ride over to the big hill an' look right over the range to where all the hands will be drivin' the cattle. We can see 'em start off on the trail drive to the town market. An'—"

"Whoa, cowboy," said Clark. "Thet shore sounds like a lot of fun all right, but I'm afraid I can't be runnin' off today. Fact is, I was thinkin' of askin' fer yer help today."

Nathan looked at his grandfather with surprise and interest. "Sure, Grandpa. I'll help ya."

Josiah cut in. "Me he'p G'an'pa."

"You're too little," Nathan answered with big-brother assurance, but Clark was quick to encourage the younger boy. "Shore ya can help. We're gonna need all the hands we can git."

Josiah beamed at being included.

"What're you up to?" asked Missie.

"Yer ma and me decided to move today."

"Move?"

"Yep."

"Stop your teasing, Pa," said Missie.

"Not jokin' around, daughter. Never been more serious."

"Then what do you mean, 'move'?"

"Well, we decided it might be kinda fun to spend the winter in the soddy."

"You *are* joking!" Missie obviously could not believe Clark was serious.

"No, I'm not."

"Whyever would you do that?"

"Why not? The soddy is snug and warm and big enough fer the two of us. It would be an adventure to talk about when we git back home."

"Oh, Pa," said Missie, exasperation in her voice. "Don't talk about anything so silly."

"Little girl," said Clark firmly, "it's not silly and I really am serious 'bout this."

Missie turned to Marty. "Tell me he's only teasing."

"No," said Marty matter-of-factly. "He's not. We talked it over last night. We decided it would be better fer all of us if we lived separate fer the winter. We'll be right nearby—"

"I don't understand one word of what you're sayin'," Missie said, rising from her chair with her face white and set. "If you're serious, I'd like to know why. Haven't we been caring for you—?"

Clark quickly interrupted her. "My dear," he said gently, "ya shore as the world have been doin' everythin' fer me . . . an fer yer ma. An' we 'preciate it . . . more'n we ever could say. But now thet I'm gittin' about an' am able to mostly care fer myself, well, yer ma an' me think it's 'bout time yer family had ya back again . . . all to themselves."

Willie's eyes widened with understanding, then he lowered his gaze. Marty knew he would say nothing, but she also knew he was aware now of their observations about the situation in his home.

"That's silly," Missie continued to fume. "My family has had me all along. Never have I been more than a few feet away from any of them. Why, they always knew right where to find me. We've *loved* having you here. Besides, it was all because you came to visit us that you lost that leg—"

"Missie," Clark interrupted again, "I don't want to ever hear ya say thet I lost my leg because I came here. It coulda happened at home jest as well as here. The place has nothin' to do with it, an' I never want ya to feel any kind of guilt or responsibility thet the accident happened because I was here."

"Well," Missie said, lowering her eyes but seeming to brush aside Clark's comment with her gesture, "I won't feel guilt—I promise—but I still don't understand your wanting to move on out. We've so enjoyed having you here. Before we know it, the winter will be over and you'll be off home again. We want you here as much as possible. Tell them, Willie," she implored her husband. But Willie merely continued eating his scrambled eggs and muffins.

"Tell them, Willie," Missie instructed again.

Willie swallowed and looked from one to the other. It was apparent that he did not wish to be involved in the discussion. Clark spoke up before Willie was obliged any further.

"We know our son-in-law would never suggest we leave his home an' his table, Missie. We really want to do this, not because we are not welcome here, but because we feel it would be good fer all of us. We'll be right nearby and can come in fer coffee whenever we need a stroll. Yer ma will be over often to borrow cups of sugar and talk 'womenfolk talk.' The boys can come an' visit us in the soddy." Clark winked. "It could be jest a heap of fun. Marty an' I have never lived all by ourselves, ya know."

"And nothing I can say will make you change your mind?" Missie said, her one last effort at persuasion.

"'Fraid not. Iffen the winter gits too tough an' we begin to get cold, we might come crawlin' back beggin' to be 'llowed in," said Clark lightly.

"I'll let ya in, Grandpa," assured Nathan, and everyone began to laugh.

"I let ya in, G'an'pa," echoed Josiah, not wanting to be outdone.

Missie moved for the coffeepot. "Well, if you are determined to do it, I guess I can't stop you, but I still don't like it."

"Look, honey," said Marty, understanding how their daughter felt, "if we didn't think it for the best, we wouldn't do it. Honest! Just give it a chance, will you, Missie? If it doesn't seem to be working for the best of all concerned, we'll move back in here. All right?"

Missie brightened some and leaned over to kiss Marty on her forehead.

"I'm sorry. It just took me off guard." She managed a smile. "If you're sure that it's what you want, my soddy is all yours. But I'm warning you, Mama, it can get awful cramped on a winter's day."

Marty laughed. "Well, I have an advantage you didn't have, my dear."

"Yes?" asked Missie.

"You," said Marty. "If I git to feelin' cramped, I can jest bundle up an' make a dash fer yer big, beautiful home. You didn't have a big house or a daughter nearby, so ya jest had to sit tight."

Missie smiled again. "Well, I hope you feel cramped real often," she said. "Then you'll visit me lots."

Clark put down his empty cup. "Well, fellas," he said to the boys, "guess we'd better git started with this here move. Got yerself a wagon we kin use?"

The boys scrambled down and led the way to the bedroom that had been known as Grandpa and Grandma's for the last few months. Clark followed, his crutch beating a rhythmic tattoo behind them.

"I'll see what I can find for rugs an' blankets," offered Missie. "You'll need some decent dishes, too. Those in the soddy are in bad shape."

"Now, don't ya fuss none," Marty warned her daughter, but she knew she might as well bid the sun not to shine. Missie was sure to fuss. Marty just shrugged her shoulders. Perhaps in the fussing Missie would find some fun. She followed Missie out, determined to make a real adventure for them all on this moving day.

✧

The nights were cooler now, and the wood fire in the old cookstove made the snug little soddy cozy and warm. Clark had encouraged Marty to visit Missie often during the first few days after their move, to assure her that indeed they had not forsaken her. Marty also invited Missie down to the soddy for afternoon tea, and Missie's many memories of the primitive dwelling gave her parents a new understanding of their daughter's first years in the West. She told of her first shocking sight of the small grass-covered mound that was to be her home, and her horror at seeing from inside the dirt roof and dirt floor, and her feeling of fear as she laid Nathan on the bed lest the chunks of earth come tumbling down on top of the wee baby. She described their first Christmas and the cowboys sitting almost toe to toe, enjoying a simple Christmas dinner. She told of Cookie holding Baby Nathan when he had the croup and helping him to breathe freely again. She talked about her first visit from Maria, her difficulty in drying her wash, her cooped-up feelings. But all the time she talked there was nostalgia in her voice, and her deep affection for the little soddy showed. Marty even began to wonder if Missie might be envying them the chance to live in it!

The boys loved to come, and Marty and Clark found themselves listening for their knock on the door and the two little voices calling, "Grandpa!" "Grandma!" They would pester Clark as he tried to study for the Sunday lessons. They coaxed to be able to add fuel to the fire. They wanted to roll on the bed, scratch marks in the dirt floor, and have their meals at the small table. They brought garden vegetables, fresh eggs, or milk from their mother. They even brought treats from Wong's kitchen.

Clark and Marty enjoyed them but always made sure they were home to greet their father when he returned at the end of the day.

Life finally had settled into a warm, comfortable, wholesome routine for all of them. Marty was thankful that Clark had proposed the move, feeling that it truly was better for all concerned. Willie looked less tense, more relaxed and happy, as well. He had needed to be master in his own home again. Even Missie took on a new glow. The past months had drained all of them, but now it was time for life to return to normal.

⚜

Marty sat in front of the soddy, knitting and soaking in the late fall sun; Clark came around the corner, expertly managing his crutch and a pail of spring water. He set the pail down and sank into a chair beside Marty, wiping his brow.

His chuckle brought Marty's head up. *Now what is he findin' so funny?* she asked herself and then repeated it to Clark.

"Nothin's funny, really. Jest thinkin' thet God really *does* make 'all things work together fer good.'"

"Meanin'?"

"This here leg—the one I ain't got no more. Ya notice which one is missin'?"

"Yah, the left one."

"Yep, the left one—but more'n thet. Look, it frees up my right hand when I'm workin'. See, I use the crutch in the left. Not only thet, but it's the left one I chopped into thet winter takin' out logs. Remember?"

Marty wondered how he thought she could forget. She still went weak and sick inside when she thought of how Clark had returned to the house with his pale face and blood-drenched foot. "I remember," she said, her voice tight.

"Well, thet's the foot thet's gone. Thet rascal has kept me awake more'n one night—'specially when the weather's 'bout to change."

"You never mentioned thet before."

"Weren't no reason to. Guess it won't keep me awake again, though."

Clark chuckled again. Marty couldn't quite bring herself to join him, but she smiled at this strong, patient man of hers who saw God's hand in all the circumstances of his life.

⁂

Clark had a visit from Juan. It had been three weeks since they had seen the de la Rosas. They had been informed that Juan and Maria had gone away, and they assumed Juan was still gathering equipment and supplies for his medical practice. He greeted Clark now with a firm handshake and clear eyes. Marty sensed that he wanted to talk to Clark in private and left the two of them alone over steaming cups of coffee.

"Well, after much prayer and struggle," began Juan immediately, "I did as you recommended."

"You have been home?"

"I have been home," Juan said with deep feeling.

"I'm glad," said Clark. "An' how did yer pa receive you?"

Juan's eyes clouded for a moment. "My father, I am sorry to say, was not there to greet me. He died seven months ago."

"I'm sorry," Clark said with sincerity.

"I am sorry, too. I should have gone sooner. I should not have let stubborn pride keep me away."

"An' yer mother?"

"My mother welcomed me with outstretched arms."

Clark smiled. "I'm sure she did."

"My father had died and left my mother all alone. Daily she prayed that if her son Juan was still living he would come back to her. Because of my foolishness, it took a long time for my mother's prayers to be answered."

"We are all foolish at times," Clark reminded him.

Juan went on. "My mother could scarcely believe her eyes when I walked into her room. She had failed much. She did not eat well or care for herself since my father died. When she saw me, she wept long for joy. Then she told me how my father had pined after sending me away. He tried for many months to find me—to ask for my forgiveness—but there was no trace of where I had gone. Before he died, he had my mother promise that she would keep trying. She did. She sent out men and offered rewards, but she could not find me."

Juan stopped to wipe a hand across his eyes. "I caused them much hurt," he murmured.

"Ya didn't know."

"No, I didn't know. I was too busy nursing hurts of my own. . . . My mother was so happy to hear that I am a doctor again. I would like you to meet her."

"I'd love to meet her. Maybe someday—"

"Not someday. Now."

"Ya mean—?"

"She's here. I left her up at the house having tea with Missie and Maria. She wants very much to meet the man who sent her son home to her."

"But I . . . *I* didn't do thet. Ya went on yer own. It was yer decision."

"Yes, you let me make the decision. You left me my dignity. But you knew when you talked to me how I would have to decide." Juan smiled.

"I'd love to meet yer mama," said Clark, picking up his crude crutch.

"An' I have something for you," said Juan, returning to the door and reaching outside for a carefully fashioned crutch with a padded arm bar. "They can make very good crutches in the city," he added.

Clark took the new crutch and handled it carefully, looking over every angle and the total length of it.

"It's a dandy," he grinned. "An' I thank ya."

Clark, with his new "store-bought" crutch, and Juan went to the house together. Juan explained as they walked, "My mother had no desire to live alone on the rancho. As I did not wish to return to ranching in that area, we decided to sell the ranch to the man who has run it for my father. Mother is insisting on using much of the money from the sale for my medical practice. She wants us to have good equipment for those who need help. She is going to live with us. We are all so happy. Maria can't remember having a mother. Hers died when she was a very young girl. We are all very happy, Mr. Clark, and we thank you."

Señora de la Rosa was a delicate, dark woman with flashing eyes and a quick smile. In spite of her years and the intense sorrow in her past, she still had a youthful spirit and vibrant outlook on life. Clark and Marty liked her immediately.

"Mama has said that we shall all come to service together," said Maria. "When God works to answer her prayers through people who worship—even though they worship in a different way than she is used to—they must have the approval of God, she says. And so God would also surely approve of us worshiping together with them. So we shall be here next Sunday—and all the Sundays—and we will be glad to help in the building of the new church."

The prayer time together before the de la Rosas left for home was full of fervent thanksgiving to God.

SIXTEEN

Winter

Nathan celebrated his sixth birthday—a big event for him at any time, but even more important on this occasion because his grandparents were there to help in the merrymaking. The Kleins and de la Rosas also came for the event, and the house rang with laughter and friendly chatter.

Josiah got his full share of attention on the occasion, coming in from the kitchen wrapped in one of Wong's big white aprons. Everyone had a good laugh, and Joey was pleased with the response.

Nathan had insisted he wanted a crutch "jest like Grandpa's" for his birthday and could not understand the objections to getting him one. He wanted to imitate his grandfather in every way, and he felt that the use of a crutch—even though he planned on keeping his leg—would be one more thing he could share with this man he loved so dearly. Missie was horrified at the thought of such a thing, fearing that Nathan's toting about a crutch might be tempting fate. She tried to talk Nathan out of it, promising him all kinds of things in its place. But he still wanted one. Clark finally had a man-to-man talk with the boy, and Nathan came away from the discussion happy that he had two good legs to walk on "like his pa."

Willie was pleased with the profits from the fall cattle sale, and he and Missie left by train for a larger city to do some shopping. Clark and Marty took charge of the two boys while the LaHayes were gone. The children begged to sleep in the soddy with their grandparents, and the four had a cozy and enjoyable time together.

The shipment of furnishings eventually arrived, and Missie now had a new dining room—splendid in its dark wood furniture, thick rug, and rich draperies. Marty complimented Missie many times on her excellent taste, but Missie laughed and replied that anyone could have good taste as long as they had good money.

Missie, too, had a birthday. Marty thoroughly enjoyed the chance to make the cake and prepare the birthday dinner after the number of years they had been apart for this event. All the ranch hands were invited for the meal. The large family dining room was almost as crowded as the little soddy had been many Christmases ago. But Missie loved it, and the cowboys all seemed to appreciate it, too.

Marty awoke one morning to the sound of the wind howling around the little soddy. The winter's first storm had moved in without warning. Clark was already up and had gotten a nice fire going before reading his Bible at the small table.

Marty snuggled under the covers again and thought about how fortunate they were. Winter might be here with all its sound and fury, but they were snug and warm and dry. Marty did not put off getting up for long. Clark had coffee perking, and the smell of it quickly enticed her from the bed. She crawled forth rather hesitantly, but the comforting heat from the fire meant the howling wind had no power in their warm shelter.

"My, thet coffee smells good! I think ya purposely made it jest to tempt me from the bed," she said, slipping her arms around Clark's shoulders and giving him a kiss on the cheek.

"Ya hear thet wind?" asked Clark. "Sounds like we're gonna find out all 'bout a western winter."

"Guess we will at thet," said Marty, "but ya know, it ain't scarin' me none."

Clark merely smiled.

"Whatcha doin'?" asked Marty.

"Well, Henry figures thet when the storms strike on a Sunday, the folks from any distance won't be able to make it here fer the service. So we talked it over an' decided to make 'em up some lesson materials they could read and study at home."

"Thet's a good idea!" Marty enthused.

"At least this'll help 'em to feel a part of the group, even iffen they can't git here. They'll be studyin' the same portion of the Word as the rest of us."

"Thet's nice," Marty encouraged again.

"But I've been at this fer what seems ages already, an' I shore could do with breakfast. I was jest sittin' here thinkin' this is the kind of a mornin' I could use a nice big stack of pancakes."

Marty laughed and went to get dressed so she could make Clark his pancakes.

⁂

The winter weather continued as it had begun. The storms moved in and out of the area, leaving behind big drifts of snow. As predicted, the Sunday crowd at the LaHayes' diminished during that time. Henry saw to it that those members of the little congregation not able to attend received Clark's Sunday lesson materials.

The church building committee worked hard at drawing up plans and arranging for the materials for spring building. All the members of the group were anxious to get into their own little church. Juan's mother sent away to the city and ordered a bell for the spire. She felt that a church of God should have a bell for calling together the worshipers.

Donations for materials and labor came in from many of the neighbors. Willie and Henry were sure that when a building was finally in evidence, the Sunday attendance would increase sharply.

Cookie often dropped in at the soddy to see Clark. Marty was sure he waited until he saw her heading for Missie's for a chat or to do some baking together, and then, in her absence, he would hobble off to have a cup of coffee with Clark. Clark did not discuss much of their conversation with her—she knew he was honoring Cookie's desire for confidence. Yet she also realized the old cowboy was deeply troubled about his past life and its effect on his eternal future. Marty wanted to hasten "the awakening" and say outright to Cookie, "Yer a sinner an' ya realize yer bad deeds can keep ya from heaven. I was a sinner, too. But one needn't stay in thet state. Christ Jesus came so every person can be forgiven and restored to all that God intended when He created us. All ya need do, Cookie, is to accept the gift of life He offers to ya. It's jest thet simple. Nothin' to it at all. No need to fret an' stew over whether it's a good idea or a bad idea. Common sense tells ya thet ya can't lose on such a deal. Jest do it an' git it taken care of."

Clark was far more patient with the man, and Marty knew he would carefully explain what Scripture had to say about mankind's fall into sin—beginning with Adam and Eve—about human selfishness, about every person's need of a Savior, and about God's solution to this need. Cookie was gradually realizing his own need and understanding what Christ had done for him, Clark quietly told Marty. He felt confident that when Cookie made his decision, there would be no turning back. Still, Marty inwardly chafed, wishing it wouldn't take the man so long.

Scottie, too, was on the Davises' prayer list. They liked and respected the foreman, and they longed to see him make his peace with God. Scottie came to the Sunday services whenever he was free to do so, but he did not seem to feel any need of a change in his life.

Lane, the one who had helped Doc de la Rosa with the surgery, was growing spiritually. Daily he sought out Clark or Willie for the answer to some question he had found as he read the Scriptures. He not only read the Bible, but he endeavored to live daily by its commands and precepts. Lane could never be accused of being a hypocrite. Even the bitter Smith began to show a grudging respect for Lane and one day admitted to Jake, "Don't hold much to religion. Always figured it was fer women an' young'uns an' men who couldn't stand on their own feet. But if I was ever to git religion, I'd want the kind thet Lane's got."

Jake looked skeptical. "Didn't know there was more'n one kind," he drawled.

"Ya didn't? Then ya ain't been watchin' Lane lately."

"So where did Lane git his special brand?" sneered Jake.

"Reckon he got it from the same place the boss an' his pa-in-law got theirs. It seems to be made of the same stuff."

Jake thought of Willie and his steadiness—even through the tough times—his fairness with his men, and his concern for his community. He also thought of Clark and his acceptance of his handicap, and he murmured under his breath, "Yah, reckon it is." Then he turned to Smith. "So, iffen they's able to pass it on an' are so anxious to share it, what's stoppin' ya from gittin' yerself some?"

Smith did not answer. He just scowled and rode away.

When Christmastime arrived, Marty's thoughts were often on her family at home, even as her thoughts had been on Missie during the Christmases they had been separated. Marty reminded herself that Kate was there to help Ellie make a Christmas for the family on the farm, and the last letter had stated that Nandry's and Clae's families would both be home for Christmas, as well. Soon after the new year, Joe and Clae and little Esther would be leaving for the city, where Joe would finally have the opportunity to get his seminary training. Marty wished she would be there to tell them good-bye, but it brought a certain joy to her heart to know they would be in the very city where Luke would eventually take his medical training. It would not be nearly so hard to let him go knowing that Clae and Joe would be there to welcome him.

Even so, Marty thought much of her other family as she made her preparations for Christmas with the family in the West.

Wong and Cookie combined their efforts to prepare a Christmas feast for all the members of the ranch family. It was bound to be a sumptuous affair, and everyone was anticipating the occasion. Marty supposed they would all eat more than they really needed, but somehow even that spoke of God's abundant blessings to them, especially this Christmas.

Nathan and Josiah had worked themselves up into a fever of excitement. Nathan knew of Christmases past and the thrill of receiving gifts. Josiah was too young to remember other Christmases, but he was willing to take his big brother's word for what would happen.

Marty had busily knitted mittens, socks, and scarves for the two boys, and Clark had been carefully fashioning a snow sled. "Shore enough," he told Marty, "with all them hills around, there must be one that a sled would work good on." Marty heartily agreed. Even though they would be many days' journey away from the rest of their family, they were happy to spend this Christmas with Missie, Willie, and the boys.

On Christmas Eve, Marty finished the last of her Christmas presents, and they packed up their gifts and themselves and went out into the starlit winter night for the short trip to Missie's house. They had planned an evening of games, Christmas carols, and popcorn over the log fire. The gifts would be exchanged the next morning.

Nathan answered their knock and squealed his delight at their arrival, and Josiah was just behind him to echo his joy.

"Hi, Grandpa! Hi, Grandma! Come in. We're havin' Christmas," shouted Nathan.

"Ch'is'mas," echoed Josiah and pulled them in by the hands.

The evening was full of love and joy. They chatted and ate and played games and sang amid laughter and lighthearted banter. They shared their memories of other Christmases. Nathan loved the stories, but finally Josiah's lids started to droop as he fought to stay awake.

Finally Missie rose to put the two children to bed. Nathan certainly was not anxious to go, afraid that he might miss out on something. Missie assured him everything would be there for him to see and share in the morning.

When the children were settled for the night and the grown-ups were having coffee and slices of Wong's Christmas cake made from one of Marty's recipes, Missie, her cheeks aglow and her eyes alight, shared her secret.

"You are going to be grandparents again in July," she said. "We're going to have another little one."

"Oh, thet's wonderful!" cried Marty, hugging her girl close. "But, my, I wish it would be sooner! We should be off home long 'fore then, an' it will be so hard to leave without seein' him—or her."

"I'm hoping for a girl this time," admitted Missie. "But a boy would be all right, too. Willie's always needing lots of cowboys on the ranch." They laughed together, and Willie looked pleased.

They talked further about their hopes and dreams concerning the new baby. Marty noted how thankful she was that Dr. de la Rosa would be there for the birthing. And perhaps by then he would also have his little medical office ready for use.

Clark and Marty, arm in arm, returned over the snow-packed path back to the little soddy. They were just about to enter when Cookie appeared, hobbling hurriedly toward the bunkhouse from the cook shack, a small lantern swinging by his side. Marty assumed he must be going to meet with the cowboys for their own Christmas celebration, but Clark said there seemed to be an urgency to Cookie's steps.

"Somethin' wrong?" he called to Cookie.

Cookie hesitated. "No, nothin' wrong, really. Least not fer you to concern yourselves with. Scottie jest came ridin' in with some stray cowpoke he found out there on the range someplace. Fella's in pretty bad shape. Looks like he ain't et in a week, an' the weather's kinda on the cold side to be sittin' out under a rock outcroppin'. Lane, he went over to see what the doc would advise fer his frostbite."

Cookie was about to move on, but Clark called to him, "I'll join ya. Don't s'pose there be much I can do, but I'll take a look-see."

He turned to Marty and spoke softly, "Ya go on in out of this cold to bed. I'll jest be a few minutes an' then I'll be in to join ya. Ya might want to check on the fire again 'fore ya turn in."

Then Clark deftly hopped along after Cookie, his crutch making strange tracks in the fresh snow.

The cowboys had put the unfortunate man to bed, Lane directing them to his bunk before he left for the doctor's. Smithie was using the only medicine he was acquainted with—a shot of whiskey. The man was sputtering and fussing, so Clark knew at least he was alive.

"Where'd ya find 'im?"

"Scottie found him someplace out there. Didn't even have a horse. Said it had died. He was walkin' somewhere—who knows where—an' the bad weather caught him. He tried to hole up in a sheltered spot and wait out the wind. He coulda been there till spring and not had the wind stop none."

Clark smiled in spite of his concern. "Is he in bad shape?"

"Don't know yet. He has some frostbite fer sure, an' he's thin as a rattler. 'Bout as mean as one, too, I'm thinkin'. All he can do is cuss an' name call. Don't seem to 'preciate much the trouble Scottie took fer 'im."

Clark moved nearer to the bed.

The man before him was heavily bearded and his eyes were only dark holes in his head. Bedraggled and dirty, he looked as though he hadn't had a meal in weeks. Yet something about him was vaguely familiar.

Clark motioned for them to move the lantern in closer, the result being a gruff complaint and a curse from the stranger. Clark looked steadily into the thin, shadowed face and finally was sure.

"Jedd," he said, shaking his head in disbelief. "Jedd Larson."

SEVENTEEN

Jedd

The sick man stirred slightly and mumbled something incoherent. All other eyes in the room turned on Clark.

"Ya know this man?" asked Scottie.

"It's Jedd Larson; there's shore no mistakin' thet. But he do look in bad shape. Last I seen 'im he was still young and strong—and a mite on the stubborn side. Marty an' me raised his two girls—though it's hard fer us to remember at times they ain't really our own flesh and blood. We think of 'em as such."

"Well, I'll be a—" exclaimed Cookie, though he was not allowed to finish his statement, for the ill man began to toss and call out in his delirium. Clark leaned over him in an effort to understand what the man was saying. He straightened as he caught the one word that was repeated over and over. Jedd was saying, "Tina."

"Understand 'im?" asked Cookie.

"He's askin' fer his wife. She's been gone fer a number of years now. Can't say thet Jedd treated her too kindly whilst she was here. Maybe he's regrettin' it now."

Clark reached out a hand and felt Jedd's brow, hot with fever. He leaned over the man again and spoke his name softly. There was no response. Clark knelt down beside the bed and took the man's hand in his. He began to talk to Jedd. The cowboys gradually moved back from the bed to allow the two men a degree of privacy.

"Jedd," Clark said clearly, "Jedd, this is Clark. Clark Davis, yer neighbor. Remember me, Jedd? Clark Davis. Clark and Marty. Ya left yer girls with us, Jedd, when ya decided to go west. Tina wanted 'em to have schoolin'. Tina asked Marty to give the girls a chance, Jedd. Remember? They are fine girls, Jedd, yer Nandry an' Clae. You'd be mighty proud of 'em. Both of 'em married. Nandry has a family of four. An' Clae's got a little girl. Yer a grandpa, Jedd. A grandpa five times over. You'd be proud of yer grandchildren, too, could ya see 'em."

The man was not responding. He stared off into space and now and then mumbled or cursed as the warmth of the room increased the pain in his frozen limbs. Clark continued to speak to him, rubbing his hand as he spoke, careful not to touch the frostbitten fingers.

"Jedd, Nandry and Clae still worry 'bout ya. Still pray fer ya daily. They want ya back, Jedd. They want to share with ya their love, their family, their God. Remember, Jedd? Tina found peace with God before she died. Well, yer girls are servin' their mother's God, too, Jedd. There's nothin' they would like better than fer you to know God, too. Ya hear me, Jedd? Yer girls love ya. Nandry an' Clae—they love ya. Tina loved ya, an' God loves ya, too, Jedd."

"Ya gotta keep holdin' on," Clark continued, speaking softly but with urgency. "Ya can't jest go an' give up now. Hang in there, Jedd."

There was hardly a pause in the low murmur of Clark's voice until Lane and the doctor arrived. Dr. de la Rosa examined Jedd carefully and gave him some medication. He shook his head as he turned to Clark and the waiting ranch hands.

"He is in bad shape. He was not well even before he was caught in the storm."

"Will he make it?" asked Clark.

"I do not know."

"Please, Doc," said Clark, "iffen there's anything at all you can do fer 'im—anything to bring him through—I'll stand the bill. This here is the father of two girls Marty an' me raised as our own. He's been bullheaded and stubborn, thoughtless and sometimes cruel, but his girls love 'im. If only Jedd can live long enough fer someone to tell 'im of God's love an' fergiveness. Thet would mean so much to his girls . . . to us. Ya think you can bring him round, Doc? I jest can't bear the thought of 'im dyin' without my bein' able to talk with him 'bout his girls and 'bout God's love for 'im."

Dr. de la Rosa looked very solemn. "I can only try," he said. "You pray that God might work a miracle."

The doctor no doubt thought Clark would go to his little soddy and kneel in prayer, but Clark saw the need as imminent. He immediately knelt beside the bed on which Jedd lay and began to pray fervently for a miracle. Around him feet shuffled as cowboys, uncertain of what to do, shifted position. But Lane knew. He crossed to the bunk and knelt down beside Clark, joining him in his prayer.

"Dear God," began Clark, "you know this here man before us. He's been sinful, God, but so have we all. He's made some bad judgments, but so have we. He needs ya, Lord, just as we all do. He has never recognized you as God an' Savior, an' he needs thet chance, Lord. He can't hear or respond in his present condition, so we need ya to do a miracle, Lord, an' help the doc bring him round so we can talk with him and read yer Word so he might have the chance to decide fer himself. We are askin' this, Lord, in the name of Jesus, yer Son, who died so each one of us—includin' Jedd here—could have life eternal. Thank ya, Lord, for hearin' the prayer of those of us who bow before ya. Amen."

Clark stood up, adjusting his crutch to support himself. The man before him still lay unconscious.

Lane reached out and touched the whiskered cheek. Then he turned to the doctor. "What's next, Doc?"

Juan looked back at the man on the bed. "I think I should take him to my home. I can put him on the cot in the office."

All eyes looked at the doctor, questioning.

The doctor continued. "He is going to need much care. We can watch him there. It will make my mother feel needed. She wishes to do something for someone, and this will be her chance. If I am able to help this man . . ." Juan hesitated, then continued. "I think it is too late to save many of his fingers and toes. Perhaps he will lose them all."

It was sobering news. Clark noticed some of the hands in the room unconsciously curl up into fists, as though defying fate to try to take their own.

Lane moved first. "Ya want me to git a team?" he asked the doctor.

"Yes. Put lots of hay in the bottom of a wagon. We'll need to make him a bed."

For the second time that Christmas Eve, Lane made the trip to the doctor's, this time driving the team that carried a critically ill man. His saddle horse tied to the rear, Dr. de la Rosa rode in the wagon with them, watching Jedd to be sure he stayed well covered in the bitter winter wind.

Clark returned to the little soddy and found that Marty had not gone to bed.

"I've been frettin' an' thinkin' all kinds of things," she said.

"You'll never believe this," said Clark, "but maybe you should sit down fer this. Thet man Scottie brought in off the range is Jedd Larson."

"*Jedd?*"

"Shore ain't in very good shape."

"Oh, Clark. Did ya tell 'im 'bout his girls? Did he say—?"

"Jedd didn't say much 'ceptin' a few cuss words, Marty. He is plumb outta his head. No, thet's not right. He did say one thing. Over an' over. He said 'Tina.'"

"Tina . . . then he remembers."

"Somehow thet one name gave me hope, Marty. Somehow it helped me to believe this wasn't jest fate thet sent Jedd this way, but God givin' him a chance to find *Him.*"

"Oh, Clark, I pray it might be so," said Marty, tears filling her eyes.

"If only I could have talked to him—made him understand me some-how."

"Can I see 'im?" asked Marty.

"He's gone."

"Gone? But how could—"

"Lane went fer Dr. de la Rosa, an' the doc decided when he checked Jedd out it would be better fer 'im to have Jedd at his house so he could watch over 'im. Lane took 'im on over in the wagon. They left jest a few minutes ago."

"Oh, Clark. I hope he makes it. I hope ya have a chance to talk to him. Was he really bad, Clark?"

Clark nodded his head solemnly.

"Oh, Clark!" cried Marty again. "Let's pray." The two knelt beside the bed and prayed long and fervently for this one from the past with such strong ties to their family.

"Please, Lord, bring him round enough to understand ya love him in spite of what he's done to his wife, to his girls," Marty prayed. "Help us know how to show him thet love."

In spite of their shock and anxiety over Jedd, Christmas Day was a time of thanksgiving and joy. With two small boys in the house, it was impossible not to feel the excitement and pleasure of this celebration of Jesus' birth. Even though they had retired late the night before and had had difficulty getting to sleep, Clark and Marty were up early and over in the big house. Nathan and Josiah were already up and filling the house with cries of happiness as they looked at the gifts under the tree that had arrived sometime during the night. They did not seem very interested in their breakfast that morning.

Nathan was thrilled with the sled that Clark had made and begged to go out and try it even before he had eaten. Clark laughed and promised the boys he would take them out on the sled just as soon as their mother approved. Missie, smiling, shrugged her shoulders and shook her head.

Nathan's favorite gift from his parents was a new halter for Spider, his pony. Willie finally gave in to his pleadings and told him they would go to the barn and make sure the halter fit. Nathan soon reappeared, bundled to his eyebrows with Marty's gift of socks, mittens, and carelessly looped scarf. Willie laughed at the sight.

"Ya shore enough look well cared fer weatherwise, 'cept fer yer feet. Ain't ya plannin' to wear any boots?"

"They won't go over my big socks," replied Nathan, which brought more laughs.

Josiah soon rounded the corner, too. Still in his nightclothes, he also had looped his long scarf over it all. One eye was hidden and he peeked out from the other one, his head tipped to give him better vision. His mittens had been pulled onto the wrong hands, and the empty thumbs stuck out to the sides like two misplaced horns. The socks, partly on but mostly off, gave Josiah the appearance of duck feet. He waddled forward, pleased with himself and ready to join his brother and pa for the trip to the barn.

Now Willie really laughed. He led the two boys back to their room, properly dressed Josiah and helped Nathan to find socks and boots that worked together. Then, with the small Josiah on his pa's shoulders and Nathan trudging along at his side with the cherished new halter, Clark joined them and they all started out for the barn.

"They do make some sight, don't they?" said Missie at the window, her voice full of emotion.

"Don't know how many times I've stood at my window an' watched yer pa an' his sons crossin' the yard," Marty responded. "If I had no other reason to love yer pa than thet single one—the seein' of his care fer his young'uns—it would be enough to make me love him as long as God grants me breath," she continued softly.

They turned back to the preparations for the day. There was much to be done, for Christmas dinner for all of the hands had become a tradition on the LaHaye ranch. Though usually busy and going many different directions, on Christmas Day they took the time to all eat together and hear the reading of the Christmas story.

Around the morning's breakfast table, the discussion often returned to the wonder at Jedd Larson turning up on the LaHaye ranch. They had not heard of Jedd since he had left his farm back home and headed west so many years ago. Marty wished there was some way she could tell Clae and Nandry the exciting news, and then she remembered that if Jedd did not make it through this Christmas Day, the news they would have to share with their girls would be bad news, not good news. Again and again throughout the day Marty quietly prayed.

After the trip to the barn, as promised, Clark took the boys for a sled ride.

At first it was difficult for him to pull the sled with the two small passengers up the nearby slope, but eventually he found that his crutch, jammed into the snow, made a good replacement for the limb he did not have.

The boys squealed with delight as Clark shoved them off and they made the short, swift trip down the hill. This time, Nathan pulled the sled back up the hill, but it was hard for little Josiah to climb back up through the deep snow on his own. Clark went to meet him and carried him up the hill piggyback. Again and again the two sped down the hill and made their slow and awkward climb back up. At last, exhausted but happy, they agreed to head back to the house and get warmed up.

"We'll have to do this again, huh, Grandpa?" said Nathan.

"'G'in," echoed his little brother.

"Shore will," puffed Clark, who had enjoyed it almost as much as the boys.

"After dinner?" asked Nathan.

"Well, I dunno 'bout thet. I think I might jest have to catch my breath a bit. And maybe yer pa an' ma might have some of their own plans fer after dinner."

"After thet, then?"

"We'll see," laughed Clark. "We'll see."

About one o'clock the cowboys began to arrive, kicking the snow from their boots and slapping their wide-brimmed hats against their sides. They laughed and joked as they filed in. Marty stood back in amazement as they stopped in the large entry and removed their boots and lined them up neatly against the wall, no doubt thinking of possible damage to Missie's fine rugs. Marty had been west only for a short while, but already she understood how important boots were to the ranch hands, how important it was not to be caught with your boots off. She smiled her appreciation for their thoughtfulness. But they seemed embarrassed and ill at ease as they stood looking down at their stockinged feet. Marty noticed that some of the socks had holes in them and wondered if she would dare offer to darn them. She said nothing now but went to the kitchen to find a worn towel. One by one she picked up the boots and carefully wiped away all traces of water and dirt. Then she handed them, pair by pair, back to the owners. The cowboys climbed back into the boots with warm grins and eloquent nods of thanks. They were now anticipating the meal that already was filling the air with delightful aromas as Wong carried dish after dish to the large dining room.

Before the meal, Willie, as the head of the home and the owner of the ranch, read to them the story of the birth of the Christ child. Some throats were self-consciously cleared and many gazes were fastened on the tops of boots or the big leathery hands in their laps, but everyone listened carefully. Willie then asked Clark to lead them in prayer.

The meal began in comparative silence, but it wasn't long until hearty laughter and good-natured teasing took over. Nathan and Josiah joined in merrily, describing in detail to the ranch hands their gifts of the morning, the trip to the barn with the new halter that "Spider liked real good," and their ride on Grandpa's sled.

After they all had eaten as much as they possibly could, the guests moved to the living room, where a friendly fire welcomed them. Henry was not there to lead them with his guitar, having decided to follow the LaHaye tradition and have a family Christmas dinner for his own hands. But in spite of the absence of Henry, they sang the Christmas carols under Willie's direction. Those who did not sing seemed to enjoy listening.

Scottie was the first who had to leave. He always took responsibility for the Christmas shift with the cattle. Usually one or two of the other hands joined him voluntarily out of respect for their boss. Today it was Jake and Charlie. Lane announced that he planned to ride over to the doctor's to see how Jedd was doing. Clark said that he would like to go with him.

The cowboys left, calling their thanks as they flipped their Stetsons back on their heads.

After dinner, the two boys were tucked in for a much-needed nap. Missie and Marty went to help Wong and Cookie clear the dishes, and the house again fell into silence.

Clark and Lane saddled up for a visit to the doc's house and Jedd. The ride through the crisp afternoon felt particularly cold, and Clark especially noticed it in the stump of his missing leg. He had not thought to provide extra protection for the area, not realizing how sensitive it was to the temperature. Lane, without saying anything, swung down from his horse and pulled a blanket from behind his saddle. Speaking of other things, he crossed to Clark's horse and tucked the blanket around the stump, making sure it was fastened securely in place and would not slip with the movement of horse and rider. Still making no reference to the missing leg or the blanket, he remounted and they moved on. Clark was much more comfortable during the remainder of the ride.

They found Jedd in much the same condition as he had been the night before. Juan's mother sat with him. Jedd had been bathed, and his beard and hair had been neatly trimmed. His feet and hands bore large bandages, and Clark was reminded of the doctor's concern for the fingers and toes that had been frozen. When the two visitors found Jedd unconscious, they did not stay long. Juan promised that if the man roused, he would send one of his ranch hands with the message. The doctor seemed encouraged that Jedd had held his own throughout the day. His pulse rate had improved, and this gave Juan some hope.

Lane and Clark left for home after sharing a cup of hot coffee and some of Maria's special Christmas goodies.

As they mounted their horses, Clark tucked Lane's blanket around himself. "Never knowed," he said simply, "jest how much the cold would bother a leg like mine. Here I was pridin' myself thet I wouldn't suffer any cold toes on this side."

Lane smiled but only said, "It'll toughen."

EIGHTEEN

From Death to Life

It was three days before a rider came from the de la Rosas' to inform them that Jedd Larson was now awake. Clark immediately saddled a horse and prepared to go to him. He tucked his Bible inside his jacket and asked Marty for an extra blanket.

"It's a trick I learned from Lane," explained Clark in answer to her unasked question. "This here short leg gets awful cold. A blanket keeps it more livable."

Marty spent the day knitting and praying. It seemed like Clark was gone forever, but at last Marty heard the sound of a horse approaching the barn. In the clear, crisp winter air, the sounds of the hoofbeats rang out clearly. Max left the yard on the run, always the first to welcome a rider.

Marty watched from the window until Clark came in sight, and then she grabbed her shawl and ran to meet him.

"Come to Missie's," she called. "She'll want to hear all 'bout it, too."

Clark changed direction and headed for the big house as Marty ran down the rutted snow-packed path to meet him there.

"Oh, I was hoping you'd come right on over here," Missie called to them from the doorway. "I just couldn't wait to hear all about it."

Missie led the way to the open fire. "We're nearly bursting," she spoke for both of them. "Tell us about it quick."

"Did Jedd know ya this time?" Marty began.

"Oh, he knew me all right. Was almost as surprised to see me as I was to see him the other night."

"What did he say?"

"He asked first thing 'bout the girls."

Marty felt her throat constrict with emotion. "I'm so glad he cares somethin' fer 'em," she said.

"He seemed right concerned. Said he'd 'bout made up his mind to go on home. He was tryin' to reach town an' the train station when he got lost in the snow an' was stranded out on the range."

"Did he mention Tina again?"

"We talked 'bout Tina quite a piece."

Marty could wait no longer. "Clark," she said, "were ya able to talk to 'im 'bout his need fer God?"

"I was. We went through the main points in the Bible—from creation to redemption to Christ's return."

"Did he understand?"

"Seemed to."

"Did he . . . did he . . . ?"

Clark put his arm around Marty and pulled her close. His voice sounded husky as he said, "Those girls of ours are gonna be happy to know their pa joined with their ma today."

"Ya mean—?"

"Jedd Larson made his peace with his Savior."

"Oh, thank ya, Father," prayed Marty aloud, happy tears running down her cheeks.

Clark cleared his throat.

"He joined Tina in another way, too." He paused for a moment, then said quietly, "Jedd didn't make it. Juan had to operate. Jedd wasn't strong enough to stand it. The frozen fingers and toes had turned bad, an' there weren't any way Juan could save 'im. He's been stayin' with him day an' night, fightin' to bring 'im through this, but—"

"But he did, Clark. He did!" exclaimed Marty. "Because of Juan's fight to save 'im, Jedd not only has life—but *everlastin'* life."

"I'm afraid it's hard for a doctor to look at things thet way," said Clark soberly.

"But it's true. And, oh, Clark, if you hadn't been here, Jedd maybe wouldn'ta decided to make his peace with God 'fore he died." Marty's eyes fell to Clark's pant leg, pinned up securely just below the knee. "If it weren't fer the accident, ya wouldn't still be here, Clark. We would've gone home long ago."

Clark pulled her closer to him and kissed her hair, and Missie joined them on the other side as they embraced and thanked the Lord together for Jedd's salvation.

During the long winter days, Marty spent much of her time in the little soddy knitting, mending, or hand-sewing for Missie and her family. She also had a basketful of socks to mend for the ranch hands, having made discreet inquiries after the boots had come off at dinnertime on Christmas. Clark used his hours to make things with his hands and his limited tools. In the long evenings, he spent hours with the Bible, preparing the Sunday lessons for the congregation.

Each Sunday after the worshipers gathered together for their service, there were discussions concerning the materials and the progress of the church building. As the committee continued planning and ordering supplies, the building was taking shape on paper and in the minds of the people, even though not a stake had been pounded or a nail driven. However, the supplies were all being stockpiled at the Newtons' as they arrived by train, and a building bee was planned as soon as the weather would permit. Folks hoped for an early spring so the work might be started.

As the weather improved, so did the Sunday attendance. Once again, the folks from the town ventured out on their long drive. But they seemed anxious to be a part of the fellowship and to keep informed about progress on the church building. Besides, they reported, though they enjoyed the Bible studies at home and it had been a good idea, it was not the same as meeting with the group and hearing Clark's insights on the truths from the Scripture portion.

During the week, when Marty felt too confined, she would toss a shawl about her shoulders and hurry over the snow-crusted path to Missie's house. On a few occasions, Missie came to visit her while the children slept. Missie said she loved to sit in the quiet, snug little soddy, sipping tea and telling stories about those first years at the ranch. Missie occasionally acknowledged aloud that the days were quickly passing and her beloved mother would all too soon return back home.

As the winter days lengthened, their visits turned to garden plans and setting hens. It was hard to stay in the house with the drifts of snow shrinking daily. The boys gamboled about like young colts finally set free in the sunshine and hints of warmth to come. Their mother had to coax and scold them to keep their warm jackets on and buttoned.

<hr/>

Clark, too, had been planning ahead, only his thoughts had taken a different turn. He thought often about the small congregation. He had enjoyed the opportunity to lead them over the winter months. He knew they were not likely to soon find a minister for the group. What would happen when he had to leave for home? Clark decided to ride over and talk about it with Henry. And so it was that Clark began to have study sessions with Henry to prepare him to take over leadership of the church. The people would know that when Clark left there would still be worship and Bible study. The building was only a small part of the requirements for a congregation.

At long last, spring did arrive. This time it did not come slowly as spring so often does. One day it was still winter, and the next day spring was unmistakably in the air.

The spring birds appeared, little flowers colored the hillsides, green grass carpeted the area by the flowing spring, and Nathan ran capless and nursed a runny nose.

Missie's mind quickly switched to her planting. She pulled out all her seeds, giving special attention to the ones Clark and Marty had brought with them. Spreading the little packages all across her table, she and her father began to sort and plan. Nathan and Josiah wanted to get in on the interesting activity, and soon her carefully sorted seeds were all mixed up again. Marty shepherded the boys to the kitchen for milk and cookies, and Clark and Missie continued their garden plans.

In spite of his crutch, it was Clark who tended to the plowing of the soil. He arranged little pots for planting seedlings inside and advised Missie as to what would grow best, as well as where and when to plant them.

After the garden was started, it was time for Missie to turn to her chickens. She had spotted six hens with a desire to nest, and she carefully selected a setting of eggs for each one of them. Clark helped her with the coops, and the hens were housed in fine style. Missie placed her settings under the mothers-to-be and marked her calendar for the coming event. Marty couldn't help smiling as she watched father and daughter work together.

❦

The date for the church building bee was set. Wagons loaded with excited families, plenty of food, and necessary tools headed for the Newtons' ranch. Cookie had to be available at home to feed the hands who were on duty with the cattle. Wong did not go, either. He was not a builder and did not feel comfortable sharing the cooking duties with several neighborhood women, so he stayed in his own kitchen and sent a big bucket of his special doughnuts to go with the morning coffee.

Juan had discovered two experienced carpenters from town who took charge of the actual construction. The neighborhood men offered their hands and skills wherever they were needed.

Within the week the church building was lifting its spire proudly toward the sky, the barren prairie and wide horizon providing a dramatic silhouette. Señora de la Rosa wept the first time she heard the bell peal, reaching across the miles and echoing from the distant hills.

The announcement of the first service in the new church brought many new faces to the congregation that day. Clark wondered, as he looked over the crowd from his place on the platform, how many were there for social reasons or idle curiosity and how many were already genuine worshipers "in spirit and in truth." Regardless of what had brought them there that day, he saw a wonderful opportunity to open the Word of God to them.

Marty sat with Missie and her family on one of the new pews, Nathan tucked in between them and Josiah snuggled on his mother's lap. *I love the smell of new wood,* thought Marty as she looked around at the families nearby and sensed their joyful anticipation. *While we've been here,* her thoughts moved on, *God has provided a doctor for their bodies' needs and a church for their spiritual needs. Thank you, Lord!*

As the Sundays continued to come and go, Clark was pleased to see quite a few of the visitors continue to come. The regular attendees made a point of keeping in contact with each new visitor to the church.

❦

Nathan and Josiah now spent much of their time outside during the lovely spring weather. With their grandfather's help, they had planted their own small garden and checked it daily, running to their grandmother with progress reports.

"It's growin'!" cried Nathan one day as he burst in upon Marty.

"What's growin'?" she asked innocently.

"My garden! Come see. Come see."

Marty hurried after him. Nathan fell on his knees and pointed to some small green plants just beginning to poke their heads out of the soil. Marty didn't have the heart to tell him just then that they were weeds. *Wait until some real garden begins to grow,* she told herself, *and then we'll take care of the weeds.*

But Josiah had his own way of looking after the weeds. He pulled them up to see how they were doing, then pushed them awkwardly into the ground again and pounded on their tender tops with his pudgy palm—even the hardy weeds did not survive his "tender" care.

Eventually the "real" gardens did begin to grow. Marty was not sure who was the most excited with their growing plants—the two small boys or Missie. Marty understood. She wished she were home planting her own garden. She missed it and wondered if Ellie and the boys would be taking care of it.

Marty took another horseback ride out with Missie and the boys to view the herds. Hundreds of spring calves scampered around their bawling mothers. Marty had never seen such a sight and tucked it away in her memory to report on when she and Clark returned home.

Nathan climbed down off his pony to pick wild flowers for his two favorite ladies. Marty's smile went from him to Missie, who sat on her horse with young Josiah astraddle in front of her. Missie's face was flushed, her figure gently rounding with the new life growing within her, and her hair, teased loose by the prairie wind, fanned about her. Behind her, the hills rolled on and on like a gently dipping sage-green sea. Beyond them, the mountains lifted silver peaks to play secret games with the fluffy clouds that hung low in the sky. The scene was lovely, full of life and warmth and love—a memory Marty would cherish for many years to come.

She was thankful now that Missie and Willie had come west. She was glad she and Clark had been able to visit. She was even glad for the extra time that Clark's accident had allowed them. Missie was happy here. As Marty looked at her contented daughter, she realized that Missie really belonged here. She was a gentle part of Willie's West. Marty looked about her with new appreciation for the ever-present hills and the openness—even the wind. This land spoke of freedom, of independence, and of strength. Marty was proud that her daughter was a part of it.

They rode home in silence . . . no doubt each thinking her own thoughts. Nathan cantered ahead on Spider, manfully "breaking trail" for his mother and grandmother. Josiah, his head resting against his mother, had nodded off to sleep.

Clark was waiting for them when they returned. He had spent the day putting new legs on Cookie's worktable.

"How did you and Cookie make out?" asked Missie. She and Marty knew that Clark had been looking for an opportunity for a heart-to-heart talk with Cookie about his relationship with God.

Clark shook his head. "We had a good talk—nice an' open—but

Cookie is still hesitant. He says he wants to be sure he is acceptin' Jesus Christ—not Clark Davis."

"I don't understand," said Missie.

Marty thought about the statement for a moment. "I think maybe I do," she said slowly.

"Well," Clark said modestly, "Cookie says he admires me . . . guess 'cause we both of us had a similar kind of accident. Not much to admire a man fer, but Cookie reasons a little different than some men do. Anyway, he listens to the Word as I give it Sunday by Sunday; he sees me able to make do with one leg . . . I don't know. He's got it all mixed up as to what I can do as a man and what I can do with the Lord's help. He's not sure yet where the difference lies. Cookie's right, ya know. I don't want him to be a follower of Clark Davis. Iffen he can't find the difference here, he should wait until he does. No good followin' a man. Nothin' I can give to Cookie he can't find in himself."

"Sounds strange to me," mused Missie. "I've never thought of anyone getting mixed up about who to be following before. Seems plain to me that Jesus is the only way to heaven."

"I left Cookie my Bible and marked some verses for 'im to read. I hope he can understand their meanin'."

"We're gonna have to do some praying," Missie said simply as Clark and Nathan moved away with the horses and she and Marty walked on to the house, Josiah asleep in her arms. "If Pa can't make Cookie see the difference, how will Willie or Henry ever do it?"

Eventually they learned that it was Lane who showed Cookie the difference. He walked into the cook shack and found Cookie frowning over Clark's Bible.

"I still don't figure it," mumbled Cookie.

"Don't figure what?" asked Lane, reaching for the ever-ready coffeepot.

"If I take on this here religion, will I be doin' it to try to become a man like Clark Davis?"

"What's wrong with bein' a man like Clark Davis?"

"Nothin'. Nothin' I can see. Only he says thet tryin' to be like 'im ain't gonna git me one step closer to those pearly gates yer always talkin' 'bout."

"Oh, thet," said Lane, understanding Cookie's dilemma. "He's right."

"But how can I be like *Jesus*?" asked Cookie in frustration. "I don't even *know* Him."

"Forgit 'bout bein' *like* Him fer now," said Lane. "Yer tryin' to start too far ahead of yerself." Cookie looked doubtful but let Lane continue.

"You've heard it preached an' read many times thet all men are sinners?"

"Yah," grunted Cookie.

"Are ya doubtin' ya fit in thet category?"

"Shucks, no," said Cookie. "I know myself better'n thet."

"Okay," said Lane, "thet's where ya start. Now ya know yer a sinner, an' I guess if yer wantin' to copy Davis, ya don't really want to stay one."

Cookie nodded his agreement.

"Well, how ya try to clean up yer act ain't gonna make a whole lot of difference. You'll never measure up, no matter how hard ya try. Oh, ya might even git to *act* as good as Clark Davis himself, but thet won't really impress God none. He still sees deeper than the skin.

"The Bible says thet man looks on the outside, but God looks on the heart. Also says thet the heart of man is 'desperately wicked.' But the good news is thet our hearts can be changed. Now, thet there's the startin' place.

"Jesus, holy an' pure, died fer every dirty, wicked heart thet ever beat. All we gotta do is see what we are, an' who He is, an' accept fer ourselves what He did. Thet's all there is to it. From there on, He does the workin' on makin' ya a follower."

Cookie's eyes opened wide at the simplicity of it. Lane gulped the last of his coffee, placed his cup on the table, and headed for the door.

When he reached the door he hesitated, turned to Cookie, and said softly, "All ya gotta do is ask Him."

After Lane was gone, Cookie did.

NINETEEN

Plans and Farewells

Clark and Marty began to talk about when they should go home, talking quietly together in the privacy of the little soddy. At first it was like a dream to be thinking of boarding the slow-moving train again and leaving behind the West that they had come to respect and the family they loved so deeply. Marty wished there was a way she could bundle them all up and take them home with her. But then she thought of Willie and his love for his spread, Missie and the sun reflecting in her eyes, and Nathan and Josiah as they rushed about their beloved hills with the wind whipping at their hair. And she knew she would not want to pick them up by their roots and try to transplant them—not really.

Marty's thoughts turned more and more to her farm-home family. *How're Clare and his young Kate doing in the little log house? Is Arnie still seeing the preacher's daughter? What is the girl really like? Is Ellie entertaining any gentleman callers? Which of the neighborhood young men will be the first one to notice our pretty young daughter who is now a woman?* She wondered if Luke still nursed his dream of going off to train as a doctor and how Dr. Watkins and the boy were getting along. Marty was anxious to get home again and have some of her questions answered.

A long letter from Ellie arrived. She told about the new grass and leaves on the flowering shrubs. She spoke of the songbirds that were back and the new colt in the pasture. She reported that Clare had plowed the garden spot and she and Kate had planted the garden—more than they would ever be using themselves, she was sure, but they just couldn't seem to stop once they had gotten started. She told of Nandry's tears of joy and sorrow upon receiving the news of her father. She wrote that Nandry had immediately sat down and penned a long letter to Clae and Joe. Ellie gave news about the neighbors, the church, and the school. But she did not say how Clare and Kate were doing in the little house, or if Arnie was still seeing the preacher's daughter, or if she, Ellie, was receiving gentleman callers, or how Luke was doing in his quest of becoming a doctor. Marty's heart yearned to know all the answers.

"Clark," she said, folding up the letter for the third time, "I think it's time we got us some tickets."

Clark ran a hand over the rope he was braiding for Nathan. "Yeah," he agreed, "I think it is. We best have us a chat with Willie an' Missie tonight."

That evening Marty expected some protests when they voiced their decision. Missie put down the cup of coffee she had just poured and took a deep breath.

"No use pretending that we didn't know it had to come," she said quietly. "No use fussing about it. You must be powerful lonesome for the ones at home. I marvel that you were able to stay away this long." She poured another cup of coffee and handed it to Willie. "Of course, I wish you could just stay on here forever. But I know better. Truth is, I'm thankful for every day we've already had."

Willie cleared his throat and ran a hand through his thick hair. "Don't know as how I'm gonna git along without yer pair of hands," he said to Clark. "Can't believe the number of little things you've seen to over the winter months—things thet none of us ever seemed to find time fer."

Clark smiled. "Got a good idea," he said. "Why don't I see iffen I can talk yer pa into comin' out fer a spell? He's awful handy round a place. Never seen a man thet could make things look better in short order than yer pa. How 'bout it?"

Willie grinned. "I'd like thet," he said sincerely. "Seems like a long time since I seen my pa."

"When do you plan on going?" asked Missie.

"I'll be ridin' into town tomorra to check out the trains," returned Clark. "No use waitin' till it gits so hot one can hardly stand the ride. It was pretty uncomfortable at times fer yer ma when we came out last year. Thought it might be a little cooler iffen we go right away."

Missie was silent.

Marty looked at her daughter and caught her blinking away tears.

"We've loved having you," Missie finally managed. "You know that. I'm so sorry we have to send you back to the rest of the family different than you came, Pa. Hope they won't hold it against us and the West."

"Why should they?" asked Clark. "Accidents aren't confined to one place. Jest before we left home, a neighbor farmer got drug by a team of horses and lost *both* his legs."

"Still," said Missie, "it's going be a shock for them when they actually see you."

"I don't think any of 'em'll take it too hard," said Clark comfortably.

"We're gonna miss ya at the church," put in Willie. "Can't believe how much interest there is since we started to have real services."

"Thet won't stop," Clark answered. "Henry is all prepared to give ya Bible lessons jest as I was doin'. He'll do a fine job. I already wrote to Joe to send Henry out some good books on the Bible fer studyin'. I expect Henry to really git into 'em. He loves studyin' the Word and will bring to the people everything he can find. I think Henry is gonna make a fine lay preacher."

"We're glad for Henry," Missie said. "He's been a great help and a good friend ever since we left home."

"Ya have some very fine neighbors here," Marty said with feeling. "I'm so relieved, Missie, to know ya have ladies to visit and share with and a good doctor close by so ya won't need to go way up to Tettsford Junction fer this next little one."

"So am I," Missie agreed, reaching out to take Willie's hand. "That was what I dreaded most 'bout havin' Nathan an' Josiah—the long months of bein' away from Willie."

767

"Well, if I'm gonna make thet ride into town tomorra, I guess I should be gittin' to bed. Thet's a long way fer a slow rider to be travelin'." Clark stood and lifted his crutch into position.

"Would ya prefer the team to a saddle horse?" asked Willie.

"Hey, thet sounds like a good idea. Might be I'll even take young Nathan along with me, if his mother agrees."

"He'd love to go," said Missie. "He's really going to miss you. Both of you. He won't know what to do with himself when you leave."

"Won't be long until Nathan will be needin' school. I know ya have been teachin' him yerself, Missie, since ya had trainin' and some experience with schoolin.' Will ya keep on with thet?" asked Marty.

"Willie and some of the neighbor men are meeting at Juan's on Wednesday night. There are several families whose children are much older than Nathan, and they are most anxious to get them some schooling before they're so old they think they don't even *need* school. I love teaching our boys, but I think they will do well in a real school with other children."

"Glad to hear thet."

"The church committee is going to tell them they can meet in the church if they want to."

"Thet's a good idea," said Clark with enthusiasm. "I sure hope it all works out fer 'em. Now, we better git. I'll be by to pick up yer son 'bout eight, if thet's all right."

"That'll be fine. He'll be up and ready to go. Why don't you both come on over and have breakfast with us first?"

"Oh no, dear, we don't want—"

"Ma," said Missie, "please. There won't be too many days for us to have a meal together. Let's make the most of the ones we have left."

Marty kissed her daughter and agreed on breakfast the next morning.

❧

Clark and Nathan enjoyed a leisurely drive into town. Nathan, curious about everything he heard and saw, kept up an excited stream of questions and comments. Clark realized that the young boy was truly ready for school.

"What ya plannin' to be when ya grow up, boy?" asked Clark.

"I don't know, Grandpa. Some days I wanna be a rancher like my pa. An' sometimes I wanna be a foreman like Scottie, an' some days I wanna be a cowboy like Lane, but most of all I think I wanna be a cook like Cookie."

Clark laughed. The ranch was really all the life the boy knew. Clark determined to send Nathan a packet of good books.

"What do you wanna be, Grandpa?"

"Ya mean when I grow up?"

"Yer already growed."

"Oh yah," said Clark, "guess I am at that."

"What ya gonna be?" asked Nathan again.

"Well," said Clark, "I'm a farmer."

"What do farmers do?"

"Much like a rancher, only they don't raise quite so many cows and horses. An' they might have pigs or sheep or even goats to go with them other animals. An' they plow fields, an' pick rock, an' pull stumps, an' plant grain thet they harvest every fall. Then they build haystacks and store feed fer their animals to eat in the winter months. And they butcher an' cure meat, an' chop wood, an' doctor sick critters, an' take in garden vegetables, an' fix fences."

"Boy," said Nathan, "farmers do lotsa stuff, huh, Grandpa?"

"Guess that's right."

"Can ya do all thet, Grandpa?"

"Shore. Don't take nobody special to do all thet."

"Boy, ya can do lots of things with only one leg, can't ya, Grandpa?"

"Well, ya see, son, when I was doin' all those things I still had me two legs. So I been thinkin' some lately of how I can still do the same things. It's gonna take some special tools. Ya know the piece of harness I made fer myself so I could balance and still handle the horse an' the plow?"

Nathan nodded and smiled. "That's kind of a funny contraption, Grandpa," he commented, and they both shared a chuckle.

"Well, I plan on makin' a lot of things like thet," Clark explained. "I couldn't start to work on them yet, 'cause they've got to be measured jest so, to fit the different things I'll be usin'—like the plow an' the rake an' the seeder. I'm gonna make 'em all when I git home. I got this here idea of how I'll fix the plow, see . . ." And Clark commenced to tell Nathan all the details of his idea while the little boy's eyes opened wide as he listened. The miles melted away as the two worked together on Clark's plans.

In town Clark discovered that the next available eastbound train was leaving the following Tuesday. He bought their tickets and then took Nathan to the general store for a treat. They also pocketed some sweets for Josiah, then headed the team for home.

The news of the upcoming departure had Marty in a flurry of plans and activities. She was sure she had much to do to prepare for the journey, but when she set about to begin, she found it wasn't much after all—not nearly what it had been in preparing for their trip west. Now there was only their own luggage to pack, since all the things they had brought with them for Missie and the family would be staying right there. Marty relaxed and enjoyed her last days, spending as much time with the boys as she could.

She cleaned up the tiny soddy and bade it a fond farewell, then moved their things back into Missie's fine house for the remaining days.

That evening Willie came home from the de la Rosas' with exciting news. The community had voted to begin the new school in the church building. Henry's Melinda had been asked to teach. Her close neighbor, Mrs. Netherton, an older woman with no children, had agreed to stay with Melinda's young son while she was at school. Since Melinda was reluctant to leave her boy too long, the first year of school would be held only for three days a week. Still, the neighborhood agreed that this arrangement was far better than no school at all.

Willie and Missie had decided that Nathan would be allowed to join the school-bound crowd. Since Melinda would be driving right by their ranch, she had agreed to pick up the young scholar.

As each final day together ticked by, Marty took special note. A little clock ran in her mind: *This is our last Friday . . . our last Saturday . . . our last service in the little church.* That Sunday she prepared for the service with extra care. Clark had already shared with her some of his thoughts on the Scripture portion for the day. Marty felt them to be most appropriate on their last day with this congregation they had learned to love. There was no better message that Clark could leave with them.

When Clark stood before the group on that last Sunday, he read solemnly, yet exultantly, from Jeremiah 9:23 and 24: "Thus saith the Lord, Let not the wise man glory in his wisdom, neither let the mighty man glory in his might, let not the rich man glory in his riches: but let him that glorieth glory in this, that he understandeth and knoweth me, that I am the Lord which exercise lovingkindness, judgment, and righteousness, in the earth: for in these things I delight, saith the Lord." As she listened, Marty prayed for the individuals who sat in the seats around her. Her desire, as well as Clark's, was that each one of them might deeply understand and live the truth of the Scriptures, and this one in particular.

After the service had ended, Clark invited Henry to speak to the congregation. It was commonly known that when Clark left, Henry would take up the reins of leadership.

With emotion in his voice, Henry expressed his thanks to Clark and Marty for their guidance and encouragement over the months they had been with them, the congregation echoing his appreciation with amens and yeses. Then Clark and Marty, taken completely by surprise, were guests of honor as the whole fellowship gathered around to give them a farewell celebration. Food was spread out on makeshift tables, and the women served the group, then joined the men and children digging in with relish.

Underlying the festivities and laughter was a feeling of sadness since in just two days the Davises would be leaving them. Clark and Marty appreciated each one who came with a special thank-you shining in his or her eyes and warm handshakes and embraces. They were special, these people. They were special because they were Christian brothers and sisters. Clark and Marty were sure they would miss them—not family by blood but by adoption into the family of God.

TWENTY

Homeward Bound

When Tuesday morning arrived, Marty was packed and ready to go. As Willie brought the team around and Missie prepared her sons for the trip to town, Clark went to say a last farewell to the ranch hands, and Marty slipped out of the house and made one last trip to the little soddy. She was not as nostalgic about it for her own sake as for Missie's. Marty had spent a winter in the soddy by choice. Missie had made it a home because it was all that was available to her.

Marty stood and gazed around the little room once again. In her fancy she could see Missie as a very young bride bending over the tiny stove with its cow-chip fire, preparing the evening meal. In the cradle at the end of the bed would rest their tiny baby, Nathan. Willie would return from his long, hard day of herding cattle to be greeted with love and concern and a simple meal.

Marty could picture, too, the growing Nathan, the Christmas gathering of ranch hands, the visits with new neighbors. Marty would cherish her own mental images of the little soddy. Her own time spent there helped her to more clearly picture Missie in it.

Yes, she and Clark had been happy in the soddy, too. Those long evenings as she sat sewing and Clark pored over his Bible, sharing with her special truths as he found them and inviting her thoughts on particular verses—these were memories to treasure. Perhaps it would be many weeks before she and Clark would have so many hours of each day to cherish as their own without interruption from the daily demands of farm and family.

Marty slowly retraced her steps to the house—Missie's beautiful home. Marty had never seen a home that was more comfortable or more tastefully furnished. She was proud of Missie and her homemaking abilities.

Marty rounded the corner to find they were loading the wagon. She stepped forward to take her place. All the ranch hands who were not on duty were there to shake her hand, and Marty spoke to each of them. Cookie was the last in the line.

The old ranch cook stepped forward, his hand outstretched.

"Cookie," said Marty, emotion choking her voice, "we are so thankful to God fer yer choosin' to follow Him. Yer jest special to us in so many ways."

Cookie changed his mind and gave Marty an affectionate hug instead.

Lane moved forward and took Clark's hand. He said nothing, but his eyes said what he could not put into words.

Just as the wagon was about to move out of the yard, Wong came running, waving a bundle in his hands. Some fresh doughnuts, a treat for the trip, he said. Marty and Clark thanked him warmly, and he beamed as he bobbed his head.

"Much thanks," he said. "Much thanks for special joy you brought this house and to Wong's kitchen. Come again, maybe?"

The wagon pulled away amid hat waving and calls, and then they were on their way.

Marty's view was blurred with tears as she looked back from the hillside where she'd had her first look at Missie's home. So much had happened there to endear so many people to her heart.

Josiah climbed on her lap, and she held him close all the way to town. Nathan chattered excitedly, voicing his perspective that Grandma and Grandpa were privileged indeed to be passengers on a real moving train.

"An' someday I'm gonna come all the way on the train to the farm an' see ya," he promised fervently.

And Josiah echoed, "See ya."

"Yeah," said Nathan, "me and Joey. We'll come an' see ya."

"That would be most wonderful," said Marty and held her Joey even closer.

When they reached the town, Clark checked their trunk through, and they gathered their hand baggage and went to get a cup of coffee while they waited for the train.

It was hard to know what should be said in their last few minutes together. It seemed like there was still so much left to be said, in spite of the fact they had spent all these months talking.

They filled the time with small talk and reminders of messages for each one of the family on the farm.

It was nearly time to get back to the station when Scottie appeared.

"I wasn't able to see ya off at the house," he said, extending his hand to Clark, "but I shore didn't want to miss sayin' good-bye. Guess I needn't say thet we're gonna miss ya round the spread. S'pose now I'll have to mend my own halters and clean my own barns."

Clark smiled. He didn't feel he had helped Scottie out that much, but he knew what he had done had been appreciated. He shook Scottie's hand firmly. "Ya'll always have a warm spot in our hearts an' prayers," he told the ranch foreman, and Scottie smiled.

They walked slowly to the train station. Already the train was sending up great puffs of smoke as the firebox was filled in preparation for the departure. Long cars were filled with bawling steers, and Marty knew they would share the ride with many cattle heading for market. She wondered if some of Willie's herd might even be on board.

It was time for the last tearful good-bye.

"Pa," said Missie, her voice choked, "do you think you could ship out some apple cuttings by train? I've been missing those trees an awful lot."

Clark was thoughtful, not sure that apple trees would grow in the area, but he nodded his head. "Why not?" he said. "It's shore worth a try. Ya can plant them down by yer spring an' make sure they git plenty of water. Might not produce too much fruit, but ya might git enough fer a pie or two."

Missie laughed through her tears. "Truth is," she stated, "I won't even care too much if I don't get fruit. It's the blossoms I miss the most. It seems to me they promise spring, and love, and happiness every time they appear."

Clark gave his daughter a long understanding hug.

They all embraced one last time and told one another again how much the visit had meant to each of them. Marty and Clark held their two grandsons for as long as they dared, and then the "all aboard" was called and they waved one last time and climbed onto the train.

Marty waved until the train turned a curve and the town and her family were left behind. She wiped her tears on her handkerchief and resolved that she would cry no more.

The traveling days moved by, measured by the rhythms of the steel wheels. Each revolution took them farther away from Willie and Missie but closer to the other members of their family.

Marty didn't find the return trip quite so difficult, nor so uncomfortably warm. Maybe now she knew what to expect and set her mind accordingly.

There were a few stops at small towns here and there—some taking far too long—but then they traveled on again, day and night. On the third day, they pulled into the town where they had switched trains on their westward journey. Again it meant an overnight stay. Clark and Marty both remembered the dirty little hotel and its bedbugs.

"Surely we can do better than thet," Clark assured Marty and made some discreet inquiries. They were pointed to the home of an elderly lady who, they were told, kept roomers on occasion. Fortunately, the woman had a vacancy and accepted them as overnight guests.

By the time they made their way back to the station the next morning, shoppers were beginning to appear on the streets. The town was again awakening as it had done the year before.

When they reached the train station, Clark held the door for Marty and she passed through and headed for some seats near the window. She would sit and wait while Clark checked out the departure time.

Clark walked closely behind her to settle the luggage he carried down beside her before going over to the ticket counter. Other passengers milled about the room.

Marty heard the loud voice of a youngster. "Ma, look—look at thet poor man."

Marty's head came up slowly and she looked around, wondering who the unfortunate person might be. She spotted no one who fit the description.

"Ya lookin' fer the man?"

At the sound of Clark's voice, Marty flushed, embarrassed to be caught staring about out of curiosity. Her eyes admitted to Clark that she had indeed been looking for "the poor man."

Clark was quick to ease her guilt. "I was, too," he confessed. "Did ya spot 'im?"

Marty shook her head.

"Me neither," said Clark and then began to chuckle.

Marty looked at him in surprise.

"Thet is," went on Clark, "till I looked at myself."

"Yerself?"

Clark chuckled again.

"He was talkin' 'bout *me*, Marty."

"You?"

Then Marty's gaze fell to the pinned-up empty pant leg and the crutch in Clark's hand. Her breath caught in a little gasp. It was true. The boy was speaking of Clark—and "the poor man" was chuckling!

Then Marty saw it—the humor of it, the glory of it. They both had completely forgotten that Clark was considered handicapped—"the poor man." They reached for each other and laughed together till tears of joy ran freely down their faces.

About the Author

Bestselling author **Janette Oke** is celebrated for her significant contribution to the Christian book industry. Her novels have sold more than thirty million copies, and she is the recipient of the ECPA President's Award, the CBA Life Impact Award, the Gold Medallion, and the Christy Award. In addition, the Hallmark Channel has made numerous films based on her books. Janette and her husband, Edward, live in Alberta, Canada.